The Mysterious Affair at Styles
Peril at End House
The ABC Murders
One, Two, Buckle My Shoe

Agatha Christie

Diamond Books
An Imprint of HarperCollins*Publishers*,
77–85 Fulham Palace Road
Hammersmith, London W6 8JB

This Diamond Books Omnibus edition first published 1993
9 8 7 6 5 4 3 2 1

The Mysterious Affair at Styles Copyright Agatha Christie 1920
Peril at End House Copyright Agatha Christie Mallowan 1932
The ABC Murders Copyright Agatha Christie Mallowan 1936
One, Two, Buckle My Shoe Copyright Agatha Christie Mallowan 1940

ISBN 1 85813 243 6 (UK)
ISBN Diamond Books 0261 661 50 7 (international edition)

Phototypeset in Plantin by Mendip Communications, Frome, Somerset

Printed in France by Maury-Eurolivres

Contents

BOOKS BY AGATHA CHRISTIE

The ABC Murders
The Adventure of the Christmas Pudding
After the Funeral
And Then There Were None
Appointment with Death
At Bertram's Hotel
The Big Four
The Body in the Library
By the Pricking of My Thumbs
Cards on the Table
A Caribbean Mystery
Cat Among the Pigeons
The Clocks
Crooked House
Curtain: Poirot's Last Case
Dead Man's Folly
Death Comes as the End
Death in the Clouds
Death on the Nile
Destination Unknown
Dumb Witness
Elephants Can Remember
Endless Night
Evil Under the Sun
Five Little Pigs
4.50 from Paddington
Hallowe'en Party
Hercule Poirot's Christmas
Hickory Dickory Dock
The Hollow
The Hound of Death
The Labours of Hercules
The Listerdale Mystery
Lord Edgware Dies
The Man in the Brown Suit
The Mirror Crack'd from Side to Side
Miss Marple's Final Cases
The Moving Finger
Mrs McGinty's Dead
The Murder at the Vicarage
Murder in Mesopotamia
Murder in the Mews
A Murder is Announced
Murder is Easy
The Murder of Roger Ackroyd
Murder on the Links
Murder on the Orient Express
The Mysterious Affair at Styles

The Mysterious Mr Quin
The Mystery of the Blue Train
Nemesis
N or M?
One, Two, Buckle My Shoe
Ordeal by Innocence
The Pale Horse
Parker Pyne Investigates
Partners in Crime
Passenger to Frankfurt
Peril at End House
A Pocket Full of Rye
Poirot Investigates
Poirot's Early Cases
Postern of Fate
Problem at Pollensa Bay
Sad Cypress
The Secret Adversary
The Secret of Chimneys
The Seven Dials Mystery
The Sittaford Mystery
Sleeping Murder
Sparkling Cyanide
Taken at the Flood
They Came to Baghdad
They Do It With Mirrors
Third Girl
The Thirteen Problems
Three-Act Tragedy
Towards Zero
Why Didn't They Ask Evans

*Novels under the Nom de Plume of 'Mary
Westmacott'*
Absent in the Spring
The Burden
A Daughter's A Daughter
Giant's Bread
The Rose and the Yew Tree
Unfinished Portrait

*Books under the name of Agatha Christie
Mallowan*
Come Tell me How You Live
Star Over Bethlehem

Autobiography
Agatha Christie: An Autobiography

The Mysterious Affair at Styles

CHAPTER I

I GO TO STYLES

The intense interest aroused in the public by what was known at the time as 'The Styles Case' has now somewhat subsided. Nevertheless, in view of the world-wide notoriety which attended it, I have been asked, both by my friend Poirot and the family themselves, to write an account of the whole story. This, we trust, will effectually silence the sensational rumours which still persist.

I will therefore briefly set down the circumstances which led to my being connected with the affair.

I had been invalided home from the Front; and, after spending some months in a rather depressing Convalescent Home, was given a month's sick leave. Having no near relations or friends, I was trying to make up my mind what to do, when I ran across John Cavendish. I had seen very little of him for some years. Indeed, I had never known him particularly well. He was a good fifteen years my senior, for one thing, though he hardly looked his forty-five years. As a boy, though, I had often stayed at Styles, his mother's place in Essex.

We had a good yarn about old times, and it ended in his inviting me down to Styles to spend my leave there.

'The mater will be delighted to see you again – after all those years,' he added.

'Your mother keeps well?' I asked.

'Oh, yes. I suppose you know that she has married again?'

I am afraid I showed my surprise rather plainly. Mrs Cavendish, who had married John's father when he was a widower with two sons, had been a handsome woman of middle-age as I remembered her. She certainly could not be a day less than seventy now. I recalled her as an energetic, autocratic personality, somewhat inclined to charitable and social notoriety, with a fondness for opening bazaars and playing the Lady Bountiful. She was a most generous woman, and possessed a considerable fortune of her own.

Their country-place, Styles Court, had been purchased by Mr Cavendish early in their married life. He had been completely under his wife's ascendancy, so much so that, on dying, he left the place to her for her lifetime, as well as the larger part of his income; an arrangement that was distinctly unfair to his two sons. Their stepmother, however, had always been most generous to them;

9

indeed, they were so young at the time of their father's remarriage that they always thought of her as their own mother.

Lawrence, the younger, had been a delicate youth. He had qualified as a doctor but early relinquished the profession of medicine, and lived at home while pursuing literary ambitions; though his verses never had any marked success.

John practised for some time as a barrister, but had finally settled down to the more congenial life of a country squire. He had married two years ago, and had taken his wife to live at Styles, though I entertained a shrewd suspicion that he would have preferred his mother to increase his allowance, which would have enabled him to have a home of his own. Mrs Cavendish, however, was a lady who liked to make her own plans, and expected other people to fall in with them, and in this case she certainly had the whip hand, namely: the purse strings.

John noticed my surprise at the news of his mother's remarriage and smiled rather ruefully.

'Rotten little bounder too!' he said savagely. 'I can tell you, Hastings, it's making life jolly difficult for us. As for Evie – you remember Evie?'

'No.'

'Oh, I suppose she was after your time. She's the mater's factotum, companion, Jack of all trades! A great sport – old Evie! Not precisely young and beautiful, but as game as they make them.'

'You were going to say –'

'Oh, this fellow! He turned up from nowhere, on the pretext of being a second cousin or something of Evie's, though she didn't seem particularly keen to acknowledge the relationship. The fellow is an absolute outsider, anyone can see that. He's got a great black beard, and wears patent leather boots in all weathers! But the mater cottoned to him at once, took him on as secretary – you know how she's always running a hundred societies?'

I nodded.

'Well, of course, the war has turned the hundreds into thousands. No doubt the fellow was very useful to her. But you could have knocked us all down with a feather when, three months ago, she suddenly announced that she and Alfred were engaged! The fellow must be at least twenty years younger than she is! It's simply bare-faced fortune hunting; but there you are – she is her own mistress, and she's married him.'

'It must be a difficult situation for you all.'

10

'Difficult! It's damnable!'

Thus it came about that, three days later, I descended from the train at Styles St Mary, an absurd little station, with no apparent reason for existence, perched up in the midst of green fields and country lanes. John Cavendish was waiting on the platform, and piloted me out to the car.

'Got a drop or two of petrol still, you see,' he remarked. 'Mainly owing to the mater's activities.'

The village of Styles St Mary was situated about two miles from the little station, and Styles Court lay a mile the other side of it. It was a still, warm day in early July. As one looked out over the flat Essex country, lying so green and peaceful under the afternoon sun, it seemed almost impossible to believe that, not so very far away, a great war was running its appointed course. I felt I had suddenly strayed into another world. As we turned in at the lodge gates, John said:

'I'm afraid you'll find it very quiet down here, Hastings.'

'My dear fellow, that's just what I want.'

'Oh, it's pleasant enough if you want to lead the idle life. I drill with the volunteers twice a week, and lend a hand at the farms. My wife works regularly "on the land". She is up at five every morning to milk, and keeps at it steadily until lunch-time. It's a jolly good life taking it all round – if it weren't for that fellow Alfred Inglethorp!' He checked the car suddenly, and glanced at his watch. 'I wonder if we've time to pick up Cynthia. No, she'll have started from the hospital by now.'

'Cynthia! That's not your wife?'

'No, Cynthia is a protégée of my mother's, the daughter of an old schoolfellow of hers, who married a rascally solicitor. He came a cropper, and the girl was left an orphan and penniless. My mother came to the rescue, and Cynthia has been with us nearly two years now. She works in the Red Cross Hospital at Tadminster, seven miles away.'

As he spoke the last words, we drew up in front of the fine old house. A lady in a stout tweed skirt, who was bending over a flower bed, straightened herself at our approach.

'Hullo, Evie, here's our wounded hero! Mr Hastings – Miss Howard.'

Miss Howard shook hands with a hearty, almost painful, grip. I had an impression of very blue eyes in a sunburnt face. She was a pleasant-looking woman of about forty, with a deep voice, almost manly in its stentorian tones, and had a large sensible square body, with feet to match – these last encased in good thick boots. Her conversation, I soon found, was couched in the telegraphic style.

'Weeds grow like house afire. Can't keep even with 'em. Shall press you in. Better be careful!'

'I'm sure I shall be only too delighted to make myself useful,' I responded.

'Don't say it. Never does. Wish you hadn't later.'

'You're a cynic, Evie,' said John, laughing. 'Where's tea today – inside or out?'

'Out. Too fine a day to be cooped up in the house.'

'Come on then, you've done enough gardening for today. "The labourer is worthy of his hire," you know. Come and be refreshed.'

'Well,' said Miss Howard, drawing off her gardening gloves, 'I'm inclined to agree with you.'

'She led the way round the house to where tea was spread under the shade of a large sycamore.

A figure rose from one of the basket chairs, and came a few steps to meet us.

'My wife, Hastings,' said John.

I shall never forget my first sight of Mary Cavendish. Her tall, slender form, outlined against the bright light; the vivid sense of slumbering fire that seemed to find expression only in those wonderful tawny eyes of hers, remarkable eyes, different from any other woman's that I have ever known; the intense power of stillness she possessed, which nevertheless conveyed the impression of a wild untamed spirit in an exquisitely civilized body – all these things are burnt into my memory. I shall never forget them.

She greeted me with a few words of pleasant welcome in a low clear voice, and I sank into a basket chair feeling distinctly glad that I had accepted John's invitation. Mrs Cavendish gave me some tea, and her few quiet remarks heightened my first impression of her as a thoroughly fascinating woman. An appreciative listener is always stimulating, and I described, in a humorous manner, certain incidents of my Convalescent Home, in a way which, I flatter myself, greatly amused my hostess. John, of course, good fellow though he is, could hardly be called a brilliant conversationalist.

At that moment a well remembered voice floated through the open french window near at hand:

'Then you'll write to the Princess after tea, Alfred? I'll write to Lady Tadminster for the second day, myself. Or shall we wait until

12

we hear from the Princess? In case of a refusal, Lady Tadminster might open it the first day, and Mrs Crosbie the second. Then there's the Duchess – about the school fête.'

There was the murmur of a man's voice, and then Mrs Inglethorp's rose in reply:

'Yes, certainly. After tea will do quite well. You are so thoughtful, Alfred dear.'

The french window swung open a little wider, and a handsome white-haired old lady, with a somewhat masterful cast of features, stepped out of it on to the lawn. A man followed her, a suggestion of deference in his manner.

Mrs Inglethorp greeted me with effusion.

'Why, if it isn't too delightful to see you again, Mr Hastings, after all these years. Alfred, darling, Mr Hastings – my husband.'

I looked with some curiosity at 'Alfred darling'. He certainly struck a rather alien note. I did not wonder at John objecting to his beard. It was one of the longest and blackest I have ever seen. He wore gold-rimmed pince-nez, and had a curious impassivity of feature. It struck me that he might look natural on a stage, but was strangely out of place in real life. His voice was rather deep and unctuous. He placed a wooden hand in mine and said:

'This is a pleasure, Mr Hastings.' Then, turning to his wife: 'Emily dearest, I think that cushion is a little damp.'

She beamed fondly at him, as he substituted another with every demonstration of the tenderest care. Strange infatuation of an otherwise sensible woman!

With the presence of Mr Inglethorp, a sense of constraint and veiled hostility seemed to settle down upon the company. Miss Howard, in particular, took no pains to conceal her feelings. Mrs Inglethorp, however, seemed to notice nothing unusual. Her volubility, which I remembered of old, had lost nothing in the intervening years, and she poured out a steady flood of conversation, mainly on the subject of the forthcoming bazaar which she was organizing and which was to take place shortly. Occasionally she referred to her husband over a question of days or dates. His watchful and attentive manner never varied. From the very first I took a firm and rooted dislike to him, and I flatter myself that my first judgments are usually fairly shrewd.

Presently Mrs Inglethorp turned to give some instructions about letters to Evelyn Howard, and her husband addressed me in his painstaking voice:

13

'Is soldiering your regular profession, Mr Hastings?'

'No, before the war I was in Lloyd's.'

'And you will return there after it is over?'

'Perhaps. Either that or a fresh start altogether.'

Mary Cavendish leant forward.

'What would you really choose as a profession, if you could just consult your inclination?'

'Well, that depends.'

'No secret hobby?' she asked. 'Tell me – you're drawn to something? Everyone is – usually something absurd.'

'You'll laugh at me.'

She smiled.

'Perhaps.'

'Well, I've always had a secret hankering to be a detective!'

'The real thing – Scotland Yard? Or Sherlock Holmes?'

'Oh, Sherlock Holmes by all means. But really, seriously, I am awfully drawn to it. I came across a man in Belgium once, a very famous detective, and he quite inflamed me. He was a marvellous little fellow. He used to say that all good detective work was a mere matter of method. My system is based on his – though of course I have progressed rather further. He was a funny little man, a great dandy, but wonderfully clever.'

'Like a good detective story myself,' remarked Miss Howard. 'Lots of nonsense written, though. Criminal discovered in last chapter. Every one dumbfounded. Real crime – you'd know at once.'

'There have been a great number of undiscovered crimes,' I argued.

'Don't mean the police, but the people that are right in it. The family. You couldn't really hoodwink them. They'd know.'

'Then,' I said, much amused, 'you think that if you were mixed up in a crime, say a murder, you'd be able to spot the murderer right off?'

'Of course I should. Mightn't be able to prove it to a pack of lawyers. But I'm certain I'd know. I'd feel it in my finger-tips if he came near me.'

'It might be a "she",' I suggested.

'Might. But murder's a violent crime. Associate it more with a man.'

'Not in a case of poisoning.' Mrs Cavendish's clear voice startled me. 'Dr Bauerstein was saying yesterday that, owing to the general ignorance of the more uncommon poisons among the medical profession, there were probably countless cases of poisoning quite unsuspected.'

'Why, Mary, what a gruesome conversation!' cried Mrs Inglethorp. 'It makes me feel as if a goose were walking over my grave. Oh, there's Cynthia!'

A young girl in VAD uniform ran lightly across the lawn.

'Why, Cynthia, you are late today. This is Mr Hastings – Miss Murdoch.'

Cynthia Murdoch was a fresh-looking young creature, full of life and vigour. She tossed off her little VAD cap, and I admired the great loose waves of her auburn hair, and the smallness and whiteness of the hand she held out to claim her tea. With dark eyes and eyelashes she would have been a beauty.

She flung herself down on the ground beside John, and as I handed her a plate of sandwiches she smiled up at me.

'Sit down here on the grass, do. It's ever so much nicer.'

I dropped down obediently.

'You work at Tadminster, don't you, Miss Murdoch?'

She nodded.

'For my sins.'

'Do they bully you, then?' I asked, smiling.

'I should like to see them!' cried Cynthia with dignity.

'I have got a cousin who is nursing,' I remarked. 'And she is terrified of "Sisters".'

'I don't wonder. Sisters *are*, you know, Mr Hastings. They simp-ly *are*! You've no idea! But I'm not a nurse, thank heaven, I work in the dispensary.'

'How many people do you poison?' I asked, smiling.

Cynthia smiled too.

'Oh, hundreds!' she said.

'Cynthia,' called Mrs Inglethorp, 'do you think you could write a few notes for me?'

'Certainly, Aunt Emily.'

She jumped up promptly, and something in her manner reminded me that her position was a dependent one, and that Mrs Inglethorp, kind as she might be in the main, did not allow her to forget it.

My hostess turned to me.

'John will show you your room. Supper is at half-past seven. We have given up late dinner for some time now. Lady Tadminster, our Member's wife – she was the late Lord Abbotsbury's daughter – does the same. She agrees with me that one must set an example of economy. We are quite a war household; nothing is wasted here – every scrap of waste paper, even, is saved and sent away in sacks.'

I expressed my appreciation, and John took me into the house and up the broad staircase, which forked right and left half-way to different wings of the building. My room was in the left wing, and looked out over the park.

John left me, and a few minutes later I saw him from my window walking slowly across the grass arm in arm with Cynthia Murdoch. I heard Mrs Inglethorp call 'Cynthia' impatiently, and the girl started and ran back to the house. At the same moment, a man stepped out from the shadow of a tree and walked slowly in the same direction. He looked about forty, very dark with a melancholy clean-shaven face. Some violent emotion seemed to be mastering him. He looked up at my window as he passed, and I recognized him, though he had changed much in the fifteen years that had elapsed since we last met. It was John's younger brother, Lawrence Cavendish. I wondered what it was that had brought that singular expression to his face.

Then I dismissed him from my mind, and returned to the contemplation of my own affairs.

The evening passed pleasantly enough; and I dreamed that night of that enigmatical woman, Mary Cavendish.

The next morning dawned bright and sunny, and I was full of the anticipation of a delightful visit.

I did not see Mrs Cavendish until lunch-time, when she volunteered to take me for a walk, and we spent a charming afternoon roaming in the woods, returning to the house about five.

As we entered the large hall, John beckoned us both into the smoking-room. I saw at once by his face that something disturbing had occurred. We followed him in, and he shut the door after us.

'Look here, Mary, there's the deuce of a mess. Evie's had a row with Alfred Inglethorp, and she's off.'

'Evie? Off?'

John nodded gloomily.

'Yes; you see she went to the mater, and – oh, here's Evie herself.'

Miss Howard entered. Her lips were set grimly together, and she carried a small suit-case. She looked excited and determined, and slightly on the defensive.

'At any rate,' she burst out, 'I've spoken my mind!'

'My dear Evelyn,' cried Mrs Cavendish, 'this can't be true!'

Miss Howard nodded grimly.

'True enough! Afraid I said some things to Emily she won't forget

16

or forgive in a hurry. Don't mind if they've only sunk in a bit. Probably water off a duck's back, though. I said right out: "You're an old woman, Emily, and there's no fool like an old fool. The man's twenty years younger than you, and don't you fool yourself as to what he married you for. Money! Well, don't let him have too much of it. Farmer Raikes has got a very pretty young wife. Just ask your Alfred how much time he spends over there." She was very angry. Natural! I went on: "I'm going to warn you, whether you like it or not. That man would as soon murder you in your bed as look at you. He's a bad lot. You can say what you like to me, but remember what I've told you. He's a bad lot!" '

'What did she say?'

Miss Howard made an extremely expressive grimace.

' "Darling Alfred" – "dearest Alfred" – "wicked calumnies" – "wicked lies" – "wicked woman" – to accuse her "dear husband"! The sooner I left her house the better. So I'm off.'

'But not now?'

'This minute!'

For a moment we sat and stared at her. Finally John Cavendish, finding his persuasions of no avail, went off to look up the trains. His wife followed him, murmuring something about persuading Mrs Inglethorp to think better of it.

As she left the room, Miss Howard's face changed. She leant towards me eagerly.

'Mr Hastings, you're honest. I can trust you?'

I was a little startled. She laid her hand on my arm, and sank her voice to a whisper.

'Look after her, Mr Hastings. My poor Emily. They're a lot of sharks – all of them. Oh, I know what I'm talking about. There isn't one of them that's not hard up and trying to get money out of her. I've protected her as much as I could. Now I'm out of the way, they'll impose upon her.'

'Of course, Miss Howard,' I said, 'I'll do everything I can, but I'm sure you're excited and overwrought.'

She interrupted me by slowly shaking her forefinger.

'Young man, trust me. I've lived in the world rather longer than you have. All I ask you is to keep your eyes open. You'll see what I mean.'

The throb of the motor came through the open window, and Miss Howard rose and moved to the door. John's voice sounded outside. With her hand on the handle, she turned her head over her shoulder,

17

and beckoned to me.

'Above all, Mr Hastings, watch that devil – her husband!'

There was no time for more. Miss Howard was swallowed up in an eager chorus of protests and goodbyes. The Inglethorps did not appear.

As the motor drove away, Mrs Cavendish suddenly detached herself from the group, and moved across the drive to the lawn to meet a tall bearded man who had been evidently making for the house. The colour rose in her cheeks as she held out her hand to him.

'Who is that?' I asked sharply, for instinctively I distrusted the man.

'That's Dr Bauerstein,' said John shortly.

'And who is Dr Bauerstein?'

'He's staying in the village doing a rest cure, after a bad nervous breakdown. He's a London specialist; a very clever man – one of the greatest living experts on poisons, I believe.'

'And he's a great friend of Mary's,' put in Cynthia, the irrepressible.

John Cavendish frowned and changed the subject.

'Come for a stroll, Hastings. This has been a most rotten business. She always had a rough tongue, but there is no stauncher friend in England than Evelyn Howard.'

He took the path through the plantation, and we walked down to the village through the woods which bordered one side of the estate.

As we passed through one of the gates on our way home again, a pretty young woman of gipsy type coming in the opposite direction bowed and smiled.

'That's a pretty girl,' I remarked appreciatively.

John's face hardened.

'That is Mrs Raikes.'

'The one that Miss Howard –'

'Exactly,' said John, with rather unnecessary abruptness.

I thought of the white-haired old lady in the big house, and that vivid wicked little face that had just smiled into ours, and a vague chill of foreboding crept over me. I brushed it aside.

'Styles is really a glorious old place,' I said to John.

He nodded rather gloomily.

'Yes, it's a fine property. It'll be mine some day – should be mine now by rights, if my father had only made a decent will. And then I shouldn't be so damned hard up as I am now.'

'Hard up, are you?'

18

'My dear Hastings, I don't mind telling you that I'm at my wits' end for money.'

'Couldn't your brother help you?'

'Lawrence? He's gone through every penny he ever had, publishing rotten verses in fancy bindings. No, we're an impecunious lot. My mother's always been awfully good to us, I must say. That is, up to now. Since her marriage, of course –' He broke off, frowning.

For the first time I felt that, with Evelyn Howard, something indefinable had gone from the atmosphere. Her presence had spelt security. Now that security was removed – and the air seemed rife with suspicion. The sinister face of Dr Bauerstein recurred to me unpleasantly. A vague suspicion of everyone and everything filled my mind. Just for a moment I had a premonition of approaching evil.

CHAPTER II

THE 16TH AND 17TH OF JULY

I had arrived at Styles on the 5th of July. I come now to the events of the 16th and 17th of that month. For the convenience of the reader I will recapitulate the incidents of those days in as exact a manner as possible. They were elicited subsequently at the trial by a process of long and tedious cross-examinations.

I received a letter from Evelyn Howard a couple of days after her departure, telling me she was working as a nurse at the big hospital in Middlingham, a manufacturing town some fifteen miles away, and begging me to let her know if Mrs Inglethorp should show any wish to be reconciled.

The only fly in the ointment of my peaceful days was Mrs Cavendish's extraordinary and, for my part, unaccountable preference for the society of Dr Bauerstein. What she saw in the man I cannot imagine, but she was always asking him up to the house, and often went off for long expeditions with him. I confess that I was quite unable to see his attraction.

The 16th of July fell on a Monday. It was a day of turmoil. The famous bazaar had taken place on Saturday, and an entertainment, in connection with the same charity, at which Mrs Inglethorp was to recite a War poem, was to be held that night. We were all busy during the morning arranging and decorating the Hall in the village where it was to take place. We had a late luncheon and spent the afternoon resting in the garden. I noticed that John's manner was somewhat unusual. He seemed very excited and restless.

After tea, Mrs Inglethorp went to lie down to rest before her efforts in the evening and I challenged Mary Cavendish to a single at tennis.

About a quarter to seven, Mrs Inglethorp called to us that we should be late as supper was early that night. We had rather a scramble to get ready in time; and before the meal was over the motor was waiting at the door.

The entertainment was a great success, Mrs Inglethorp's recitation receiving tremendous applause. There were also some tableaux in which Cynthia took part. She did not return with us, having been asked to a supper party, and to remain the night with some friends who had been acting with her in the tableaux.

The following morning, Mrs Inglethorp stayed in bed to break-fast, as she was rather over-tired; but she appeared in her briskest mood about 12.30, and swept Lawrence and myself off to a luncheon party.

'Such a charming invitation from Mrs Rolleston. Lady Tad-minster's sister, you know. The Rollestons came over with the Conqueror – one of our oldest families.'

Mary had excused herself on the plea of an engagement with Dr Bauerstein.

We had a pleasant luncheon, and as we drove away Lawrence suggested that we should return by Tadminster, which was barely a mile out of our way, and pay a visit to Cynthia in her dispensary. Mrs Inglethorp replied that this was an excellent idea, but as she had several letters to write she would drop us there, and we could come back with Cynthia in the pony-trap.

We were detained under suspicion by the hospital porter, until Cynthia appeared to vouch for us, looking very cool and sweet in her long white overall. She took us up to her sanctum, and introduced us to her fellow dispenser, a rather awe-inspiring individual, whom Cynthia cheerily addressed as 'Nibs'.

'What a lot of bottles!' I exclaimed, as my eye travelled round the small room. 'Do you really know what's in them all?'

'Say something original,' groaned Cynthia. 'Every single person who comes up here says that. We are really thinking of bestowing a prize on the first individual who does *not* say: "What a lot of bottles!" And I know the next thing you're going to say is: "How many people have you poisoned?" '

I pleaded guilty with a laugh.

'If you people only knew how fatally easy it is to poison someone by mistake, you wouldn't joke about it. Come on, let's have tea. We've got all sorts of secret stores in that cupboard. No, Lawrence – that's the poison cupboard. The big cupboard – that's right.'

We had a very cheery tea, and assisted Cynthia to wash up afterwards. We had just put away the last teaspoon when a knock came at the door. The countenances of Cynthia and Nibs were suddenly petrified into a stern and forbidding expression.

'Come in,' said Cynthia, in a sharp professional tone.

A young and rather scared-looking nurse appeared with a bottle which she proffered to Nibs, who waved her towards Cynthia with the somewhat enigmatical remark:

'*I*'m not really here today.'

21

Cynthia took the bottle and examined it with the severity of a judge.

'This should have been sent up this morning.'

'Sister is very sorry. She forgot.'

'Sister should read the rules outside the door.'

I gathered from the little nurse's expression that there was not the least likelihood of her having the hardihood to retail this message to the dreaded 'Sister'.

'So now it can't be done until tomorrow,' finished Cynthia.

'Don't you think you could possibly let us have it tonight?'

'Well,' said Cynthia graciously, 'we are very busy, but if we have time it shall be done.'

The little nurse withdrew, and Cynthia promptly took a jar from the shelf, refilled the bottle and placed it on the table outside the door.

I laughed.

'Discipline must be maintained?'

'Exactly. Come out on our little balcony. You can see all the outside wards there.'

I followed Cynthia and her friend and they pointed out the different wards to me. Lawrence remained behind, but after a few moments Cynthia called to him over her shoulder to come and join us. Then she looked at her watch.

'Nothing more to do, Nibs?'

'No.'

'All right. Then we can lock up and go.'

I had seen Lawrence in quite a different light that afternoon. Compared to John, he was an astoundingly difficult person to get to know. He was the opposite of his brother in almost every respect, being unusually shy and reserved. Yet he had a certain charm of manner, and I fancied that, if one really knew him well, one could have a deep affection for him. I had always fancied that his manner to Cynthia was rather constrained, and that she on her side was inclined to be shy of him. But they were both gay enough this afternoon, and chatted together like a couple of children.

As we drove through the village, I remembered that I wanted some stamps, so accordingly we pulled up at the post office.

As I came out again, I cannoned into a little man who was just entering. I drew aside and apologized, when suddenly, with a loud exclamation, he clasped me in his arms and kissed me warmly.

'*Mon ami* Hastings!' he cried. 'It is indeed *mon ami* Hastings!'

22

'Poirot!' I exclaimed.

I turned to the pony-trap.

'This is a very pleasant meeting for me, Miss Cynthia. This is my old friend, Monsieur Poirot, whom I have not seen for years.'

'Oh, we know Monsieur Poirot,' said Cynthia gaily. 'But I had no idea he was a friend of yours.'

'Yes, indeed,' said Poirot seriously. 'I know Mademoiselle Cynthia. It is by the charity of that good Mrs Inglethorp that I am here.' Then, as I looked at him inquiringly: 'Yes, my friend, she had kindly extended hospitality to seven of my country-people who, alas, are refugees from their native land. We Belgians will always remember her with gratitude.'

Poirot was an extraordinary-looking little man. He was hardly more than five feet four inches, but carried himself with great dignity. His head was exactly the shape of an egg, and he always perched it a little on one side. His moustache was very stiff and military. The neatness of his attire was almost incredible; I believe a speck of dust would have caused him more pain than a bullet wound. Yet this quaint dandified little man who, I was sorry to see, now limped badly, had been in his time one of the most celebrated members of the Belgian police. As a detective, his *flair* had been extraordinary, and he had achieved triumphs by unravelling some of the most baffling cases of the day.

He pointed out to me the little house inhabited by him and his fellow Belgians, and I promised to go and see him at an early date. Then he raised his hat with a flourish to Cynthia and we drove away.

'He's a dear little man,' said Cynthia. 'I'd no idea you knew him.'

'You've been entertaining a celebrity unawares,' I replied.

And, for the rest of the way home, I recited to them the various exploits and triumphs of Hercule Poirot.

We arrived back in a very cheerful mood. As we entered the hall, Mrs Inglethorp came out of her boudoir. She looked flushed and upset.

'Oh, it's you,' she said.

'Is there anything the matter, Aunt Emily?' asked Cynthia.

'Certainly not,' said Mrs Inglethorp sharply. 'What should there be?' Then catching sight of Dorcas, the parlourmaid, going into the dining-room, she called to her to bring some stamps into the boudoir.

'Yes, m'm.' The old servant hesitated, then added diffidently: 'Don't you think, m'm, you'd better get to bed? You're looking

23

very tired.'

'Perhaps you're right, Dorcas – yes – no – not now. I've some letters I must finish by post-time. Have you lighted the fire in my room as I told you?'

'Yes, m'm.'

'Then I'll go to bed directly after supper.'

She went into her boudoir again, and Cynthia stared after her.

'Goodness gracious! I wonder what's up?' she said to Lawrence.

He did not seem to have heard her, for without a word he turned on his heel and went out of the house.

I suggested a quick game of tennis before supper and, Cynthia agreeing, I ran upstairs to fetch my racquet.

Mrs Cavendish was coming down the stairs. It may have been my fancy, but she, too, was looking odd and disturbed.

'Had a good walk with Dr Bauerstein?' I asked, trying to appear as indifferent as I could.

'I didn't go,' she replied abruptly. 'Where is Mrs Inglethorp?'

'In the boudoir.'

Her hand clenched itself on the banisters, then she seemed to nerve herself for some encounter, and went rapidly past me down the stairs across the hall to the boudoir, the door of which she shut behind her.

As I ran out to the tennis court a few moments later, I had to pass the open boudoir window, and was unable to help overhearing the following scrap of dialogue. Mary Cavendish was saying in the voice of a woman desperately controlling herself: 'Then you won't show it to me?'

To which Mrs Inglethorp replied:

'My dear Mary, it has nothing to do with that matter.'

'Then show it to me.'

'I tell you it is not what you imagine. It does not concern you in the least.'

To which Mary Cavendish replied, with a rising bitterness: 'Of course, I might have known you would shield him.'

Cynthia was waiting for me, and greeted me eagerly with:

'I say! There's been the most awful row! I've got it all out of Dorcas.'

'What kind of row?'

'Between Aunt Emily and *him*. I do hope she's found him out at last!'

'Was Dorcas there, then?'

'Of course not. She "happened to be near the door". It was a real old bust-up. I do wish I knew what it was all about.'

I thought of Mrs Raikes's gipsy face, and Evelyn Howard's warnings, but wisely decided to hold my peace, whilst Cynthia exhausted every possible hypothesis, and cheerfully hoped, 'Aunt Emily will send him away, and will never speak to him again.'

I was anxious to get hold of John, but he was nowhere to be seen. Evidently something very momentous had occurred that afternoon. I tried to forget the few words I had overheard; but, do what I would, I could not dismiss them altogether from my mind. What was Mary Cavendish's concern in the matter?

Mr Inglethorp was in the drawing-room when I came down to supper. His face was impassive as ever, and the strange unreality of the man struck me afresh.

Mrs Inglethorp came down at last. She still looked agitated, and during the meal there was a somewhat constrained silence. Inglethorp was unusually quiet. As a rule, he surrounded his wife with little attentions, placing a cushion at her back, and altogether playing the part of the devoted husband. Immediately after supper, Mrs Inglethorp retired to her boudoir again.

'Send my coffee in here, Mary,' she called. 'I've just five minutes to catch the post.'

Cynthia and I went and sat by the open window in the drawing-room. Mary Cavendish brought our coffee to us. She seemed excited.

'Do you young people want lights, or do you enjoy the twilight?' she asked. 'Will you take Mrs Inglethorp her coffee, Cynthia? I will pour it out.'

'Do not trouble, Mary,' said Inglethorp. 'I will take it to Emily.' He poured it out, and went out of the room carrying it carefully.

Lawrence followed him, and Mrs Cavendish sat down by us.

We three sat for some time in silence. It was a glorious night, hot and still. Mrs Cavendish fanned herself gently with a palm leaf.

'It's almost too hot,' she murmured. 'We shall have a thunderstorm.'

Alas, that these harmonious moments can never endure! My paradise was rudely shattered by the sound of a well-known, and heartily disliked, voice in the hall.

'Dr Bauerstein!' exclaimed Cynthia. 'What a funny time to come.'

I glanced jealously at Mary Cavendish, but she seemed quite undisturbed, the delicate pallor of her cheeks did not vary.

In a few moments, Alfred Inglethorp had ushered the doctor in, the latter laughing, and protesting that he was in no fit state for a drawing-room. In truth, he presented a sorry spectacle, being literally plastered with mud.

'What have you been doing, doctor?' cried Mrs Cavendish.

'I must make my apologies,' said the doctor. 'I did not really mean to come in, but Mr Inglethorp insisted.'

'Well, Bauerstein, you are in a plight,' said John, strolling in from the hall. 'Have some coffee, and tell us what you have been up to.'

'Thank you, I will.' He laughed rather ruefully, as he described how he had discovered a very rare species of fern in an inaccessible place, and in his efforts to obtain it had lost his footing, and slipped ignominiously into a neighbouring pond.

'The sun soon dried me off,' he added, 'but I'm afraid my appearance is very disreputable.'

At this juncture, Mrs Inglethorp called to Cynthia from the hall, and the girl ran out.

'Just carry up my despatch-case, will you, dear? I'm going to bed.'

The door into the hall was a wide one. I had risen when Cynthia did, John was close by me. There were, therefore, three witnesses who could swear that Mrs Inglethorp was carrying her coffee, as yet untasted, in her hand. My evening was utterly and entirely spoilt by the presence of Dr Bauerstein. It seemed to me the man would never go. He rose at last, however, and I breathed a sigh of relief.

'I'll walk down to the village with you,' said Mr Inglethorp. 'I must see our agent over those estate accounts.' He turned to John. 'No one need sit up. I will take the latch-key.'

26

CHAPTER III

THE NIGHT OF THE TRAGEDY

To make this part of my story clear, I append the following plan of
the first floor of Styles. The servants' rooms are reached through the
door B. They have no communication with the right wing, where the
Inglethorps' rooms were situated.

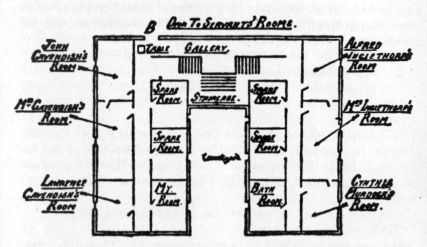

It seemed to be the middle of the night when I was awakened by
Lawrence Cavendish. He had a candle in his hand, and the agitation
of his face told me at once that something was seriously wrong.

'What's the matter?' I asked, sitting up in bed, and trying to
collect my scattered thoughts.

'We are afraid my mother is very ill. She seems to be having some
kind of fit. Unfortunately she has locked herself in.'

'I'll come at once.'

I sprang out of bed, and pulling on a dressing-gown, followed
Lawrence along the passage and the gallery to the right wing of the
house.

John Cavendish joined us, and one or two of the servants were
standing round in a state of awe-stricken excitement. Lawrence
turned to his brother.

'What do you think we had better do?'

Never, I thought, had his indecision of character been

27

more apparent.

John rattled the handle of Mrs Inglethorp's door violently, but with no effect. It was obviously locked or bolted on the inside. The whole household was aroused by now. The most alarming sounds were audible from the interior of the room. Clearly something must be done.

'Try going through Mr Inglethorp's room, sir,' cried Dorcas. 'Oh, the poor mistress!'

Suddenly I realized that Alfred Inglethorp was not with us – that he alone had given no sign of his presence. John opened the door of his room. It was pitch dark, but Lawrence was following with the candle, and by its feeble light we saw that the bed had not been slept in, and that there was no sign of the room having been occupied.

We went straight to the connecting door. That, too, was locked or bolted on the inside. What was to be done?

'Oh, dear, sir,' cried Dorcas, wringing her hands, 'whatever shall we do?'

'We must try and break the door in, I suppose. It'll be a tough job, though. Here, let one of the maids go down and wake Baily and tell him to go for Dr Wilkins at once. Now then, we'll have a try at the door. Half a moment, though, isn't there a door into Miss Cynthia's room?'

'Yes, sir, but that's always bolted. It's never been undone.'

'Well, we might just see.'

He ran rapidly down the corridor to Cynthia's room. Mary Cavendish was there, shaking the girl – who must have been an unusually sound sleeper – and trying to wake her.

In a moment or two he was back.

'No good. That's bolted too. We must break in the door. I think this one is a shade less solid than the one in the passage.'

We strained and heaved together. The framework of the door was solid, and for a long time it resisted our efforts, but at last we felt it give beneath our weight, and finally, with a resounding crash, it was burst open.

We stumbled in together, Lawrence still holding his candle. Mrs Inglethorp was lying on the bed, her whole form agitated by violent convulsions, in one of which she must have overturned the table beside her. As we entered, however, her limbs relaxed, and she fell back upon the pillows.

John strode across the room and lit the gas. Turning to Annie, one of the housemaids, he sent her downstairs to the dining-room for

28

brandy. Then he went across to his mother whilst I unbolted the door that gave on the corridor.

I turned to Lawrence, to suggest that I had better leave them now that there was no further need of my services, but the words were frozen on my lips. Never have I seen such a ghastly look on any man's face. He was white as chalk, the candle he held in his shaking hand was sputtering on to the carpet, and his eyes, petrified with terror, or some such kindred emotion, stared fixedly over my head at a point on the further wall. It was as though he had seen something that turned him to stone. I instinctively followed the direction of his eyes, but I could see nothing unusual. The still feebly flickering ashes in the grate, and the row of prim ornaments on the mantelpiece, were surely harmless enough.

The violence of Mrs Inglethorp's attack seemed to be passing. She was able to speak in short gasps.

'Better now – very sudden – stupid of me – to lock myself in.'

A shadow fell on the bed and, looking up, I saw Mary Cavendish standing near the door with her arm around Cynthia. She seemed to be supporting the girl, who looked utterly dazed and unlike herself. Her face was heavily flushed, and she yawned repeatedly.

'Poor Cynthia is quite frightened,' said Mrs Cavendish in a low clear voice. She herself, I noticed, was dressed in her white land smock. Then it must be later than I thought. I saw that a faint streak of daylight was showing through the curtains of the windows, and that the clock on the mantelpiece pointed to close upon five o'clock.

A strangled cry from the bed startled me. A fresh access of pain seized the unfortunate old lady. The convulsions were of a violence terrible to behold. Everything was confusion. We thronged round her, powerless to help or alleviate. A final convulsion lifted her from the bed, until she appeared to rest upon her head and her heels, with her body arched in an extraordinary manner. In vain Mary and John tried to administer more brandy. The moments flew. Again the body arched itself in that peculiar fashion.

At that moment, Dr Bauerstein pushed his way authoritatively into the room. For one instant he stopped dead, staring at the figure on the bed, and, at the same instant, Mrs Inglethorp cried out in a strangled voice, her eyes fixed on the doctor:

'Alfred – Alfred –' Then she fell back motionless on the pillows.

With a stride, the doctor reached the bed, and seizing her arms worked them energetically, applying what I knew to be artificial respiration. He issued a few short sharp orders to the servants. An

29

imperious wave of his hand drove us all to the door. We watched him, fascinated, though I think we all knew in our hearts that it was too late, and that nothing could be done now. I could see by the expression on his face that he himself had little hope.

Finally he abandoned his task, shaking his head gravely. At that moment, we heard footsteps outside, and Dr Wilkins, Mrs Inglethorp's own doctor, a portly, fussy little man, came bustling in.

In a few words Dr Bauerstein explained how he had happened to be passing the lodge gates as the car came out, and had run up to the house as fast as he could, whilst the car went on to fetch Dr Wilkins. With a faint gesture of the hand, he indicated the figure on the bed.

'Ve – ry sad. Ve – ry sad,' murmured Dr Wilkins. 'Poor dear lady. Always did far too much – far too much – against my advice. I warned her, 'Take – it – easy.' But no – her zeal for good works was too great. Nature rebelled. Na – ture – re – belled.'

Dr Bauerstein, I noticed, was watching the local doctor narrowly. He still kept his eyes fixed on him as he spoke.

'The convulsions were of a peculiar violence, Dr Wilkins. I am sorry you were not here in time to witness them. They were quite – tetanic in character.'

'Ah!' said Dr Wilkins wisely.

'I should like to speak to you in private,' said Dr Bauerstein. He turned to John. 'You do not object?'

'Certainly not.'

We all trooped out into the corridor, leaving the two doctors alone, and I heard the key turned in the lock behind us.

We went slowly down the stairs. I was violently excited. I have a certain talent for deduction, and Dr Bauerstein's manner had started a flock of wild surmises in my mind. Mary Cavendish laid her hand upon my arm.

'What is it? Why did Dr Bauerstein seem so – peculiar?'

I looked at her.

'Do you know what I think?'

'What?'

'Listen!' I looked round, the others were out of earshot. I lowered my voice to a whisper. 'I believe she has been poisoned! I'm certain Dr Bauerstein suspects it.'

'*What?*' She shrank against the wall, the pupils of her eyes dilating wildly. Then, with a sudden cry that startled me, she cried out: 'No, no – not that – not that!' And breaking from me, fled up the stairs. I followed her, afraid that she was going to faint. I found her leaning

30

against the banisters, deadly pale. She waved me away impatiently.

'No, no – leave me. I'd rather be alone. Let me just be quiet for a minute or two. Go down to the others.'

I obeyed her reluctantly. John and Lawrence were in the dining-room. I joined them. We were all silent, but I suppose I voiced the thoughts of us all when I at last broke it by saying:

'Where is Mr Inglethorp?'

John shook his head.

'He's not in the house.'

Our eyes met. Where *was* Alfred Inglethorp? His absence was strange and inexplicable. I remembered Mrs Inglethorp's dying words. What lay beneath them? What more could she have told us, if she had had time?

At last we heard the doctors descending the stairs. Dr Wilkins was looking important and excited, and trying to conceal an inward exultation under a manner of decorous calm. Dr Bauerstein remained in the background, his grave bearded face unchanged. Dr Wilkins was the spokesman for the two. He addressed himself to John:

'Mr Cavendish, I should like your consent to a post-mortem.'

'Is that necessary?' asked John gravely. A spasm of pain crossed his face.

'Absolutely,' said Dr Bauerstein.

'You mean by that –?'

'That neither Dr Wilkins nor myself could give a death certificate under the circumstances.'

John bent his head.

'In that case, I have no alternative but to agree.'

'Thank you,' said Dr Wilkins briskly. 'We propose that it should take place tomorrow night – or rather tonight.' And he glanced at the daylight. 'Under the circumstances, I am afraid an inquest can hardly be avoided – these formalities are necessary, but I beg that you won't distress yourselves.'

There was a pause, and then Dr Bauerstein drew two keys from his pocket, and handed them to John.

'These are the keys of the two rooms. I have locked them and, in my opinion, they would be better kept locked for the present.'

The doctors then departed.

I had been turning over an idea in my head, and I felt that the moment had now come to broach it. Yet I was a little chary of doing so. John, I knew, had a horror of any kind of publicity, and was an

31

easy-going optimist, who preferred never to meet trouble half-way. It might be difficult to convince him of the soundness of my plan. Lawrence, on the other hand, being less conventional, and having more imagination, I felt I might count upon as an ally. There was no doubt that the moment had come for me to take the lead.

'John,' I said, 'I am going to ask you something.'

'Well?'

'You remember my speaking of my friend Poirot? The Belgian who is here? He has been a most famous detective.'

'Yes.'

'I want you to let me call him in – to investigate this matter.'

'What – now? Before the post-mortem?'

'Yes, time is an advantage if – if – there has been foul play.'

'Rubbish!' cried Lawrence angrily. 'In my opinion the whole thing is a mare's nest of Bauerstein's! Wilkins hadn't an idea of such a thing, until Bauerstein put it into his head. But, like all specialists, Bauerstein's got a bee in his bonnet. Poisons are his hobby, so, of course, he sees them everywhere.'

I confess that I was surprised by Lawrence's attitude. He was so seldom vehement about anything.

John hesitated.

'I can't feel as you do, Lawrence,' he said at last, 'I'm inclined to give Hastings a free hand, though I should prefer to wait a bit. We don't want any unnecessary scandal.'

'No, no,' I cried eagerly, 'you need have no fear of that. Poirot is discretion itself.'

'Very well then, have it your own way. I leave it in your hands. Though, if it is as we suspect, it seems a clear enough case. God forgive me if I am wronging him!'

I looked at my watch. It was six o'clock. I determined to lose no time.

Five minutes' delay, however, I allowed myself. I spent it in ransacking the library until I discovered a medical book which gave a description of strychnine poisoning.

CHAPTER IV

POIROT INVESTIGATES

The house which the Belgians occupied in the village was quite close to the park gates. One could save time by taking a narrow path through the long grass, which cut off the detours of the winding drive. So I, accordingly, went that way. I had nearly reached the lodge, when my attention was arrested by the running figure of a man approaching me. It was Mr Inglethorp. Where had he been? How did he intend to explain his absence?

He accosted me eagerly.

'My God! This is terrible! My poor wife! I have only just heard.'

'Where have you been?' I asked.

'Denby kept me late last night. It was one o'clock before we'd finished. Then I found that I'd forgotten the latch-key after all. I didn't want to arouse the household, so Denby gave me a bed.'

'How did you hear the news?' I asked.

'Wilkins knocked Denby up to tell him. My poor Emily! She was so self-sacrificing – such a noble character. She overtaxed her strength.'

A wave of revulsion swept over me. What a consummate hypocrite the man was!

'I must hurry on,' I said, thankful that he did not ask me whither I was bound.

In a few minutes I was knocking at the door of Leastways Cottage. Getting no answer, I repeated my summons impatiently. A window above me was cautiously opened, and Poirot himself looked out.

He gave an exclamation of surprise at seeing me. In a few brief words, I explained the tragedy that had occurred, and that I wanted his help.

'Wait, my friend, I will let you in, and you shall recount to me the affairs whilst I dress.'

In a few moments he had unbarred the door, and I followed him up to his room. There he installed me in a chair, and I related the whole story, keeping back nothing, and omitting no circumstance, however insignificant, whilst he himself made a careful and deliberate toilet.

I told him of my awakening, of Mrs Inglethorp's dying words, of her husband's absence, of the quarrel the day before, of the scrap of conversation between Mary and her mother-in-law that I had overheard, of the former quarrel between Mrs Inglethorp and Evelyn Howard, and of the latter's innuendoes.

I was hardly as clear as I could wish. I repeated myself several times, and occasionally had to go back to some detail that I had forgotten. Poirot smiled kindly on me.

'The mind is confused? Is it not so? Take time, *mon ami*. You are agitated; you are excited – it is but natural. Presently, when we are calmer, we will arrange the facts, neatly, each in his proper place. We will examine – and reject. Those of importance we will put on one side; those of no importance, pouf!' – he screwed up his cherub-like face, and puffed comically enough – 'blow them away!'

'That's all very well,' I objected, 'but how are you going to decide what is important, and what isn't? That always seems the difficulty to me.'

Poirot shook his head energetically. He was now arranging his moustache with exquisite care.

'No so. *Voyons*! One fact leads to another – so we continue. Does the next fit in with that? *A merveille*! Good! We can proceed. This next little fact – no! Ah, that is curious! There is something missing – a link in the chain that is not there. We examine. We search. And that little curious fact, that possibly paltry little detail that will not tally, we put it here!' He made an extravagant gesture with his hand. 'It is significant! It is tremendous!'

'Y – es –'

'Ah!' Poirot shook his forefinger so fiercely at me that I quailed before it. 'Beware! Peril to the detective who says: "It is so small – it does not matter. It will not agree. I will forget it." That way lies confusion! Everything matters.'

'I know. You always told me that. That's why I have gone into all the details of this thing whether they seemed to me relevant or not.'

'And I am pleased with you. You have a good memory, and you have given me the facts faithfully. Of the order in which you present them, I say nothing – truly, it is deplorable! But I make allowances – you are upset. To that I attribute the circumstances that you have omitted one fact of paramount importance.'

'What is that?' I asked.

'You have not told me if Mrs Inglethorp ate well last night.'

I stared at him. Surely the war had affected the little man's brain. He was carefully engaged in brushing his coat before putting it on,

34

and seemed wholly engrossed in the task.

'I don't remember,' I said. 'And, anyway, I don't see –'

'You do not see? But it is of the first importance.'

'I can't see why,' I said, rather nettled. 'As far as I can remember, she didn't eat much. She was obviously upset, and it had taken her appetite away. That was only natural.'

'Yes,' said Poirot thoughtfully, 'it was only natural.'

He opened a drawer, and took out a small despatch-case, then turned to me.

'Now I am ready. We will proceed to the château, and study matters on the spot. Excuse me, *mon ami*, you dressed in haste, and your tie is on one side. Permit me.' With a deft gesture, he rearranged it.

'Ça y est! Now, shall we start?'

We hurried up the village, and turned in at the lodge gates. Poirot stopped for a moment, and gazed sorrowfully over the beautiful expanse of park, still glittering with morning dew.

'So beautiful, so beautiful, and yet, the poor family, plunged in sorrow, prostrated with grief.'

He looked at me keenly as he spoke, and I was aware that I reddened under his prolonged gaze.

Was the family prostrated by grief? Was the sorrow at Mrs Inglethorp's death so great? I realized that there was an emotional lack in the atmosphere. The dead woman had not the gift of commanding love. Her death was a shock and a distress, but she would not be passionately regretted.

Poirot seemed to follow my thoughts. He nodded his head gravely.

'No, you are right,' he said, 'it is not as though there was a blood tie. She has been kind and generous to these Cavendishes, but she was not their own mother. Blood tells – always remember that – blood tells.'

'Poirot,' I said, 'I wish you would tell me why you wanted to know if Mrs Inglethorp ate well last night? I have been turning it over in my mind, but I can't see how it has anything to do with the matter.'

He was silent for a minute or two as we walked along, but finally he said:

'I do not mind telling you – though, as you know, it is not my habit to explain until the end is reached. The present contention is that Mrs Inglethorp died of strychnine poisoning, presumably administered in her coffee.'

'Yes?'

'Well, what time was the coffee served?'

'About eight o'clock.'

'Therefore she drank it between then and half-past eight – certainly not much later. Well, strychnine is a fairly rapid poison. Its effects would be felt very soon, probably in about an hour. Yet, in Mrs Inglethorp's case, the symptoms do not manifest themselves until five o'clock the next morning: nine hours! But a heavy meal, taken at about the same time as the poison, might retard its effects, though hardly to that extent. Still, it is a possibility to be taken into account. But, according to you, she ate very little for supper, and yet the symptoms do not develop until early the next morning! Now that is a curious circumstance, my friend. Something may arise at the autopsy to explain it. In the meantime, remember it.'

As we neared the house, John came out and met us. His face looked weary and haggard.

'This is a very dreadful business, Monsieur Poirot,' he said. 'Hastings has explained to you that we are anxious for no publicity?'

'I comprehend perfectly.'

'You see, it is only suspicion so far. We have nothing to go upon.'

'Precisely. It is a matter of precaution only.'

John turned to me, taking out his cigarette-case, and lighting a cigarette as he did so.

'You know that fellow Inglethorp is back?'

'Yes. I met him.'

John flung the match into an adjacent flower bed, a proceeding which was too much for Poirot's feelings. He retrieved it, and buried it neatly.

'It's jolly difficult to know how to treat him.'

'That difficulty will not exist long,' pronounced Poirot quietly.

John looked puzzled, not quite understanding the portent of this cryptic saying. He handed the two keys which Dr Bauerstein had given him to me.

'Show Monsieur Poirot everything he wants to see.'

'The rooms are locked?' asked Poirot.

'Dr Bauerstein considered it advisable.'

Poirot nodded thoughtfully.

'Then he is very sure. Well, that simplifies matters for us.'

We went up together to the room of the tragedy. For convenience I append a plan of the room and the principal articles of furniture in it.

Poirot locked the door on the inside, and proceeded to a minute inspection of the room. He darted from one object to the other with

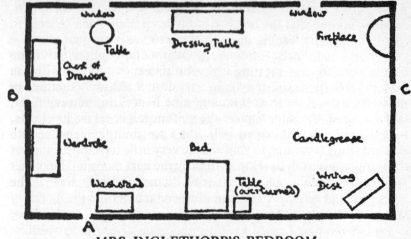

MRS INGLETHORP'S BEDROOM
A.—Door into Passage
B.—Door into Mr Inglethorp's Room
C.—Door into Cynthia's Room

the agility of a grasshopper. I remained by the door, fearing to obliterate any clues. Poirot, however, did not seem grateful to me for my forbearance.

'What have you, my friend?' he cried, 'that you remain there like – how do you say? – ah, yes, the stuck pig?'

I explained that I was afraid of obliterating any footmarks.

'Footmarks? But what an idea! There has already been practically an army in the room! What footmarks are we likely to find? No, come here and aid me in my search. I will put down my little case until I need it.'

He did so, on the round table by the window, but it was an ill-advised proceeding; for, the top of it being loose, it tilted up, and precipitated the despatch-case on to the floor.

'*En voilà une table!*' cried Poirot. 'Ah, my friend, one may live in a big house and yet have no comfort.'

After which piece of moralizing, he resumed his search.

A small purple despatch-case, with a key in the lock, on the writing table, engaged his attention for some time. He took out the key from the lock, and passed it to me to inspect. I saw nothing peculiar, however. It was an ordinary key of the Yale type, with a bit of twisted wire through the handle.

Next, he examined the framework of the door we had broken in, assuring himself that the bolt had really been shot. Then he went to the door opposite leading into Cynthia's room. That door was also bolted, as I had stated. However, he went to the length of unbolting it, and opening and shutting it several times; this he did with the utmost precaution against making any noise. Suddenly something in the bolt itself seemed to rivet his attention. He examined it carefully, and then, nimbly whipping out a pair of small forceps from his case, he drew out some minute particle which he carefully sealed up in a tiny envelope.

On the chest of drawers there was a tray with a spirit lamp and a small saucepan on it. A small quantity of a dark fluid remained in the saucepan, and an empty cup and saucer that had been drunk out of stood near it.

I wondered how I could have been so unobservant as to overlook this. Here was a clue worth having. Poirot delicately dipped his finger into the liquid, and tasted it gingerly. He made a grimace.

'Cocoa – with – I think – rum in it.'

He passed on to the debris on the floor, where the table by the bed had been overturned. A reading-lamp, some books, matches, a bunch of keys, and the crushed fragments of a coffee-cup lay scattered about.

'Ah, this is curious,' said Poirot.

'I must confess that I see nothing particularly curious about it.'

'You do not? Observe the lamp – the chimney is broken in two places; they lie there as they fell. But see, the coffee-cup is absolutely smashed to powder.'

'Well,' I said wearily. 'I suppose someone must have stepped on it.'

'Exactly,' said Poirot, in an odd voice. 'Someone stepped on it.'

He rose from his knees, and walked slowly across to the mantelpiece, where he stood abstractedly fingering the ornaments, and straightening them – a trick of his when he was agitated.

'*Mon ami*,' he said, turning to me, 'somebody stepped on that cup, grinding it to powder, and the reason they did so was either because it contained strychnine or – which is far more serious – because it did not contain strychnine!'

I made no reply. I was bewildered, but I knew that it was no good asking him to explain. In a moment or two he roused himself, and went on with his investigations. He picked up the bunch of keys from the floor, and twirling them round in his fingers finally selected one,

38

very bright and shining, which he tried in the lock of the purple despatch-case. It fitted, and he opened the box, but after a moment's hesitation, closed and relocked it, and slipped the bunch of keys, as well as the key that had originally stood in the lock, into his own pocket.

'I have no authority to go through these papers. But it should be done – at once!'

He then made a very careful examination of the drawers of the wash-stand. Crossing the room to the left-hand window, a round stain, hardly visible on the dark brown carpet, seemed to interest him particularly. He went down on his knees, examining it minutely – even going so far as to smell it.

Finally, he poured a few drops of the cocoa into a test tube, sealing it up carefully. His next proceeding was to take out a little notebook.

'We have found in this room,' he said, writing busily, 'six points of interest. Shall I enumerate them, or will you?'

'Oh, you,' I replied hastily.

'Very well, then. One, a coffee-cup that has been ground into powder; two, a despatch-case with a key in the lock; three, a stain on the floor.'

'That may have been done some time ago,' I interrupted.

'No, for it is still perceptibly damp and smells of coffee. Four, a fragment of some dark green fabric – only a thread or two, but recognizable.'

'Ah!' I cried. 'That was what you sealed up in the envelope.'

'Yes. It may turn out to be a piece of one of Mrs Inglethorp's own dresses, and quite unimportant. We shall see. Five, *this!*' With a dramatic gesture, he pointed to a large splash of candle grease on the floor by the writing-table. 'It must have been done since yesterday, otherwise a good housemaid would have at once removed it with blotting-paper and a hot iron. One of my best hats once – but that is not to the point.'

'It was very likely done last night. We were very agitated. Or perhaps Mrs Inglethorp herself dropped her candle.'

'You brought only one candle into the room?'

'Yes. Lawrence Cavendish was carrying it. But he was very upset. He seemed to see something over here' – I indicated the mantelpiece – 'that absolutely paralysed him.'

'That is interesting,' said Poirot quickly. 'Yes, it is suggestive' – his eye sweeping the whole length of the wall – 'But it was not his candle that made this great patch, for you perceive that this is white grease; whereas Monsieur Lawrence's candle, which is still on the dressing-table, is pink. On the other hand, Mrs Inglethorp had no candlestick in the room, only a reading lamp.'

'Then,' I said, 'what do you deduce?'

To which my friend only made a rather irritating reply, urging me to use my own natural faculties.

'And the sixth point?' I asked. 'I suppose it is the sample of cocoa.'

'No,' said Poirot thoughtfully, 'I might have included that in the six, but I did not. No, the sixth point I will keep to myself for the present.'

He looked quickly round the room. 'There is nothing more to be done here, I think, unless' – he stared earnestly and long at the dead ashes in the grate. 'The fire burns – and it destroys. But by chance – there might be – let us see!'

Deftly, on hands and knees, he began to sort the ashes from the grate into the fender, handling them with the greatest caution. Suddenly, he gave a faint exclamation.

'The forceps, Hastings!'

I quickly handed them to him, and with skill he extracted a small piece of half-charred paper.

'There, *mon ami!*' he cried. 'What do you think of that?'

I scrutinized the fragment. This is an exact reproduction of it:

I was puzzled. It was unusually thick, quite unlike ordinary notepaper. Suddenly an idea struck me.

'Poirot!' I cried. 'This is a fragment of a will!'

'Exactly.'

I looked at him sharply.

'You are not surprised?'

'No,' he said gravely, 'I expected it.'

I relinquished the piece of paper, and watched him put it away in

40

his case, with the same methodical care that he bestowed on everything. My brain was in a whirl. What was this complication of a will? Who had destroyed it? The person who had left the candle grease on the floor? Obviously. But how had anyone gained admission? All the doors had been bolted on the inside.

'Now, my friend,' said Poirot briskly, 'we will go. I should like to ask a few questions of the parlourmaid – Dorcas, her name is, is it not?'

We passed through Alfred Inglethorp's room, and Poirot delayed long enough to make a brief but fairly comprehensive examination of it. We went out through that door, locking both it and that of Mrs Inglethorp's room as before.

I took him down to the boudoir which he had expressed a wish to see, and went myself in search of Dorcas.

When I returned with her, however, the boudoir was empty.

'Poirot,' I cried, 'where are you?'

'I am here, my friend.'

He had stepped outside the french window, and was standing, apparently lost in admiration, before the various shaped flower beds.

'Admirable!' he murmured. 'Admirable! What symmetry! Observe that crescent; and those diamonds – their neatness rejoices the eye. The spacing of the plants, also, is perfect. It has been recently done; is it not so?'

'Yes, I believe they were at it yesterday afternoon. But come in – Dorcas is here.'

'*Eh bien, eh bien!* Do not grudge me a moment's satisfaction of the eye.'

'Yes, but this affair is more important.'

'And how do you know that these fine begonias are not of equal importance?'

I shrugged my shoulders. There was really no arguing with him if he chose to take that line.

'You do not agree? But such things have been. Well, we will come in and interview the brave Dorcas.'

Dorcas was standing in the boudoir, her hands folded in front of her, and her grey hair rose in stiff waves under her white cap. She was the very model and picture of a good old-fashioned servant.

In her attitude towards Poirot, she was inclined to be suspicious, but he soon broke down her defences. He drew forward a chair.

'Pray be seated mademoiselle.'

'Thank you, sir.'

'You have been with your mistress many years, is it not so?'

'Ten years, sir.'

'That is a long time, and very faithful service. You were much attached to her, were you not?'

'She was a very good mistress to me, sir.'

'Then you will not object to answering a few questions. I put them to you with Mr Cavendish's full approval.'

'Oh, certainly, sir.'

'Then I will begin by asking you about the events of yesterday afternoon. Your mistress had a quarrel?'

'Yes, sir. But I don't know that I ought –' Dorcas hesitated.

Poirot looked at her keenly.

'My good Dorcas, it is necessary that I should know every detail of that quarrel as fully as possible. Do not think you are betraying your mistress's secrets. Your mistress lies dead, and it is necessary that we should know all – if we are to avenge her. Nothing can bring her back to life, but we do hope, if there has been foul play, to bring the murderer to justice.'

'Amen to that,' said Dorcas fiercely. 'And, naming no names, there's *one* in this house that none of us could ever abide! And an ill day it was when first *he* darkened the threshold.'

Poirot waited for her indignation to subside, and then, resuming his business-like tone, he asked:

'Now, as to this quarrel? What is the first you heard of it?'

'Well, sir, I happened to be going along the hall outside yesterday –'

'What time was that?'

'I couldn't say exactly, sir, but it wasn't teatime by a long way. Perhaps four o'clock – or it may have been a bit later. Well, sir, as I said, I happened to be passing along, when I heard voices very loud and angry in here. I didn't exactly mean to listen, but – well, there it is. I stopped. The door was shut, but the mistress was speaking very sharp and clear, and I heard what she said quite plainly. "You have lied to me, and deceived me," she said. I didn't hear what Mr Inglethorp replied. He spoke a good bit lower than she did – but she answered: "How dare you? I have kept you and clothed you and fed you! You owe everything to me! And this is how you repay me! By bringing disgrace upon our name!" Again I didn't hear what he said, but she went on: "Nothing that you can say will make any difference. I see my duty clearly. My mind is made up. You need not think that any fear of publicity, or scandal between husband and wife will deter me." Then I thought I heard them coming out, so I went off quickly.'

'You are sure it was Mr Inglethorp's voice you heard?'

'Oh, yes, sir, whose else's could it be?'

'Well, what happened next?'

'Later, I came back to the hall; but it was all quiet. At five o'clock, Mrs Inglethorp rang the bell and told me to bring her a cup of tea – nothing to eat – to the boudoir. She was looking dreadful – so white and upset. "Dorcas," she says, "I've had a great shock." "I'm sorry for that, m'm," I says. "You'll feel better after a nice hot cup of tea, m'm." She had something in her hand. I don't know if it was a letter, or just a piece of paper, but it had writing on it, and she kept staring at it, almost as if she couldn't believe what was written there. She whispered to herself, as though she had forgotten I was there: "These few words – and everything's changed." And then she says to me: "Never trust a man, Dorcas, they're not worth it!" I hurried off, and got her a good strong cup of tea, and she thanked me, and said she'd feel better when she'd drunk it. "I don't know what to do," she says. "Scandal between husband and wife is a dreadful thing, Dorcas. I'd rather hush it up if I could." Mrs Cavendish came in just then, so she didn't say any more.'

'She still had the letter, or whatever it was, in her hand?'

'Yes, sir.'

'What would she be likely to do with it afterwards?'

'Well, I don't know, sir, I expect she would lock it up in that purple case of hers.'

'Is that where she usually kept important papers?'

'Yes, sir. She brought it down with her every morning, and took it up every night.'

'When did she lose the key of it?'

'She missed it yesterday at lunch-time, sir, and told me to look carefully for it. She was very much put out about it.'

'But she had a duplicate key?'

'Oh, yes, sir.'

Dorcas was looking very curiously at him and, to tell the truth, so was I. What was all this about a lost key? Poirot smiled.

'Never mind, Dorcas, it is my business to know things. Is this the key that was lost?' He drew from his pocket the key that he had found in the lock of the despatch-case upstairs.

Dorcas's eyes looked as though they would pop out of her head.

'That's it, sir, right enough. But where did you find it? I looked everywhere for it.'

'Ah, but you see it was not in the same place yesterday as it was to-day. Now, to pass to another subject, had your mistress a dark green dress in her wardrobe?'

Dorcas was rather startled by the unexpected question.

'No, sir.'

'Are you quite sure?'

'Oh, yes, sir.'

'Has anyone else in the house got a green dress?'

Dorcas reflected.

'Miss Cynthia has a green evening dress.'

'Light or dark green?'

'A light green, sir; a sort of chiffon, they call it.'

'Ah, that is not what I want. And nobody else has anything green?'

'No, sir – not that I know of.'

Poirot's face did not betray a trace of whether he was disappointed or otherwise. He merely remarked:

'Good, we will leave that and pass on. Have you any reason to believe that your mistress was likely to take a sleeping powder last night?'

'Not *last* night, sir, I know she didn't.'

'Why do you know so positively?'

'Because the box was empty. She took the last one two days ago, and she didn't have any more made up.'

'You are quite sure of that?'

'Positive, sir.'

'Then that is cleared up? By the way, your mistress didn't ask you to sign any paper yesterday?'

'To sign a paper? No, sir.'

'When Mr Hastings and Mr Lawrence came in yesterday evening, they found your mistress busy writing letters. I suppose you can give me no idea to whom these letters were addressed?'

'I'm afraid I couldn't, sir. I was out in the evening. Perhaps Annie could tell you, though she's a careless girl. Never cleared the coffee-cups away last night. That's what happens when I'm not here to look after things.'

Poirot lifted his hand.

'Since they have been left, Dorcas, leave them a little longer, I pray you. I should like to examine them.'

'Very well, sir.'

'What time did you go out last evening?'

'About six o'clock, sir.'

44

'Thank you, Dorcas, that is all I have to ask you.' He rose and strolled to the window. 'I have been admiring these flower beds. How many gardeners are employed here, by the way?'

'Only three now, sir. Five, we had, before the war, when it was kept as a gentleman's place should be. I wish you could have seen it then, sir. A fair sight it was. But now there's only old Manning, and young William, and a new-fashioned woman gardener in breeches and such-like. Ah, these are dreadful times!'

'The good times will come again, Dorcas. At least, we hope so. Now, will you send Annie to me here?'

'Yes, sir. Thank you, sir.'

'How did you know that Mrs Inglethorp took sleeping powders?' I asked, in lively curiosity, as Dorcas left the room. 'And about the lost key and the duplicate?'

'One thing at a time. As to the sleeping powders, I knew by this.' He suddenly produced a small carboard box, such as chemists use for powders.

'Where did you find it?'

'In the wash-stand drawer in Mrs Inglethorp's bedroom. It was Number Six of my catalogue.'

'But I suppose, as the last powder was taken two days ago, it is not of much importance?'

'Probably not, but do you notice anything that strikes you as peculiar about this box?'

I examined it closely.

'No, I can't say that I do.'

'Look at the label.'

I read the label carefully: One powder to be taken at bedtime, if required. Mrs Inglethorp. 'No, I see nothing unusual.'

'Not the fact that there is no chemist's name?'

'Ah?' I exclaimed. 'To be sure, that is odd!'

'Have you ever known a chemist to send out a box like that, without his printed name?'

'No, I can't say that I have.'

I was becoming quite excited, but Poirot damped my ardour by remarking:

'Yet the explanation is quite simple. So do not intrigue yourself, my friend.'

An audible creaking proclaimed the approach of Annie, so I had no time to reply.

Annie was a fine, strapping girl, and was evidently labouring under intense excitement, mingled with a certain ghoulish enjoyment of the tragedy.

Poirot came to the point at once, with a business-like briskness.

'I sent for you, Annie, because I thought you might be able to tell me something about the letters Mrs Inglethorp wrote last night. How many were there? And can you tell me any of the names and addresses?'

Annie considered.

'There were four letters, sir. One was to Miss Howard, and one was to Mr Wells, the lawyer, and the other two I don't think I remember, sir – oh, yes, one was to Ross's, the caterers in Tadminster. The other one, I don't remember.'

'Think,' urged Poirot.

Annie racked her brains in vain.

'I'm sorry, sir, but it's clean gone. I don't think I can have noticed it.'

'It does not matter,' said Poirot, not betraying any sign of disappointment. 'Now I want to ask you about something else. There is a saucepan in Mrs Inglethorp's room with some cocoa in it. Did she have that every night?'

'Yes, sir, it was put in her room every evening, and she warmed it up in the night – whenever she fancied it.'

'What was it? Plain cocoa?'

'Yes, sir, made with milk, with a teaspoonful of sugar, and two teaspoonfuls of rum in it.'

'Who took it to her room?'

'I did, sir.'

'Always?'

'Yes, sir.'

'At what time?'

'When I went to draw the curtains, as a rule, sir.'

'Did you bring it straight up from the kitchen then?'

'No, sir, you see there's not much room on the gas stove, so cook used to make it early, before putting the vegetables on for supper. Then I used to bring it up, and put it on the table by the swing door, and take it into her room later.'

'The swing door is in the left wing, is it not?'

'Yes, sir.'

'And the table, is it on this side of the door, or on the farther – servants' side?'

'It's this side, sir.'

'What time did you bring it up last night?'

'About quarter-past seven, I should say, sir.'

'And when did you take it into Mrs Inglethorp's room?'

'When I went to shut up, sir. About eight o'clock. Mrs Inglethorp came up to bed before I'd finished.'

'Then, between 7.15 and 8 o'clock, the cocoa was standing on the table in the left wing?'

'Yes, sir.' Annie had been growing redder and redder in the face, and now she blurted out unexpectedly:

'And if there *was* salt in it, sir, it wasn't me. I never took the salt near it.'

'What makes you think there was salt in it?' asked Poirot.

'Seeing it on the tray, sir.'

'You saw some salt on the tray?'

'Yes. Coarse kitchen salt, it looked. I never noticed it when I took the tray up, but when I came to take it into the mistress's room I saw it at once, and I suppose I ought to have taken it down again, and asked Cook to make some fresh. But I was in a hurry, because Dorcas was out, and I thought maybe the cocoa itself was all right, and the salt had only gone on the tray. So I dusted it off with my apron, and took it in.'

I had the utmost difficulty in controlling my excitement. Unknown to herself, Annie had provided us with an important piece of evidence. How she would have gaped if she had realized that her 'coarse kitchen salt' was strychnine, one of the most deadly poisons known to mankind. I marvelled at Poirot's calm. His self-control was astonishing. I awaited his next question with impatience, but it disappointed me.

'When you went into Mrs Inglethorp's room, was the door leading into Miss Cynthia's room bolted?'

'Oh! Yes, sir; it always was. It had never been opened.'

'And the door into Mr Inglethorp's room? Did you notice if that was bolted too?'

Annie hesitated.

'I couldn't rightly say, sir; it was shut but I couldn't say whether it was bolted or not.'

'When you finally left the room, did Mrs Inglethorp bolt the door after you?'

'No, sir, not then, but I expect she did later. She usually did lock it at night. The door into the passage, that is.'

'Did you notice any candle grease on the floor when you did the

47

room yesterday?'

'Candle grease? Oh, no, sir. Mrs Inglethorp didn't have a candle, only a reading-lamp.'

'Then, if there had been a large patch of candle grease on the floor, you think you would have been sure to have seen it?'

'Yes, sir, and I would have taken it out with a piece of blotting-paper and a hot iron.'

Then Poirot repeated the question he had put to Dorcas:

'Did your mistress ever have a green dress?'

'No, sir.'

'Nor a mantle, nor a cape, nor a – how do you call it? – a sports coat?'

'Not green, sir.'

'Nor anyone else in the house?'

Annie reflected.

'No, sir.'

'You are sure of that?'

'Quite sure.'

'*Bien!* That is all I want to know. Thank you very much.'

With a nervous giggle, Annie took herself creakingly out of the room. My pent-up excitement burst forth.

'Poirot,' I cried, 'I congratulate you! This is a great discovery.'

'What is a great discovery?'

'Why, that it was the cocoa and not the coffee that was poisoned. That explains everything! Of course, it did not take effect until the early morning, since the cocoa was only drunk in the middle of the night.'

'So you think that the cocoa – mark well what I say, Hastings, the *cocoa* – contained strychnine?'

'Of course! That salt on the tray, what else could it have been?'

'It might have been salt,' replied Poirot placidly.

I shrugged my shoulders. If he was going to take the matter that way, it was no good arguing with him. The idea crossed my mind, not for the first time, that poor old Poirot was growing old. Privately I thought it lucky that he had associated with him someone of a more receptive type of mind.

Poirot was surveying me with quietly twinkling eyes.

'You are not pleased with me, *mon ami?*'

'My dear Poirot,' I said coldly, 'it is not for me to dictate to you. You have a right to your own opinion, just as I have to mine.'

'A most admirable sentiment,' remarked Poirot, rising briskly to his feet. 'Now I have finished with this room. By the way, whose is the smaller desk in the corner?'

'Mr Inglethorp's.'

'Ah!' he tried the roll top tentatively. 'Locked, But perhaps one of Mrs Inglethorp's keys would open it.' He tried several, twisting and turning them with a practised hand, and finally uttering an ejaculation of satisfaction. '*Voila!* It is not the key, but it will open it at a pinch.' He slid back the roll top, and ran a rapid eye over the neatly filed papers. To my surprise, he did not examine them, merely remarking approvingly as he relocked the desk: 'Decidedly, he is a man of method, this Mr Inglethorp!'

A 'man of method' was, in Poirot's estimation, the highest praise that could be bestowed on any individual.

I felt that my friend was not what he had been as he rambled on disconnectedly:

'There were no stamps in his desk, but there might have been, eh, *mon ami*? There might have been? Yes' – his eyes wandered round the room – 'this boudoir has nothing more to tell us. It did not yield much. Only this.'

He pulled a crumpled envelope out of his pocket, and tossed it over to me. It was rather a curious document. A plain, dirty-looking old envelope with a few words scrawled across it, apparently at random. The following is a facsimile of it:

CHAPTER V

'IT ISN'T STRYCHNINE, IS IT?'

'Where did you find this?' I asked Poirot, in lively curiosity.

'In the waste-paper basket. You recognize the handwriting?'

'Yes, it is Mrs Inglethorp's. But what does it mean?'

Poirot shrugged his shoulders.

'I cannot say – but it is suggestive.'

A wild idea flashed across me. Was it possible that Mrs Inglethorp's mind was deranged? Had she some fantastic idea of demoniacal possession? And, if that were so, was it not also possible that she might have taken her own life?

I was about to expound these theories to Poirot, when his own words distracted me.

'Come,' he said, 'now to examine the coffee-cups!'

'My dear Poirot! What on earth is the good of that, now that we know about the cocoa?'

'Oh, *là là!* That miserable cocoa!' cried Poirot flippantly.

He laughed with apparent enjoyment, raising his arms to heaven in mock despair, in what I could not but consider the worst possible taste.

'And, anyway,' I said, with increasing coldness, 'as Mrs Inglethorp took her coffee upstairs with her, I do not see what you expect to find, unless you consider it likely that we shall discover a packet of strychnine on the coffee tray!'

Poirot was sobered at once.

'Come, come my friend,' he said, slipping his arm through mine. '*Ne vous fâchez pas!* Allow me to interest myself in my coffee cups, and I will respect your cocoa. There! Is it a bargain?'

He was so quaintly humorous that I was forced to laugh; and we went together to the drawing-room, where the coffee cups and tray remained undisturbed as we had left them.

Poirot made me recapitulate the scene of the night before, listening very carefully, and verifying the position of the various cups.

'So Mrs Cavendish stood by the tray – and poured out. Yes. Then she came across to the window where you sat with Mademoiselle Cynthia. Yes. Here are the three cups. And the cup on the mantelpiece, half drunk, that would be Mr Lawrence Cavendish's.

And the one on the tray?'

'John Cavendish's. I saw him put it down there.'

'Good. One, two, three, four, five – but where, then, is the cup of Mr Inglethorp?'

'He does not take coffee.'

'Then all are accounted for. One moment, my friend.'

With infinite care, he took a drop or two from the grounds in each cup, sealing them up in separate test tubes, tasting each in turn as he did so. His physiognomy underwent a curious change. An expression gathered there that I can only describe as half puzzled, and half relieved.

'*Bien!*' he said at last. 'It is evident! I had an idea – but clearly I was mistaken. Yes, altogether I was mistaken. Yet it is strange. But no matter!'

And, with a characteristic shrug, he dismissed whatever it was that was worrying him from his mind. I could have told him from the beginning that this obsession of his over the coffee was bound to end in a blind alley, but I restrained my tongue. After all, though he was old, Poirot had been a great man in his day.

'Breakfast is ready,' said John Cavendish, coming in from the hall, 'You will breakfast with us, Monsieur Poirot?'

Poirot acquiesced. I observed John. Already he was almost restored to his normal self. The shock of the events of the last night had upset him temporarily, but his equable poise soon swung back to the normal. He was a man of very little imagination, in sharp contrast with his brother, who had, perhaps, too much.

Ever since the early hours of the morning, John had been hard at work, sending telegrams – one of the first had gone to Evelyn Howard – writing notices for the papers, and generally occupying himself with the melancholy duties that a death entails.

'May I ask how things are proceeding?' he said. 'Do your investigations point to my mother having died a natural death – or – or must we prepare ourselves for the worst?'

'I think, Mr Cavendish,' said Poirot gravely, 'that you would do well not to buoy yourself up with any false hopes. Can you tell me the views of the other members of the family?'

'My brother Lawrence is convinced that we are making a fuss over nothing. He says that everything points to its being a simple case of heart failure.'

'He does, does he? That is very interesting – very interesting,' murmured Poirot softly. 'And Mrs Cavendish?'

51

A faint cloud passed over John's face.

'I have not the least idea what my wife's views on the subject are.'

The answer brought a momentary stiffness in its train. John broke the rather awkward silence by saying with a slight effort:

'I told you, didn't I, that Mr Inglethorp has returned?'

Poirot bent his head.

'It's an awkward position for all of us. Of course, one has to treat him as usual – but, hang it all, one's gorge does rise at sitting down to eat with a possible murderer!'

Poirot nodded sympathetically.

'I quite understand. It is a very difficult situation for you, Mr Cavendish. I would like to ask you one question. Mr Inglethorp's reason for not returning last night was, I believe, that he had forgotten the latch-key. Is not that so?'

'Yes.'

'I suppose you are quite sure that the latch-key *was* forgotten – that he did not take it after all?'

'I have no idea. I never thought of looking. We always keep it in the hall drawer. I'll go and see if it's there now.'

Poirot held up his hand with a faint smile.

'No, no, Mr Cavendish, it is too late now. I am certain that you will find it. If Mr Inglethorp did take it, he has had ample time to replace it by now.'

'But do you think –'

'I think nothing. If anyone had chanced to look this morning before his return, and seen it there, it would have been a valuable point in his favour. That is all.'

John looked perplexed.

'Do not worry,' said Poirot smoothly. 'I assure you that you need not let it trouble you. Since you are so kind, let us go and have some breakfast.'

Everyone was assembled in the dining-room. Under the circumstances, we were naturally not a cheerful party. The reaction after a shock is always trying, and I think we were suffering from it. Decorum and good breeding naturally enjoined that our demeanour should be much as usual, yet I could not help wondering if this self-control were really a matter of great difficulty. There were no red eyes, no signs of secretly indulged grief. I felt that I was right in my opinion that Dorcas was the person most affected by the personal side of the tragedy.

I pass over Alfred Inglethorp, who acted the bereaved widower in a manner that I felt to be disgusting in its hypocrisy. Did he know that we suspected him, I wondered. Surely he could not be unaware of the fact, conceal it as we would. Did he feel some secret stirring of fear, or was he confident that his crime would go unpunished? Surely the suspicion in the atmosphere must warn him that he was already a marked man.

But did everyone suspect him? What about Mrs Cavendish? I watched her as she sat at the head of the table, graceful, composed, enigmatic. In her soft grey frock, with white ruffles at the wrists falling over her slender hands, she looked very beautiful. When she chose, however, her face could be sphinx-like in its inscrutability. She was very silent, hardly opening her lips, and yet in some queer way I felt that the great strength of her personality was dominating us all.

And little Cynthia? Did she suspect? She looked very tired and ill, I thought. The heaviness and languor of her manner were very marked. I asked her if she were feeling ill, and she answered frankly:

'Yes, I've got the most beastly headache.'

'Have another cup of coffee, mademoiselle?' said Poirot solicitously. 'It will revive you. It is unparalleled for the *mal de tête*.' He jumped up and took her cup.

'No sugar,' said Cynthia, watching him, as he picked up the sugar-tongs.

'No sugar? You abandon it in the war-time, eh?'

'No, I never take it in coffee.'

'*Sacré!*' murmured Poirot to himself, as he brought back the replenished cup.

Only I heard him, and glancing up curiously at the little man I saw that his face was working with suppressed excitement, and his eyes were as green as a cat's. He had heard or seen something that had affected him strongly – but what was it? I do not usually label myself as dense, but I must confess that nothing out of the ordinary had attracted *my* attention.

In another moment, the door opened and Dorcas appeared. 'Mr Wells to see you, sir,' she said to John.

I remembered the name as being that of the lawyer to whom Mrs Inglethorp had written the night before.

John rose immediately.

'Show him into my study.' Then he turned to us. 'My mother's lawyer,' he explained. And in a lower voice: 'He is also Coroner – you understand. Perhaps you would like to come with me?'

We acquiesced and followed him out of the room. John strode on ahead and I took the opportunity of whispering to Poirot:

'There will be an inquest then?'

Poirot nodded absently. He seemed absorbed in thought; so much so that my curiosity was aroused.

'What is it? You are not attending to what I say.'

'It is true, my friend. I am much worried.'

'Why?'

'Because Mademoiselle Cynthia does not take sugar in her coffee.'

'What? You cannot be serious?'

'But I am most serious. Ah, there is something there that I do not understand. My instinct was right.'

'What instinct?'

'The instinct that led me to insist on examining those coffee cups. *Chut!* no more now!'

We followed John into his study, and he closed the door behind us.

Mr Wells was a pleasant man of middle-age, with keen eyes, and the typical lawyer's mouth. John introduced us both, and explained the reason of our presence.

'You will understand, Wells,' he added, 'that this is all strictly private. We are still hoping that there will turn out to be no need for investigation of any kind.'

'Quite so, quite so,' said Mr Wells soothingly. 'I wish we could have spared you the pain and publicity of an inquest, but, of course, it's quite unavoidable in the absence of a doctor's certificate.'

'Yes, I suppose so.'

'Clever man, Bauerstein. Great authority on toxicology, I believe.'

'Indeed,' said John with a certain stiffness in his manner. Then he added rather hesitatingly: 'Shall we have to appear as witnesses – all of us, I mean?'

'You, of course – and ah – er – Mr – er – Inglethorpe.'

A slight pause ensued before the lawyer went on in his soothing manner:

'Any other evidence will be simply confirmatory, a mere matter of form.'

'I see.'

A faint expression of relief swept over John's face. It puzzled me, for I saw no occasion for it.

'If you know of nothing to the contrary,' pursued Mr Wells, 'I had thought of Friday. That will give us plenty of time for the doctor's report. The post-mortem is to take place tonight, I believe?'

'Yes.'

'Then the arrangement will suit you?'

'Perfectly.'

'I need not tell you, my dear Cavendish, how distressed I am at this most tragic affair.'

'Can you give us no help in solving it, monsieur?' interposed Poirot, speaking for the first time since we had entered the room.

'I?'

'Yes, we heard that Mrs Inglethorp wrote to you last night. You should have received the letter this morning.'

'I did, but it contains no information. It is merely a note asking me to call upon her this morning, as she wanted my advice on a matter of great importance.'

'She gave you no hint as to what that matter might be?'

'Unfortunately, no.'

'That is a pity,' said John.

'A great pity,' agreed Poirot gravely.

There was a silence. Poirot remained lost in thought for a few minutes. Finally he turned to the lawyer again.

'Mr Wells, there is one thing I should like to ask you – that is, if it is not against professional etiquette. In the event of Mrs Inglethorp's death, who would inherit her money?'

The lawyer hesitated a moment, and then replied:

'The knowledge will be public property very soon, so if Mr Cavendish does not object –'

'Not at all,' interpolated John.

'I do not see any reason why I should not answer your question. By her last will, dated August of last year, after various unimportant legacies to servants, etc., she gave her entire fortune to her stepson, Mr John Cavendish.'

'Was not that – pardon the question, Mr Cavendish – rather unfair to her other stepson, Mr Lawrence Cavendish?'

'No, I do not think so. You see, under the terms of their father's will, while John inherited the property, Lawrence, at his step-mother's death, would come into a considerable sum of money. Mrs Inglethorp left her money to her elder stepson, knowing that he would have to keep up Styles. It was, to my mind, a very fair and equitable distribution.'

Poirot nodded thoughtfully.

'I see. But I am right in saying, am I not, that by your English law that will was automatically revoked when Mrs

55

Inglethorp remarried?'

Mr Wells bowed his head.

'As I was about to proceed, Monsieur Poirot, that document is now null and void.'

'*Hein!*' said Poirot. He reflected for a moment, and then asked: 'Was Mrs Inglethorp herself aware of that fact?'

'I do not know. She may have been.'

'She was,' said John unexpectedly. 'We were discussing the matter of wills being revoked by marriage only yesterday.'

'Ah! One more question, Mr Wells. You say "her last will". Had Mrs Inglethorp, then, made several former wills?'

'On an average, she made a new will at least once a year,' said Mr Wells imperturbably. 'She was given to changing her mind as to her testamentary dispositions, now benefiting one, now another member of her family.'

'Suppose,' suggested Poirot, 'that, unknown to you, she had made a new will in favour of someone who was not, in any sense of the word, a member of the family – we will say Miss Howard, for instance – would you be surprised?'

'Not in the least.'

'Ah!' Poirot seemed to have exhausted his questions.

I drew close to him, while John and the lawyer were debating the question of going through Mrs Inglethorp's papers.

'Do you think Mrs Inglethorp made a will leaving all her money to Miss Howard?' I asked in a low voice, with some curiosity.

Poirot smiled.

'No.'

'Then why did you ask?'

'Hush!'

John Cavendish had turned to Poirot.

'Will you come with us, Monsieur Poirot? We are going through my mother's papers. Mr Inglethorp is quite willing to leave it entirely to Mr Wells and myself.'

'Which simplifies matters very much,' murmured the lawyer. 'As technically, of course, he was entitled –' He did not finish the sentence.

'We will look through the desk in the boudoir first,' explained John, 'and go up to her bedroom afterwards. She kept her most important papers in a purple despatch-case, which we must look through carefully.'

'Yes,' said the lawyer, 'it is quite possible that there may be a later

56

will than the one in my possession.'

'There *is* a later will.' It was Poirot who spoke.

'What?' John and the lawyer looked at him startled.

'Or rather,' pursued my friend imperturbably, 'there *was* one.'

'What do you mean – there was one? Where is it now?'

'Burnt!'

'Burnt?'

'Yes. See here.' He took out the charred fragment we had found in the grate in Mrs Inglethorp's room, and handed it to the lawyer with a brief explanation of when and where he had found it.

'But possibly this is an old will?'

'I do not think so. In fact I am almost certain that it was made no earlier than yesterday afternoon.'

'What?' 'Impossible!' broke simultaneously from both men.

Poirot turned to John.

'If you will allow me to send for your gardener, I will prove it to you.'

'Oh, of course – but I don't see –'

Poirot raised his hand.

'Do as I ask you. Afterwards you shall question as much as you please.'

'Very well.' He rang the bell.

Dorcas answered it in due course.

'Dorcas, will you tell Manning to come round and speak to me here.'

'Yes, sir.'

Dorcas withdrew.

We waited in a tense silence. Poirot alone seemed perfectly at his ease, and dusted a forgotten corner of the bookcase.

The clumping of hobnailed boots on the gravel outside proclaimed the approach of Manning. John looked questioningly at Poirot. The latter nodded.

'Come inside, Manning,' said John, 'I want to speak to you.'

Manning came slowly and hesitatingly through the french window, and stood as near it as he could. He held his cap in his hands, twisting it very carefully round and round. His back was much bent, though he was probably not as old as he looked, but his eyes were sharp and intelligent, and belied his slow and rather cautious speech.

'Manning,' said John, 'this gentleman will put some questions to you which I want you to answer.'

'Yessir,' mumbled Manning.

57

Poirot stepped forward briskly. Manning's eye swept over him with a faint contempt.

'You were planting a bed of begonias round by the south side of the house yesterday afternoon, were you not, Manning?'

'Yes, sir, me and Willum.'

'And Mrs Inglethorp came to the window and called you, did she not?'

'Yes, sir, she did.'

'Tell me in your own words exactly what happened after that.'

'Well, sir, nothing much. She just told Willum to go on his bicycle down to the village, and bring back a form of will, or such-like – I don't know what exactly – she wrote it down for him.'

'Well?'

'Well, he did, sir.'

'And what happened next?'

'We went on with the begonias, sir.'

'Did not Mrs Inglethorp call you again?'

'Yes, sir, both me and Willum, she called.'

'And then?'

'She made us come right in, and sign our names at the bottom of a long paper – under where she'd signed.'

'Did you see anything of what was written above her signature?' asked Poirot sharply.

'No, sir, there was a bit of blotting paper over that part.'

'And you signed where she told you?'

'Yes, sir, first me and then Willum.'

'What did she do with it afterwards?'

'Well, sir, she slipped it into a long envelope, and put it inside a sort of purple box that was standing on the desk.'

'What time was it when she first called you?'

'About four, I should say, sir.'

'Not earlier? Couldn't it have been about half-past three?'

'No, I shouldn't say so, sir. It would be more likely to be a bit after four – not before it.'

'Thank you, Manning, that will do,' said Poirot pleasantly.

The gardener glanced at his master, who nodded, whereupon Manning lifted a finger to his forehead with a low mumble, and backed cautiously out of the window.

We all looked at each other.

'Good heavens!' murmured John. 'What an extraordinary coincidence.'

'How – a coincidence?'

'That my mother should have made a will on the very day of her death!'

Mr Wells cleared his throat and remarked drily:

'Are you so sure it is a coincidence, Cavendish?'

'What do you mean?'

'Your mother, you tell me, had a violent quarrel with – someone yesterday afternoon –'

'What do you mean?' cried John again. There was a tremor in his voice, and he had gone very pale.

'In consequence of that quarrel, your mother very suddenly and hurriedly makes a new will. The contents of that will we shall never know. She told no one of its provisions. This morning, no doubt, she would have consulted me on the subject – but she had no chance. The will disappears, and she takes its secret with her to her grave. Cavendish, I much fear there is no coincidence there. Monsieur Poirot, I am sure you agree with me that the facts are very suggestive.'

'Suggestive, or not,' interrupted John, 'we are most grateful to Monsieur Poirot for elucidating the matter. But for him, we should never have known of this will. I suppose I may not ask you, monsieur, what first led you to suspect the fact?'

Poirot smiled and answered:

'A scribbled-over old envelope, and a freshly planted bed of begonias.'

John, I think, would have pressed his questions further, but at that moment the loud purr of a motor was audible, and we all turned to the window as it swept past.

'Evie!' cried John. 'Excuse me, Wells.' He went hurriedly out into the hall.

Poirot looked inquiringly at me.

'Miss Howard,' I explained.

'Ah, I am glad she has come. There is a woman with a head and a heart too, Hastings. Though the good God gave her no beauty!'

I followed John's example, and went out into the hall, where Miss Howard was endeavouring to extricate herself from the voluminous mass of veils that enveloped her head. As her eyes fell on me, a sudden pang of guilt shot through me. This was the woman who had warned me so earnestly, and to whose warning I had, alas, paid no heed! How soon, and how contemptuously, I had dismissed it from my mind. Now that she had been proved justified in so tragic a manner, I felt ashamed. She had known Alfred Inglethorp only too well. I wondered whether, if she had remained at Styles, the tragedy would have taken place, or would the man have feared her watchful eyes?

I was relieved when she shook me by the hand, with her well remembered painful grip. The eyes that met mine were sad, but not reproachful; that she had been crying, bitterly, I could tell by the redness of her eyelids, but her manner was unchanged from its old blunt gruffness.

'Started the moment I got the wire. Just come off night duty. Hired car. Quickest way to get here.'

'Have you had anything to eat this morning, Evie?' asked John.

'No.'

'I thought not. Come along, breakfast's not cleared away yet, and they'll make you some fresh tea.' He turned to me. 'Look after her, Hastings, will you? Wells is waiting for me. Oh, here's Monsieur Poirot. He's helping us, you know, Evie.'

Miss Howard shook hands with Poirot, but glanced suspiciously over her shoulder at John.

'What do you mean – helping us?'

'Helping us to investigate.'

'Nothing to investigate. Have they taken him to prison yet?'

'Taken who to prison?'

'Who? Alfred Inglethorp, of course!'

'My dear Evie, do be careful. Lawrence is of the opinion that my mother died from heart seizure.'

'More fool, Lawrence!' retorted Miss Howard. 'Of course Alfred Inglethorp murdered poor Emily – as I always told you he would.'

'My dear Evie, don't shout so. Whatever we may think or suspect, it is better to say as little as possible for the present. The inquest isn't until Friday.'

'Not until fiddlesticks!' The snort Miss Howard gave was truly magnificent. 'You're all off your heads. The man will be out of the country by then. If he's any sense, he won't stay here tamely and wait to be hanged.'

John Cavendish looked at her helplessly.

'I know what it is,' she accused him, 'you've been listening to the doctors. Never should. What do they know? Nothing at all – or just enough to make them dangerous. I ought to know – my own father was a doctor. That little Wilkins is about the greatest fool that even I have ever seen. Heart seizure! Sort of thing he would say. Anyone with any sense could see at once that her husband had poisoned her. I always said he'd murder her in her bed, poor soul. Now he's done it. And all you can do is to murmur silly things about "heart seizure" and "inquest on Friday". You ought to be ashamed of yourself, John Cavendish.'

'What do you want me to do?' asked John, unable to help a faint smile. 'Dash it all, Evie, I can't haul him down to the local police station by the scruff of his neck.'

'Well, you might do something. Find out how he did it. He's a crafty beggar. Dare say he soaked fly papers. Ask Cook if she's missed any.'

It occurred to me very forcibly at that moment that to harbour Miss Howard and Alfred Inglethorp under the same roof, and keep the peace between them, was likely to prove a Herculean task, and I did not envy John. I could see by the expression of his face that he fully appreciated the difficulty of the position. For the moment, he sought refuge in retreat, and left the room precipitately.

Dorcas brought in fresh tea. As she left the room, Poirot came over from the window where he had been standing, and sat down facing Miss Howard.

'Mademoiselle,' he said gravely, 'I want to ask you something.'

'Ask away,' said the lady, eyeing him with some disfavour.

'I want to be able to count upon your help.'

'I'll help you to hang Alfred with pleasure,' she replied gruffly. 'Hanging's too good for him. Ought to be drawn and quartered, like in good old times.'

'We are at one then,' said Poirot, 'for I, too, want to hang the criminal.'

'Alfred Inglethorp?'

'Him, or another.'

'No question of another. Poor Emily was never murdered until *he* came along. I don't say she wasn't surrounded by sharks – she was. But it was only her purse they were after. Her life was safe enough. But along comes Mr Alfred Inglethorp – and within two months – hey presto!'

'Believe me, Miss Howard,' said Poirot very earnestly, 'if Mr Inglethorp is the man, he shall not escape me. On my honour, I will hang him as high as Haman!'

'That's better,' said Miss Howard more enthusiastically.

'But I must ask you to trust me. Now your help may be very valuable to me. I will tell you why. Because, in all this house of mourning, yours are the only eyes that have wept.'

Miss Howard blinked, and a new note crept into the gruffness of her voice.

'If you mean that I was fond of her – yes, I was. You know, Emily was a selfish old woman in her way. She was very generous, but she always wanted a return. She never let people forget what she had done for them – and, that way, she missed love. Don't think she ever realized it, though, or felt the lack of it. Hope not, anyway. I was on a different footing. I took my stand from the first. "So many pounds a year I'm worth to you. Well and good. But not a penny piece besides – not a pair of gloves, nor a theatre ticket." She didn't understand – was very offended sometimes. Said I was foolishly proud. It wasn't that – but I couldn't explain. Anyway, I kept my self-respect. And so, out of the whole bunch, I was the only one who could allow myself to be fond of her. I watched over her. I guarded her from the lot of them. And then a glib-tongued scoundrel comes along, and pooh! all my years of devotion go for nothing.'

Poirot nodded sympathetically.

'I understand, mademoiselle, I understand all you feel. It is most natural. You think that we are lukewarm – that we lack fire and energy – but trust me, it is not so.'

John stuck his head in at this juncture, and invited us both to come up to Mrs Inglethorp's room, as he and Mr Wells had finished looking through the desk in the boudoir.

As we went up the stairs, John looked back to the dining-room, and lowered his voice confidentially:

'Look here, what's going to happen when these two meet?'

I shook my head helplessly.

'I've told Mary to keep them apart if she can.'

'Will she be able to do so?'

'The Lord only knows. There's one thing, Inglethorp himself won't be too keen on meeting her.'

'You've got the keys still, haven't you, Poirot?' I asked, as we reached the door of the locked room.

Taking the keys from Poirot, John unlocked it, and we all passed in. The lawyer went straight to the desk, and John followed him.

'My mother kept most of her important papers in this despatch-case, I believe,' he said.

Poirot drew out the small bunch of keys.

'Permit me. I locked it, out of precaution, this morning.'

'But it's not locked now.'

'Impossible!'

'See.' And John lifted the lid as he spoke.

'*Mille tonnerres!*' cried Poirot, dumbfounded. 'And I – who have both the keys in my pocket!' He flung himself upon the case. Suddenly he stiffened. '*En voilà une affaire!* This lock has been forced!'

'What?'

Poirot laid down the case again.

'But who forced it? Why should they? When? But the door was locked!' These exclamations burst from us disjointedly.

Poirot answered them categorically – almost mechanically.

'Who? That is the question. Why? Ah, if I only knew. When? Since I was here an hour ago. As to the door being locked, it is a very ordinary lock. Probably any other of the doorkeys in this passage would fit it.'

We stared at one another blankly. Poirot had walked over to the mantelpiece. He was outwardly calm, but I noticed his hands, which from long force of habit were mechanically straightening the spill vases on the mantelpiece, were shaking violently.

'See here, it was like this,' he said at last. 'There was something in that case – some piece of evidence, slight in itself perhaps, but still enough of a clue to connect the murderer with the crime. It was vital to him that it should be destroyed before it was discovered and its significance appreciated. Therefore, he took the risk, the great risk, of coming in here. Finding the case locked, he was obliged to force it, thus betraying his presence. For him to take that risk, it must have been something of great importance.'

'But what was it?'

'Ah!' cried Poirot, with a gesture of anger. 'That, I do not know! A document of some kind, without doubt, possibly the scrap of paper Dorcas saw in her hand yesterday afternoon. And I' – his anger burst forth freely – 'miserable animal that I am! I guessed nothing! I have behaved like an imbecile! I should never have left that case here. I should have carried it away with me. Ah, triple pig! And now it is gone. It is destroyed – but is it destroyed? Is there not yet a chance – we must leave no stone unturned –'

He rushed like a madman from the room, and I followed him as soon as I had sufficiently recovered my wits. But, by the time I had reached the top of the stairs, he was out of sight.

Mary Cavendish was standing where the staircase branched, staring down into the hall in the direction in which he had disappeared.

'What has happened to your extraordinary little friend, Mr Hastings? He has just rushed past me like a mad bull.'

'He's rather upset about something,' I remarked feebly. I really did not know how much Poirot would wish me to disclose. As I saw a faint smile gather on Mrs Cavendish's expressive mouth, I endeavoured to try and turn the conversation by saying: 'They haven't met yet, have they?'

'Who?'

'Mr Inglethorp and Miss Howard.'

She looked at me in rather a disconcerting manner.

'Do you think it would be such a disaster if they did meet?'

'Well, don't you?' I said, rather taken aback.

'No.' She was smiling in her quiet way. 'I should like to see a good flare up. It would clear the air. At present we are all thinking so much, and saying so little.'

'John doesn't think so,' I remarked. 'He's anxious to keep them apart.'

'Oh, John!'

Something in her tone fired me, and I blurted out:

'Old John's an awfully good sort.'

She studied me curiously for a minute or two, and then said, to my great surprise:

'You are loyal to your friend. I like you for that.'

'Aren't you my friend, too?'

'I am a very bad friend.'

'Why do you say that?'

'Because it is true. I am charming to my friends one day, and forget all about them the next.'

I don't know what impelled me, but I was nettled, and I said foolishly and not in the best of taste:

'Yet you seem to be invariably charming to Dr Bauerstein!'

Instantly I regretted my words. Her face stiffened. I had the impression of a steel curtain coming down and blotting out the real woman. Without a word, she turned and went swiftly up the stairs, whilst I stood like an idiot gaping after her.

I was recalled to other matters by a frightful row going on below. I could hear Poirot shouting and expounding. I was vexed to think that my diplomacy had been in vain. The little man appeared to be taking the whole house into his confidence, a proceeding of which I, for one, doubted the wisdom. Once again I could not help regretting that my friend was so prone to lose his head in moments of excitement. I stepped briskly down the stairs. The sight of me calmed Poirot almost immediately. I drew him aside.

'My dear fellow,' I said, 'is this wise? Surely you don't want the whole house to know of this occurrence? You are actually playing into the criminal's hands.'

'You think so, Hastings?'

'I am sure of it.'

'Well, well, my friend, I will be guided by you.'

'Good. Although, unfortunately, it is a little too late now.'

'True.'

He looked so crestfallen and abashed that I felt quite sorry, though I still thought my rebuke a just and wise one.

'Well,' he said at last, 'let us go, *mon ami*.'

'You have finished here?'

'For the moment, yes. You will walk back with me to the village?'

'Willingly.'

He picked up his little suit-case, and we went out through the open window in the drawing-room. Cynthia Murdoch was just coming in, and Poirot stood aside to let her pass.

'Excuse me, mademoiselle, one minute.'

'Yes?' she turned inquiringly.

'Did you ever make up Mrs Inglethorp's medicines?'

A slight flush rose in her face, as she answered rather constrainedly:

'No.'

'Only her powders?'

The flush deepened as Cynthia replied:

'Oh, yes, I did make up some sleeping powders for her once.'

'These?'

Poirot produced the empty box which had contained powders. She nodded.

'Can you tell me what they were? Sulphonal? Veronal?'

'No, they were bromide powders.'

'Ah! Thank you, mademoiselle; good morning.'

As we walked briskly away from the house, I glanced at him more than once. I had often before noticed that, if anything excited him, his eyes turned green like a cat's. They were shining like emeralds now.

'My friend,' he broke out at last, 'I have a little idea, a very strange, and probably utterly impossible idea. And yet – it fits in.'

65

I shrugged my shoulders. I privately thought that Poirot was rather too much given to these fantastic ideas. In this case, surely, the truth was only too plain and apparent.

'So that is the explanation of the blank label on the box,' I remarked. 'Very simple, as you said, I really wonder that I did not think of it myself.'

Poirot did not appear to be listening to me.

'They have made one more discovery, *là-bas*,' he observed, jerking his thumb over his shoulder in the direction of Styles. 'Mr Wells told me as we were going upstairs.'

'What was it?'

'Locked up in the desk in the boudoir, they found a will of Mrs Inglethorp's, dated before her marriage, leaving her fortune to Alfred Inglethorp. It must have been made just at the time they were engaged. It came quite as a surprise to Wells – and to John Cavendish also. It was written on one of those printed will forms, and witnessed by two of the servants – not Dorcas.'

'Did Mr Inglethorp know of it?'

'He says not.'

'One might take that with a grain of salt,' I remarked sceptically. 'All these wills are very confusing. Tell me, how did those scribbled words on the envelope help you to discover that a will was made yesterday afternoon?'

Poirot smiled.

'*Mon ami*, have you ever, when writing a letter, been arrested by the fact that you did not know how to spell a certain word?'

'Yes, often. I suppose everyone has.'

'Exactly. And have you not, in such a case, tried the word once or twice on the edge of the blotting-paper, or a spare scrap of paper, to see if it looked right? Well, that is what Mrs Inglethorp did. You will notice that the word "possessed" is spelt first with one "s" and subsequently with two – correctly. To make sure, she had further tried it in a sentence, thus: "I am possessed." Now, what did that tell me? It told me that Mrs Inglethorp had been writing the word "possessed" that afternoon, and, having the fragment of paper found in the grate fresh in my mind, the possibility of a will – a document almost certain to contain that word – occurred to me at once. This possibility was confirmed by a further circumstance. In the general confusion, the boudoir had not been swept that morning, and near the desk were several traces of brown mould and earth. The weather had been perfectly fine for some days, and no ordinary boots would

66

have left such a heavy deposit.

'I strolled to the window, and saw at once that the begonia beds had been newly planted. The mould in the beds was exactly similar to that on the floor of the boudoir, and also I learnt from you that they *had* been planted yesterday afternoon. I was now sure that one, or possibly both of the gardeners – for there were two sets of footprints in the bed – had entered the boudoir, for if Mrs Inglethorp had merely wished to speak to them she would in all probability have stood at the window, and they would not have come into the room at all. I was now quite convinced that she had made a fresh will, and had called the two gardeners in to witness her signature. Events proved that I was right in my supposition.'

'That was very ingenious,' I could not help admitting. 'I must confess that the conclusions I drew from those few scribbled words were quite erroneous.'

He smiled.

'You gave too much rein to your imagination. Imagination is a good servant, and a bad master. The simplest explanation is always the most likely.'

'Another point – how did you know that the key of the despatch-case had been lost?'

'I did not know it. It was a guess that turned out to be correct. You observed that it had a piece of twisted wire through the handle. That suggested to me at once that it had possibly been wrenched off a flimsy key-ring. Now, if it had been lost and recovered, Mrs Inglethorp would at once have replaced it on her bunch; but on her bunch I found what was obviously the duplicate key, very new and bright, which led me to the hypothesis that somebody else had inserted the original key in the lock of the despatch-case.'

'Yes,' I said, 'Alfred Inglethorp, without a doubt.'

Poirot looked at me curiously.

'You are very sure of his guilt?'

'Well, naturally. Every fresh circumstance seems to establish it more clearly.'

'On the contrary,' said Poirot quietly, 'there are several points in his favour.'

'Oh, come now!'

'Yes.'

'I see only one.'

'And that?'

'That he was not in the house last night.'

' "Bad shot!" as you English say! You have chosen the one point that to my mind tells against him.'

'How is that?'

'Because if Mr Inglethorp knew that his wife would be poisoned last night, he would certainly have arranged to be away from the house. His excuse was an obviously trumped up one. That leaves us two possibilities: either he knew what was going to happen or he had a reason of his own for his absence.'

'And that reason?' I asked sceptically.

Poirot shrugged his shoulders.

'How should I know? Discreditable, without doubt. This Mr Inglethorp, I should say, is somewhat of a scoundrel – but that does not of necessity make him a murderer.'

I shook my head, unconvinced.

'We do not agree, eh?' said Poirot. 'Well, let us leave it. Time will show which of us is right. Now let us turn to other aspects of the case. What do you make of the fact that all the doors of the bedroom were bolted on the inside?'

'Well –' I considered. 'One must look at it logically.'

'True.'

'I should put it this way. The doors *were* bolted – our own eyes have told us that – yet the presence of the candle grease on the floor, and the destruction of the will, prove that during the night someone entered the room. You agree so far?'

'Perfectly. Put with admirable clearness. Proceed.'

'Well,' I said, encouraged, 'as the person who entered did not do so by the window, nor by miraculous means, it follows that the door must have been opened from inside by Mrs Inglethorp herself. That strengthens the conviction that the person in question was her husband. She would naturally open the door to her own husband.'

Poirot shook his head.

'Why should she? She had bolted the door leading into his room – a most unusual proceeding on her part – she had had a most violent quarrel with him that very afternoon. No, he was the last person she would admit.'

'But you agree with me that the door must have been opened by Mrs Inglethorp herself?'

'There is another possibility. She may have forgotten to bolt the door into the passage when she went up to bed, and have got up later, towards morning, and bolted it then.'

'Poirot, is that seriously your opinion?'

68

'No, I do not say it is so, but it might be. Now, turn to another feature, what do you make of the scrap of conversation you overheard between Mrs Cavendish and her mother-in-law?'

'I had forgotten that,' I said thoughtfully. 'That is as enigmatical as ever. It seems incredible that a woman like Mrs Cavendish, proud and reticent to the last degree, should interfere so violently in what was certainly not her affair.'

'Precisely. It was an astonishing thing for a woman of her breeding to do.'

'It is certainly curious,' I agreed. 'Still, it is unimportant, and need not be taken into account.'

A groan burst from Poirot.

'What have I always told you? Everything must be taken into account. If the fact will not fit the theory – let the theory go.'

'Well, we shall see,' I said, nettled.

'Yes, we shall see.'

We had reached Leastways Cottage, and Poirot ushered me upstairs to his own room. He offered me one of the tiny Russian cigarettes he himself occasionally smoked. I was amused to notice that he stowed away the used matches most carefully in a little china pot. My momentary annoyance vanished.

Poirot had placed our two chairs in front of the open window which commanded a view of the village street. The fresh air blew in warm and pleasant. It was going to be a hot day.

Suddenly my attention was arrested by a weedy-looking young man rushing down the street at a great pace. It was the expression on his face that was extraordinary – a curious mingling of terror and agitation.

'Look, Poirot!' I said.

He leant forward. '*Tiens!*' he said. 'It is Mr Mace, from the chemist's shop. He is coming here.'

The young man came to a halt before Leastways Cottage, and, after hesitating a moment, pounded vigorously at the door.

'A little minute,' cried Poirot from the window. 'I come.'

Motioning to me to follow him, he ran swiftly down the stairs and opened the door. Mr Mace began at once.

'Oh, Mr Poirot, I'm sorry for the inconvenience, but I heard that you'd just come back from the Hall?'

'Yes, we have.'

The young man moistened his dry lips. His face was working curiously.

69

'It's all over the village about old Mrs Inglethorp dying so suddenly. They do say –' he lowered his voice cautiously – 'that it's poison?'

Poirot's face remained quite impassive.

'Only the doctors can tell us that, Mr Mace.'

'Yes, exactly – of course –' The young man hesitated, and then his agitation was too much for him. He clutched Poirot by the arm, and sank his voice to a whisper: 'Just tell me this, Mr Poirot, it isn't – it isn't strychnine, is it?'

I hardly heard what Poirot replied. Something evidently of a non-committal nature. The young man departed, and as he closed the door Poirot's eyes met mine.

'Yes,' he said, nodding gravely. 'He will have evidence to give at the inquest.'

We went slowly upstairs again. I was opening my lips, when Poirot stopped me with a gesture of his hand.

'Not now, not now, *mon ami*. I have need of reflection. My mind is in some disorder – which is not well.'

For about ten minutes he sat in dead silence, perfectly still, except for several expressive motions of his eyebrows, and all the time his eyes grew steadily greener. At last he heaved a deep sigh.

'It is well. The bad moment has passed. Now all is arranged and classified. One must never permit confusion. The case is not clear yet – no. For it is of the most complicated! It puzzles *me*. Me, Hercule Poirot! There are two facts of significance.'

'And what are they?'

'The first is the state of the weather yesterday. That is very important.'

'But it was a glorious day!' I interrupted. 'Poirot, you're pulling my leg!'

'Not at all. The thermometer registered 80° in the shade. Do not forget that, my friend. It is the key to the whole riddle!'

'And the second point?' I asked.

'The important fact that Monsieur Inglethorp wears very peculiar clothes, has a black beard, and uses glasses.'

'Poirot, I cannot believe you are serious.'

'I am absolutely serious, my friend.'

'But this is childish!'

'No, it is very momentous.'

'And supposing the Coroner's jury returns a verdict of Wilful Murder against Alfred Inglethorp. What becomes of your theories, then?'

'They would not be shaken because twelve stupid men had happened to make a mistake! But that will not occur. For one thing, a country jury is not anxious to take responsibility upon itself, and Mr Inglethorp stands practically in the position of local squire. Also,' he added placidly, '*I* should not allow it!'

'*You* would not allow it?'

'No.'

I looked at the extraordinary little man, divided between annoyance and amusement. He was so tremendously sure of himself. As though he read my thoughts, he nodded gently.

'Oh, yes, *mon ami*, I would do what I say.' He got up and laid his hand on my shoulder. His physiognomy underwent a complete change. Tears came into his eyes. 'In all this, you see, I think of the poor Mrs Inglethorp who is dead. She was not extravagantly loved – no. But she was very good to us Belgians – I owe her a debt.'

I endeavoured to interrupt, but Poirot swept on.

'Let me tell you this, Hastings. She would never forgive me if I let Alfred Inglethorp, her husband, be arrested *now* – when a word from me could save him!'

CHAPTER VI

THE INQUEST

In the interval before the inquest, Poirot was unfailing in his activity. Twice he closeted with Mr Wells. He also took long walks into the country. I rather resented his not taking me into his confidence, the more so as I could not in the least guess what he was driving at.

It occurred to me that he might have been making inquiries at Raikes's farm; so, finding him out when I called at Leastways Cottage on Wednesday evening, I walked over there by the fields, hoping to meet him. But there was no sign of him, and I hesitated to go right up to the farm itself. As I walked away, I met an aged rustic, who leered at me cunningly.

'You'm from the Hall, bain't you?' he asked.

'Yes. I'm looking for a friend of mine whom I thought might have walked this way.'

'A little chap? As waves his hands when he talks? One of them Belgies from the village?'

'Yes,' I said eagerly. 'He has been here, then?'

'Oh, ay, he's been here, right enough. More'n once too. Friend of yours, is he? Ah, you gentlemen from the Hall – you'm a pretty lot!' And he leered more jocosely than ever.

'Why, do the gentlemen from the Hall come here often?' I asked, as carelessly as I could.

He winked at me knowingly.

'*One* does, mister. Naming no names, mind. And a very liberal gentleman too! Oh, thank you, sir, I'm sure.'

I walked on sharply. Evelyn Howard had been right then, and I experienced a sharp twinge of disgust, as I thought of Alfred Inglethorp's liberality with another woman's money. Had that piquant gipsy face been at the bottom of the crime, or was it the base mainspring of money? Probably a judicious mixture of both.

On one point, Poirot seemed to have a curious obsession. He once or twice observed to me that he thought Dorcas must have made an error fixing the time of the quarrel. He suggested to her repeatedly that it was 4.30, and not 4 o'clock when she heard the voices.

But Dorcas was unshaken. Quite an hour, or even more, had elapsed between the time when she had heard the voices and 5 o'clock, when she had taken tea to her mistress.

The inquest was held on Friday at the Stylites Arms in the village. Poirot and I sat together, not being required to give evidence.

The preliminaries were gone through. The jury viewed the body, and John Cavendish gave evidence of identification.

Further questioned, he described his awakening in the early hours of the morning, and the circumstances of his mother's death.

The medical evidence was next taken. There was a breathless hush, and every eye was fixed on the famous London specialist, who was known to be one of the greatest authorities of the day on the subject of toxicology.

In a few brief words, he summed up the result of the post-mortem. Shorn of its medical phraseology and technicalities, it amounted to the fact that Mrs Inglethorp had met her death as a result of strychnine poisoning. Judging from the quantity recovered, she must have taken not less than three-quarters of a grain of strychnine, but probably one grain or slightly over.

'Is it possible that she could have swallowed the poison by accident?' asked the Coroner.

'I should consider it very unlikely. Strychnine is not used for domestic purposes, as some poisons are, and there are restrictions placed on its sale.'

'Does anything in your examination lead you to determine how the poison was administered?'

'No.'

'You arrived at Styles before Dr Wilkins, I believe?'

'That is so. The motor met me just outside the lodge gates, and I hurried there as fast as I could.'

'Will you relate to us exactly what happened next?'

'I entered Mrs Inglethorp's room. She was at that moment in a typical tetanic convulsion. She turned towards me, and gasped out: "Alfred – Alfred –"'

'Could the strychnine have been administered in Mrs Inglethorp's after-dinner coffee which was taken to her by her husband?'

'Possibly, but strychnine is a fairly rapid drug in its action. The symptoms appear from one to two hours after it has been swallowed. It is retarded under certain conditions, none of which, however, appear to have been present in this case. I presume Mrs Inglethorp took the coffee after dinner about eight o'clock, whereas the symptoms did not manifest themselves until the early hours of the morning, which, on the face of it, points to the drug having been taken much later in the evening.'

73

'Mrs Inglethorp was in the habit of drinking a cup of cocoa in the middle of the night. Could the strychnine have been administered in that?'

'No, I myself took a sample of the cocoa remaining in the saucepan and had it analysed. There was no strychnine present.'

I heard Poirot chuckle softly beside me.

'How did you know?' I whispered.

'Listen.'

'I should say' – the doctor was continuing – 'that I would have been considerably surprised at any other result.'

'Why?'

'Simply because strychine has an unusually bitter taste. It can be detected in a solution of 1 in 70,000, and can only be disguised by some strongly flavoured substance. Cocoa would be quite powerless to mask it.'

One of the jury wanted to know if the same objection applied to coffee.

'No. Coffee has a bitter taste of its own which would probably cover the taste of the strychnine.'

'Then you consider it more likely that the drug was administered in the coffee, but that for some unknown reason its action was delayed?'

'Yes, but, the cup being completely smashed, there is no possibility of analysing its contents.'

This concluded Dr Bauerstein's evidence. Dr Wilkins corroborated it on all points. Sounded as to the possibility of suicide, he repudiated it utterly. The deceased, he said, suffered from a weak heart, but otherwise enjoyed perfect health, and was of a cheerful and well-balanced disposition. She would be one of the last people to take her own life.

Lawrence Cavendish was next called. His evidence was quite unimportant, being a mere repetition of that of his brother. Just as he was about to step down, he paused, and said hesitatingly:

'I should like to make a suggestion if I may?'

He glanced deprecatingly at the Coroner, who replied briskly:

'Certainly, Mr Cavendish, we are here to arrive at the truth of this matter, and welcome anything that may lead to further elucidation.'

'It is just an idea of mine,' explained Lawrence. 'Of course I may be quite wrong, but it still seems to me that my mother's death might be accounted for by natural means.'

'How do you make that out, Mr Cavendish?'

'My mother, at the time of her death, and for some time before it, was taking a tonic containing strychnine.'

'Ah!' said the Coroner.

The jury looked up, interested.

'I believe,' continued Lawrence, 'that there have been cases where the cumulative effect of the drug, administered for some time, has ended by causing death. Also, is it not possible that she may have taken an overdose of her medicine by accident?'

'This is the first we have heard of the deceased taking strychnine at the time of her death. We are much obliged to you, Mr Cavendish.'

Dr Wilkins was recalled and ridiculed the idea.

'What Mr Cavendish suggests is quite impossible. Any doctor would tell you the same. Strychnine is, in a certain sense, a cumulative poison, but it would be quite impossible for it to result in sudden death in this way. There would have to be a long period of chronic symptoms which would at once have attracted my attention. The whole thing is absurd.'

'And the second suggestion? That Mrs Inglethorp may have inadvertently taken an overdose?'

'Three, or even four doses, would not have resulted in death. Mrs Inglethorp always had an extra large amount of medicine made up at a time, as she dealt with Coot's, the Cash Chemists in Tadminster. She would have had to take very nearly the whole bottle to account for the amount of strychnine found at the post-mortem.'

'Then you consider that we may dismiss the tonic as not being in any way instrumental in causing her death?'

'Certainly. The supposition is ridiculous.'

The same juryman who had interrupted before here suggested that the chemist who made up the medicine might have committed an error.

'That, of course, is always possible,' replied the doctor.

But Dorcas, who was the next witness called, dispelled even that possibility. The medicine had not been newly made up. On the contrary, Mrs Inglethorp had taken the last dose on the day of her death.

So the question of the tonic was finally abandoned, and the Coroner proceeded with his task. Having elicited from Dorcas how she had been awakened by the violent ringing of her mistress's bell, and had subsequently roused the household, he passed to the subject of the quarrel on the preceding afternoon.

Dorcas's evidence on this point was substantially what Poirot and I had already heard, so I will not repeat it here.

The next witness was Mary Cavendish. She stood very upright, and spoke in a low, clear, and perfectly composed voice. In answer to the Coroner's question, she told how, her alarm clock having aroused her at 4.30 as usual, she was dressing, when she was startled by the sound of something heavy falling.

'That would have been the table by the bed?' commented the Coroner.

'I opened my door,' continued Mary, 'and listened. In a few minutes a bell rang violently, Dorcas came running down and woke my husband, and we all went to my mother-in-law's room, but it was locked –'

The Coroner interrupted her.

'I really do not think we need trouble you further on that point. We know all that can be known of the subsequent happenings. But I should be obliged if you would tell us all you overheard of the quarrel the day before.'

'I?'

There was a faint insolence in her voice. She raised her hand and adjusted the ruffle of lace at her neck, turning her head a little as she did so. And quite spontaneously the thought flashed across my mind: 'She is gaining time!'

'Yes. I understand,' continued the Coroner deliberately, 'that you were sitting reading on the bench just outside the long window of the boudoir. That is so, is it not?'

This was news to me and glancing sideways at Poirot, I fancied that it was news to him as well.

There was the faintest pause, the mere hesitation of a moment, before she answered:

'Yes, that is so.'

'And the boudoir window was open, was it not?'

Surely her face grew a little paler as she answered:

'Yes.'

'Then you cannot have failed to hear the voices inside, especially as they were raised in anger. In fact, they would be more audible where you were than in the hall.'

'Possibly.'

'Will you repeat to us what you overheard of the quarrel?'

'I really do not remember hearing anything.'

'Do you mean to say you did not hear voices?'

'Oh, yes, I heard the voices, but I did not hear what they said.' A faint spot of colour came into her cheek. 'I am not in the habit of listening to private conversations.'

The Coroner persisted.

'And you remember nothing at all? *Nothing*, Mrs Cavendish? Not one stray word or phrase to make you realize that it *was* a private conversation?'

She paused, and seemed to reflect, still outwardly as calm as ever.

'Yes; I remember, Mrs Inglethorp said something – I do not remember exactly what – about causing scandal between husband and wife.'

'Ah!' The Coroner leant back satisfied. 'That corresponds with what Dorcas heard. But excuse me, Mrs Cavendish, although you realized it was a private conversation, you did not move away? You remained where you were?'

I caught the momentary gleam of her tawny eyes as she raised them. I felt certain that at that moment she would willingly have torn the little lawyer, with his insinuations, into pieces, but she replied quietly enough:

'No. I was comfortable where I was. I fixed my mind on my book.'

'And that is all you can tell us?'

'That is all.'

The examination was over, though I doubted if the Coroner was entirely satisfied with it. I think he suspected that Mary Cavendish could tell more if she chose.

Amy Hill, shop assistant, was next called, and deposed to having sold a will form on the afternoon of the 17th to William Earl, under-gardener at Styles.

William Earl and Manning succeeded her, and testified to witnessing a document. Manning fixed the time at about 4.30, William was of the opinion that it was rather earlier.

Cynthia Murdoch came next. She had, however, little to tell. She had known nothing of the tragedy, until awakened by Mrs Cavendish.

'You did not hear the table fall?'

'No. I was fast asleep.'

The Coroner smiled.

'A good conscience makes a sound sleeper,' he observed. 'Thank you, Miss Murdoch, that is all.'

'Miss Howard.'

Miss Howard produced the letter written to her by Mrs Inglethorp on the evening of the 17th. Poirot and I had, of course, already seen it. It added nothing to our knowledge of the tragedy. The following is a facsimile:

July 17th Styles Court
Essex

My dear Evelyn

Can we not bury the hatchet? I have found it hard to forgive the things you said against my dear husband but I am an old woman very fond of you

Yours affectionately

Emily Inglethorpe

It was handed to the jury who scrutinized it attentively.

'I fear it does not help us much,' said the Coroner, with a sigh. 'There is no mention of any of the events of that afternoon.'

'Plain as a pikestaff to me,' said Miss Howard shortly. 'It shows clearly enough that my poor old friend had just found out she'd been made a fool of!'

'It says nothing of the kind in the letter,' the Coroner pointed out.

'No, because Emily never could bear to put herself in the wrong. But *I* know her. She wanted me back. But she wasn't going to own that I'd been right. She went round about. Most people do. Don't believe in it myself.'

Mr Wells smiled faintly. So, I noticed, did several of the jury. Miss Howard was obviously quite a public character.

'Anyway, all this tomfoolery is a great waste of time,' continued the lady, glancing up and down the jury disparagingly. 'Talk – talk – talk! When all the time we know perfectly well –'

The Coroner interrupted her in an agony of apprehension:

'Thank you, Miss Howard, that is all.'

I fancy he breathed a sigh of relief when she complied.

Then came the sensation of the day. The Coroner called Albert Mace, chemist's assistant.

It was our agitated young man of the pale face. In answer to the Coroner's questions, he explained that he was a qualified pharmacist, but had only recently come to this particular shop, as the assistant formerly there had just been called up for the army.

These preliminaries completed, the Coroner proceeded to business.

'Mr Mace, have you lately sold strychnine to any unauthorized person?'

'Yes, sir.'

'When was this?'

'Last Monday night.'

'Monday? Not Tuesday?'

'No, sir, Monday, the 16th.'

'Will you tell us to whom you sold it?'

You could have heard a pin drop.

'Yes, sir. It was Mr Inglethorp.'

Every eye turned simultaneously to where Alfred Inglethorp was sitting, impassive and wooden. He started slightly, as the damning words fell from the young man's lips. I half thought he was going to rise from his chair, but he remained seated, although a remarkably well acted expression of astonishment rose on his face.

'You are sure of what you say?' asked the Coroner sternly.

'Quite sure, sir.'

'Are you in the habit of selling strychnine indiscriminately over the counter?'

79

The wretched young man wilted visibly under the Coroner's frown.

'Oh, no, sir – of course not. But, seeing it was Mr Inglethorp of the Hall, I thought there was no harm in it. He said it was to poison a dog.'

Inwardly I sympathized. It was only human nature to endeavour to please 'The Hall' – especially when it might result in custom being transferred from Coot's to the local establishment.

'Is it not customary for anyone purchasing poison to sign a book?'

'Yes, sir, Mr Inglethorp did so.'

'Have you got the book here?'

'Yes, sir.'

It was produced; and, with a few words of stern censure, the Coroner dismissed the wretched Mr Mace.

Then, amidst a breathless silence, Alfred Inglethorp was called. Did he realize, I wondered, how closely the halter was being drawn around his neck?

The Coroner went straight to the point.

'On Monday evening last, did you purchase strychnine for the purpose of poisoning a dog?'

Inglethorp replied with perfect calmness:

'No, I did not. There is no dog at Styles, except an outdoor sheepdog, which is in perfect health.'

'You deny absolutely having purchased strychnine from Albert Mace on Monday last?'

'I do.'

'Do you also deny *this*?'

The Coroner handed him the register in which his signature was inscribed.

'Certainly I do. The handwriting is quite different from mine. I will show you.'

He took an old envelope out of his pocket, and wrote his name on it, handing it to the jury. It was certainly utterly dissimilar.

'Then what is your explanation of Mr Mace's statement?'

Alfred Inglethorp replied imperturbably:

'Mr Mace must have been mistaken.'

The Coroner hesitated for a moment, and then said:

'Mr Inglethorp, as a mere matter of form, would you mind telling us where you were on the evening of Monday, July 16th?'

'Really – I cannot remember.'

'That is absurd, Mr Inglethorp,' said the Coroner sharply.

'Think again.'

Inglethorp shook his head.

'I cannot tell you. I have an idea that I was out walking.'

'In what direction?'

'I really can't remember.'

The Coroner's face grew graver.

'Were you in company with anyone?'

'No.'

'Did you meet anyone on your walk?'

'No.'

'That is a pity,' said the Coroner dryly. 'I am to take it then that you decline to say where you were at the time that Mr Mace positively recognized you as entering the shop to purchase strychnine?'

'If you like to take it that way, yes.'

'Be careful, Mr Inglethorp.'

Poirot was fidgeting nervously.

'*Sacré!*' he murmured. 'Does this imbecile of a man *want* to be arrested?'

Inglethorp was indeed creating a bad impression. His futile denials would not have convinced a child. The Coroner, however, passed briskly to the next point, and Poirot drew a deep breath of relief.

'You had a discussion with your wife on Tuesday afternoon?'

'Pardon me,' interrupted Alfred Inglethorp, 'you have been misinformed. I had no quarrel with my dear wife. The whole story is absolutely untrue. I was absent from the house the entire afternoon.'

'Have you anyone who can testify to that?'

'You have my word,' said Inglethorp haughtily.

The Coroner did not trouble to reply.

'There are two witnesses who will swear to having heard your disagreement with Mrs Inglethorp.'

'Those witnesses were mistaken.'

I was puzzled. The man spoke with such quiet assurance that I was staggered. I looked at Poirot. There was an expression of exultation on his face which I could not understand. Was he at last convinced of Alfred Inglethorp's guilt?

'Mr Inglethorp,' said the Coroner, 'you have heard your wife's dying words repeated here. Can you explain them in any way?'

'Certainly I can.'

'You can?'

'It seems very simple. The room was dimly lighted. Dr Bauerstein

81

is much of my height and build, and, like me, wears a beard. In the dim light, and suffering as she was, my poor wife mistook him for me.'

'Ah!' murmured Poirot to himself. 'But it is an idea, that!'

'You think it is true?' I whispered.

'I do not say that. But it is truly an ingenious supposition.'

'You read my wife's last words as an accusation' – Inglethorp was continuing – 'they were, on the contrary, an appeal to me.'

The Coroner reflected a moment, then he said:

'I believe, Mr Inglethorp, that you yourself poured out the coffee, and took it to your wife that evening?'

'I poured it out, yes. But I did not take it to her. I meant to do so, but I was told that a friend was at the hall door, so I laid down the coffee on the hall table. When I came through the hall again a few minutes later, it was gone.'

This statement might, or might not, be true, but it did not seem to me to improve matters much for Inglethorp. In any case, he had had ample time to introduce the poison.

At that point, Poirot nudged me gently, indicating two men who were sitting together near the door. One was a little, sharp, dark, ferret-faced man, the other was tall and fair.

I questioned Poirot mutely. He put his lips to my ear.

'Do you know who that little man is?'

I shook my head.

'That is Detective-Inspector James Japp of Scotland Yard – Jimmy Japp. The other man is from Scotland Yard, too. Things are moving quickly, my friend.'

I stared at the two men intently. There was certainly nothing of the policeman about them. I should never have suspected them of being official personages.

I was still staring, when I was startled and recalled by the verdict being given:

'Wilful Murder against some person or persons unknown.'

CHAPTER VII

POIROT PAYS HIS DEBTS

As we came out of the Stylites Arms, Poirot drew me aside by a gentle pressure of the arm. I understood his object. He was waiting for the Scotland Yard men.

In a few moments, they emerged, and Poirot at once stepped forward, and accosted the shorter of the two.

'I fear you do not remember me, Inspector Japp.'

'Why, if it isn't Mr Poirot!' cried the Inspector. He turned to the other man. 'You've heard me speak of Mr Poirot? It was in 1904 he and I worked together – the Abercrombie forgery case – you remember, he was run down in Brussels. Ah, those were great days, moosier. Then, do you remember "Baron" Altara? There was a pretty rogue for you! He eluded the clutches of half the police in Europe. But we nailed him in Antwerp – thanks to Mr Poirot here.'

As these friendly reminiscences were being indulged in, I drew nearer, and was introduced to Detective-Inspector Japp, who is his turn introduced us both to his companion, Superintendent Summerhaye.

'I need hardly ask what you are doing here, gentlemen,' remarked Poirot.

Japp closed one eye knowingly.

'No, indeed. Pretty clear case I should say.'

But Poirot answered gravely:

'There I differ from you.'

'Oh, come!' said Summerhaye, opening his lips for the first time. 'Surely the whole thing is clear as daylight. The man's caught red-handed. How he could be such a fool beats me!'

But Japp was looking attentively at Poirot.

'Hold your fire, Summerhaye,' he remarked jocularly.

'Me and moosier here have met before – and there's no man's judgement I'd sooner take than his. If I'm not greatly mistaken, he's got something up his sleeve. Isn't that so, moosier?'

Poirot smiled.

'I have drawn certain conclusions – yes.'

Summerhaye was still looking rather sceptical, but Japp continued his scrutiny of Poirot.

'It's this way,' he said, 'so far, we've only seen the case from the

83

outside. That's where the Yard's at a disadvantage in a case of this kind, where the murder's only out, so to speak, after the inquest. A lot depends on being on the spot first thing, and that's where Mr Poirot's had the start of us. We shouldn't have been here as soon as this even, if it hadn't been for the fact that there was a smart doctor on the spot, who gave us the tip through the Coroner. But you've been on the spot from the first, and you may have picked up some little hints. From the evidence at the inquest, Mr Inglethorp murdered his wife as sure as I stand here, and if anyone but you hinted the contrary I'd laugh in his face. I must say I was surprised the jury didn't bring it in Wilful Murder against him right off. I think they would have, if it hadn't been for the Coroner – he seemed to be holding them back.'

'Perhaps, though, you have a warrant for his arrest in your pocket now,' suggested Poirot.

A kind of wooden shutter of officialdom came down over Japp's expressive countenance.

'Perhaps I have, and perhaps I haven't,' he remarked dryly.

Poirot looked at him thoughtfully.

'I am very anxious, Messieurs, that he should not be arrested.'

'I dare say,' observed Summerhaye sarcastically.

Japp was regarding Poirot with comical perplexity.

'Can't you go a little further, Mr Poirot? A wink's as good as a nod – from you. You've been on the spot – and the Yard doesn't want to make any mistakes, you know.'

Poirot nodded gravely.

'That is exactly what I thought. Well, I will tell you this. Use your warrant: arrest Mr Inglethorp. But it will bring you no kudos – the case against him will be dismissed at once! *Comme ça!*' And he snapped his fingers expressively.

Japp's face grew grave, though Summerhaye gave an incredulous snort.

As for me, I was literally dumb with astonishment. I could only conclude that Poirot was mad.

Japp had taken out a handkerchief, and was gently dabbing his brow.

'I daren't do it, Mr Poirot. I'd take your word, but there's others over me who'll be asking what the devil I mean by it. Can't you give me a little more to go on?'

Poirot reflected a moment.

'It can be done,' he said at last. 'I admit I do not wish it. It forces my hand. I would have preferred to work in the dark just for the present, but what you say is very just – the word of a Belgian policeman, whose day is past, is not enough! And Alfred Inglethorp must not be arrested. That I have sworn, as my friend Hastings here knows. See, then, my good Japp, you go at once to Styles?'

'Well, in about half an hour. We're seeing the Coroner and the doctor first.'

'Good. Call for me in passing – the last house in the village. I will go with you. At Styles, Mr Inglethorp will give you, or if he refuses – as is probable – I will give you such proofs that shall satisfy you that the case against him could not possibly be sustained. Is that a bargain?'

'That's a bargain,' said Japp heartily. 'And, on behalf of the Yard, I'm much obliged to you, though I'm bound to confess I can't at present see the faintest possible loophole in the evidence, but you always were a marvel! So long, then, moosier.'

The two detectives strode away, Summerhaye with an incredulous grin on his face.

'Well, my friend,' cried Poirot, before I could get in a word, 'what do you think? *Mon dieu!* I had some warm moments in that court; I did not figure to myself that the man would be so pig-headed as to refuse to say anything at all. Decidely, it was the policy of an imbecile.'

'H'm! There are other explanations besides that of imbecility,' I remarked. 'For, if the case against him is true, how could he defend himself except by silence?'

'Why, in a thousand ingenious ways,' cried Poirot. 'See; say that it is I who have committed this murder, I can think of seven most plausible stories! Far more convincing than Mr Inglethorp's stony denials!'

I could not help laughing.

'My dear Poirot, I am sure you are capable of thinking of seventy! But, seriously, in spite of what I heard you say to the detectives, you surely cannot still believe in the possibility of Alfred Inglethorp's innocence?'

'Why not now as much as before? Nothing has changed.'

'But the evidence is so conclusive.'

'Yes, too conclusive.'

We turned in at the gate of Leastways Cottage, and proceeded up the now familiar stairs.

'Yes, yes, too conclusive,' continued Poirot, almost to himself.

'Real evidence is usually vague and unsatisfactory. It has to be examined – sifted. But here the whole thing is cut and dried. No, my friend, this evidence has been very cleverly manufactured – so cleverly that it has defeated its own ends.'

'How do you make that out?'

'Because, so long as the evidence against him was vague and intangible, it was very hard to disprove. But, in his anxiety, the criminal has drawn the net so closely that one cut will set Inglethorp free.'

I was silent. And in a minute or two, Poirot continued:

'Let us look at the matter like this. Here is a man, let us say, who sets out to poison his wife. He has lived by his wits as the saying goes. Presumably, therefore, he has some wits. He is not altogether a fool. Well, how does he set about it? He goes boldly to the village chemist's and purchases strychnine under his own name, with a trumped-up story about a dog which is bound to be proved absurd. He does not employ the poison that night. No, he waits until he has had a violent quarrel with her, of which the whole household is cognizant, and which naturally directs their suspicions upon him. He prepares no defence – no shadow of an alibi, yet he knows the chemist's assistant must necessarily come forward with the facts. Bah! Do not ask me to believe that any man could be so idiotic! Only a lunatic, who wished to commit suicide by causing himself to be hanged, would act so!'

'Still – I do not see –' I began.

'Neither do I see. I tell you, *mon ami*, it puzzles me. *Me* – Hercule Poirot!'

'But if you believe him innocent, how do you explain his buying the strychnine?'

'Very simply. He did *not* buy it.'

'But Mace recognized him!'

'I beg your pardon, he saw a man with a black beard like Mr Inglethorp's and wearing glasses like Mr Inglethorp, and dressed in Mr Inglethorp's rather noticeable clothes. He could not recognize a man whom he had probably only seen in the distance, since, you remember, he himself had only been in the village a fortnight, and Mrs Inglethorp dealt principally with Coot's in Tadminster.'

'Then you think –'

'*Mon ami*, do you remember the two points I laid stress upon? Leave the first one for the moment, what was the second?'

'The important fact that Alfred Inglethorp wears peculiar clothes, has a black beard, and uses glasses,' I quoted.

'Exactly. Now suppose anyone wished to pass himself off as John or Lawrence Cavendish. Would it be easy?'

'No,' I said thoughtfully. 'Of course an actor –'

But Poirot cut me short ruthlessly.

'And why would it not be easy? I will tell you, my friend: Because they are both clean-shaven men. To make up successfully as one of these two in broad daylight, it would need an actor of genius, and a certain initial facial resemblance. But in the case of Alfred Inglethorp, all that is changed. His clothes, his beard, the glasses which hide his eyes – those are the salient points about his personal appearance. Now, that is the first instinct of the criminal? To divert suspicion from himself, is it not so? And how can he best do that? By throwing it on someone else. In this instance, there was a man ready to his hand. Everybody was predisposed to believe in Mr Inglethorp's guilt. It was a foregone conclusion that he would be suspected; but, to make it a sure thing there must be tangible proof – such as the actual buying of the poison, and that, with a man of the peculiar appearance of Mr Inglethorp, was not difficult. Remember, this young Mace had never actually spoken to Mr Inglethorp. How should he doubt that the man in his clothes, with his beard and his glasses, was not Alfred Inglethorp?'

'It may be so,' I said, fascinated by Poirot's eloquence. 'But, if that was the case, why does he not say where he was at six o'clock on Monday evening?'

'Ah, why indeed?' said Poirot, calming down. 'If he were arrested, he probably would speak, but I do not want it to come to that. I must make him see the gravity of his position. There is, of course, something discreditable behind his silence. If he did not murder his wife, he is, nevertheless, a scoundrel, and has something of his own to conceal; quite apart from the murder.'

'What can it be?' I mused, won over to Poirot's views for the moment, although still retaining a faint conviction that the obvious deduction was the correct one.

'Can you not guess?' asked Poirot, smiling.

'No, can you?'

'Oh, yes, I had a little idea some time ago – and it has turned out to be correct.'

'You never told me,' I said reproachfully.

Poirot spread out his hands apologetically.

'Pardon me, *mon ami*, you were not precisely *sympathique*.' He turned to me earnestly. 'Tell me – you see now that he must not be arrested?'

'Perhaps,' I said doubtfully, for I was really indifferent to the fate of Alfred Inglethorp, and thought that a good fright would do him no harm.

Poirot, who was watching me intently, gave a sigh.

'Come, my friend,' he said changing the subject, 'apart from Mr Inglethorp, how did the the evidence at the inquest strike you?'

'Oh, pretty much what I expected.'

'Did nothing strike you as peculiar about it?'

My thoughts flew to Mary Cavendish, and I hedged:

'In what way?'

'Well, Mr Lawrence Cavendish's evidence for instance?'

I was relieved.

'Oh, Lawrence! No, I don't think so. He's always a nervous chap.'

'His suggestion that his mother might have been poisoned accidentally by means of the tonic she was taking, that did not strike you as strange – *hein?*'

'No, I can't say it did. The doctors ridiculed it of course. But it was quite a natural suggestion for a layman to make.'

'But Monsieur Lawrence is not a layman. You told me yourself that he had started by studying medicine, and that he had taken his degree.'

'Yes, that's true. I never thought of that.' I was rather startled. 'It *is* odd.'

Poirot nodded.

'From the first, his behaviour has been peculiar. Of all the household, he alone would be likely to recognize the symptoms of strychnine poisoning, and yet we find him the only member of the family to uphold strenuously the theory of death from natural causes. If it had been Monsieur John, I could have understood it. He has no technical knowledge, and is by nature unimaginative. But Monsieur Lawrence – no! And now, today, he puts forward a suggestion that he himself must have known was ridiculous. There is food for thought in this, *mon ami!*'

'It's very confusing,' I agreed.

'Then there is Mrs Cavendish,' continued Poirot. 'That is another who is not telling all she knows! What do you make of her attitude?'

'I don't know what to make of it. It seems inconceivable that she should be shielding Alfred Inglethorp. Yet that is what it looks like.'

Poirot nodded reflectively.

'Yes, it is queer. One thing is certain, she overheard a good deal more of that "private conversation" than she was willing to admit.'

'And yet she is the last person one would accuse of stooping to eavesdrop!'

'Exactly. One thing her evidence *has* shown me. I made a mistake. Dorcas was quite right. The quarrel did take place earlier in the afternoon, about four o'clock, as she said.'

I looked at him curiously. I had never understood his insistence on that point.

'Yes, a good deal that was peculiar came out today,' continued Poirot. 'Dr Bauerstein, now, what was *he* doing up and dressed at that hour in the morning? It is astonishing to me that no one commented on the fact.'

'He has insomnia, I believe,' I said doubtfully.

'Which is a very good, or a very bad explanation,' remarked Poirot. 'It covers everything, and explains nothing. I shall keep my eye on our clever Dr Bauerstein.'

'Any more faults to find with the evidence?' I inquired satirically.

'*Mon ami*,' replied Poirot gravely, 'when you find that people are not telling you the truth – look out! Now, unless I am much mistaken, at this inquest today only one – at most, two persons were speaking the truth without reservation or subterfuge.'

'Oh, come now, Poirot! I won't cite Lawrence, or Mrs Cavendish. But there's John – and Miss Howard, surely they were speaking the truth?'

'Both of them, my friend? One, I grant you, but both – !'

His words gave me an unpleasant shock. Miss Howard's evidence, unimportant as it was, had been given in such a downright straightforward manner that it had never occurred to me to doubt her sincerity. Still, I had a great respect for Poirot's sagacity – except on the occasions when he was what I described to myself as 'foolish pig-headed'.

'Do you really think so?' I asked. 'Miss Howard had always seemed to me so essentially honest – almost uncomfortably so.'

Poirot gave me a curious look, which I could not quite fathom. He seemed about to speak, and then checked himself.

'Miss Murdoch too,' I continued, 'there's nothing untruthful about *her*.'

'No. But it was strange that she never heard a sound, sleeping next door; whereas Mrs Cavendish, in the other wing of the building, distinctly heard the table fall.'

'Well, she's young. And she sleeps soundly.'

'Ah, yes, indeed! She must be a famous sleeper, that one!'

I did not quite like the tone of his voice, but at that moment a smart knock reached our ears, and looked out of the window we perceived the two detectives waiting for us below.

Poirot seized his hat, gave a ferocious twist to his moustache, and, carefully brushing an imaginary speck of dust from his sleeve, motioned me to precede him down the stairs; there we joined the detectives and set out for Styles.

I think the appearance of the two Scotland Yard men was rather a shock – especially to John, though, of course, after the verdict, he had realized that it was only a matter of time. Still, the presence of the detectives brought the truth home to him more than anything else could have done.

Poirot had conferred with Japp in a low tone on the way up, and it was the latter functionary who requested that the household, with the exception of the servants, should be assembled together in the drawing-room. I realized the significance of this. It was up to Poirot to make his boast good.

Personally, I was not sanguine. Poirot might have excellent reasons for his belief in Inglethorp's innocence, but a man of the type of Summerhaye would require tangible proofs, and these I doubted if Poirot could supply.

Before very long we had all trooped into the drawing-room, the door of which Japp closed. Poirot politely set chairs for everyone. The Scotland Yard men were the cynosure of all eyes. I think that for the first time we realized that the thing was not a bad dream, but a tangible reality. We had read of such things – now we ourselves were actors in the drama. Tomorrow the daily papers, all over England, would blazon out the news in staring headlines:

'MYSTERIOUS TRAGEDY IN ESSEX'
'WEALTHY LADY POISONED'

There would be pictures of Styles, snap-shots of 'The family leaving the Inquest' – the village photographer had not been idle! All the things that one had read a hundred times – things that happen to other people, not to oneself. And now, in this house, a murder had been committed. In front of us were 'the detectives in charge of the case'. The well-known glib phraseology passed rapidly through my mind in the interval before Poirot opened the proceedings.

I think everyone was a little surprised that it should be he and not one of the official detectives who took the initiative.

'*Mesdames* and *messieurs*,' said Poirot, bowing as though he were a celebrity about to deliver a lecture, 'I have asked you to come here all together, for a certain object. That object, it concerns Mr Alfred Inglethorp.'

Inglethorp was sitting a little by himself – I think, unconsciously, everyone had drawn his chair slightly away from him – and he gave a faint start as Poirot pronounced his name.

'Mr Inglethorp,' said Poirot, addressing him directly, 'a very dark shadow is resting on this house – the shadow of murder.'

Inglethorp shook his head sadly.

'My poor wife,' he murmered. 'Poor Emily! It is terrible.'

'I do not think, monsieur,' said Poirot pointedly, 'that you quite realize how terrible it may be – for you.' And as Inglethorp did not appear to understand, he added: 'Mr Inglethorp, you are standing in very grave danger.'

The two detectives fidgeted. I saw the official caution 'Anything you say will be used in evidence against you,' actually hovering on Summerhaye's lips. Poirot went on:

'Do you understand now, monsieur?'

'No. What do you mean?'

'I mean,' said Poirot deliberately, 'that you are suspected of poisoning your wife.'

A little gasp ran round the circle at this plain speaking.

'Good heavens!' cried Inglethorp, starting up. 'What a monstrous idea! I – poison my dearest Emily!'

'I do not think' – Poirot watched him narrowly – 'that you quite realize the unfavourable nature of your evidence at the inquest. Mr Inglethorp, knowing what I have now told you, do you still refuse to say where you were at six o'clock on Monday afternoon?'

With a groan, Alfred Inglethorp sank down again and buried his face in his hands. Poirot approached and stood over him.

'Speak!' he cried menacingly.

With an effort, Inglethorp raised his face from his hands. Then, slowly and deliberately, he shook his head.

'You will not speak?'

'No. I do not believe that anyone could be so monstrous as to accuse me of what you say.'

Poirot nodded thoughtfully, like a man whose mind is made.

'*Soit!*', he said. 'Then I must speak for you.'

Alfred Inglethorp sprang up again.

'You? How can you speak? You do not know –' he broke off abruptly.

Poirot turned to face us. '*Mesdames* and *messieurs!* I speak! Listen! I, Hercule Poirot, affirm that the man who entered the chemist's shop, and purchased strychnine at six o'clock on Monday last, was not Mr Inglethorp, for at six o'clock on that day Mr Inglethorp was escorting Mrs Raikes back to her home from a neighbouring farm. I can produce not less than five witnesses to swear to having seen them together, either at six or just after and, as you may know, the Abbey Farm, Mrs Raikes's home, is at least two and a half miles distant from the village. There is absolutely no question as to the alibi!'

CHAPTER VIII

FRESH SUSPICIONS

There was a moment's stupefied silence. Japp, who was the least surprised of any of us, was the first to speak.

'My word,' he cried, 'you're the goods! And no mistake, Mr Poirot! These witnesses of yours are all right, I suppose?'

'*Voilà!* I have prepared a list of them – names and addresses. You must see them, of course. But you will find it all right.'

'I'm sure of that.' Japp lowered his voice. 'I'm much obliged to you. A pretty mare's nest arresting him would have been.' He turned to Inglethorp. 'But, if you'll excuse me, sir, why couldn't you say all this at the inquest?'

'I will tell you why,' interrupted Poirot. 'There was a certain rumour –'

'A most malicious and utterly untrue one,' interrupted Alfred Inglethorp in an agitated voice.

'And Mr Inglethorp was anxious to have no scandal revived just at present. Am I right?'

'Quite right.' Inglethorp nodded. 'With my poor Emily not yet buried, can you wonder I was anxious that no more lying rumours should be started?'

'Between you and me, sir,' remarked Japp, 'I'd sooner have any amount of rumours than be arrested for murder. And I venture to think that your poor lady would have felt the same. And, if it hadn't been for Mr Poirot here, arrested you would have been, as sure as eggs is eggs!'

'I was foolish, no doubt,' murmured Inglethorp. 'But you do not know, inspector, how I have been persecuted and maligned.' And he shot a baleful glance at Evelyn Howard.

'Now, sir,' said Japp, turning briskly to John, 'I should like to see the lady's bedroom, please, and after that I'll have a little chat with the servants. Don't you bother about anything. Mr Poirot, here, will show me the way.'

As they all went out of the room, Poirot turned and made me a sign to follow him upstairs. There he caught me by the arm, and drew me aside.

'Quick, go to the other wing. Stand there – just this side of the baize door. Do not move till I come.' Then, turning rapidly, he rejoined the two detectives.

I followed his instructions, taking up my position by the baize door, and wondering what on earth lay behind the request. Why was I to stand in this particular spot on guard? I looked thoughtfully down the corridor in front of me. An idea struck me. With the exception of Cynthia Murdoch's, every room was in this left wing. Had that anything to do with it? Was I to report who came or went? I stood faithfully at my post. The minutes passed. Nobody came. Nothing happened.

It must have been quite twenty minutes before Poirot rejoined me.

'You have not stirred?'

'No, I've stuck here like a rock. Nothing's happened.'

'Ah!' Was he pleased, or disappointed? 'You've seen nothing at all?'

'No.'

'But you have probably heard something? A big bump – eh, *mon ami?*'

'No.'

'Is it possible? Ah, but I am vexed with myself! I am not usually clumsy. I made but a slight gesture' – I know Poirot's gestures – 'with the left hand, and over went the table by the bed!'

He looked so childishly vexed and crestfallen that I hastened to console him.

'Never mind, old chap. What does it matter? Your triumph downstairs excited you. I can tell you, that was a surprise to us all. There must be more in this affair of Inglethorp's with Mrs Raikes than we thought, to make him hold his tongue so persistently. What are you going to do now? Where are the Scotland Yard fellows?'

'Gone down to interview the servants. I showed them all our exhibits. I am disappointed in Japp. He has no method!'

'Hullo!' I said, looking out of the window. 'Here's Dr Bauerstein. I believe you're right about that man, Poirot. I don't like him.'

'He is clever,' observed Poirot meditatively.

'Oh, clever as the devil! I must say I was overjoyed to see him in the plight he was in on Tuesday. You never saw such a spectacle!' And I described the doctor's adventure. 'He looked a regular scarecrow! Plastered with mud from head to foot.'

'You saw him, then?'

'Yes. Of course, he didn't want to come in – it was just after dinner – but Mr Inglethorp insisted.'

'What?' Poirot caught me violently by the shoulders.

'Was Dr Bauerstein here on Tuesday evening? Here? And you never told me? Why did you not tell me? Why? Why?'

He appeared to be in an absolute frenzy.

'My dear Poirot,' I expostulated, 'I never thought it would interest you. I didn't know it was of any importance.'

'Importance? It is of the first importance! So Dr Bauerstein was here on Tuesday night – the night of the murder. Hastings, do you not see? That alters everything – everything!'

I had never seen him so upset. Loosening his hold of me, he mechanically straightened a pair of candlesticks, still murmuring to himself: 'Yes, that alters everything – everything.'

Suddenly he seemed to come to a decision.

'*Allons!*' he said. 'We must act at once. Where is Mr Cavendish?'

John was in the smoking-room. Poirot went straight to him.

'Mr Cavendish, I have some important business in Tadminster. A new clue. May I take your motor?'

'Why, of course. Do you mean at once?'

'If you please.'

John rang the bell, and ordered round the car. In another ten minutes, we were racing down the park and along the high road to Tadminster.

'Now, Poirot,' I remarked resignedly, 'perhaps you will tell me what all this is about?'

'Well, *mon ami*, a good deal you can guess for yourself. Of course, you realize that, now Mr Inglethorp is out of it, the whole position is greatly changed. We are face to face with an entirely new problem. We know now that there is one person who did not buy the poison. We have cleared away the manufactured clues. Now for the real ones. I have ascertained that anyone in the household, with the exception of Mrs Cavendish, who was playing tennis with you, could have personated Mr Inglethorp on Monday evening. In the same way, we have his statement that he put the coffee down in the hall. No one took much notice of that at the inquest – but now it has a very different significance. We must find out who did take that coffee to Mrs Inglethorp eventually, or who passed through the hall whilst it was standing there. From your account, there are only two people whom we can positively say did not go near the coffee – Mrs Cavendish, and Mademoiselle Cynthia.'

'Yes, that is so.' I felt an inexpressible lightening of the heart. Mary Cavendish could certainly not rest under suspicion.

'In clearing Alfred Inglethorp,' continued Poirot, 'I have been obliged to show my hand sooner than I intended. As long as I might be thought to be pursuing him, the criminal would be off his guard. Now, he will be doubly careful. Yes – doubly careful.' He turned to me abruptly. 'Tell me, Hastings, you yourself – have you no suspicions of anybody?'

I hesitated. To tell the truth, an idea, wild and extravagant in itself, had once or twice that morning flashed through my brain. I had rejected it as absurd, nevertheless it persisted.

'You couldn't call it a suspicion,' I murmured. 'It's so utterly foolish.'

'Come now,' urged Poirot encouragingly. 'Do not fear. Speak your mind. You should always pay attention to your instincts.'

'Well then,' I blurted out, 'it's absurd – but I suspect Miss Howard of not telling all she knows!'

'Miss Howard?'

'Yes – you'll laugh at me –'

'Not at all. Why should I?'

'I can't help feeling,' I continued blunderingly, 'that we've rather left her out of the possible suspects, simply on the strength of her having been away from the place. But, after all, she was only fifteen miles away. A car would do it in half an hour. Can we say positively that she was away from Styles on the night of the murder?'

'Yes, my friend,' said Poirot unexpectedly, 'we can. One of my first actions was to ring up the hospital where she was working.'

'Well?'

'Well, I learnt that Miss Howard had been on afternoon duty on Tuesday, and that – a convoy coming in unexpectedly – she had kindly offered to remain on night duty, which offer was gratefully accepted. That disposes of that.'

'Oh!' I said, rather nonplussed. 'Really,' I continued, 'It's her extraordinary vehemence against Inglethorp that started me off suspecting her. I can't help feeling she'd do anything against him. And I had an idea she might know something about the destroying of the will. She might have burnt the new one, mistaking it for the earlier one in his favour. She is so terribly bitter against him.'

'You consider her vehemence unnatural?'

'Y – es. She is so very violent. I wonder really whether she is quite sane on that point.'

Poirot shook his head energetically.

'No, no, you are on a wrong track there. There is nothing weak-minded or degenerate about Miss Howard. She is an excellent specimen of well balanced English beef and brawn. She is sanity itself.'

'Yet her hatred of Inglethorp seems almost a mania. My idea was – a very ridiculous one, no doubt – that she had intended to poison him – and that, in some way, Mrs Inglethorp got hold of it by mistake. But I don't at all see how it could have been done. The whole thing is absurd and ridiculous to the last degree.'

'Still you are right in one thing. It is always wise to suspect everybody until you can prove logically, and to your own satisfaction, that they are innocent. Now, what reasons are there against Miss Howard's having deliberately poisoned Mrs Inglethorp?'

'Why, she was devoted to her!' I exclaimed.

'Tcha! Tcha!' cried Poirot irritably. 'You argue like a child. If Miss Howard were capable of poisoning the old lady, she would be quite equally capable of simulating devotion. No, we must look elsewhere. You are perfectly correct in your assumption that her vehemence against Alfred Inglethorp is too violent to be natural; but you are quite wrong in the deduction you draw from it. I have drawn my own deductions, which I believe to be correct, but I will not speak of them at present.' He paused a minute, then went on. 'Now, to my way of thinking, there is one insuperable objection to Miss Howard's being the murderess.'

'And that is?'

'That in no possible way could Mrs Inglethorp's death benefit Miss Howard. Now there is no murder without a motive.'

I reflected.

'Could not Mrs Inglethorp have made a will in her favour?'

Poirot shook his head.

'But you yourself suggested that possibility to Mr Wells?'

Poirot smiled.

'That was for a reason. I did not want to mention the name of the person who was actually in my mind. Miss Howard occupied very much the same position, so I used her name instead.'

'Still, Mrs Inglethorp might have done so. Why, that will made on the afternoon of her death may –'

But Poirot's shake of the head was so energetic that I stopped.

'No, my friend. I have certain little ideas of my own about that will. But I can tell you this much – it was not in Miss Howard's favour.'

I accepted his assurance, though I did not really see how he could be so positive about the matter.

'Well,' I said, with a sigh, 'we will acquit Miss Howard, then. It is partly your fault that I ever came to suspect her. It was what you said about her evidence at the inquest that set me off.'

Poirot looked puzzled.

'What did I say about her evidence at the inquest?'

'Don't you remember? When I cited her and John Cavendish as being above suspicion?'

'Oh – ah – yes.' He seemed a little confused, but recovered himself. 'By the way, Hastings, there is something I want you to do for me.'

'Certainly. What is it?'

'Next time you happen to be alone with Lawrence Cavendish, I want you to say this to him. 'I have a message for you from Poirot. He says: "Find the extra coffee-cup, and you can rest in peace!" Nothing more. Nothing less.'

' "Find the extra coffee-cup, and you can rest in peace!" Is that right?' I asked, much mystified.

'Excellent.'

'But what does it mean?'

'Ah, that I will leave you to find out. You have access to the facts. Just say that to him, and see what he says.'

'Very well – but it's all extremely mysterious.'

We were running into Tadminster now, and Poirot directed the car to the 'Analytical Chemist'.

Poirot hopped down briskly, and went inside. In a few minutes he was back again.

'There,' he said. 'That is all my business.'

'What were you doing there?' I asked in lively curiosity.

'I left something to be analysed.'

'Yes, but what?'

'The sample of cocoa I took from the saucepan in the bedroom.'

'But that has already been tested!' I cried, stupefied. 'Dr Bauerstein had it tested, and you yourself laughed at the possibility of there being strychnine in it.'

'I know Dr Bauerstein had it tested,' replied Poirot quietly.

'Well, then?'

'Well, I have a fancy for having it analysed again, that is all.'

And not another word on the subject could I drag out of him.

This proceeding of Poirot's, in respect of the cocoa, puzzled me intensely. I could see neither rhyme nor reason in it. However, my confidence in him, which at one time had rather waned, was fully

98

restored since his belief in Alfred Inglethorp's innocence had been so triumphantly vindicated.

The funeral of Mrs Inglethorp took place the following day, and on Monday, as I came down to a late breakfast, John drew me aside, and informed me that Mr Inglethorp was leaving that morning, to take up his quarters at the Stylites Arms, until he should have completed his plans.

'And really it's a great relief to think he's going, Hastings,' continued my honest friend. 'It was bad enough before, when we thought he'd done it, but I'm hanged if it isn't worse now, when we all feel guilty for having been so down on the fellow. The fact is, we've treated him abominably. Of course, things did look black against him. I don't see how anyone could blame us for jumping to the conclusions we did. Still, there it is, we were in the wrong, and now there's a beastly feeling that one ought to make amends; which is difficult, when one doesn't like the fellow a bit better than one did before. The whole thing's damned awkward! And I'm thankful he's had the tact to take himself off. It's a good thing Styles wasn't the mater's to leave to him. Couldn't bear to think of the fellow lording it here. He's welcome to her money.'

'You'll be able to keep up the place all right?' I asked.

'Oh, yes. There are the death duties, of course, but half my father's money goes with the place, and Lawrence will stay with us for the present, so there is his share as well. We shall be pinched at first, of course, because, as I once told you, I am in a bit of a hole financially myself. Still, the Johnnies will wait now.'

In the general relief at Inglethorp's approaching departure, we had the most genial breakfast we had experienced since the tragedy. Cynthia, whose young spirits were naturally buoyant, was looking quite her pretty self again, and we all, with the exception of Lawrence, who seemed unalterably gloomy and nervous, were quietly cheerful, at the opening of a new and hopeful future.

The papers, of course, had been full of the tragedy. Glaring headlines, sandwiched biographies of every member of the household, subtle innuendoes, the usual familiar tag about the police having a clue. Nothing was spared us. It was a slack time. The war was momentarily inactive, and the newspapers seized with avidity on this crime in fashionable life: 'The Mysterious Affair at Styles' was the topic of the moment.

Naturally it was very annoying for the Cavendishes. The house was constantly besieged by reporters, who were consistently denied admission, but who continued to haunt the village and the grounds, where they lay in wait with cameras, for any unwary members of the household. We all lived in a blast of publicity. The Scotland Yard men came and went, examining, questioning, lynx-eyed and reserved of tongue. Towards what end they were working, we did not know. Had they any clue, or would the whole thing remain in the category of undiscovered crimes?

After breakfast, Dorcas came up to me rather myseriously, and asked if she might have a few words with me.

'Certainly. What is it, Dorcas?'

'Well, it's just this, sir. You'll be seeing the Belgian gentleman today perhaps?' I nodded. 'Well, sir, you know how he asked me so particular if the mistress, or anyone else, had a green dress?'

'Yes, yes. You have found one?' My interest was aroused.

'No, not that, sir. But since then I've remembered what the young gentlemen' – John and Lawrence were still the 'young gentlemen' to Dorcas – 'call the "dressing-up box". It's up in the front attic, sir. A great chest, full of old clothes and fancy dresses, and what not. And it came to me sudden like that there might be a green dress amongst them. So, if you'd tell the Belgian gentleman –'

'I will tell him, Dorcas,' I promised.

'Thank you very much, sir. A very nice gentleman he is, sir. And quite a different class from them two detectives from London, what goes prying about, and asking questions. I don't hold with foreigners as a rule, but from what the newspapers says I make out as how these brave Belgies isn't the ordinary run of foreigners and certainly he's a most polite spoken gentleman.'

Dear old Dorcas! As she stood there, with her honest face upturned to mine, I thought what a fine specimen she was of the old-fashioned servant that is so fast dying out.

I thought I might as well go down to the village at once, and look up Poirot; but I met him half-way, coming up to the house, and at once gave him Dorcas's message.

'Ah, the brave Dorcas! We will look at the chest, although – but no matter – we will examine it all the same.'

We entered the house by one of the windows. There was no one in the hall, and we went straight up to the attic.

Sure enough, there was the chest, a fine old piece, all studded with brass nails, and full to overflowing with every imaginable type of garment.

Poirot bundled everything out on the floor with scant ceremony.

There were one or two green fabrics of varying shades; but Poirot shook his head over them all. He seemed somewhat apathetic in the search, as though he expected no great results from it. Suddenly he gave an exclamation.

'What is it?'

'Look!'

The chest was nearly empty, and there, reposing right at the bottom, was a magnificent black beard.

'*Ohó!*' said Poirot. '*Ohó!*' He turned it over in his hands, examining it closely. 'New,' he remarked. 'Yes, quite new.'

After a moment's hesitation, he replaced it in the chest, heaped all the other things on top of it as before, and made his way briskly downstairs. He went straight to the pantry, where we found Dorcas busily polishing her silver.

Poirot wished her good morning with Gallic politeness, and went on:

'We have been looking through that chest, Dorcas. I'm much obliged to you for mentioning it. There is, indeed, a fine collection there. Are they often used, may I ask?'

'Well, sir, not very often nowadays, though from time to time we do have what the young gentlemen call "a dress-up night". And very funny it is sometimes, sir. Mr Lawrence, he's wonderful. Most comic! I shall never forget the night he came down as the Char of Persia, I think he called it – a sort of Eastern King it was. He had the big paper knife in his hand, and "Mind, Dorcas," he says, "you'll have to be very respectful. This is my specially sharpened scimitar, and it's off with your head if I'm at all displeased with you!" Miss Cynthia, she was what they call an Apache, or some such name – a Frenchified sort of cut-throat, I take it to be. A real sight she looked. You'd never have believed a pretty young lady like that could have made herself into such a ruffian. Nobody would have known her.'

'These evenings must have been great fun,' said Poirot genially. 'I suppose Mr Lawrence wore that fine black beard in the chest upstairs, when he was Shah of Persia?'

'He did have a beard, sir,' replied Dorcas, smiling. 'And well I know it, for he borrowed two skeins of my black wool to make it with! And I'm sure it looked wonderfully natural at a distance. I didn't know as there was a beard up there at all. It must have been got quite lately, I think. There was a red wig, I know, but nothing else in the way of hair. Burnt corks they use mostly – though 'tis messy getting it off again. Miss Cynthia was a Negress once, and, oh, the trouble she had.'

'So Dorcas knows nothing about that black beard,' said Poirot thoughtfully, as we walked out into the hall again.

'Do you think it is *the* one?' I whispered eagerly.

Poirot nodded.

'I do. You noticed it had been trimmed?'

'No.'

'Yes. It was cut exactly the shape of Mr Inglethorp's and I found one or two snipped hairs. Hastings, this affair is very deep.'

'Who put it in the chest, I wonder?'

'Someone with a good deal of intelligence,' remarked Poirot drily. 'You realize that he chose the one place in the house to hide it where its presence would not be remarked? Yes, he is intelligent. But we must be more intelligent. We must be so intelligent that he does not suspect us of being intelligent at all.'

I acquiesced.

'There, *mon ami*, you will be of great assistance to me.'

I was pleased with the compliment. There had been times when I hardly thought that Poirot appreciated me at my true worth.

'Yes,' he continued, staring at me thoughtfully, 'you will be invaluable.'

This was naturally gratifying, but Poirot's next words were not so welcome.

'I must have an ally in the house,' he observed reflectively.

'You have me,' I protested.

'True, but you are not sufficient.'

I was hurt, and showed it. Poirot hurried to explain himself.

'You do not quite take my meaning. You are known to be working with me. I want somebody who is not associated with us in any way.'

'Oh, I see. How about John?'

'No, I think not.'

'The dear fellow isn't perhaps very bright,' I said thoughtfully.

'Here comes Miss Howard,' said Poirot suddenly. 'She is the very person. But I am in her black books, since I cleared Mr Inglethorp. Still, we can but try.'

With a nod that was barely civil, Miss Howard assented to Poirot's request for a few minutes' conversation.

We went into the little morning-room, and Poirot closed the door.

'Well, Monsieur Poirot,' said Miss Howard impatiently, 'what is it? Out with it. I'm busy.'

'Do you remember, mademoiselle, that I once asked you to

help me?'

'Yes, I do.' The lady nodded. 'And I told you I'd help you with pleasure – to hang Alfred Inglethorp.'

'Ah!' Poirot studied her seriously. 'Miss Howard, I will ask you one question. I beg of you to reply to it truthfully.'

'Never tell lies,' replied Miss Howard.

'It is this. Do you still believe that Mrs Inglethorp was poisoned by her husband?'

'What do you mean?' she asked sharply. 'You needn't think your pretty explanations influence me in the slightest. I'll admit that it wasn't he who bought strychnine at the chemist's shop. What of that? I dare say he soaked fly paper, as I told you at the beginning.'

'That is arsenic – not strychnine,' said Poirot mildly.

'What does that matter? Arsenic would put poor Emily out of the way just as well as strychnine. If I'm convinced he did it, it doesn't matter a jot to me *how* he did it.'

'Exactly. If you are convinced he did it,' said Poirot quietly. 'I will put my question in another form. Did you ever in your heart of hearts believe that Mrs Inglethorp was poisoned by her husband?'

'Good heavens!' cried Miss Howard. 'Haven't I always told you the man is a villain? Haven't I always told you he would murder her in her bed? Haven't I always hated him like poison?'

'Exactly,' said Poirot. 'That bears out my little idea entirely.'

'What little idea?'

'Miss Howard, do you remember a conversation that took place on the day of my friend's arrival here? He repeated it to me, and there is a sentence of yours that has impressed me very much. Do you remember affirming that if a crime had been committed, and anyone you loved had been murdered, you felt certain that you would know by instinct who the criminal was, even if you were quite unable to prove it?'

'Yes, I remember saying that. I believe it, too. I suppose you think it nonsense?'

'Not at all.'

'And yet you will pay no attention to my instinct against Alfred Inglethorp?'

'No,' said Poirot curtly. 'Because your instinct is not against Mr Inglethorp.'

'What?'

'No. You wish to believe he committed the crime. You believe him capable of committing it. But your instinct tells you he did not

103

commit it. It tells you more – shall I go on?'

She was staring at him, fascinated, and made a slight affirmative movement of the hand.

'Shall I tell you why you have been so vehement against Mr Inglethorp? It is because you have been trying to believe what you wish to believe. It is because you are trying to drown and stifle your instinct, which tells you another name –'

'No, no, no!' cried Miss Howard, wildly, flinging up her hands. 'Don't say it! Oh, don't say it! It isn't true! It can't be true. I don't know what put such a wild – such a dreadful – idea into my head!'

'I am right, am I not?' asked Poirot.

'Yes, yes; you must be a wizard to have guessed. But it can't be so – it's so monstrous, too impossible. It *must* be Alfred Inglethorp.'

Poirot shook his head gravely.

'Don't ask me about it,' continued Miss Howard, 'because I shan't tell you. I won't admit it, even to myself. I must be mad to think of such a thing.'

Poirot nodded, as if satisfied.

'I will ask you nothing. It is enough for me that it is as I thought. And I – I, too, have an instinct. We are working together towards a common end.'

'Don't ask me to help you, because I won't. I wouldn't lift a finger to – to –' She faltered.

'You will help me in spite of yourself. I ask you nothing – but you will be my ally. You will not be able to help yourself. You will do the only thing that I want of you.'

'And that is?'

'You will watch!'

Evelyn Howard bowed her head.

'Yes, I can't help doing that. I am always watching – always hoping I shall be proved wrong.'

'If we are wrong, well and good,' said Poirot. 'No one will be more pleased than I shall. But, if we are right? If we are right, Miss Howard, on whose side are you then?'

'I don't know, I don't know –'

'Come now.'

'It could be hushed up.'

'There must be no hushing up.'

'But Emily herself –' She broke off.

'Miss Howard,' said Poirot gravely, 'this is unworthy of you.'

Suddenly she took her face from her hands.

'Yes,' she said quietly, 'that was not Evelyn Howard who spoke!' She flung her head up proudly. '*This* is Evelyn Howard! And she is on the side of Justice! Let the cost be what it may.' And with these words, she walked firmly out of the room.

'There,' said Poirot, looking after her, 'goes a very valuable ally. That woman, Hastings, has got brains as well as a heart.'

I did not reply.

'Instinct is a marvellous thing,' mused Poirot. 'It can neither be explained nor ignored.'

'You and Miss Howard seem to know what you are talking about,' I observed coldly. 'Perhaps you don't realize that I am still in the dark.'

'Really? Is that so, *mon ami?*'

'Yes. Enlighten me, will you?'

Poirot studied me attentively for a moment or two. Then, to my intense surprise, he shook his head decidedly.

'No, my friend.'

'Oh, look here, why not?'

'Two is enough for a secret.'

'Well, I think it is very unfair to keep back facts from me.'

'I am not keeping back facts. Every fact that I know is in your possession. You can draw your own deductions from them. This time it is a question of ideas.'

'Still, it would be interesting to know.'

Poirot looked at me very earnestly, and again shook his head.

'You see,' he said sadly, '*you* have no instincts.'

'It was intelligence you were requiring just now,' I pointed out.

'The two often go together,' said Poirot enigmatically.

The remark seemed so utterly irrelevant that I did not even take the trouble to answer it. But I decided that if I made any interesting and important discoveries – as no doubt I should – I would keep them to myself, and surprise Poirot with the ultimate result.

There are times when it is one's duty to assert oneself.

CHAPTER IX

DR BAUERSTEIN

I had no opportunity as yet of passing on Poirot's message to Lawrence. But now, as I strolled out on the lawn, still nursing a grudge against my friend's high-handedness, I saw Lawrence on the croquet lawn, aimlessly knocking a couple of very ancient balls about, with a still more ancient mallet.

It struck me that it would be a good opportunity to deliver my message. Otherwise, Poirot himself might relieve me of it. It was true that I did not quite gather its purport, but I flattered myself that by Lawrence's reply, and perhaps a little skilful cross-examination on my part, I should soon perceive its significance. Accordingly I accosted him.

'I've been looking for you,' I remarked untruthfully.

'Have you?'

'Yes. The truth is, I've got a message for you – from Poirot.'

'Yes?'

'He told me to wait until I was alone with you,' I said, dropping my voice significantly, and watching him intently out of the corner of my eye. I have always been rather good at what is called, I believe, creating an atmosphere.

'Well?'

There was no change of expression in the dark melancholic face. Had he any idea of what I was about to say?

'This is the message.' I dropped my voice still lower. ' "Find the extra coffee-cup, and you can rest in peace." '

'What on earth does he mean?' Lawrence stared at me in quite unaffected astonishment.

'Don't you know?'

'Not in the least. Do you?'

I was compelled to shake my head.

'What extra coffee-cup?'

'I don't know.'

'He'd better ask Dorcas, or one of the maids, if he wants to know about coffee-cups. It's their business, not mine. I don't know anything about the coffee-cups, except that we've got some that are never used, which are a perfect dream! Old Worcester. You're not a connoisseur, are you, Hastings?'

I shook my head.

'You miss a lot. A really perfect bit of old china – it's pure delight to handle it, or even to look at it.'

'Well, what am I to tell Poirot?'

'Tell him I don't know what he's talking about. It's double Dutch to me.'

'All right.'

I was moving off towards the house again when he suddenly called me back.

'I say, what was the end of the message? Say it over again, will you?'

' "Find the extra coffee-cup, and you can rest in peace." Are you sure you don't know what it means?' I asked him earnestly.

He shook his head.

'No,' he said musingly, 'I don't. I – I wish I did.'

The boom of the gong sounded from the house, and we went in together. Poirot had been asked by John to remain to lunch, and was already seated at the table.

By tacit consent, all mention of the tragedy was barred. We conversed on the war, and other outside topics. But after the cheese and biscuits had been handed round, and Dorcas had left the room, Poirot suddenly leant forward to Mrs Cavendish.

'Pardon me, madame, for recalling unpleasant memories, but I have a little idea' – Poirot's 'little ideas' were becoming a perfect byword – 'and would like to ask one or two questions.'

'Of me? Certainly.'

'You are too aimable, madame. What I want to ask is this: the door leading into Mrs Inglethorp's room from that of Mademoiselle Cynthia, it was bolted, you say?'

'Certainly it was bolted,' replied Mary Cavendish, rather surprised. 'I said so at the inquest.'

'Bolted?'

'Yes.' She looked perplexed.

'I mean,' explained Poirot, 'you are sure it was bolted, and not merely locked?'

'Oh, I see what you mean. No, I don't know. I said bolted, meaning that it was fastened, and I could not open it, but I believe all the doors were found bolted on the inside.'

'Still, as far as you are concerned, the door might equally well have been locked?'

'Oh, yes.'

'You yourself did not happen to notice, madame, when you entered Mrs Inglethorp's room, whether that door was bolted or not?'

'I – I believe it was.'

'But you did not see it?'

'No. I – never looked.'

'But I did,' interrupted Lawrence suddenly. 'I happened to notice that it *was* bolted.'

'Ah, that settles it.' And Poirot looked crestfallen.

I could not help rejoicing that, for once, one of his 'little ideas' had come to naught.

After lunch Poirot begged me to accompany him home. I consented rather stiffly.

'You are annoyed, is it not so?' he asked anxiously, as we walked through the park.

'Not at all,' I said coldly.

'That is well. That lifts a great load from my mind.'

This was not quite what I had intended. I had hoped that he would have observed the stiffness of my manner. Still, the fervour of his words went towards the appeasing of my just displeasure. I thawed.

'I gave Lawrence your message,' I said.

'And what did he say? He was entirely puzzled?'

'Yes. I am quite sure he had no idea of what you meant.'

I had expected Poirot to be disappointed; but, to my surprise, he replied that that was as he had thought, and that he was very glad. My pride forbade me to ask any questions.

Poirot switched off on another tack.

'Mademoiselle Cynthia was not at lunch today? How was that?'

'She is at the hospital again. She resumed work today.'

'Ah, she is an industrious little demoiselle. And pretty too. She is like pictures I have seen in Italy. I would rather like to see that dispensary of hers. Do you think she would show it to me?'

'I am sure she would be delighted. It's an interesting little place.'

'Does she go there every day?'

'She has all Wednesdays off, and comes back to lunch on Saturdays. Those are her only times off.'

'I will remember. Women are doing great work nowadays, and Mademoiselle Cynthia is clever – oh, yes, she has brains, that little one.'

'Yes. I believe she has passed quite a stiff exam.'

'Without doubt. After all, it is very responsible work. I suppose they have very strong poisons there?'

'Yes, she showed them to us. They are kept locked up in a little cupboard. I believe they have to be very careful. They always take out the key before leaving the room.'

'Indeed. It is near the window, this cupboard?'

'No, right the other side of the room. Why?'

Poirot shrugged his shoulders.

'I wondered. That is all. Will you come in?'

We had reached the cottage.

'No. I think I'll be getting back. I shall go round the long way through the woods.'

The woods round Styles were very beautiful. After the walk across the open park, it was pleasant to saunter lazily through the cool glades. There was hardly a breath of wind, the very chirp of the birds was faint and subdued. I strolled on a little way, and finally flung myself down at the foot of a grand old beech-tree. My thoughts of mankind were kindly and charitable. I even forgave Poirot for his absurd secrecy. In fact, I was at peace with the world. Then I yawned.

I thought about the crime, and it struck me as being very unreal and far off.

I yawned again.

Probably, I thought, it really never happened. Of course, it was all a bad dream. The truth of the matter was that it was Lawrence who had murdered Alfred Inglethorp with a croquet mallet. But it was absurd of John to make such a fuss about it, and to go shouting out: 'I tell you I won't have it!'

I woke up with a start.

At once I realized that I was in a very awkward predicament. For, about twelve feet away from me, John and Mary Cavendish were standing facing each other, and they were evidently quarrelling. And, quite as evidently, they were unaware of my vicinity, for before I could move or speak John repeated the words which had aroused me from my dream.

'I tell you, Mary, I won't have it.'

Mary's voice came, cool and liquid:

'Have *you* any right to criticize my actions?'

'It will be the talk of the village! My mother was only buried on Saturday, and here you are gadding about with the fellow.'

'Oh,' she shrugged her shoulders, 'if it is only village gossip that you mind!'

'But it isn't. I've had enough of the fellow hanging about. He's a Polish Jew, anyway.'

'A tinge of Jewish blood is not a bad thing. It leavens the' – she looked at him – 'stolid stupidity of the ordinary Englishman.'

Fire in her eyes, ice in her voice. I did not wonder that the blood rose to John's face in a crimson tide.

'Mary!'

'Well?' Her tone did not change.

The pleading died out of his voice.

'Am I to understand that you will continue to see Bauerstein against my express wishes?'

'If I choose.'

'You defy me?'

'No, but I deny your right to criticize my actions. Have *you* no friends of whom I should disapprove?'

John fell back a pace. The colour ebbed slowly from his face.

'What do you mean?' he said, in an unsteady voice.

'You see!' said Mary quietly. 'You *do* see, don't you, that *you* have no right to dictate to *me* as to the choice of my friends?'

John glanced at her pleadingly, a stricken look in his face.

'No right? Have I *no* right, Mary?' he said unsteadily. He stretched out his hands. 'Mary –'

For a moment, I thought she wavered. A softer expression came over her face, then suddenly she turned almost fiercely away.

'None!'

She was walking away when John sprang after her, and caught her by the arm.

'Mary' – his voice was very quiet now – 'are you in love with this fellow Bauerstein?'

She hesitated, and suddenly there swept across her face a strange expression, old as the hills, yet with something eternally young about it. So might some Egyptian sphinx have smiled.

She freed herself quietly from his arm, and spoke over her shoulder.

'Perhaps,' she said; and then swiftly passed out of the little glade, leaving John standing there as though he had been turned to stone.

Rather ostentatiously, I stepped forward, crackling some dead branches with my feet as I did so. John turned. Luckily, he took if for granted that I had only just come upon the scene.

'Hullo, Hastings. Have you seen the little fellow safely back to his cottage? Quaint little chap! Is he any good, though, really?'

110

'He was considered one of the finest detectives of his day.'

'Oh, well, I suppose there must be something in it, then. What a rotten world it is, though!'

'You find it so?' I asked.

'Good Lord, yes! There's this terrible business to start with. Scotland Yard men in and out of the house like a jack-in-the-box! Never know where they won't turn up next. Screaming headlines in every paper in the country – damn all journalists, I say! Do you know there was a whole crowd staring in at the lodge gates this morning. Sort of Madame Tussaud's chamber of horrors business that can be seen for nothing. Pretty thick, isn't it?'

'Cheer up, John!' I said soothingly. 'It can't last for ever.'

'Can't it, though? It can last long enough for us never to be able to hold up our heads again.'

'No, no, you're getting morbid on the subject.'

'Enough to make a man morbid, to be stalked by beastly journalists and stared at by gaping moon-faced idiots, wherever he goes! But there's worse than that.'

'What?'

John lowered his voice.

'Have you ever thought, Hastings – it's a nightmare to me – who did it? I can't help feeling sometimes it must have been an accident. Because – because – who could have done it? Now Inglethorp's out of the way, there's no one else; no one, I mean, except – one of us.'

Yes, indeed, that was nightmare enough for any man! One of us? Yes, surely it must be so, unless –

A new idea suggested itself to my mind. Rapidly, I considered it. The light increased. Poirot's mysterious doings, his hints – they all fitted in. Fool that I was not to have thought of this possibility before, and what a relief for us all.

'No, John,' I said, 'it isn't one of us. How could it be?'

'I know, but, still, who else is there?'

'Can't you guess?'

'No.'

I looked cautiously round, and lowered my voice.

'Dr Bauerstein!' I whispered.

'Impossible!'

'Not at all.'

'But what earthly interest could he have in mother's death?'

'That I don't see,' I confessed, 'but I'll tell you this: Poirot thinks so.'

'Poirot? Does he? How do you know?'

I told him of Poirot's intense excitement on hearing that Dr Bauerstein had been at Styles on the fatal night, and added:

'He said twice: "That alters everything." And I've been thinking. You know Inglethorp said he had put down the coffee in the hall? Well, it was just then that Bauerstein arrived. Isn't is possible that, as Inglethorp brought him through the hall, the doctor dropped something into the coffee in passing?'

'H'm,' said John. 'It would have been very risky.'

'Yes, but it was possible.'

'And then, how could he know it was her coffee? No, old fellow, I don't think that will wash.'

But I had remembered something else.

'You're quite right. That wasn't how it was done. Listen.' And then I told him of the cocoa sample which Poirot had taken to be analysed.

John interrupted just as I had done.

'But, look here, Bauerstein had had it analysed already?'

'Yes, yes, that's the point. I didn't see it either until now. Don't you understand? Bauerstein had it analysed – that's just it! If Bauerstein's the murderer, nothing could be simpler than for him to substitute some ordinary cocoa for his sample, and send that to be tested. And of course they would find no strychnine! But no one would dream of suspecting Bauerstein, or think of taking another sample – except Poirot,' I added, with belated recognition.

'Yes, but what about the bitter taste that cocoa won't disguise?'

'Well, we've only his word for that. And there are other possibilities. He's admittedly one of the world's greatest toxicologists –'

'One of the world's greatest what? Say it again.'

'He knows more about poisons than almost anybody,' I explained. 'Well, my idea is, that perhaps he's found some way of making strychnine tasteless. Or it may not have been strychnine at all, but some obscure drug no one has ever heard of, which produces much the same symptoms.'

'H'm, yes, that might be,' said John. 'But look here, how could he have got at the cocoa? That wasn't downstairs?'

'No, it wasn't,' I admitted reluctantly.

And then, suddenly, a dreadful possibility flashed through my mind. I hoped and prayed it would not occur to John also. I glanced sideways at him. He was frowning perplexedly, and I drew a deep

112

breath of relief, for the terrible thought that had flashed across my mind was this: that Dr Bauerstein might have had an accomplice.

Yet surely it could not be! Surely no woman as beautiful as Mary Cavendish could be a murderess. Yet beautiful women had been known to poison.

And suddenly I remembered that first conversation at tea on the day of my arrival, and the gleam in her eyes as she had said that poison was a woman's weapon. How agitated she had been on that fatal Tuesday evening! Had Mrs Inglethorp discovered something between her and Bauerstein, and threatened to tell her husband? Was it to stop that denunciation that the crime had been committed?

Then I remembered that enigmatical conversation between Poirot and Evelyn Howard. Was this what they had meant? Was this the monstrous possibility that Evelyn had tried not to believe?

Yes, it all fitted in.

No wonder Miss Howard has suggested 'hushing it up'. Now I understood that unfinished sentence of hers: 'Emily herself –' And in my heart I agreed with her. Would not Mrs Inglethorp have preferred to go unavenged rather than have such terrible dishonour fall upon the name of Cavendish?

'There's another thing,' said John suddenly, and the unexpected sound of his voice made me start guiltily. 'Something which makes me doubt if what you say can be true.'

'What's that?' I asked, thankful that he had gone away from the subject of how the poison could have been introduced into the cocoa.

'Why, the fact that Bauerstein demanded a post-mortem. He needn't have done so. Little Wilkins would have been quite content to let it go at heart disease.'

'Yes,' I said doubtfully. 'But we don't know. Perhaps he thought it safer in the long run. Someone might have talked afterwards. Then the Home Office might have ordered exhumation. The whole thing would have come out, then, and he would have been in an awkward position, for no one would have believed that a man of his reputation could have been deceived into calling it heart disease.'

'Yes, that's possible,' admitted John. 'Still,' he added, 'I'm blest if I can see what his motive could have been.'

I trembled.

'Look here,' I said, 'I may be altogether wrong. And, remember, all this is in confidence.'

'Oh, of course – that goes without saying.'

We had walked, as we talked, and now we passed through the little gate into the garden. Voices rose near at hand, for tea was spread out under the sycamore-tree, as it had been on the day of my arrival.

Cynthia was back from the hospital, and I placed my chair beside her, and told her of Poirot's wish to visit the dispensary.

'Of course! I'd love him to see it. He'd better come to tea there one day. I must fix it up with him. He's such a dear little man! But he *is* funny. He made me take the brooch out of my tie the other day, and put it in again, because he said it wasn't straight.'

I laughed.

'It's quite a mania with him.'

'Yes, isn't it?'

We were silent for a minute or two, and then, glancing in the direction of Mary Cavendish, and dropping her voice, Cynthia said:

'Mr Hastings.'

'Yes?'

'After tea, I want to talk to you.'

Her glance at Mary had set me thinking. I fancied that between these two there existed very little sympathy. For the first time, it occurred to me to wonder about the girl's future. Mrs Inglethorp had made no provision of any kind for her, but I imagined that John and Mary would probably insist on her making her home with them – at any rate until the end of the war. John, I knew, was very fond of her, and would be sorry to let her go.

John, who had gone into the house, now reappeared. His good-natured face wore an unaccustomed frown of anger.

'Confound those detectives! I can't think what they're after! They've been in every room in the house – turning things inside out, and upside down. It really is too bad! I suppose they took advantage of our all being out. I shall go for that fellow Japp, when I next see him!'

'Lot of Paul Prys,' grunted Miss Howard.

Lawrence opined that they had to make a show of doing something.

Mary Cavendish said nothing.

After tea, I invited Cynthia to come for a walk, and we sauntered off into the woods together.

'Well?' I inquired, as soon as we were protected from prying eyes by the leafy screen.

With a sigh, Cynthia flung herself down, and tossed off her hat. The sunlight, piercing through the branches, turned the auburn of her hair to quivering gold.

114

'Mr Hastings – you are always so kind, and you know such a lot.'

It struck me at this moment that Cynthia was really a very charming girl! Much more charming than Mary, who never said things of that kind.

'Well?' I asked benignantly, as she hesitated.

'I want to ask your advice. What shall I do?'

'Do?'

'Yes. You see, Aunt Emily always told me I should be provided for. I suppose she forgot, or didn't think she was likely to die – anyway, I am *not* provided for! And I don't know what to do. Do you think I ought to go away from here at once?'

'Good heavens, no! They don't want to part with you, I'm sure.'

Cynthia hesitated a moment, plucking up the grass with her tiny hands. Then she said: 'Mrs Cavendish does. She hates me.'

'Hates you?' I cried, astonished.

Cynthia nodded.

'Yes. I don't know why, but she can't bear me and *he* can't either.'

'There I know you're wrong,' I said warmly. 'On the contrary, John is very fond of you.'

'Oh, yes – *John*. I meant Lawrence. Not, of course, that I care whether Lawrence hates me or not. Still, it's rather horrid when no one loves you, isn't it?'

'But they do, Cynthia dear,' I said earnestly. 'I'm sure you are mistaken. Look, there is John – and Miss Howard –'

Cynthia nodded rather gloomily. 'Yes, John likes me, I think, and of course Evie, for all her gruff ways, wouldn't be unkind to a fly. But Lawrence never speaks to me if he can help it, and Mary can hardly bring herself to be civil to me. She wants Evie to stay on, is begging her to, but she doesn't want me, and – and – I don't know what to do.' Suddenly the poor child burst out crying.

I don't know what possessed me. Her beauty, perhaps, as she sat there, with the sunlight glinting down on her head; perhaps the sense of relief at encountering someone who so obviously could have no connection with the tragedy; perhaps honest pity for her youth and loneliness. Anyway, I leant forward, and taking her little hand, I said awkwardly:

'Marry me, Cynthia.'

Unwittingly, I had hit upon a sovereign remedy for her tears. She sat up at once, drew her hand away, and said, with some asperity:

'Don't be silly!'

I was a little annoyed.

'I'm not being silly. I am asking you to do me the honour of becoming my wife.'

To my intense surprise, Cynthia burst out laughing, and called me a 'funny bear'.

'It's perfectly sweet of you,' she said, 'but you know you don't want to!'

'Yes, I do. I've got –'

'Never mind what you've got. You don't really want to – and I don't either.'

'Well, of course, that settles it,' I said stiffly. 'But I don't see anything to laugh at. There's nothing funny about a proposal.'

'No, indeed,' said Cynthia. 'Somebody might accept you next time. Good-bye, you've cheered me up *very* much.'

And, with a final uncontrollable burst of merriment, she vanished through the trees.

Thinking over the interview, it struck me as being profoundly unsatisfactory.

It occurred to me suddenly that I would go down to the village, and look up Bauerstein. Somebody ought to be keeping an eye on the fellow. At the same time, it would be wise to allay any suspicions he might have as to his being suspected. I remembered how Poirot had relied on my diplomacy. Accordingly, I went to the little house with the 'Apartments' card inserted in the window, where I knew he lodged, and tapped on the door.

An old woman came and opened it.

'Good afternoon,' I said pleasantly. 'Is Dr Bauerstein in?'

She stared at me.

'Haven't you heard?'

'Heard what?'

'About him.'

'What about him?'

'He's took.'

'Took? Dead?'

No, took by the perlice.'

'By the police!' I gasped. 'Do you mean they've arrested him?'

'Yes, that's it, and –'

I wanted to hear no more, but tore up the village to find Poirot.

CHAPTER X

THE ARREST

To my extreme annoyance, Poirot was not in, and the old Belgian who answered my knock informed me that he believed he had gone to London.

I was dumbfounded. What on earth could Poirot be doing in London? Was it a sudden decision on his part, or had he already made up his mind when he parted from me a few hours earlier?

I retraced my steps to Styles in some annoyance. With Poirot away, I was uncertain how to act. Had he foreseen this arrest? Had he not, in all probability, been the cause of it? Those questions I could not resolve. But in the meantime what was I to do? Should I announce the arrest openly at Styles, or not? Though I did not acknowledge it to myself, the thought of Mary Cavendish was weighing on me. Would it not be a terrible shock to her? For the moment, I set aside utterly any suspicions of her. She could not be implicated – otherwise I should have heard some hint of it.

Of course, there was no possibility of being able permanently to conceal Dr Bauerstein's arrest from her. It would be announced in every newspaper on the morrow. Still, I shrank from blurting it out. If only Poirot had been accessible, I could have asked his advice. What possessed him to go posting off to London in this unaccountable way?

In spite of myself, my opinion of his sagacity was immeasurably heightened. I would never have dreamt of suspecting the doctor, had not Poirot put it into my head. Yes, decidedly, the little man was clever.

After some reflecting, I decided to take John into my confidence, and leave him to make the matter public or not, as he thought fit.

He gave vent to a prodigious whistle, as I imparted the news.

'Great Scot! You *were* right, then. I couldn't believe it at the time.'

'No, it is astonishing until you get used to the idea, and see how it makes everything fit in. Now, what are we to do? Of course, it will be generally known tomorrow.'

John reflected.

'Never mind,' he said at last, 'we won't say anything at present. There is no need. As you say, it will be known soon enough.'

But to my intense surprise, on getting down early the next

morning, and eagerly opening the newspapers, there was not a word about the arrest! There was a column of mere padding about 'The Styles Poisoning Case,' but nothing further. It was rather inexplicable, but I supposed that, for some reason or other, Japp wished to keep it out of the papers. It worried me just a little, for it suggested the possibility that there might be further arrests to come.

After breakfast, I decided to go down to the village, and see if Poirot had returned yet; but, before I could start, a well-known face blocked one of the windows, and the well-known voice said:

'*Bon jour, mon ami!*'

'Poirot,' I exclaimed, with relief, and seizing him by both hands I dragged him into the room. 'I was never so glad to see anyone. Listen, I have said nothing to anybody but John. Is that right?'

'My friend,' replied Poirot, 'I do not know what you are talking about.'

'Dr Bauerstein's arrest, of course,' I answered impatiently.

'Is Bauerstein arrested, then?'

'Did you not know it?'

'Not the least in the world.' But, pausing a moment, he added: 'Still, it does not surprise me. After all, we are only four miles from the coast.'

'The coast?' I asked puzzled. 'What has that got to do with it?'

Poirot shrugged his shoulders.

'Surely, it is obvious!'

'Not to me. No doubt I am very dense, but I cannot see what the proximity of the coast has got to do with the murder of Mrs Inglethorp.'

'Nothing at all, of course,' replied Poirot, smiling. 'But we were speaking of the arrest of Dr Bauerstein.'

'Well, he is arrested for the murder of Mrs Inglethorp –'

'What?' cried Poirot, in apparently lively astonishment. 'Dr Bauerstein arrested for the murder of Mrs Inglethorp?'

'Yes.'

'Impossible! That would be too good a farce! Who told you that, my friend?'

'Well no one exactly told me,' I confessed. 'But he is arrested.'

'Oh, yes, very likely. But for espionage, *mon ami*.'

'Espionage?' I gasped.

'Precisely.'

'Not for poisoning Mrs Inglethorp?'

'Not unless our friend Japp has taken leave of his senses,' replied

Poirot placidly.

'But – but I thought you thought so too?'

Poirot gave me one look, which conveyed a wondering pity, and his full sense of the utter absurdity of such an idea.

'Do you mean to say,' I asked, slowly adapting myself to the new idea, 'that Dr Bauerstein is a spy?'

Poirot nodded.

'Have you never suspected it?'

'It never entered my head.'

'It did not strike you as peculiar that a famous London doctor should bury himself in a little village like this, and should be in the habit of walking about at all hours of the night, fully dressed?'

'No,' I confessed, 'I never thought of such a thing.'

'He is, of course, a German by birth,' said Poirot thoughtfully, 'though he has practised so long in this country that nobody thinks of him as anything but an Englishman. He was naturalized about fifteen years ago. A very clever man – a Jew of course.'

'The blackguard!' I cried indignantly.

'Not at all. He is, on the contrary, a patriot. Think what he stands to lose. I admire the man myself.'

But I could not look at it in Poirot's philosophical way.

'And this is the man with whom Mrs Cavendish has been wandering about all over the country!' I cried indignantly.

'Yes. I should fancy he had found her very useful,' remarked Poirot. 'So long as gossip busied itself in coupling their names together, any other vagaries of the doctor's passed unobserved.'

'Then you think he never really cared for her?' I asked eagerly – rather too eagerly, perhaps, under the circumstances.

'That, of course, I cannot say, but – shall I tell you my own private opinion, Hastings?'

'Yes.'

'Well, it is this: Mrs Cavendish does not care, and never has cared one little jot about Dr Bauerstein!'

'Do you really think so?' I could not disguise my pleasure.

'I am quite sure of it. And I will tell you why.'

'Yes?'

'Because she cares for someone else, *mon ami*.'

'Oh!' What did he mean? In spite of myself, an agreeable warmth spread over me. I am not a vain man where women are concerned, but I remembered certain evidences, too lightly thought of at the time, perhaps, but which certainly seemed to indicate –

My pleasing thoughts were interrupted by the sudden entrance of Miss Howard. She glanced round hastily to make sure there was no one else in the room, and quickly produced an old sheet of brown paper. This she handed to Poirot, murmuring as she did so the cryptic words:

'On top of the wardrobe.' Then she hurriedly left the room.

Poirot unfolded the sheet of paper eagerly, and uttered an exclamation of satisfaction. He spread it out on the table.

'Come here, Hastings. Now tell me, what is that initial – J. Or L.?'

It was a medium-sized sheet of paper, rather dusty, as though it had lain by for some time. But it was the label that was attracting Poirot's attention. At the top, it bore the printed stamp of Messrs Parkson's, the well-known theatrical costumiers, and it was addressed to '– (the debatable initial) Cavendish, Esq., Styles Court, Styles St Mary, Essex.'

'It might be T. Or it might be L.,' I said, after studying the thing for a minute or two. 'It certainly isn't a J.'

'Good,' replied Poirot, folding up the paper again. 'I, also, am of your way of thinking. It is an L., depend upon it!'

'Where did it come from?' I asked curiously. 'Is it important?'

'Moderately so. It confirms a surmise of mine. Having deduced its existence, I set Miss Howard to search for it, and, as you see, she has been successful.'

'What did she mean by "On top of the wardrobe"?'

'She meant,' replied Poirot promptly, 'that she found it on top of a wardrobe.'

'A funny place for a piece of brown paper,' I mused.

'Not at all. The top of a wardrobe is an excellent place for brown paper and cardboard boxes. I have kept them there myself. Neatly arranged, there is nothing to offend the eye.'

'Poirot,' I asked earnestly, 'have you made up your mind about this crime?'

'Yes – that is to say, I believe I know how it was committed.'

'Ah!'

'Unfortunately, I have no proof beyond my surmise, unless –' With sudden energy, he caught me by the arm, and whirled me down the hall, calling out in French in his excitement: 'Mademoiselle Dorcas, Mademoiselle Dorcas, *un moment, s'il vous plaît!*'

Dorcas, quite flurried by the noise, came hurrying out of the pantry.

'My good Dorcas, I have an idea – a little idea – if it should prove justified, what magnificent chance! Tell me, on Monday, not Tuesday, Dorcas, but Monday, the day before the tragedy, did anything go wrong with Mrs Inglethorp's bell?'

Dorcas looked very surprised.

'Yes, sir, now you mention it, it did; though I don't know how you came to hear of it. A mouse, or some such, must have nibbled the wire through. The man came and put it right on Tuesday morning.'

With a long-drawn exclamation of ecstasy, Poirot led the way back to the morning-room.

'See you, one should not ask for outside proof – no, reason should be enough. But the flesh is weak, it is consolation to find that one is on the right track. Ah, my friend, I am like a giant refreshed. I run! I leap.'

And, in very truth, run and leap he did, gambolling wildly down the stretch of lawn outside the long window.

'What is your remarkable little friend doing?' asked a voice behind me, and I turned to find Mary Cavendish at my elbow.

She smiled, and so did I. 'What is it all about?'

'Really, I can't tell you. He asked Dorcas some question about a bell, and appeared so delighted with her answer that he is capering about as you see!'

Mary laughed.

'How ridiculous! He's going out of the gate. Isn't he coming back today?'

'I don't know. I've given up trying to guess what he'll do next.'

'Is he quite mad, Mr Hastings?'

'I honestly don't know. Sometimes, I feel sure he is as mad as a hatter; and then, just as he is at his maddest, I find there is method in his madness.'

'I see.'

In spite of her laugh, Mary was looking thoughtful this morning. She seemed grave, almost sad.

It occurred to me that it would be a good opportunity to tackle her on the subject of Cynthia. I began rather tactfully, I thought, but I had not gone far before she stopped me authoritatively.

'You are an excellent advocate, I have no doubt, Mr Hastings, but in this case your talents are quite thrown away. Cynthia will run no risk of encountering any unkindness from me.'

I began to stammer feebly that I hoped she hadn't thought – But again she stopped me, and her words were so unexpected that they quite drove Cynthia, and her troubles, out of my mind.

121

'Mr Hastings,' she said, 'do you think I and my husband are happy together?'

I was considerably taken aback, and murmured something about it not being my business to think anything of the sort.

'Well,' she said quietly, 'whether it is your business or not, I will tell you that we are *not* happy.'

I said nothing, for I saw that she had not finished.

She began slowly, walking up and down the room, her head a little bent, and that slim, supple figure of hers swaying gently as she walked. She stopped suddenly, and looked up at me.

'You don't know anything about me, do you?' she asked. 'Where I come from, who I was before I married John – anything, in fact? Well, I will tell you. I will make a father confessor of you. You are kind, I think – yes, I am sure you are kind.'

Somehow, I was not quite as elated as I might have been. I remembered that Cynthia had begun her confidences in much the same way. Besides, a father confessor should be elderly, it is not at all the role for a young man.

'My father was English,' said Mrs Cavendish, 'but my mother was a Russian.'

'Ah,' I said, 'now I understand –'

'Understand what?'

'A hint of something foreign – different – that there has always been about you.'

'My mother was very beautiful, I believe. I don't know, because I never saw her. She died when I was quite a little child. I believe there was some tragedy connected with her death – she took an overdose of some sleeping draught by mistake. However that may be, my father was broken-hearted. Shortly afterwards, he went into the Consular Service. Everywhere he went, I went with him. When I was twenty-three, I had been nearly all over the world. It was a splendid life – I loved it.'

There was a smile on her face, and her head was thrown back. She seemed living in the memory of those old glad days.

'Then my father died. He left me very badly off. I had to go and live with some old aunts in Yorkshire.' She shuddered. 'You will understand me when I say that it was a deadly life for a girl brought up as I had been. The narrowness, the deadly monotony of it, almost drove me mad.' She paused a minute, and added in a different tone: 'And then I met John Cavendish.'

'Yes?'

'You can imagine that, from my aunts' point of view, it was a very good match for me. But I can honestly say it was not this fact which weighed with me. No, he was simply a way of escape from the insufferable monotony of my life.'

I said nothing, and after a moment, she went on:

'Don't misunderstand me. I was quite honest with him. I told him, what was true, that I liked him very much, that I hoped to come to like him more, but that I was not in any way what the world calls "in love" with him. He declared that that satisfied him, and so – we were married.'

She waited a long time, a little frown had gathered on her forehead. She seemed to be looking back earnestly into those past days.

'I think – I am sure – he cared for me at first. But I suppose we were not well matched. Almost at once, we drifted apart. He – it is not a pleasant thing for my pride, but it is the truth – tired of me very soon.' I must have made some murmur of dissent, for she went on quickly: 'Oh, yes, he did! Not that it matters now – now that we've come to the parting of the ways.'

'What do you mean?'

She answered quietly:

'I mean that I am not going to remain at Styles.'

'You and John are not going to live here?'

'John may live here, but I shall not.'

'You are going to leave him?'

'Yes.'

'But why?'

She paused a long time, and said at last:

'Perhaps – because I want to be – free!'

And, as she spoke, I had a sudden vision of broad spaces, virgin tracts of forests, untrodden lands – and a realization of what freedom would mean to such a nature as Mary Cavendish. I seemed to see her for a moment as she was, a proud wild creature, as untamed by civilization as some shy bird of the hills. A little cry broke from her lips:

'You don't know, you don't know, how this hateful place has been prison to me!'

'I understand,' I said, 'but – but don't do anything rash.'

'Oh, rash!' Her voice mocked at my prudence.

Then suddenly I said a thing I could have bitten out my tongue for:

'You know that Dr Bauerstein has been arrested?'

123

An instant coldness passed like a mask over her face, blotting out all expression.

'John was so kind as to break that to me this morning.'

'Well, what do you think?' I asked feebly.

'Of what?'

'Of the arrest?'

'What should I think? Apparently he is a German spy; so the gardener had told John.'

Her face and voice were absolutely cold and expressionless. Did she care, or did she not?'

She moved away a step or two, and fingered one of the flower vases. 'These are quite dead. I must do them again. Would you mind moving – thank you, Mr Hastings.' And she walked quietly past me out of the window, with a cool little nod of dismissal.

No, surely she could not care for Bauerstein. No woman could act her part with that icy unconcern.

Poirot did not make his appearance the following morning, and there was no sign of the Scotland Yard men.

But, at lunch-time, there arrived a new piece of evidence – or rather lack of evidence. We had vainly tried to trace the fourth letter which Mrs Inglethorp had written on the evening preceding her death. Our efforts having been in vain, we had abandoned the matter, hoping that it might turn up of itself one day. And this is just what did happen, in the shape of a communication, which arrived by the second post from a firm of French music publishers, acknowledging Mrs Inglethorp's cheque, and regretting they had been unable to trace a certain series of Russian folk songs. So the last hope of solving the mystery, by means of Mrs Inglethorp's correspondence on the fatal evening, had to be abandoned.

Just before tea, I strolled down to tell Poirot of the new disappointment, but found, to my annoyance, that he was once more out.

'Gone to London again?'

'Oh, no, monsieur, he has but taken the train to Tadminster. "To see a young lady's dispensary," he said.'

'Silly ass!' I ejaculated. 'I told him Wednesday was the one day she wasn't there! Well, tell him to look us up tomorrow morning, will you?'

'Certainly, monsieur.'

But, on the following day, no sign of Poirot. I was getting angry. He was really treating us in the most cavalier fashion.

After lunch, Lawrence drew me aside, and asked if I was going down to see him.

'No, I don't think I shall. He can come up here if he wants to see us.'

'Oh!' Lawrence looked indeterminate. Something unusually nervous and excited in his manner roused my curiosity.

'What is it?' I asked. 'I could go if there's anything special.'

'It's nothing much, but – well, if you are going, will you tell him' – he dropped his voice to a whisper – 'I think I've found the extra coffee-cup!'

I had almost forgotten that enigmatical message of Poirot's but now my curiosity was aroused afresh.

Lawrence would say no more, so I decided that I would descend from my high horse, and once more seek out Poirot at Leastways Cottage.

This time I was received with a smile. Monsieur Poirot was within. Would I mount? I mounted accordingly.

Poirot was sitting by the table, his head buried in his hands. He sprang up at my entrance.

'What is it?' I asked solicitously. 'You are not ill, I trust?'

'No, no, not ill. But I decide an affair of great moment.'

'Whether to catch the criminal or not?' I asked facetiously.

But to my great surprise, Poirot nodded gravely.

' "To speak or not to speak," as your so great Shakespeare says, "that is the question".'

I did not trouble to correct the quotation.

'You are not serious, Poirot?'

'I am of the most serious. For the most serious of all things hangs in the balance.'

'And that is?'

'A woman's happiness, *mon ami*,' he said gravely.

I did not quite know what to say.

'The moment has come,' said Poirot thoughtfully, 'and I do not know what to do. For, see you, it is a big stake for which I play. No one but I, Hercule Poirot, would attempt it!' And he tapped himself proudly on the breast.

After pausing a few minutes respectfully, so as not to spoil his effect, I gave him Lawrence's message.

'Aha!' he cried. 'So he has found the extra coffee-cup. That is good. He has more intelligence than would appear, this long-faced Monsieur Lawrence of yours!'

I did not myself think very highly of Lawrence's intelligence; but I forbore to contradict Poirot, and gently took him to task for forgetting my instructions as to which were Cynthia's days off.

'It is true. I have the head of a sieve. However, the other young lady was most kind. She was sorry for my disappointment, and showed me everything in the kindest way.'

'Oh, well, that's all right, then, and you must go to tea with Cynthia another day.'

I told him about the letter.

'I am sorry for that,' he said. 'I always had hopes of that letter. But, no, it was not to be. This affair must all be unravelled from within.' He tapped his forehead. 'These little grey cells. It is "up to them" – as you say over here.' Then, suddenly, he asked: 'Are you a judge of finger-marks, my friend?'

'No,' I said, rather surprised, 'I know that there are no two finger-marks alike, but that's as far as my science goes.'

'Exactly.'

He unlocked a little drawer, and took out some photographs which he laid on the table.

'I have numbered, them, 1, 2, 3. Will you describe them to me?'

I studied the proofs attentively.

'All greatly magnified, I see. No. 1, I should say, are a man's finger-prints; thumb and first finger. No. 2 are a lady's; they are much smaller, and quite different in every way. No. 3' – I paused for some time – 'there seems to be a lot of confused finger-marks, but here, very distinctly, are No. 1's.'

'Overlapping the others?'

'Yes.'

'You recognize them beyond fail?'

'Oh, yes; they are identical.'

Poirot nodded, and gently taking the photographs from me locked them up again.

'I suppose,' I said, 'that as usual, you are not going to explain?'

'On the contrary. No. 1 were the finger-prints of Monsieur Lawrence. No. 2 were those of Mademoiselle Cynthia. They are not important. I merely obtained them for comparison. No. 3 is a little more complicated.'

'Yes?'

'It is, as you see, highly magnified. You may have noticed a sort of blur extending all across the picture. I will not describe to you the special apparatus, dusting powder, etc., which I used. It is a

126

well-known process to the police, and by means of it you can obtain a photograph of the finger-prints on any object in a very short space of time. Well, my friend, you have seen the finger-marks – it remains to tell you the particular object on which they had been left.'

'Go on – I am really excited.'

'*Eh bien!* Photo No. 3 represents the highly magnified surface of a tiny bottle in the top poison cupboard of the dispensary in the Red Cross Hospital at Tadminster – which sounds like the house that Jack built!'

'Good heavens!' I exclaimed. 'But what were Lawrence Cavendish's finger-marks doing on it? He never went near the poison cupboard the day we were there?'

'Oh, yes, he did!'

'Impossible! We were all together the whole time.'

Poirot shook his head.

'No, my friend, there was a moment when you were not all together. There was a moment when you could not have been all together, or it would not have been necessary to call to Monsieur Lawrence to come and join you on the balcony.'

'I'd forgotten that,' I admitted. 'But it was only for a moment.'

'Long enough.'

'Long enough for what?'

Poirot's smile became rather enigmatical.

'Long enough for a gentleman who had once studied medicine to gratify a very natural interest and curiosity.'

Our eyes met. Poirot's were pleasantly vague. He got up and hummed a little tune. I watched him suspiciously.

'Poirot,' I said, 'what was in this particular little bottle?'

Poirot looked out of the window.

'Hydro-chloride of strychnine,' he said, over his shoulder, continuing to hum.

'Good heavens!' I said it quite quietly. I was not surprised. I had expected that answer.

'They use the pure hydro-chloride of strychnine very little – only occasionally for pills. It is the official solution, Liq. Strychnine Hydro-clor. that is used in most medicines. That is why the finger-marks have remained undisturbed since then.'

'How did you manage to take this photograph?'

'I dropped my hat from the balcony,' explained Poirot simply. 'Visitors were not permitted below at that hour, so, in spite of my many apologies, Mademoiselle Cynthia' colleague had to go down and fetch it for me.'

'Then you knew what you were going to find?'

'No, not at all. I merely realized that it was possible, from your story, for Monsieur Lawrence to go to the poison cupboard. The possibility had to be confirmed, or eliminated.'

'Poirot,' I said, 'your gaiety does not deceive me. This is a very important discovery.'

'I do not know,' said Poirot. 'But one thing does strike me. No doubt it has struck you too.'

'What is that?'

'Why, that there is altogether too much strychnine about this case. This is the third time we run up against it. There was strychnine in Mrs Ingelthorp's tonic. There is the strychnine sold across the counter at Styles St Mary by Mace. Now we have more strychnine, handled by one of the household. It is confusing; and, as you know, I do not like confusion.'

Before I could reply, one of the other Belgians opened the door and stuck his head in.

'There is a lady below, asking for Mr Hastings.'

'A lady?'

I jumped up. Poirot followed me down the stairs. Mary Cavendish was standing in the doorway.

'I have been visiting an old woman in the village,' she explained, 'and as Lawrence told me you were with Monsieur Poirot I thought I would call for you.'

'Alas, madame,' said Poirot, 'I thought you had come to honour me with a visit!'

'I will some day, if you ask me,' she promised him, smiling.

'That is well. If you should need a father confessor, madame' – she started ever so slightly – 'remember, Papa Poirot is always at your service.'

She stared at him for a few minutes, as though seeking to read some deeper meaning into his words. Then she turned abruptly away.

'Come, will you not walk back with us too, Monsieur Poirot?'

'Enchanted, madame.'

All the way to Styles, Mary talked fast and feverishly. It struck me that in some way she was nervous of Poirot's eyes.

The weather had broken, and the sharp wind was almost autumnal in its shrewishness. Mary shivered a little, and buttoned her black sports coat closer. The wind through the trees made a mournful

128

noise, like some giant sighing.

We walked up to the great door of Styles, and at once the knowledge came to us that something was wrong.

Dorcas came running out to meet us. She was crying and wringing her hands. I was aware of other servants huddled together in the background, all eyes and ears.

'Oh, m'am! Oh, m'am! I don't know how to tell you –'

'What is it, Dorcas?' I asked impatiently. 'Tell us at once.'

'It's those wicked detectives. They've arrested him – they've arrested Mr Cavendish!'

'Arrested Lawrence?' I gasped.

I saw a strange look come into Dorcas's eyes.

'No, sir. Not Mr Lawrence – Mr John.'

Behind me, with a wild cry, Mary Cavendish fell heavily against me, and as I turned to catch her I met the quiet triumph in Poirot's eyes.

CHAPTER XI

THE CASE FOR THE PROSECUTION

The trial of John Cavendish for the murder of his step-mother took place two months later.

Of the intervening weeks I will say little, but my admiration and sympathy went out unfeignedly to Mary Cavendish. She ranged herself passionately on her husband's side, scorning the mere idea of his guilt, and fought for him tooth and nail.

I expressed my admiration to Poirot, and he nodded thoughtfully. 'Yes, she is of those women who show at their best in adversity. It brings out all that is sweetest and truest in them. Her pride and her jealousy have –'

'Jealousy?' I queried.

'Yes. Have you not realized that she is an unusually jealous woman? As I was saying, her pride and jealousy have been laid aside. She thinks of nothing but her husband, and the terrible fate that is hanging over him.'

He spoke very feelingly, and I looked at him earnestly, remembering that last afternoon, when he had been deliberating whether or not to speak. With his tenderness for 'a woman's happiness', I felt glad that the decision had been taken out of his hands.

'Even now,' I said, 'I can hardly believe it. You see, up to the very last minute, I thought it was Lawrence!'

Poirot grinned.

'I know you did.'

'But John! My old friend John!'

'Every murderer is probably somebody's old friend,' observed Poirot philosophically. 'You cannot mix up sentiment and reason.'

'I must say I think you might have given me a hint.'

'Perhaps, *mon ami*, I did not do so, just because he *was* your old friend.'

I was rather disconcerted by this, remembering how I had busily passed on to John what I believed to be Poirot's views concerning Bauerstein. He, by the way, had been acquitted of the charge brought against him. Nevertheless, although he had been too clever for them this time, and the charge of espionage could not be brought home to him, his wings were pretty well clipped for the future.

I asked Poirot whether he thought John would be condemned. To my intense surprise, he replied that, on the contrary, he was extremely likely to be acquitted.

'But Poirot –' I protested.

'Oh, my friend, have I not said to you all along that I have no proofs. It is one thing to know that a man is guilty, it is quite another matter to prove him so. And, in this case, there is terribly little evidence. That is the whole trouble. I, Hercule Poirot, know, but I lack the last link in my chain. And unless I can find that missing link –' He shook his head gravely.

'When did you first suspect John Cavendish?' I asked, after a minute or two.

'Did you not suspect him at all?'

'No, indeed.'

'Not after that fragment of conversation you overheard between Mrs Cavendish and her mother-in-law, and her subsequent lack of frankness at the inquest?'

'No.'

'Did you not put two and two together, and reflect that if it was not Alfred Inglethorp who was quarrelling with his wife – and you remember, he strenuously denied it at the inquest – it must be either Lawrence or John? Now, if it was Lawrence, Mary Cavendish's conduct was just as inexplicable. But if, on the other hand, it was John, the whole thing was explained quite naturally.'

'So,' I cried, a light breaking in upon me, 'it was John who quarrelled with his mother that afternoon?'

'Exactly.'

'And you have known this all along?'

'Certainly. Mrs Cavendish's behaviour could only be explained that way.'

'And yet you say he may be acquitted?'

Poirot shrugged his shoulders.

'Certainly I do. At the police court proceedings, we shall hear the case for the prosecution, but in all probability his solicitors will advise him to reserve his defence. That will be sprung upon us at the trial. And – ah, by the way, I have a word of caution to give you, my friend. I must not appear in the case.'

'What?'

'No. Officially, I have nothing to do with it. Until I have found that last link in my chain, I must remain behind the scenes. Mrs Cavendish must think I am working for her husband, not against him.'

'I say, that's playing it a bit low down,' I protested.

'Not at all. We have to deal with a most clever and unscrupulous man, and we must use any means in our power – otherwise he will slip through our fingers. That is why I have been careful to remain in the background. All the discoveries have been made by Japp, and Japp will take all the credit. If I am called upon to give evidence at all' – he smiled broadly – 'it will probably be as witness for the defence.'

I could hardly believe my ears.

'It is quite *en règle*,' continued Poirot. 'Strangely enough, I can give evidence that will demolish one contention of the prosecution.'

'Which one?'

'The one that relates to the destruction of the will. John Cavendish did not destroy that will.'

Poirot was a true prophet. I will not go into the details of the police court proceedings, as it involves many tiresome repetitions. I will merely state baldly that John Cavendish reserved his defence, and was duly committed for trial.

September found us all in London. Mary took a house in Kensington, Poirot being included in the family party.

I myself had been given a job at the War Office, so was able to see them continually.

As the weeks went by, the state of Poirot's nerves grew worse and worse. That 'last link' he talked about was still lacking. Privately, I hoped it might remain so, for what happiness could there be for Mary, if John were not acquitted?

On September 15th John Cavendish appeared in the dock of the Old Bailey, charged with 'The Wilful Murder of Emily Agnes Inglethorp', and pleaded 'Not Guilty'.

Sir Ernest Heavywether, the famous K.C., had been engaged to defend him.

Mr Philips, K.C., opened the case for the Crown.

The murder, he said, was a most premeditated and cold-blooded one. It was neither more nor less than the deliberate poisoning of a fond and trusting woman by the stepson to whom she had been more than a mother. Ever since his boyhood, she had supported him. He and his wife had lived at Styles Court in every luxury, surrounded by her care and attention. She had been their kind and generous benefactress.

He proposed to call witnesses to show how the prisoner, a profligate and spendthrift, had been at the end of his financial tether, and had also been carrying on an intrigue with a certain Mrs Raikes, a

132

neighbouring farmer's wife. This having come to his stepmother's ears, she taxed him with it on the afternoon before her death, and a quarrel ensued, part of which was overheard. On the previous day, the prisoner had purchased strychnine at the village chemist's shop, wearing a disguise by means of which he hoped to throw the onus of the crime upon another man – to wit, Mrs Inglethorp's husband, of whom he had been bitterly jealous. Luckily for Mr Inglethorp, he had been able to produce an unimpeachable alibi.

On the afternoon of July 17th, continued Counsel, immediately after the quarrel with her son, Mrs Inglethorp made a new will. This will was found destroyed in the grate of her bedroom the following morning, but evidence had come to light which showed that it had been drawn up in favour of her husband. Deceased had already made a will in his favour before her marriage, but – and Mr Philips wagged an expressive forefinger – the prisoner was not aware of that. What had induced the deceased to make a fresh will, with the old one still extant, he could not say. She was an old lady, and might possibly have forgotten the former one; or – this seemed to him more likely – she may have had an idea that it was revoked by her marriage, as there had been some conversation on the subject. Ladies were not always very well versed in legal knowledge. She had, about a year before, executed a will in favour of the prisoner. He would call evidence to show that it was the prisoner who ultimately handed his stepmother her coffee on the fatal night. Later in the evening, he had sought admission to her room, on which occasion, no doubt, he found an opportunity of destroying the will which, as far as he knew, would render the one in his favour valid.

The prisoner had been arrested in consequence of the discovery, in his room, by Detective-Inspector Japp – a most brilliant officer – of the identical phial of strychnine which had been sold at the village chemist's to the supposed Mr Inglethorp on the day before the murder. It would be for the jury to decide whether or no these damning facts constituted an overwhelming proof of the prisoner's guilt.

And, subtly implying that a jury which did not so decide was quite unthinkable, Mr Philips sat down and wiped his forehead.

The first witnesses for the prosecution were mostly those who had been called at the inquest, the medical evidence being again taken first.

Sir Ernest Heavywether, who was famous all over England for the unscrupulous manner in which he bullied witnesses, only asked two questions.

'I take it, Dr Bauerstein, that strychnine, as a drug, acts quickly?'

'Yes.'

'And that you are unable to account for the delay in this case?'

'Yes.'

'Thank you.'

Mr Mace identified the phial handed him by Counsel as that sold by him to 'Mr Inglethorp'. Pressed, he admitted that he only knew Mr Inglethorp by sight. He had never spoken to him. The witness was not cross-examined.

Alfred Inglethorp was called, and denied having purchased the poison. He also denied having quarrelled with his wife. Various witnesses testified to the accuracy of these statements.

The gardeners' evidence as to the witnessing of the will was taken, and then Dorcas was called.

Dorcas, faithful to her 'young gentlemen', denied strenuously that it could have been John's voice she heard, and resolutely declared, in the teeth of everything, that it was Mr Inglethorp who had been in the boudoir with her mistress. A rather wistful smile passed across the face of the prisoner in the dock. He knew only too well how useless her gallant defiance was, since it was not the object of the defence to deny this point. Mrs Cavendish, of course, could not be called upon to give evidence against her husband.

After various questions on other matters, Mr Philips asked:

'In the month of June last, do you remember a parcel arriving for Mr Lawrence Cavendish from Parkson's?'

Dorcas shook her head.

'I don't remember, sir. It may have done, but Mr Lawrence was away from home part of June.'

'In the event of a parcel arriving for him whilst he was away, what would be done with it?'

'It would either be put in his room or sent on after him.'

'By you?'

'No, sir, I should leave it on the hall table. It would be Miss Howard who would attend to anything like that.'

Evelyn Howard was called and, after being examined on other points, was questioned as to the parcel.

'Don't remember. Lots of parcels come. Can't remember one special one.'

'You do not know if it was sent after Mr Lawrence Cavendish to Wales, or whether it was put in his room?'

'Don't think it was sent after him. Should have remembered if it was.'

'Supposing a parcel arrived addressed to Mr Lawrence Cavendish, and afterwards it disappeared, should you remark its absence?'

'No, don't think so. I should think someone had taken charge of it.'

'I believe, Miss Howard, that it was you who found this sheet of brown paper?' He held up the same dusty piece which Poirot and I had examined in the morning room at Styles.

'Yes, I did.'

'How did you come to look for it.'

'The Belgian detective who was employed on the case asked me to search for it.'

'Where did you eventually discover it?'

'On the top of – of – a wardrobe.'

'On the top of the prisoner's wardrobe?'

'I believe so.'

'Did you not find it yourself?'

'Yes.'

'Then you must know where you found it?'

'Yes, it was on the prisoner's wardrobe.'

'That is better.'

An assistant from Parkson's Theatrical Costumiers, testified that on June 29th they had supplied a black beard to Mr L. Cavendish, as requested. It was ordered by letter, and a postal order was enclosed. No, they had not kept the letter. All transactions were entered in their books. They had sent the beard, as directed, to 'L. Cavendish, Esq., Styles Court.'

Sir Ernest Heavywether rose ponderously.

'Where was the letter written from?'

'From Styles Court.'

'The same address to which you sent the parcel?'

'Yes.'

Like a beast of prey, Heavywether fell upon him:

'How do you know?'

'I – I don't understand.'

'How do you know that letter came from Styles? Did you notice the postmark?'

'No – but –'

'Ah, you did *not* notice the postmark! And yet you affirm so confidently that it came from Styles. It might, in fact, have been any postmark?'

'Y – es.'

'In fact, the letter, though written on stamped notepaper, might have been posted from anywhere? From Wales, for instance?'

The witness admitted that such might be the case, and Sir Ernest signified that he was satisfied.

Elizabeth Wells, second housemaid at Styles, stated that after she had gone to bed she remembered that she had bolted the front door, instead of leaving it on the latch as Mr Inglethorp had requested. She had accordingly gone downstairs again to rectify her error. Hearing a slight noise in the West wing, she had peeped along the passage, and had seen Mr John Cavendish knocking at Mrs Inglethorp's door.

Sir Ernest Heavywether made short work of her, and under his unmerciful bullying she contradicted herself hopelessly, and Sir Ernest sat down again with a satisfied smile on his face.

With the evidence of Annie, as to the candle grease on the floor, and as to seeing the prisoner take the coffee into the boudoir, the proceedings were adjourned until the following day.

As we went home, Mary Cavendish spoke bitterly against the prosecuting counsel.

'That hateful man! What a net he has drawn around my poor John! How he twisted every little fact until he made it seem what it wasn't!'

'Well,' I said consolingly, 'it will be the other way about tomorrow.'

'Yes,' she said meditatively; then suddenly dropped her voice. 'Mr Hastings, you do not think – surely it could not have been Lawrence – oh, no, that could not be !'

But I myself was puzzled, and as soon as I was alone with Poirot I asked him what he thought Sir Ernest was driving at.

'Ah!' said Poirot appreciatively. 'He is a clever man, that Sir Ernest.'

'Do you think he believes Lawrence guilty?'

'I do not think he believes or cares anything! No, what he is trying for is to create such confusion in the minds of the jury that they are divided in their opinion as to which brother did it. He is endeavouring to make out that there is quite as much evidence against Lawrence as against John – and I am not at all sure that he will not succeed.'

Detective-Inspector Japp was the first witness called when the trial was reopened, and gave his evidence succinctly and briefly. After relating the earlier events, he proceeded:

'Acting on information received, Superintendent Summerhaye and myself searched the prisoner's room, during his temporary absence from the house. In his chest of drawers, hidden beneath some underclothing, we found: first, a pair of gold-rimmed pince-nez similar to those worn by Mr Inglethorp' – these were exhibited – 'secondly, this phial.'

The phial was that already recognized by the chemist's assistant, a tiny bottle of blue glass, containing a few grains of a white crystalline powder, and labelled: 'Strychnine Hydro-chloride. POISON.'

A fresh piece of evidence discovered by the detectives since the police court proceedings was a long, almost new piece of blotting-paper. It had been found in Mrs Inglethorp's cheque book, and on being reversed at a mirror, showed clearly the words: '. . . everything of which I die possessed I leave to my beloved husband Alfred Ing . . .' This placed beyond question the fact that the destroyed will had been in favour of the deceased lady's husband. Japp then produced the charred fragment of paper recovered from the grate, and this, with the discovery of the beard in the attic, completed his evidence.

But Sir Ernest's cross-examination was yet to come.

'What day was it when you searched the prisoner's room?'

'Tuesday, the 24th of July.'

'Exactly a week after the tragedy?'

'Yes.'

'You found these two objects, you say, in the chest of drawers. Was the drawer unlocked?'

'Yes.'

'Does it not strike you as unlikely that a man who had committed a crime should keep the evidence of it in an unlocked drawer for anyone to find?'

'He might have stowed them there in a hurry.'

'But you have just said it was a whole week since the crime. He would have had ample time to remove them and destroy them.'

'Perhaps.'

'There is no perhaps about it. Would he, or would he not have had plenty of time to remove and destroy them?'

'Yes.'

'Was the pile of underclothes under which the things were hidden heavy or light?'

'Heavyish.'

'In other words, it was winter underclothing. Obviously, the prisoner would not be likely to go to that drawer?'

137

'Perhaps not.'

'Kindly answer my question. Would the prisoner, in the hottest week of a hot summer, be likely to go to a drawer containing winter underclothing? Yes, or no?'

'No.'

'In that case, is it not possible that the articles in question might have been put there by a third person, and that the prisoner was quite unaware of their presence?'

'I should not think it likely.'

'But it is possible?'

'Yes.'

'That is all.'

More evidence followed. Evidence as to the financial difficulties in which the prisoner had found himself at the end of July. Evidence as to his intrigue with Mrs Raikes – poor Mary, that must have been bitter hearing for a woman of her pride. Evelyn Howard had been right in her facts, though her animosity against Alfred Inglethorp had caused her to jump to the conclusion that he was the person concerned.

Lawrence Cavendish was then put into the box. In a low voice, in answer to Mr Philips' questions, he denied having ordered anything from Parkson's in June. In fact, on June 29th, he had been staying away, in Wales.

Instantly, Sir Ernest's chin was shooting pugnaciously forward.

'You deny having ordered a black beard from Parkson's on June 29th?'

'I do.'

'Ah! In the event of anything happening to your brother, who will inherit Styles Court?'

The brutality of the question called a flush to Lawrence's pale face. The Judge gave vent to a faint murmur of disapprobation, and the prisoner in the dock leant forward angrily.

Heavywether cared nothing for his client's anger.

'Answer my question, if you please.'

'I suppose,' said Lawrence quietly, 'that I should.'

'What do you mean by you "suppose"? Your brother has no children. You *would* inherit it, wouldn't you?'

'Yes.'

'Ah, that's better,' said Heavywether, with ferocious geniality. 'And you'd inherit a good slice of money too, wouldn't you?'

'Really, Sir Ernest,' protested the Judge, 'these questions are not relevant.'

Sir Ernest bowed, and having shot his arrow proceeded.

'On Tuesday, the 17th July, you went, I believe, with another guest, to visit the dispensary at the Red Cross Hospital in Tadminster?'

'Yes.'

'Did you – while you happened to be alone for a few seconds – unlock the poison cupboard, and examine some of the bottles?'

'I – I may have done so.'

'I put it to you that you did so?'

'Yes.'

Sir Ernest fairly shot the next question at him.

'Did you examine one bottle in particular?'

'No, I do not think so.'

'Be careful, Mr Cavendish, I am referring to a little bottle of Hydro-chloride of Strychnine.'

Lawrence was turning a sickly greenish colour.

'N – o – I am sure I didn't.'

'Then how do you account for the fact that you left the unmistakable impress of your finger-prints on it?'

The bullying manner was highly efficacious with a nervous disposition.

'I – I suppose I must have taken up the bottle.'

'I suppose so too! Did you abstract any of the contents of the bottle?'

'Certainly not.'

'Then why did you take it up?'

'I once studied to be a doctor. Such things naturally interest me.'

'Ah! So poisons "naturally interest" you, do they? Still, you waited to be alone before gratifying that "interest" of yours?'

'That was pure chance. If the others had been there, I should have done just the same.'

'Still, as it happens, the others were not there?'

'No, but –'

'In fact, during the whole afternoon, you were only alone for a couple of minutes, and it happened – I say, it happened – to be during those two minutes that you displayed your "natural interest" in Hydro-chloride of Strychnine?'

Lawrence stammered pitiably.

'I – I –'

With a satisfied and expressive countenance, Sir Ernest observed:

139

'I have nothing more to ask you, Mr Cavendish.'

This bit of cross-examination had caused great excitement in court. The heads of the many fashionably attired women present were busily laid together, and their whispers became so loud that the Judge angrily threatened to have the court cleared if there was not immediate silence.

There was little more evidence. The handwriting experts were called upon for their opinion of the signature of 'Alfred Inglethorp' in the chemist's poison register. They all declared unanimously that it was certainly not his handwriting, and gave it as their view that it might be that of the prisoner disguised. Cross-examined, they admitted that it might be the prisoner's handwriting cleverly counterfeited.

Sir Ernest Heavywether's speech in opening the case for the defence was not a long one, but it was backed by the full force of his emphatic manner. Never, he said, in the course of his long experience, had he known a charge of murder rest on slighter evidence. Not only was it entirely circumstantial, but the greater part of it was practically unproved. Let them take the testimony they had heard and sift it impartially. The strychnine had been found in a drawer in the prisoner's room. That drawer was an unlocked one, as he had pointed out, and he submitted that there was no evidence to prove that it was the prisoner who had concealed the poison there. It was, in fact, a wicked and malicious attempt on the part of some third person to fix the crime on the prisoner. The prosecution had been unable to produce a shred of evidence in support of their contention that it was the prisoner who ordered the black beard from Parkson's. The quarrel which had taken place between the prisoner and his stepmother was freely admitted, but both it and his financial embarrassments had been grossly exaggerated.

His learned friend – Sir Ernest nodded carelessly at Mr Philips – had stated that if prisoner were an innocent man, he would have come forward at the inquest to explain that it was he, and not Mr Inglethorp, who had been the participator in the quarrel. He thought the facts had been misrepresented. What had actually occurred was this. The prisoner, returning to the house on Tuesday evening, had been authoritatively told that there had been a violent quarrel between Mr and Mrs Inglethorp. No suspicion had entered the prisoner's head that anyone could possibly have mistaken his voice for that of Mr Inglethorp. He naturally concluded that his stepmother had had two quarrels.

140

The prosecution averred that on Monday, July 16th, the prisoner had entered the chemist's shop in the village, disguised as Mr Inglethorp. The prisoner, on the contrary, was at that time at a lonely spot called Marston's Spinney, where he had been summoned by an anonymous note, couched in blackmailing terms, and threatening to reveal certain matters to his wife unless he complied with its demands. The prisoner had, accordingly, gone to the appointed spot, and after waiting there vainly for half an hour he returned home. Unfortunately, he had met with no one on the way there or back who could vouch for the truth of his story, but luckily he had kept the note, and it would be produced as evidence.

As for the statement relating to the destruction of the will, the prisoner had formerly practised at the Bar, and was perfectly well aware that the will made in his favour a year before was automatically revoked by his stepmother's re-marriage. He would call evidence to show who did destroy the will, and it was possible that that might open up quite a new view of the case.

Finally, he would point out to the jury that there was evidence against other people besides John Cavendish. He would direct their attention to the fact that the evidence against Mr Lawrence Cavendish was quite as strong, if not stronger than that against his brother.

He would now call the prisoner.

John acquitted himself well in the witness-box. Under Sir Ernest's skilful handling, he told his tale credibly and well. The anonymous note received by him was produced, and handed to the jury to examine. The readiness with which he admitted his financial difficulties, and the disagreement with his stepmother, lent value to his denials.

At the close of his examination, he paused, and said:

'I should like to make one thing clear. I utterly reject and disapprove of Sir Ernest Heavywether's insinuations against my brother. My brother, I am convinced, had no more to do with the crime than I have.'

Sir Ernest merely smiled, and noted with a sharp eye that John's protest had produced a very favourable impression on the jury.

Then the cross-examination began.

'I understand you to say that it never entered your head that the witnesses at the inquest could possibly have mistaken your voice for that of Mr Inglethorp. Is not that very surprising?'

'No, I don't think so. I was told there had been a quarrel between

141

my mother and Mr Inglethorp, and it never occurred to me that such was not really the case.'

'Not when the servant Dorcas repeated certain fragments of the conversation – fragments which you must have recognized?'

'I did not recognize them.'

'Your memory must be unusually short!'

'No, but we were both angry, and, I think, said more than we meant. I paid very little attention to my mother's actual words.'

Mr Philips' incredulous sniff was a triumph of forensic skill. He passed on to the subject of the note.

'You have produced this note very opportunely. Tell me, is there nothing familiar about the handwriting of it?'

'Not that I know of.'

'Do you not think that it bears a marked resemblance to your own handwriting – carelessly disguised?'

'No, I do not think so.'

'I put it to you that it is your handwriting!'

'No.'

'I put it to you that, anxious to prove an alibi, you conceived the idea of a fictitious and rather incredible appointment, and wrote this note yourself in order to bear out your statement!'

'No.'

'Is it not a fact that, at the time you claim to have been waiting about at a solitary and unfrequented spot, you were really in the chemist's shop in Styles St Mary, where you purchased strychnine in the name of Alfred Inglethorp?'

'No, that is a lie.'

'I put it to you that, wearing a suit of Mr Inglethorp's clothes, with a black beard trimmed to resemble his, you were there – and signed the register in his name!'

'That is absolutely untrue.'

'Then I will leave the remarkable similarity of handwriting between the note, the register, and your own, to the consideration of the jury,' said Mr Philips, and sat down with the air of a man who had done his duty, but who was nevertheless horrified by such deliberate perjury.

After this, as it was growing late, the case was adjourned till Monday.

Poirot, I noticed, was looking profoundly discouraged. He had that little frown between the eyes that I knew so well.

'What is it, Poirot?' I inquired.

142

'Ah, *mon ami*, things are going badly, badly.'

In spite of myself, my heart gave a leap of relief. Evidently there was a likelihood of John Cavendish being acquitted.

When we reached the house, my little friend waved aside Mary's offer of tea.

'No, I thank you, madame. I will mount to my room.'

I followed him. Still frowning, he went across to the desk and took out a small pack of patience cards. Then he drew up a chair to the table, and to my utter amazement, began solemnly to build card houses!

My jaw dropped involuntarily, and he said at once:

'No, *mon ami*, I am not in my second childhood! I steady my nerves, that is all. This employment requires precision of the fingers. With precision of the fingers goes precision of the brain. And never have I needed that more than now!'

'What is the trouble?' I asked.

With a great thump on the table, Poirot demolished his carefully built-up edifice.

'It is this, *mon ami!* That I can build card houses seven stories high, but I cannot' – thump – 'find' – thump – 'that last link of which I spoke to you.'

I could not quite tell what to say, so I held my peace, and he began slowly building up the cards again, speaking in jerks as he did so.

'It is done – so! By placing – one card – on another – with mathematical – precision!'

I watched the card house rising under his hands, story by story. He never hesitated or faltered. It was really almost like a conjuring trick.

'What a steady hand you've got,' I remarked. 'I believe I've only seen your hand shake once.'

'On an occasion when I was enraged, without doubt,' observed Poirot, with great placidity.

'Yes, indeed! You were in a towering rage. Do you remember? It was when you discovered that the lock of the despatch-case in Mrs Inglethorp's bedroom had been forced. You stood by the mantel-piece, twiddling the things on it in your usual fashion, and your hand shook like a leaf! I must say –'

But I stopped suddenly. For Poirot, uttering a hoarse and inarticulate cry, again annihilated his masterpiece of cards, and putting his hands over his eyes swayed backwards and forwards, apparently suffering the keenest agony.

'Good heavens, Poirot!' I cried. 'What is the matter? Are you

143

taken ill?'

'No, no,' he gasped. 'It is – it is – that I have an idea!'

'Oh!' I exclaimed, much relieved. 'One of your "little ideas"?'

'Ah, *ma foi*, no!' replied Poirot frankly. 'This time it is an idea gigantic! Stupendous! And you – *you*, my friend, have given it to me!'

Suddenly clasping me in his arms, he kissed me warmly on both cheeks, and before I had recovered from my surprise ran headlong from the room.

Mary Cavendish entered at that moment.

'What *is* the matter with Monsieur Poirot? He rushed past me crying out: "A garage! For the love of Heaven, direct me to a garage, madame!" And, before I could answer, he had dashed out into the street.'

I hurried to the window. True enough, there he was, tearing down the street, hatless, and gesticulating as he went. I turned to Mary with a gesture of despair.

'He'll be stopped by a policeman in another minute. There he goes, round the corner!'

Our eyes met, and we stared helplessly at one another.

'What can be the matter?'

I shook my head.

'I don't know. He was building card houses, when suddenly he said he had an idea, and rushed off as you saw.'

'Well,' said Mary, 'I expect he will be back before dinner.'

But night fell, and Poirot had not returned.

CHAPTER XII

THE LAST LINK

Poirot's abrupt departure had intrigued us all greatly. Sunday morning wore away, and still he did not reappear. But about three o'clock a ferocious and prolonged hooting outside drove us to the window, to see Poirot alighting from a car, accompanied by Japp and Summerhaye. The little man was transformed. He radiated an absurd complacency. He bowed with exaggerated respect to Mary Cavendish.

'Madame, I have your permission to hold a little *réunion* in the *salon?* It is necessary for every one to attend.'

Mary smiled sadly.

'You know, Monsieur Poirot, that you have *carte blanche* in every way.'

'You are too amiable, madame.'

Still beaming, Poirot marshalled us all into the drawing-room, bringing forward chairs as he did so.

'Miss Howard – here. Mademoiselle Cynthia. Monsieur Lawrence. The good Dorcas. And Annie. *Bien!* We must delay our proceedings a few minutes more until Mr Inglethorp arrives. I have sent him a note.'

Miss Howard rose immediately from her seat.

'If that man comes into the house, I leave it!'

'No, no!' Poirot went up to her and pleaded in a low voice.

Finally Miss Howard consented to return to her chair. A few minutes later Alfred Inglethorp entered the room.

The company once assembled, Poirot rose from his seat with the air of a popular lecturer, and bowed politely to his audience.

'*Messieurs, mesdames,* as you all know, I was called in by Monsieur John Cavendish to investigate this case. I at once examined the bedroom of the deceased which, by the advice of the doctors, had been kept locked, and was consequently exactly as it had been when the tragedy occurred. I found: first, a fragment of green material; secondly, a stain on the carpet near the window, still damp; thirdly, an empty box of bromide powders.

'To take the fragment of green material first, I found it caught in the bolt of the communicating door between that room and the adjoining one occupied by Mademoiselle Cynthia. I handed the fragment over to the police who did not consider it of much importance. Nor did they recognize it for what it was – a piece torn from a green land armlet.'

There was a little stir of excitement.

'Now there was only one person at Styles who worked on the land – Mrs Cavendish. Therefore it must have been Mrs Cavendish who entered deceased's room through the door communicating with Mademoiselle Cynthia's room.'

'But that door was bolted on the inside!' I cried.

'When I examined the room, yes. But in the first place we have only her word for it, since it was she who tried that particular door and reported it fastened. In the ensuing confusion she would have had ample opportunity to shoot the bolt across. I took an early opportunity of verifying my conjectures. To begin with, the fragment corresponds exactly with a tear in Mrs Cavendish's armlet. Also, at the inquest, Mrs Cavendish declared that she had heard, from her own room, the fall of the table by the bed. I took an early opportunity of testing that statement by stationing my friend Monsieur Hastings, in the left wing of the building, just outside Mrs Cavendish's door. I myself, in company with the police, went to the deceased's room, and whilst there I, apparently accidentally, knocked over the table in question, but found that, as I had expected, Monsieur Hastings had heard no sound at all. This confirmed my belief that Mrs Cavendish was not speaking the truth when she declared that she had been dressing in her room at the time of the tragedy. In fact, I was convinced that, far from having been in her own room, Mrs Cavendish was actually in the deceased's room when the alarm was given.'

I shot a quick glance at Mary. She was very pale, but smiling.

'I proceeded to reason on that assumption. Mrs Cavendish is in her mother-in-law's room. We will say that she is seeking for something and has not yet found it. Suddenly Mrs Inglethorp awakens and is seized with an alarming paroxysm. She flings out her arm, overturning the bed table, and then pulls desperately at the bell. Mrs Cavendish, startled, drops her candle, scattering the grease on the carpet. She picks it up, and retreats quickly to Mademoiselle Cynthia's room, closing the door behind her. She hurries out into the passage, for the servants must not find her where she is. But it is too late! Already footsteps are echoing along the gallery which connects the two wings. What can she do? Quick as thought, she hurries back to the young girl's room, and starts shaking her awake. The hastily

146

aroused household come trooping down the passage. They are all busily battering at Mrs Inglethorp's door. It occurs to nobody that Mrs Cavendish has not arrived with the rest, but – and this is significant – I can find no one who saw her come from the other wing.' He looked at Mary Cavendish. 'Am I right, madame?'

She bowed her head.

'Quite right, monsieur. You understand that, if I had thought I would do my husband any good by revealing these facts, I would have done so. But it did not seem to me to bear upon the question of his guilt or innocence.'

'In a sense, that is correct, madame. But it cleared my mind of many misconceptions, and left me free to see other facts in their true significance.'

'The will!' cried Lawrence. 'Then it was you, Mary, who destroyed the will?'

She shook her head, and Poirot shook his also.

'No,' she said quietly. 'There is only one person who could possibly have destroyed that will – Mrs Inglethorp herself!'

'Impossible!' I exclaimed. 'She had only made it out that very afternoon!'

'Nevertheless, *mon ami*, it was Mrs Inglethorp. Because, in no other way can you account for the fact that, on one of the hottest days of the year, Mrs Inglethorp ordered a fire to be lighted in her room.'

I gave a gasp. What idiots we had been never to think of that fire as being incongruous! Poirot was continuing.

'The temperature on that day, messieurs, was 80° in the shade. Yet Mrs Inglethorp ordered a fire! Why? Because she wished to destroy something, and could think of no other way. You will remember that, in consequence of the War economies practised at Styles, no waste paper was thrown away. There was, therefore, no means of destroying a thick document such as a will. The moment I heard of a fire being lighted in Mrs Inglethorp's room, I leaped to the conclusion that it was to destroy some important document – possibly a will. So the discovery of the charred fragment in the grate was no surprise to me. I did not, of course, know at the time that the will in question had only been made that afternoon, and I will admit that, when I learnt that fact, I fell into a grievous error. I came to the conclusion that Mrs Inglethorp's determination to destroy her will arose as a direct consequence of the quarrel she had that afternoon, and that therefore the quarrel took place after, and not before, the making of the will.

'Here, as we know, I was wrong, and I was forced to abandon the idea. I faced the problem from a new standpoint. Now, at 4 o'clock, Dorcas overheard her mistress saying angrily: "You need not think that any fear of publicity, or scandal between husband and wife will deter me." I conjectured, and conjectured rightly, that these words were addressed, not to her husband, but to Mr John Cavendish. At 5 o'clock, an hour later, she uses almost the same words, but the standpoint is different. She admits to Dorcas, "I don't know what to do; scandal between husband and wife is a dreadful thing." At 4 o'clock she has been angry, but completely mistress of herself. At 5 o'clock she is in violent distress, and speaks of having had "a great shock".

'Looking at the matter psychologically, I drew one deduction which I was convinced was correct. The second "scandal" she spoke of was not the same as the first — and it concerned herself!

'Let us reconstruct. At 4 o'clock, Mrs Inglethorp quarrels with her son, and threatens to denounce him to his wife — who, by the way, overheard the greater part of the conversation. At 4.30, Mrs Inglethorp, in consequence of a conversation on the validity of wills, makes a will in favour of her husband, which the two gardeners witness. At 5 o'clock, Dorcas finds her mistress in a state of considerable agitation, with a slip of paper — "a letter", Dorcas thinks — in her hand, and it is then that she orders the fire in her room to be lighted. Presumably, then, between 4.30 and 5 o'clock, something has occurred to occasion a complete revolution of feeling, since she is now as anxious to destroy the will, as she was before to make it. What was that something?

'As far as we know, she was quite alone during that half-hour. Nobody entered or left that boudoir. What then occasioned this sudden change of sentiment?

'One can only guess, but I believe my guess to be correct. Mrs Inglethorp had no stamps in her desk. We know this, because later she asked Dorcas to bring her some. Now in the opposite corner of the room stood her husband's desk — locked. She was anxious to find some stamps, and, according to my theory, she tried her own keys in the desk. That one of them fitted I know. She therefore opened the desk, and in searching for the stamps she came across something else — that slip of paper which Dorcas saw in her hand, and which assuredly was never meant for Mrs Inglethorp's eyes. On the other hand, Mrs Cavendish believed that the slip of paper to which her mother-in-law clung so tenaciously was a written proof of her own

148

husband's infidelity. She demanded it from Mrs Inglethrop who assured her, quite truly, that it had nothing to do with that matter. Mrs Cavendish did not believe her. She thought that Mrs Inglethorp was shielding her stepson. Now Mrs Cavendish is a very resolute woman, and, behind her mask of reserve, she was madly jealous of her husband. She determined to get hold of that paper at all costs, and in this resolution chance came to her aid. She happened to pick up the key of Mrs Inglethorp's despatch-case, which had been lost that morning. She knew that her mother-in-law invariably kept all important papers in this particular case.

'Mrs Cavendish, therefore, made her plans as only a woman driven desperate through jealously could have done. Some time in the evening she unbolted the door leading into Mademoiselle Cynthia's room. Possibly she applied oil to the hinges, for I found that it opened quite noiselessly when I tried it. She put off her project until the early hours of the morning as being safer, since the servants were accustomed to hearing her move about her room at that time. She dressed completely in her land kit, and made her way quietly through Mademoiselle Cynthia's room into that of Mrs Inglethorp.'

He paused a moment, and Cynthia interrupted:

'But I should have woken up if anyone had come through my room?'

'Not if you were drugged, mademoiselle.'

'Drugged?'

'*Mais, oui!*'

'You remember' – he addressed us collectively again – 'that through all the tumult and noise next door Mademoiselle Cynthia slept. That admitted of two possibilities. Either her sleep was feigned – which I did not believe – or her unconsciousness was induced by artificial means.

'With this latter idea in my mind, I examined all the coffee-cups most carefully, remembering that it was Mrs Cavendish who had brought Mademoiselle Cynthia her coffee the night before. I took a sample from each cup, and had them analysed – with no result. I had counted the cups carefully, in the event of one having been removed. Six persons had taken coffee, and six cups were duly found. I had to confess myself mistaken.

'Then I discovered that I had been guilty of a very grave oversight. Coffee had been brought in for seven persons, not six, for Dr Bauerstein had been there that evening. This changed the face of the whole affair, for there was now one cup missing. The servants

149

noticed nothing, since Annie, the housemaid, who took in the coffee, brought in seven cups, not knowing that Mr Inglethorp never drank it, whereas Dorcas, who cleared them away the following morning, found six as usual – or strictly speaking she found five, the sixth being the one found broken in Mrs Inglethorp's room.

'I was confident that the missing cup was that of Mademoiselle Cynthia. I had an additional reason for that belief in the fact that all the cups found contained sugar, which Mademoiselle Cynthia never took in her coffee. My attention was attracted by the story of Annie about some "salt" on the tray of cocoa which she took every night to Mrs Inglethorp's room. I accordingly secured a sample of that cocoa, and sent it to be analysed.'

'But that had already been done by Dr Bauerstein,' said Lawrence quickly.

'Not exactly. The analyst was asked by him to report whether strychnine was, or was not, present. He did not have it tested, as I did, for a narcotic.'

'For a narcotic?'

'Yes. Here is the analyst's report. Mrs Cavendish administered a safe, but effectual, narcotic to both Mrs Inglethorp and Mademoiselle Cynthia. And it is possible that she had a *mauvais quart d'heure* in consequence! Imagine her feelings when her mother-in-law is suddenly taken ill and dies, and immediately after she hears the word "Poison"! She has believed that the sleeping draught she administered was perfectly harmless, but there is no doubt that for one terrible moment she must have feared that Mrs Inglethorp's death lay at her door. She is seized with panic, and under its influence she hurries downstairs, and quickly drops the coffee-cup and saucer used by Mademoiselle Cynthia into a large brass vase, where it is discovered later by Monsieur Lawrence. The remains of the cocoa she dare not touch. Too many eyes are upon her. Guess at her relief when strychnine is mentioned, and she discovers that after all the tragedy is not her doing.

'We are now able to account for the symptoms of strychnine poisoning being so long in making their appearance. A narcotic taken with strychnine will delay the action of the poison for some hours.'

Poirot paused. Mary looked up at him, the colour slowly rising in her face.

'All you have said is quite true, Monsieur Poirot. It was the most awful hour of my life. I shall never forget it. But you are wonderful. I understand now –'

'What I meant when I told you that you could safely confess to Papa Poirot, eh? But you would not trust me.'

'I see everything now,' said Lawrence. 'The drugged cocoa, taken on top of the poisoned coffee, amply accounts for the delay.'

'Exactly. But was the coffee poisoned, or was it not? We come to a little difficulty here, since Mrs Inglethorp never drank it.'

'What?' The cry of surprise was universal.

'No. You will remember my speaking of a stain on the carpet in Mrs Inglethorp's room? There were some peculiar points about that stain. It was still damp, it exhaled a strong odour of coffee, and imbedded in the nap of the carpet I found some little splinters of china. What had happened was plain to me, for not two minutes before I had placed my little case on the table near the window, and the table, tilting up, had deposited it upon the floor on precisely the identical spot. In exactly the same way, Mrs Inglethorp had laid down her cup of coffee on reaching her room the night before, and the treacherous table had played her the same trick.

'What happened next is mere guesswork on my part, but I should say that Mrs Inglethorp picked up the broken cup and placed it on the table by the bed. Feeling in need of a stimulant of some kind, she heated up her cocoa, and drank it off then and there. Now we are faced with a new problem. We know the cocoa contained no strychnine. The coffee was never drunk. Yet the strychnine must have been administered between seven and nine o'clock that evening. What third medium was there – a medium so suitable for disguising the taste of strychnine that it is extraordinary no one has thought of it?' Poirot looked around the room, and then answered himself impressively. 'Her medicine!'

'Do you mean that the murderer introduced the strychnine into her tonic?' I cried.

'There was no need to introduce it. It was already there – in the mixture. The strychnine that killed Mrs Inglethorp was the identical strychnine prescribed by Dr Wilkins. To make that clear to you, I will read you an extract from a book on dispensing which I found in the Dispensary of the Red Cross Hospital at Tadminster:

'The following prescription has become famous in textbooks:

Strychninae Sulph	gr. 1
Potass Bromide	3vi
Aqua ad	3viii
Fiat Mistura	

This solution deposits in a few hours the greater part of the strychnine salt as an insoluble bromide in transparent crystals. A lady in England lost her life by taking a similar mixture: the precipitated strychnine collected at the bottom, and in taking the last dose she swallowed nearly all of it!

'Now there was, of course, no bromide in Dr Wilkins' prescription, but you will remember that I mentioned an empty box of bromide powders. One or two of those powders introduced into the full bottle of medicine would effectually precipitate the strychnine, as the book describes, and cause it to be taken in the last dose. You will learn later that the person who usually poured out Mrs Inglethorp's medicine was always extremely careful not to shake the bottle, but to leave the sediment at the bottom of it undisturbed.

'Throughout the case, there have been evidences that the tragedy was intended to take place on Monday evening. On that day, Mrs Inglethorp's bell wire was neatly cut, and on Monday evening Mademoiselle Cynthia was spending the night with friends, so that Mrs Inglethorp would have been quite alone in the right wing, completely shut off from help of any kind, and would have died, in all probability, before medical aid could have been summoned. But in her hurry to be in time for the village entertainment Mrs Inglethorp forgot to take her medicine, and the next day she lunched away from home, so that the last – and fatal – dose was actually taken twenty-four hours later than had been anticipated by the murderer; and it is owing to that delay that the final proof – the last link of the chain – is now in my hands.'

Amid breathless excitement, he held out three thin strips of paper.

'A letter in the murderer's own handwriting, *mes amis!* Had it been a little clearer in its terms, it is possible that Mrs Inglethorp, warned in time, would have escaped. As it was, she realized her danger, but not the manner of it.'

In the deathly silence, Poirot pieced together the slips of paper and, clearing his throat, read:

DEAREST EVELYN,

You will be anxious at hearing nothing. It is all right – only it will be tonight instead of last night. You understand. There's a good time coming once the old woman is dead and out of the way. No one can possibly bring home the crime to me. That idea of yours about the bromides was a stroke of genius! But we must be very circumspect. A false step –

152

'Here, my friends, the letter breaks off. Doubtless the writer was interrupted; but there can be no question as to his identity. We all know his handwriting and –'

A howl that was almost a scream broke the silence.

'You devil! How did you get it?'

A chair was overturned. Poirot skipped nimbly aside. A quick movement on his part, and his assailant fell with a crash.

'*Messieurs, mesdames*,' said Poirot, with a flourish, 'let me introduce you to the murderer, Mr Alfred Inglethorp!'

CHAPTER XIII

POIROT EXPLAINS

'Poirot, you old villain,' I said, 'I've half a mind to strangle you! What do you mean by deceiving me as you have done?'

We were sitting in the library. Several hectic days lay behind us. In the room below, John and Mary were together once more, while Alfred Inglethorp and Miss Howard were in custody. Now at last, I had Poirot to myself, and could relieve my still burning curiosity.

Poirot did not answer me for a moment, but at last he said:

'I did not deceive you, *mon ami*. At most, I permitted you to deceive yourself.'

'Yes, but why?'

'Well, it is difficult to explain. You see, my friend, you have a nature so honest, and a countenance so transparent, that – *enfin*, to conceal your feelings is impossible! If I had told you my ideas, the very first time you saw Mr Alfred Inglethorp that astute gentleman would have – in your so expressive idiom – "smelt a rat"! And then, *bon jour* to our chances of catching him!'

'I think that I have more diplomacy than you give me credit for.'

'My friend,' besought Poirot, 'I implore you, do not enrage yourself! Your help has been of the most invaluable. It is but the extremely beautiful nature that you have which made me pause.'

'Well,' I grumbled, a little mollified, 'I still think you might have given me a hint.'

'But I did, my friend. Several hints. You would not take them. Think now, did I ever say to you that I believed John Cavendish guilty? Did I not, on the contrary, tell you that he would almost certainly be acquitted?'

'Yes, but –'

'And did I not immediately afterwards speak of the difficulty of bringing the murderer to justice? Was it not plain to you that I was speaking of two entirely different persons?'

'No,' I said, 'it was not plain to me!'

'Then again,' continued Poirot, 'at the beginning, did I not repeat to you several times that I didn't want Mr Inglethorp arrested *now?* That should have conveyed something to you.'

'Do you mean to say you suspected him as long ago as that?'

'Yes. To begin with, whoever else might benefit by Mrs Inglethorp's death, her husband would benefit the most. There was no getting away from that. When I went up to Styles with you that first day, I had no idea as to how the crime had been committed, but from what I knew of Mr Inglethorp I fancied that it would be very hard to find anything to connect him with it. When I arrived at the château, I realized at once that it was Mrs Inglethorp who had burnt the will; and there, by the way, you cannot complain, my friend, for I tried my best to force on you the significance of that bedroom fire in midsummer.'

'Yes, yes,' I said impatiently. 'Go on.'

'Well, my friend, as I say, my views as to Mr Inglethorp's guilt were very much shaken. There was, in fact, so much evidence against him that I was inclined to believe that he had not done it.'

'When did you change your mind?'

'When I found that the more efforts I made to clear him, the more efforts he made to get himself arrested. Then, when I discovered that Inglethorp had nothing to do with Mrs Raikes, and that in fact it was John Cavendish who was interested in that quarter, I was quite sure.'

'But why?'

'Simply this. If it had been Inglethorp who was carrying on an intrigue with Mrs Raikes, his silence was perfectly comprehensible. But, when I discovered that it was known all over the village that it was John who was attracted by the farmer's pretty wife, his silence bore quite a different interpretation. It was nonsense to pretend that he was afraid of the scandal, as no possible scandal could attach to him. This attitude of his gave me furiously to think, and I was slowly forced to the conclusion that Alfred Inglethorp wanted to be arrested. *Eh bien!* from that moment, I was equally determined that he should not be arrested.'

'Wait a moment. I don't see why he wished to be arrested?'

'Because, *mon ami*, it is the law of your country that a man once acquitted can never be tried again for the same offence. Aha! but it was clever – his idea! Assuredly, he is a man of method. See here, he knew that in his position he was bound to be suspected, so he conceived the exceedingly clever idea of preparing a lot of manufactured evidence against himself. He wished to be suspected. He wished to be arrested. He would then produce his irreproachable alibi – and, hey presto, he was safe for life!'

'But I still don't see how he managed to prove his alibi, and yet go to the chemist's shop?'

Poirot stared at me in surprise.

'Is it possible? My poor friend! You have not yet realized that it was Miss Howard who went to the chemist's shop?'

'Miss Howard?'

'But, certainly. Who else? It was most easy for her. She is of a good height, her voice is deep and manly; moreover, remember, she and Inglethorp are cousins, and there is a distinct resemblance between them, especially in their gait and bearing. It was simplicity itself. They are a clever pair!'

'I am still a little fogged as to how exactly the bromide business was done,' I remarked.

'*Bon!* I will reconstruct for you as far as possible. I am inclined to think that Miss Howard was the master mind in that affair. You remember her once mentioning that her father was a doctor? Possibly she dispensed his medicines for him, or she may have taken the idea from one of the many books lying about when Mademoiselle Cynthia was studying for her exam. Anyway, she was familiar with the fact that the addition of a bromide to a mixture containing strychnine would cause the precipitation of the latter. Probably the idea came to her quite suddenly. Mrs Inglethorp had a box of bromide powders, which she occasionally took at night. What could be more easier than quietly to dissolve one or more of those powders in Mrs Inglethorp's large-sized bottle of medicine when it came from Coot's? The risk is practically nil. The tragedy will not take place until nearly a fortnight later. If anyone has seen either of them touching the medicine, they will have forgotten it by that time. Miss Howard will have engineered her quarrel, and departed from the house. The lapse of time, and her absence, will defeat all suspicion. Yes, it was a clever idea! If they had left it alone, it is possible the crime might never have been brought home to them. But they were not satisfied. They tried to be too clever – and that was their undoing.'

Poirot puffed at his tiny cigarette, his eyes fixed on the ceiling.

'They arranged a plan to throw suspicion on John Cavendish, by buying strychnine at the village chemist's, and signing the register in his handwriting.

'On Monday Mrs Inglethorp will take the last dose of her medicine. On Monday, therefore, at six o'clock, Alfred Inglethorp arranges to be seen by a number of people at a spot far removed from the village. Miss Howard has previously made up a cock-and-bull story about him and Mrs Raikes to account for his holding his tongue afterwards. At six o'clock, Miss Howard, disguised as Alfred

Inglethorp, enters the chemist's shop, with her story about a dog, obtains the strychnine, and writes the name of Alfred Inglethorp in John's handwriting, which she had previously studied carefully.

'But, as it will never do if John, too, can prove an alibi, she writes him an anonymous note – still copying his handwriting – which takes him to a remote spot where it is exceedingly unlikely that anyone will see him.

'So far, all goes well. Miss Howard goes back to Middlingham. Alfred Inglethorp returns to Styles. There is nothing that can compromise him in any way, since it is Miss Howard who has the strychnine, which, after all, is only wanted as a blind to throw suspicion on John Cavendish.

'But now a hitch occurs. Mrs Inglethorp does not take her medicine that night. The broken bell, Cynthia's absence – arranged by Inglethorp through his wife – all these are wasted. And then – he makes his slip.

'Mrs Inglethorp is out, and he sits down to write to his accomplice, who, he fears, may be in a panic at the non-success of their plan. It is probable that Mrs Inglethorp returned earlier than he expected. Caught in the act, and somewhat flurried, he hastily shuts and locks his desk. He fears that if he remains in the room he may have to open it again, and that Mrs Inglethorp might catch sight of the letter before he could snatch it up. So he goes out and walks in the woods, little dreaming that Mrs Inglethorp will open his desk, and discover the incriminating document.

'But this, as we know, is what happened. Mrs Inglethorp reads it, and becomes aware of the perfidy of her husband and Evelyn Howard, though, unfortunately, the sentence about the bromide conveys no warning to her mind. She knows that she is in danger – but is ignorant of where the danger lies. She decides to say nothing to her husband, but sits down and writes to her solicitor, asking him to come on the morrow, and she also determines to destroy immediately the will which she has just made. She keeps the fatal letter.'

'It was to discover that letter, then, that her husband forced the lock of the despatch-case?'

'Yes, and from the enormous risk he ran we can see how fully he realized its importance. That letter excepted, there was absolutely nothing to connect him with the crime.'

'There's only one thing I can't make out, why didn't he destroy it at once when he got hold of it?'

'Because he did not dare take the biggest risk of all – that of

157

keeping it on his own person.'

'I don't understand.'

'Look at it from his point of view. I have discovered that there were only five short minutes in which he could have taken it – the five minutes immediately before our own arrival on the scene, for before that time Annie was brushing the stairs, and would have seen anyone who passed going to the right wing. Figure to yourself the scene! He enters the room, unlocking the door by means of one of the other door-keys – they were all much alike. He hurries to the despatch-case – it is locked, and the keys are nowhere to be seen. That is a terrible blow to him, for it means that his presence in the room cannot be concealed as he had hoped. But he sees clearly that everything must be risked for the sake of that damning piece of evidence. Quickly, he forces the lock with a penknife, and turns over the papers until he finds what he is looking for.

'But now a fresh dilemma arises: he dare not keep that piece of paper on him. He may be seen leaving the room – he may be searched. If the paper is found on him, it is certain doom. Probably, at this minute, too, he hears the sounds below of Mr Wells and John leaving the boudoir. He must act quickly. Where can he hide this terrible slip of paper? The contents of the waste-paper basket are kept and, in any case, are sure to be examined. There are no means of destroying it; and he dare not keep it. He looks round, and he sees – what do you think, *mon ami?*'

'In a moment he has torn the letter into long thin strips, and rolling them up into spills he thrusts them hurriedly in amongst the other spills in the vase on the mantelpiece.'

I uttered an exclamation.

'No one would think of looking there,' Poirot continued. 'And he will be able, at his leisure, to come back and destroy this solitary piece of evidence against him.'

'Then, all the time, it was in the spill vase in Mrs Inglethorp's bedroom, under our very noses?' I cried.

Poirot nodded.

'Yes, my friend. That is where I discovered my "last link", and I owe that very fortunate discovery to you.'

'To me?'

'Yes. Do you remember telling me that my hand shook as I was straightening the ornaments on the mantelpiece?'

'Yes, but I don't see –'

'No, but I saw. Do you know, my friend, I remembered that

158

earlier in the morning, when we had been there together, I had straightened all the objects on the mantelpiece. And, if they were already straightened, there would be no need to straighten them again, unless, in the meantime, someone else had touched them.'

'Dear me,' I murmured, 'so that is the explanation of your extraordinary behaviour. You rushed down to Styles, and found it still there?'

'Yes, and it was a race for time.'

'But I still can't understand why Inglethorp was such a fool to leave it there when he had plenty of opportunity to destroy it.'

'Ah, but he had no opportunity. I saw to that.'

'You?'

'Yes. Do you remember reproving me for taking the household into my confidence on the subject?'

'Yes.'

'Well, my friend, I saw there was just one chance. I was not sure then if Inglethorp was the criminal or not, but if he was I reasoned that he would not have the paper on him, but would have hidden it somewhere, and by enlisting the sympathy of the household I could effectually prevent his destroying it. He was already under suspicion, and by making the matter public I secured the services of about ten amateur detectives, who would be watching him unceasingly, and being himself aware of their watchfulness he would not dare seek further to destroy the document. He was, therefore, forced to depart from the house, leaving it in the spill vase.'

'But surely Miss Howard had ample opportunities of aiding him.'

'Yes, but Miss Howard did not know of the paper's existence. In accordance with their pre-arranged plan, she never spoke to Alfred Inglethorp. They were supposed to be deadly enemies, and until John Cavendish was safely convicted they neither of them dared risk a meeting. Of course, I had a watch kept on Mr Inglethorp, hoping that sooner or later he would lead me to the hiding-place. But he was too clever to take any chances. The paper was safe where it was; since no one had thought of looking there in the first week, it was not likely they would do so afterwards. But for your lucky remark, we might never have been able to bring him to justice.'

'I understand that now; but when did you first begin to suspect Miss Howard.'

'When I discovered that she had told a lie at the inquest about the letter she had received from Mrs Inglethorp.'

'Why, what was there to lie about?'

159

'You saw that letter? Do you recall its general appearance.'

'Yes – more or less.'

'You will recollect, then, that Mrs Inglethorp wrote a very distinctive hand, and left large clear spaces between her words. But if you look at the date at the top of the letter you will notice that "July 17th" is quite different in this respect. Do you see what I mean?'

'No,' I confessed, 'I don't.'

'You do not see that that letter was not written on the 17th, but on the 7th – the day after Miss Howard's departure? The "1" was written in before the "7" to turn it into the "17th".'

'But why?'

'That is exactly what I asked myself. Why does Miss Howard suppress the letter written on the 17th, and produce this faked one instead? Because she did not wish to show the letter of the 17th. Why, again? And at once a suspicion dawned in my mind. You will remember my saying that it was wise to beware of people who were not telling the truth.'

'And yet,' I cried indignantly, 'after that, you gave me two reasons why Miss Howard could not have committed the crime!'

'And very good reasons too,' replied Poirot. 'For a long time they were a stumbling-block to me until I remembered a very significant fact: that she and Alfred Inglethorp were cousins. She could not have committed the crime single-handed, but the reasons against that did not debar her from being an accomplice. And, then, there was that rather overvehement hatred of hers! It concealed a very opposite emotion. There was, undoubtedly, a tie of passion between them long before he came to Styles. They had already arranged their infamous plot – that he should marry this rich, but rather foolish old lady, induce her to make a will leaving her money to him, and then gain their ends by a very cleverly conceived crime. If all had gone as they planned, they would probably have left England, and lived together on their poor victim's money.

'They are a very astute and unscrupulous pair. While suspicion was to be directed against him, she would be making quiet preparations for a very different *dénouement*. She arrives from Middlingham with all the compromising items in her possession. No suspicion attaches to her. No notice is paid to her coming and going in the house. She hides the strychnine and glasses in John's room. She puts the beard in the attic. She will see to it that sooner or later they are duly discovered.'

'I don't quite see why they tried to fix the blame on John,' I remarked. 'It would have been much easier for them to bring the crime home to Lawrence.'

'Yes, but that was mere chance. All the evidence against him arose out of pure accident. It must, in fact, have been distinctly annoying to the pair of schemers.'

'His manner was unfortunate,' I observed thoughtfully.

'Yes. You realize, of course, what was the back of that?'

'No.'

'You did not understand that he believed Mademoiselle Cynthia guilty of the crime?'

'No,' I exclaimed, astonished. 'Impossible!'

'Not at all. I myself nearly had the same idea. It was in my mind when I asked Mr Wells that first question about the will. Then there were the bromide powders which she had made up, and her clever male impersonations, as Dorcas recounted them to us. There was really more evidence against her than anyone else.'

'You are joking, Poirot!'

'No. Shall I tell you what made Monsieur Lawrence turn so pale when he first entered his mother's room on the fatal night? It was because, whilst his mother lay there, obviously poisoned, he saw, over your shoulder, that the door into Mademoiselle Cynthia's room was unbolted.'

'But he declared that he saw it bolted!' I cried.

'Exactly,' said Poirot dryly. 'And that was just what confirmed my suspicion that it was not. He was shielding Mademoiselle Cynthia.'

'But why should he shield her?'

'Because he is in love with her.'

I laughed.

'There, Poirot, you are quite wrong! I happen to know for a fact that, far from being in love with her, he positively dislikes her.'

'Who told you that, *mon ami?*'

'Cynthia herself.'

'*La pauvre petite!* And she was concerned?'

'She said that she did not mind at all.'

'Then she certainly did mind very much,' remarked Poirot. 'They are like that – *les femmes!*'

'What you say about Lawrence is a great surprise to me,' I said.

'But why? It was most obvious. Did not Monsieur Lawrence make the sour face every time Mademoiselle Cynthia spoke and laughed with his brother? He had taken it into his long head that Mademoiselle Cynthia was in love with Monsieur John. When he entered his

161

mother's room and saw her obviously poisoned, he jumped to the conclusion that Mademoiselle Cynthia knew something about the matter. He was nearly driven desperate. First he crushed the coffee-cup to powder under his feet, remembering that *she* had gone up with his mother the night before, and he determined that there should be no chance of testing its contents. Thenceforward, he strenuously, and quite uselessly, upheld the theory of "Death from natural causes".'

'And what about the "extra coffee-cup"?'

'I was fairly certain that it was Mrs Cavendish who had hidden it, but I had to make sure. Monsieur Lawrence did not know at all what I meant; but, on reflection, he came to the conclusion that if he could find an extra coffee-cup anywhere his lady love would be cleared of suspicion. And he was perfectly right.'

'One thing more. What did Mrs Inglethorp mean by her dying words?'

'They were, of course, an accusation against her husband.'

'Dear me, Poirot,' I said with a sigh, 'I think you have explained everything. I am glad it has all ended so happily. Even John and his wife are reconciled.'

'Thanks to me.'

'How do you mean – thanks to you?'

'My dear friend, do you realize that it was simply and solely the trial which has brought them together again? That John Cavendish still loved his wife, I was convinced. Also, that she was equally in love with him. But they had drifted very far apart. It all arose from a misunderstanding. She married him without love. He knew it. He is a sensitive man in his way, he would not force himself upon her if she did not want him. And, as he withdrew, her love awoke. But they are both unusually proud, and their pride held them inexorably apart. He drifted into an entanglement with Mrs Raikes, and she deliberately cultivated the friendship of Dr Bauerstein. Do you remember the day of John Cavendish's arrest, when you found me deliberating over a big decision?'

'Yes, I quite understood your distress.'

'Pardon me, *mon ami*, but you did not understand it in the least. I was trying to decide whether or not I would clear John Cavendish at once. I could have cleared him – though it might have meant a failure to convict the real criminals. They were entirely in the dark as to my real attitude up to the very last moment – which partly accounts for my success.'

'Do you mean that you could have saved John Cavendish from being brought to trial?'

'Yes, my friend. But I eventually decided in favour of "a woman's happiness". Nothing but the great danger through which they have passed could have brought these two proud souls together again.'

I looked at Poirot in silent amazement. The colossal cheek of the little man! Who on earth but Poirot would have thought of a trial for murder as a restorer of conjugal happiness!

'I perceive your thoughts, *mon ami*,' said Poirot, smiling at me. 'No one but Hercule Poirot would have attempted such a thing! And you are wrong in condemning it. The happiness of one man and woman is the greatest thing in all the world.'

His words took me back to earlier events. I remembered Mary as she lay white and exhausted on the sofa, listening, listening. There had come the sound of the bell below. She had started up. Poirot had opened the door, and meeting her agonized eyes had nodded gently. 'Yes, madame,' he said. 'I have brought him back to you.' He had stood aside, and as I went out I had seen the look in Mary's eyes, as John Cavendish had caught his wife in his arms.

'Perhaps you are right, Poirot,' I said gently. 'Yes, it is the greatest thing in the world.'

Suddenly, there was a tap at the door, and Cynthia peeped in.

'I – I – only –'

'Come in,' I said, springing up.

She came in, but did not sit down.

'I – only wanted to tell you something –'

'Yes?'

Cynthia fidgeted with a little tassel for some moments, then, suddenly exclaiming: 'You dears!' kissed first me and then Poirot, and rushed out of the room again.

'What on earth does this mean?' I asked, surprised.

It was very nice to be kissed by Cynthia, but the publicity of the salute rather impaired the pleasure.

'It means that she has discovered Monsieur Lawrence does not dislike her as much as she thought,' replied Poirot philosophically.

'But –'

'Here he is.'

Lawrence at that moment passed the door.

'Eh! Monsieur Lawrence,' called Poirot. 'We must congratulate you, is it not so?'

Lawrence blushed, and then smiled awkwardly. A man in love is a

163

sorry spectacle. Now Cynthia had looked charming.

I sighed.

'What is it, *mon ami?*'

'Nothing,' I said sadly. 'They are two delightful women!'

'And neither of them is for you?' finished Poirot. 'Never mind. Console yourself, my friend. We may hunt together again, who knows? And then –'

Peril at End House

To Eden Philpotts

*to whom I shall always be grateful for his friendship
and the encouragement he gave me many years ago*

Contents

CHAPTER ONE

The Majestic Hotel

No seaside town in the south of England is, I think, as attractive as St Loo. It is well named the Queen of Watering Places and reminds one forcibly of the Riviera. The Cornish coast is to my mind every bit as fascinating as that of the south of France.

I remarked as much to my friend, Hercule Poirot. 'So it said on our menu in the restaurant car yesterday, *mon ami*. Your remark is not original.'

'But don't you agree?'

He was smiling to himself and did not at once answer my question. I repeated it.

'A thousand pardons, Hastings. My thoughts were wandering. Wandering indeed to that part of the world you mentioned just now.'

The south of France?'

'Yes. I was thinking of that last winter that I spent there and of the events which occurred.'

I remembered. A murder had been committed on the Blue Train, and the mystery – a complicated and baffling one – had been solved by Poirot with his usual unerring acumen.

'How I wish I had been with you,' I said with deep regret.

'I too,' said Poirot. 'Your experience would have been invaluable to me.'

I looked at him sideways. As a result of long habit, I distrust his compliments, but he appeared perfectly serious. And after all, why not? I have a very long experience of the methods he employs.

'What I particularly missed was your vivid imagination, Hastings,' he went on dreamily. 'One needs a certain amount of light relief. My valet, Georges, an admirable man with whom I sometimes permitted myself to discuss a point, has no imagination whatever.' This remark seemed to me quite irrelevant.

'Tell me, Poirot,' I said. 'Are you never tempted to renew your activities? This passive life –'

'Suits me admirably, my friend. To sit in the sun – what could be more charming? To step from your pedestal at the zenith of your fame – what could be a grander gesture? They say of me: "*That is Hercule Poirot! – The great – the unique! – There was never any one like him, there never will be!*" *Eh bien* – I am satisfied. I ask no more.

169

I am modest.'

'I should not myself have used the word modest. It seemed to me that my little friend's egotism had certainly not declined with his years. He leaned back in his chair, caressing his moustache and almost purring with self-satisfaction.

We were sitting on one of the terraces of the Majestic Hotel. It is the biggest hotel in St Loo and stands in its own grounds on a headland overlooking the sea. The gardens of the hotel lay below us freely interspersed with palm trees. The sea was of a deep and lovely blue, the sky clear and the sun shining with all the single-hearted fervour an August sun should (but in England so often does not) have. There was a vigorous humming of bees, a pleasant sound – and altogether nothing could have been more ideal.

We had only arrived last night, and this was the first morning of what we proposed should be a week's stay. If only these weather conditions continued, we should indeed have a perfect holiday.

I picked up the morning paper which had fallen from my hand and resumed my perusal of the morning's news. The political situation seemed unsatisfactory, but uninteresting, there was trouble in China, there was a long account of a rumoured City swindle, but on the whole there was no news of a very thrilling order.

'Curious thing this parrot disease,' I remarked, as I turned the sheet.

'Very curious.'

'Two more deaths at Leeds, I see.'

'Most regrettable.'

I turned a page.

'Still no news of that flying fellow, Seton, in his round-the-world flight. Pretty plucky, these fellows. That amphibian machine of his, the *Albatross*, must be a great invention. Too bad if he's gone west. Not that they've given up hope yet. He may have made one of the Pacific islands.'

'The Solomon islanders are still cannibals, are they not?' inquired Poirot pleasantly.

'Must be a fine fellow. That sort of thing makes one feel it's a good thing to be an Englishman after all.'

'It consoles for the defeats at Wimbledon,' said Poirot.

'I – I didn't mean,' I began.

My friend waved my attempted apology aside gracefully.

'Me,' he announced. 'I am not amphibian, like the machine of the poor Captain Seton, but I am cosmopolitan. And for the English I

170

have always had, as you know, a great admiration. The thorough way, for instance, in which they read the daily paper.'

My attention had strayed to political news.

'They seem to be giving the Home Secretary a pretty bad time of it,' I remarked with a chuckle.

'The poor man. He has his troubles, that one. Ah! yes. So much so that he seeks for help in the most improbable quarters.'

I stared at him.

With a slight smile, Poirot drew from the pocket his morning's correspondence, neatly secured by a rubber band. From this he selected one letter which he tossed across at me.

'It must have missed us yesterday,' he said.

I read the letter with a pleasurable feeling of excitement.

'But Poirot,' I cried. 'This is most flattering!'

'You think so, my friend?'

'He speaks in the warmest terms of your ability.'

'He is right,' said Poirot, modestly averting his eyes.

'He begs you to investigate this matter for him – puts it as a personal favour.'

'Quite so. It is unnecessary to repeat all this to me. You understand, my dear Hastings. I have read the letter myself.'

'It is too bad,' I cried. 'This will put an end to our holiday.'

'No, no, *calmez vous* – there is no question of that.'

'But the Home Secretary says the matter is urgent.'

'He may be right – or again he may not. These politicians, they are easily excited. I have seen myself, in the Chambre des Deputés in Paris –'

'Yes, yes, but Poirot, surely we ought to be making arrangements? The express to London has gone – it leaves at twelve o'clock. The next –'

'Calm yourself, Hastings, calm yourself, I pray of you! Always the excitement, the agitation. We are not going to London today – nor yet tomorrow.'

'But this summons –'

'Does not concern me. I do not belong to your police force, Hastings. I am asked to undertake a case as a private investigator. I refuse.'

'You *refuse?*'

'Certainly. I write with perfect politeness, tender my regrets, my apologies, explain that I am completely desolated – but what will you? I have retired – I am finished.'

'You are not finished,' I exclaimed warmly.

Poirot patted my knee.

'There speaks the good friend – the faithful dog. And you have reason, too. The grey cells, they still function – the order, the method – it is still there. But when I have retired, my friend, I have retired! It is finished! I am not a stage favourite who gives the world a dozen farewells. In all generosity I say: let the young men have a chance. They may possibly do something creditable. I doubt it, but they may. Anyway they will do well enough for this doubtless tiresome affair of the Home Secretary's.'

'But, Poirot, the compliment!'

'Me, I am above compliments. The Home Secretary, being a man of sense, realizes that if he can only obtain my services all will be successful. What will you? He is unlucky. Hercule Poirot has solved his last case.'

I looked at him. In my heart of hearts I deplored his obstinacy. The solving of such a case as was indicated might add still further lustre to his already world-wide reputation. Nevertheless I could not but admire his unyielding attitude.

Suddenly a thought struck me and I smiled.

'I wonder,' I said, 'that you are not afraid. Such an emphatic pronouncement will surely tempt the gods.'

'Impossible,' he replied, 'that anyone should shake the decision of Hercule Poirot.'

'*Impossible*, Poirot?'

'You are right, *mon ami*, one should not use such a word. *Eh, ma foi*, I do not say that if a bullet should strike the wall by my head, I would not investigate the matter! One is human after all!'

I smiled. A little pebble had just struck the terrace beside us, and Poirot's fanciful analogy from it tickled my fancy. He stooped down and picked up the pebble as he went on.

'Yes – one is human. One is the sleeping dog – well and good, but the sleeping dog can be roused. There is a proverb in your language that says so.'

'In fact,' I said, 'if you find a dagger planted by your pillow tomorrow morning – let the criminal who put it there beware!'

He nodded, but rather absently.

Suddenly, to my surprise, he rose and descended the couple of steps that led from the terrace to the garden. As he did so, a girl came into sight hurrying up towards us.

I had just registered the impression that she was a decidedly pretty

172

girl when my attention was drawn to Poirot who, not looking where he was going, had stumbled over a root and fallen heavily. He was just abreast of the girl at the time and she and I between us helped him to his feet. My attention was naturally on my friend, but I was conscious of an impression of dark hair, an impish face and big dark-blue eyes.

'A thousand pardons,' stammered Poirot. 'Mademoiselle, you are most kind. I regret exceedingly – ouch! – my foot he pains me considerably. No, no, it is nothing really – the turned ankle, that is all. In a few minutes all will be well. But if you could help me, Hastings – you and Mademoiselle between you, if she will be so very kind. I am ashamed to ask it of her.'

With me on the one side and the girl on the other we soon got Poirot on to a chair on the terrace. I then suggested fetching a doctor, but this my friend negatived sharply.

'It is nothing, I tell you. The ankle turned, that is all. Painful for the moment, but soon over.' He made a grimace. 'See, in a little minute I shall have forgotten. Mademoiselle, I thank you a thousand times. You were most kind. Sit down, I beg of you.'

The girl took a chair.

'It's nothing,' she said. 'But I wish you would let it be seen to.'

'Mademoiselle, I assure you, it is a *bagatelle*! In the pleasure of your society the pain passes already.'

The girl laughed.

'That's good.'

'What about a cocktail?' I suggested. 'It's just about the time.'

'Well –' She hesitated. 'Thanks very much.'

'Martini?'

'Yes, please – dry Martini.'

I went off. On my return, after having ordered the drinks, I found Poirot and the girl engaged in animated conversation.

'Imagine, Hastings,' he said, 'that house there – the one on the point – that we have admired so much, it belongs to Mademoiselle here.'

'Indeed?' I said, though I was unable to recall having expressed any admiration. In fact I had hardly noticed the house. 'It looks rather eerie and imposing standing there by itself far from anything.'

'It's called End House,' said the girl. 'I love it – but it's a tumble-down old place. Going to rack and ruin.'

'You are the last of an old family, Mademoiselle?'

'Oh! we're nothing important. But there have been Buckleys here

173

for two or three hundred years. My brother died three years ago, so I'm the last of the family.'

'That is sad. You live there alone, Mademoiselle?'

'Oh! I'm away a good deal and when I'm at home there's usually a cheery crowd coming and going.'

'That is so modern. Me, I was picturing you in a dark mysterious mansion, haunted by a family curse.'

'How marvellous! What a picturesque imagination you must have. No, it's not haunted. Or if so, the ghost is a beneficent one. I've had three escapes from sudden death in as many days, so I must bear a charmed life.'

Poirot sat up alertly.

'Escapes from death? That sounds interesting, Mademoiselle.'

'Oh! they weren't very thrilling. Just accidents you know.' She jerked her head sharply as a wasp flew past. 'Curse these wasps. There must be a nest of them round here.'

'The bees and the wasps – you do not like them, Mademoiselle? You have been stung – yes?'

'No – but I hate the way they come right past your face.'

'The bee in the bonnet,' said Poirot. 'Your English phrase.'

At that moment the cocktails arrived. We all held up our glasses and made the usual inane observations.

'I'm due in the hotel for cocktails, really,' said Miss Buckley. 'I expect they're wondering what has become of me.'

Poirot cleared his throat and set down his glass.

'Ah! for a cup of good rich chocolate,' he murmured. 'But in England they make it not. Still, in England you have some very pleasing customs. The young girls, their hats come on and off – so prettily – so easily –'

The girl stared at him.

'What do you mean? Why shouldn't they?'

'You ask that because you are young – so young, Mademoiselle. But to me the natural thing seems to have a coiffure high and rigid – so – and the hat attached with many hat pins – *là – là – là – et là*.'

He executed four vicious jabs in the air.

'But how frightfully uncomfortable!'

'Ah! I should think so,' said Poirot. No martyred lady could have spoken with more feeling. 'When the wind blew it was the agony – it gave you the *migraine*.'

Miss Buckley dragged off the simple wide-brimmed felt she was wearing and cast it down beside her.

'And now we do this,' she laughed.

'Which is sensible and charming,' said Poirot, with a little bow.

I looked at her with interest. Her dark hair was ruffled and gave her an elfin look. There was something elfin about her altogether. The small, vivid face, pansy shaped, the enormous dark-blue eyes, and something else – something haunting and arresting. Was it a hint of recklessness? There were dark shadows under the eyes.

The terrace on whch we were sitting was a little-used one. The main terrace where most people sat was just round the corner at a point where the cliff shelved directly down to the sea.

From round this corner now there appeared a man, a red-faced man with a rolling carriage who carried his hands half clenched by his side. There was something breezy and carefree about him – a typical sailor.

'I can't think where the girl's got to,' he was saying in tones that easily carried to where we sat. 'Nick – Nick.'

Miss Buckley rose.

'I knew they'd be getting in a state. Attaboy – George – here I am.'

'Freddie's frantic for a drink. Come on, girl.'

He cast a glance of frank curiosity at Poirot, who must have differed considerably from most of Nick's friends.

The girl performed a wave of introduction.

'This is Commander Challenger – er –'

But to my surprise Poirot did not supply the name for which she was waiting. Instead he rose, bowed very ceremoniously and murmured:

'Of the English Navy. I have a great regard for the English Navy.'

This type of remark is not one that an Englishman acclaims most readily. Commander Challenger flushed and Nick Buckley took command of the situation.

'Come on, George. Don't gape. Let's find Freddie and Jim.'

She smiled at Poirot.

'Thanks for the cocktail. I hope the ankle will be all right.'

With a nod to me she slipped her hand through the sailor's arm and they disappeared round the corner together.

'So that is one of Mademoiselle's friends,' murmured Poirot thoughtfully. 'One of her cheery crowd. What about him? Give me your expert judgement, Hastings. Is he what you call a good fellow – yes?'

Pausing for a moment to try and decide exactly what Poirot thought I should mean by a 'good fellow', I gave a doubtful assent.

'He seems all right – yes,' I said. 'So far as one can tell by a cursory glance.'

'I wonder,' said Poirot.

The girl had left her hat behind. Poirot stooped to pick it up and twirled it round absent-mindedly on his finger.

'Has he a *tendresse* for her? What do you think, Hastings?'

'My dear Poirot! How *can* I tell? Here – give me that hat. The lady will want it. I'll take it to her.'

Poirot paid no attention to my request. He continued to revolve the hat slowly on his finger.

'*Pas encore. Ça m'amuse.*'

'Really, Poirot!'

'Yes, my friend, I grow old and childish, do I not?'

This was so exactly what I was feeling that I was somewhat disconcerted to have it put into words. Poirot gave a little chuckle, then leaning forward he laid a finger against the side of his nose.

'But no – I am not so completely imbecile as you think! We will return the hat – but assuredly – but later! We will return it to End House and thus we shall have the opportunity of seeing the charming Miss Nick again.'

'Poirot,' I said. 'I believe you have fallen in love.'

'She is a pretty girl – eh?'

'Well – you saw for yourself. Why ask me?'

'Because, alas! I cannot judge. To me, nowadays, anything young is beautiful. *Jeunesse – jeunesse* . . . It is the tragedy of my years. But you – I appeal to you! Your judgement is not up-to-date, naturally, having lived in the Argentine so long. You admire the figure of five years ago, but you are at any rate more modern than I am. She is pretty – yes? She has the appeal to the sexes?'

'One sex is sufficient, Poirot. The answer, I should say, is very much in the affirmative. Why are you so interested in the lady?'

'Am I interested?'

'Well – look at what you've just being saying.'

'You are under a misapprehension, *mon ami*. I may be interested in the lady – yes – but I am much more interested in her hat.'

I stared at him, but he appeared perfectly serious.

He nodded his head at me.

'Yes, Hastings, that very hat.' He held it towards me. 'You see the reason for my interest?'

'It's a nice hat,' I said, bewildered. 'But quite an ordinary hat. Lots of girls have hats like it.'

176

'Not like this one.'

I looked at it more closely.

'You see, Hastings?'

'A perfectly plain fawn felt. Good style –'

'I did not ask you to describe the hat. It is plain that you do *not* see. Almost incredible, my poor Hastings, how you hardly ever *do* see! It amazes me every time anew! But regard, my dear old imbecile – it is not necessary to employ the grey cells – the eyes will do. Regard – regard –'

And then at last I saw to what he had been trying to draw my attention. The slowly turning hat was revolving on his finger, and that finger was stuck neatly through a hole in the brim of the hat. When he saw that I had realized his meaning, he drew his finger out and held the hat towards me. It was a small neat hole, quite round, and I could not imagine its purpose, if purpose it had.

'Did you observe the way Mademoiselle Nick flinched when a bee flew past? The bee in the bonnet – the hole in the hat.'

'But a bee couldn't make a hole like that.'

'Exactly, Hastings! What acumen! It could not. *But a bullet could, mon cher!*'

'A bullet?'

'*Mai oui!* A bullet like *this.*'

He held out his hand with a small object in the palm of it.

'A spent bullet, *mon ami.* It was that which hit the terrace just now when we were talking. A spent bullet!'

'You mean –'

'*I mean that one inch of a difference and that hole would not be through the hat but through the head.* Now do you see why I am interested, Hastings? You were right, my friend when you told me not to use the word "impossible". Yes – one is human! Ah! but he made a grave mistake, that would-be murderer, when he shot at his victim within a dozen yards of Hercule Poirot! For him, it is indeed *la mauvaise chance.* But you see now why we must make our entry into End House and get into touch with Mademoiselle? *Three near escapes from death in three days.* That is what she said. We must act quickly, Hastings. The peril is very close at hand.'

CHAPTER TWO

End House

'Poirot,' I said. 'I have been thinking.'

'An admirable exercise, my friend. Continue it.'

We were sitting facing each other at lunch at a small table in the window.

'This shot must have been fired quite close to us. And yet we did not hear it.'

'And you think that in the peaceful stillness, with the rippling waves the only sound, we should have done so?'

'Well, it's odd.'

'No, it is not odd. Some sounds – you get used to them so soon that you hardly notice they are there. All this morning, my friend, speedboats have been making trips in the bay. You complained at first – soon, you did not even notice. But, *ma foi*, you could fire a machine gun almost and not notice it when one of those boats is on the sea.'

'Yes, that's true.'

'Ah! *voilà*,' murmured Poirot. 'Mademoiselle and her friends. They are to lunch here, it seems. And therefore I must return the hat. But no matter. The affair is sufficiently serious to warrant a visit all on its own.'

He leaped up nimbly from his seat, hurried across the room, and presented the hat with a bow just as Miss Buckley and her companions were seating themselves at table.

They were a party of four, Nick Buckley, Commander Challenger, another man and another girl. From where we sat we had a very imperfect view of them. From time to time the naval man's laugh boomed out. He seemed a simple, likeable soul, and I had already taken a fancy to him.

My friend was silent and distrait during our meal. He crumbled his bread, made strange little ejaculations to himself and straightened everything on the table. I tried to talk, but meeting with no encouragement soon gave up.

He continued to sit on at the table long after he had finished his cheese. As soon as the other party had left the room, however, he too rose to his feet. They were just settling themselves at a table in the lounge when Poirot marched up to them in his most military fashion,

178

and addressed Nick directly.

'Mademoiselle, may I crave one little word with you.'

The girl frowned. I realized her feelings clearly enough. She was afraid that this queer little foreigner was going to be a nuisance. I could not but sympathize with her, knowing how it must appear in her eyes. Rather unwillingly, she moved a few steps aside.

Almost immediately I saw an expression of surprise pass over her face at the low hurried words Poirot was uttering.

In the meantime, I was feeling rather awkward and ill at ease. Challenger with ready tact came to my rescue, offering me a cigarette and making some commonplace observation. We had taken each other's measure and were inclined to be sympathetic to each other. I fancied that I was more his own kind than the man with whom he had been lunching. I now had the opportunity of observing the latter. A tall, fair, rather exquisite young man, with a rather fleshy nose and over-emphasized good looks. He had a supercilious manner and a tired drawl. There was a sleekness about him that I especially disliked.

Then I looked at the woman. She was sitting straight opposite me in a big chair and had just thrown off her hat. She was an unusual type – a weary Madonna describes it best. She had fair, almost colourless hair, parted in the middle and drawn straight down over her ears to a knot in the neck. Her face was dead white and emaciated – yet curiously attractive. Her eyes were very light grey with large pupils. She had a curious look of detachment. She was staring at me. Suddenly she spoke.

'Sit down – till your friend has finished with Nick.'

She had an affected voice, languid and artificial – yet which had a curious attraction – a kind of resonant lingering beauty. She impressed me, I think, as the most tired person I had ever met. Tired in mind, not in body, as though she had found everything in the world to be empty and valueless.

'Miss Buckley very kindly helped my friend when he twisted his ankle this morning,' I explained as I accepted her offer.

'So Nick said.' Her eyes considered me, still detachedly. 'Nothing wrong with his ankle now, is there?'

I felt myself blushing.

'Just a momentary sprain,' I explained.

'Oh! well – I'm glad to hear Nick didn't invent the whole thing. She's the most heaven-sent little liar that ever existed, you know. Amazing – it's quite a gift.'

179

I hardly knew what to say. My discomfiture seemed to amuse her.

'She's one of my oldest friends,' she said, 'and I always think loyalty's such a tiresome virtue, don't you? Principally practised by the Scots – like thrift and keeping the Sabbath. But Nick is a liar, isn't she, Jim? That marvellous story about the brakes of the car – and Jim says there was nothing in it at all.'

The fair man said in a soft rich voice:

'I know something about cars.'

He half turned his head. Outside amongst other cars was a long, red car. It seemed longer and redder than any car could be. It had a long gleaming bonnet of polished metal. A super car!

'Is that your car?' I asked on a sudden impulse.

He nodded.

'Yes.'

I had an insane desire to say, 'It would be!'

Poirot rejoined us at that moment. I rose, he took me by the arm, gave a quick bow to the party, and drew me rapidly away.

'It is arranged, my friend. We are to call on Mademoiselle at End House at half-past six. She will be returned from the motoring by then. Yes, yes, surely she will have returned – in safety.'

His face was anxious and his tone was worried.

'What did you say to her?'

'I asked her to accord me an interview – as soon as possible. She was a little unwilling – naturally. She thinks – I can see the thoughts passing through her mind: 'Who is he – this little man? Is he the bounder, the upstart, the Moving Picture director?' If she could have refused she would – but it is difficult – asked like that on the spur of the moment it is easier to consent. She admits that she will be back by six-thirty. *Ça y est!*'

I remarked that that seemed to be all right then, but my remark met with little favour. Indeed Poirot was as jumpy as the proverbial cat. He walked about our sitting-room all the afternoon, murmuring to himself and ceaselessly rearranging and straightening the ornaments. When I spoke to him, he waved his hands and shook his head.

In the end we started out from the hotel at barely six o'clock.

'It seems incredible,' I remarked, as we descended the steps of the terrace. 'To attempt to shoot anyone in a hotel garden. Only a madman would do such a thing.'

'I disagree with you. Given one condition, it would be quite a reasonably safe affair. To begin with the garden is deserted. The people who come to hotels are like a flock of sheep. It is customary to

180

sit on the terrace overlooking the bay – *eh bien*, so everyone sits on the terrace. Only, I who am an original, sit overlooking the garden. And even then, I *saw* nothing. There is plenty of cover, you observe – trees, groups of palms, flowering shrubs. Anyone could hide himself comfortably and be unobserved whilst he waited for Mademoiselle to pass this way. And she would come this way. To come round by the road from End House would be much longer. Mademoiselle Nick Buckley, she would be of those who are always late and taking the short cut!'

'All the same, the risk was enormous. He might have been seen – and you can't make shooting look like an accident.'

'Not like an *accident* – no.'

'What do you mean?'

'Nothing – a little idea. I may or may not be justified. Leaving it aside for a moment, there is what I mentioned just now – an essential *condition*.'

'Which is?'

'Surely you can tell me, Hastings.'

'I wouldn't like to deprive you of the pleasure of being clever at my expense!'

'Oh! the sarcasm! The irony! Well, what leaps to the eye is this: *the motive cannot be obvious.* If it *were* – why, then, truly the risk would indeed be too great to be taken! People would say: "I wonder if it were So-and-So. Where was So-and-So when the shot was fired?" No, the murderer – the would-be murderer, I should say – cannot be obvious. And that, Hastings is why I am afraid! Yes, at this minute I am afraid. I reassure myself. I say: "There are four of them." I say: "Nothing can happen when they are all together." I say: "It would be madness!" And all the time I am afraid. These "accidents" – I want to hear about them!'

He turned back abruptly.

'It is still early. We will go the other way by the road. The garden has nothing to tell us. Let us inspect the orthodox approach to End House.'

Our way led out of the front gate of the hotel and up a sharp hill to the right. At the top of it was a small lane with a notice on the wall: 'TO END HOUSE ONLY.'

We followed it and after a few hundred yards the lane gave an abrupt turn and ended in a pair of dilapidated entrance gates, which would have been the better for a coat of paint.

Inside the gates, to the right, was a small lodge. This lodge

181

presented a piquant contrast to the gates and to the condition of the grass-grown drive. The small garden round it was spick and span, the window frames and sashes had been lately painted and there were clean bright curtains at the windows.

Bending over a flower-bed was a man in a faded Norfolk jacket. He straightened up as the gate creaked and turned to look at us. He was a man of about sixty, six foot at least, with a powerful frame and a weather-beaten face. His head was almost completely bald. His eyes were a vivid blue and twinkled. He seemed a genial soul.

'Good-afternoon,' he observed as we passed.

I responded in kind and as we went on up the drive I was conscious of those blue eyes raking our backs inquisitively.

'I wonder,' said Poirot, thoughtfully.

He left it at that without vouchsafing any explanation of what it was that he wondered.

The house itself was large and rather dreary looking. It was shut in by trees, the branches of which actually touched the roof. It was clearly in bad repair. Poirot swept it with an appraising glance before ringing the bell – an old-fashioned bell that needed a Herculean pull to produce any effect and which once started, echoed mournfully on and on.

The door was opened by a middle-aged woman – 'a decent woman in black' – so I felt she should be described. Very respectable, rather mournful, completely uninterested.

Miss Buckley, she said, had not yet returned. Poirot explained that we had an appointment. He had some little difficulty in gaining his point, she was the type that is apt to be suspicious of foreigners. Indeed I flatter myself that it was *my* appearance which turned the scale. We were admitted and ushered into the drawing-room to await Miss Buckley's return.

There was no mournful note here. The room gave on the sea and was full of sunshine. It was shabby and betrayed conflicting styles – ultra modern of a cheap variety superimposed on solid Victorian. The curtains were of faded brocade, but the covers were new and gay and the cushions were positively hectic. On the walls were hung family portraits. Some of them, I thought, looked remarkably good. There was a gramophone and there were some records lying idly about. There were a portable wireless, practically no books, and one newspaper flung open on the end of the sofa. Poirot picked it up – then laid it down with a grimace. It was the St Loo *Weekly Herald and Directory*. Something impelled him to pick it up a second time, and he was glancing at a column when the door opened and Nick Buckley came into the room.

'Bring the ice, Ellen,' she called over her shoulder, then addressed herself to us.

'Well, here I am – and I've shaken off the others. I'm devoured with curiosity. Am I the long-lost heroine that is badly wanted for the Talkies? You were so very solemn' – she addressed herself to Poirot – 'that I feel it can't be anything else. Do make me a handsome offer.'

'Alas! Mademoiselle –' began Poirot.

'Don't say it's the opposite,' she begged him. 'Don't say you paint miniatures and want me to buy one. But no – with that moustache and staying at the Majestic, which has the nastiest food and the highest prices in England – no, it simply can't be.'

The woman who had opened the door to us came into the room with ice and a tray of bottles. Nick mixed cocktails expertly, continuing to talk. I think at last Poirot's silence (so unlike him) impressed itself upon her. She stopped in the very act of filling the glasses and said sharply:

'Well?'

'That is what I wish it to be – well, Mademoiselle.' He took the cocktail from her hand. 'To your good health, Mademoiselle – to your continued good health.'

The girl was no fool. The significance of his tone was not lost on her.

'Is – anything the matter?'

'Yes, Mademoiselle. This . . .'

He held out his hand to her with the bullet on the palm of it. She picked it up with a puzzled frown.

'You know what that is?'

'Yes, of course I know. It's a bullet.'

'Exactly. Mademoiselle – it was not a wasp that flew past your face this morning – it was this bullet.'

'Do you mean – was some criminal idiot shooting bullets in a hotel garden?'

'It would seem so.'

'Well, I'm damned,' said Nick frankly. 'I do seem to bear a charmed life. That's number four.'

'Yes,' said Poirot. 'That is number four. I want, Mademoiselle, to hear about the other three – accidents.'

She stared at him.

'I want to be very sure, Mademoiselle, that they were – *accidents*.'

183

'Why, of course! What else could they be?'

'Mademoiselle, prepare yourself, I beg, for a great shock. What if someone is attempting your life?'

All Nick's response to this was a burst of laughter. The idea seemed to amuse her hugely.

'What a marvellous idea! My dear man, who on earth do you think would attempt my life? I'm not the beautiful young heiress whose death releases millions. I wish somebody *was* trying to kill me – that *would* be a thrill, if you like – but I'm afraid there's not a hope!'

'Will you tell me, Mademoiselle, about those accidents?'

'Of course – but there's nothing in it. They were just stupid things. There's a heavy picture hangs over my bed. It fell in the night. Just by pure chance I had happened to hear a door banging somewhere in the house and went down to find it and shut it – and so I escaped. It would probably have bashed my head in. That's No. 1.'

Poirot did not smile.

'Continue, Mademoiselle. Let us pass to No. 2.'

'Oh, that's weaker still. There's a scrambly cliff path down to the sea. I go down that way to bathe. There's a rock you can dive off. A boulder got dislodged somehow and came roaring down just missing me. The third thing was quite different. Something went wrong with the brakes of the car – I don't know quite what – the garage man explained, but I didn't follow it. Anyway if I'd gone through the gate and down the hill, they wouldn't have held and I suppose I'd have gone slap into the Town Hall and there would have been the devil of a smash. Slight defacement of the Town Hall, complete obliteration of me. But owing to my *always* leaving something behind, I turned back and merely ran into the laurel hedge.'

'And you cannot tell me what the trouble was?'

'You can go and ask them at Mott's Garage. They'll know. It was something quite simple and mechanical that had been unscrewed, I think. I wondered if Ellen's boy (my stand-by who opened the door to you, has got a small boy) had tinkered with it. Boys do like messing about with cars. Of course Ellen swore he'd never been near the car. I think something must just have worked loose in spite of what Mott said.'

'Where is your garage, Mademoiselle?'

'Round the other side of the house.'

'Is it kept locked?'

Nick's eyes widened in surprise.

'Oh! *no*. Of course not.'

184

'Anyone could tamper with the car unobserved?'

'Well – yes – I suppose so. But it's so silly.'

'No, Mademoiselle. It is not silly. You do not understand. You are in danger – grave danger. I tell it to you. I! And you do not know who I am?'

'No.' said Nick, breathlessly.

'I am Hercule Poirot.'

'Oh!' said Nick, in rather a flat tone. 'Oh, yes.'

'You know my name, eh?'

'Oh, yes.'

She wriggled uncomfortably. A hunted look came into her eyes. Poirot observed her keenly.

'You are not at ease. That means, I suppose, that you have not read my books.'

'Well – no – not all of them. But I know the name, of course.'

'Mademoiselle, you are a polite little liar.' (I started, remembering the words spoken at the Majestic Hotel that day after lunch.) 'I forget – you are only a child – you would not have heard. So quickly does fame pass. My friend there – he will tell you.'

Nick looked at me. I cleared my throat, somewhat embarrassed.

'Monsieur Poirot is – er – was – a great detective,' I explained.

'Ah! my friend,' cried Poirot. 'Is that all you can find to say? *Mais dis donc!* Say then to Mademoiselle that I am a detective unique, unsurpassed, the greatest that ever lived!'

'That is now unnecessary,' I said coldly. 'You have told her yourself.'

'Ah, yes, but it is more agreeable to have been able to preserve the modesty. One should not sing one's own praises.'

'One should not keep a dog and have to bark oneself,' agreed Nick, with mock sympathy. 'Who is the dog, by the way? Dr Watson, I presume.'

'My name is Hastings,' I said coldly.

'Battle of – 1066,' said Nick. 'Who said I wasn't educated? Well, this is all too, *too* marvellous! Do you think someone really wants to do away with me? It would be thrilling. But, of course, that sort of thing doesn't really happen. Only in books. I expect Monsieur Poirot is like a surgeon who's invented an operation or a doctor who's found an obscure disease and wants everyone to have it.'

'*Sacré tonnerre!*' thundered Poirot. 'Will you be serious? You young people of today, will nothing make you serious? It would not have been a joke, Mademoiselle, if you had been lying in the hotel

185

garden a pretty little corpse with a nice little hole through your head instead of your hat. You would not have laughed then – eh?'

'Unearthly laughter heard at a *séance*,' said Nick. 'But seriously, M. Poirot – it's very kind of you and all that – but the whole thing *must* be an accident.'

'You are as obstinate as the devil!'

'That's where I got my name from. My grandfather was popularly supposed to have sold his soul to the devil. Everyone round here called him Old Nick. He was a wicked old man – but great fun. I adored him. I went everywhere with him and so they called us Old Nick and Young Nick. My real name is Magdala.'

'That is an uncommon name.'

'Yes, it's a kind of family one. There have been lots of Magdalas in the Buckley family. There's one up there.'

She nodded at a picture on the wall.

'Ah!' said Poirot. Then looking at a portrait hanging over the mantelpiece, he said:

'Is that your grandfather, Mademoiselle?'

'Yes, rather an arresting portrait, isn't it? Jim Lazarus offered to buy it, I wouldn't sell. I've got an affection for Old Nick.'

'Ah!' Poirot was silent for a minute, then he said very earnestly:

'*Revenons à nos moutons*. Listen, Mademoiselle. I implore you to be serious. You are in danger. Today, somebody shot at you with a Mauser pistol –'

'A Mauser pistol? –'

For a moment she was startled.

'Yes, why? Do you know of anyone who has a Mauser pistol?'

She smiled.

'I've got one myself.'

'You have?'

'Yes – it was Dad's. He brought it back from the War. It's been knocking round here ever since. I saw it only the other day in that drawer.'

She indicated an old-fashioned bureau. Now, as though suddenly struck by an idea, she crossed to it and pulled the drawer open. She turned rather blankly. Her voice held a new note.

'Oh!' she said. 'It's – it's gone.'

CHAPTER THREE

Accidents?

It was from that moment that the conversation took on a different tone. Up to now, Poirot and the girl had been at cross-purposes. They were separated by a gulf of years. His fame and reputation meant nothing to her – she was of the generation that knows only the great names of the immediate moment. She was, therefore, unimpressed by his warnings. He was to her only a rather comic elderly foreigner with an amusingly melodramatic mind.

And this attitude baffled Poirot. To begin with, his vanity suffered. It was his constant dictum that all the world knew Hercule Poirot. Here was someone who did not. Very good for him, I could not but feel – but not precisely helpful to the object in view!

With the discovery of the missing pistol, however, the affair took on a new phase. Nick ceased to treat it as a mildly amusing joke. She still treated the matter lightly, because it was her habit and her creed to treat all occurrences lightly, but there was a distinct difference in her manner.

She came back and sat down on the arm of a chair, frowning thoughtfully.

'That's odd,' she said.

Poirot whirled round on me.

'You remember, Hastings, the little idea I mentioned? Well, it was correct, my little idea! Supposing Mademoiselle had been found shot lying in the hotel garden? She might not have been found for some hours – few people pass that way. And *beside her hand* – just fallen from it – *is her own pistol*. Doubtless the good Madame Ellen would identify it. There would be suggestions, no doubt, of worry or of sleeplessness –'

Nick moved uneasily.

'That's true. I have been worried to death. Everybody's been telling me I'm nervy. Yes – they'd say all that . . .'

'And bring in a verdict of suicide. Mademoiselle's fingerprints conveniently on the pistol and nobody else's – but yes, it would be very simple and convincing.'

'How terribly amusing!' said Nick, but not, I was glad to note, as though she were terribly amused.

Poirot accepted her words in the conventional sense in which they

187

were uttered.

'*N'est ce pas?* But you understand, Mademoiselle, there must be no more of this. Four failures – yes – but the fifth time there may be a success.'

'Bring out your rubber-tyred hearses,' murmured Nick.

'But we are here, my friend and I, to obviate all that!' I felt grateful for the 'we'. Poirot has a habit of sometimes ignoring my existence.

'Yes,' I put in. 'You mustn't be alarmed, Miss Buckley. We will protect you.'

'How frightfully nice of you,' said Nick. 'I think the whole thing is perfectly marvellous. Too, too thrilling.'

She still preserved her airy detached manner, but her eyes, I thought, looked troubled.

'And the first thing to do,' said Poirot, 'is to have the consultation.'

He sat down and beamed upon her in a friendly manner.

'To begin with, Mademoiselle, a conventional question – but – have you any enemies?'

Nick shook her head rather regretfully.

'I'm afraid not,' she said apologetically.

'*Bon.* We will dismiss that possibility then. And now we ask the question of the cinema, of the detective novel – Who profits by your death, Mademoiselle?'

'I can't imagine,' said Nick. 'That's why it all seems such nonsense. There's this beastly old barn, of course, but it's mortgaged up to the hilt, the roof leaks and there can't be a coal mine or anything exciting like that hidden in the cliff.'

'It is mortgaged – *hein?*'

'Yes. I had to mortgage it. You see there were two lots of death duties – quite soon after each other. First my grandfather died – just six years ago, and then my brother. That just about put the lid on the financial position.'

'And your father?'

'He was invalided home from the War, then got pneumonia and died in 1919. My mother died when I was a baby. I lived here with grandfather. He and Dad didn't get on (I don't wonder), so Dad found it convenient to park me and go roaming the world on his own account. Gerald – that was my brother – didn't get on with grandfather either. I dare say I shouldn't have got on with him if I'd been a boy. Being a girl saved me. Grandfather used to say I was a chip off the old block and had inherited his spirit.' She laughed. 'He was an awful old rip, I believe. But frightfully lucky. There was a saying round here that everything he touched turned to gold. He was a gambler, though, and gambled it away again. When he died he left hardly anything beside the house and land. I was sixteen when he died and Gerald was twenty-two. Gerald was killed in a motor accident just three years ago and the place came to me.'

'And after you, Mademoiselle? Who is your nearest realtion?'

'My cousin, Charles. Charles Vyse. He's a lawyer down here. Quite good and worthy but very dull. He gives me good advice and tries to restrain my extravagant tastes.'

'He manages your affairs for you – eh?'

'Well – yes, if you like to put it that way. I haven't many affairs to manage. He arranged the mortgage for me and made me let the lodge.'

'Ah! – the lodge. I was going to ask you about that. It is let?'

'Yes – to some Australians. Croft their name is. Very hearty, you know – and all that sort of thing. Simply oppressively kind. Always bringing up sticks of celery and early peas and things like that. They're shocked at the way I let the garden go. They're rather a nuisance, really – at least he is. Too terribly friendly for words. She's a cripple, poor thing, and lies on a sofa all day. Anyway they pay the rent and that's the great thing.'

'How long have they been here?'

'Oh! about six months.'

'I see. Now, beyond this cousin of yours – on your father's side or your mother's, by the way?'

'Mother's. My mother was Amy Vyse.'

'*Bien!* Now, beyond this cousin, as I was saying, have you any other relatives?'

'Some very distant cousins in Yorkshire – Buckleys.'

'No one else?'

'No.'

'That is lonely.'

Nick stared at him.

'Lonely? What a funny idea. I'm not down here much, you know. I'm usually in London. Relations are too devastating as a rule. They fuss and interfere. It's much more fun to be on one's own.'

'I will not waste the sympathy. You are a modern, I see, Mademoiselle. Now – your household.'

'How grand that sounds! Ellen's the household. And her husband, who's a sort of gardener – not a very good one. I pay them frightfully little because I let them have the child here. Ellen does for me when

189

I'm down here and if I have a party we get in who and what we can to help. I'm giving a party on Monday. It's Regatta week, you know.'

'Monday – and today is Saturday. Yes. Yes. And now, Mademoiselle, your friends – the ones with whom you were lunching today, for instance?'

'Well, Freddie Rice – the fair girl – is practically my greatest friend. She's had a rotten life. Married to a beast – a man who drank and drugged and was altogether a queer of the worst description. She had to leave him a year or two ago. Since then she's drifted round. I wish to goodness she'd get a divorce and marry Jim Lazarus.'

'Lazarus? The art dealer in Bond Street?'

'Yes. Jim's the only son. Rolling in money, of course. Did you see that car of his? He's a Jew, of course, but a frightfully decent one. And he's devoted to Freddie. They go about everywhere together. They are staying at the Majestic over the week-end and are coming to me on Monday.'

'And Mrs Rice's husband?'

'The mess? Oh! he's dropped out of everything. Nobody knows where he is. It makes it horribly awkward for Freddie. You can't divorce a man when you don't know where he is.'

'*Evidemment!*'

'Poor Freddie,' said Nick, pensively. 'She's had rotten luck. The thing was all fixed once. She got hold of him and put it to him, and he said he was perfectly willing, but he simply hadn't got the cash to take a woman to a hotel. So the end of it all was she forked out – and he took it and off he went and has never been heard of from that day to this. Pretty mean, I call it.'

'Good heavens,' I exclaimed.

'My friend Hastings is shocked,' remarked Poirot. 'You must be more careful, Mademoiselle. He is out of date, you comprehend. He has just returned from those great clear open spaces, etc., and he has yet to learn the language of nowadays.'

'Well, there's nothing to get shocked about,' said Nick, opening her eyes very wide. 'I mean, everybody knows, don't they, that there are such people. But I call it a low-down trick all the same. Poor old Freddie was so damned hard up at the time that she didn't know where to turn.'

'Yes, yes, not a very pretty affair. And your other friend, Mademoiselle. The good Commander Challenger?'

'George? I've known George all my life – well, for the last five years anyway. He's a good scout, George.'

'He wishes you to marry him – eh?'

'He does mention it now and again. In the small hours of the morning or after the second glass of port.'

'But you remain hard-hearted.'

'What would be the use of George and me marrying one another? We've neither of us got a bean. And one would get terribly bored with George. That "playing for one's side," "good old school" manner. After all, he's forty if he's a day.'

The remark made me wince slightly.

'In fact he has one foot in the grave,' said Poirot. 'Oh! do not mind me, Mademoiselle. I am a grandpapa – a nobody. And now tell me more about these accidents. The picture, for instance?'

'It's been hung up again – on a new cord. You can come and see it if you like.'

She led the way out of the room and we followed her. The picture in question was an oil painting in a heavy frame. It hung directly over the bed-head.

With a murmured, 'You permit, Mademoiselle,' Poirot removed his shoes and mounted upon the bed. He examined the picture and the cord, and gingerly tested the weight of the painting. With an elegant grimace he descended.

'To have that descend on one's head – no, it would not be pretty. The cord by which it was hung, Mademoiselle, was it, like this one, a wire cable?'

'Yes, but not so thick. I got a thicker one this time.'

'That is comprehensible. And you examined the break – the edges were frayed?'

'I think so – but I didn't notice particularly. Why should I?'

'Exactly. As you say, why should you? All the same, I should much like to look at that piece of wire. Is it about the house anywhere?'

'It was still on the picture. I expect the man who put the new wire on just threw the old one away.'

'A pity. I should like to have seen it.'

'You don't think it was just an accident after all? Surely it couldn't have been anything else.'

'It may have been an accident. It is impossible to say. But the damage to the brakes of your car – that was not an accident. And the stone that rolled down the cliff – I should like to see the spot where that accident occurred.'

Nick took us out in the garden and led us to the cliff edge. The sea glittered blue below us. A rough path led down the face of the rock. Nick described just where the accident occurred and Poirot nodded thoughtfully. Then he asked:

'How many ways are there into your garden, Mademoiselle?'

'There's the front way – past the lodge. And a tradesman's entrance – a door in the wall half-way up that lane. Then there's a gate just along here on the cliff edge. It leads out on to a zig zag path that leads up from that beach to the Majestic Hotel. And then, of course, you can go straight through a gap in the hedge into the Majestic garden – that's the way I went this morning. To go through the Majestic garden is a short cut to the town anyway.'

'And your gardener – where does he usually work?'

'Well, he usually potters round the kitchen garden, or else he sits in the potting-shed and pretends to be sharpening the shears.'

'Round the other side of the house, that is to say?'

'So that if anyone were to come in here and dislodge a boulder he would be very unlikely to be noticed.'

Nick gave a sudden little shiver.

'Do you – do you really think that is what happened?' she asked, 'I can't believe it somehow. It seems so perfectly futile.'

Poirot drew the bullet from his pocket again and looked at it.

'That was not futile, Mademoiselle,' he said gently.

'It must have been some madman.'

'Possibly. It is an interesting subject of after-dinner conversation – are all criminals really madmen? There may be a malformation in their little grey cells – yes, it is very likely. That, it is the affair of the doctor. For me – I have different work to perform. I have the innocent to think of, not the guilty – the victim, not the criminal. It is you I am considering now, Mademoiselle, not your unknown assailant. You are young and beautiful, and the sun shines and the world is pleasant, and there is life and love ahead of you. It is all that of which I think, Mademoiselle. Tell me, these friends of yours, Mrs Rice and Mr Lazarus – they have been down here, how long?'

'Freddie came down on Wednesday to this part of the world. She stopped with some people near Tavistick for a couple of nights. She came on here yesterday. Jim has been touring round about, I believe.'

'And Commander Challenger?'

'He's at Devonport. He comes over in his car whenever he can – week-ends mostly.'

Poirot nodded. We were walking back to the house. There was a

192

silence, and then he said suddenly:

'Have you a friend whom you can trust, Mademoiselle?'

'There's Freddie.'

'Other than Mrs Rice.'

'Well, I don't know. I suppose I have. Why?'

'Because I want you to have a friend to stay with you – immediately.'

'Oh!'

Nick seemed rather taken aback. She was silent a moment or two, thinking. Then she said doubtfully:

'There's Maggie. I could get hold of her, I expect.'

'Who is Maggie?'

'One of my Yorkshire cousins. There's a large family of them. He's a clergyman, you know. Maggie's about my age, and I usually have her to stay sometime or other in the summer. She's no fun, though – one of those painfully pure girls, with the kind of hair that has just become fashionable by accident. I was hoping to get out of having her this year.'

'Not at all. Your cousin, Mademoiselle, will do admirably. Just the type of person I had in mind.'

'All right,' said Nick, with a sigh. 'I'll wire her. I certainly don't know who else I could get hold of just now. Everyone's fixed up. But if it isn't the Choirboys' Outing or the Mothers' Beanfeast she'll come all right. Though what you expect her to *do* . . .'

'Could you arrange for her to sleep in your room?'

'I suppose so.'

'She would not think that an odd request?'

'Oh, no, Maggie never thinks. She just *does* – earnestly, you know. Christian works – with faith and perseverance. All right, I'll wire her to come on Monday.'

'Why not tomorrow?'

'With Sunday trains? She'll think I'm dying if I suggest that. No, I'll say Monday. Are you going to tell her about the awful fate hanging over me?'

'*Nous verrons*. You still make a jest of it? You have courage, I am glad to see.'

'It makes a diversion anyway,' said Nick.

Something in her tone struck me and I glanced at her curiously. I had a feeling that there was something she had left untold. We had re-entered the drawing-room. Poirot was fingering the newspaper on the sofa.

193

'You read this, Mademoiselle?' he asked, suddenly.

'The St Loo *Herald*? Not seriously. I opened it to see the tides. It gives them every week.'

'I see. By the way, Mademoiselle, have you ever made a will?'

'Yes, I did. About six months ago. Just before my op.'

'*Qu'est ce que vous dites*? Your *op*?'

'Operation. For appendicitis. Someone said I ought to make a will, so I did. It made me feel quite important.'

'And the terms of that will?'

'I left End House to Charles. I hadn't much else to leave, but what there was I left to Freddie. I should think probably the – what do you call them – liabilities would have exceeded the assets, really.'

Poirot nodded absently.

'I will take my leave now. *Au revoir, Mademoiselle*. Be careful.'

'What of?' asked Nick.

'You are intelligent. Yes, that is the weak point – in which direction are you to be careful? Who can say? But have confidence, Mademoiselle. In a few days I shall have discovered the truth.'

'Until then beware of poison, bombs, revolver shots, motor accidents and arrows dipped in the secret poison of the South American Indians,' finished Nick glibly.

'Do not mock yourself, Mademoiselle,' said Poirot gravely.

He paused as he reached the door.

'By the way,' he said. 'What price did M. Lazarus offer you for the portrait of your grandfather?'

'Fifty pounds.'

'Ah!' said Poirot.

He looked earnestly back at the dark saturnine face above the mantelpiece.

'But, as I told you, I don't want to sell the old boy.'

'No,' said Poirot, thoughtfully. 'No, I understand.'

CHAPTER FOUR

There Must Be Something!

'Poirot,' I said, as soon as we were out upon the road. 'There is one thing I think you ought to know.'

'And what is that, *mon ami?*'

I told him of Mrs Rice's version of the trouble with the motor.

'*Tiens! C'est intéressant, ça.* There is, of course, a type, vain, hysterical, that seeks to make itself interesting by having marvellous escapes from death and which will recount to you surprising histories that never happened! Yes, it is well known, that type there. Such people will even do themselves grave bodily injury to sustain the fiction.'

'You don't think that –'

'That Mademoiselle Nick is of that type? No, indeed. You observed, Hastings, that we had great difficulty in convincing her of her danger. And right to the end she kept up the farce of a half-mocking disbelief. She is of her generation, that little one. All the same, it is interesting – what Madame Rice said. Why should she say it? Why say it even if it were true? It was unnecessary – almost *gauche.*'

'Yes,' I said. 'That's true. She dragged it into the conversation neck and crop – for no earthly reason that I could see.'

'That is curious. Yes, that is curious. The little facts that are curious, I like to see them appear. They are significant. They point the way.'

'The way – where?'

'You put your finger on the weak spot, my excellent Hastings. Where? Where indeed! Alas, we shall not know till we get there.'

'Tell me, Poirot,' I said. 'Why did you insist on her getting this cousin to stay?'

Poirot stopped and waved an excited forefinger at me.

'Consider,' he cried. 'Consider for one little moment, Hastings. How we are handicapped! How are our hands tied! To hunt down a murderer after a crime has been committed – *c'est tout simple!* Or at least it is simple to one of my ability. The murderer has, so to speak, signed his name by committing the crime. But here there is no crime – and what is more we do not want a crime. To detect a crime before it had been committed – that is indeed of a rare difficulty.

'What is our first aim? The safety of Mademoiselle. And that is not easy. No, it is not easy, Hastings. We cannot watch over her day and night – we cannot even send a policeman in big boots to watch over her. We cannot pass the night in a young lady's sleeping chamber. The affair bristles with difficulties.

'But we can do one thing. We can make it more difficult for our assassin. We can put Mademoiselle upon her guard and we can introduce a perfectly impartial witness. It will take a very clever man to get round those two circumstances.'

He paused, and then said in an entirely different tone of voice:

'But what I am afraid of, Hastings –'

'Yes?'

'What I am afraid of is – that he *is* a very clever man. And I am not easy in my mind. No, I am not easy at all.'

'Poirot,' I said. 'You're making me feel quite nervous.'

'So am I nervous. Listen, my friend, that paper, the St Loo *Weekly Herald*. It was open and folded back at – where do you think? A little paragraph which said, "*Among the guests staying at the Majestic Hotel are M. Hercule Poirot and Captain Hastings.*" Supposing – just supposing that someone had read that paragraph. They know my name – everyone knows my name –'

'Miss Buckley didn't,' I said, with a grin.

'She is a scatterbrain – she does not count. A serious man – a criminal – would know my name. And he would be afraid ! He would wonder! He would ask himself questions. Three times he has attempted the life of Mademoiselle and now Hercule Poirot arrives in the neighbourhood. "Is that coincidence?" he would ask himself. And he would fear that it might *not* be coincidence. What would he do then?'

'Lie low and hide his tracks,' I suggested.

'Yes – yes – or else – if he had real audacity, he would strike *quickly* – without loss of time. Before I had time to make inquiries – *pouf*, Mademoiselle is dead. This is what a man of audacity would do.'

'But why do you think that somebody read that paragraph other than Miss Buckley?'

'It was not Miss Buckley who read that paragraph. When I mentioned my name it meant nothing to her. It was not even familiar. Her face did not change. Besides she told us – she opened the paper to look at the tides – nothing else. Well, there was no tide table on that page.'

'You think someone in the house –'

196

'Someone in the house or who has access to it. And that last is easy – the window stands open. Without doubt Miss Buckley's friends pass in and out.'

'Have you any idea? Any suspicion?'

Poirot flung out his hands.

'Nothing. Whatever the motive, it is, as I predicted, not an obvious one. That is the would-be murderer's security – that is why he could act so daringly this morning. On the face of it, no one seems to have any reason for desiring the little Nick's death. The property? End House? That passes to the cousin – but does he particularly want a heavily mortgaged and very dilapidated old house? It is not even a family place so far as he is concerned. He is not a Buckley, remember. We must see this Charles Vyse, certainly, but the idea seems fantastic.

'Then there is Madame – the bosom friend – with her strange eyes and her air of a lost Madonna –'

'You felt that too? I asked, startled.

'What is her concern in the business? She tells you that her friend is a liar. *C'est gentil ça!* Why does she tell you? Is she afraid of something that Nick may say? Is that something connected with the car? Or did she use that as an insurance, and was her real fear of something else? Did anyone tamper with the car, and if so, who? And does she know about it?

'Then the handsome blond, M. Lazarus. Where does he fit in? With his marvellous automobile and his money. Can he possibly be concerned in any way? Commander Challenger –'

'He's all right,' I put in quickly. 'I'm sure of that. A real pukka sahib.'

'Doubtless he has been to what you consider the right school. Happily, being a foreigner, I am free from these prejudices, and can make investigations unhampered by them. But I will admit that I find it hard to connect Commander Challenger with the case. In fact, I do not see that he can be connected.'

'Of course he can't,' I said warmly.

Poirot looked at me meditatively.

'You have an extraordinary effect on me, Hastings. You have so strongly the *flair* in the wrong direction that I am almost tempted to go by it! You are that wholly admirable type of man, honest, credulous, honourable, who is invariably taken in by any scoundrel. You are the type of man who invests in doubtful oil fields, and non-existent gold mines. From hundreds like you, the swindler

197

makes his daily bread. Ah, well – I shall study this Commander Challenger. You have awakened my doubts.'

'My dear Poirot,' I cried, angrily. 'You are perfectly absurd. A man who has knocked about the world like I have –'

'Never learns,' said Poirot, sadly. 'It is amazing – but there it is.'

'Do you suppose I'd have made a success of my ranch out in the Argentine if I were the kind of credulous fool you make out?'

'Do not enrage yourself, *mon ami*. You have made a great success of it – you and your wife.'

'Bella.' I said, 'always goes by my judgement.'

'She is as wise as she is charming,' said Poirot. 'Let us not quarrel my friend. See, there ahead of us, it says Mott's Garage. That, I think, is the garage mentioned by Mademoiselle Buckley. A few inquiries will soon give us the truth of that little matter.'

We duly entered the place and Poirot introduced himself by explaining that he had been recommended there by Miss Buckley. He made some inquiries about hiring a car for some afternoon drives and from there slid easily into the topic of the damage sustained by Miss Buckley's car not long ago.

Immediately the garage proprietor waxed voluble. Most extraordinary thing he'd ever seen. He proceeded to be technical. I, alas, am not mechanically minded. Poirot, I should imagine, is even less so. But certain facts did emerge unmistakably. The car had been tampered with. And the damage had been something quite easily done, occupying very little time.

'So that is that,' said Poirot, as we strolled away. 'The little Nick was right, and the rich M. Lazarus was wrong. Hastings, my friend, all this is very interesting.'

'What do we do now?'

'We visit the post office and send off a telegram if it is not too late.'

'A telegram?' I said hopefully.

'Yes,' said Poirot thoughtfully. 'A telegram.'

The post office was still open. Poirot wrote out his telegram and despatched it. He vouchsafed me no information as to its contents. Feeling that he wanted me to ask him, I carefully refrained from doing so.

'It is annoying that tomorrow is Sunday,' he remarked, as we strolled back to the hotel. 'We cannot now call upon M. Vyse till Monday morning.'

'You could get hold of him at his private address.'

'Naturally. But that is just what I am anxious not to do. I would

198

prefer, in the first place, to consult him professionally and to form my judgement of him from that aspect.'

'Yes,' I said thoughtfully. 'I suppose that would be best.'

'The answer to one simple little question, for instance, might make a great difference. If M. Charles Vyse was in his office at twelve-thirty this morning, then it was not he who fired that shot in the garden of the Majestic Hotel.'

'Ought we not to examine the *alibis* of the three at the hotel?'

'That is much more difficult. It would be easy enough for one of them to leave the others for a few minutes, a hasty egress from one of the innumerable windows – lounge, smoking-room, drawing-room, writing-room, quickly under cover to the spot where the girl must pass – the shot fired and a rapid retreat. But as yet, *mon ami*, we are not even sure that we have arrived at all the *dramatis personae* in the drama. There is the respectable Ellen – and her so far unseen husband. Both inmates of the house and possibly, for all we know, with a grudge against our little Mademoiselle. There are even the unknown Australians at the lodge. And there may be others, friends and intimates of Miss Buckley's whom she has no reason for suspecting and consequently has not mentioned. I cannot help feeling, Hastings, that there is something *behind* this – *something* that has not yet come to light. I have a little idea that Miss Buckley knows more than she told us.'

'You think she is keeping something back?'

'Yes.'

'Possibly with an idea of shielding whoever it is?'

Poirot shook his head with the utmost energy.

'No, no. As far as that goes, she gave me the impression of being utterly frank. I am convinced that as regards these attempts on her life, she was telling all she knew. But there is something else – something that she believes has nothing to do with that at all. And I should like to know what that something is. For I – I say it in all modesty – am a great deal more intelligent than *une petite comme ça*. I, Hercule Poirot, might see a connection where she sees none. It might give me the clue I am seeking. For I announce to you, Hastings, quite frankly and humbly, that I am as you express it, all on the sea. Until I can get some glimmering of the *reason* behind all this, I am in the dark. There must be *something* – some factor in the case that I do not grasp. What is it? *Je me demande ça sans cesse. Qu'est-ce que c'est?*'

'You will find out,' I said, soothingly.

'So long,' he said sombrely, 'as I do not find out too late.'

199

CHAPTER FIVE

Mr and Mrs Croft

There was dancing that evening at the hotel. Nick Buckley dined there with her friends and waved a gay greeting to us.

She was dressed that evening in floating scarlet chiffon that dragged on the floor. Out of it rose her white neck and shoulders and her small impudent dark head.

'An engaging young devil,' I remarked.

'A contrast to her friend – eh?'

Frederica Rice was in white. She danced with a languorous weary grace that was as far removed from Nick's animation as anything could be.

'She is very beautiful,' said Poirot suddenly.

'Who? Our Nick?'

'No – the other. Is she evil? Is she good? Is she merely unhappy? One cannot tell. She is a mystery. She is, perhaps, nothing at all. But I tell you, my friend, she is an *allumeuse*.'

'What do you mean?' I ask curiously.

He shook his head, smiling.

'You will feel it sooner or later. Remember my words.'

Presently to my surprise, he rose. Nick was dancing with George Challenger. Frederica and Lazarus had just stopped and had sat down at their table. Then Lazarus got up and went away. Mrs Rice was alone. Poirot went straight to her table. I followed him.

His methods were direct and to the point.

'You permit?' He laid a hand on the back of a chair, then slid into it. 'I am anxious to have a word with you while your friend is dancing.'

'Yes?' Her voice sounded cool, uninterested.

'Madame, I do not know whether your friend has told you. If not, I will. Today her life has been attempted.'

Her great grey eyes widened in horror and surprise. The pupils, dilated black pupils, widened too.

'What do you mean?'

'Mademoiselle Buckley was shot at in the garden of this hotel.'

She smiled suddenly – a gentle, pitying, incredulous smile.

'Did Nick tell you so?'

'No, Madame, I happened to see it with my own eyes. Here is the bullet.'

200

He held it out to her and she drew back a little.

'But, then – but, then –'

'It is no fantasy of Mademoiselle's imagination, you understand I vouch for that. And there is more. Several very curious accidents have happened in the last few days. You will have heard – no, perhaps you will not. You only arrived yesterday, did you not?'

'Yes – yesterday.'

'Before that you were staying with friends, I understand. At Tavistock.'

'Yes.'

'I wonder, Madame, what were the names of the friends with whom you were staying.'

She raised her eyebrows.

'Is there any reason why I should tell you that?' she asked coldly.

Poirot was immediately all innocent surprise.

'A thousand pardons, Madame. I was most *maladroit*. But I myself, having friends at Tavistock, fancied that you might have met them there . . . Buchanan – that is the name of my friends.'

Mrs Rice shook her head.

'I don't remember them. I don't think I can have met them.' Her tone now was quite cordial. 'Don't let us talk about boring people. Go on about Nick. Who shot at her? Why?'

'I do not know who – *as yet*,' said Poirot. 'But I shall find out. Oh! yes, I shall find out. I am, you know, a detective. Hercule Poirot is my name.'

'A very famous name.'

'Madame is too kind.'

She said slowly:

'What do you want me to do?'

I think she surprised us both there. We had not expected just that.

'I will ask you, Madame, to watch over your friend.'

'I will.'

'That is all.'

He got up, made a quick bow, and we returned to our own table.

'Poirot,' I said, 'aren't you showing your hand very plainly?'

'*Mon ami*, what else can I do? It lacks subtlety, perhaps, but it makes for safety. *I can take no chances*. At any rate one thing emerges plain to see.'

'What is that?'

'*Mrs Rice was not at Tavistock*. Where was she? Ah! but I will find out. Impossible to keep information from Hercule Poirot. See – the

201

handsome Lazarus has returned. She is telling him. He looks over at us. He is clever, that one. Note the shape of his head. Ah! I wish I knew –'

'What?' I asked, as he came to a stop.

'What I shall know on Monday,' he returned, ambiguously.

I looked at him but said nothing. He sighed.

'You have no longer the curiosity, my friend. In the old days –'

'There are some pleasures,' I said, coldly, 'that it is good for you to do without.'

'You mean –?'

'The pleasure of refusing to answer questions.'

'*Ah c'est malin.*'

'Quite so.'

'Ah, well, well,' murmured Poirot. 'The strong silent man beloved of novelists in the Edwardian age.'

His eyes twinkled with their old glint.

Nick passed our table shortly afterwards. She detached herself from her partner and swooped down on us like a gaily-coloured bird.

'Dancing on the edge of death,' she said lightly.

'It is a new sensation, Mademoiselle?'

'Yes. Rather fun.'

She was off again, with a wave of her hand.

'I wish she hadn't said that,' I said, slowly. 'Dancing on the edge of death. I don't like it.'

'I know. It is too near the truth. She has courage, that little one. Yes, she has courage. But unfortunately it is not courage that is needed at this moment. Caution, not courage – *voilà ce qu'il nous faut!*'

The following day was Sunday. We were sitting on the terrace in front of the hotel, and it was about half-past eleven when Poirot suddenly rose to his feet.

'Come, my friend. We will try a little experiment. I have ascertained that M. Lazarus and Madame have gone out in the car and Mademoiselle with them. The coast is clear.'

'Clear for what?'

'You shall see.'

We walked down the steps and across a short stretch of grass to the sea. A couple of bathers were coming up it. They passed us laughing and talking.

When they had gone, Poirot walked to the point where an inconspicuous small gate, rather rusty on its hinges, bore the words in half obliterated letters, 'End House. Private.' There was no one in sight. We passed quietly through.

In another minute we came out on the stretch of lawn in front of the house. There was no one about. Poirot strolled to the edge of the cliff and looked over. Then he walked towards the house itself. The French windows on to the verandah were open and we passed straight into the drawing-room. Poirot wasted no time there. He opened the door and went out into the hall. From there he mounted the stairs, I at his heels. He went straight to Nick's bedroom – sat down on the edge of the bed and nodded to me with a twinkle.

'You see, my friends, how easy it is. No one has seen us come. No one will see us go. We could do any little affair we had to do in perfect safety. We would, for instance, fray through a picture wire so that it would be bound to snap before many hours had passed. And supposing that by chance anyone did happen to be in front of the house and see us coming. Then we would have a perfectly natural excuse – providing that we were known as friends of the house.'

'You mean that we can rule out a stranger?'

'That is what I mean, Hastings. It is no stray lunatic who is at the bottom of this. We must look nearer home than that.'

He turned to leave the room and I followed him. We neither of us spoke. We were both, I think, troubled in mind.

And then, at the bend of the staircase, we both stopped abruptly. A man was coming up.

He too stopped. His face was in shadow but his attitude was one of one completely taken aback. He was the first to speak, in a loud, rather bullying voice.

'What the hell are you doing here, I'd like to know?'

'Ah!' said Poirot. 'Monsieur – Croft, I think?'

'That's my name, but what –'

'Shall we go into the drawing-room to converse? It would be better, I think.'

The other gave way, turned abruptly and descended, we following close on his heels. In the drawing-room, with the door shut, Poirot made a little bow.

'I will introduce myself. Hercule Poirot at your service.'

The other's face cleared a little.

'Oh!' he said slowly. 'You're the detective chap. I've read about you.'

'In the St Loo *Herald*?'

'Eh? I've read about you way back in Australia. French, aren't

203

you?'

'Belgian. It makes no matter. This is my friend, Captain Hastings.'

'Glad to meet you. But look, what's the big idea? What are you doing here? Anything – wrong?'

'It depends what you call – wrong?'

The Australian nodded. He was a fine-looking man in spite of his bald head and advancing years. His physique was magnificent. He had a heavy, rather underhung face – a crude face, I called it to myself. The piercing blue of his eyes was the most noticeable thing about him.

'See here,' he said. 'I came round to bring little Miss Buckley a handful of tomatoes and a cucumber. That man of hers is no good – bone idle – doesn't grow a thing. Lazy hound. Mother and I – why, it makes us mad, and we feel it's only neighbourly to do what we can! We've got a lot more tomatoes than we can eat. Neighbours should be matey, don't you think? I came in, as usual, through the window and dumped the basket down. I was just going off again when I heard footsteps and men's voices overhead. That struck me as odd. We don't deal much in burglars round here – but after all it was possible. I thought I'd just make sure everything was all right. Then I met you two on the stairs coming down. It gave me a bit of a surprise. And now you tell me you're a bonza detective. What's it all about?'

'It is very simple,' said Poirot, smiling. 'Mademoiselle had a rather alarming experience the other night. A picture fell above her bed. She may have told you of it?'

'She did. A mighty fine escape.'

'To make all secure I promised to bring her some special chain – it will not do to repeat the occurence, eh? She tells me she is going out this morning, but I may come and measure what amount of chain will be needed. *Voilà* – it is simple.'

He flung out his hands with a childlike simplicity and his most engaging smile.

Croft drew a deep breath.

'So that's all it is?'

'Yes – you have had the scare for nothing. We are very law-abiding citizens, my friend and I.'

'Didn't I see you yesterday?' said Croft, slowly. 'Yesterday evening it was. You passed our little place.'

'Ah! yes, you were working in the garden and were so polite as to say good-afternoon when we passed.'

'That's right. Well – well. And you're the Monsieur Hercule Poirot I've heard so much about. Tell me, are you busy, Mr Poirot? Because if not, I wish you'd come back with me now – have a cup of morning tea, Australian fashion, and meet my old lady. She's read all about you in the newspapers.'

'You are too kind, M. Croft. We have nothing to do and shall be delighted.'

'That's fine.'

'You have the measurements correctly, Hastings?' asked Poirot, turning to me.

I assured him that I had the measurements correctly and we accompanied our new friend.

Croft was a talker; we soon realized that. He told us of his home near Melbourne, of his early struggles, of his meeting with his wife, of their combined efforts and of his final good fortune and success.

'Right away we made up our minds to travel,' he said. 'We'd always wanted to come to the old country. Well, we did. We came down to this part of the world – tried to look up some of my wife's people – they came from round about here. But we couldn't trace any of them. Then we took a trip on the Continent – Paris, Rome, the Italian Lakes, Florence – all those places. It was while we were in Italy that we had the train accident. My poor wife was badly smashed up. Cruel, wasn't it? I've taken her to the best doctors and they all say the same – there's nothing for it but time – time and lying up. It's an injury to the spine.'

'What a misfortune!'

'Hard luck, isn't it? Well, there it was. And she'd only got one kind of fancy – to come down here. She kind of felt if we had a little place of our own – something small – it would make all the difference. We saw a lot of messy-looking shacks, and then by good luck we found this. Nice and quiet and tucked away – no cars passing, or gramophones next door. I took it right away.'

With the last words we had come to the lodge itself. He sent his voice echoing forth in a loud 'Cooee,' to which came an answering 'Cooee.'

'Come in,' said Mr Croft. He passed through the open door and up the short flight of stairs to a pleasant bedroom. There, on a sofa, was a stout middle-aged woman with pretty grey hair and a very sweet smile.

'Who do you think this is, mother?' said Mr Croft. 'The extra-special, world-celebrated detective, Mr Hercule Poirot. I brought him right along to have a chat with you.'

'If that isn't too exciting for words,' cried Mrs Croft, shaking Poirot warmly by the hand. 'Read about that Blue Train business, I did, and you just happening to be on it, and a lot about your other cases. Since this trouble with my back. I've read all the detective stories that ever were, I should think. Nothing else seems to pass the time away so quick. Bert, dear, call out to Edith to bring the tea along.'

'Right you are, mother.'

'She's a kind of nurse attendant, Edith is,' Mrs Croft explained. 'She comes along each morning to fix me up. We're not bothering with servants. Bert's as good a cook and a house-parlourman as you'd find anywhere, and it gives him occupation – that and the garden.'

'Here we are,' cried Mr Croft, reappearing with a tray. 'Here's the tea. This is a great day in our lives, mother.'

'I suppose you're staying down here, Mr Poirot?' Mrs Croft asked, as she leaned over a little and wielded the teapot.

'Why, yes, Madame, I take the holiday.'

'But surely I read that you had retired – that you'd taken a holiday for good and all.'

'Ah! Madame, you must not believe everything you read in the papers.'

'Well, that's true enough. So you still carry on business?'

'When I find a case that interests me.'

'Sure you're not down here on work?' inquired Mr Croft, shrewdly. 'Calling it a holiday might be all part of the game.'

'You mustn't ask him embarrassing questions, Bert,' said Mrs Croft. 'Or he won't come again. We're simple people, Mr Poirot, and you're giving us a great treat coming here today – you and your friend. You really don't know the pleasure you're giving us.'

She was so natural and so frank in her gratification that my heart quite warmed to her.

'That was a bad business about that picture,' said Mr Croft.

'That poor little girl might have been killed,' said Mrs Croft, with deep feeling. 'She *is* a live wire. Livens the place up when she comes down here. Not much liked in the neighbourhood, so I've heard. But that's the way in these stuck English places. They don't like life and gaiety in a girl. I don't wonder she doesn't spend much time down here, and that long-nosed cousin of hers has no more chance of persuading her to settle down here for good and all than – than – well, I don't know what.'

'Don't gossip, Milly,' said her husband.

'Aha!' said Poirot. 'The wind is in that quarter. Trust the instinct of Madame! So M. Charles Vyse is in love with our little friend?'

'He's silly about her,' said Mrs Croft. 'But she won't marry a country lawyer. And I don't blame her. He's a poor stick, anyway. I'd like her to marry that nice sailor – what's his name, Challenger. Many a smart marriage might be worse than that. He's older than she is, but what of that? Steadying – that's what she needs. Flying about all over the place, the Continent even, all alone or with that queer-looking Mrs Rice. She's a sweet girl, Mr Poirot – I know that well enough. But I'm worried about her. She's looked none too happy lately. She's had what I call a haunted kind of look. And that worries me! I've got my reasons for being interested in that girl, haven't I, Bert?'

Mr Croft got up from his chair rather suddenly.

'No need to go into that, Milly,' he said. 'I wonder, Mr Poirot, if you'd care to see some snapshots of Australia?'

The rest of our visit passed uneventfully. Ten minutes later we took our leave.

'Nice people,' I said. 'So simple and unassuming. Typical Australians.'

'You liked them?'

'Didn't you?'

'They were very pleasant – very friendly.'

'Well, what is it, then? There's something, I can see.'

'They were, perhaps, just a shade too "typical",' said Poirot, thoughtfully. 'That cry of Cooee – that insistence on showing us snapshots – was it not playing a part just a little too thoroughly?'

'What a suspicious old devil you are!'

'You are right, *mon ami*. I am suspicious of everyone – of everything. I am afraid, Hastings – afraid.'

CHAPTER SIX

A Call Upon Mr Vyse

Poirot clung firmly to the Continental breakfast. To see me consuming eggs and bacon upset and distressed him – so he always said. Consequently he breakfasted in bed upon coffee and rolls and I was free to start the day with the traditional Englishman's breakfast of bacon and eggs and marmalade.

I looked into his room on Monday morning as I went downstairs. He was sitting up in bed arrayed in a very marvellous dressing-gown.

'*Bonjour*, Hastings. I was just about to ring. This note that I have written, will you be so good as to get it taken over to End House and delivered to Mademoiselle at once.'

I held out my hand for it. Poirot looked at me and sighed.

'If only – if only, Hastings, you would part your hair in the middle instead of at the side! What a difference it would make to the symmetry of your appearance. And your moustache. If you *must* have a moustache, let it be a real moustache – a thing of beauty such as mine.'

Repressing a shudder at the thought, I took the note firmly from Poirot's hand and left the room.

I had rejoined him in our sitting-room when word was sent up to say Miss Buckley had called. Poirot gave the order for her to be shown up.

She came in gaily enough, but I fancied that the circles under her eyes were darker than usual. In her hand she held a telegram which she handed to Poirot.

'There,' she said. 'I hope that will please you!'

Poirot read it aloud.

'Arrive 5.30 today. Maggie.'

'My nurse and guardian!' said Nick. 'But you're wrong, you know. Maggie's got no kind of brains. Good works is about all she's fit for. That and never seeing the point of jokes. Freddie would be ten times better at spotting hidden assassins. And Jim Lazarus would be better still. I never feel one has got to the bottom of Jim.'

'And the Commander Challenger?'

'Oh! George! He'd never see anything till it was under his nose. But he'd let them have it when he did see. Very useful when it came to a show-down, George would be.'

208

She tossed off her hat and went on:

'I gave orders for the man you wrote about to be let in. It sounds mysterious. Is he installing a dictaphone or something like that?'

Poirot shook his head.

'No, no, nothing scientific. A very simple little matter of opinion, Mademoiselle. Something I wanted to know.'

'Oh, well,' said Nick. 'It's all great fun, isn't it?'

'Is it, Mademoiselle?' asked Poirot, gently.

She stood for a minute with her back to us, looking out of the window. Then she turned. All the brave defiance had gone out of her face. It was childishly twisted awry, as she struggled to keep back the tears.

'No,' she said. 'It – it isn't, really. I'm afraid – I'm afraid. Hideously afraid. And I always thought I was brave.'

'So you are, *mon enfant*, so you are. Both Hastings and I, we have both admired your courage.'

'Yes, indeed,' I put in warmly.

'No,' said Nick, shaking her head. 'I'm not brave. It's – it's the *waiting*. Wondering the whole time if anything more's going to happen. And *how* it'll happen! And *expecting* it to happen.'

'Yes, yes – it is the strain.'

'Last night I pulled my bed out into the middle of the room. And fastened my window and bolted my door. When I came here this morning, I came round by the road. I couldn't – I simply couldn't come through the garden. It's as though my nerve had gone all of a sudden. It's this thing coming on top of everything else.'

'What do you mean exactly by that, Mademoiselle? On top of everything else?'

There was a momentary pause before she replied.

'I don't mean anything particular. What the newspapers call "the strain of modern life", I suppose. Too many cocktails, too many cigarettes – all that sort of thing. It's just that I've got into a ridiculous – sort of – of state.'

She had sunk into a chair and was sitting there, her small fingers curling and uncurling themselves nervously.

'You are not being frank with me, Mademoiselle. There is something.'

'There isn't – there really isn't.'

'There is something you have not told me.'

'I've told you every single smallest thing.'

She spoke sincerely and earnestly.

209

'About these accidents – about the attacks upon you, yes.'

'Well – then?'

'But you have not told me everything that is in your heart – in your life ...'

She said slowly:

'Can anyone do that ...?'

'Ah! then,' said Poirot, with triumph. 'You admit it!'

She shook her head. He watched her keenly.

'Perhaps,' he suggested, shrewdly. 'It is not *your* secret?'

I thought I saw a momentary flicker of her eyelids. But almost immediately she jumped up.

'Really and truly, M. Poirot, I've told every single thing I know about this stupid business. If you think I know something about someone else, or have suspicions, you are wrong. It's having *no* suspicions that's driving me mad! Because I'm not a fool. I can see that if those "accidents" weren't accidents, they must have been engineered by somebody very near at hand – somebody who – knows me. And that's what is so awful. Because I haven't the least idea – not the very least – who that somebody might be.'

She went over once more to the window and stood looking out. Poirot signed to me not to speak. I think he was hoping for some further revelation, now that the girl's self-control had broken down.

When she spoke, it was in a different tone of voice, a dreamy far-away voice.

'Do you know a queer wish I've always had? I love End House. I've always wanted to produce a play there. It's got an – an atmosphere of drama about it. I've seen all sorts of plays staged there in my mind. And now it's as though a drama were being acted there. Only I'm not producing it ... I'm *right* in it! I'm *right* in it! I am, perhaps, the person who – dies in the first act.'

Her voice broke.

'Now, now, Mademoiselle.' Poirot's voice was resolutely brisk and cheerful. 'This will not do. This is hysteria.'

She turned and looked at him sharply.

'Did Freddie tell you I was hysterical?' she asked. 'She says I am, sometimes. But you mustn't always believe what Freddie says. There are times, you know when – when she isn't quite herself.'

There was a pause, then Poirot asked a totally irrelevant question:

'Tell me, Mademoiselle,' he said. 'Have you ever received an offer for End House?'

'To sell it, do you mean?'

'That is what I meant.'

'No.'

'Would you consider selling it if you got a good offer?'

Nick considered for a moment.

'No, I don't think so. Not, I mean, unless it was such a ridiculously good offer that it would be perfectly foolish not to.'

'*Précisément.*'

'I don't want to sell it, you know, because I'm fond of it.'

'Quite so. I understand.'

Nick moved slowly towards the door.

'By the way, there are fireworks tonight. Will you come? Dinner at eight o'clock. The fireworks begin at nine-thirty. You can see them splendidly from the garden where it overlooks the harbour.'

'I shall be enchanted.'

'Both of you, of course,' said Nick.

'Many thanks,' I said.

'Nothing like a party for reviving the drooping spirits,' remarked Nick. And with a little laugh she went out.

'*Pauvre enfant*,' said Poirot.

He reached for his hat and carefully flicked an infinitesimal speck of dust from its surface.

'We are going out?' I asked.

'*Mais oui*, we have legal business to transact, *mon ami*.'

'Of course. I understand.'

'One of your brilliant mentality could not fail to do so, Hastings.'

The offices of Messrs Vyse, Trevannion & Wynnard were situated in the main street of the town. We mounted the stairs to the first floor and entered a room where three clerks were busily writing. Poirot asked to see Mr Charles Vyse.

A clerk murmured a few words down a telephone, received, apparently, an affirmative reply, and remarking that Mr Vyse would see us now, he led us across the passage, tapped on a door and stood aside for us to pass in.

From behind a large desk covered with legal papers, Mr Vyse rose up to greet us.

He was a tall young man, rather pale, with impassive features. He was going a little bald on either temple and wore glasses. His colouring was fair and indeterminate.

Poirot had come prepared for the encounter. Fortunately he had with him an agreement, as yet unsigned, and so on some technical points in connection with this, he wanted Mr Vyse's advice.

Mr Vyse, speaking carefully and correctly, was soon able to allay Poirot's alleged doubts, and to clear up some obscure points of the wording.

'I am very much obliged to you,' murmured Poirot. 'As a foreigner, you comprehend, these legal matters and phrasing are most difficult.'

It was then that Mr Vyse asked who had sent Poirot to him.

'Miss Buckley,' said Poirot, promptly. 'Your cousin, is she not? A most charming young lady. I happened to mention that I was in perplexity and she told me to come to you. I tried to see you on Saturday morning – about half-past twelve – but you were out.'

'Yes, I remember. I left early on Saturday.'

'Mademoiselle your cousin must find that large house very lonely? She lives there alone, I understand.'

'Quite so.'

'Tell me, Mr Vyse, if I may ask, is there any chance of that property being in the market?'

'Not the least, I should say.'

'You understand, I do not ask idly. I have a reason! I am in search, myself, of just such a property. The climate of St Loo enchants me. It is true that the house appears to be in bad repair, there has not been, I gather, much money to spend upon it. Under those circumstances, is it not possible that Mademoiselle would consider an offer?'

'Not the least likelihood of it.' Charles Vyse shook his head with the utmost decision. 'My cousin is absolutely devoted to the place. Nothing would induce her to sell, I know. It is, you understand, a family place.'

'I comprehend that, but –'

'It is absolutely out of the question. I know my cousin. She has a fanatical devotion to the house.'

A few minutes later we were out in the street again.

'Well, my friend,' said Poirot. 'And what impression did this M. Charles Vyse makes upon you?'

I considered.

'A very negative one,' I said at last. 'He is a curiously negative person.'

'Not a strong personality, you would say?'

'No, indeed. The kind of man you would never remember on meeting him again. A mediocre person.'

'His appearance is certainly not striking. Did you notice any discrepancy in the course of our conversation with him?'

'Yes,' I said slowly, 'I did. With regard to the selling of End House.'

'Exactly. Would you have described Mademoiselle Buckley's attitude towards End House as one of "fanatical devotion"?'

'It is a very strong term.'

'Yes – and Mr Vyse is not given to using strong terms. His normal attitude – a legal attitude – is to under, rather than over, state. Yet he says that Mademoiselle has a fanatical devotion to the home of her ancestors.'

'She did not convey that impression this morning,' I said. 'She spoke about it very sensibly, I thought. She's obviously fond of the place – just as anyone in her position would be – but certainly nothing more.'

'So, in fact, one of the two is lying,' said Poirot, thoughtfully.

'One would not suspect Vyse of lying.'

'Clearly a great asset if one has any lying to do,' remarked Poirot. 'Yes, he has quite the air of a George Washington, that one. Did you notice another thing, Hastings?'

'What was that?'

'*He was not in his office at half-past twelve on Saturday.*'

CHAPTER SEVEN

Tragedy

The first person we saw when we arrived at End House that evening was Nick. She was dancing about the hall wrapped in a marvellous kimono covered with dragons.

'Oh! it's only you!'

'Mademoiselle – I am desolated!'

'I know. It did sound rude. But you see, I'm waiting for my dress to arrive. They promised – the brutes – promised faithfully!'

'Ah! if it is a matter of *la toilette*! There is a dance tonight, is there not?'

'Yes. We are all going on to it after the fireworks. That is, I suppose we are.'

There was a sudden drop in her voice. But the next minute she was laughing.

'Never give in! That's my motto. Don't think of trouble and trouble won't come! I've got my nerve back tonight. I'm going to be gay and enjoy myself.'

There was a footfall on the stairs. Nick turned.

'Oh! here's Maggie. Maggie, here are the sleuths that are protecting me from the secret assassin. Take them into the drawing-room and let them tell you about it.'

In turn we shook hands with Maggie Buckley, and, as requested, she took us into the drawing-room. I formed an immediate favourable opinion of her.

It was, I think, her appearance of calm good sense that so attracted me. A quiet girl, pretty in the old-fashioned sense – certainly not smart. Her face was innocent of make-up and she wore a simple, rather shabby, black evening dress. She had frank blue eyes, and a pleasant slow voice.

'Nick has been telling me the most amazing things,' she said. 'Surely she must be exaggerating? Who ever would want to harm Nick? She can't have an enemy in the world.'

Incredulity showed strongly in her voice. She was looking at Poirot in a somewhat unflattering fashion. I realized that to a girl like Maggie Buckley, foreigners were always suspicious.

'Nevertheless, Miss Buckley, I assure you that it is the truth,' said Poirot quietly.

She made no reply, but her face remained unbelieving.

'Nick seems quite fey tonight,' she remarked. 'I don't know what's the matter with her. She seems in the wildest spirits.'

That word – fey! It sent a shiver through me. Also, something in the intonation of her voice had set me wondering.

'Are you Scotch, Miss Buckley?' I asked, abruptly.

'My mother was Scottish,' she explained.

She viewed me, I noticed, with more approval than she viewed Poirot. I felt that my statement of the case would carry more weight with her than Poirot's would.

'Your cousin is behaving with great bravery,' I said. 'She's determined to carry on as usual.'

'It's the only way, isn't it?' said Maggie. 'I mean – whatever one's inward feelings are – it is no good making a fuss about them. That's only uncomfortable for everyone else.' She paused and then added in a soft voice: 'I'm very fond of Nick. She's been good to me always.'

We could say nothing more for at that moment Frederica Rice drifted into the room. She was wearing a gown of Madonna blue and looked very fragile and ethereal. Lazarus soon followed her and then Nick danced in. She was wearing a black frock, and round her was wrapped a marvellous old Chinese shawl of vivid lacquer red.

'Hello, people,' she said. 'Cocktail?'

We all drank, and Lazarus raised his glass to her.

'That's a marvellous shawl, Nick,' he said. 'It's an old one, isn't it?'

'Yes – brought back by Great-Great-Great-Uncle Timothy from his travels.'

'It's a beauty – a real beauty. You wouldn't find another to match it if you tried.'

'It's warm,' said Nick. 'It'll be nice when we're watching the fireworks. And it's gay. I – I hate black.'

'Yes,' said Frederica. 'I don't believe I've ever seen you in a black dress before, Nick. Why did you get it?'

'Oh! I don't know.' The girl flung aside with a petulant gesture, but I had caught a curious curl of her lips as though of pain. 'Why does one do anything?'

We went in to dinner. A mysterious manservant had appeared – hired, I presume, for the occasion. The food was indifferent. The champagne, on the other hand, was good.

'George hasn't turned up,' said Nick. 'A nuisance his having to go back to Plymouth last night. He'll get over this evening sometime or other, I expect. In time for the dance anyway. I've got a man for Maggie. Presentable, if not passionately interesting.'

A faint roaring sound drifted in through the window.

'Oh! curse the speedboat,' said Lazarus. 'I get so tired of it.'

'That's not the speedboat,' said Nick. 'That's a seaplane.'

'I believe you're right.'

'Of course I'm right. The sound's quite different.'

'When are you going to get your Moth, Nick?'

'When I can raise the money,' laughed Nick.

'And then, I suppose you'll be off to Australia like that girl – what's her name?'

'I'd love to –'

'I admire her enormously,' said Mrs Rice, in her tired voice. 'What marvellous nerve! All by herself too.'

'I admire all these flying people,' said Lazarus. 'If Michael Seton had succeeded in his flight round the world he'd have been the hero of the day – and rightly so. A thousand pities he's come to grief. He's the kind of man England can't afford to lose.'

'He may still be all right,' said Nick.

'Hardly. It's a thousand to one against by now. Poor Mad Seton.'

'They always called him Mad Seton, didn't they?' asked Frederica.

Lazarus nodded.

'He comes of rather a mad family,' he said. 'His uncle, Sir Matthew Seton, who died about a week ago – he was as mad as a hatter.'

'He was the mad millionaire who ran bird sanctuaries, wasn't he?' asked Frederica.

'Yes. Used to buy up islands. He was a great woman-hater. Some girl chucked him once, I believe, and he took to Natural History by way of consoling himself.'

'Why do you say Michael Seton is dead?' persisted Nick. 'I don't see any reason for giving up hope – yet.'

'Of course, you knew him, didn't you?' said Lazarus. 'I forgot.'

'Freddie and I met him at Le Touquet last year,' said Nick. 'He was too marvellous, wasn't he, Freddie?'

'Don't ask me, darling. He was your conquest, not mine. He took you up once, didn't he?'

'Yes – at Scarborough. It was simply too wonderful.'

'Have you done any flying, Captain Hastings?' Maggie asked of me in polite conversational tones.

216

I had to confess that a trip to Paris and back was the extent of my acquaintance with air travel.

Suddenly, with an exclamation, Nick sprang up.

'There's the telephone. Don't wait for me. It's getting late. And I've asked lots of people.'

She left the room. I glanced at my watch. It was just nine o'clock. Dessert was brought, and port. Poirot and Lazarus were talking Art. Pictures, Lazarus was saying, were a great drug in the market just now. They went on to discuss new ideas in furniture and decoration.

I endeavoured to do my duty by talking to Maggie Buckley, but I had to admit that the girl was heavy in hand. She answered pleasantly, but without throwing the ball back. It was uphill work.

Frederica Rice sat dreamily silent, her elbows on the table and the smoke from her cigarette curling round her fair head. She looked like a meditative angel.

It was just twenty past nine when Nick put her head round the door.

'Come out of it, all of you! The animals are coming in two by two.'

We rose obediently. Nick was busy greeting arrivals. About a dozen people had been asked. Most of them were rather uninteresting. Nick, I noticed, made a good hostess. She sank her modernisms and made everyone welcome in an old-fashioned way. Among the guests I noticed Charles Vyse.

Presently we all moved out into the garden to a place overlooking the sea and the harbour. A few chairs had been placed there for the elderly people, but most of us stood. The first rocket flamed to Heaven.

At that moment I heard a loud familiar voice, and turned my head to see Nick greeting Mr Croft.

'It's too bad,' she was saying, 'that Mrs Croft can't be here too. We ought to have carried her on a stretcher or something.'

'It's bad luck on poor mother altogether. But she never complains – that woman's got the sweetest nature – Ha! that's a good one.' This as a shower of gold rain showed up in the sky.

The night was a dark one – there was no moon– the new moon being due in three day's time. It was also, like most summer evenings, cold. Maggie Buckley, who was next to me, shivered.

'I'll just run in and get a coat,' she murmured.

'Let me.'

'No, you wouldn't know where to find it.'

She turned towards the house. At that moment Frederica Rice's voice called:

'Oh, Maggie, get mine too. It's in my room.'

'She didn't hear,' said Nick. 'I'll get it, Freddie. I want my fur one – this shawl isn't nearly hot enough. It's this wind.'

There was, indeed, a sharp breeze blowing off the sea.

Some set pieces started down on the quay. I fell into conversation with an elderly lady standing next to me who put me through a rigorous catechism as to life, career, tastes and probable length of stay.

Bang! A shower of green stars filled the sky. They changed to blue, then red, then silver.

Another and yet another.

'"Oh!" and then "Ah!" that is what one says,' observed Poirot suddenly close to my ear. 'At the end it becomes monotonous, do you not find? Brrr! The grass, it is damp to the feet! I shall suffer for this – a chill. And no possibility of obtaining a proper *tisane*!'

'A chill? On a lovely night like this?'

'A lovely night! A lovely night! You say that, because the rain it does not pour down in sheets! Always when the rain does not fall, it is a lovely night. But I tell you, my friend, if there were a little thermometer to consult you would see.'

'Well,' I admitted, 'I wouldn't mind putting on a coat myself.'

'You are very sensible. You have come from a hot climate.'

'I'll bring yours.'

Poirot lifted first one, then the other foot from the ground with a cat-like motion.

'It is the dampness of the feet I fear. Would it, think you, be possible to lay hands on a pair of goloshes?'

I repressed a smile.

'Not a hope,' I said. 'You understand, Poirot, that it is no longer done.'

'Then I shall sit in the house,' he declared. 'Just for the Guy Fawkes show, shall I want only *enrhumer* myself? And catch, perhaps, a *fluxion de poitrine?*'

Poirot still murmuring indignantly, we bent our footsteps towards the house. Loud clapping drifted up to us from the quay below where another set piece was being shown – a ship, I believe, with *Welcome to Our Visitors* displayed across it.

'We are all children at heart,' said Poirot, thoughtfully. '*Les Feus D'Artifices*, the party, the games with balls – yes, and even the conjurer, the man who deceives the eye, however carefully it watches

218

– mais qu'est-ce que vous avez?'

I had caught him by the arm, and was clutching him with one hand, while with the other I pointed.

We were within a hundred yards of the house, and just in front of us, between us and the open French window, *there lay a huddled figure wrapped in a scarlet Chinese shawl* . . .

'*Mon Dieu!*' whispered Poirot. '*Mon Dieu* . . .'

CHAPTER EIGHT

The Fatal Shawl

I suppose it was not more than forty seconds that we stood there, frozen with horror, unable to move, but it seemed like an hour. Then Poirot moved forward, shaking off my hand. He moved stiffly like an automaton.

'It has happened,' he murmured, and I can hardly describe the anguished bitterness of his voice. 'In spite of everything – in spite of my precautions, it has happened. Ah! miserable criminal that I am, why did I not guard her better. I should have foreseen. Not for one instant should I have left her side.'

'You mustn't blame yourself,' I said.

My tongue stuck to the roof of my mouth, and I could hardly articulate.

Poirot only responded with a sorrowful shake of his head. He knelt down by the body.

And at that moment we received a second shock.

For Nick's voice rang out, clear and gay, and a moment later Nick appeared in the square of the window silhouetted against the lighted room behind.

'Sorry I've been so long, Maggie,' she said. 'But –'

Then she broke off – staring at the scene before her.

With a sharp exclamation, Poirot turned over the body on the lawn and I pressed forward to see.

I looked down into the dead face of Maggie Buckley.

In another minute Nick was beside us. She gave a sharp cry.

'Maggie – Oh! Maggie – it – it can't –'

Poirot was still examining the girl's body. At last very slowly he rose to his feet.

'Is she – is –' Nick's voice broke off.

'Yes, Mademoiselle. She is dead.'

'But why? But why? Who could have wanted to kill *her*?'

Poirot's reply came quickly and firmly.

'It was not her they meant to kill, Mademoiselle! It was *you*! They were misled by the shawl.'

A great cry broke from Nick.

'Why couldn't it have been me?' she wailed. 'Oh! why couldn't it have been me? I'd so much rather. I don't want to live – *now*. I'd be glad – willing – happy – to die.'

She flung up her arms wildly and then staggered slightly. I passed an arm round her quickly to support her.

'Take her into the house, Hastings,' said Poirot. 'Then ring up the police.'

'The police?'

'*Mais oui!* Tell them someone has been shot. And afterwards stay with Mademoiselle Nick. *On no account leave her.*'

I nodded comprehension of these instructions, and supporting the half-fainting girl, made my way through the drawing-room window. I laid the girl on the sofa there, with a cushion under her head, and then hurried out into the hall in search of the telephone.

I gave a slight start on almost running into Ellen. She was standing there with a most peculiar expression on her meek, respectable face. Her eyes were glittering and she was passing her tongue repeatedly over her dry lips. Her hands were trembling, as though with excitement. As soon as she saw me, she spoke.

'Has – has anything happened, sir?'

'Yes,' I said curtly. 'Where's the telephone?'

'Nothing – nothing wrong, sir?'

'There's been an accident,' I said evasively. 'Somebody hurt. I must telephone.'

'Who has been hurt, sir?'

There was a positive eagerness in her face.

'Miss Buckley. Miss Maggie Buckley.'

'Miss Maggie? Miss *Maggie*? Are you sure, sir – I mean are you sure that – that it's Miss Maggie?'

'I'm quite sure,' I said. 'Why?'

'Oh! – nothing. I – I thought it might be one of the other ladies. I thought perhaps it might be – Mrs Rice.'

'Look here,' I said. 'Where's the telephone?'

'It's in the little room here, sir.' She opened the door for me and indicated the instrument.

'Thanks,' I said. And, as she seemed disposed to linger, I added: 'That's all I want, thank you.'

'If you want Dr Graham –'

'No, no,' I said. 'That's all. Go, please.'

She withdrew reluctantly, as slowly as she dared. In all probability she would listen outside the door, but I could not help that. After all, she would soon know all there was to be known.

I got the police station and made my report. Then, on my own

221

initiative, I rang up the Dr Graham Ellen had mentioned. I found his number in the book. Nick, at any rate, should have medical attention, I felt – even though a doctor could do nothing for that poor girl lying out there. He promised to come at once and I hung up the receiver and came out into the hall again.

If Ellen had been listening outside the door she had managed to disappear very swiftly. There was no one in sight when I came out. I went back into the drawing-room. Nick was trying to sit up.

'Do you think – could you get me – some brandy?'

'Of course.'

I hurried into the dining-room, found what I wanted and came back. A few sips of the spirit revived the girl. The colour began to come back into her cheeks. I rearranged the cushion for her head.

'It's all – so awful.' She shivered. 'Everything – everywhere.'

'I know, my dear, I know.'

'No, you don't! You can't. And it's all such a *waste*. If it were only me. It would be all over . . .'

'You mustn't,' I said, 'be morbid.'

She only shook her head, reiterating: 'You don't know! You don't *know*!'

Then, suddenly, she began to cry. A quiet, hopeless sobbing like a child. That, I thought, was probably the best thing for her, so I made no effort to stem her tears.

When their first violence had died down a little, I stole across to the window and looked out. I had heard an outcry of voices a few minutes before. They were all there by now, a semi-circle round the scene of the tragedy, with Poirot like a fantastical sentinel, keeping them back.

As I watched, two uniformed figures came striding across the grass. The police had arrived.

I went quietly back to my place by the sofa. Nick lifted her tear-stained face.

'Oughtn't I to be doing something?'

'No, my dear. Poirot will see to it. Leave it to him.' Nick was silent for a minute or two, then she said:

'Poor Maggie. Poor dear old Maggie. Such a good sort who never harmed a soul in her life. That this should happen to *her*. I feel as though I'd killed her – bringing her down in the way that I did.'

I shook my head sadly. How little one can foresee the future. When Poirot insisted on Nick's inviting a friend, how little did he think that he was signing an unknown girl's death warrant.

222

We sat in silence. I longed to know what was going on outside, but I loyally fulfilled Poirot's instructions and stuck to my post.

It seemed hours later when the door opened and Poirot and a police inspector entered the room. With them came a man who was evidently Dr Graham. He came over at once to Nick.

'And how are you feeling, Miss Buckley? This must have been a terrible shock.' His fingers were on her pulse.

'Not too bad.'

He turned to me.

'Has she had anything?'

'Some brandy,' I said.

'I'm all right,' said Nick, bravely.

'Able to answer a few questions, eh?'

'Of course.'

The police inspector moved forward with a preliminary cough. Nick greeted him with the ghost of a smile.

'Not impeding the traffic this time,' she said.

I gathered they were not strangers to each other.

'This is a terrible business, Miss Buckley,' said the inspector. 'I'm very sorry about it. Now Mr Poirot here, whose name I'm very familiar with (and proud we are to have him with us, I'm sure), tells me that to the best of his belief you were shot at in the grounds of the Majestic Hotel the other morning?'

Nick nodded.

'I thought it was just a wasp,' she explained. 'But it wasn't.'

'And you'd had some rather peculiar accidents before that?'

'Yes – at least it was odd their happening so close together.'

She gave a brief account of the various circumstances.

'Just so. Now how came it that your cousin was wearing your shawl tonight?'

'We came in to fetch her coat – it was rather cold watching the fireworks. I flung off the shawl on the sofa here. Then I went upstairs and put on the coat I'm wearing now – a light nutria one. I also got a wrap for my friend Mrs Rice out of her room. There it is on the floor by the window. Then Maggie called out that she couldn't find her coat. I said it must be downstairs. She went down and called up she still couldn't find it. I said it must have been left in the car – it was a tweed coat she was looking for – she hasn't got an evening furry one – and I said I'd bring her down something of mine. But she said it didn't matter – she'd take my shawl if I didn't want it. And I said of course but would that be enough? And she said Oh, yes, because she

223

really didn't feel it particularly cold after Yorkshire. She just wanted *something*. And I said all right, I'd be out in a minute. And when I did – did come out –'

She stopped, her voice breaking . . .

'Now, don't distress yourself, Miss Buckley. Just tell me this. Did you hear a shot – or two shots?'

Nick shook her head.

'No – only just the fireworks popping and the squibs going off.'

'That's just it,' said the inspector. 'You'd never notice a shot with all that going on. It's no good asking you, I suppose, if you've any clue to who it is making these attacks upon you?'

'I haven't the least idea,' said Nick. 'I can't imagine.'

'And you wouldn't be likely to,' said the inspector. 'Some homicidal maniac – that's what it looks like to me. Nasty business. Well, I won't need to ask you any more questions to-night, miss. I'm more sorry about this than I can say.'

Dr Graham stepped forward.

'I'm going to suggest, Miss Buckley, that you don't stay here. I've been talking it over with M. Poirot. I know of an excellent nursing home. You've had a shock, you know. What you need is complete rest –'

Nick was not looking at him. Her eyes had gone to Poirot.

'Is it – because of the shock?' she asked.

He came forward.

'I want you to feel safe, *mon enfant*. And *I* want to feel, too, that you *are* safe. There will be a nurse there – a nice practical unimaginative nurse. She will be near you all night. When you wake up and cry out – she will be there, close at hand. You understand?'

'Yes,' said Nick, 'I understand. But *you* don't. I'm not afraid any longer. I don't care one way or another. If anyone wants to murder me, they can.'

'Hush, hush,' I said. 'You're over-strung.'

'You don't know. None of you know!'

'I really think M. Poirot's plan is a good one,' the doctor broke in soothingly. 'I will take you in my car. And we will give you a little something to ensure a good night's rest. Now what do you say?'

'I don't mind,' said Nick. 'Anything you like. It doesn't matter.'

Poirot laid his hand on hers.

'I know, Mademoiselle. I know what you must feel. I stand before you ashamed and stricken to the heart. I, who promised protection, have not been able to protect. I have failed. I am a miserable. But believe me, Mademoiselle, my heart is in agony because of that failure. If you know what I am suffering you would forgive, I am sure.'

'That's all right,' said Nick, still in the same dull voice. 'You mustn't blame yourself. I'm sure you did the best you could. Nobody could have helped it – or done more, I'm sure. Please don't be unhappy.'

'You are very generous, Mademoiselle.'

'No, I –'

There was an interruption. The door flew open and George Challenger rushed into the room.

'What's all this?' he cried. 'I've just arrived. To find a policeman at the gate and a rumour that somebody's dead. What is it all about? For God's sake, tell me. Is it – is it – Nick?'

The anguish in his tone was dreadful to hear. I suddenly realized that Poirot and the doctor between them completely blotted out Nick from his sight.

Before anyone had time to answer, he repeated his question.

'Tell me – it can't be true – Nick isn't *dead*?'

'No, *mon ami*,' said Poirot, gently. 'She is alive.'

And he drew back so that Challenger could see the little figure on the sofa.

For a moment or two Challenger stared at her incredulously. Then, staggering a little, like a drunken man, he muttered:

'Nick – Nick.'

And suddenly dropping on his knees beside the sofa and hiding his head in his hands, he cried in a muffled voice:

'Nick – my darling – I thought that you were dead.'

Nick tried to sit up.

'It's all right, George. Don't be an idiot. I'm quite safe.'

He raised his head and looked round wildly.

'But *somebody's* dead? The policeman said so.'

'Yes,' said Nick. 'Maggie. Poor old Maggie. Oh! –'

A spasm twisted her face. The doctor and Poirot came forward. Graham helped her to her feet. He and Poirot, one on each side, helped her from the room.

'The sooner you get to your bed the better,' remarked the doctor. 'I'll take you along at once in my car. I've asked Mrs Rice to pack a few things ready for you to take.'

They disappeared through the door. Challenger caught my arm.

'I don't understand. Where are they taking her?'

225

I explained.

'Oh! I see. Now, then, Hastings, for God's sake give me the hang of this thing. What a ghastly tragedy! That poor girl.'

'Come and have a drink,' I said. 'You're all to pieces.'

'I don't mind if I do.'

We adjourned to the dining-room.

'You see,' he explained, as he put away a stiff whisky and soda, 'I thought it was Nick.'

There was very little doubt as to the feelings of Commander George Challenger. A more transparent lover never lived.

CHAPTER NINE

A. to J.

I doubt if I shall ever forget the night that followed. Poirot was a prey to such an agony of self-reproach that I was really alarmed. Ceaselessly he strode up and down the room heaping anathemas on his own head and deaf to my well-meant remonstrances.

'What it is to have too good an opinion of oneself. I am punished – yes, I am punished. I, Hercule Poirot. I was too sure of myself.'

'No, no,' I interpolated.

'But who would imagine – who could imagine – such unparalleled audacity? I had taken, as I thought, all possible precautions. I had warned the murderer –'

'Warned the murderer?'

'*Mais oui*. I had drawn attention to myself. I had let him see that I suspected – someone. I had made it, or so I thought, too dangerous for him to dare to repeat his attempts at murder. I had drawn a cordon round Mademoiselle. And he slips through it! Boldly – under our very eyes almost, he slips through it! In spite of us all – of everyone being on the alert, he achieves his object.'

'Only he doesn't,' I reminded him.

'That is the chance only! From my point of view, it is the same. A human life has been taken, Hastings – whose life is non-essential?'

'Of course,' I said. 'I didn't mean that.'

'But on the other hand, what you say is true. And that makes it worse – ten times worse. For the murderer is still as far as ever from achieving his object. Do you understand, my friend? The position is changed – for the worse. It may mean that not one life – but two – will be sacrificed.'

'Not while you're about,' I said stoutly.

He stopped and wrung my hand.

'*Merci, mon ami! Merci!* You still have confidence in the old one – you still have the faith. You put new courage into me. Hercule Poirot will not fail again. No second life shall be taken. I will rectify my error – for, see you, there must have been an error! Somewhere there has been a lack of order and method in my usually so well arranged ideas. I will start again. Yes, I will start at the beginning. And this time – I will not fail.'

'You really think then,' I said, 'that Nick Buckley's life is still in

227

danger?'

'My friend, for what other reason did I send her to this nursing home?'

'Then it wasn't the shock –'

'The shock! Pah! One can recover from shock as well in one's own home as in a nursing home – better, for that matter. It is not amusing there, the floors of green linoleum, the conversation of the nurses – the meals on trays, the ceaseless washing. No, no, it is for safety and safety only. I take the doctor into my confidence. He agrees. He will make all arrangements. No one, *mon ami, not even her dearest friend*, will be admitted to see Miss Buckley. You and I are the only ones permitted. *Pour les autres – eh bien!* "Doctor's orders," they will be told. A phrase very convenient and one not to be gainsayed.'

'Yes,' I said. 'Only –'

'Only what, Hastings?'

'That can't go on for ever.'

'A very true observation. But it gives us a little breathing space. And you realize, do you not, that the character of our operations has changed.'

'In what way?'

'Our original task was to ensure the safety of Mademoiselle. Our task now is a much simpler one – a task with which we are well acquainted. It is neither more nor less than the hunting down of a murderer.'

'You call that simpler?'

'Certainly it is simpler. The murderer has, as I said the other day, *signed his name to the crime*. He has come out into the open.'

'You don't think –' I hesitated, then went on. 'You don't think that the police are right? That this is the work of a madman, some wandering lunatic with homicidal mania?'

'I am more than ever convinced that such is not the case.'

'You really think that –'

I stopped. Poirot took up my sentence, speaking very gravely.

'That the murderer is someone in Mademoiselle's own circle? Yes, *mon ami*, I do.'

'But surely last night must almost rule out that possibility. We were all together and –'

He interrupted.

'Could you swear, Hastings, that any particular person had never left our little company there on the edge of the cliff? Is there any one person there whom you could swear you had seen *all* the time?'

228

'No,' I said slowly, struck by his words. 'I don't think I could. It was dark. We all moved about, more or less. On different occasions I noticed Mrs Rice, Lazarus, you, Croft, Vyse – but all the time – no.'

Poirot nodded his head.

'Exactly. It would be a matter of a very few minutes. The two girls go to the house. The murderer slips away unnoticed, hides behind that sycamore tree in the middle of the lawn. Nick Buckley, or so he thinks, comes out of the window, passes within a foot of him, he fires three shots in rapid succession –'

'Three?' I interjected.

'Yes. He was taking no chances this time. We found three bullets in the body.'

'That was risky, wasn't it?'

'Less risky in all probability than one shot would have been. A Mauser pistol does not make a great deal of noise. It would resemble more or less the popping of the fireworks and blend in very well with the noise of them.'

'Did you find the pistol?' I asked.

'No. And there, Hastings, lies to my mind the indisputable proof that no stranger is responsible for this. We agree, do we not, that Miss Buckley's own pistol was taken in the first place for one reason only – to give her death the appearance of suicide.'

'Yes.'

'That is the only possible reason, is it not? But now, you observe, there is no pretence of suicide. *The murderer knows that we should not any longer be deceived by it.* He knows, in fact, what we know!'

I reflected, admitting to myself the logic of Poirot's deduction.

'What did he do with the pistol do you think?'

Poirot shrugged his shoulders.

'For that, it is difficult to say. But the sea was exceedingly handy. A good toss of the arm, and the pistol sinks, never to be recovered. We cannot, of course, be absolutely sure – but that is what *I* should have done.'

His matter-of-fact tone made me shiver a little.

'Do you think – do you think he realized that he'd killed the wrong person?'

'I am quite sure he did not,' said Poirot, grimly. 'Yes, that must have been an unpleasant little surprise for him when he learnt the truth. To keep his face and betray nothing – it cannot have been easy.'

At that moment I bethought me of the strange attitude of the maid,

229

Ellen. I gave Poirot an account of her peculiar demeanour. He seemed very interested.

'She betrayed surprise, did she, that it was Maggie who was dead?'

'Great surprise.'

'That is curious. And yet, the fact of a tragedy was clearly *not* a surprise to her. Yes, there is something there that must be looked into. Who is she, this Ellen? So quiet, so respectable in the English manner? Could it be she who –?' He broke off.

'If you're going to include the accidents,' I said, 'surely it would take a man to have rolled that heavy boulder down the cliff.'

'Not necessarily. It is very largely a question of leverage. Oh, yes, it could be done.'

He continued his slow pacing up and down the room.

'Anyone who was at End House last night comes under suspicion. But those guests – no, I do not think it was one of them. For the most part, I should say, they were mere acquaintances. There was no intimacy between them and the young mistress of the house.'

'Charles Vyse was there,' I remarked.

'Yes, we must not forget him. He is, logically, our strongest suspect.' He made a gesture of despair and threw himself into a chair opposite mine. '*Voilà* – it is always that we come back to! Motive! We must find the motive if we are to understand this crime. And it is there, Hastings, that I am continually baffled. Who can possibly have a motive for doing away with Mademoiselle Nick? I have let myself go to the most absurd suppositions. I, Hercule Poirot, have descended to the most ignominious flights of fancy. I have adopted the mentality of the cheap thriller. The grandfather – the 'Old Nick' – he who is supposed to have gambled his money away. Did he really do so, I have asked myself? Did he, on the contrary, hide it away? Is it hidden somewhere in End House? Buried somewhere in the grounds? With that end in view (I am ashamed to say it) I inquired of Mademoiselle Nick whether there had ever been any offers to buy the house.'

'Do you know, Poirot,' I said, 'I call that rather a bright idea. There may be something in it.'

Poirot groaned.

'You would say that! It would appeal, I knew, to your romantic but slightly mediocre mind. Buried treasure – yes, you would enjoy that idea.'

'Well – I don't see why not –'

'Because, my friend, the more prosaic explanation is nearly always

230

more probable. Then Mademoiselle's father – I have played with even more degrading ideas concerning him. He was a traveller. Supposing, I say to myself, that he has stolen a jewel – the eye of a God. Jealous priests are on his tracks. Yes, I, Hercule Poirot, have descended to depths such as these.

'I have had other ideas concerning this father,' he went on. 'Ideas at once more dignified and more probable. Did he, in the course of his wanderings, contract a second marriage? Is there a nearer heir than M. Charles Vyse? But again, that leads nowhere, for we are up against the same difficulty – that there is really nothing of value to inherit.

'I have neglected no possibility. Even that chance reference of Mademoiselle Nick's to the offer made her by M. Lazarus. You remember? The offer to purchase her grandfather's portrait. I telegraphed on Saturday for an expert to come down and examine that picture. He was the man about whom I wrote to Mademoiselle this morning. Supposing, for instance, it were worth several thousand pounds?'

'You surely don't think a rich man like young Lazarus –?'

'Is he rich? Appearances are not everything. Even an old-established firm with palatial showrooms and every appearance of prosperity may rest on a rotten basis. And what does one do then? Does one run about crying out that times are hard? No, one buys a new and luxurious car. One spends a little more money than usual. One lives a little more ostentatiously. For credit, see you, is everything! But sometimes a monumental business has crashed – for no more than a few thousand pounds – *of ready money*.

'Oh! I know,' he continued, forestalling my protests. 'It is far-fetched – but it is not so bad as revengeful priests or buried treasure. It bears, at any rate, some relationship to things as they happen. And we can neglect nothing – nothing that might bring us nearer the truth.'

With careful fingers he straightened the objects on the table in front of him. When he spoke, his voice was grave and, for the first time, calm.

'*Motive!*' he said. 'Let us come back to that, and regard this problem calmly and methodically. To begin with, how many kinds of motive are there for murder? What are the motives which lead one human being to take another human being's life?

'We exclude for the moment homicidal mania. Because I am absolutely convinced that the solution of our problem does not lie there. We also exclude killing done on the spur of the moment under the impulse of an ungovernable temper. This is cold-blooded deliberate murder. What are the motives that actuate such a murder as that?'

'There is, first, *Gain*. Who stood to gain by Mademoiselle Buckley's death? Directly or indirectly. Well, we can put down Charles Vyse. He inherits a property that, from the financial point of view, is probably not worth inheriting. He might, perhaps, pay off the mortgage, build small villas on the land and eventually make a small profit. It is possible. The place might be worth something to him if he had any deeply cherished love of it – if, it were, for instance, a family place. That is, undoubtedly, an instinct very deeply implanted in some human beings, and it has, in cases I have known, actually led to crime. But I cannot see any such motive in M. Vyse's case.

'The only other person who would benefit at all by Mademoiselle Buckley's death is her friend, Madame Rice. But the amount would clearly be a very small one. Nobody else, as far as I can see, *gains* by Mademoiselle Buckley's death.

'What is another motive? Hate – or love that has turned to hate. The *crime passionnel*. Well, there again we have the word of the observant Madame Croft that both Charles Vyse and Commander Challenger are in love with the young lady.'

'I think we can say that we have observed the latter phenomenon for ourselves,' I remarked, with a smile.

'Yes – he tends to wear his heart on his sleeve, the honest sailor. For the other, we rely on the word of Madame Croft. Now, if Charles Vyse felt that he were supplanted, would he be so powerfully affected that he would kill his cousin rather than let her become the wife of another man?'

'It sounds very melodramatic,' I said, doubtfully.

'It sounds, you would say, un-English. I agree. But even the English have emotions. And a type such as Charles Vyse, is the most likely to have them. He is a repressed young man. One who does not show his feelings easily. Such often have the most violent feelings. I would never suspect the Commander Challenger of murder for emotional reasons. No, no, he is not the type. But with Charles Vyse – yes, it is possible. But it does not entirely satisfy me.

'Another motive for crime – Jealousy. I separate it from the last, because jealousy may not, necessarily, be a sexual emotion. There is envy – envy of possession – of supremacy. Such a jealousy as drove the Iago of your great Shakespeare to one of the cleverest crimes (speaking from the professional point of view) that has ever been committed.'

'Why was it so clever?' I asked, momentarily diverted.

'*Parbleu* – because he got others to execute it. Imagine a criminal nowadays on whom one was unable to put the handcuffs because he had never done anything himself. But this is not the subject we were discussing. Can jealousy, of any kind, be responsible for this crime? Who has reason to envy Mademoiselle? Another woman? There is only Madame Rice, and as far as we can see, there was no rivalry between the two women. But again, that is only "as far as we can see". There may be something there.

'Lastly – Fear. Does Mademoiselle Nick, by any chance, hold somebody's secret in her power? Does she know something which, if it were known, might ruin another life? If so, I think we can say very definitely, *that she herself is unaware of it*. But that might be, you know. That might be. And if so, it makes it very difficult. Because, whilst she holds the clue in her hands, she holds it unconsciously and will be quite unable to tell us what it is.'

'You really think that is possible?'

'It is a hypothesis. I am driven to it by the difficulty of finding a reasonable theory elsewhere. When you have eliminated other possibilities you turn to the one that is left and say – since the other is not – *this must be so* . . .'

He was silent a long time.

At last, rousing himself from his absorption, he drew a sheet of paper towards him and began to write.

'What are you writing?' I asked, curiously.

'*Mon ami*, I am composing a list. It is a list of people surrounding Mademoiselle Buckley. Within that list, if my theory is correct, there must be the name of the murderer.'

He continued to write for perhaps twenty minutes – then shoved the sheets of paper across to me.

'*Voilà, mon ami*. See what you make of it.'

The following is a reproduction of the paper:

A. Ellen.
B. Her gardener husband.
C. Their child.
D. Mr Croft.
E. Mrs Croft.

F. Mrs Rice.
G. Mr Lazarus.
H. Commander Challenger.
I. Mr Charles Vyse.
J.

Remarks:
A. *Ellen.* – Suspicious circumstances. Her attitude and words on hearing of the crime. Best opportunity of anyone to have staged accidents and to have known of pistol, *but* unlikely to have tampered with car, and general mentality of crime seems above her level.
Motive. – None – unless hate arising out of some incident unknown.
Note. – Further inquiries as to her antecedents and general relations with NB.

B. *Her Husband.* – Same as above. More likely to have tampered with car.
Note. Should be interviewed.

C. *Child.* – Can be ruled out.
Note. – Should be interviewed. Might give valuable information.

D. *Mr Croft.* – Only suspicious circumstance the fact that we met him mounting the stair to bedroom floor. Had ready explanation which may be true. But it may not!
Nothing known of antecedents.
Motive. – None.

E. *Mrs Croft.* – Suspicious circumstances. – None.
Motive. – None.

F. *Mrs Rice.* – Suspicious circumstances. Full opportunity. Asked N. B. to fetch wrap. Has deliberately tried to create impression that N. B. is a liar and her account of 'accidents' not to be relied on. Was not at Tavistock when accidents occurred. Where was she?
Motive. – *Gain?* Very slight. *Jealousy?* Possible, but nothing known. *Fear?* Also possible, but nothing known.

234

Note. – Converse with N. B. on subject. See if any light is thrown upon matter. Possibly something to do with F. R.'s marriage.

G. *Mr Lazarus.* – Suspicious circumstances. General opportunity. Offer to buy picture. Said brakes of car were quite all right (according to F. R.). May have been in neighbourhood prior to Friday.
Motive. – None – unless profit on picture. *Fear?* – unlikely.
Note. – Find out where J. L. was before arriving at St Loo. Find out financial position of Aaron Lazarus & Son.

H. *Commander Challenger.* – Suspicious circumstances. None. Was in neighbourhood all last week, so opportunity for 'accidents' good. Arrived half an hour after murder.
Motive. – None.

I. *Mr Vyse.* –Suspicious circumstances. Was absent from office at time when shot was fired in garden of hotel. Opportunity good. Statement about selling of End House open to doubt. Of a repressed temperament. Would probably know about pistol.
Motive. – *Gain?* (slight) *Love or Hate?* Possible with one of his temperament. *Fear?* Unlikely.
Note. – Find out who held mortgage. Find out position of Vyse's firm.

J. ? – There *could* be a J., *e.g.* an outsider. *But* with a link in the form of one of the foregoing. If so, probably connected with A. D. and E. or F. The existence of J. would explain (1) Ellen's lack of surprise at crime and her pleasurable satisfaction. (But that might be due to natural pleasurable excitement of her class over deaths.) (2) The reason for Croft and his wife coming to live in lodge. (3) Might supply motive for F. R.'s *fear* of secret being revealed or for *jealousy*.

Poirot watched me as I read.

'It is very English, is it not?' he remarked, with pride. 'I am more English when I write than when I speak.'

'It's an excellent piece of work,' I said, warmly. 'It sets all the possibilities out most clearly.'

'Yes,' he said, thoughtfully, as he took it back from me. 'And one name leaps to the eye, my friend. *Charles Vyse.* He has the best opportunities. We have given him the choice of two motives. *Ma foi* – if that was a list of racehorses, he would start favourite, *n'est-ce pas?*'

'He is certainly the most likely suspect.'

'You have a tendency, Hastings, to prefer the least likely. That, no doubt, is from reading too many detective stories. In real life, nine times out of ten, it is the most likely and the most obvious person who commits the crime.'

'But you don't really think that is so this time?'

'There is only one thing that is against it. The boldness of the crime! That has stood out from the first. Because of that, as I say, the motive *cannot be obvious*.'

'Yes, that is what you said at first.'

'And that is what I say again.'

With a sudden brusque gesture he crumpled the sheets of paper and threw them on the floor.

'No,' he said, as I uttered an exclamation of protest. 'That list has been in vain. Still, it has cleared my mind. *Order and method!* That is the first stage. To arrange the facts with neatness and precision. The next stage –'

'Yes.'

'The next stage is that of the psychology. The correct employment of the little grey cells! I advise you, Hastings, to go to bed.'

'No,' I said. 'Not unless you do. I'm not going to leave you.'

'Most faithful of dogs! But see you, Hastings, you cannot assist me to think. That is all I am going to do – think.'

I still shook my head.

'You might want to discuss some point with me.'

'Well – well – you are a loyal friend. Take at least, I beg of you, the easy-chair.'

That proposal I did accept. Presently the room began to swim and dip. The last thing I remember was seeing Poirot carefully retrieving the crumpled sheets of paper from the floor and putting them away tidily in the wastepaper basket.

Then I must have fallen asleep.

CHAPTER TEN

Nick's Secret

It was daylight when I awoke.

Poirot was still sitting where he had been the night before. His attitude was the same, but in his face was a difference. His eyes were shining with that queer cat-like green light that I knew so well.

I struggled to an upright position, feeling very stiff and uncomfortable. Sleeping in a chair is a proceeding not to be recommended at my time of life. Yet one thing at least resulted from it – I awoke not in that pleasant state of lazy somnolence but with a mind and brain as active as when I fell asleep.

'Poirot,' I cried. 'You have thought of something.'

He nodded. He leaned forward, tapping the table in front of him.

'Tell me, Hastings, the answer to these three questions. *Why has Mademoiselle Nick been sleeping badly lately? Why did she buy a black evening dress – she never wears black? Why did she say last night, "I have nothing to live for – now"?*'

I stared. The questions seemed beside the point.

'Answer those questions, Hastings, answer them.'

'Well – as to the first – she said she had been worried lately.'

'Precisely. What has she been worried about?'

'And the black dress – well, everybody wants a change sometimes.'

'For a married man, you have very little appreciation of feminine psychology. If a woman thinks she does not look well in a colour, she refuses to wear it.'

'And the last – well, it was a natural thing to say after that awful shock.'

'No, *mon ami*, it was *not* a natural thing to say. To be horror-struck by her cousin's death, to reproach herself for it – yes, all that is natural enough. But the other, no. She spoke of life with weariness – as of a thing no longer dear to her. Never before had she displayed that attitude. She had been defiant – yes – she had snapped the fingers, yes – and then, when that broke down, she was afraid. Afraid, mark you, because life was sweet and she did not wish to die. But weary of life – no! That never! Even before dinner that was not so. We have there, Hastings, a *psychological change*. And that is interesting. What was it caused her point of view to change?'

'The shock of her cousin's death.'

'I wonder. It was the shock that loosed her tongue. But suppose the change was before that. Is there anything else could account for it?'

'I don't know of anything.'

'Think, Hastings. Use your little grey cells.'

'Really –'

'What was the last moment we had the opportunity of observing her?'

'Well, actually, I suppose, at dinner.'

'Exactly. After that, we only saw her receiving guests, making them welcome – purely a formal attitude. What happened at the end of dinner, Hastings?'

'She went to telephone,' I said, slowly.

'*A la bonne heure.* You have got there at last. She went to telephone. And she was absent a long time. Twenty minutes at least. That is a long time for a telephone call. Who spoke to her over the telephone? What did they say? Did she really telephone? We have to find out, Hastings, what happened in that twenty minutes. For there, or so I fully believe, we shall find the clue we seek.'

'You really think so?'

'*Mais oui, mais oui!* All along, Hastings, I have told you that Mademoiselle has been keeping something back. She doesn't think it has any connection with the murder – but I, Hercule Poirot, know better! It *must* have a connection. For, all along, I have been conscious that there is a factor lacking. If there were not a factor lacking – why then, the whole thing would be plain to me! And as it is not plain to me – *eh bien* – then the missing factor is the keystone of the mystery! I know I am right, Hastings.

'I must know the answer to those three questions. And, then – and then – I shall begin *to see* . . .'

'Well,' I said, stretching my stiffened limbs, 'I think a bath and a shave are indicated.'

By the time I had had a bath and changed into day clothing I felt better. The stiffness and weariness of a night passed in uncomfortable conditions passed off. I arrived at the breakfast table feeling that one drink of hot coffee would restore me to my normal self.

I glanced at the paper, but there was little news in it beyond the fact that Michael Seton's death was now definitely confirmed. The intrepid airman had perished. I wondered whether, tomorrow, new headlines would have sprung into being: 'GIRL MURDERED DURING

238

FIREWORK PARTY. MYSTERIOUS TRAGEDY.' Something like that.

I had just finished breakfast when Frederica Rice came up to my table. She was wearing a plain little frock of black marocain with a little soft pleated white collar. Her fairness was more evident than ever.

'I want to see M. Poirot, Captain Hastings. Is he up yet, do you know?'

'I will take you up with me now,' I said. 'We shall find him in the sitting-room.'

'Thank you.'

'I hope,' I said, as we left the dining-room together, 'that you didn't sleep too badly?'

'It was a shock,' she said, in a meditative voice. 'But, of course, I didn't know the poor girl. It's not as though it had been Nick.'

'I suppose you'd never met this girl before?'

'Once – at Scarborough. She came over to lunch with Nick.'

'It will be a terrible blow to her father and mother,' I said.

'Dreadful.'

But she said it very impersonally. She was, I fancied, an egoist. Nothing was very real to her that did not concern herself.

Poirot had finished his breakfast and was sitting reading the morning paper. He rose and greeted Frederica with all his customary Gallic politeness.

'Madame,' he said. '*Enchanté!*'

He drew forward a chair.

She thanked him with a very faint smile and sat down. Her two hands rested on the arms of the chair. She sat there very upright, looking straight in front of her. She did not rush into speech. There was something a little frightening about her stillness and aloofness.

'M. Poirot,' she said at last. 'I suppose there is no doubt that this – sad business last night was all part and parcel of the same thing? I mean – that the intended victim was really Nick?'

'I should say, Madame, that there was no doubt at all.'

Frederica frowned a little.

'Nick bears a charmed life,' she said.

There was some curious undercurrent in her voice that I could not understand.

'Luck, they say, goes in cycles,' remarked Poirot.

'Perhaps. It is certainly useless to fight against it.'

Now there was only weariness in her tone. After a moment or two, she went on.

'I must beg your pardon, M. Poirot. Nick's pardon, too. Up till last night I did not believe. I never dreamed that the danger was – serious.'

'Is that so, Madame?'

'I see now that everything will have to be gone into – carefully. And I imagine that Nick's immediate circle of friends will not be immune from suspicion. Ridiculous, of course, but there it is. Am I right, M. Poirot?'

'You are very intelligent, Madame.'

'You asked me some questions about Tavistock the other day, M. Poirot. As you will find out sooner or later, I might as well tell you the truth now. I was not at Tavistock.'

'No, Madame.'

'I motored down to this part of the world with Mr Lazarus early last week. We did not wish to arouse more comment than necessary. We stayed at a little place called Shellacombe.'

'That is, I think, about seven miles from here, Madame?'

'About that – yes.'

Still that quiet far-away weariness.

'May I be impertinent, Madame?'

'Is there such a thing – in these days?'

'Perhaps you are right, Madame. How long have you and M. Lazarus been friends?'

'I met him six months ago.'

'And you – care for him, Madame.'

Frederica shrugged her shoulders.

'He is – rich.'

'Oh! *là là*,' cried Poirot. 'That is an ugly thing to say.'

She seemed faintly amused.

'Isn't it better to say it myself – than to have you say it for me?'

'Well – there is always that, of course. May I repeat, Madame, that you are *very* intelligent.'

'You will give me a diploma soon,' said Frederica, and rose.

'There is nothing more you wish to tell me, Madame?'

'I do not think so – no. I am going to take some flowers round to Nick and see how she is.'

'Ah, that is very *aimable* of you. Thank you, Madame, for your frankness.'

She glanced at him sharply, seemed about to speak, then thought better of it and went out of the room, smiling faintly at me as I held the door open for her.

'She is intelligent,' said Poirot. 'Yes, but so is Hercule Poirot!'

'What do you mean?'

'That it is all very well and very pretty to force the richness of M. Lazarus down my throat –'

'I must say that rather disgusted me.'

'*Mon cher*, always you have the right reaction in the wrong place. It is not, for the moment, a question of good taste or otherwise. If Madame Rice has a devoted friend who is rich and can give her all she needs – why then obviously Madame Rice would not need to murder her dearest friend for a mere pittance.'

'Oh!' I said.

'*Précisément!* "Oh!" '

'Why didn't you stop her going to the nursing home?'

'Why should I show my hand? Is it Hercule Poirot who prevents Mademoiselle Nick from seeing her friends? *Quelle idée!* It is the doctors and the nurses. Those tiresome nurses! So full of rules and regulations and "doctor's' orders".'

'You're not afraid that they may let her in after all? Nick may insist.'

'Nobody will be let in, my dear Hastings, but you and me. And for that matter, the sooner we make our way there, the better.'

The sitting-room door flew open and George Challenger barged in. His tanned face was alive with indignation.

'Look here, M. Poirot,' he said. 'What's the meaning of this? I rang up that damned nursing home where Nick is. Asked how she was and what time I could come round and see her. And they say the doctor won't allow any visitors. I want to know the meaning of that. To put it plainly, is this your work? Or is Nick really ill from shock?'

'I assure you, Monsieur, that I do not lay down rules for nursing homes. I would not dare. Why not ring up the good doctor – what was his name now? – Ah, yes, Graham.'

'I have. He says she's going on as well as could be expected – usual stuff. But I know all the tricks – my uncle's a doctor. Harley Street. Nerve specialist. Psycho-analysis – all the rest of it. Putting relations and friends off with soothing words. I've heard about it all. I don't believe Nick isn't up to seeing any one. I believe you're at the bottom of this, M. Poirot.'

Poirot smiled at him in a very kindly fashion. Indeed, I have always observed that Poirot has a kindly feeling for a lover.

'Now listen to me, *mon ami*,' he said. 'If one guest is admitted, others cannot be kept out. You comprehend? It must be all or none.

We want Mademoiselle's safety, you and I, do we not? Exactly. Then, you understand – it must be *none*.'

'I get you,' said Challenger, slowly. 'But then –'

'*Chut!* We will say no more. We will forget even what we have said. The prudence, the extreme prudence, is what is needed at present.'

'I can hold my tongue,' said the sailor quietly.

He turned away to the door, pausing as he went out to say:

'No embargo on flowers, is there? So long as they are not white ones.'

Poirot smiled.

'And now,' he said, as the door shut behind the impetuous Challenger, 'whilst M. Challenger and Madame and perhaps M. Lazarus all encounter each other in the flower shop, you and I will drive quietly to our destination.'

'And ask for the answer to the three questions?' I said.

'Yes. We will ask. Though, as a matter of fact, I know the answer.'

'What?' I exclaimed.

'Yes.'

'But when did you find out?'

'Whilst I was eating my breakfast, Hastings. It stared me in the face.'

'Tell me.'

'No, I will leave you to hear it from Mademoiselle.'

Then, as if to distract my mind, he pushed an open letter across to me.

It was a report by the expert Poirot had sent to examine the picture of old Nicholas Buckley. It stated definitely that the picture was worth at most twenty pounds.

'So that is one matter cleared up,' said Poirot.

'No mouse in that mousehole,' I said, remembering a metaphor of Poirot's on one past occasion.

'Ah! you remember that? No, as you say, no mouse in that mousehole. Twenty pounds and M. Lazarus offered fifty. What an error of judgement for a seemingly astute young man. But there, there, we must start on our errand.'

The nursing home was set high on a hill overlooking the bay. A white-coated orderly received us. We were put into a little room downstairs and presently a brisk-looking nurse came to us.

One glance at Poirot seemed to be enough. She had clearly received her instructions from Dr Graham together with a minute description of the little detective. She even concealed a smile.

'Miss Buckley has passed a very fair night,' she said. 'Come up, will you?'

In a pleasant room with the sun streaming into it, we found Nick. In the narrow iron bed, she looked like a tired child. Her face was white and her eyes were suspiciously red, and she seemed listless and weary.

'It's good of you to come,' she said in a flat voice.

Poirot took her hand in both of his.

'Courage, Mademoiselle. There is always something to live for.'

The words startled her. She looked up in his face.

'Oh!' she said. 'Oh!'

'Will you not tell me now, Mademoiselle, what it was that has been worrying you lately? Or shall I guess? And may I offer you, Mademoiselle, my very deepest sympathy.'

Her face flushed.

'So you know. Oh, well, it doesn't matter who knows now. Now that it's all over. Now that I shall never see him again.'

Her voice broke.

'Courage, Mademoiselle.'

'I haven't got any courage left. I've used up every bit in these last weeks. Hoping and hoping and – just lately – hoping against hope.'

I stared. I could not understand one word.

'Regard the poor Hastings,' said Poirot. 'He does not know what we are talking about.'

Her unhappy eyes met mine.

'Michael Seton, the airman,' she said. 'I was engaged to him – and he's dead.'

CHAPTER ELEVEN

The Motive

I was dumbfounded.

I turned on Poirot.

'Is this what you meant?'

'Yes, *mon ami*. This morning – I knew.'

'How did you know? How did you guess? You said it stared you in the face at breakfast.'

'So it did, my friend. From the front page of the newspaper. I remembered the conversation at dinner last night – and I saw everything.'

He turned to Nick again.

'You heard the news last night?'

'Yes. On the wireless. I made an excuse about the telephone. I wanted to hear the news alone – in case ...' She swallowed hard. 'And I heard it ...'

'I know, I know.' He took her hand in both of his.

'It was – pretty ghastly. And all the people arriving. I don't know how I got through it. It all felt like a dream. I could see myself from outside – behaving just as usual. It was queer somehow.'

'Yes, yes, I understand.'

'And then, when I went to fetch Freddie's wrap – I broke down for a minute. I pulled myself together quite quickly. But Maggie kept calling up about her coat. And then at last she took my shawl and went, and I put on some powder and some rouge and followed her out. And there she was – dead ...'

'Yes, yes, it must have been a terrible shock.'

'You don't understand. I was angry! I wished it had been *me!* I wanted to be dead – and there I was – alive and perhaps to live for years! And Michael dead – drowned far away in the Pacific.'

'*Pauvre enfant,*'

'I don't want to be alive. I don't want to live, I tell you!' she cried, rebelliously.

'I know – I know. To all of us, Mademoiselle, there comes a time when death is preferable to life. But it passes – sorrow passes and grief. You cannot believe that now, I know. It is useless for an old man like me to talk. Idle words – that is what you think – idle words.'

'You think I'll forget – and marry someone else? Never!'

244

She looked rather lovely as she sat up in bed, her two hands clenched and her cheeks burning.

Poirot said gently:

'No, no. I am not thinking anything of the kind. You are very lucky, Mademoiselle. You have been loved by a brave man – a hero. How did you come to meet him?'

'It was at Le Touquet – last September. Nearly a year ago.'

'And you became engaged – when?'

'Just after Christmas. But it had to be a secret.'

'Why was that?'

'Michael's uncle – old Sir Matthew Seton. He loved birds and hated women.'

'*Ah! ce n'est pas raisonnable!*'

'Well – I don't mean quite that. He was a complete crank. Thought women ruined a man's life. And Michael was absolutely dependent on him. He was frightfully proud of Michael and it was he who financed the building of the *Albatross* and the expenses of the round-the-world flight. It was the dearest dream of his life as well as of Michael's. If Michael had pulled it off – well, then he could have asked his uncle anything. And even if old Sir Matthew had still cut up rough, well, it wouldn't have really mattered. Michael would have been made – a kind of world hero. His uncle would have come round in the end.'

'Yes, yes, I see.'

'But Michael said it would be fatal if anything leaked out. We must keep it a dead secret. And I did. I never told anyone – not even Freddie.'

Poirot groaned.

'If only you had told me, Mademoiselle,'

Nick stared at him.

'But what difference would it have made? It couldn't have anything to do with these mysterious attacks on me? No, I'd promised Michael – and I kept my word. But it was awful – the anxiety, wondering and getting in a state the whole time. And everyone saying one was so nervy. And being unable to explain.'

'Yes, I comprehend all that.'

'He was missing once before, you know. Crossing the desert on the way to India. That was pretty awful, and then after all, it was all right. His machine was damaged, but it was put right, and he went on. And I kept saying to myself that it would be the same this time. Everyone said he must be dead – and I kept telling myself that he

245

must be all right, really. And then – last night . . .'

Her voice trailed away.

'You had hoped up till then?'

'I don't know. I think it was more that I refused to believe. It was awful never being able to talk to anyone.'

'Yes, I can imagine that. Were you never tempted to tell Madame Rice, for instance?'

'Sometimes I wanted to frightfully.'

'You do not think she – guessed?'

'I don't think so.' Nick considered the idea carefully. 'She never said anything. Of course she used to hint things sometimes. About our being great friends and all that.'

'You never considered telling her when M. Seton's uncle died? You know that he died about a week ago?'

'I know. He had an operation or something. I suppose I might have told anybody then. But it wouldn't have been a nice way of doing it, would it? I mean, it would have seemed rather boastful – to do it just then – when all the papers were full of Michael. And reporters would have come and interviewed me. It would all have been rather cheap. And Michael would have hated it.'

'I agree with you, Mademoiselle. You could not have announced it publicly. I only meant that you could have spoken of it privately to a friend.'

'I did sort of hint to one person,' said Nick. 'I – thought it was only fair. But I don't know how much he – the person took in.'

Poirot nodded.

'Are you on good terms with your cousin M. Vyse?' he asked, with a rather abrupt change of subject.

'Charles? What put him into you head?'

'I was just wondering – that was all.'

'Charles means well,' said Nick. 'He's a frightful stick, of course. Never moves out of this place. He disapproves of me, I think.'

'Oh! Mademoiselle, Mademoiselle. And I hear that he has laid all his devotion at your feet!'

'Disapproving of a person doesn't keep you from having a pash for them. Charles thinks my mode of life is reprehensible and he disapproves of my cocktails, my complexion, my friends and my conversation. But he still feels my fatal fascination. He always hopes to reform me, I think.'

She paused and then said, with a ghost of a twinkle:

'Who have you been pumping to get the local information?'

246

'You must not give me away, Mademoiselle. I had a little conversation with the Australian lady, Madame Croft.'

'She's rather an old dear – when one has time for her. Terribly sentimental. Love and home and children – you know the sort of thing.'

'I am old-fashioned and sentimental myself, Mademoiselle.'

'Are you? I should have said that Captain Hastings was the sentimental one of you two.'

I blushed indignantly.

'He is furious,' said Poirot, eying my discomfiture with a good deal of pleasure. 'But you are right, Mademoiselle. Yes, you are right.'

'Not at all,' I said, angrily.

'Hastings has a singularly beautiful nature. It has been the greatest hindrance to me at times.'

'Don't be absurd, Poirot.'

'He is, to begin with, reluctant to see evil anywhere, and when he does see it his righteous indignation is so great that he is incapable of dissembling. Altogether a rare and beautiful nature. No, *mon ami*, I will not permit you to contradict me. It is as I say.'

'You've both been very kind to me,' said Nick, gently.

'*Là, là*, Mademoiselle. That is nothing. We have much more to do. To begin with, you will remain here. You will obey orders. You will do what I tell you. At this juncture I must not be hampered.'

Nick sighed wearily.

'I'll do anything you like. I don't care what I do.'

'You will see no friends for the present.'

'I don't care. I don't want to see anyone.'

'For you the passive part – for us the active one. Now, Mademoiselle, I am going to leave you. I will not intrude longer upon your sorrow.'

He moved towards the door, pausing with his hand on the handle to say over his shoulder:

'By the way, you once mentioned a will you made. Where is it, this will?'

'Oh! it's knocking round somewhere.'

'At End House?'

'Yes.'

'In a safe? Locked up in your desk?'

'Well, I really don't know. It's somewhere about.' She frowned. 'I'm frightfully untidy, you know. Papers and things like that would be mostly in the writing-table in the library. That's where most of the bills are. The will is probably with them. Or it might be in my bedroom.'

'You permit me to make the search – yes?'

'If you want to – yes. Look at anything you like.'

'*Merci*, Mademoiselle. I will avail myself of your permission.'

CHAPTER TWELVE

Ellen

Poirot said no word till we had emerged from the nursing home into the outer air. Then he caught me by the arm.

'You see, Hastings? You see? Ah! *Sacré tonnerre!* I was right! I was right! Always I knew there was something lacking – some piece of the puzzle that was not there. And without that missing piece the whole thing was meaningless.'

His almost despairing triumph was double-Dutch to me. I could not see that anything very epoch-making had occurred.

'It was there all the time. And I could not see it. But how should I? To know there is *something* – that, yes – but to know what that something is. *Ah! Ça c'est bien plus difficile.*'

'Do you mean that this has some direct bearing on the crime?'

'*Ma foi*, do you not see?'

'As a matter of fact, I don't.'

'Is it possible? Why, it gives us what we have been looking for – the motive – the hidden obscure motive!'

'I may be very dense, but I can't see it. Do you mean jealousy of some kind?'

'Jealousy? No, no, my friend. The usual motive – the inevitable motive. Money, my friend, money!'

I stared. He went on, speaking more calmly.

'Listen, *mon ami*. Just over a week ago Sir Matthew Seton dies. And Sir Matthew Seton was a millionaire – one of the richest men in England.'

'Yes, but –'

'*Attendez*. One step at a time. He has a nephew whom he idolizes and to whom, we may safely assume, he has left his vast fortune.'

'But –'

'*Mais oui* – legacies, yes, an endowment to do with his hobby, yes, but the bulk of the money would go to Michael Seton. Last Tuesday, Michael Seton is reported missing – *and on Wednesday the attacks on Mademoiselle's life begin.* Supposing, Hastings, that Michael Seton made a will before he started on his flight, and that in that will he left all he had to his fiancée.'

'That's pure supposition.'

'It is supposition – yes. *But it must be so*. Because, if it is not so,

249

there is no meaning in anything that has happened. It is no paltry inheritance that is at stake. It is an enormous fortune.'

I was silent for some minutes, turning the matter over in my mind. It seemed to me that Poirot was leaping to conclusions in a most reckless manner, and yet I was secretly convinced that he was right. It was his extraordinary flair for being right that influenced me. Yet it seemed to me that there was a good deal to be proved still.

'But if nobody knew of the engagement,' I argued.

'Pah! Somebody *did* know. For the matter of that, somebody always *does* know. If they do not know, they guess. Madame Rice suspected. Mademoiselle Nick admitted as much. She may have had means of turning those suspicions into certainties.'

'How?'

'Well, for one thing, there must have been letters from Michael Seton to Mademoiselle Nick. They had been engaged some time. And her best friend could not call that young lady anything but careless. She leaves things here and there, and everywhere. I doubt if she has ever locked up anything in her life. Oh, yes, there would be means of making sure.'

'And Frederica Rice would know about the will that her friend had made?'

'Doubtless. Oh, yes, it narrows down now. You remember my list – a list of persons numbered from A. to J. It has narrowed down to only two persons. I dismiss the servants. I dismiss the Commander Challenger – even though he did take one hour and a half to reach here from Plymouth – and the distance is only thirty miles. I dismiss the long-nosed M. Lazarus who offered fifty pounds for a picture that was only worth twenty (it is odd, that, when you come to think of it. Most uncharacteristic of his race). I dismiss the Australians – so hearty and so pleasant. I keep two people on my list still.'

'One is Frederica Rice,' I said slowly.

I had a vision of her face, the golden hair, the white fragility of the features.

'Yes. She is indicated very clearly. However carelessly worded Mademoiselle's will may have been, she would be plainly indicated as residuary legatee. Apart from End House, everything was to go to her. If Mademoiselle Nick instead of Mademoiselle Maggie had been shot last night, Madame Rice would be a rich woman today.'

'I can hardly believe it!'

'You mean that you can hardly believe that a beautiful woman can be a murderess? One often has a little difficulty with members of a

250

jury on that account. But you may be right. There is still another
suspect.'

'Who?'

'Charles Vyse.'

'But he only inherits the house.'

'Yes – but he may not know that. Did he make Mademoiselle's will
for her? I think not. If so, it would be in his keeping, not "knocking
around somewhere", or whatever the phrase was that Mademoiselle
used. So, you see, Hastings, *it is quite probable that he knows nothing
about that will*. He may believe that she has never made a will and
that, in that case, he will inherit as next of kin.'

'You know,' I said, 'that really seems to me much more probable.'

'That is your romantic mind, Hastings. The wicked solicitor. A
familiar figure in fiction. If as well as being a solicitor he has an
impassive face, it makes the matter almost certain. It is true that, in
some ways, he is more in the picture than Madame. He would be
more likely to know about the pistol and more likely to use one.'

'And to send the boulder crashing down.'

'Perhaps. Though, as I have told you, much can be done by
leverage. And the fact that the boulder was dislodged at the wrong
minute, and consequently missed Mademoiselle, is more suggestive
of feminine agency. The idea of tampering with the interior of a car
seems masculine in conception – though many women are as good
mechanics as men nowadays. On the other hand, there are one or two
gaps in the theory against M. Vyse.'

'Such as –?'

'He is less likely to have known of the engagement than Madame.
And there is another point. His action was rather precipitate.'

'What do you mean?'

'Well, until last night there was no *certitude* that Seton was dead.
To act rashly, without due assurance, seems very uncharacteristic of
the legal mind.'

'Yes,' I said. 'A woman would jump to conclusions.'

'Exactly. *Ce que femme veut, Dieu veut.* That is the attitude.'

'It's really amazing the way Nick has escaped. It seems almost
incredible.'

And suddenly I remembered the tone in Frederica's voice as she
had said: 'Nick bears a charmed life.'

I shivered a little.

'Yes,' said Poirot, thoughtfully. 'And I can take no credit to
myself. Which is humiliating.'

251

'Providence,' I murmured.

'Ah! *mon ami*, I would not put on the shoulders of the good God the burden of men's wrongdoing. You say that in your Sunday morning voice of thankfulness – without reflecting that what you are really saying is that *le bon Dieu* has killed Miss Maggie Buckley.'

'Really, Poirot!'

'Really, my friend! But I will not sit back and say "*le bon Dieu* has arranged everything, I will not interfere". Because I am convinced that *le bon Dieu* created Hercule Poirot for the express purpose of interfering. It is my *métier*.'

We had been slowly ascending the zig-zag path up the cliff. It was at this juncture that we passed through the little gate into the grounds of End House.

'Pouf!' said Poirot. 'That ascent is a steep one. I am hot. My moustaches are limp. Yes, as I was saying just now, I am on the side of the innocent. I am on the side of Mademoiselle Nick because she was attacked. I am on the side of Mademoiselle Maggie because she has been killed.'

'And you are against Frederica Rice and Charles Vyse.'

'No, no, Hastings. I keep an open mind. I say only that at the moment one of those two is indicated. Chut!'

We had come out on the strip of lawn by the house, and a man was driving a mowing machine. He had a long, stupid face and lack-lustre eyes. Beside him was a small boy of about ten, ugly but intelligent-looking.

It crossed my mind that we had not heard the mowing machine in action, but I presumed that the gardener was not overworking himself. He had probably been resting from his labours, and had sprung into action on hearing our voices approaching.

'Good morning,' said Poirot.

'Good morning, sir.'

'You are the gardener, I suppose. The husband of Madame who works in the house.'

'He's my Dad,' said the small boy.

'That's right, sir,' said the man. 'You'll be the foreign gentleman, I take it, that's really a detective. Is there any news of the young mistress, sir?'

'I come from seeing her at the immediate moment. She has passed a satisfactory night.'

'We've had policemen here,' said the small boy. 'That's where the lady was killed. Here by the steps. I seen a pig killed once, haven't I,

252

Dad?'

'Ah!' said his father, unemotionally.

'Dad used to kill pigs when he worked on a farm. Didn't you, Dad? I seen a pig killed. I liked it.'

'Young 'uns like to see pigs killed,' said the man, as though stating one of the unalterable facts of nature.

'Shot with a pistol, the lady was,' continued the boy. 'She didn't have her throat cut. No!'

We passed on to the house, and I felt thankful to get away from the ghoulish child.

Poirot entered the drawing-room, the windows of which were open, and rang the bell. Ellen, neatly attired in black, came in answer to the bell. She showed no surprise at seeing us.

Poirot explained that we were here by permission of Miss Buckley to make a search of the house.

'Very good sir.'

'The police have finished?'

'They said they had seen everything they wanted, sir. They've been about the garden since very early in the morning. I don't know whether they've found anything.'

She was about to leave the room when Poirot stopped her with a question.

'Were you very surprised last night when you heard Miss Buckley had been shot?'

'Yes, sir, very surprised. Miss Maggie was a nice young lady, sir. I can't imagine anyone being so wicked as to want to harm her.'

'If it had been anyone else, you would not have been so surprised – eh?'

'I don't know what you mean, sir?'

'When I came into the hall last night,' he said, 'you asked at once whether anyone had been hurt. Were you expecting anything of the kind?'

She was silent. Her fingers pleated a corner of her apron. She shook her head and murmured:

'You gentlemen wouldn't understand.'

'Yes, yes,' said Poirot, 'I would understand. However fantastic what you may say, I would understand.'

She looked at him doubtfully, then seemed to make up her mind to trust him.

'You see, sir,' she said, 'this isn't a good house.'

I was surprised and a little contemptuous. Poirot, however,

seemed to find the remark not in the least unusual.

'You mean it is an old house.'

'Yes, sir, not a good house.'

'You have been here long?'

'Six years, sir. But I was here as a girl. In the kitchen as kitchen-maid. That was in the time of old Sir Nicholas. It was the same then.'

Poirot looked at her attentively.

'In an old house,' she said, 'there is sometimes an atmosphere of evil.'

'That's it, sir,' said Ellen, eagerly. 'Evil. Bad thoughts and bad deeds too. It's like dry rot in a house, sir, you can't get it out. It's a sort of feeling in the air. I always knew something bad would happen in this house, some day.'

'Well, you have been proved right.'

'Yes, sir.'

There was a very slight underlying satisfaction in her tone, the satisfaction of one whose gloomy prognostications have been shown to be correct.

'But you didn't think it would be Miss Maggie.'

'No, indeed, I didn't, sir. Nobody hated *her* – I'm sure of it.'

It seemed to me that in those words was a clue. I expected Poirot to follow it up, but to my surprise he shifted to quite a different subject.

'You didn't hear the shots fired?'

'I couldn't have told with the fireworks going on. Very noisy they were.'

'You weren't out watching them?'

'No, I hadn't finished clearing up dinner.'

'Was the waiter helping you?'

'No, sir, he'd gone out into the garden to have a look at the fireworks.'

'But you didn't go.'

'No, sir.'

'Why was that?'

'I wanted to get finished.'

'You don't care for fireworks?'

'Oh, yes, sir, it wasn't that. But you see, there's two nights of them, and William and I get the evening off tomorrow and go down into the town and see them from there.'

'I comprehend. And you heard Mademoiselle Maggie asking for her coat and unable to find it?'

254

'I heard Miss Nick run upstairs, sir, and Miss Buckley call up from the front hall saying she couldn't find something and I heard her say, "All right – I'll take the shawl –" '

'Pardon,' Poirot interrupted. 'You did not endeavour to search for the coat for her – or get it from the car where it had been left?'

'I had my work to do, sir.'

'Quite so – and doubtless neither of the two young ladies asked you because they thought you were out looking at the fireworks?'

'Yes, sir.'

'So that, other years, you *have* been out looking at the fireworks?'

A sudden flush came into her pale cheeks.

'I don't know what you mean, sir. We're always allowed to go out into the garden. If I didn't feel like it this year, and would rather get on with my work and go to bed, well, that's my business, I imagine.'

'*Mais oui. Mais oui.* I did not intend to offend you. Why should you not do as you prefer. To make a change, it is pleasant.'

He paused and then added:

'Now another little matter in which I wonder whether you can help me. This is an old house. Are there, do you know, any secret chambers in it?'

'Well – there's a kind of sliding panel – in this very room. I remember being shown it as a girl. Only I can't remember just now where it is. Or was it in the library? I can't say, I'm sure.'

'Big enough for a person to hide in?'

'Oh, no indeed, sir! A little cupboard place – a kind of niche. About a foot square, sir, not more than that.'

'Oh! that is not what I mean at all.'

The blush rose to her face again.

'If you think I was hiding anywhere – I wasn't! I heard Miss Nick run down the stairs and out and I heard her cry out – and I came into the hall to see if – if anything was the matter. And that's the gospel truth, sir. That's the gospel truth.'

255

CHAPTER THIRTEEN

Letters

Having successfully got rid of Ellen, Poirot turned a somewhat thoughtful face towards me.

'I wonder now – did she hear those shots? I think she did. She heard them, she opened the kitchen door. She heard Nick rush down the stairs and out, and she herself came into the hall to find out what had happened. That is natural enough. But why did she not go out and watch the fireworks that evening? That is what I should like to know, Hastings.'

'What was your idea in asking about a secret hiding place?'

'A mere fanciful idea that, after all, we might not have disposed of J.'

'J?'

'Yes. The last person on my list. The problematical outsider. Supposing for some reason connected with Ellen, that J. had come to the house last night. He (I assume a he) conceals himself in a secret chamber in this room. A girl passes through whom he takes to be Nick. He follows her out – and shoots her. *Non – c'est idiot!* And anyway, we know that there is no hiding place. Ellen's decision to remain in the kitchen last night was a pure hazard. Come, let us search for the will of Mademoiselle Nick.'

There were no papers in the drawing-room. We adjourned to the library, a rather dark room looking out on the drive. Here there was a large old-fashioned walnut bureau-writing-table.

It took us some time to go through it. Everything was in complete confusion. Bills and receipts were mixed up together. Letters of invitation, letters pressing for payment of accounts, letters from friends.

'We will arrange these papers,' said Poirot, sternly, 'with order and method.'

He was as good as his word. Half an hour later, he sat back with a pleased expression on his face. Everything was neatly sorted, docketed and filed.

'*C'est bien, ça.* One thing is at least to the good. We have had to go through everything so thoroughly that there is no possibility of our having missed anything.'

'No, indeed. Not that there's been much to find.'

'Except possibly this.'

He tossed across a letter. It was written in large sprawling handwriting, almost indecipherable.

'*Darling*, – Party was too too marvellous. Feel rather a worm today. You were wise not to touch that stuff – don't ever start, darling. It's too damned hard to give up. I'm writing the boy friend to hurry up the supply. What Hell life is!

'Yours,
'FREDDIE.'

'Dated last February,' said Poirot thoughtfully. 'She takes drugs, of course, I knew that as soon as I looked at her.'

'Really? I never suspected such a thing.'

'It is fairly obvious. You have only to look at her eyes. And then there are her extraordinary variations of mood. Sometimes she is all on edge, strung up – sometimes she is lifeless – inert.'

'Drug-taking affects the moral sense, does it not?'

'Inevitably. But I do not think Madame Rice is a real addict. She is at the beginning – not the end.'

'And Nick?'

'There are no signs of it. She may have attended a dope party now and then for fun, but she is no taker of drugs.'

'I'm glad of that.'

I remembered suddenly what Nick had said about Frederica: that she was not always herself. Poirot nodded and tapped the letter he held.

'This is what she was referring to, undoubtedly. Well, we have drawn the blank, as you say, here. Let us go up to Mademoiselle's room.'

There was a desk in Nick's room also, but comparatively little was kept in it. Here again, there was no sign of a will. We found the registration book of her car and a perfectly good dividend warrant of a month back. Otherwise there was nothing of importance.

Poirot sighed in an exasperated fashion.

'The young girls – they are not properly trained nowadays. The order, the method, it is left out of their bringing up. She is charming, Mademoiselle Nick, but she is a feather-head. Decidedly, she is a feather-head.'

He was now going through the contents of a chest of drawers.

'Surely, Poirot,' I said, with some embarrassment, 'those are underclothes.'

He paused in surprise.

'And why not, my friend?'

'Don't you think – I mean – we can hardly –'

He broke into a roar of laughter.

'Decidedly, my poor Hastings, you belong to the Victorian era. Mademoiselle Nick would tell you so if she were here. In all probability she would say that you had the mind like the sink! Young ladies are not ashamed of their underclothes nowadays. The camisole, the cami-knicker, it is no longer a shameful secret. Every day, on the beach, all these garments will be discarded within a few feet of you. And why not?'

'I don't see any need for what you are doing.'

'*Ecoutez*, my friend. Clearly, she does not lock up her treasures, Mademoiselle Nick. If she wished to hide any thing from sight – where would she hide it? Underneath the stockings and the petticoats. Ah! what have we here?'

He held up a packet of letters tied with a faded pink ribbon.

'The love letters of M. Michael Seton, if I mistake not.'

Quite calmly he untied the ribbon and began to open out the letters.

'Poirot,' I cried, scandalized. 'You really can't do that. It isn't playing the game.'

'I am not playing a game, *mon ami*.' His voice range out suddenly harsh and stern. 'I am hunting down a murderer.'

'Yes, but private letters –'

'May have nothing to tell me – on the other hand, they may. I must take every chance, my friend. Come, you might as well read them with me. Two pairs of eyes are no worse than one pair. Console yourself with the thought that the staunch Ellen probably knows them by heart.'

I did not like it. Still I realized that in Poirot's position he could not afford to be squeamish, and I consoled myself by the quibble that Nick's last word had been, 'Look at anything you like.'

The letters spread over several dates, beginning last winter.

New Year's Day.

'*Darling*, – The New Year is in and I'm making good resolutions. It seems too wonderful to be true – that you should actually love me. You've made all the difference to my life. I believe we both knew –

from the very first moment we met. Happy New Year, my lovely girl.

'Yours for ever, MICHAEL.'

February 8th.

'*Dearest Love*, – How I wish I could see you more often. This is pretty rotten, isn't it? I hate all this beastly concealment, but I explained to you how things are. I know how much you hate lies and concealment. I do too. But honestly, it might upset the whole apple cart. Uncle Matthew has got an absolute bee in his bonnet about early marriages and the way they wreck a man's career. As though you could wreck mine, you dear angel!

'Cheer up, darling. Everything will come right.

'Yours,
'MICHAEL.'

March 2nd.

'I oughtn't to write to you two days running, I know. But I must. When I was up yesterday I thought of you. I flew over Scarborough. Blessed, blessed, blessed Scarborough – the most wonderful place in the world. Darling, you don't know how I love you!

'Yours,
'MICHAEL.'

April 18th.

'*Dearest*, – The whole thing is fixed up. Definitely. If I pull this off (and I shall pull it off) I shall be able to take a firm line with Uncle Matthew – and if he doesn't like it – well, what do I care? It's adorable of you to be so interested in my long technical descriptions of the *Albatross*. How I long to take you up in her. Some day! Don't, for goodness' sake, worry about me. The thing isn't half so risky as it sounds. I simply couldn't get killed now that I know you care for me. Everything will be all right, sweetheart. Trust your Michael.'

April 20th.

'*You Angel*, – Every word you say is true and I shall treasure that letter always. I'm not half good enough for you. You are so different from everybody else. I adore you.

'Your
'MICHAEL.'

The last was undated.

259

'*Dearest*, – Well – I'm off tomorrow. Feeling tremendously keen and excited and absolutely certain of success. The old *Albatross* is all tuned up. She won't let me down.

'Cheer up, sweetheart, and don't worry. There's a risk, of course, but all life's a risk really. By the way, somebody said I ought to make a will (tactful fellow – but he meant well), so I have – on a half sheet of notepaper – and sent it to old Whitfield. I'd no time to go round there. Somebody once told me that a man made a will of three words, "All to Mother", and it was legal all right. My will was rather like that – I remembered your name was really Magdala, which was clever of me! A couple of the fellows witnessed it.

'Don't take all this solemn talk about wills to heart, will you? (I didn't mean that pun. An accident.) I shall be as right as rain. I'll send you telegrams from India and Australia and so on. And keep up heart. *It's going to be all right.* See?

'Good night and God bless you,

'MICHAEL.'

Poirot folded the letters together again.

'You see, Hastings? I had to read them – to make sure. It is as I told you.'

'Surely you could have found out some other way?'

'No, *mon cher*, that is just what I could not do. It had to be this way. We have now some very valuable evidence.'

'In what way?'

'We now know that the fact of Michael's having made a will in favour of Mademoiselle Nick is actually recorded in writing. Anyone who had read those letters would know the fact. And with letters carelessly hidden like that, anyone could read them.'

'Ellen?'

'Ellen, almost certainly, I should say. We will try a little experiment on her before passing out.'

'There is no sign of the will.'

'No, that is curious. But in all probability it is thrown on top of a bookcase, or inside a china jar. We must try to awaken Mademoiselle's memory on that point. At any rate, there is nothing more to be found here.'

Ellen was dusting the hall as we descended.

Poirot wished her good morning very pleasantly as we passed. He turned back from the front door to say:

'You knew, I suppose, that Miss Buckley was engaged to the airman, Michael Seton?'

She stared.

'What? The one there's all the fuss in the papers about?'

'Yes.'

'Well, I never. To think of that. Engaged to Miss Nick.'

'Complete and absolute surprise registered very convincingly,' I remarked, as we got outside.

'Yes. It really seemed genuine.'

'Perhaps it was,' I suggested.

'And that packet of letters reclining for months under the *lingerie*! No, *mon ami*.'

'All very well,' I thought to myself. 'But we are not all Hercule Poirots. We do not all go nosing into what does not concern us.'

But I said nothing.

'This Ellen – she is an enigma,' said Poirot. 'I do not like it. There is something here that I do not understand.'

CHAPTER FOURTEEN

The Mystery of the Missing Will

We went straight back to the nursing home.

Nick looked rather surprised to see us.

'Yes, Mademoiselle,' said Poirot, answering her look. 'I am like the Jack in the Case. I pop up again. To begin with I will tell you that I have put the order in your affairs. Everything is now neatly arranged.'

'Well, I expect it was about time,' said Nick, unable to help smiling. 'Are you *very* tidy, M. Poirot?'

'Ask my friend Hastings here.'

The girl turned an inquiring gaze on me.

I detailed some of Poirot's minor peculiarities – toast that had to be made from a square loaf – eggs matching in size – his objection to golf as a game 'shapeless and haphazard', whose only redeeming feature was the tee boxes! I ended by telling her the famous case which Poirot had solved by his habit of straightenting ornaments on the mantelpiece.

Poirot sat by smiling.

'He makes the good tale of it, yes,' he said, when I had finished. 'But on the whole it is true. Figure to yourself, Mademoiselle, that I never cease trying to persuade Hastings to part his hair in the middle instead of on the side. See what an air, lop-sided and unsymmetrical, it gives him.'

'Then you must disapprove of me, M. Poirot,' said Nick. 'I wear a side parting. And you must approve of Freddie who parts her hair in the middle.'

'He was certainly admiring her the other evening,' I put in maliciously. 'Now I know the reason.'

'*C'est assez*,' said Poirot. 'I am here on serious business. Mademoiselle, this will of yours, I find it not.'

'Oh!' She wrinkled her brows. 'But does it matter so much? After all, I'm not dead. And wills aren't really important till you are dead, are they?'

'That is correct. All the same, I interest myself in this will of yours. I have various little ideas concerning it. Think Mademoiselle. Try to remember where you placed it – where you saw it last?'

'I don't suppose I put it anywhere particular,' said Nick. 'I never do put things in places. I probably shoved it into a drawer.'

'You did not put it in the secret panel by any chance?'

'The secret *what*?'

'Your maid, Ellen, says that there is a secret panel in the drawing-room or the library.'

'Nonsense,' said Nick. I've never heard of such a thing. *Ellen* said so?'

'*Mais oui*. It seems she was in service at End House as a young girl. The cook showed it to her.'

'It's the first I've ever heard of it. I suppose Grandfather must have known about it, but, if so, he didn't tell me. And I'm sure he *would* have told me. M. Poirot, are you sure Ellen isn't making it all up?'

'No, Mademoiselle, I am not at all sure! *Il me semble* that there is something – odd about this Ellen of yours.'

'Oh! I wouldn't call her odd. William's a half-wit, and the child is a nasty little brute, but Ellen's all right. The essence of respectability.'

'Did you give her leave to go out and see the fireworks last night, Mademoiselle?'

'Of course. They always do. They clear up afterwards.'

'Yet she did not go out.'

'Oh, yes, she did.'

'How do you know, Mademoiselle?'

'Well – well – I suppose I don't know. I told her to go and she thanked me – and so, of course, I assumed that she did go.'

'On the contrary – she remained in the house.'

'But – how very odd!'

'You think it odd?'

'Yes, I do. I'm sure she's never done such a thing before. Did she say why?'

'She did not tell me the real reason – of that I am sure.'

Nick looked at him questioningly.

'Is it – important?'

Poirot flung out his hands.

'That is just what I cannot say, Mademoiselle. *C'est curieux*. I leave it like that.'

'This panel business too,' said Nick, reflectively. 'I can't help thinking that's frightfully queer – and unconvincing. Did she show you where it was?'

'She said she couldn't remember.'

'I don't believe there is such a thing.'

'It certainly looks like it.'

263

'She must be going batty, poor thing.'

'She certainly recounts the histories! She said also that End House was not a good house to live in.'

Nick gave a little shiver.

'Perhaps she's right there,' she said slowly. 'Sometimes I've felt that way myself. There's a queer feeling in that house . . .'

Her eyes grew large and dark. They had a fated look. Poirot hastened to recall her to other topics.

'We have wandered from our subject, Mademoiselle. The will. The last will and testament of Magdala Buckley.'

'I put that,' said Nick, with some pride. 'I remember putting that, and I said pay all debts and testamentary expenses. I remembered that out of a book I'd read.'

'You did not use a will form, then?'

'No, there wasn't time for that. I was just going off to the nursing home, and besides Mr Croft said will forms were very dangerous. It was better to make a simple will and not try to be too legal.'

'M. Croft? He was there?'

'Yes. It was he who asked me if I'd made one. I'd never have thought of it myself. He said if you died in – in –'

'Intestate,' I said.

'Yes, that's it. He said if you died intestate, the Crown pinched a lot and that would be a pity.'

'Very helpful, the excellent M. Croft!'

'Oh, he was,' said Nick warmly. 'He got Ellen in and her husband to witness it. Oh! of course! What an idiot I've been!'

We looked at her inquiringly.

'I've been a perfect idiot. Letting you hunt round End House. Charles has got it, of course! My cousin, Charles Vyse.'

'Ah! so that is the explanation.'

'Mr Croft said a lawyer was the proper person to have charge of it.'

'*Très correct, ce bon M. Croft.*'

'Men are useful sometimes,' said Nick. 'A lawyer or the Bank – that's what he said. And I said Charles would be best. So we stuck it in an envelope and sent it off to him straight away.'

She lay back on her pillows with a sigh.

'I'm sorry I've been so frightfully stupid. But it is all right now. Charles has got it, and if you really want to see it, of course he'll show it to you.'

'Not without an authorization from you,' said Poirot, smiling.

'How silly.'

'No, Mademoiselle. Merely prudent.'

'Well, I think it's silly.' She took a piece of paper from a little stack that lay beside her bed. 'What shall I say? Let the dog see the rabbit?'

'*Comment?*'

I laughed at his startled face.

He dictated a form of words, and Nick wrote obediently.

'Thank you, Mademoiselle,' said Poirot, as he took it.

'I'm sorry to have given you such a lot of trouble. But I really had forgotten. You know how one forgets things almost at once?'

'With order and method in the mind one does not forget.'

'I'll have to have a course of some kind,' said Nick. 'You're giving me quite an inferiority complex.'

'That is impossible. *Au revoir, Mademoiselle.*' He looked round the room. 'Your flowers are lovely.'

'Aren't they? The carnations are from Freddie and the roses from George and the lilies from Jim Lazarus. And look here –'

She pulled the wrapping from a large basket of hothouse grapes by her side.

Poirot's face changed. He stepped forward sharply.

'You have not eaten any of them?'

'No. Not yet.'

'Do not do so. You must eat nothing, Mademoiselle, that comes in from outside. *Nothing.* You comprehend?'

'Oh!'

She stared at him, the colour ebbing slowly from her face.

'I see. You think – you think it isn't over yet. You think they're still trying?' she whispered.

He took her hand.

'Do not think of it. You are safe here. But remember – nothing that comes in from outside.'

I was conscious of that white frightened face on the pillow as we left the room.

Poirot looked at his watch.

'*Bon.* We have just time to catch M. Vyse at his office before he leaves it for lunch.'

On arrival we were shown into Charles Vyse's office after the briefest of delays.

The young lawyer rose to greet us. He was as formal and unemotional as ever.

'Good morning, M. Poirot. What can I do for you?'

Without more ado Poirot presented the letter Nick had written.

He took it and read it, then gazed over the top of it in a perplexed manner.

'I beg your pardon. I really am at a loss to understand?'

'Has not Mademoiselle Buckley made her meaning clear?'

'In this letter,' he tapped it with his finger-nail, 'she asks me to hand over to you a will made by her and entrusted to my keeping in February last.'

'Yes, Monsieur.'

'But, my dear sir, no will has been entrusted to my keeping!'

'*Comment?*'

'As far as I know my cousin never made a will. I certainly never made one for her.'

'She wrote this herself, I understand, on a sheet of notepaper and posted it to you.'

The lawyer shook his head.

'In that case all I can say is that I never received it.'

'Really, M. Vyse –'

'I never received anything of the kind, M. Poirot.'

There was a pause, then Poirot rose to his feet.

'In that case, M. Vyse, there is nothing to be said. There must be some mistake.'

'Certainly there must be some mistake.'

He rose also.

'Good day, M. Vyse.'

'Good day, M. Poirot.'

'And that is that,' I remarked, when we were out in the street once more.

'*Précisément.*'

'Is he lying, do you think?'

'Impossible to tell. He has the good poker face, M. Vyse, besides looking as though he had swallowed one. One thing is clear, he will not budge from the position he has taken up. *He never received the will.* That is his point.'

'Surely Nick will have a written acknowledgement of its receipt.'

'*Cette petite*, she would never bother her head about a thing like that. She despatched it. It was off her mind. *Voilà.* Besides, on the very day, she went into a nursing home to have her appendix out. She had her emotions, in all probability.'

'Well, what do we do now?'

'*Parbleu*, we go and see M. Croft. Let us see what he can remember about this business. It seems to have been very much his

266

doing.'

'He didn't profit by it in any way,' I said, thoughtfully.

'No. No, I cannot see anything in it from his point of view. He is probably merely the busybody – the man who likes to arrange his neighbour's affairs.'

Such an attitude was indeed typical of Mr Croft, I felt. He was the kindly knowall who causes so much exasperation in this world of ours.

We found him busy in his shirt sleeves over a steaming pot in the kitchen. A most savoury smell pervaded the little lodge.

He relinquished his cookery with enthusiasm, being clearly eager to talk about the murder.

'Half a jiffy,' he said. 'Walk upstairs. Mother will want to be in on this. She'd never forgive us for talking down here. Cooee – Milly. Two friends coming up.'

Mrs Croft greeted us warmly and was eager for news of Nick. I liked her much better than her husband.

'That poor dear girl,' she said. 'In a nursing home, you say? Had a complete breakdown, I shouldn't wonder. A dreadful business, M. Poirot – perfectly dreadful. An innocent girl like that shot dead. It doesn't bear thinking about – it doesn't indeed. And no lawless wild part of the world either. Right here in the heart of the old country. Kept me awake all night, it did.'

'It's made me nervous about going out and leaving you, old lady,' said her husband, who had put on his coat and joined us. 'I don't like to think of your having been left all alone here yesterday evening. It give me the shivers.'

'You're not going to leave me again, I can tell you,' said Mrs Croft. 'Not after dark, anyway. And I'm thinking I'd like to leave this part of the world as soon as possible. I shall never feel the same about it. I shouldn't think poor Nicky Buckley could ever bear to sleep in that house again.'

It was a little difficult to reach the object of our visit. Both Mr and Mrs Croft talked so much and were so anxious to know all about everything. Were the poor dead girl's relations coming down? When was the funeral? Was there to be an inquest? What did the police think? Had they any clue yet? Was it true that a man had been arrested in Plymouth?

Then, having answered all these questions, they were insistent on offering us lunch. Only Poirot's mendacious statement that we were obliged to hurry back to lunch with the Chief Constable saved us.

267

At last a momentary pause occurred and Poirot got in the question he had been waiting to ask.

'Why, of course,' said Mr Croft. He pulled the blind cord up and down twice, frowning at it abstractedly. 'I remember all about it. Must have been when we first came here. I remember. Appendicitis – that's what the doctor said –'

'And probably not appendicitis at all,' interrupted Mrs Croft. 'These doctors – they always like cutting you up if they can. It wasn't the kind you *have* to operate on anyhow. She'd had indigestion and one thing and another, and they'd X-rayed her and they said out it had better come. And there she was, poor little soul, just going off to one of those nasty Homes.'

'I just asked her,' said Mr Croft, 'if she'd made a will. More as a joke than anything else.'

'Yes?'

'And she wrote it out then and there. Talked about getting a will form at the post office – but I advised her not to. Lot of trouble they cause sometimes, so a man told me. Anyway, her cousin is a lawyer. He could draw her out a proper one afterwards if everything was all right – as, of course, I knew it would be. This was just a precautionary matter.'

'Who witnessed it?'

'Oh! Ellen, the maid, and her husband.'

'And afterwards? What was done with it?'

'Oh! we posted it to Vyse. The lawyer, you know.'

'You know that it was posted?'

'My dear M. Poirot, I posted it myself. Right in this box here by the gate.'

'So if M. Vyse says he never got it –'

Croft stared.

'Do you mean that it got lost in the post? Oh! but surely that's impossible.'

'Anyway, you are certain that you posted it.'

'Certain sure,' said Mr Croft, heartily. 'I'll take my oath on that any day.'

'Ah! well,' said Poirot. 'Fortunately it does not matter. Mademoiselle is not likely to die just yet awhile.'

'*Et voilà!*' said Poirot, when we were out of earshot and walking down to the hotel. 'Who is lying? M. Croft? Or M. Charles Vyse? I must confess I see no reason why M. Croft should be lying. To suppress the will would be of no advantage to him – especially when

268

he had been instrumental in getting it made. No, his statement seems clear enough and tallies exactly with what was told us by Mademoiselle Nick. But all the same –'

'Yes?'

'All the same, I am glad that M. Croft was doing the cooking when we arrived. He left an excellent impression of a greasy thumb and first finger on a corner of the newspaper that covered the kitchen table. I managed to tear it off unseen by him. We will send it to our good friend Inspector Japp of Scotland Yard. There is just a chance that he might know something about it.'

'Yes?'

'You know, Hastings, I cannot help feeling that our genial M. Croft is a little too good to be genuine.'

'And now,' he added. '*Le déjeuner*. I faint with hunger.'

CHAPTER FIFTEEN

Strange Behaviour of Frederica

Poirot's inventions about the Chief Constable were proved not to
have been so mendacious after all. Colonel Weston called upon us
soon after lunch.

He was a tall man of military carriage with considerable good-
looks. He had a suitable reverence for Poirot's achievements, with
which he seemed to be well acquainted.

'Marvellous piece of luck for us having you down here, M. Poirot,'
he said again and again.

His one fear was that he should be compelled to call in the
assistance of Scotland Yard. He was anxious to solve the mystery and
catch the criminal without their aid. Hence his delight at Poirot's
presence in the neighbourhood.

Poirot, so far as I could judge, took him completely into his
confidence.

'Deuced odd business,' said the Colonel. 'Never heard of anything
like it. Well, the girl ought to be safe enough in a nursing home. Still,
you can't keep her there for ever!'

'That, M. le Colonel, is just the difficulty. There is only one way of
dealing with it.'

'And that is?'

'We must lay our hands on the person responsible.'

'If what you suspect is true, that isn't going to be so easy.'

'*Ah! je le sais bien.*'

'Evidence! Getting evidence is going to be the devil.'

He frowned abstractedly.

'Always difficult, these cases, where there's no routine work. If we
could get hold of the pistol –'

'In all probability it is at the bottom of the sea. That is, if the
murderer had any sense.'

'Ah!' said Colonel Weston. 'But often they haven't. You'd be
surprised at the fool things people do. I'm not talking of murders –
we don't have many murders down in these parts, I'm glad to say –
but in ordinary police court cases. The sheer damn foolishness of
these people would surprise you.'

'They are of a different mentality, though,'

'Yes – perhaps. If Vyse is the chap, well, we'll have our work cut out. He's a cautious man and a sound lawyer. He'll not give himself away. The woman – well, there would be more hope there. Ten to one she'll try again. Women have no patience.'

He rose.

'Inquest tomorrow morning. Coroner will work in with us and give away as little as possible. We want to keep things dark at present.'

He was turning towards the door when he suddenly came back.

'Upon my soul, I'd forgotten the very thing that will interest you most, and that I want your opinion about.'

Sitting down again, he drew from his pocket a torn scrap of paper with writing on it and handed it to Poirot.

'My police found this when they were searching the grounds. Not far from where you were all watching the fireworks. It's the only suggestive thing they did find.'

Poirot smoothed it out. The writing was large and straggling.

'. . . *must have money at once. If not you . . . what will happen. I'm warning you.*'

Poirot frowned. He read and re-read it.

'This is interesting,' he said. 'I may keep it?'

'Certainly. There are no finger-prints on it. I'll be glad if you can make anything of it.'

Colonel Weston got to his feet again.

'I really must be off. Inquest tomorrow, as I said. By the way, you are not being called as witness – only Captain Hastings. Don't want the newspaper people to get wise to your being on the job.'

'I comprehend. What of the relations of the poor young lady?'

'The father and mother are coming from Yorkshire today. They'll arrive about half-past five. Poor souls. I'm heartily sorry for them. They are taking the body back with them the following day.'

He shook his head.

'Unpleasant business. I'm not enjoying this, M. Poirot.'

'Who could, M. le Colonel? It is, as you say, an unpleasant business.'

When he had gone, Poirot examined the scrap of paper once more.

'An important clue?' I asked.

He shrugged his shoulders.

'How can one tell? There is a hint of blackmail about it! Someone of our party that night was being pressed for money in a very unpleasant way. Of course, it is possible that it was one of

271

the strangers.'

He looked at the writing through a little magnifying glass.

'Does this writing look at all familiar to you, Hastings?'

'It reminds me a little of something – Ah! I have it – that note of Mrs Rice's.'

'Yes,' said Poirot, slowly. 'There are resemblances. Decidedly there are resemblances. It is curious. Yet I do not think that this is the writing of Madame Rice. Come in,' he said, as a knock came at the door.

It was Commander Challenger.

'Just looked in,' he explained. 'Wanted to know if you were any further forward.'

'*Parbleu*,' said Poirot. 'At this moment I am feeling that I am considerably further back. I seem to progress *en reculant*.'

'That's bad. But I don't really believe it, M. Poirot. I've been hearing all about you and what a wonderful chap you are. Never had a failure, they say.'

'That is not true,' said Poirot. 'I had a bad failure in Belgium in 1893. You recollect, Hastings? I recounted it to you. The affair of the box of chocolates.'

'I remember,' I said.

And I smiled, for at the time that Poirot told me that tale, he had instructed me to say 'chocolate box' to him if ever I should fancy he was growing conceited! He was then bitterly offended when I used the magical words only a minute and a quarter later.

'Oh, well,' said Challenger, 'that is such a long time ago it hardly counts. You are going to get to the bottom of this, aren't you?'

'That I swear. On the word of Hercule Poirot. I am the dog who stays on the scent and does not leave it.'

'Good. Got any ideas?'

'I have suspicions of two people.'

'I suppose I mustn't ask you who they are?'

'I should not tell you! You see, I might possibly be in error.'

'My *alibi* is satisfactory, I trust,' said Challenger, with a faint twinkle.

Poirot smiled indulgently at the bronzed face in front of him. 'You left Devonport at a few minutes past 8.30. You arrived here at five minutes past ten – twenty minutes after the crime had been committed. But the distance from Devonport is only just over thirty miles, and you have often done it in an hour since the road is good. So, you see, your alibi is not good at all!'

'Well, I'm –'

'You comprehend, I inquire into everything. Your *alibi*, as I say, is not good. But there are other things beside alibis. You would like, I think, to marry Mademoiselle Nick?'

The sailor's face flushed.

'I've always wanted to marry her,' he said huskily.

'Precisely. *Eh bien* – Mademoiselle Nick was engaged to another man. A reason, perhaps, for killing the other man. But that is unnecessary – he dies the death of a hero.'

'So it *is* true – that Nick was engaged to Michael Seton? There's a rumour to that effect all over the town this morning.'

'Yes – it is interesting how soon news spreads. You never suspected it before?'

'I knew Nick was engaged to someone – she told me so two days ago. But she didn't give me a clue as to whom it was.'

'It was Michael Seton. *Entre nous*, he has left her, I fancy, a very pretty fortune. Ah! assuredly, it is not a moment for killing Mademoiselle Nick – from your point of view. She weeps for her lover now, but the heart consoles itself. She is young. And I think, Monsieur, that she is very fond of you . . .'

Challenger was silent for a moment or two.

'If it should be . . .' he murmured.

There was a tap on the door.

It was Frederica Rice.

'I've been looking for you,' she said to Challenger. 'They told me you were here. I wanted to know if you'd got my wrist-watch back yet.'

'Oh, yes, I called for it this morning.'

He took it from his pocket and handed it to her. It was a watch of rather an unusual shape – round, like a globe, set on a strap of plain black moiré. I remembered that I had seen one much the same shape on Nick Buckley's wrist.

'I hope it will keep better time now.'

'It's rather a bore. Something is always going wrong with it.'

'It is for beauty, Madame, and not for utility,' said Poirot.

'Can't one have both?' She looked from one to the other of us. 'Am I interrupting a conference?'

'No, indeed, Madame. We were talking gossip – not the crime. We were saying how quickly news spreads – how that everyone now knows that Mademoiselle Nick was engaged to that brave airman who perished.'

273

'So Nick *was* engaged to Michael Seton!' exclaimed Frederica.

'It surprises you, Madame?'

'It does a little. I don't know why. Certainly I did think he was very taken with her last autumn. They went about a lot together. And then, after Christmas, they both seemed to cool off. As far as I know, they hardly met.'

'The secret, they kept it very well.'

'That was because of old Sir Matthew, I suppose. He was really a little off his head, I think.'

'You had no suspicion, Madame? And yet Mademoiselle was such an intimate friend.'

'Nick's a close little devil when she likes,' murmured Frederica. 'But I understand now why she's been so nervy lately. Oh! and I ought to have guessed from something she said only the other day.'

'Your little friend is very attractive, Madame.'

'Old Jim Lazarus used to think so at one time,' said Challenger, with his loud, rather tactless laugh.

'Oh! Jim –' She shrugged her shoulders, but I thought she was annoyed.

She turned to Poirot.

'Tell me, M. Poirot, did you –'

She stopped. Her tall figure swayed and her face turned whiter still. Her eyes were fixed on the centre of the table.

'You are not well, Madame.'

I pushed forward a chair, helped her to sink into it. She shook her head, murmured, 'I'm all right,' and leaned forward, her face between her hands. We watched her awkwardly.

She sat up in a minute.

'How absurd! George, darling, don't look so worried. Let's talk about murders. Something exciting. I want to know if M. Poirot is on the track.'

'It is early to say, Madame,' said Poirot, non-committally.

'But you have ideas – yes?'

'Perhaps. But I need a great deal more evidence.'

'Oh!' She sounded uncertain.

Suddenly she rose.

'I've got a head. I think I'll go and lie down. Perhaps tomorrow they'll let me see Nick.'

She left the room abruptly. Challenger frowned.

'You never know what that woman's up to. Nick may have been fond of her, but I don't believe she was fond of Nick. But there, you

274

can't tell with women. It's darling – darling – darling – all the time – and "damn you" would probably express it much better. Are you going out, M. Poirot?' For Poirot had risen and was carefully brushing a speck off his hat.

'Yes, I am going into the town.'

'I've got nothing to do. May I come with you.'

'Assuredly. It will be a pleasure.'

We left the room. Poirot, with an apology, went back.

'My stick,' he explained, as he rejoined us.

Challenger winced slightly. And indeed the stick, with its embossed gold band, was somewhat ornate.

Poirot's first visit was to a florist.

'I must send some flowers to Mademoiselle Nick,' he explained.

He proved difficult to suit.

In the end he chose an ornate gold basket to be filled with orange carnations. The whole to be tied up with a large blue bow.

The shopwoman gave him a card and he wrote on it with a flourish: 'With the Compliments of Hercule Poirot.'

'I sent her some flowers this morning,' said Challenger. 'I might send her some fruit.'

'*Inutile!*' said Poirot.

'What?'

'I said it was useless. The eatable – it is not permitted.'

'Who says so?'

'I say so. I have made the rule. It has already been impressed on Mademoiselle Nick. She understands.'

'Good Lord' said Challenger.

He looked thoroughly startled. He stared at Poirot curiously.

'So that's it, is it?' he said. 'You're still – afraid.'

CHAPTER SIXTEEN

Interview with Mr Whitfield

The inquest was a dry proceeding – mere bare bones. There was
evidence of identification, then I gave evidence of the finding of the
body. Medical evidence followed.

The inquest was adjourned for a week.

The St Loo murder had jumped into prominence in the daily
press. It had, in fact, succeeded 'Seton Still Missing. Unknown Fate
of Missing Airman.'

Now that Seton was dead and due tribute had been paid to his
memory, a new sensation was due. The St Loo Mystery was a
godsend to papers at their wits' end for news in the month of August.

After the inquest, having successfully dodged reporters, I met
Poirot, and we had an interview with the Rev. Giles Buckley and his
wife.

Maggie's father and mother were a charming pair, completely
unworldly and unsophisticated.

Mrs Buckley was a woman of character, tall and fair and showing
very plainly her northern ancestry. Her husband was a small man,
grey-haired, with a diffident appealing manner.

Poor souls, they were completely dazed by the misfortune that had
overtaken them and robbed them of a well-beloved daughter. 'Our
Maggie', as they called her.

'I can scarcely realize it even now,' said Mr Buckley. 'Such a dear
child, M. Poirot. So quiet and unselfish – always thinking of others.
Who could wish to harm her?'

'I could hardly understand the telegram,' said Mrs Buckley. 'Why
it was only the morning before that we had seen her off.'

'In the midst of life we are in death,' murmured her husband.

'Colonel Weston has been very kind,' said Mrs Buckley. 'He
assures us that everything is being done to find the man who did this
thing. He must be a madman. No other explanation is possible.'

'Madame, I cannot tell you how I sympathize with you in your loss
– and how I admire your bravery!'

'Breaking down would not bring Maggie back to us,' said Mrs
Buckley, sadly.

'My wife is wonderful,' said the clergyman. 'Her faith and courage
are greater than mine. It is all so – so bewildering, M. Poirot.'

'I know – I know, Monsieur.'

'You are a great detective, M. Poirot?' said Mrs Buckley.

'It has been said, Madame.'

'Oh! I know. Even in our remote country village we have heard of you. You are going to find out the truth, M. Poirot?'

'I shall not rest until I do, Madame.'

'It will be revealed to you, M. Poirot,' quavered the clergyman. 'Evil cannot go unpunished.'

'Evil never goes unpunished, Monsieur. But the punishment is sometimes secret.'

'What do you mean by that, M. Poirot?'

Poirot only shook his head.

'Poor little Nick,' said Mrs Buckley. 'I am really sorriest of all for her. I had a most pathetic letter. She says she feels she asked Maggie down here to her death.'

'That is morbid,' said Mr Buckley.

'Yes, but I know how she feels. I wish they would let me see her. It seems so extraordinary not to let her own family visit her.'

'Doctors and nurses are very strict,' said Poirot, evasively. 'They make the rules – so – and nothing will change them. And doubtless they fear for her the emotion – the natural emotion – she would experience on seeing you.'

'Perhaps,' said Mrs Buckley, doubtfully. 'But I don't hold with nursing homes. Nick would do much better if they let her come back with me – right away from this place.'

'It is possible – but I fear they will not agree. It is long since you have seen Mademoiselle Buckley?'

'I haven't seen her since last autumn. She was at Scarborough. Maggie went over and spent the day with her and then she came back and spent a night with us. She's a pretty creature – though I can't say I like her friends. And the life she leads – well, it's hardly her fault, poor child. She's had no upbringing of any kind.'

'It is a strange house – End House,' said Poirot thoughtfully.

'I don't like it,' said Mrs Buckley. 'I never have. There's something all wrong about that house. I disliked old Sir Nicholas intensely. He made me shiver.'

'Not a good man, I'm afraid,' said her husband. 'But he had a curious charm.'

'*I* never felt it,' said Mrs Buckley. 'There's an evil feeling about that house. I wish we'd never let our Maggie go there.'

'Ah! wishing,' said Mr Buckley, and shook his head.

'Well,' said Poirot. 'I must not intrude upon you any longer. I only wished to proffer to you my deep sympathy.'

'You have been very kind, M. Poirot. And we are indeed grateful for all you are doing.'

'You return to Yorkshire – when?'

'Tomorrow. A sad journey. Goodbye, M. Poirot, and thank you again.'

'Very simple delightful people,' I said, after we had left.

Poirot nodded.

'It makes the heart ache, does it not, *mon ami*? A tragedy so useless – so purposeless. *Cette jeune fille* – Ah! but I reproach myself bitterly. I, Hercule Poirot, was on the spot and I did not prevent the crime!'

'Nobody could have prevented it.'

'You speak without reflection, Hastings. No ordinary person could have prevented it – but of what good is it to be Hercule Poirot with grey cells of a finer quality than other people's, if you do not manage to do what ordinary people cannot?'

'Well, of course,' I said. 'If you are going to put it like that –'

'Yes, indeed. I am abased, downhearted – completely abased.'

I reflected that Poirot's abasement was strangely like other people's conceit, but I prudently forebore from making any remark.

'And now,' he said, '*en avant. To London.*'

'London?'

'*Mais oui.* We shall catch the two o'clock train very comfortably. All is peaceful here. Mademoiselle is safe in the nursing home. No one can harm her. The watchdogs, therefore, can take leave of absence. There are one or two little pieces of information that I require.'

Our first proceeding on arriving in London was to call upon the late Captain Seton's solicitors, Messrs Whitfield, Pargiter & Whitfield.

Poirot had arranged for an appointment beforehand, and although it was past six o'clock, we were soon closeted with Mr Whitfield, the head of the firm.

He was a very urbane and impressive person. He had in front of him a letter from the Chief Constable and another from some high official at Scotland Yard.

'This is all very irregular and unusual, M. – ah – Poirot,' he said, as he polished his eyeglasses.

'Quite so, M. Whitfield. But then murder is also irregular – and, I am glad to say, sufficiently unusual.'

'True. True. But rather far-fetched – to make a connection between this murder and my late client's bequest – eh?'

'I think not.'

'Ah! you think not. Well – under the circumstances – and I must admit that Sir Henry puts it very strongly in his letter – I shall be – er – happy to do anything that is in my power.'

'You acted as legal adviser to the late Captain Seton?'

'To all the Seton family, my dear sir. We have done so – our firm have done so, I mean – for the last hundred years.'

'*Parfaitement.* The late Sir Matthew Seton made a will?'

'We made it for him.'

'And he left his fortune – how?'

'There were several bequests – one to the Natural History Museum – but the bulk of his large – his, I may say, *very large fortune* – he left to Captain Michael Seton absolutely. He had no other near relations.'

'A very large fortune, you say?'

'The late Sir Matthew was the second richest man in England,' replied Mr Whitfield, composedly.

'He had somewhat peculiar views, had he not?' Mr Whitfield looked at him severely.

'A millionaire, M. Poirot, is allowed to be eccentric. It is almost expected of him.'

Poirot received his correction meekly and asked another question.

'His death was unexpected, I understand?'

'*Most* unexpected. Sir Matthew enjoyed remarkably good health. He had an internal growth, however, which no one had suspected. It reached a vital tissue and an immediate operation was necessary. The operation was, as always on these occasions, completely successful. But Sir Matthew died.'

'And his fortune passed to Captain Seton.'

'That is so.'

'Captain Seton had, I understand, made a will before leaving England?'

'If you can call it a will – yes,' said Mr Whitfield, with strong distaste.

'It is legal?'

'It is perfectly legal. The intention of the testator is plain and it is properly witnessed. Oh, yes, it is legal.'

'But you do not approve of it?'

'My dear sir, what are *we* for?'

I had often wondered. Having once had occasion to make a perfectly simple will myself. I had been appalled at the length and verbiage that resulted from my solicitor's office.

'The truth of the matter was,' continued Mr Whitfield, 'that at the time Captain Seton had little or nothing to leave. He was dependent on the allowance he received from his uncle. He felt, I suppose, that anything would do.'

And had thought correctly, I whispered to myself.

'And the terms of this will?' asked Poirot.

'He leaves everything of which he dies possessed to his affianced wife, Miss Magdala Buckley absolutely. He names me as his executor.

'Then Miss Buckley inherits?'

'Certainly Miss Buckley inherits.'

'And if Miss Buckley had happened to die last Monday?'

'Captain Seton having predeceased her, the money would go to whomever she had named in her will as residuary legatee – or failing a will to her next of kin.'

'I may say,' added Mr Whitfield, with an air of enjoyment, 'that death duties would have been enormous. Enormous! Three deaths, remember, in rapid succession.' He shook his head. 'Enormous!'

'But there would have been something left?' murmured Poirot, meekly.

'My dear sir, as I told you, Sir Matthew was the second richest man in England.'

Poirot rose.

'Thank you, Mr Whitfield, very much for the information that you have given me.'

'Not at all. Not at all. I may say that I shall be in communication with Miss Buckley – indeed, I believe the letter has already gone. I shall be happy to be of any service I can to her.'

'She is a young lady,' said Poirot, 'who could do with some sound legal advice.'

'There will be fortune hunters, I am afraid,' said Mr Whitfield, shaking his head.

'It seems indicated,' agreed Poirot. 'Good day, Monsieur.'

'Goodbye, M. Poirot. Glad to have been of service to you. Your name is – ah! – familiar to me.'

He said this kindly – with an air of one making a valuable admission.

'It is all exactly as you thought, Poirot,' I said, when we

were outside.

'*Mon ami*, it was bound to be. *It could not be any other way.* We will go now to the Cheshire Cheese where Japp meets us for an early dinner.'

We found Inspector Japp of Scotland Yard awaiting us at the chosen rendezvous. He greeted Poirot with every sign of warmth.

'Years since I've seen you, Moosior Poirot. Thought you were growing vegetable marrows in the country.'

'I tried, Japp, I tried. But even when you grow vegetable marrows you cannot get away from murder.'

He sighed. I knew of what he was thinking – that strange affair at Fernley Park. How I regretted that I had been far away at that time.

'And Captain Hastings too,' said Japp. 'How are you, sir?'

'Very fit, thanks,' I said.

'And now there are more murders?' continued Japp, facetiously.

'As you say – more murders.'

'Well, you mustn't be depressed, old cock,' said Japp. 'Even if you can't see your way clear – well – you can't go about at your time of life and expect to have the success you used to do. We all of us get stale as the years go by. Got to give the young 'uns a chance, you know.'

'And yet the old dog is the one who knows the tricks,' murmured Poirot. 'He is cunning. He does not leave the scent.'

'Oh! well – we're talking about human beings, not dogs.'

'Is there so much difference?'

'Well, it depends how you look at things. But you're a caution, isn't he, Captain Hastings? Always was. Looks much the same – hair a bit thinner on top but the face fungus fuller than ever.'

'Eh?' said Poirot. 'What is that?'

'He's congratulating you on your moustaches,' I said, soothingly.

'They are luxuriant, yes,' said Poirot, complacently caressing them.

Japp went off into a roar of laughter.

'Well,' he said, after a minute or two, 'I've done your bit of business. Those finger-prints you sent me –'

'Yes?' said Poirot, eagerly.

'Nothing doing. Whoever the gentleman may be – he hasn't passed through *our* hands. On the other hand, I wired to Melbourne and nobody of that description or name is known there.'

'Ah!'

'So there may be something fishy after all. But he's not one of the lads.'

281

'As to the other business,' went on Japp.

'Yes?'

'Lazarus and Son have a good reputation. Quite straight and honourable in their dealings. Sharp, of course – but that's another matter. You've got to be sharp in business. But they're all right. They're in a bad way, though – financially, I mean.'

'Oh! – is that so?'

'Yes – the slump in pictures has hit them badly. And antique furniture too. All this modern continental stuff coming into fashion. They built new premises last year and – well – as I say, they're not far from Queer Street.'

'I am much obliged to you.'

'Not at all. That sort of thing isn't my line, as you know. But I made a point of finding out as you wanted to know. We can always get information.'

'My good Japp, what should I do without you?'

'Oh! that's all right. Always glad to oblige an old friend. I let you in on some pretty good cases in the old days, didn't I?'

This, I realized, was Japp's way of acknowledging indebtedness to Poirot, who had solved many a case which had baffled the inspector.

'They were the good days – yes.'

'I wouldn't mind having a chat with you now and again even in these days. Your methods may be old-fashioned but you've got your head screwed on the right way, M. Poirot.'

'What about my other question. The Dr MacAllister?'

'Oh, him! He's a woman's doctor. I don't mean a gynaecologist. I mean one of these nerve doctors – tell you to sleep in purple walls and orange ceiling – talk to you about your libido, whatever that is – tell you to let it rip. He's a bit of a quack, if you ask me – but he gets the women all right. They flock to him. Goes abroad a good deal – does some kind of medical work in Paris, I believe.'

'Why Dr MacAllister?' I asked, bewildered. I had never heard of the name. 'Where does he come in?'

'Dr MacAllister is the uncle of Commander Challenger,' explained Poirot. 'You remember he referred to an uncle who was a doctor?'

'How thorough you are,' I said. 'Did you think he had operated on Sir Matthew?'

'He's not a surgeon,' said Japp.

'*Mon ami*,' said Poirot, 'I like to inquire into everything. Hercule Poirot is a good dog. The good dog follows the scent, and if, regrettably, there is no scent to follow, he noses around – seeking

282

always something that is not very nice. So also, does Hercule Poirot. And often – Oh! so often – does he find it!'

'It's not a nice profession, ours,' said Japp. 'Stilton, did you say? I don't mind if I do. No, it's not a nice profession. And yours is worse than mine – not official, you see, and therefore a lot more worming yourself into places in underhand ways.'

'I do not disguise myself, Japp. Never have I disguised myself.'

'You couldn't,' said Japp. 'You're unique. Once seen, never forgotten.'

Poirot looked at him rather doubtfully.

'Only my fun,' said Japp. 'Don't mind me. Glass of port? Well, if you say so.'

The evening became thoroughly harmonious. We were soon in the middle of reminiscences. This case, that case, and the other. I must say that I, too, enjoyed talking over the past. Those had been good days. How old and experienced I felt now!

'Poor old Poirot. He was perplexed by this case – I could see that. His powers were not what they were. I had the feeling that he was going to fail – that the murderer of Maggie Buckley would never be brought to book.

'Courage, my friend,' said Poirot, slapping me on the shoulder. 'All is not lost. Do not pull the long face, I beg of you.'

'That's all right. I'm all right.'

'And so am I. And so is Japp.'

'We're all all right,' declared Japp, hilariously.

And on this pleasant note we parted.

The following morning we journeyed back to St Loo. On arrival at the hotel Poirot rang up the nursing home and asked to speak to Nick.

Suddenly I saw his face change – he almost dropped the instrument.

'*Comment?* What is that? Say it again, I beg.'

He waited for a minute or two listening. Then he said:

'Yes, yes, I will come at once.'

He turned a pale face to me.

'Why did I go away, Hastings? *Mon Dieu!* Why did I go away?'

'What has happened?'

'Mademoiselle Nick is dangerously ill. Cocaine poisoning. They have got at her after all. *Mon Dieu! Mon Dieu! Why did I go away?*'

CHAPTER SEVENTEEN

A Box of Chocolates

All the way to the nursing home Poirot murmured and muttered to himself. He was full of self-reproach.

'I should have known,' he groaned. 'I should have known! And yet, what could I do? I took every precaution. It is impossible – impossible. *No one* could get to her! Who has disobeyed my orders?'

At the nursing home we were shown into a little room downstairs, and after a few minutes Dr Graham came to us. He looked exhausted and white.

'She'll do,' he said. 'It's going to be all right. The trouble was knowing how much she'd taken of the damned stuff.'

'What was it?'

'Cocaine.'

'She will live?'

'Yes, yes, she'll live.'

'But how did it happen? How did they get at her? Who has been allowed in?' Poirot fairly danced with impotent excitement.

'Nobody has been allowed in.'

'Impossible.'

'It's true.'

'But then–'

'It was a box of chocolates.'

'Ah! *sacré*. And I told her to eat *nothing – nothing –* that came from outside.'

'I don't know about that. It's hard work keeping a girl from a box of chocolates. She only ate one, thank goodness.'

'Was the cocaine in all the chocolates?'

'No. The girl ate one. There were two others in the top layer. The rest were all right.

'How was it done?'

'Quite clumsily. Chocolate cut in half – the cocaine mixed with the filling and the chocolate stuck together again. Amateurishly. What you might call a home-made job.'

Poirot groaned.

'Ah! if I knew – if I knew. Can I see Mademoiselle?'

'If you come back in an hour I think you can see her,' said the doctor. 'Pull yourself together, man. She isn't going to die.'

For another hour we walked the streets of St Loo. I did my best to distract Poirot's mind – pointing out to him that all was well, that, after all, no mischief had been done.

But he only shook his head, and repeated at intervals:

'*I am afraid, Hastings, I am afraid ...*'

And the strange way he said it made me, too, feel afraid.

Once he caught me by the arm.

'Listen, my friend. *I am all wrong.* I have been all wrong from the beginning.'

'You mean it isn't the money –'

'No, no, I am right about that. Oh, yes. But those two – it is too simple – too easy, that. There is another twist still. Yes, there is something!'

And then in an outburst of indignation:

'*Ah! cette petite!* Did I not *forbid* her? Did I not say, "Do not touch anything from outside?" And she disobeys me – me, Hercule Poirot. Are not four escapes from death enough for her? Must she take a fifth chance? *Ah, c'est inouï!*'

At last we made our way back. After a brief wait we were conducted upstairs.

Nick was sitting up in bed. The pupils of her eyes were widely dilated. She looked feverish and her hands kept twitching violently.

'At it again,' she murmured.

Poirot experienced real emotion at the sight of her. He cleared his throat and took her hand in his.

'Ah! Mademoiselle – Mademoiselle.'

'I shouldn't care,' she said, defiantly, 'if they *had* got me this time. I'm sick of it all – sick of it!'

'*Pauvre petite!*'

'Something in me doesn't like to give them best!'

'That is the spirit – *le sport* – you must be the good sport, Mademoiselle.'

'Your old nursing home hasn't been so safe after all,' said Nick.

'If you had obeyed orders, Mademoiselle –'

She looked faintly astonished.

'But I have.'

'Did I not impress upon you that you were to eat nothing that came from outside?'

'No more I did.'

'But these chocolates –'

'Well, they were all right. *You* sent them.'

285

'What is that you say, Mademoiselle?'

'*You* sent them!'

'Me? Never. Never anything of the kind.'

'But you *did*. Your card was in the box.'

'What?'

Nick made a spasmodic gesture towards the table by the bed. The nurse came forward.

'You want the card that was in the box?'

'Yes, please, nurse.'

There was a moment's pause. The nurse returned to the room with it in her hand.

'Here it is.'

I gasped. So did Poirot. For on the card, in flourishing handwriting, were written the same words that I had seen Poirot inscribe on the card that accompanied the basket of flowers.

'With the Compliments of Hercule Poirot.'

'*Sacré tonnerre!*'

'You see,' said Nick, accusingly.

'I did not write this!' cried Poirot.

'What?'

'And yet,' murmured Poirot, 'and yet it is my handwriting.'

'I know. It's exactly the same as the card that came with the orange carnations. I never doubted that the chocolates came from you.'

Poirot shook his head.

'How should you doubt? Oh! the devil! The clever, cruel devil! To think of *that*! Ah! but he has genius, this man, genius! "*With the Compliments of Hercule Poirot.*" So simple. Yes, but one had to think of it. And I – I did not *think*. I omitted to foresee this move.'

Nick moved restlessly.

'Do not agitate yourself, Mademoiselle. You are blameless – blameless. It is I that am to blame, miserable imbecile that I am! I should have foreseen this move. Yes, I should have foreseen it.'

His chin dropped on his breast. He looked the picture of misery.

'I really think –' said the nurse.

She had been hovering nearby, a disapproving expression on her face.

'Eh? Yes, yes, I will go. Courage, Mademoiselle. This is the last mistake I will make. I am ashamed, desolated – I have been tricked, outwitted – as though I were a little schoolboy. *But it shall not happen again*. No. I promise you. Come, Hastings.'

Poirot's first proceeding was to interview the matron. She was, naturally, terribly upset over the whole business.

'It seems incredible to me, M. Poirot, absolutely incredible. That a thing like that should happen in my nursing home.'

Poirot was sympathetic and tactful. Having soothed her sufficiently, he began to inquire into the circumstance of the arrival of the fatal packet. Here, the matron declared, he would do best to interview the orderly who had been on duty at the time of its arrival.

The man in question, whose name was Hood, was a stupid but honest-looking young fellow of about twenty-two. He looked nervous and frightened. Poirot put him at his ease, however.

'No blame can be attached to you,' he said kindly. 'But I want you to tell me exactly when and how this parcel arrived.'

The orderly looked puzzled.

'It's difficult to say, sir,' he said, slowly. 'Lots of people come and inquire and leave things for the different patients.'

'The nurse says this came last night,' I said. 'About six o'clock.'

The lad's face brightened.

'I do remember, now, sir. A gentleman brought it.'

'A thin-faced gentleman – fair-haired?'

'He was fair-haired – but I don't know about thin-faced.'

'Would Charles Vyse bring it himself?' I murmured to Poirot.

I had forgotten that the lad would know a local name.

'It wasn't Mr Vyse,' he said. 'I know him. It was a bigger gentleman – handsome-looking – came in a big car.'

'Lazarus,' I exclaimed.

Poirot shot me a warning glance and I regretted my precipitance.

'He came in a large car and he left this parcel. It was addressed to Miss Buckley?'

'Yes, sir.'

'And what did you do with it?'

'I didn't touch it, sir. Nurse took it up.'

'Quite so, but you touched it when you took it from the gentleman, *n'est ce pas?*'

'Oh! that, yes, of course, sir. I took it from him and put it on the table.'

'Which table? Show me, if you please.'

The orderly led us into the hall. The front door was open. Close to it, in the hall, was a long marble-topped table on which lay letters and parcels.

'Everything that comes is put on here, sir. Then the nurses take things up to the patients.'

'Do you remember what time this parcel was left?'

'Must have been about five-thirty, or a little after. I know the post had just been, and that's usually at about half-past five. It was a pretty busy afternoon, a lot of people leaving flowers and coming to see patients.'

'Thank you. Now, I think, we will see the nurse who took up the parcel.'

This proved to be one of the probationers, a fluffy little person all agog with excitement. She remembered taking the parcel up at six o'clock when she came on duty.

'Six o'clock,' murmured Poirot. 'Then it must have been twenty minutes or so that the parcel was lying on the table downstairs.'

'Pardon?'

'Nothing, Mademoiselle. Continue. You took the parcel to Miss Buckley?'

'Yes, there were several things for her. There was this box and some flowers also – sweet peas – from a Mr and Mrs Croft, I think. I took them up at the same time. And there was a parcel that had come by post – and curiously enough *that* was a box of Fuller's chocolates also.'

'*Comment?* A second box?'

'Yes, rather a coincidence. Miss Buckley opened them both. She said— "Oh! what a shame. I'm not allowed to eat them." Then she opened the lids to look inside and see if they were both just the same, and your card was in one and she said, "Take the other impure box away, nurse. I might have got them mixed up." Oh! dear, whoever would have thought of such a thing? Seems like an Edgar Wallace, doesn't it?'

Poirot cut short this flood of speech.

'Two boxes, you say? From whom was the other box?'

'There was no name inside.'

'And which was the one that came – that had the appearance of coming – from me? The one by post or the other?'

'I declare now – I can't remember. Shall I go up and ask Miss Buckley?'

'If you would be so amiable.'

She ran up the stairs.

'Two boxes,' murmured Poirot. 'There is confusion for you.'

The nurse returned breathless.

'Miss Buckley isn't sure. She unwrapped them both before she looked inside. But she thinks it wasn't the box that came by post.'

'Eh?' said Poirot, a little confused.

'The box from you was the one that didn't come by post. At least she thinks so, but she isn't quite sure.'

'*Diable!*' said Poirot, as we walked away. 'Is no one ever quite sure? In detective books – yes. But life – real life – is always full of muddle. Am I sure, myself, about anything at all? No, no – a thousand times, no.'

'Lazarus,' I said.'

'Yes, that is a surprise, is it not?'

'Shall you say anything to him about it?'

'Assuredly. I shall be interested to see how he takes it. By the way, we might as well exaggerate the serious condition of Mademoiselle. It will do no harm to let it be assumed that she is at death's door. You comprehend? The solemn face – yes, admirable. You resemble closely an undertaker. *C'est tout à fait bien.*'

We were lucky in finding Lazarus. He was bending over the bonnet of his car outside the hotel.

Poirot went straight up to him.

'Yesterday evening, Monsieur Lazarus, you left a box of chocolates for Mademoiselle,' he began without preamble.

Lazarus looked rather surprised.

'Yes.'

'That was very amiable of you.'

'As a matter of fact they were from Freddie, from Mrs Rice. She asked me to get them.'

'Oh! I see.'

'I took them round in the car.'

'I comprehend.'

He was silent for a minute or two and then said:

'Madame Rice, where is she?'

'I think she's in the lounge.'

We found Frederica having tea. She looked up at us with an anxious face.

'What is this I hear about Nick being taken ill?'

'It is a most mysterious affair, Madame. Tell me, did you send her a box of chocolates yesterday?'

'Yes. At least she asked me to get them for her.'

'*She* asked you to get them for her?'

'Yes.'

'But she was not allowed to see anyone. How did you see her?'

'I didn't. She telephoned.'

289

'Ah! And she said – what?'

'Would I get her a two-pound box of Fuller's chocolates.'

'How did her voice sound – weak?'

'No – not at all. Quite strong. But different somehow. I didn't realize it was she speaking at first.'

'Until she told you who she was?'

'Yes.'

'Are you sure, Madame, that it *was* your friend?'

Frederica looked startled.

'I – I – why, of course it was. Who else could it have been?'

'That is an interesting question, Madame.'

'You don't mean –'

'*Could you swear*, Madame, that it was your friend's voice – apart from what she said?'

'No,' said Frederica, slowly, 'I couldn't. Her voice was certainly different. I thought it was the phone – or perhaps being ill . . .'

'If she had not told you who she was, you would not have recognized it?'

'No, no, I don't think I should. Who was it, M. Poirot? Who was it?'

'That is what I mean to know, Madame.'

The graveness of his face seemed to awaken her suspicions.

'Is Nick – has anything happened?' she asked, breathlessly.

Poirot nodded.

'She is ill – dangerously ill. Those chocolates, Madame – were poisoned.'

'The chocolates *I* sent her? But that's impossible – impossible!'

'Not impossible, Madame, since Mademoiselle is at death's door.'

'Oh, my God.' She hid her face in her hands, then raised it white and quivering. 'I don't understand – I don't understand. The other, yes, but not this. They couldn't be poisoned. Nobody ever touched them but me and Jim. You're making some dreadful mistake, M. Poirot.'

'It is not I that make a mistake – even though my name was in the box.'

She stared at him blankly.

'If Mademoiselle Nick dies –' he said, and made a threatening gesture with his hand.

She gave a low cry.

He turned away, and taking me by the arm, went up to the sitting-room.

He flung his hat on the table.

'I understand nothing – but nothing! I am in the dark. I am a little child. Who stands to gain by Mademoiselle's death? Madame Rice. Who buys the chocolates and admits it and tells a story of being rung up on the telephone that cannot hold water for a minute? Madame Rice. It is too simple – too stupid. And she is not stupid – no.'

'Well, then –'

'But she takes cocaine, Hastings. I am certain she takes cocaine. There is no mistaking it. And there was cocaine in those chocolates. And what did she mean when she said, "*The other, yes, but not this.*" It needs explaining, that! And the sleek M. Lazarus – what is *he* doing in all this? What does she know, Madame Rice? She knows something. But I cannot make her speak. She is not of those you can frighten into speech. But she knows something, Hastings. Is her tale of the telephone true, or did she invent it? If it is true whose voice was it?

'I tell you, Hastings. This is all very black – very black.'

'Always darkest before dawn,' I said reassuringly.

He shook his head.

'Then the other box – that came by post. Can we rule that out? No, we cannot, because Mademoiselle is not sure. It is an annoyance, that!'

He groaned.

I was about to speak when he stopped me.

'No, no. Not another proverb. I cannot bear it. If you would be the good friend – the good helpful friend –'

'Yes,' I said eagerly.

'Go out, I beg of you, and buy me some playing cards.'

I stared.

'Very well,' I said coldly.

I could not but suspect that he was making a deliberate excuse to get rid of me.

Here, however, I misjudged him. That night, when I came into the sitting-room about ten o'clock, I found Poirot carefully building card houses – and I remembered!

It was an old trick of his – soothing his nerves. He smiled at me.

'Yes – you remember. One needs the precision. One card on another – so – in exactly the right place and that supports the weight of the card on top and so on, up and up. Go to bed, Hastings. Leave me here, with my house of cards. I clear the mind.'

It was about five in the morning when I was shaken awake.

Poirot was standing by my bedside. He looked pleased and happy.

'It was very just what you said, *mon ami*. Oh! it was very just. More, it was *spirituel*!'

I blinked at him, being imperfectly awake.

'Always darkest before dawn – that is what you said. It has been very dark – and now it is dawn.'

I looked at the window. He was perfectly right.

'No, no, Hastings. In the head! The mind! The little grey cells!'

He paused and then said quietly:

'You see, Hastings, Mademoiselle is dead.'

'What?' I cried, suddenly wide awake.

'Hush – hush. It is as I say. Not really – *bien entendu* – but it can be arranged. Yes, for twenty-four hours it can be arranged. I arrange it with the doctor, with the nurses.

'You comprehend, Hastings? *The murderer has been successful.* Four times he has tried and failed. The fifth time he has succeeded.'

'*And now, we shall see what happens next* . . .

'It will be very interesting.'

CHAPTER EIGHTEEN

The Face at the Window

The events of the next day are completely hazy in my memory. I was unfortunate enough to awake with fever on me. I have been liable to these bouts of fever at inconvenient times ever since I once contracted malaria.

In consequence, the events of that day take on in my memory the semblance of a nightmare – with Poirot coming and going as a kind of fantastic clown, making a periodic appearance in a circus.

He was, I fancy, enjoying himself to the full. His poise of baffled despair was admirable. How he achieved the end he had in view and which he had disclosed to me in the early hours of the morning, I cannot say. But achieve it he did.

It cannot have been easy. The amount of deception and subterfuge involved must have been colossal. The English character is averse to lying on a wholesale scale and that, no less, was what Poirot's plan required. He had, first, to get Dr Graham converted to the scheme. With Dr Graham on his side, he had to persuade the Matron and some members of the staff of the nursing home to conform to the plan. There again, the difficulties must have been immense. It was probably Dr Graham's influence that turned the scale.

Then there was the Chief Constable and the police. Here, Poirot would be up against officialdom. Nevertheless he wrung at last an unwilling consent out of Colonel Weston. The Colonel made it clear that it was in no way his responsibility. Poirot and Poirot alone was responsible for the spreading abroad of these lying reports. Poirot agreed. He would have agreed to anything so long as he was permitted to carry out his plan.

I spent most of the day dozing in a large armchair with a rug over my knees. Every two or three hours or so, Poirot would burst in and report progress.

'*Comment ça va, mon ami?* How I commiserate you. But it is as well, perhaps. The farce, you do not play it as well as I do. I come this moment from ordering a wreath – a wreath immense – stupendous. Lilies, my friend – large quantities of lilies. "*With heartfelt regret. From Hercule Poirot.*" Ah! what a comedy.'

He departed again.

'I come from a most poignant conversation with Madame Rice,'

293

was his next piece of information. 'Very well dressed in black, that one. Her poor friend – what a tragedy! I groan sympathetically. Nick, she says, was so joyous, so full of life. Impossible to think of her as dead. I agree. "It is," I say, "the irony of death that it takes one like that. The old and useless are left." Oh! *là là!* I groan again.'

'How you are enjoying this,' I murmured feebly.

'*Du tout.* It is part of my plan, that is all. To play the comedy successfully, you must put the heart into it. Well, then, the conventional expressions of regret over, Madame comes to matters nearer home. All night she has lain awake wondering about those sweets. It is impossible – impossible. "Madame," I say, "it is not impossible. You can see the analyst's report." Then she says, and her voice is far from steady, "It was – *cocaine*, you say?" I assent. And she says, "Oh, my God. I don't understand." '

'Perhaps that's true.'

'She understands well enough that she is in danger. She is intelligent. I told you that before. Yes, she is in danger, and she knows it.'

'And yet it seems to me that for the first time you don't believe her guilty.'

Poirot frowned. The excitement of his manner abated.

'It is profound what you say there, Hastings. No – it seems to me that – somehow – the facts no longer fit. These crimes – so far what has marked them most – the subtlety, is it not? And here is no subtlety at all – only the crudity, pure and simple. No, it does not fit.'

He sat down at the table.

'*Voilà* – let us examine the facts. There are three possibilities. There are the sweets bought by Madame and delivered by M. Lazarus. And in that case the guilt rests with one or the other or *both*. And the telephone call, supposedly from Mademoiselle Nick, that is an invention pure and simple. That is the straightforward – the obvious solution.

'Solution 2: The *other* box of sweets – that which came by post. Anyone may have sent those. Any of the suspects on our list from A. to J. (You remember? A very wide field.) But, if that were the guilty box, *what is the point of the telephone call?* Why complicate matters with a second box?'

I shook my head feebly. With a temperature of 102, any complication seemed to me quite unnecessary and absurd.

'Solution 3: A poisoned box was substituted for the innocent box bought by Madame. In that case the telephone call is ingenious and understandable. Madame is to be what you call the kitten's paw. She is to pull the roasting chestnuts out of the fire. So Solution 3 is the most logical – but, alas, it is also the most difficult. How be sure of substituting a box at the right moment? The orderly might take the box straight upstairs – a hundred and one possibilities might prevent the substitution being effected. No, it does not seem sense.'

'Unless it were Lazarus,' I said.

Poirot looked at me.

'You have the fever, my friend. It mounts, does it not?'

I nodded.

'Curious how a few degrees of heat should stimulate the intellect. You have uttered there an observation of profound simplicity. So simple, was it, that I had failed to consider it. But it would suppose a very curious state of affairs. M. Lazarus, the dear friend of Madame, doing his best to get her hanged. It opens up possibilities of a very curious nature. But complex – very complex.'

I closed my eyes. I was glad I had been brilliant, but I did not want to think of anything complex. I wanted to go to sleep.

Poirot, I think, went on talking, but I did not listen. His voice was vaguely soothing . . .

It was late afternoon when I saw him next.

'My little plan, it has made the fortune of flower shops,' he announced. 'Everybody orders wreaths. M. Croft, M. Vyse, Commander Challenger –'

The last name awoke a chord of compunction in my mind.

'Look here, Poirot,' I said. 'You must let him in on this. Poor fellow, he will be distracted with grief. It isn't fair.'

'You have always the tenderness for him, Hastings.'

'I like him. He's a thoroughly decent chap. You've got to take him into the secret.'

Poirot shook his head.

'No, *mon ami*. I do not make the exceptions.'

'But you don't suspect him to have anything to do with it?'

'I do not make the exceptions.'

'Think how he must be suffering.'

'On the contrary, I prefer to think of what a joyful surprise I prepare for him. To think the loved one dead – and find her alive! It is a sensation unique – stupendous.'

'What a pig-headed old devil you are. He'd keep the secret all right.'

'I am not so sure.'

295

'He's the soul of honour. I'm certain of it.'

'That makes it all the more difficult to keep a secret. Keeping a secret is an art that requires many lies magnificently told, and a great aptitude for playing the comedy and enjoying it. Could he dissemble, the Commander Challenger? If he is what you say he is, he certainly could *not*.'

'Then you won't tell him?'

'I certainly refuse to imperil my little idea for the sake of the sentiment. It is life and death we lay with, *mon cher*. Anyway, the suffering, it is good for the character. Many of your famous clergymen have said so – even a Bishop if I am not mistaken.'

I made no further attempt to shake his decision. His mind, I could see, was made up.

'I shall not dress for dinner,' he murmured. 'I am too much the broken old man. That is my part, you understand. All my self-confidence has crashed – I am broken. I have failed. I shall eat hardly any dinner – the food untasted on the plate. That is the attitude, I think. In my own apartment I will consume some brioches and some chocolate *éclairs* (so called) which I had the foresight to buy at a confectioners. *Et vous?*'

'Some more quinine, I think,' I said, sadly.

'Alas, my poor Hastings. But courage, all will be well to-morrow.'

'Very likely. These attacks often last only twenty-four hours.'

I did not hear him return to the room. I must have been asleep. When I awoke, he was sitting at the table writing. In front of him was a crumpled sheet of paper smoothed out. I recognized it for the paper on which he had written that list of people – A. to J. – which he had afterwards crumpled up and thrown away.

He nodded in answer to my unspoken thought.

'Yes, my friend. I have resurrected it. I am at work upon it from a different angle. I compile a list of questions concerning each person. The questions may have no bearing on the crime – they are just things that I do not know – things that remain unexplained, and for which I seek to supply the answer from my own brain.'

'How far have you got?'

'I have finished. You would like to hear? You are strong enough?'

'Yes, as a matter of fact, I am feeling a great deal better.'

'*A la bonne heure!* Very well, I will read them to you. Some of them, no doubt, you will consider puerile.'

He cleared his throat.

'A. *Ellen.* – Why did she remain in the house and not go out to see

296

fireworks? (Unusual, as Mademoiselle's evidence and surprise make clear.) What did she think or suspect might happen? Did she admit anyone (J. for instance) to the house? Is she speaking the truth about the secret panel? If there is such a thing why is she unable to remember where it is? (Mademoiselle seems very certain there is no such thing – and she would surely know.) If she invented it, why did she invent it? Had she read Michael Seton's love letters or was her surprise at Mademoiselle Nick's engagement genuine?

'B. *Her Husband.* – Is he as stupid as he seems? Does he share Ellen's knowledge, whatever it is, or does he not? Is he, in any respect, a mental case?

'C. *The Child.* – Is his delight in blood a natural instinct common to his age and development, or is it morbid, and is that morbidity inherited from either parent? Has he ever shot with a toy pistol?

'D. *Who is Mr Croft?* – Where does he really come from? Did he post the will as he swears he did? What motive could he have in *not* posting it?

'E. *Mrs Croft. Same as above.* – Who *are* Mr and Mrs Croft? Are they in hiding for some reason – and if so, what reason? Have they any connection with the Buckley family?

'F. *Mrs Rice.* – Was she really aware of the engagement between Nick and Michael Seton? Did she merely guess it, or had she actually read the letters which passed between them? (In that case she would know Mademoiselle was Seton's heir.) Did she know that she herself was Mademoiselle's residuary legatee? (This, I think, is likely. Mademoiselle would probably tell her so, adding perhaps that she would not get much out of it.) Is there any truth in Commander Challenger's suggestion that Lazarus was attracted by Mademoiselle Nick? (This might explain a certain lack of cordiality between the two friends which seems to have shown itself in the last few months.) Who is the 'boy friend' mentioned in her note as supplying the drug? *Could this possibly be J.?* Why did she turn faint one day in this room? Was it something that had been said – or was it something she *saw*? Is her account of the telephone message asking her to buy chocolates correct – or is it a deliberate lie? What did she mean by "I can understand the other – but not this"? If she is not herself guilty, what knowledge has she got that she is keeping to herself?'

297

'You perceive,' said Poirot, suddenly breaking off, 'that the questions concerning Madame Rice are almost innumerable. From beginning to end, she is an enigma. And that forces me to a conclusion. Either Madame Rice is guilty – or she knows – or shall we say, thinks she knows – who *is* guilty. But is she right? Does she know or does she merely suspect? And how is it possible to make her speak?'

He sighed.

'Well, I will go on with my list of questions.

'G. *Mr. Lazarus.* – Curious – there are practically no questions to ask concerning him – except the crude one, 'Did he substitute the poisoned sweets?' Otherwise I find only one totally irrelevant question. But I have put it down. 'Why did M. Lazarus offer fifty pounds for a picture that was only worth twenty?'

'He wanted to do Nick a good turn,' I suggested.

'He would not do it that way. He is a dealer. He does not buy to sell at a loss. If he wished to be amiable he would lend her money as a private individual.'

'It can't have any bearing on the crime, anyway.'

'No, that is true – but all the same, I should like to know. I am a student of the psychology, you understand.'

'Now we come to H.'

'H. *Commander Challenger.* – Why did Mademoiselle Nick tell him she was engaged to someone else? What necessitated her having to tell him that? She told no one else. Had he proposed to her? What are his relations with his uncle?'

'His uncle, Poirot?'

'Yes, the doctor. That rather questionable character. Did any private news of Michael Seton's death come through to the Admiralty before it was announced publicly?'

'I don't quite see what you're driving at Poirot. Even if Challenger knew beforehand about Seton's death, it does not seem to get us anywhere. It provides no earthly motive for killing the girl he loved.'

'I quite agree. What you say is perfectly reasonable. But these are just things I should like to know. I am still the dog, you see, nosing about for the things that are not very nice!'

'I. *M. Vyse.* – Why did he say what he did about his cousin's fanatical devotion to End House? What possible motive could he have in saying that? Did he, or did he not, receive the will? Is he, in fact, an honest man – or is he not an honest man?

'*And now J.* – *Eh bien*, J. is what I put down before – a giant question mark. Is there such a person, or is there not –

'*Mon Dieu!* my friend, what have you?'

I had started from my chair with a sudden shriek. With a shaking hand I pointed at the window.

'A face, Poirot!' I cried. 'A face pressed against the glass. A dreadful face! It's gone now – but I saw it.'

Poirot strode to the window and pushed it open. He leant out.

'There is no one there now,' he said, thoughtfully. 'You are sure you did not imagine it, Hastings?'

'Quite sure. It was a horrible face.'

'There is a balcony, of course, Anyone could reach there quite easily if they wanted to hear what we were saying. When you say a dreadful face, Hastings, just what do you mean?'

'A white, staring face, hardly human.'

'*Mon ami*, that is the fever. A face, yes. An unpleasant face, yes. But a face hardly human – *no*. What you saw was the effect of a face pressed closely against the glass – that allied to the shock of seeing it there at all.'

'It was a dreadful face,' I said, obstinately.

'It was not the face of – anyone you know?'

'No, indeed.'

'H'm – it might have been, though! I doubt if you would recognize it under these circumstances. I wonder now – yes, I very much wonder . . .'

He gathered up his papers thoughtfully.

'One thing at least is to the good. If the owner of that face overheard our conversation we did not mention that Mademoiselle Nick was alive and well. Whatever else our visitor may have heard, that at least escaped him.'

'But surely,' I said, 'the results of this – eh – brilliant manoeuvre of yours have been slightly disappointing up to date. Nick is dead and no startling developments have occurred!'

'I did not expect them yet awhile. Twenty-fours hours, I said. *Mon ami, tomorrow, if I am not mistaken, certain things will arise. Otherwise* – otherwise I am wrong from start to finish. There is the post, you

299

see. I have hopes of tomorrow's post.'

I awoke in the morning feeling weak but with the fever abated. I also felt hungry. Poirot and I had breakfast served in our sitting-room.

'Well?' I said, maliciously, as he sorted his letters. 'Has the post done what you expected of it?'

Poirot, who had just opened two envelopes which patently contained bills, did not reply. I thought he looked rather cast down and not his usual cock-a-hoop self.

I opened my own mail. The first was a notice of a spiritualist meeting.

'If all else fails, we must go to the spiritualists,' I remarked. 'I often wonder that more tests of this kind aren't made. The spirit of the victim comes back and names the murderer. That would be a proof.'

'It would hardly help us,' said Poirot, absently. 'I doubt if Maggie Buckley knew whose hand it was shot her down. Even if she could speak she would have nothing of value to tell us. *Tiens!* that is odd.'

'What is?'

'You talk of the dead speaking, and at that moment I open this letter.'

He tossed it across to me. It was from Mrs Buckley and ran as follows:

> '*Langley Rectory.*
> '*Dear Monsieur Poirot*, – On my return here I found a letter written by my poor child on her arrival at St Loo. There is nothing in it of interest to you, I'm afraid, but I thought perhaps you would care to see it.
> 'Thanking you for your kindness,
> 'Your sincerely,
> 'JEAN BUCKLEY.'

The enclosure brought a lump to my throat. It was so terribly commonplace and so completely untouched by any apprehension of tragedy:

> '*Dear Mother*, – I arrived safely. Quite a comfortable journey. Only two people in the carriage all the way to Exeter.
> 'It is lovely weather here. Nick seems very well and gay – a little restless, perhaps, but I cannot see why she should have telegraphed for me in the way she did. Tuesday would have done just as well.

300

'No more now. We are going to have tea with some neighbours. They are Australians and have rented the lodge. Nick says they are kind but rather awful. Mrs Rice and Mr Lazarus are coming to stay. He is the art dealer. I will post this in the box by the gate, then it will catch the post. Will write to-morrow.

'Your loving daughter,

'MAGGIE.'

'P.S. – Nick says there *is* a reason for her wire. She will tell me after tea. She is very queer and jumpy.'

'The voice of the dead,' said Poirot, quietly. 'And it tells us – nothing.'

'The box by the gate,' I remarked idly. 'That's where Croft said he posted the will.'

'Said so – yes. I wonder. How I wonder!'

'There is nothing else of interest among your letters?'

'Nothing. Hastings, I am very unhappy. I am in the dark. Still in the dark. I comprehend nothing.'

At that moment the telephone rang. Poirot went to it.

Immediately I saw a change come over her face. His manner was very restrained, nevertheless he could not disguise from my eyes his intense excitement.

His own contributions to the conversation were entirely non-committal so that I could not gather what it was all about.

Presently, however, with a '*Très bien. Je vous remercie*,' he put back the receiver and came back to where I was sitting. His eyes were sparkling with excitement.

'*Mon ami*,' he said. '*What did I tell you?* Things have begun to happen.'

'What was it?'

'That was M. Charles Vyse on the telephone. He informs me that this morning, through the post, he has received a will signed by his cousin, Miss Buckley, and dated the 25th February last.'

'What? *The* will?'

'*Evidemment.*'

'It has turned up?'

'Just at the right moment, *n'est-ce pas?*'

'Do you think he is speaking the truth?'

'Or do I think he has had the will all along? Is that what you would say? Well, it is all a little curious. But one thing is certain; I told you that, if Mademoiselle Nick were supposed to be dead, we should have developments – and sure enough here they are!'

'Extraordinary,' I said. 'You were right. I suppose this is the will making Frederica Rice residuary legatee?'

'M. Vyse said nothing about the contents of the will. He was far too correct. But there seems very little reason to doubt that this is the same will. It is witnessed, he tells me, by Ellen Wilson and her husband.'

'So we are back at the old problem,' I said. 'Frederica Rice.'

'The enigma!'

'Frederica Rice,' I murmured, inconsequently. 'It's a pretty name.'

'Prettier than what her friends call her. Freddie' – he made a face – 'ce n'est pas joli – for a young lady.'

'There aren't many abbreviations of Frederica,' I said. 'It's not like Margaret where you can have half a dozen – Maggie, Margot, Madge, Peggie –'

'True. Well, Hastings, are you happier now? That things have begun to happen?'

'Yes, of course. Tell me – did you expect *this* to happen?'

'No – not exactly. I had formulated nothing very precise to myself. All I had said was that given a certain result, the causes of that result must make themselves evident.'

'Yes,' I said, respectfully.

'What was it that I was going to say just as that telephone rang?' mused Poirot. 'Oh, yes, that letter from Mademoiselle Maggie. I wanted to look at it once again. I have an idea in the back of my mind that something in it struck me as rather curious.'

I picked it up from where I had tossed it, and handed it to him.

He read it over to himself. I moved about the room, looking out of the window and observing the yachts racing on the bay.

Suddenly an exclamation startled me. I turned round. Poirot was holding his head in his hands and rocking himself to and fro, apparently in an agony of woe.

'Oh!' he groaned. 'But I have been blind – blind.'

'What's the matter?'

'Complex, I have said? Complicated? *Mais non*. Of a simplicity extreme – extreme. And miserable one that I am, I saw nothing – nothing.'

'Good gracious, Poirot, what is this light that has suddenly burst upon you?'

'Wait – wait – do not speak! I must arrange my ideas. Rearrange them in the light of this discovery so stupendous.'

Seizing his list of questions, he ran over them silently, his lips moving busily. Once or twice he nodded his head emphatically.

Then he laid them down and leaning back in his chair he shut his eyes. I thought at last that he had gone to sleep.

Suddenly he sighed and opened his eyes.

'But yes!' he said. 'It all fits in! All the things that have puzzled me. All the things that have seemed to me a little unnatural. They all have their place.'

'You mean – you know everything?'

'Nearly everything. All that matters. In some respects I have been right in my deductions. In other ways ludicrously far from the truth. But now it is all clear. I shall send today a telegram asking two questions – but the answers to them I know already – I know *here*!' He tapped his forehead.

'And when you receive the answers?' I asked, curiously.

He sprang to his feet.

'My friend, do you remember that Mademoiselle Nick said she wanted to stage a play at End House? Tonight, we stage such a play in End House. But it will be a play produced by Hercule Poirot. Mademoiselle Nick will have a part to play in it,' He grinned suddenly. 'You comprehend, Hastings, *there will be a ghost in this play*. Yes, a ghost. End House has never seen a ghost. It will have one tonight. No' – as I tried to ask a question – 'I will say no more. Tonight, Hastings, we will produce our comedy – and reveal the truth. But now, there is much to do – much to do.'

He hurried from the room.

CHAPTER NINETEEN

Poirot Produces a Play

It was a curious gathering that met that night at End House.

I had hardly seen Poirot all day. He had been out for dinner but had left me a message that I was to be at End House at nine o'clock. Evening dress, he had added, was not necessary.

The whole thing was like a rather ridiculous dream.

On arrival I was ushered into the dining-room and when I looked round I realized that every person on Poirot's list from A. to I. (J. was necessarily excluded, being in the Mrs Harris-like position of 'there ain't no such person') was present.

Even Mrs Croft was there in a kind of invalid chair. She smiled and nodded at me.

'This is a surprise, isn't it?' she said, cheerfully. 'It makes a change for me, I must say. I think I shall try and get out now again. All M. Poirot's idea. Come and sit by me, Captain Hastings. Somehow I feel this is rather a gruesome business – but Mr Vyse made a point of it.'

'My Vyse?' I said, rather surprised.

Charles Vyse was standing by the mantelpiece. Poirot was beside him talking earnestly to him in an undertone.

I looked round the room. Yes, they were all there. After showing me in (I had been a minute or two late) Ellen had taken her place on a chair just beside the door. On another chair, sitting painfully straight and breathing hard, was her husband. The child, Alfred, squirmed uneasily between his father and mother.

The rest sat round the dining-table. Frederica in her black dress, Lazarus beside her, George Challenger and Croft on the other side of the table. I sat a little away from it near Mrs Croft. And now Charles Vyse, a final nod of the head, took his place at the end of the table, and Poirot slipped unobtrusively into a seat next to Lazarus.

Clearly the producer, as Poirot had styled himself, did not propose to take a prominent part in the play. Charles Vyse was apparently in charge of the proceedings. I wondered what surprises Poirot had in store for him.

The young lawyer cleared his throat and stood up. He looked just the same as ever, impassive, formal and unemotional.

'This is rather an unconventional gathering we have here to-night,' he said. 'But the circumstances are very peculiar. I refer, of course, to the circumstances surrounding the death of my cousin, Miss Buckley. There will have, of course, to be an autopsy – there seems to be no doubt that she met her death by poison, and that that poison was administered with the intent to kill. This is police business and I need not go into it. The police would doubtless prefer me not to do so.

'In an ordinary case, the will of a deceased person is read after the funeral, but in deference to M. Poirot's special wish, I am proposing to read it before the funeral takes place. In fact, I am proposing to read it here and now. That is why everyone has been asked to come here. As I said just now, the circumstances are unusual and justify a departure from precedent.

'The will itself came into my possession in a somewhat unusual manner. Although dated last February, it only reached me by post this morning. However, it is undoubtedly in the handwriting of my cousin – I have no doubt on that point, and though a most informal document, it is properly attested.'

He paused and cleared his throat once more.

Every eye was upon his face.

From a long envelope in his hand, he drew out an enclosure. It was, as we could see, an ordinary piece of End House notepaper with writing on it.

'It is quite short,' said Vyse. He made a suitable pause, then began to read:

'*This is the last Will and Testament of Magdala Buckley. I direct that all my funeral expenses should be paid and I appoint my cousin Charles Vyse as my executor. I leave everything of which I die possessed to Mildred Croft in grateful recognition of the services rendered by her to my father, Philip Buckley, which services nothing can ever repay.*

'*Signed* – MAGDALA BUCKLEY,
'*Witnesses* – ELLEN WILSON.

'WILLIAM WILSON.'

I was dumbfounded! So I think was everyone else. Only Mrs Croft nodded her head in quiet understanding.

'It's true,' she said, quietly. 'Not that I ever meant to let on about it. Philip Buckley was out in Australia, and if it hadn't been for me – well, I'm not going into that. A secret it's been and a secret it had better remain. She knew about it, though. Nick did, I mean. Her father must have told her. We came down here because we wanted to have a look at the place. I'd always been curious about this End

House Philip Buckley talked of. And that dear girl knew all about it, and couldn't do enough for us. Wanted us to come and live with her, she did. But we wouldn't do that. And so she insisted on our having the lodge – and not a penny of rent would she take. We pretended to pay it, of course, so as not to cause talk, but she handed it back to us. And now – this! Well, if anyone says there is no gratitude in the world, I'll tell them they're wrong! This proves it.'

There was still an amazed silence. Poirot looked at Vyse.

'Had you any idea of this?'

Vyse shook his head.

'I knew Philip Buckley had been in Australia. But I never heard any rumours of a scandal there.'

He looked inquiringly at Mrs Croft.

She shook her head.

'No, you won't get a word out of me. I never have said a word and I never shall. The secret goes to the grave with me.'

Vyse said nothing. He sat quietly tapping the table with a pencil.

'I presume, M. Vyse' – Poirot leaned forward – 'that as next of kin you could contest that will? There is, I understand, a vast fortune at stake which was not the case when the will was made.'

Vyse looked at him coldly.

'The will is perfectly valid. I should not dream of contesting my cousin's disposal of her property.'

'You're an honest fellow,' said Mrs Croft, approvingly. 'And I'll see you don't lose by it.'

Charles sank a little from this well-meant but slightly embarrassing remark.

'Well, Mother,' said Mr Croft, with an elation he could not quite keep out of his voice. 'This *is* a surprise! Nick didn't tell *me* what she was doing.'

'The dear sweet girl,' murmured Mrs Croft, putting her handkerchief to her eyes. 'I wish she could look down and see us now. Perhaps she does – who knows?'

'Perhaps,' agreed Poirot.

Suddenly an idea seemed to strike him. He looked round.

'An idea! We are all here seated round a table. Let us hold a *séance*.'

'A *séance?*' said Mrs Croft, somewhat shocked. 'But surely –'

'Yes, yes, it will be most interesting. Hastings, here, has pronounced mediumistic powers.' (Why fix on *me*, I thought.) 'To get through a message from the other world – the opportunity is unique! I feel the conditions are propitious. You feel the same, Hastings.'

'Yes,' I said resolutely, playing up.

'Good. I knew it. Quick, the lights.'

In another minute he had risen and switched them off. The whole thing had been rushed on the company before they had had the energy to protest had they wanted to do so. As a matter of fact they were, I think, still dazed with astonishment over the will.

The room was not quite dark. The curtains were drawn back and the window was open for it was a hot night, and through those windows came a faint light. After a minute or two, as we sat in silence, I began to be able to make out the faint outlines of the furniture. I wondered very much what I was supposed to do and cursed Poirot heartily for not having given me my instructions beforehand.

However, I closed my eyes and breathed in a rather stertorous manner.

Presently Poirot rose and tiptoed to my chair. Then returning to his own, he murmured.

'Yes, he is already in a trance. Soon – things will begin to happen.'

There is something about sitting in the dark, waiting, that fills one with unbearable apprehension. I know that I myself was a prey to nerves and so, I was sure, was everyone else. And yet I had at least an idea of what was about to happen. I knew the one vital fact that no one else knew.

And yet, in spite of all that, my heart leapt into my mouth as I saw the dining-room door slowly opening.

It did so quite soundlessly (it must have been oiled) and the effect was horribly grisly. It swung slowly open and for a minute or two that was all. With its opening a cold blast of air seemed to enter the room. It was, I suppose, a common or garden draught owing to the open window, but it *felt* like the icy chill mentioned in all the ghost stories I have ever read.

And then we all saw it! Framed in the doorway was a white shadowy figure. Nick Buckley . . .

She advanced slowly and noiselessly – with a kind of floating ethereal motion that certainly conveyed the impression of nothing human . . .

I realized then what an actress the world had missed. Nick had wanted to play a part at End House. Now she was playing it, and I felt convinced that she was enjoying herself to the core. She did it

307

perfectly.

She floated forward into the room – and the silence was broken. There was a gasping cry from the invalid chair beside me. A kind of gurgle from Mr Croft. A startled oath from Challenger. Charles Vyse drew back his chair, I think. Lazarus leaned forward. Frederica alone made no sound or movement.

And then a scream rent the room. Ellen sprang up from her chair. 'It's her!' she shrieked. 'She's come back. She's walking! Them that's murdered always walks. It's her! It's her!'

And then, with a click the lights went on.

I saw Poirot standing by them, the smile of the ringmaster on his face. Nick stood in the middle of the room in her white draperies.

It was Frederica who spoke first. She stretched out an unbelieving hand – touched her friend.

'Nick,' she said. 'You're – you're *real*!'

It was almost a whisper.

Nick laughed. She advanced.

'Yes,' she said. 'I'm real enough. Thank you so much for what you did for my father, Mrs Croft. But I'm afraid you won't be able to enjoy the benefit of that will just yet.'

'Oh, my God,' gasped Mrs Croft. 'Oh, my God.' She twisted to and fro in her chair. 'Take me away, Bert. Take me away. It was all a joke, my dear – all a joke, that's all it was. Honest.'

'A queer sort of joke,' said Nick.

The door had opened again and a man had entered so quietly that I had not heard him. To my surprise I saw that it was Japp. He exchanged a quick nod with Poirot as though satisfying him of something. Then his face suddenly lit up and he took a step forward towards the squirming figure in the invalid chair.

'Hello-ello-ello,' he said. 'What's this? An old friend! Milly Merton, I declare! And at your old tricks again, my dear.'

He turned round in an explanatory way to the company disregarding Mrs Croft's shrill protests.

'Cleverest forger we've ever had, Milly Merton. We knew there had been an accident to the car they made their last getaway in. But there! Even an injury to the spine wouldn't keep Milly from her tricks. She's an artist, she is!'

'Was that will a forgery?' said Vyse.

He spoke in tones of amazement.

'Of course it was a forgery,' said Nick scornfully. 'You don't think I'd make a silly will like that, do you? I left you End House, Charles, and everything else to Frederica.'

She crossed as she spoke and stood by her friend, and just at that moment *it happened!*

A spurt of flame from the window and the hiss of a bullet. Then another and the sound of a groan and a fall outside . . .

And Frederica on her feet with a thin trickle of blood running down her arm . . .

CHAPTER TWENTY

J.

It was all so sudden that for a moment no one knew what had happened.

Then, with a violent exclamation, Poirot ran to the window. Challenger was with him.

A moment later they reappeared, carrying with them the limp body of a man. As they lowered him carefully into a big leather armchair and his face came into view, I uttered a cry.

'*The face* – the face at the window . . .'

It was the man I had seen looking in on us the previous evening. I recognized him at once. I realized that when I had said he was hardly human I had exaggerated as Poirot had accused me of doing.

Yet there was something about his face that justified my impression. It was a lost face – the face of one removed from ordinary humanity.

White, weak, depraved – it seemed a mere mask – as though the spirit within had fled long ago.

Down the side of it there trickled a stream of blood.

Frederica came slowly forward till she stood by the chair.

Poirot intercepted her.

'You are hurt, Madame?'

She shook her head.

'The bullet grazed my shoulder – that is all.'

She put him aside with a gentle hand and bent down.

The man's eyes opened and he saw her looking down at him.

'I've done for you this time, I hope,' he said in a low vicious snarl, and then, his voice changing suddenly till it sounded like a child's, 'Oh! Freddie, I didn't mean it. I didn't mean it. You've always been so decent to me . . .'

'It's all right –'

She knelt down beside him.

'I didn't mean –'

His head dropped. The sentence was never finished.

Frederica looked up at Poirot.

'Yes, Madame, he is dead,' he said, gently.

She rose slowly from her knees and stood looking down at him. With one hand she touched his forehead – pitifully, it seemed. Then she signed and turned to the rest of us.

'He was my husband,' she said, quietly.

'J.,' I murmured.

Poirot caught my remark, and nodded a quick assent.

'Yes,' he said softly. 'Always I felt that there was a J. I said so from the beginning, did I not?'

'He was my husband,' said Frederica again. Her voice was terribly tired. She sank into a chair that Lazarus brought for her. 'I might as well tell you everything – now.'

'He was – completely debased. He was a drug fiend. He taught me to take drugs. I have been fighting the habit ever since I left him. I think – at last – I am nearly cured. But it has been difficult. Oh! so horribly difficult. Nobody knows how difficult!'

'I could never escape from him. He used to turn up and demand money – with threats. A kind of blackmail. If I did not give him money he would shoot himself. That was always his threat. Then he took to threatening to shoot *me*. He was not responsible. He was mad – crazy . . .'

'I suppose it was he who shot Maggie Buckley. He didn't mean to shoot her, of course. He must have thought it was me.

'I ought to have said, I suppose. But, after all, I wasn't *sure*. And those queer accidents Nick had – that made me feel that perhaps it wasn't him after all. It might have been someone quite different.

'And then – one day – I saw a bit of his handwriting on a torn piece of paper on M. Poirot's table. It was part of a letter he had sent me. I knew then that M. Poirot was on the track.

'Since then I have felt that it was only a matter of time . . .'

'But I don't understand about the sweets. He wouldn't have wanted to poison *Nick*. And anyway, I don't see how he *could* have had anything to do with that. I've puzzled and puzzled.'

She put both hands to her face, then took them away and said with a queer pathetic finality:

'That's all . . .'

CHAPTER TWENTY-ONE

The Person – K.

Lazarus came quickly to her side.

'My dear,' he said. 'My dear.'

Poirot went to the sideboard, poured out a glass of wine and brought it to her, standing over her while she drank it.

She handed the glass back to him and smiled.

'I'm all right now,' she said. 'What – what had we better do next?'

She looked at Japp, but the Inspector shook his head. 'I'm on a holiday, Mrs Rice. Just obliging an old friend – that's all I'm doing. The St Loo police are in charge of the case.'

She looked at Poirot.

'And M. Poirot is in charge of the St Loo Police?'

'Oh! *quelle idée, Madame!* I am a mere humble adviser.'

'M. Poirot,' said Nick. 'Can't we hush it up?'

'You wish that, Mademoiselle?'

'Yes. After all – I'm the person most concerned. And there will be no more attacks on me – now.'

'No, that is true. There will be no more attacks on you now.'

'You're thinking of Maggie. But, M. Poirot, nothing will bring Maggie back to life again! If you make all this public, you'll only bring a terrible lot of suffering and publicity on Frederica – and she hasn't deserved it.'

'You say she has not deserved it?'

'Of course she hasn't! I told you right at the beginning that she had a brute of a husband. You've seen tonight – what he was. Well, he's dead. Let that be the end of things. Let the police go on looking for the man who shot Maggie. They just won't find him, that's all.'

'So that is what you say, Mademoiselle? *Hush it all up.*'

'Yes. Please. Oh! *Please.* Please, *dear* M. Poirot.'

Poirot looked slowly round.

'What do you all say?'

Each spoke in turn.

'I agree,' I said, as Poirot looked at me.

'I, too,' said Lazarus.

'Best thing to do,' from Challenger.

'Let's forget everything that's passed in this room tonight.' This very determinedly from Croft.

'You *would* say that!' interpolated Japp.

'Don't be hard on me, dearie,' his wife sniffed to Nick, who looked at her scornfully but made no reply.

'Ellen?'

'Me and William won't say a word, sir. Least said, soonest mended.'

'And you, M. Vyse?'

'A thing like this can't be hushed up,' said Charles Vyse. 'The facts must be made known in the proper quarter.'

'Charles!' cried Nick.

'I'm sorry, dear. I look at it from the legal aspect.'

Poirot gave a sudden laugh.

'So you are seven to one. The good Japp is neutral.'

'I'm on holiday,' said Japp, with a grin. 'I don't count.'

'Seven to one. Only M. Vyse holds out – on the side of law and order! You know, M. Vyse, you are a man of character!'

Vyse shrugged his shoulders.

'The position is quite clear. There is only one thing to do.'

'Yes – you are an honest man. *Eh bien* – I, too, range myself on the side of the minority. *I, too, am for the truth.*'

'M. Poirot!' cried Nick.

'Mademoiselle – you dragged me into the case. I came into it at your wish. You cannot silence me now.'

He raised a threatening forefinger in a gesture that I knew well.

'Sit down – all of you, and I will tell you – the truth.'

Silenced by his imperious attitude, we sat down meekly and turned attentive faces towards him.

'*Ecoutez!* I have a list here – a list of persons connected with the crime. I numbered them with the letters of the alphabet including the letter J. J. stood for a person unknown – linked to the crime by one of the others. I did not know who J. was until tonight, *but I knew that there was such a person.* The events of tonight have proved that I was right.

'But yesterday, I suddenly realized that I had made a grave error. I had made an omission. I added another letter to my list. The letter K.'

'Another person unknown?' asked Vyse, with a slight sneer.

'Not exactly. I adopted J. as the symbol for a person unknown. Another person unknown would be merely another J. K. has a different significance. *It stands for a person who should have been included in the original list, but who was overlooked.*'

He bent over Frederica.

'Reassure yourself, Madame. *Your husband was not guilty of murder.* It was the person K. who shot Mademoiselle Maggie.'

She stared.

'But who is K.?'

Poirot nodded to Japp. He stepped forward and spoke in tones reminiscent of the days when he had given evidence in police courts.

'Acting on information received, I took up a position here early in the evening, having been introduced secretly into the house by M. Poirot. I was concealed behind the curtains in the drawing-room. When everyone was assembled in this room, a young lady entered the drawing-room and switched on the light. She made her way to the fireplace and opened a small recess in the panelling that appeared to be operated with a spring. She took from the recess a pistol. With this in her hand she left the room. I followed her and opening the door a crack I was able to observe her further movements. Coats and wraps had been left in the hall by the visitors on arrival. The young lady carefully wiped the pistol with a handkerchief and then placed it in the pocket of a grey wrap, the property of Mrs Rice –'

A cry burst from Nick.

'This is untrue – every word of it!'

Poirot pointed a hand at her.

'*Voilà!*' he said. '*The person K.! It was Mademoiselle Nick who shot her cousin, Maggie Buckley.*'

'Are you mad?' cried Nick. 'Why should I kill Maggie?'

'In order to inherit the money left to her by Michael Seton! Her name too was Magdala Buckley – and it was to her he was engaged – not you.'

'You – you –'

She stood there trembling – unable to speak. Poirot turned to Japp.

'You telephoned to the police?'

'Yes, they are waiting in the hall now. They've got the warrant.'

'You're all mad!' cried Nick, contemptuously. She moved swiftly to Frederica's side. 'Freddie, give me your wrist-watch as – as a souvenir, will you?'

Slowly Frederica unclasped the jewelled watch from her wrist and handed it to Nick.

'Thanks. And now – I suppose we must go through with this perfectly ridiculous comedy.'

'The comedy you planned and produced in End House. Yes – but

314

you should not have given the star part to Hercule Poirot. That, Mademoiselle, was your mistake – your very grave mistake.'

CHAPTER TWENTY-TWO

The End of the Story

'You want me to explain?'

Poirot looked round with a gratified smile and the air of mock humility I knew so well.

We had moved into the drawing-room and our numbers had lessened. The domestics had withdrawn tactfully, and the Crofts had been asked to accompany the police. Frederica, Lazarus, Challenger, Vyse and I remained.

'*Eh bien* – I confess it – I was fooled – fooled completely and absolutely. The little Nick, she had me where she wanted me, as your idiom so well expresses it. Ah! Madame, when you said that your friend was a clever little liar – how right you were! How right!'

'Nick always told lies,' said Frederica, composedly. 'That's why I didn't really believe in these marvellous escapes of hers.'

'And I – imbecile that I was – did!'

'Didn't they really happen?' I asked. I was, I admit, still hopelessly confused.

'They were invented – very cleverly – to give just the impression they did.'

'What was that?'

'They gave the impression that Mademoiselle Nick's life was in danger. But I will begin earlier than that. I will tell you the story as I have pieced it out – not as it came to me imperfectly and in flashes.

'At the beginning of the business then, we have this girl, this Nick Buckley, young and beautiful, unscrupulous, and passionately and fanatically devoted to her home.'

Charles Vyse nodded.

'I told you that.'

'And you were right. Mademoiselle Nick loved End House. But she had no money. The house was mortgaged. She wanted money – she wanted it feverishly – and she could not get it. She meets this young Seton at Le Touquet, he is attracted by her. She knows that in all probability he is his uncle's heir and that that uncle is worth millions. Good, her star is in the ascendant, she thinks. But he is not really seriously attracted. He thinks her good fun, that is all. They meet at Scarborough, he takes her up in his machine and then – the catastrophe occurs. He meets Maggie and falls in love with her at first

316

sight.

'Mademoiselle Nick is dumbfounded. Her cousin Maggie whom she has never considered pretty! But to young Seton she is "different". The one girl in the world for him. They become secretly engaged. Only one person knows – has to know. That person is Mademoiselle Nick. The poor Maggie – she is glad that there is one person she can talk to. Doubtless she reads to her cousin parts of her financé's letters. So it is that Mademoiselle gets to hear of the will. She pays no attention to it at the time. But it remains in her mind.

'Then comes the sudden and unexpected death of Sir Matthew Seton, and hard upon that the rumours of of Michael Seton's being missing. And straightaway an outrageous plan comes into our young lady's head. Seton does not know that her name is Magdala also. He only knows her as Nick. His will is clearly quite informal – a mere mention of a name. But in the eyes of the world Seton is her friend! It is with *her* that his name has been coupled. If she were to claim to be engaged to him, no one would be surprised. *But to do that successfully Maggie must be out of the way*.

'Time is short. She arranges for Maggie to come and stay in a few days' time. Then she has her escapes from death. The picture whose cord she cuts through. The brake of the car that she tampers with. The boulder – that perhaps was natural and she merely invented the story of being underneath on the path.

'And then – she sees *my* name in the paper. (I told you, Hastings, everyone knew Hercule Poirot!) and she has the audacity to make *me* an accomplice! The bullet through the hat that falls at my feet. Oh! the pretty comedy. And I am taken in! I believe in the peril that menaces her! *Bon!* She has got a valuable witness on her side. I play into her hands by asking her to send for a friend.

'She seizes the chance and sends for Maggie to come a day earlier.

'How easy the crime is actually! She leaves us at the dinner table and after hearing on the wireless that Seton's death is a fact, she starts to put her plan into action. She has plenty of time, then, to take Seton's letters to Maggie – look through them and select the few that will answer her purpose. These she places in her own room. Then, later, she and Maggie leave the fireworks and go back to the house. She tells her cousin to put on her shawl. Then stealing out after her, she shoots her. Quick, into the house, the pistol concealed in the secret panel (of whose existence she thinks nobody knows). Then upstairs. There she waits till voices are heard. The body is discovered. It is her cue.

317

'Down she rushes and out through the window.

'How well she played her part! Magnificently! Oh, yes, she staged a fine drama here. The maid, Ellen, said this was an evil house. I am inclined to agree with her. It was from the house that Mademoiselle Nick took her inspiration.'

'But those poisoned sweets,' said Frederica. 'I still don't understand about that.'

'It was all part of the same scheme. Do you not see that if Nick's life was attempted *after* Maggie was dead that absolutely settled the question that Maggie's death had been a mistake.

'When she thought the time was ripe she rang up Madame Rice and asked her to get her a box of chocolates.'

'Then it *was* her voice?'

'But, yes! How often the simple explanation is the true one! *N'est ce pas?* She made her voice sound a little different – that was all. So that you might be in doubt when questioned. Then, when the box arrived – again how simple. She fills three of the chocolates with cocaine (she had cocaine with her, cleverly concealed), eats one of them and is ill – but not *too* ill. She knows very well how much cocaine to take and just what symptoms to exaggerate.

'And the card – *my* card! Ah! *Sapristi* – she has a nerve! It *was* my card – the one I sent with the flowers. Simple, was it not? Yes, but it had to be thought of ...'

There was a pause and then Frederica asked:

'Why did she put the pistol in my coat?'

'I thought you would ask me that, Madame. It was bound to occur to you in time. Tell me – had it ever entered your head that Mademoiselle Nick no longer liked you? Did you ever feel that she might – hate you?'

'It's difficult to say,' said Frederica, slowly. 'We lived an insincere life. She *used* to be fond of me.'

'Tell me, M. Lazarus – it is not a time for false modesty, you understand – was there ever anything between you and her?'

'No.' Lazarus shook his head. 'I was attracted to her at one time. And then – I don't know why – I went off her.'

'Ah!' said Poirot, nodding his head sagely. 'That was her tragedy. She attracted people – and then they "went off her". Instead of liking her better and better you fell in love with her friend. She began to hate Madame – Madame who had a rich friend behind her. Last winter when she made a will, she was fond of Madame. Later it was different.

318

'She remembered that will. She did not know that Croft had suppressed it – that it had never reached its destination. Madame (or so the world would say) had got a motive for desiring her death. So it was to Madame she telephoned asking her to get the chocolates. Tonight, the will would have been read, naming Madame her residuary legatee – and then the pistol would be found in her coat – *the pistol with which Maggie Buckley was shot.* If Madame found it, she might incriminate herself by trying to get rid of it.'

'She must have hated me,' murmured Frederica.

'Yes, Madame. You had what she had not – the knack of winning love, and *keeping* it.'

'I'm rather dense,' said Challenger, 'but I haven't quite fathomed the will business yet.'

'No? That's a different business altogether – a very simple one. The Crofts are lying low down here. Mademoiselle Nick has to have an operation. She has made no will. The Crofts see a chance. They persuade her to make one and take charge of it for the post. Then, if anything happens to her – if she dies – they produce a cleverly forged will – leaving the money to Mrs Croft with a reference to Australia and Philip Buckley whom they know once visited the country.

'But Mademoiselle Nick has her appendix removed quite satisfactorily so the forged will is no good. For the moment, that is. Then the attempts on her life begin. The Crofts are hopeful once more. Finally, I announce her death. The chance is too good to be missed. The forged will is immediately posted to M. Vyse. Of course, to begin with, they naturally thought her much richer than she is. They knew nothing about the mortgage.'

'What I really want to know, M. Poirot,' said Lazarus, 'is how you actually got wise to all this. When did you begin to suspect?'

'Ah! there I am ashamed. I was so long – so long. There were things that worried me – yes. Things that seemed not quite right. Discrepancies between what Mademoiselle Nick told me and what other people told me. Unfortunately, I always believed Mademoiselle Nick.

'And then, suddenly, I got a revelation. Mademoiselle Nick made one mistake. She was too clever. When I urged her to send for a friend she promised to do so – and suppressed the fact that she had already sent for Mademoiselle Maggie. It seemed to her less suspicious – *but it was a mistake.*'

'For Maggie Buckley wrote a letter home immediately on arrival, and in it she used one innocent phrase that puzzled me: "*I don't see why Nick should have telegraphed for me the way she did. Tuesday would have done just as well.*" What did that mention of Tuesday mean? *It could only mean one thing.* Maggie had been coming to stay on Tuesday anyway. But in that case Mademoiselle Nick had lied – or had at any rate suppressed the truth.

'And for the first time I looked at her in a different light. I criticized her statements. Instead of believing them, I said, "Suppose this were not true." I remembered the discrepancies. "How would it be if every time it was Mademoiselle Nick who was lying and not the other person?"

'I said to myself: "Let us be simple. What has *really* happened?"

'And I saw that what had really happened was that *Maggie Buckley* had been killed. Just that! But who could want Maggie Buckley dead?

'And then I thought of something else – a few foolish remarks that Hastings had made not five minutes before. He had said that there were plenty of abbreviations for Margaret – Maggie, Margot, etc. And it suddenly occurred to me to wonder what was Mademoiselle Maggie's real name?

'Then, *tout d'un coup*, it came to me! Supposing her name was *Magdala*! It was a Buckley name, Mademoiselle Nick had told me so. Two Magdala Buckleys. Supposing . . .

'In my mind I ran over the letters of Michael Seton's that I had read. Yes – there was nothing impossible. There was a mention of Scarborough – but Maggie had been in Scarborough with Nick – her mother had told me so.

'And it explained one thing which had worried me. Why were there so *few* letters? If a girl keeps her love letters at all, she keeps *all* of them. Why these select few? Was there any peculiarity about them?

'And I remembered that there was no *name* mentioned in them. They all began differently – but they began with a term of endearment. Nowhere in them was there the name – *Nick*.

'And there was something else, something that I ought to have seen at once – that cried the truth aloud.'

'What was that?'

'Why – this. Mademoiselle Nick underwent an operation for appendicitis on February 27th last. There is a letter of Michael Seton's dated March 2nd, and no mention of anxiety, of illness or anything unusual. That ought to have shown me that the letters were written to a *different person altogether*.

320

'Then I went through a list of questions that I had made. And I answered them in the light of my new idea.

'In all but a few isolated questions the result was simple and convincing. And I answered, too, another question which I had asked myself earlier. *Why did Mademoiselle Nick buy a black dress?* The answer was that she and her cousin had to be dressed alike, with the scarlet shawl as an additional touch. That was the true and convincing answer, *not* the other. A girl would not buy mourning before she knew her lover was dead. She would be unreal – unnatural.

'And so I, in turn, staged my little drama. And the thing I hoped for happened! Nick Buckley had been very vehement about the question of a secret panel. She had declared there was no such thing. But if there were – and I did not see why Ellen should have invented it – *Nick must know of it.* Why was she so vehement? Was it possible that she had hidden the pistol there? With the secret intention of using it to throw suspicion on somebody later?

'I let her see that appearances were very black against Madame. That was as she had planned. As I foresaw, she was unable to resist the crowning proof. Besides it was safer for herself. That secret panel might be found by Ellen and the pistol in it!

'We are all safely in here. She is waiting outside for her cue. It is absolutely safe, she thinks, to take the pistol from its hiding place and put it in Madame's coat . . .

'And so – at the last – she failed . . .'

Frederica shivered.

'All the same,' she said. 'I'm glad I gave her my watch.'

'Yes, Madame.'

She looked up at him quickly.

'You know about that too?'

'What about Ellen?' I asked, breaking in. 'Did she know or suspect anything?'

'No. I asked her. She told me that she decided to stay in the house that night because in her own phrase she "thought something was up". Apparently Nick urged her to see the fireworks rather too decisively. She had fathomed Nick's dislike of Madame. She told me that "she felt in her bones something was going to happen", but she thought it was going to happen to Madame. She knew Miss Nick's temper, she said, and she was always a queer little girl.'

'Yes,' murmured Frederica. 'Yes, let us think of her like that. A queer little girl. A queer little girl who couldn't help herself . . . I

321

shall – anyway.'

Poirot took her hand and raised it gently to his lips.

Charles Vyse stirred uneasily.

'It's going to be a very unpleasant business,' he said, quietly. 'I must see about some kind of defence for her, I suppose.'

'There will be no need, I think,' said Poirot, gently. 'Not if I am correct in my assumptions.'

He turned suddenly on Challenger.

'That's where you put the stuff, isn't it?' he said. 'In those wrist-watches.'

'I – I –' The sailor stammered – at a loss.

'Do not try and deceive me – with your hearty good-fellow manner. It has deceived Hastings – but it does not deceive *me*. You make a good thing out of it, do you not – the traffic in drugs – you and your uncle in Harley Street.'

'M. Poirot.'

Challenger rose to his feet.

My little friend blinked up at him placidly.

'You are the useful "boy friend". Deny it, if you like. But I advise you, if you do not want the facts put in the hands of the police – to go.'

And to my utter amazement, Challenger did go. He went from the room like a flash. I stared after him open-mouthed.

Poirot laughed.

'I told you so, *mon ami*. Your instincts are always wrong. *C'est épatant!*'

'Cocaine was in the wrist-watch –' I began.

'Yes, yes. That is how Mademoiselle Nick had it with her so conveniently at the nursing home. And having finished her supply in the chocolate box she asked Madame just now for hers *which was full*.'

'You mean she can't do without it?'

'*Non, non.* Mademoiselle Nick is not an addict. Sometimes – for fun – that is all. But tonight she needed it for a different purpose. It will be a full dose this time.'

'You mean –?' I gasped.

'It is the best way. Better than the hangman's rope. But pst! we must not say so before M. Vyse who is all for law and order. Officially I know nothing. The contents of the wrist-watch – it is the merest guess on my part.'

'Your guesses are always right, M. Poirot,' said Frederica.

'I must be going,' said Charles Vyse, cold disapproval in his attitude as he left the room.

Poirot looked from Frederica to Lazarus.

'You are going to get married – eh?'

'As soon as we can.'

'And indeed, M. Poirot,' said Frederica. 'I am not the drug-taker you think. I have cut myself down to a tiny dose. I think now – with happiness in front of me – I shall not need a wrist-watch any more.'

'I hope you will have happiness, Madame,' said Poirot, gently. 'You have suffered a great deal. And in spite of everything you have suffered, you have still the quality of mercy in your heart ...'

'I will look after her,' said Lazarus. 'My business is in a bad way, but I believe I shall pull through. And if I don't – well, Frederica does not mind being poor – with me.'

She shook her head, smiling.

'It is late,' said Poirot, looking at the clock.

We all rose.

'We have spent a strange night in this strange house,' Poirot went on. 'It is, I think, as Ellen says, an evil house ...'

He looked up at the picture of old Sir Nicholas.

Then, with a sudden gesture, he drew Lazarus aside.

'I ask your pardon, but, of all my questions, there is one still unanswered. Tell me, why did you offer fifty pounds for that picture? It would give me much pleasure to know – so as, you comprehend, to leave nothing unanswered.'

Lazarus looked at him with an impassive face for a minute or two. Then he smiled.

'You see, M. Poirot,' he said. 'I am a dealer.'

'Exactly.'

'That picture is not worth a penny more than twenty pounds. I knew that if I offered Nick fifty, she would immediately suspect it was worth more and would get it valued elsewhere. Then she would find that I had offered her far more than it was worth. The next time I offered to buy a picture she would not have got it valued.'

'Yes, and then?'

'The picture on the far wall is worth at least five thousand pounds,' said Lazarus drily.

'Ah!' Poirot drew a long breath.

'Now I know everything,' he said happily.

THE END

The ABC Murders

Foreword

By Captain Arthur Hastings, O.B.E.

In this narrative of mine I have departed from my usual practice of relating only those incidents and scenes at which I myself was present. Certain chapters, therefore, are written in the third person.

I wish to assure my readers that I can vouch for the occurrences related in these chapters. If I have taken a certain poetic licence in describing the thoughts and feelings of various persons, it is because I believe I have set them down with a reasonable amount of accuracy. I may add that they have been 'vetted' by my friend Hercule Poirot himself.

In conclusion, I will say that if I have described at too great length some of the secondary personal relationships which arose as a consequence of this strange series of crimes, it is because the human and personal elements can never be ignored. Hercule Poirot once taught me in a very dramatic manner that romance can be a by-product of crime.

As to solving of the ABC mystery, I can only say that in my opinion Poirot showed real genius in the way he tackled a problem entirely unlike any which had previously come his way.

Contents

To James Watts

One of my most sympathetic readers

CHAPTER ONE

The Letter

It was in June of 1935 that I came home from my ranch in South America for a stay of about six months. It had been a difficult time for us out there. Like everyone else, we had suffered from world depression. I had various affairs to see to in England that I felt could only be successful if a personal touch was introduced. My wife remained to manage the ranch.

I need hardly say that one of my first actions on reaching England was to look up my old friend, Hercule Poirot.

I found him installed in one of the newest type of service flats in London. I accused him (and he admitted the fact) of having chosen this particular building entirely on account of its strictly goemetrical appearance and proportions.

'But yes, my friend, it is of a most pleasing symmetry, do you not find it so?'

I said that I thought there could be too much squareness and, alluding to an old joke, I asked if in this super-modern hostelry they managed to induce hens to lay square eggs.

Poirot laughed heartily.

'Ah, you remember that? Alas! no – science has not yet induced the hens to conform to modern tastes, they still lay eggs of different size and colours!'

I examined my old friend with an affectionate eye. He was looking wonderfully well – hardly a day older than when I had last seen him.

'You're looking in fine fettle, Poirot,' I said. 'You've hardly aged at all. In fact, if it were possible, I should say that you had fewer grey hairs than when I saw you last.'

Poirot beamed on me.

'And why is that not possible? It is quite true.'

'Do you mean your hair is turning from grey to black instead of from black to grey?'

'Precisely.'

'But surely that's a scientific impossibility!'

'Not at all.'

'But that's very extraordinary. It seems against nature.'

'As usual, Hastings, you have the beautiful and unsuspicious mind. Years do not change that in you! You perceive a fact and mention the solution of it in the same breath without noticing that you are doing so!'

I stared at him, puzzled.

Without a word he walked into his bedroom and returned with a bottle in his hand which he handed to me.

I took it, for the moment uncomprehending.

It bore the words:

REVIVIT. – *To bring back the natural tone of the hair.* REVIVIT *is* NOT *a dye. In five shades, Ash, Chestnut, Titian, Brown, Black.*

'Poirot,' I cried. 'You have dyed your hair!'

'Ah, the comprehension comes to you!'

'So *that's* why your hair looks so much blacker than it did last time I was back.'

'Exactly.'

'Dear me,' I said, recovering from the shock. 'I suppose next time I come home I shall find you wearing false moustaches – or are you doing so now?'

Poirot winced. His moustaches had always been his sensitive point. He was inordinately proud of them. My words touched him on the raw.

'No, no, indeed, *mon ami.* That day, I pray the good God, is still far off. The false moustache! *Quel horreur!*'

He tugged at them vigorously to assure me of their genuine character.

'Well, they are very luxuriant still,' I said.

'*N'est ce pas?* Never, in the whole of London, have I seen a pair of moustaches to equal mine.'

A good job too, I thought privately. But I would not for the world have hurt Poirot's feelings by saying so.

Instead I asked if he still practised his profession on occasion.

'I know,' I said, 'that you actually retired years ago –'

'*C'est vrai.* To grow the vegetable marrows! And immediately a murder occurs – and I send the vegetable marrows to promenade themselves to the devil. And since then – I know very well what you will say – I am like the prima donna who makes positively the farewell performance! That farewell performance, it repeats itself an indefinite number of times!'

I laughed.

'In truth, it has been very like that. Each time I say: this is the end.

330

But no, something else arises! And I will admit it, my friend, the retirement I care for it not at all. If the little grey cells are not exercised, they grow the rust.'

'I see,' I said. 'You exercise them in moderation.'

'Precisely. I pick and choose. For Hercule Poirot nowadays only the cream of crime.'

'Has there been much cream about?'

'*Pas mal*. Not long ago I had a narrow escape.'

'Of failure?'

'No, no.' Poirot looked shocked. 'But I – *I, Hercule Poirot*, was nearly exterminated.'

I whistled.

'An enterprising murderer!'

'Not so much enterprising as careless,' said Poirot. 'Precisely that – careless. But let us not talk of it. You know, Hastings, in many ways I regard you as my mascot.'

'Indeed?' I said. 'In what ways?'

Poirot did not answer my question directly. He went on:

'As soon as I heard you were coming over I said to myself: something will arise. As in former days we will hunt together, we two. But if so it must be no common affair. It must be something' – he waved his hands excitedly – 'something *recherché* – delicate – *fine* . . .' He gave the last untranslatable word its full flavour.

'Upon my word, Poirot,' I said. 'Anyone would think you were ordering a dinner at the Ritz.'

'Whereas one cannot command a crime to order? Very true.' He sighed. 'But I believe in luck – in destiny, if you will. It is your destiny to stand beside me and prevent me from committing the unforgivable error.'

'What do you call the unforgivable error?'

'Overlooking the obvious.'

I turned this over in my mind without quite seeing the point.

'Well,' I said presently, smiling, 'has this super crime turned up yet?'

'*Pas encore*. At least – that is –'

He paused. A frown of perplexity creased his forehead. His hands automatically straightened an object or two that I had inadvertently pushed awry.

'I am not sure,' he said slowly.

There was something so odd about his tone that I looked at him in surprise.

The frown still lingered.

Suddenly with a brief decisive nod of the head he crossed the room to a desk near the window. Its contents, I need hardly say, were all neatly docketed and pigeon-holed so that he was able at once to lay his hand upon the paper he wanted.

He came slowly across to me, an open letter in his hand. He read it through himself, then passed it to me.

'Tell me, *mon ami*,' he said. 'What do you make of this?'

I took it from him with some interest.

It was written on thickish white notepaper in printed characters:

MR HERCULE POIROT, – You fancy yourself, don't you, at solving mysteries that are too difficult for our poor thick-headed British police? Let us see, Mr Clever Poirot, just how clever you can be. Perhaps you'll find this nut too hard to crack. Look out for Andover, on the 21st of the month.

Yours, etc.,

A B C

I glanced at the envelope. That also was printed.

'Postmarked WC1,' said Poirot as I turned my attention to the postmark. 'Well, what is your opinion?'

I shrugged my shoulders as I handed it back to him.

'Some madman or other, I suppose.'

'That is all you have to say?'

'Well – doesn't it sound like a madman to you?'

'Yes, my friend, it does.'

His tone was grave. I looked at him curiously.

'You take this very seriously, Poirot.'

'A madman, *mon ami*, is to be taken seriously. A madman is a very dangerous thing.'

'Yes, of course, that is true ... I hadn't considered that point ... But what I meant was, it sounds more like a rather idiotic kind of hoax. Perhaps some convivial idiot who had had one over the eight.'

'*Comment?* Nine? Nine what?'

'Nothing – just an expression. I meant a fellow who was tight. No, damn it, a fellow who had had a spot too much to drink.'

'*Merci*, Hastings – the expression "tight" I *am* acquainted with it. As you say, there may be nothing more to it than that ...'

'But you think there is?' I asked, struck by the dissatisfaction of his tone.

Poirot shook his head doubtfully, but he did not speak.

'What have you done about it?' I inquired.

'What can one do? I showed it to Japp. He was of the same opinion as you – a stupid hoax – that was the expression he used. They get these things every day at Scotland Yard. I, too, have had my share ...'

'But you take this one seriously?'

Poirot replied slowly.

'There is something about that letter, Hastings, that I do not like ...'

In spite of myself, his tone impressed me.

'You think – what?'

He shook his head, and picking up the letter, put it away again in the desk.

'If you really take it seriously, can't you do something?' I asked.

'As always, the man of action! But what is there to do? The county police have seen the letter but they, too, do not take it seriously. There are no fingerprints on it. There are no local clues as to the possible writer.'

'In fact there is only your own instinct?'

'Not instinct, Hastings. Instinct is a bad word. It is my *knowledge* – my *experience* – that tells me that something about that letter is wrong –'

He gesticulated as words failed him, then shook his head again.

'I may be making the mountain out of the anthill. In any case there is nothing to be done but wait.'

'Well, the 21st is Friday. If a whacking great robbery takes place near Andover then –'

'Ah, what a comfort that would be –!'

'*A comfort?*' I stared. The word seemed to be a very extraordinary one to use.

'A robbery may be a *thrill* but it can hardly be a comfort!' I protested.

Poirot shook his head energetically.

'You are in error, my friend. You do not understand my meaning. A robbery would be a relief since it would dispossess my mind of the fear of something else.'

'Of what?'

'*Murder*,' said Hercule Poirot.

333

CHAPTER TWO

(Not from Captain Hastings' Personal Narrative)

Mr Alexander Bonaparte Cust rose from his seat and peered near-sightedly round the shabby bedroom. His back was stiff from sitting in a cramped position and as he stretched himself to his full height an onlooker would have realized that he was, in reality, quite a tall man. His stoop and his near-sighted peering gave a delusive impression.

Going to a well-worn overcoat hanging on the back of the door, he took from the pocket a packet of cheap cigarettes and some matches. He lit a cigarette and then returned to the table at which he had been sitting. He picked up a railway guide and consulted it, then he returned to the consideration of a typewritten list of names. With a pen, he made a tick against one of the first names on the list.

It was Thursday, June 20th.

CHAPTER THREE

Andover

I had been impressed at the time by Poirot's forebodings about the anonymous letter he had received, but I must admit that the matter had passed from my mind when the 21st actually arrived and the first reminder of it came with a visit paid to my friend by Chief Inspector Japp of Scotland Yard. The CID inspector had been known to us for many years and he gave me a hearty welcome.

'Well, I never,' he exclaimed. 'If it isn't Captain Hastings back from the wilds of the what do you call it! Quite like old days seeing you here with Monsieur Poirot. You're looking well, too. Just a little bit thin on top, eh? Well, that's what we're all coming to. I'm the same.'

I winced slightly. I was under the impression that owing to the careful way I brushed my hair across the top of my head the thinness referred to by Japp was quite unnoticeable. However, Japp had never been remarkable for tact where I was concerned, so I put a good face upon it and agreed that we were none of us getting any younger.

'Except Monsieur Poirot here,' said Japp. 'Quite a good advertisement for a hair tonic, he'd be. Face fungus sprouting finer than ever. Coming out into the limelight, too, in his old age. Mixed up in all the celebrated cases of the day. Train mysteries, air mysteries, high society deaths – oh, he's here, there and everywhere. Never been so celebrated as since he retired.'

'I have already told Hastings that I am like the prima donna who makes always one more appearance,' said Poirot, smiling.

'I shouldn't wonder if you ended by detecting your own death,' said Japp, laughing heartily. 'That's an idea, that is. Ought to be put in a book.'

'It will be Hastings who will have to do that,' said Poirot, twinkling at me.

'Ha ha! That would be a joke that would,' laughed Japp.

I failed to see why the idea was so extremely amusing, and in any case I thought the joke was in poor taste. Poirot, poor old chap, is getting on. Jokes about his approaching demise can hardly be agreeable to him.

Perhaps my manner showed my feelings, for Japp changed the

subject.

'Have you heard about Monsieur Poirot's anonymous letter?'

'I showed it to Hastings the other day,' said my friend.

'Of course,' I exclaimed. 'It had quite slipped my memory. Let me see, what was the date mentioned?'

'The 21st,' said Japp. 'That's what I dropped in about. Yesterday was the 21st and just out of curiosity I rang up Andover last night. It was a hoax all right. Nothing doing. One broken shop window – kid throwing stones – and a couple of drunk and disorderlies. So just for once our Belgian friend was barking up the wrong tree.'

'I am relieved, I must confess,' acknowledged Poirot.

'You'd quite got the wind up about it, hadn't you?' said Japp affectionately. 'Bless you, we get dozens of letters like that coming in every day! People with nothing better to do and a bit weak in the top storey sit down and write 'em. They don't mean any harm! Just a kind of excitement.'

'I have indeed been foolish to take the matter so seriously,' said Poirot. 'It is the nest of the horse that I put my nose into there.'

'You're mixing up mares and wasps,' said Japp.

'*Pardon?*'

'Just a couple of proverbs. Well, I must be off. Got a little business in the next street to see to – receiving stolen jewellery. I thought I'd just drop in on my way and put your mind at rest. Pity to let those grey cells function unnecessarily.'

With which words and a hearty laugh, Japp departed.

'He does not change much, the good Japp, eh?' asked Poirot.

'He looks much older,' I said. 'Getting as grey as a badger,' I added vindictively.

Poirot coughed and said:

'You know, Hastings, there is a little device – my hairdresser is a man of great ingenuity – one attaches it to the scalp and brushes one's own hair over it – it is not a wig, you comprehend – but –'

'Poirot,' I roared. 'Once and for all I will have nothing to do with the beastly inventions of your confounded hairdresser. What's the matter with the top of my head?'

'Nothing – nothing at all.'

'It's not as though I were going *bald*.'

'Of course not! Of course not!'

'The hot summers out there naturally cause the hair to fall out a bit. I shall take back a really good hair tonic.'

'*Précisément.*'

336

'And, anyway, what business is it of Japp's? He always was an offensive kind of devil. And no sense of humour. The kind of man who laughs when a chair is pulled away just as a man is about to sit down.'

'A great many people would laugh at that.'

'It's utterly senseless.'

'From the point of view of the man about to sit, certainly it is.'

'Well,' I said, slightly recovering my temper. (I admit that I am touchy about the thinness of my hair.) 'I'm sorry that anonymous letter business came to nothing.'

'I have indeed been in the wrong over that. About that letter, there was, I thought, the odour of the fish. Instead a mere stupidity. Alas, I grow old and suspicious like the blind watchdog who growls when there is nothing there.'

'If I'm going to co-operate with you, we must look about for some other "creamy" crime,' I said with a laugh.

'You remember your remark of the other day? If you could order a crime as one orders a dinner, what would you choose?'

I fell in with his humour.

'Let me see now. Let's review the menu. Robbery? Forgery? No, I think not. Rather too vegetarian. It must be murder – red-blooded murder – with trimmings, of course.'

'Naturally. The *hors d'oeuvres*.'

'Who shall the victim be – man or woman? Man, I think. Some big-wig. American millionaire. Prime Minister. Newspaper proprietor. Scene of the crime – well, what's wrong with the good old library? Nothing like it for atmosphere. As for the weapon – well, it might be a curiously twisted dagger – or some blunt instrument – a carved stone idol –'

Poirot sighed.

'Or, of course,' I said, 'there's poison – but that's always so technical. Or a revolver shot echoing in the night. Then there must be a beautiful girl or two –'

'With auburn hair,' murmured my friend.

'Your same old joke. One of the beautiful girls, of course, must be unjustly suspected – and there's some misunderstanding between her and the young man. And then, of course, there must be some other suspects – an older woman – dark, dangerous type – and some friend or rival of the dead man's – and a quiet secretary – dark horse – and a hearty man with a bluff manner – and a couple of discharged servants or gamekeepers or something – and a damn fool of a detective rather like Japp – and well – that's about all.'

'That is your idea of the cream, eh?'

'I gather you don't agree.'

Poirot looked at me sadly.

'You have made there a very pretty résumé of nearly all the detective stories that have ever been written.'

'Well,' I said. 'What would *you* order?'

Poirot closed his eyes and leaned back in his chair. His voice came purringly from between his lips.

'A very simple crime. A crime with no complications. A crime of quiet domestic life ... very unimpassioned – very *intime*.'

'How can a crime be *intime*?'

'Supposing,' murmured Poirot, 'that four people sit down to play bridge and one, the odd man out, sits in a chair by the fire. And the end of the evening the man by the fire is found dead. One of the four, while he is dummy, has gone over and killed him, and intent on the play of the hand, the other three have not noticed. Ah, there would be a crime for you! *Which of the four was it?*'

'Well,' I said. 'I can't see *any* excitement in that!'

Poirot threw me a glance of reproof.

'No, because there are no curiously twisted daggers, no blackmail, no emerald that is the stolen eye of a god, no untraceable Eastern poisons. You have the melodramatic soul, Hastings. You would like, not one murder, but a series of murders.'

'I admit,' I said, 'that a second murder in a book often cheers things up. If the murder happens in the first chapter, and you have to follow up everybody's alibi until the last page but one – well, it does get a bit tedious.'

The telephone rang and Poirot rose to answer.

''Allo,' he said. ''Allo. Yes, it is Hercule Poirot speaking.'

He listened for a minute or two and then I saw his face change. His own side of the conversation was short and disjointed.

'*Mais oui* ...'

'Yes, of course ...'

'But yes, we will come ...'

'Naturally ...'

'It may be as you say ...'

'Yes, I will bring it. *A tout à l'heure* then.'

He replaced the receiver and came across the room to me.

'That was Japp speaking, Hastings.'

'Yes?'

'He had just got back to the Yard. There was a message from Andover . . .'

'Andover?' I cried excitedly.

Poirot said slowly:

'An old woman of the name of Ascher who keeps a little tobacco and newspaper shop has been found murdered.'

I think I felt ever so slightly damped. My interest, quickened by the sound of Andover, suffered a faint check. I had expected something fantastic – out of the way! The murder of an old woman who kept a little tobacco shop seemed, somehow, sordid and uninteresting.

Poirot continued in the same slow, grave voice:

'The Andover police believe they can put their hand on the man who did it –'

I felt a second throb of disappointment.

'It seems the woman was on bad terms with her husband. He drinks and is by way of being rather a nasty customer. He's threatened to take her life more than once.

'Nevertheless,' continued Poirot, 'in view of what has happened, the police there would like to have another look at the anonymous letter I received. I have said that you and I will go down to Andover at once.'

My spirits revived a little. After all, sordid as this crime seemed to be, it was a *crime*, and it was a long time since I had had any association with crime and criminals.

I hardly listened to the next words Poirot said. But they were to come back to me with significance later.

'This is the beginning,' said Hercule Poirot.

CHAPTER FOUR

Mrs Ascher

We were received at Andover by Inspector Glen, a tall fair-haired man with a pleasant smile.

For the sake of conciseness I think I had better give a brief résumé of the bare facts of the case.

The crime was discovered by Police Constable Dover at 1 am on the morning of the 22nd. When on his round he tried the door of the shop and found it unfastened, he entered and at first thought the place was empty. Directing his torch over the counter, however, he caught sight of the huddled-up body of the old woman. When the police surgeon arrived on the spot it was elicited that the woman had been struck down by a heavy blow on the back of the head, probably while she was reaching down a packet of cigarettes from the shelf behind the counter. Death must have occurred about nine to seven hours previously.

'But we've been able to get it down a bit nearer than that,' explained the inspector. 'We've found a man who went in and bought some tobacco at 5.30. And a second man went in and found the shop empty, as he thought, at five minutes past six. That puts the time at between 5.30 and 6.05. So far I haven't been able to find anyone who saw this man Ascher in the neighbourhood, but, of course, it's early as yet. He was in the Three Crowns at nine o'clock pretty far gone in drink. When we get hold of him he'll be detained on suspicion.'

'Not a very desirable character, inspector?' asked Poirot.

'Unpleasant bit of goods.'

'He didn't live with his wife?'

'No, they separated some years ago. Ascher's a German. He was a waiter at one time, but he took to drink and gradually became unemployable. His wife went into service for a bit. Her last place was as cook-housekeeper to an old lady, Miss Rose. She allowed her husband so much out of her wages to keep himself, but he was always getting drunk and coming round and making scenes at the places where she was employed. That's why she took the post with Miss Rose at The Grange. It's three miles out of Andover, dead in the country. He couldn't get at her there so well. When Miss Rose died, she left Mrs Ascher a small legacy, and the woman started this tobacco and newsagent business – quite a tiny place – just cheap cigarettes and a few newspapers – that sort of thing. She just about managed to keep going. Ascher used to come round and abuse her now and again and she used to give him a bit to get rid of him. She allowed him fifteen shillings a week regular.'

'Had they any children?' asked Poirot.

'No. There's a niece. She's in service near Overton. Very superior, steady young woman.'

'And you say this man Ascher used to threaten his wife?'

'That's right. He was a terror when he was in drink – cursing and swearing that he'd bash her head in. She had a hard time, did Mrs Ascher.'

'What age of woman was she?'

'Close on sixty – respectable and hard-working.'

Poirot said gravely:

'It is your opinion, inspector, that this man Ascher committed the crime?'

The inspector coughed cautiously.

'It's a bit early to say that, Mr Poirot, but I'd like to hear Franz Ascher's own account of how he spent yesterday evening. If he can give a satisfactory account of himself, well and good – if not –'

His pause was a pregnant one.

'Nothing was missing from the shop?'

'Nothing. Money in the till quite undisturbed. No signs of robbery.'

'You think that this man Ascher came into the shop drunk, started abusing his wife and finally struck her down?'

'It seems the most likely solution. But I must confess, sir, I'd like to have another look at that very odd letter you received. I was wondering if it was just possible that it came from this man Ascher.'

Poirot handed over the letter and the inspector read it with a frown.

'It doesn't read like Ascher,' he said at last. 'I doubt if Ascher would use the term "our" British police – not unless he was trying to be extra cunning – and I doubt if he's got the wits for that. Then the man's a wreck – all to pieces. His hand's too shaky to print letters clearly like this. It's good quality notepaper and ink, too. It's odd that the letter should mention the 21st of the month. Of course it *might* be coincidence.'

'That is possible – yes.'

'But I don't like this kind of coincidence, Mr Poirot. It's a bit too

341

pat.'

He was silent for a minute or two – a frown creasing his forehead.

'A B C. Who the devil could A B C be? We'll see if Mary Drower (that's the niece) can give us any help. It's an odd business. But for this letter I'd have put my money on Franz Ascher for a certainty.'

'Do you know anything of Mrs Ascher's past?'

'She's a Hampshire woman. Went into service as a girl up in London – that's where she met Ascher and married him. Things must have been difficult for them during the war. She actually left him for good in 1922. They were in London then. She came back here to get away from him, but he got wind of where she was and followed her down here, pestering her for money –' A constable came in. 'Yes, Briggs, what is it?'

'It's the man Ascher, sir. We've brought him in.'

'Right. Bring him in here. Where was he?'

'Hiding in a truck on the railway siding.'

'He was, was he? Bring him along.'

Franz Ascher was indeed a miserable and unprepossessing specimen. He was blubbering and cringing and blustering alternately. His bleary eyes moved shiftily from one face to another.

'What do you want with me? I have not done nothing. It is a shame and a scandal to bring me here! You are swine, how dare you?' His manner changed suddenly. 'No, no, I do not mean that – you would not hurt a poor old man – not be hard on him. Everyone is hard on poor old Franz. Poor old Franz.'

Mr Ascher started to weep.

'That'll do, Ascher,' said the inspector. 'Pull yourself together. I'm not charging you with anything – yet. And you're not bound to make a statement unless you like. On the other hand, if you're *not* concerned in the murder of your wife –'

Ascher interrupted him – his voice rising to a scream.

'I did not kill her! I did not kill her! It is all lies! You are goddamned English pigs – all against me. I never kill her – never.'

'You threatened to often enough, Ascher.'

'No, no. You do not understand. That was just a joke – a good joke between me and Alice. She understood.'

'Funny kind of joke! Do you care to say where you were yesterday evening, Ascher?'

'Yes, yes – I tell you everything. I did not go near Alice. I am with friends – good friends. We are at the Seven Stars – and then we are at the Red Dog –'

He hurried on, his words stumbling over each other.

'Dick Willows – he was with me – and old Curdie – and George – and Platt and lots of the boys. I tell you I do not never go near Alice. Ach Gott, it is the truth I am telling you.'

His voice rose to a scream. The inspector nodded to his underling.

'Take him away. Detained on suspicion.'

'I don't know what to think,' he said as the unpleasant, shaking old man with the malevolent, mouthing jaw was removed. 'If it wasn't for the letter, I'd say he did it.'

'What about the men he mentions?'

'A bad crowd – not one of them would stick at perjury. I've no doubt he *was* with them the greater part of the evening. A lot depends on whether any one saw him near the shop between half-past five and six.'

Poirot shook his head thoughtfully.

'You are sure nothing was taken from the shop?'

The inspector shrugged his shoulders.

'That depends. A packet or two of cigarettes might have been taken – but you'd hardly commit murder for that.'

'And there was nothing – how shall I put it – introduced into the shop? Nothing that was odd there – incongruous?'

'There was a railway guide,' said the inspector.

'A railway guide?'

'Yes. It was open and turned face downward on the counter. Looked as though someone had been looking up the trains from Andover. Either the old woman or a customer.'

'Did she sell that type of thing?'

The inspector shook his head.

'She sold penny time-tables. This was a big one – kind of thing only Smith's or a big stationer would keep.'

A light came into Poirot's eyes. He leant forward.

A light came into the inspector's eye also.

'A railway guide, you say. A Bradshaw – *or an A B C?*'

'By the lord,' he said. 'It *was* an A B C.'

343

CHAPTER FIVE

Mary Drower

I think that I can date my interest in the case from that first mention
of the A B C railway guide. Up till then I had not been able to raise
much enthusiasm. This sordid murder of an old woman in a
back-street shop was so like the usual type of crime reported in the
newspapers that it failed to strike a significant note. In my own mind
I had put down the anonymous letter with its mention of the 21st as a
mere coincidence. Mrs Ascher, I felt reasonably sure, had been the
victim of her drunken brute of a husband. But now the mention of
the railway guide (so familiarly known by its abbreviation of A B C,
listing as it did all railway stations in their alphabetical order) sent a
quiver of excitement through me. Surely – surely this could not be a
second coincidence?

The sordid crime took on a new aspect.

Who was the mysterious individual who had killed Mrs Ascher
and left an A B C railway guide behind him?

When we left the police station our first visit was to the mortuary
to see the body of the dead woman. A strange feeling came over me as
I gazed down on that wrinkled old face with the scanty grey hair
drawn back tightly from the temples. It looked so peaceful, so
incredibly remote from violence.

'Never knew who or what struck her,' observed the sergeant.
'That's what Dr Kerr says. I'm glad it was that way, poor old soul. A
decent woman she was.'

'She must have been beautiful once,' said Poirot.

'Really?' I murmured incredulously.

'But yes, look at the line of the jaw, the bones, the moulding of the
head.'

He sighed as he replaced the sheet and we left the mortuary.

Our next move was a brief interview with the police surgeon.

Dr Kerr was a competent-looking middle-aged man. He spoke
briskly and with decision.

'The weapon wasn't found,' he said. 'Impossible to say what it
may have been. A weighted stick, a club, a form of sandbag – any of
those would fit the case.'

'Would much force be needed to strike such a blow?'

The doctor shot a keen glance at Poirot.

'Meaning, I suppose, could a shaky old man of seventy do it? Oh, yes, it's perfectly possible – given sufficient weight in the head of the weapon, quite a feeble person could achieve the desired result.'

'The the murderer could just as well be a woman as a man?'

The suggestion took the doctor somewhat aback.

'A woman, eh? Well, I confess it never occurred to me to connect a woman with this type of crime. But of course it's possible – perfectly possible. Only, psychologically speaking, I shouldn't say this was a woman's crime.'

Poirot nodded his head in eager agreement.

'Perfectly, perfectly. On the face of it, highly improbable. But one must take all possibilities into account. The body was lying – how?'

The doctor gave us a careful description of the position of the victim. It was his opinion that she had been standing with her back to the counter (and therefore to her assailant) when the blow had been struck. She had slipped down in a heap behind the counter quite out of sight of anyone entering the shop casually.

When we had thanked Dr Kerr and taken our leave, Poirot said:

'You perceive, Hastings, that we have already one further point in favour of Ascher's innocence. If he had been abusing his wife and threatening her, she would have been *facing* him over the counter. Instead she had her *back* to her assailant – obviously she is reaching down tobacco or cigarettes for a *customer*.'

I gave a little shiver.

'Pretty gruesome.'

Poirot shook his head gravely.

'*Pauvre femme*,' he murmured.

Then he glanced at his watch.

'Overton is not, I think, many miles from here. Shall we run over there and have an interview with the niece of the dead woman?'

'Surely you will go first to the shop where the crime took place?'

'I prefer to do that later. I have a reason.'

He did not explain further, and a few minutes later we were driving on the London road in the direction of Overton.

The address which the inspector had given us was that of a good-sized house about a mile on the London side of the village.

Our ring at the bell was answered by a pretty dark-haired girl whose eyes were red with recent weeping.

Poirot said gently:

'Ah! I think it is you who are Miss Mary Drower, the parlourmaid here?'

345

'Yes, sir, that's right. I'm Mary, sir.'

'Then perhaps I can talk to you for a few minutes if your mistress will not object. It is about your aunt, Mrs Ascher.'

'The mistress is out, sir. She wouldn't mind, I'm sure, if you came in here.'

She opened the door of a small morning-room. We entered and Poirot, seating himself on a chair by the window, looked up keenly into the girl's face.

'You have heard of your aunt's death, of course?'

The girl nodded, tears coming once more into her eyes.

'This morning, sir. The police came over. Oh! it's terrible! Poor auntie! Such a hard life as she'd had, too. And now this – it's too awful.'

'The police did not suggest your returning to Andover?'

'They said I must come to the inquest – that's on Monday, sir. But I've nowhere to go there – I couldn't fancy being over the shop – now – and what with the housemaid being away, I didn't want to put the mistress out more than may be.'

'You were fond of your aunt, Mary?' said Poirot gently.

'Indeed I was, sir. Very good she's been to me always, auntie has. I went to her in London when I was eleven years old, after mother died. I started in service when I was sixteen, but I usually went along to auntie's on my day out. A lot of trouble she went through with that German fellow. "My old devil," she used to call him. He'd never let her be in peace anywhere. Sponging, cadging old beast.'

The girl spoke with vehemence.

'Your aunt never thought of freeing herself by legal means from this persecution?'

'Well, you see, he was her husband, sir, you couldn't get away from that.'

The girl spoke simply but with finality.

'Tell me, Mary, he threatened her, did he not?'

'Oh, yes, sir, it was awful the things he used to say. That he'd cut her throat, and such like. Cursing and swearing too – both in German and in English. And yet auntie says he was a fine handsome figure of a man when she married him. It's dreadful to think, sir, what people come to.'

'Yes, indeed. And so, I suppose, Mary, having actually heard these threats, you were not so very surprised when you learnt what had happened?'

'Oh, but I was, sir. You see, sir, I never thought for one moment that he meant it. I thought it was just nasty talk and nothing more to it. And it isn't as though auntie was afraid of him. Why, I've seen him slink away like a dog with its tail between its legs when she turned on him. *He* was afraid of *her* if you like.'

'And yet she gave him money?'

'Well, he was her husband, you see, sir.'

'Yes, so you said before.' He paused for a minute or two. Then he said: 'Suppose that, after all, he did *not* kill her.'

'Didn't kill her?'

She stared.

'That is what I said. Supposing someone else killed her . . . Have you any idea who that someone else could be?'

She stared at him with even more amazement.

'I've no idea, sir. It doesn't seem likely, though, does it?'

'There was no one your aunt was afraid of?'

Mary shook her head.

'Auntie wasn't afraid of people. She'd a sharp tongue and she'd stand up to anybody.'

'You never heard her mention anyone who had a grudge against her?'

'No, indeed, sir.'

'Did she ever get anonymous letters?'

'What kind of letters did you say, sir?'

'Letters that weren't signed – or only signed by something like A B C.' He watched her narrowly, but plainly she was at a loss. She shook her head wonderingly.

'Has your aunt any relations except you?'

'Not now, sir. One of ten she was, but only three lived to grow up. My Uncle Tom was killed in the war, and my Uncle Harry went to South America and no one's heard of him since, and mother's dead, of course, so there's only me.'

'Had your aunt any savings? Any money put by?'

'She'd a little in the Savings Bank, sir – enough to bury her proper, that's what she always said. Otherwise she didn't more than just make ends meet – what with her old devil and all.'

Poirot nodded thoughtfully. He said – perhaps more to himself than to her:

'At present one is in the dark – there is no direction – if things get clearer –' He got up. 'If I want you at any time, Mary, I will write to you here.'

'As a matter of fact, sir, I'm giving in my notice. I don't like the

347

country. I stayed here because I fancied it was a comfort to auntie to have me near by. But now' – again the tears rose in her eyes – 'there's no reason I should stay, and so I'll go back to London. It's gayer for a girl there.'

'I wish that, when you do go, you would give me your address. Here is my card.'

He handed it to her. She looked at it with a puzzled frown.

'Then you're not – anything to do with the police, sir?'

'I am a private detective.'

She stood there looking at him for some moments in silence. She said at last:

'Is there anything – queer going on, sir?'

'Yes, my child. There is – something queer going on. Later you may be able to help me.'

'I – I'll do anything, sir. It – it wasn't *right*, sir, auntie being killed.'

A strange way of putting it – but deeply moving.

A few seconds later we were driving back to Andover.

CHAPTER SIX

The Scene of the Crime

The street in which the tragedy had occurred was a turning off the main street. Mrs Ascher's shop was situated about half-way down it on the right-hand side.

As we turned into the street Poirot glanced at his watch and I realized why he had delayed his visit to the scene of the crime until now. It was just on half-past five. He had wished to reproduce yesterday's atmosphere as closely as possible.

But if that had been his purpose it was defeated. Certainly at this moment the road bore very little likeness to its appearance on the previous evening. There were a certain number of small shops interspersed between private houses of the poorer class. I judged that ordinarily there could be a fair number of people passing up and down – mostly people of the poorer classes, with a good sprinkling of children playing on the pavements and in the road.

At this moment there was a solid mass of people standing staring at one particular house or shop and it took little perspicuity to guess which that was. What we saw was a mass of average human beings looking with intense interest at the spot where another human being had been done to death.

As we drew nearer this proved to be indeed the case. In front of a small dingy-looking shop with its shutters now closed stood a harassed-looking young policeman who was stolidly adjuring the crowd to 'pass along there.' By the help of a colleague, displacements took place – a certain number of people grudgingly sighed and betook themselves to their ordinary vocations, and almost immediately other persons came along and took up their stand to gaze their fill on the spot where murder had been committed.

Poirot stopped a little distance from the main body of the crowd. From where we stood the legend painted over the door could be read plainly enough. Poirot repeated it under his breath.

'A. Ascher. *Oui, c'est peut-être là –*'

He broke off.

'Come, let us go inside, Hastings.'

I was only too ready.

We made our way through the crowd and accosted the young policeman. Poirot produced the credentials which the inspector had given him. The constable nodded, and unlocked the door to let us pass within. We did so and entered to the intense interest of the lookers-on.

Inside it was very dark owing to the shutters being closed. The constable found and switched on the electric light. The bulb was a low-powered one so that the interior was still dimly lit.

I looked about me.

A dingy little place. A few cheap magazines strewn about, and yesterday's newspapers – all with a day's dust on them. Behind the counter a row of shelves reaching to the ceiling and packed with tobacco and packets of cigarettes. There were also a couple of jars of peppermint humbugs and barley sugar. A commonplace little shop, one of many thousand such others.

The constable in his slow Hampshire voice was explaining the *mise en scène*.

'Down in a heap behind the counter, that's where she was. Doctor says as how she never knew what hit her. Must have been reaching up to one of the shelves.'

'There was nothing in her hand?'

'No, sir. but there was a packet of Player's down beside her.'

Poirot nodded. His eyes swept round the small space observing – noting.

'And the railway guide was – where?'

'Here, sir.' The constable pointed out the spot on the counter. 'It was open at the right page for Andover and lying face down. Seems as though he must have been looking up the trains to London. If so, it mightn't have been an Andover man at all. But then, of course, the railway guide might have belonged to someone else what had nothing to do with the murder at all, but just forgot it here.'

'Fingerprints?' I suggested.

The man shook his head.

'The whole place was examined straight away, sir. There weren't none.'

'Not on the counter itself?' asked Poirot.

'A long sight too many, sir! All confused and jumbled up.'

'Any of Ascher's among them?'

'Too soon to say, sir.'

Poirot nodded, then asked if the dead woman lived over the shop.

'Yes, sir, you go through that door at the back, sir. You'll excuse me not coming with you, but I've got to stay –'

Poirot passed through the door in question and I followed him.

Behind the shop was a microscopic sort of parlour and kitchen combined – it was neat and clean but very dreary looking and scantily furnished. On the mantelpiece were a few photographs. I went up and looked at them and Poirot joined me.

The photographs were three in all. One was a cheap portrait of the girl we had been with that afternoon, Mary Drower. She was obviously wearing her best clothes and had the self-conscious, wooden smile on her face that so often disfigures the expression in posed photography, and makes a snapshot preferable.

The second was a more expensive type of picture – an artistically blurred reproduction of an elderly woman with white hair. A high fur collar stood up round the neck.

I guessed that this was probably the Miss Rose who had left Mrs Ascher the small legacy which had enabled her to start in business.

The third photograph was a very old one, now faded and yellow. It represented a young man and woman in somewhat old-fashioned clothes standing arm in arm. The man had a button-hole and there was an air of bygone festivity about the whole pose.

'Probably a wedding picture,' said Poirot. 'Regard, Hastings, did I not tell you that she had been a beautiful woman?'

He was right. Disfigured by old-fashioned hairdressing and weird clothes, there was no disguising the handsomeness of the girl in the picture with her clear-cut features and spirited bearing. I looked closely at the second figure. It was almost impossible to recognise the seedy Ascher in this smart young man with the military bearing.

I recalled the leering drunken old man, and the toil-worn face of the dead woman – and I shivered a little at the remorselessness of time . . .

From the parlour a stair led to two upstairs rooms. One was empty and unfurnished, the other had evidently been the dead woman's bedroom. After being searched by the police it had been left as it was. A couple of old worn blankets on the bed – a little stock of well-darned underwear in a drawer – cookery recipes in another – a paper-backed novel entitled *The Green Oasis* – a pair of new stockings – pathetic in their cheap shininess – a couple of china ornaments – a Dresden shepherd much broken, and a blue and yellow spotted dog – a black raincoat and a woolly jumper hanging on pegs – such were the worldly possessions of the late Alice Ascher.

If there had been any personal papers, the police had taken them.

'*Pauvre femme*,' murmured Poirot. 'Come, Hastings, there is nothing for us here.'

When we were once more in the street, he hesitated for a minute or two, then crossed the road. Almost exactly opposite Mrs Ascher's was a greengrocer's shop – of the type that has most of its stock outside rather than inside.

In a low voice Poirot gave me certain instructions. Then he himself entered the shop. After waiting a minute or two I followed him in. He was at the moment negotiating for a lettuce. I myself bought a pound of strawberries.

Poirot was talking animatedly to the stout lady who was serving him.

'It was just opposite you, was it not, that this murder occurred? What an affair! What a sensation it must have caused you!'

The stout lady was obviously tired of talking about the murder. She must have had a long day of it. She observed:

'It would be as well if some of that gaping crowd cleared off. What is there to look at, I'd like to know?'

'It must have been very different last night,' said Poirot. 'Possibly you even observed the murderer enter the shop – a tall, fair man with a beard, was he not? A Russian, so I have heard.'

'What's that?' The woman looked up sharply. 'A Russian did it, you say?'

'I understand that the police have arrested him.'

'Did you ever know?' The woman was excited, voluble. 'A foreigner.'

'*Mais oui*. I thought perhaps you might have noticed him last night?'

'Well, I don't get much chance of noticing, and that's a fact. The evening's our busy time and there's always a fair few passing along and getting home after their work. A tall, fair man with a beard – no, I can't say I saw anyone of that description anywhere about.'

I broke in on my cue.

'Excuse me, sir,' I said to Poirot. 'I think you have been misinformed. A short *dark* man I was told.'

An interested discussion intervened in which the stout lady, her lank husband and a hoarse-voiced shop-boy all participated. No less than four short dark men had been observed, and the hoarse boy had seen a tall fair one, 'but he hadn't got no beard,' he added regretfully.

Finally, our purchases made, we left the establishment, leaving our falsehoods uncorrected.

'And what was the point of all that, Poirot?' I demanded somewhat reproachfully.

352

'*Parbleu*, I wanted to estimate the chances of a stranger being noticed entering the shop opposite.'

'Couldn't you simply have asked – without all that tissue of lies?'

'No, *mon ami*. If I had "simply asked", as you put it, I should have got no answer at all to my questions. You yourself are English and yet you do not seem to appreciate the quality of the English reaction to a direct question. It is invariably one of suspicion and the natural result is reticence. If I had asked those people for information they would have shut up like oysters. But by making a statement (and a somewhat out of the way and preposterous one) and by your contradiction of it, tongues are immediately loosened. We know also that that particular time was a "busy time" – that is, that everyone would be intent on their own concerns and that there would be a fair number of people passing along the pavements. Our murderer chose his time well, Hastings.'

He paused and then added on a deep note of reproach:

'Is it that you have not in any degree the common sense, Hastings? I say to you: "Make a purchase *quelconque*" – and you deliberately choose the strawberries! Already they commence to creep through their bag and endanger your good suit.'

With some dismay, I perceived that this was indeed the case.

I hastily presented the strawberries to a small boy who seemed highly astonished and faintly suspicious.

Poirot added the lettuce, thus setting the seal on the child's bewilderment.

He continued to drive the moral home.

'At a cheap greengrocer's – *not* strawberries. A strawberry, unless fresh picked, is bound to exude juice. A banana – some apples – even a cabbage – but *strawberries* –'

'It was the first thing I thought of,' I explained by way of excuse.

'That is unworthy of your imagination,' returned Poirot sternly.

He paused on the sidewalk.

The house and shop on the right of Mrs Ascher's was empty. A 'To Let' sign appeared in the windows. On the other side was a house with somewhat grimy muslin curtains.

To this house Poirot betook himself and, there being no bell, executed a series of sharp flourishes with the knocker.

The door was opened after some delay by a very dirty child with a nose that needed attention.

'Good evening,' said Poirot. 'Is your mother within?'

'Ay?' said the child.

It stared at us with disfavour and deep suspicion.

'Your mother,' said Poirot.

This took some twelve seconds to sink in, then the child turned and, bawling up the stairs 'Mum, you're wanted,' retreated to some fastness in the dim interior.

A sharp-faced woman looked over the balusters and began to descend.

'No good you wasting your time –' she began, but Poirot interrupted her.

He took off his hat and bowed magnificently.

'Good evening, madame. I am on the staff of the *Evening Flicker*. I want to persuade you to accept a fee of five pounds and let us have an article on your late neighbour, Mrs Ascher.'

The irate words arrested on her lips, the woman came down the stairs smoothing her hair and hitching at her skirt.

'Come inside, please – on the left there. Won't you sit down, sir.'

The tiny room was heavily over-crowded with a massive pseudo-Jacobean suite, but we managed to squeeze ourselves in and on to a hard-seated sofa.

'You must excuse me,' the woman was saying. 'I am sure I'm sorry I spoke so sharp just now, but you'd hardly believe the worry one has to put up with – fellows coming along selling this, that and the other – vacuum cleaners, stockings, lavender bags and such-like foolery – and all so plausible and civil spoken. Got your name, too, pat they have. It's Mrs Fowler this, that and the other.'

Seizing adroitly on the name, Poirot said:

'Well, Mrs Fowler, I hope you're going to do what I ask.'

'I don't know, I'm sure.' The five pounds hung alluringly before Mrs Fowler's eyes. 'I *knew* Mrs Ascher, of course, but as to *writing* anything.'

Hastily Poirot reassured her. No labour on her part was required. He would elicit the facts from her and the interview would be written up.

Thus encouraged, Mrs Fowler plunged willingly into reminiscence, conjecture and hearsay.

Kept herself to herself, Mrs Ascher had. Not what you'd call really *friendly*, but there, she'd had a lot of trouble, poor soul, everyone knew that. And by rights Franz Ascher ought to have been locked up years ago. Not that Mrs Ascher had been afraid of him – real tartar she could be when roused! Give as good as she got any day. But there it was – the pitcher could go to the well once too often. Again and again, she, Mrs Fowler, had said to her: 'One of these days that man will do for you. Mark my words.' And he had done, hadn't he? And there had she, Mrs Fowler, been right next door and never heard a sound.

In a pause Poirot managed to insert a question.

Had Mrs Ascher ever received any peculiar letters – letters without a proper signature – just something like A B C?

Regretfully, Mrs Fowler returned a negative answer.

'I know the kind of thing you mean – anonymous letters they call them – mostly full of words you'd blush to say out loud. Well, I don't know, I'm sure, if Franz Ascher ever took to writing those. Mrs Ascher never let on to me if he did. What's that? A railway guide, an A B C? No, I never saw such a thing about – and I'm sure if Mrs Ascher had been sent one I'd have heard about it. I declare you could have knocked me down with a feather when I heard about this whole business. It was my girl Edie what came to me. "Mum," she says, "there's ever so many policemen next door." Gave me quite a turn, it did. "Well," I said, when I heard about it, "it does show that she ought never to have been alone in the house – that niece of hers ought to have been with her. A man in drink can be like a ravening wolf," I said, "and in my opinion a wild beast is neither more nor less than what that old devil of a husband of hers is. I've warned her," I said, "many times and now my words have come true. He'll do for you," I said. And he has done for her! You can't rightly estimate what a man will do when he's in drink and this murder's a proof of it.'

She wound up with a deep gasp.

'Nobody saw this man Ascher go into the shop, I believe?' said Poirot.

Mrs Fowler sniffed scornfully.

'Naturally he wasn't going to show himself,' she said.

How Mr Ascher had got there without showing himself she did not deign to explain.

She agreed that there was no back way into the house and that Ascher was quite well known by sight in the district.

'But he didn't want to swing for it and he kept himself well hid.'

Poirot kept the conversational ball rolling some little time longer, but when it seemed certain that Mrs Fowler had told all that she knew not once but many times over, he terminated the interview, first paying out the promised sum.

'Rather a dear five pounds' worth, Poirot,' I ventured to remark when we were once more in the street.

355

'So far, yes.'

'You think she knows more than she has told?

'My friend, we are in the peculiar position of *not knowing what questions to ask*. We are like little children playing *cache-cache* in the dark. We stretch out our hands and grope about. Mrs Fowler has told us all that she *thinks* she knows – and has thrown in several conjectures for good measure! In the future, however, her evidence may be useful. It is for the future that I have invested that sum of five pounds.'

I did not quite understand the point, but at this moment we ran into Inspector Glen.

CHAPTER SEVEN

Mr Partridge and Mr Riddell

Inspector Glen was looking rather gloomy. He had, I gathered, spent the afternoon trying to get a complete list of persons who had been noticed entering the tobacco shop.

'And nobody has seen anyone?' Poirot inquired.

'Oh, yes, they have. Three tall men with furtive expressions – four short men with black moustaches – two beards – three fat men – all strangers – and all, if I'm to believe witnesses, with sinister expressions! I wonder somebody didn't see a gang of masked men with revolvers while they were about it!'

Poirot smiled sympathetically.

'Does anybody claim to have seen the man Ascher?'

'No, they don't. And that's another point in his favour. I've just told the Chief Constable that I think this is a job for Scotland Yard. I don't believe it's a local crime.'

Poirot said gravely:

'I agree with you.'

The inspector said:

'You know, Monsieur Poirot, it's a nasty business – a nasty business . . . I don't like it . . .'

We had two more interviews before returning to London.

The first was with Mr James Partridge. Mr Partridge was the last person known to have seen Mrs Ascher alive. He had made a purchase from her at 5.30.

Mr Partridge was a small man, a bank clerk by profession. He wore pince-nez, was very dry and spare-looking and extremely precise in all his utterances. He lived in a small house as neat and trim as himself.

'Mr – er – Poirot,' he said, glancing at the card my friend had handed to him. 'From Inspector Glen? What can I do for you, Mr Poirot?'

'I understand, Mr Partridge, that you were the last person to see Mrs Ascher alive.'

Mr Partridge placed his finger-tips together and looked at Poirot as though he were a doubtful cheque.

'That is a very debatable point, Mr Poirot,' he said. 'Many people may have made purchases from Mrs Ascher after I did so.'

357

'If so, they have not come forward to say so.'

Mr Partridge coughed.

'Some people, Mr Poirot, have no sense of public duty.'

He looked at us owlishly through his spectacles.

'Exceedingly true,' murmured Poirot. 'You, I understand, went to the police of your own accord?'

'Certainly I did. As soon as I heard of the shocking occurrence I perceived that my statement might be helpful and came forward accordingly.'

'A very proper spirit,' said Poirot solemnly. 'Perhaps you will be so kind as to repeat your story to me.'

'By all means. I was returning to this house and at 5.30 precisely –'

'Pardon, how was it that you knew the time so accurately?'

Mr Partridge looked a little annoyed at being interrupted.

'The church clock chimed. I looked at my watch and found I was a minute slow. That was just before I entered Mrs Ascher's shop.'

'Were you in the habit of making purchases there?'

'Fairly frequently. It was on my way home. About once or twice a week I was in the habit of purchasing two ounces of John Cotton mild.'

'Did you know Mrs Ascher at all? Anything of her circumstances or her history?'

'Nothing whatever. Beyond my purchase and an occasional remark as to the state of the weather, I had never spoken to her.'

'Did you know she had a drunken husband who was in the habit of threatening her life?'

'No, I knew nothing whatever about her.'

'You knew her by sight, however. Did anything about her appearance strike you as unusual yesterday evening? Did she appear flurried or put out in any way?'

Mr Partridge considered.

'As far as I noticed, she seemed exactly as usual,' he said.

Poirot rose.

'Thank you, Mr Partridge, for answering these questions. Have you, by any chance, an A B C in the house? I want to look up my return train to London.'

'On the shelf just behind you,' said Mr Partridge.

On the shelf in question were an A B C, a Bradshaw, the Stock Exchange Year Book, Kelly's Directory, a Who's Who and a local directory.

Poirot took down the A B C, pretended to look up a train, then thanked Mr Partridge and took his leave.

Our next interview was with Mr Albert Riddell and was of a highly different character. Mr Albert Riddell was a platelayer and our conversation took place to the accompaniment of the clattering of plates and dishes by Mr Riddell's obviously nervous wife, the growling of Mr Riddell's dog and the undisguised hostility of Mr Riddell himself.

He was a big clumsy giant of a man with a broad face and small suspicious eyes. He was in the act of eating meat-pie, washed down by exceedingly black tea. He peered at us angrily over the rim of his cup.

'Told all I've got to tell once, haven't I?' he growled. 'What's it to do with me, anyway? Told it to the blarsted police, I 'ave, and now I've got to spit it all out again to a couple of blarsted foreigners.'

Poirot gave a quick, amused glance in my direction and then said:

'In truth I sympathize with you, but what will you? It is a question of murder, is it not? One has to be very, very careful.'

'Best tell the gentleman what he wants, Bert,' said the woman nervously.

'You shut your blarsted mouth,' roared the giant.

'You did not, I think, go to the police of your own accord.' Poirot slipped the remark in neatly.

'Why the hell should I? It were no business of mine.'

'A matter of opinion,' said Poirot indifferently. 'There has been a murder – the police want to know who has been in the shop – I myself think it would have – what shall I say? – looked more natural if you had come forward.'

'I've got my work to do. Don't say I shouldn't have come forward in my own time -'

'But as it was, the police were given your name as that of a person seen to go into Mrs Ascher's and they had to come to you. Were they satisfied with your account?'

'Why shouldn't they be?' demanded Bert truculently.

Poirot merely shrugged his shoulders.

'What are you getting at, mister? Nobody's got anything against me? Everyone knows who did the old girl in, that b – of a husband of hers.'

'But he was not in the street that evening and you were.'

'Trying to fasten it on me, are you? Well, you won't succeed. What reason had I got to do a thing like that? Think I wanted to pinch a tin of her bloody tobacco? Think I'm a bloody homicidal maniac as they call it? Think I –?'

He rose threateningly from his seat. His wife bleated out:

'Bert, Bert – don't say such things. Bert – they'll think –'

'Calm yourself, monsieur,' said Poirot. 'I demand only your account of your visit. That you refuse it seems to me – what shall we say – a little odd?'

'Who said I refused anything?' Mr Riddell sank back again into his seat. 'I don't mind.'

'It was six o'clock when you entered the shop?'

'That's right – a minute or two after, as a matter of fact. Wanted a packet of Gold Flake. I pushed open the door –'

'It was closed, then?'

'That's right. I thought shop was shut, maybe. But it wasn't. I went in, there wasn't anyone about. I hammered on the counter and waited a bit. Nobody came, so I went out again. That's all, and you can put it in your pipe and smoke it.'

'You didn't see the body fallen down behind the counter?'

'No, no more would you have done – unless you was looking for it, maybe.'

'Was there a railway guide lying about?'

'Yes, there was – face downwards. It crossed my mind like that the old woman might have had to go off sudden by train and forgot to lock shop up.'

'Perhaps you picked up the railway guide or moved it along the counter?'

'Didn't touch the b – thing. I did just what I said.'

'And you did not see anyone leaving the shop before you yourself got there?'

'Didn't see any such thing. What I say is, why pitch on me –?'

Poirot rose.

'Nobody is pitching upon you – yet. Bonsoir, monsieur.'

He left the man with his mouth open and I followed him.

In the street he consulted his watch.

'With great haste, my friend, we might manage to catch the 7.02. Let us despatch ourselves quickly.'

CHAPTER EIGHT

The Second Letter

'Well?' I demanded eagerly.

We were seated in a first-class carriage which we had to ourselves. The train, an express, had just drawn out of Andover.

'The crime,' said Poirot, 'was committed by a man of medium height with red hair and a cast in the left eye. He limps slightly on the right foot and has a mole just below the shoulder-blade.'

'Poirot?' I cried.

For the moment I was completely taken in. Then the twinkle in my friend's eye undeceived me.

'Poirot!' I said again, this time in reproach.

'*Mon ami*, what will you? You fix upon me a look of doglike devotion and demand of me a pronouncement à la Sherlock Holmes! Now for the truth – *I do not know what the murderer looks like, nor where he lives, nor how to set hands upon him.*'

'If only he had left some clue,' I murmured.

'Yes, the clue – it is always the clue that attracts you. Alas that he did not smoke the cigarette and leave the ash, and then step in it with a shoe that has nails of a curious pattern. No – he is not so obliging. But at least, my friend, you have the *railway guide*. The A B C, that is a clue for you!'

'Do you think he left it by mistake then?'

'Of course not. He left it on purpose. The fingerprints tell us that.'

'But there weren't any on it.'

'That is what I mean. What was yesterday evening? A warm June night. Does a man stroll about on such an evening in *gloves*? Such a man would certainly have attracted attention. Therefore since there are no fingerprints on the A B C, it must have been carefully wiped. An innocent man would have left prints – a guilty man would not. So our murderer left it there for a purpose – but for all that it is none the less a clue. That A B C was bought by someone – it was carried by someone – there is a possibility there.'

'You think we may learn something that way?'

'Frankly, Hastings, I am not particularly hopeful. This man, this unknown X, obviously prides himself on his abilities. He is not likely to blaze a trail that can be followed straight away.'

'So that really the ABC isn't helpful at all.'

'Not in the sense you mean.'

'In any sense?'

Poirot did not answer at once. Then he said slowly:

'The answer to that is yes. We are confronted here by an unknown personage. He is in the dark and seeks to remain in the dark. But in the very nature of things *he cannot help throwing light upon himself*. In one sense we know nothing about him – in another sense we know already a good deal. I see his figure dimly taking shape – a man who prints clearly and well – who buys good-quality paper – who is at great need to express his personality. I see him as a child possibly ignored and passed over – I see him growing up with an inward sense of inferiority – warring with a sense of injustice . . . I see that inner urge – to assert himself – to focus attention on himself ever becoming stronger, and events, circumstances – crushing it down – heaping, perhaps, more humiliations on him. And inwardly the match is set to the powder train . . .'

'That's all pure conjecture,' I objected. 'It doesn't give you any practical help.'

'You prefer the match end, the cigarette ash, the nailed boots! You always have. But at least we can ask ourselves some practical questions. Why the A B C? Why Mrs Ascher? Why Andover?'

'The woman's past life seems simple enough,' I mused. 'The interviews with those two men were disappointing. They couldn't tell us anything more than we knew already.'

'To tell the truth, I did not expect much in that line. But we could not neglect two possible candidates for the murder.'

'Surely you don't think –'

'There is at least a possibility that the murderer lives in or near Andover. That is a possible answer to our question: "Why Andover?" Well, here were two men known to have been in the shop at the requisite time of day. Either of them *might* be the murderer. And there is nothing as yet to show that one or other of them is *not* the murderer.'

'That great hulking brute, Riddell, perhaps,' I admitted.

'Oh, I am inclined to acquit Riddell off-hand. He was nervous, blustering, obviously uneasy –'

'But surely that just shows –'

'A nature diametrically opposed to that which penned the A B C letter. Conceit and self-confidence are the characteristics that we must look for.'

'Someone who throws his weight about?'

362

'Possibly. But some people, under a nervous and self-effacing manner, conceal a great deal of vanity and self-satisfaction.'

'You don't think that little Mr Partridge –'

'He is more *le type*. One cannot say more than that. He acts as the writer of the letter would act – goes at once to the police – pushes himself to the fore – enjoys his position.'

'Do you really think –?'

'No, Hastings. Personally I believe that the murderer came from outside Andover, but we must neglect no avenue of research. And although I say "he" all the time, we must not exclude the possibility of a woman being concerned.'

'Surely not!'

'The method of attack is that of a man, I agree. But anonymous letters are written by women rather than by men. We must bear that in mind.'

I was silent for a few minutes, then I said:

'What do we do next?'

'My energetic Hastings,' Poirot said and smiled at me.

'No, but what do we do?'

'Nothing.'

'Nothing?' My disappointment rang our clearly.

'Am I the magician? The sorcerer? What would you have me do?'

Turning the matter over in my mind I found it difficult to give an answer. Nevertheless I felt convinced that something ought to be done and that we should not allow the grass to grow under our feet.

I said:

'There is the A B C – and the notepaper and envelope –'

'Naturally everything is being done in that line. The police have all the means at their disposal for that kind of inquiry. If anything is to be discovered on those lines have no fear but that they will discover it.'

With that I was forced to rest content.

In the days that followed I found Poirot curiously disinclined to discuss the case. When I tried to reopen the subject he waved it aside with an impatient hand.

In my own mind I was afraid that I fathomed his motive. Over the murder of Mrs Ascher, Poirot had sustained a defeat. A B C had challenged him – and A B C had won. My friend, accustomed to an unbroken line of successes, was sensitive to his failure – so much so that he could not even endure discussion of the subject. It was, perhaps, a sign of pettiness in so great a man, but even the most sober

363

of us is liable to have his head turned by success. In Poirot's case the head-turning process had been going on for years. Small wonder if its effects became noticeable at long last.

Understanding, I respected my friend's weakness and I made no further reference to the case. I read in the paper the account of the inquest. It was very brief, no mention was made of the A B C letter, and a verdict was returned of murder by some person or persons unknown. The crime attracted very little attention in the press. It had no popular or spectacular features. The murder of an old woman in a side street was soon passed over in the press for more thrilling topics.

Truth to tell, the affair was fading from my mind also, partly, I think, because I disliked to think of Poirot as being in any way associated with a failure, when on July 25th it was suddenly revived.

I had not seen Poirot for a couple of days as I had been away in Yorkshire for the weekend. I arrived back on Monday afternoon and the letter came by the six o'clock post. I remember the sudden, sharp intake of breath that Poirot gave as he slit open that particular envelope.

'It has come,' he said.

I stared at him – not understanding.

'What has come?'

'The second chapter of the A B C business.'

For a minute I looked at him uncomprehendingly. The matter had really passed from my memory.

'Read,' said Poirot and passed me over the letter.

As before, it was printed on good-quality paper.

> DEAR MR POIROT, – Well, what about it? First game to me, I think. The Andover business went with a swing, didn't it?
>
> But the fun's only just beginning. Let me draw your attention to Bexhill-on-Sea. Date, the 25th inst.
>
> What a merry time we are having! Yours etc.
>
> A B C

'Good God, Poirot,' I cried. 'Does this mean that this fiend is going to attempt another crime?'

'Naturally, Hastings. What else did you expect? Did you think that the Andover business was an isolated case? Do you not remember my saying: "This is the beginning"?'

'But this is horrible!'

'Yes, it is horrible.'

'We're up against a homicidal maniac.'

'Yes.'

His quietness was more impressive than any heroics could have been. I handed back the letter with a shudder.

The following morning saw us at a conference of powers. The Chief Constable of Sussex, the Assistant Commissioner of the CID, Inspector Glen from Andover, Superintendent Carter of the Sussex police, Japp and a younger inspector called Crome, and Dr Thompson, the famous alienist, were all assembled together. The postmark on this letter was Hampstead, but in Poirot's opinion little importance could be attached to this fact.

The matter was discussed fully. Dr Thompson was a pleasant middle-aged man who, in spite of his learning, contented himself with homely language, avoiding the technicalities of his profession.

'There's no doubt,' said the Assistant Commissioner, 'that the two letters are in the same hand. Both were written by the same person.'

'And we can fairly assume that that person was responsible for the Andover murder.'

'Quite. We've now got definite warning of a second crime scheduled to take place on the 25th – the day after tomorrow – at Bexhill. What steps can be taken?'

The Sussex Chief Constable looked at his superintendent.

'Well, Carter, what about it?'

The superintendent shook his head gravely.

'It's difficult, sir. There's not the least clue towards whom the victim may be. Speaking fair and square, what steps *can* we take?'

'A suggestion,' murmured Poirot.

Their faces turned to him.

'I think it possible that the surname of the intended victim will begin with the letter B.'

'That would be something,' said the superintendent doubtfully.

'An alphabetical complex,' said Dr Thompson thoughtfully.

'I suggest it as a possibility – no more. It came into my mind when I saw the name Ascher clearly written over the shop door of the unfortunate woman who was murdered last month. When I got the letter naming Bexhill it occurred to me as a possibility that the victim as well as the place might be selected by an alphabetical system.'

'It's possible,' said the doctor. 'On the other hand, it may be that the name Ascher was a coincidence – that the victim this time, no matter what her name is, will again be an old woman who keeps a shop. We're dealing, remember, with a madman. So far he hasn't given us any clue as to motive.'

'Has a madman any motive, sir?' asked the superintendent sceptically.

'Of course he has, man. A deadly logic is one of the special characteristics of acute mania. A man may believe himself divinely appointed to kill clergymen – or doctors – or old women in tobacco shops – and there's always some perfectly coherent reason behind it. We musn't let the alphabetical business run away with us. Bexhill succeeding to Andover *may* be a mere coincidence.'

'We can at least take certain precautions, Carter, and make a special note of the B's, especially small shopkeepers, and keep a watch on all small tobacconists and newsagents looked after by a single person. I don't think there's anything more we can do than that. Naturally, keep tabs on all strangers as far as possible.'

The superintendent uttered a groan.

'With the schools breaking up and the holidays beginning? People are fairly flooding into the place this week.'

'We must do what we can,' the Chief Constable said sharply.

Inspector Glen spoke in his turn.

'I'll have a watch kept on anyone connected with the Ascher business. Those two witnesses, Partridge and Riddell, and of course Ascher himself. If they show any sign of leaving Andover they'll be followed.'

The conference broke up after a few more suggestions and a little desultory conversation.

'Poirot,' I said as we walked along by the river. 'Surely this crime can be prevented?'

He turned a haggard face to me.

'The sanity of a city full of men against the insanity of one man? I fear, Hastings – I very much fear. Remember the long-continued success of Jack the Ripper.'

'It's horrible,' I said.

'Madness, Hastings, is a terrible thing . . . *I am afraid . . . I am very much afraid . . .*'

CHAPTER NINE

The Bexhill-on-Sea Murder

I still remember my awakening on the morning of the 25th of July. It must have been about seven-thirty.

Poirot was standing by my bedside gently shaking me by the shoulder. One glance at his face brought me from semi-consciousness into the full possession of my faculties.

'What is it?' I demanded, sitting up rapidly.

His answer came quite simply, but a wealth of emotion lay behind the three words he uttered.

'*It has happened.*'

'What?' I cried. 'You mean – but *today* is the 25th.'

'It took place last night – or rather in the early hours of this morning.'

As I sprang from bed and made a rapid toilet, he recounted briefly what he had just learnt over the telephone.

'The body of a young girl has been found on the beach at Bexhill. She has been identified as Elizabeth Barnard, a waitress in one of the cafés, who lived with her parents in a little recently built bungalow. Medical evidence gave the time of death as between 11.30 and 1 am.'

'They're quite sure that this is *the* crime?' I asked, as I hastily lathered my face.

'*An ABC open at the trains to Bexhill was found actually under the body.*'

I shivered.

'This is horrible!'

'*Faites attention*, Hastings, I do not want a second tragedy in my rooms!'

I wiped the blood from my chin rather ruefully.

'What is our plan of campaign?' I asked.

'The car will call for us in a few moments' time. I will bring you a cup of coffee here so that there will be no delay in starting.'

Twenty minutes later we were in a fast police car crossing the Thames on our way out of London.

With us was Inspector Crome, who had been present at the conference the other day, and who was officially in charge of the case.

Crome was a very different type of officer from Japp. A much younger man, he was the silent, superior type. Well educated and well read, he was, for my taste, several shades too pleased with himself. He had lately gained kudos over a series of child murders, having patiently tracked down the criminal who was now in Broadmoor.

He was obviously a suitable person to undertake the present case, but I thought that he was just a little too aware of the fact himself. His manner to Poirot was a shade patronising. He deferred to him as a younger man to an older one – in a rather self-conscious, 'public school' way.

'I've had a good long talk with Dr Thompson,' he said. 'He's very interested in the "chain" or "series" type of murder. It's the product of a particular distorted type of mentality. As a layman one can't, of course, appreciate the finer points as they present themselves to a medical point of view.' He coughed. 'As a matter of fact – my last case – I don't know whether you read about it – the Mabel Homer case, the Muswell Hill schoolgirl, you know – that man Capper was extraordinary. Amazingly difficult to pin the crime on to him – it was his third, too! Looked as sane as you or I. But there are various tests – verbal traps, you know – quite modern, of course, there was nothing of that kind in your day. Once you can induce a man to give himself away, you've got him! He knows that you know and his nerve goes. He starts giving himself away right and left.'

'Even in my day that happened sometimes,' said Poirot.

Inspector Crome looked at him and murmured conversationally: 'Oh, yes?'

There was silence between us for some time. As we passed New Cross Station, Crome said:

'If there's anything you want to ask me about the case, pray do so.'

'You have not, I presume, a description of the dead girl?'

'She was twenty-three years of age, engaged as a waitress at the Ginger Cat café –'

'*Pas ça.* I wondered – if she were pretty?'

'As to that I've no information,' said Inspector Crome with a hint of withdrawal. His manner said: 'Really – these foreigners! All the same!'

A faint look of amusement came into Poirot's eyes.

'It does not seem to you important, that? Yet, *pour une femme*, it is of the first importance. Often it decides her destiny!'

Another silence fell.

It was not until we were nearing Sevenoaks that Poirot opened the conversation again.

'Were you informed, by any chance, how and with what the girl was strangled?'

Inspector Crome replied briefly.

'Strangled with her own belt – a thick, knitted affair, I gather.'

Poirot's eyes opened very wide.

'Aha,' he said. 'At last we have a piece of information that is very definite. That tells one something, does it not?'

'I haven't seen it yet,' said Inspector Crome coldly.

I felt impatient with the man's caution and lack of imagination.

'It gives us the hallmark of the murderer,' I said. 'The girl's own belt. It shows the particular beastliness of his mind!'

Poirot shot me a glance I could not fathom. On the face of it it conveyed humorous impatience. I thought that perhaps it was a warning not to be too outspoken in front of the inspector.

I relapsed into silence.

At Bexhill we were greeted by Superintendent Carter. He had with him a pleasant-faced, intelligent-looking young inspector called Kelsey. The latter was detailed to work in with Crome over the case.

'You'll want to make your own inquiries, Crome,' said the superintendent. 'So I'll just give you the main heads of the matter and then you can get busy right away.'

'Thank you, sir,' said Crome.

'We've broken the news to her father and mother,' said the superintendent. 'Terrible shock to them, of course. I left them to recover a bit before questioning them, so you can start from the beginning there.'

'There are other members of the family – yes?' asked Poirot.

'There's a sister – a typist in London. She's been communicated with. And there's a young man – in fact, the girl was supposed to be out with him last night, I gather.'

'Any help from the A B C guide?' asked Chrome.

'It's there,' the superintendent nodded towards the table. 'No fingerprints. Open at the page for Bexhill. A new copy, I should say – doesn't seem to have been opened much. Not bought anywhere round here. I've tried all the likely stationers.'

'Who discovered the body, sir?'

'One of these fresh-air, early-morning colonels. Colonel Jerome. He was out with his dog about 6 am. Went along the front in the direction of Cooden, and down on to the beach. Dog went off and sniffed at something. Colonel called it. Dog didn't come. Colonel had a look and thought something queer was up. Went over and looked. Behaved very properly. Didn't touch her at all and rang us up immediately.'

'And the time of death was round about midnight last night?'

'Between midnight and 1 am – that's pretty certain. Our homidical joker is a man of his word. If he says the 25th it is the 25th – though it may have been only by a few minutes.'

Crome nodded.

'Yes, that's his mentality all right. There's nothing else? Nobody saw anything helpful?'

'Not as far as we know. But it's early yet. Everyone who saw a girl in white walking with a man last night will be along to tell us about it soon, and as I imagine there were about four or five hundred girls in white walking with young men last night, it ought to be a nice business.'

'Well, sir, I'd better get down to it,' said Crome. 'There's the café and there's the girl's home. I'd better go to both of them. Kelsey can come with me.'

'And Mr Poirot?' asked the superintendent.

'I will accompany you,' said Poirot to Crome with a little bow.

Crome, I thought, looked slightly annoyed. Kelsey, who had not seen Poirot before, grinned broadly.

It was an unfortunate circumstance that the first time people saw my friend they were always disposed to consider him as a joke of the first water.

'What about this belt she was strangled with?' asked Crome. 'Mr Poirot is inclined to think it's a valuable clue. I expect he'd like to see it.'

'*Du tout*,' said Poirot quickly. 'You misunderstood me.'

'You'll get nothing from that,' said Carter. 'It wasn't a leather belt – might have got fingerprints if it had been. Just a thick sort of knitted silk – ideal for the purpose.'

I gave a shiver.

'Well,' said Crome, 'we'd better be getting along.'

We set out forthwith.

Our first visit was to the Ginger Cat. Situated on the sea front, this was the usual type of small tearoom. It had little tables covered with orange-checked cloths and basket-work chairs of exceeding discomfort with orange cushions on them. It was the kind of place that specialized in morning coffee, five different kinds of teas (Devonshire, Farmhouse, Fruit, Carlton and Plain), and a few sparing lunch dishes for females such as scrambled eggs and shrimps and macaroni

370

au gratin.

The morning coffees were just getting under way. The manageress ushered us hastily into a very untidy back sanctum.

'Miss – eh – Merrion?' inquired Crome.

Miss Merrion bleated out in a high, distressed-gentlewoman voice:

'That is my name. This is a most distressing business. Most distressing. How it will affect our business I really cannot *think*!'

Miss Merrion was a very thin woman of forty with wispy orange hair (indeed she was astonishingly like a ginger cat herself). She played nervously with various fichus and frills that were part of her official costume.

'You'll have a boom,' said Inspector Kelsey encouragingly. 'You'll see! You won't be able to serve teas fast enough!'

'Disgusting,' said Miss Merrion. 'Truly disgusting. It makes one despair of human nature.'

But her eyes brightened nevertheless.

'What can you tell me about the dead girl, Miss Merrion?'

'Nothing,' said Miss Merrion positively. 'Absolutely nothing!'

'How long had she been working here?'

'This was the second summer.'

'You were satisfied with her?'

'She was a good waitress – quick and obliging.'

'She was pretty, yes?' inquired Poirot.

Miss Merrion, in her turn, gave him an 'Oh, these foreigners' look.

'She was a nice, clean-looking girl,' she said distantly.

'What time did she go off duty last night?' asked Crome.

'Eight o'clock. We close at eight. We do not serve dinners. There is no demand for them. Scrambled eggs and tea (Poirot shuddered) people come in for up to seven o'clock and sometimes after, but our rush is over by 6.30.'

'Did she mention to you how she proposed to spend her evening?'

'Certainly not,' said Miss Merrion emphatically. 'We were not on those terms.'

'No one came in and called for her? Anything like that?'

'No.'

'Did she seem quite her ordinary self? Not excited or depressed?'

'Really I could not say,' said Miss Merrion aloofly.

'How many waitresses do you employ?'

'Two normally, and an extra two after the 20th July until the end of August.'

'But Elizabeth Barnard was not one of the extras?'

'Miss Barnard was one of the regulars.'

'What about the other one?'

'Miss Higley? She is a very nice young lady.'

'Were she and Miss Barnard friends?'

'Really I could not say.'

'Perhaps we'd better have a word with her.'

'Now?'

'If you please.'

'I will send her to you,' said Miss Merrion, rising. 'Please keep her as short a time as possible. This is the morning coffee rush hour.'

The feline and gingery Miss Merrion left the room.

'Very refined,' remarked Inspector Kelsey. He mimicked the lady's mincing tone. '*Really I could not say.*'

A plump girl, slightly out of breath, with dark hair, rosy cheeks and dark eyes goggling with excitement, bounced in.

'Miss Merrion sent me,' she announced breathlessly.

'Miss Higley?'

'Yes, that's me.'

'You knew Elizabeth Barnard?'

'Oh, yes, I knew Betty. Isn't it *awful*? It's just too awful! I can't believe it's true. I've been saying to the girls all the morning I just *can't* believe it! "You know, girls," I said, "it just doesn't seem *real*. Betty! I mean, Betty Barnard, who's been here all along, *murdered*! I just can't believe it." I said. Five or six times I've pinched myself just to see if I wouldn't wake up. Betty murdered ... It's – well, you know what I mean – it doesn't seem *real*.'

'You knew the dead girl well?' asked Crome.

'Well, she's worked here longer than I have. I only came this March. She was here last year. She was rather quiet, if you know what I mean. She wasn't one to joke or laugh a lot. I don't mean that she was exactly *quiet* – she'd plenty of fun in her and all that – but she didn't – well, she was quiet and she wasn't quiet, if you know what I mean.'

I will say for Inspector Crome that he was exceedingly patient. As a witness the buxom Miss Higley was persistently maddening. Every statement she made was repeated and qualified half a dozen times. The net result was meagre in the extreme.

She had not been on terms of intimacy with the dead girl. Elizabeth Barnard, it could be guessed, had considered herself a cut

372

above Miss Higley. She had been friendly in working hours, but the girls had not seen much of her out of them. Elizabeth Barnard had had a 'friend' who worked at the estate agents near the station. Court & Brunskill. No, he wasn't Mr Court nor Mr Brunskill. He was a clerk there. She didn't know his name. But she knew him by sight well. Good-looking – oh, very good-looking, and always so nicely dressed. Clearly, there was a tingle of jealousy in Miss Higley's heart.

In the end it boiled down to this. Elizabeth Barnard had not confided in anyone in the café as to her plans for the evening, but in Miss Higley's opinion she had been going to meet her 'friend'. She had had on a new white dress, 'ever so sweet with one of the new necks.'

We had a word with each of the other two girls but with no further results. Betty Barnard had not said anything as to her plans and no one had noticed her in Bexhill during the course of the evening.

CHAPTER TEN

The Barnards

Elizabeth Barnard's parents lived in a minute bungalow, one of fifty or so recently run up by a speculative builder on the confines of the town. The name of it was Llandudno. Mr Barnard, a stout, bewildered-looking man of fifty-five or so, had noticed our approach and was standing waiting in the doorway.

'Come in, gentleman,' he said.

Inspector Kelsey took the initiative.

'This is Inspector Crome of Scotland Yard, sir,' he said. 'He's come down to help us over this business.'

'Scotland Yard?' said Mr Barnard hopefully. 'That's good. This murdering villain's got to be laid by the heels. My poor little girl –' His face was distorted by a spasm of grief.

'And this is Mr Hercule Poirot, also from London, and er –'

'Captain Hastings,' said Poirot.

'Pleased to meet you, gentlemen,' said Mr Barnard mechanically. 'Come into the snuggery. I don't know that my poor wife's up to seeing you. All broken up, she is.'

However, by the time that we were ensconced in the living room of the bungalow, Mrs Barnard had made her appearance. She had evidently been crying bitterly, her eyes were reddened and she walked with the uncertain gait of a person who had had a great shock.

'Why, mother, that's fine,' said Mr Barnard. 'You're sure you're all right – eh?'

He patted her shoulder and drew her down into a chair.

'The superintendent was very kind,' said Mr Barnard. 'After he'd broken the news to us, he said he'd leave any questions till later when we'd got over the first shock.'

'It is too cruel. Oh, it is too cruel,' cried Mrs Barnard tearfully. 'The cruellest thing that ever was, it is.'

Her voice had a faintly sing-song intonation that I thought for a moment was foreign till I remembered the name on the gate and realized that the 'effer wass' of her speech was in reality proof of her Welsh origin.

'It's very painful, madam, I know,' said Inspector Crome. 'And we've every sympathy for you, but we want to know all the facts we can so as to get to work as quick as possible.'

'That's sense, that is,' said Mr Barnard, nodding approval.

'Your daughter was twenty-three, I understand. She lived here with you and worked at the Ginger Cat Café, is that right?'

'That's it.'

'This is a new place, isn't it? Where did you live before?'

'I was in the ironmongery business in Kennington. Retired two years ago. Always meant to live near the sea.'

'You have two daughters?'

'Yes. My elder daughter works in an office in London.'

'Weren't you alarmed when your daughter didn't come home last night?'

'We didn't know she hadn't,' said Mrs Barnard tearfully. 'Dad and I always go to bed early. Nine o'clock's our time. We never knew Betty hadn't come home till the police officer came and said – and said –'

She broke down.

'Was your daughter in the habit of – er – returning home late?'

'You know what girls are nowadays, inspector,' said Barnard. 'Independent, that's what they are. These summer evenings they're not going to rush home. All the same, Betty was usually in by eleven.'

'How did she get in? Was the door open?'

'Left the key under the mat – that's what we always did.'

'There is some rumour, I believe, that your daughter was engaged to be married?'

'They don't put it as formally as that nowadays,' said Mr Barnard.

'Donald Fraser his name is, and I liked him. I liked him very much,' said Mrs Barnard. 'Poor fellow, it'll be trouble for him – this news. Does he know yet, I wonder?'

'He works in Court & Brunskill's, I understand?'

'Yes, they're the estate agents.'

'Was he in the habit of meeting your daughter most evenings after her work?'

'Not every evening. Once or twice a week would be nearer.'

'Do you know if she was going to meet him yesterday?'

'She didn't say. Betty never said much about what she was doing or where she was going. But she was a good girl, Betty was. Oh, I can't believe –'

Mrs Barnard started sobbing again.

'Pull yourself together, old lady. Try to hold up, mother,' urged her husband. 'We've got to get to the bottom of this.'

'I'm sure Donald would never – would never –' sobbed

375

Mrs Barnard.

'Now just you pull yourself together,' repeated Mr Barnard.

'I wish to God I could give you some help – but the plain fact is I know nothing – nothing at all that can help you to find the dastardly scoundrel who did this. Betty was just a merry, happy girl – with a decent young fellow that she was – well, we'd have called it walking out with in my young days. Why anyone should want to murder her simply beats me – it doesn't make sense.'

'You're very near the truth there, Mr Barnard,' said Crome. 'I tell you what I'd like to do – have a look over Miss Barnard's room. There may be something – letters – or a diary.'

'Look over it and welcome,' said Mr Barnard, rising.

He led the way. Crome followed him, then Poirot, then Kelsey, and I brought up the rear.

I stopped for a minute to retie my shoelaces, and as I did so a taxi drew up outside and a girl jumped out of it. She paid the driver and hurried up the path to the house, carrying a small suitcase. As she entered the door she saw me and stopped dead.

There was something so arresting in her pose that it intrigued me

'Who are you?' she said.

I came down a few steps. I felt embarrassed as to how exactly to reply. Should I give my name? Or mention that I had come here with the police? The girl, however, gave me no time to make a decision.

'Oh, well,' she said, 'I can guess.'

She pulled off the little white woollen cap she was wearing and threw it on the ground. I could see her better now as she turned a little so that the light fell on her.

My first impression was of the Dutch dolls that my sisters used to play with in my childhood. Her hair was black and cut in a straight bob and a bang across the forehead. Her cheekbones were high and her whole figure had a queer modern angularity that was not, somehow, unattractive. She was not good-looking – plain rather – but there was an intensity about her, a forcefulness that made her a person quite impossible to overlook.

'You are Miss Barnard?' I asked.

'I am Megan Barnard. You belong to the police, I suppose?'

'Well,' I said. 'Not exactly –'

She interrupted me.

'I don't think I've got anything to say to you. My sister was a nice bright girl with no men friends. Good morning.'

She gave me a short laugh as she spoke and regarded

me challengingly.

'That's the correct phrase, I believe?' she said.

'I'm not a reporter, if that's what you're getting at.'

'Well, what are you?' She looked around. 'Where's mum and dad?'

'Your father is showing the police your sister's bedroom. Your mother's in there. She's very upset.'

The girl seemed to make a decision.

'Come in here,' she said.

She pulled open a door and passed through. I followed her and found myself in a small, neat kitchen.

I was about to shut the door behind me – but found an unexpected resistance. The next moment Poirot had slipped quietly into the room and shut the door behind him.

'Mademoiselle Barnard?' he said with a quick bow.

'This is M. Hercule Poirot,' I said.

Megan Barnard gave him a quick, appraising glance.

'I've heard of you,' she said. 'You're the fashionable private sleuth, aren't you?'

'Not a pretty description – but it suffices,' said Poirot.

The girl sat down on the edge of the kitchen table. She felt in her bag for a cigarette. She placed it between her lips, lighted it, and then said in between two puffs of smoke:

'Somehow, I don't see what M. Hercule Poirot is doing in our humble little crime.'

'Mademoiselle,' said Poirot. 'What you do not see and what I do not see would probably fill a volume. But all that is of no practical importance. What *is* of practical importance is something that will not be easy to find.'

'What's that?'

'Death, mademoiselle, unfortunately creates a *prejudice*. A prejudice in favour of the deceased. I heard what you said just now to my friend Hastings. "A nice bright girl with no men friends." You said that in mockery of the newspapers. And it is very true – when a young girl is dead, that is the kind of thing that is said. She was bright. She was happy. She was sweet-tempered. She had not a care in the world. She had no undesirable acquaintances. There is a great charity always to the dead. Do you know what I should like this minute? I should like to find someone who knew Elizabeth Barnard *and who does not know she is dead*! Then, perhaps, I should hear what is useful to me – the truth.'

377

Megan Barnard looked at him for a few minutes in silence whilst she smoked. Then, at last, she spoke. Her words made me jump. 'Betty,' she said, 'was an unmitigated little ass!'

CHAPTER ELEVEN

Megan Barnard

As I said, Megan Barnard's words, and still more the crisp businesslike tone in which they were uttered, made me jump.

Poirot, however, merely bowed his head gravely.

'*A la bonne heure*,' he said. 'You are intelligent, mademoiselle.'

Megan Barnard said, still in the same detached tone:

'I was extremely fond of Betty. But my fondness didn't blind me from seeing exactly the kind of silly little fool she was – and even telling her so upon occasions! Sisters are like that.'

'And did she pay any attention to your advice?'

'Probably not,' said Megan cynically.

'Will you, mademoiselle, be precise.'

The girl hesitated for a minute or two.

Poirot said with a slight smile:

'I will help you. I heard what you said to Hastings. That your sister was a bright, happy girl with no men friends. It was – *un peu* – the *opposite* that was true, was it not?'

Megan said slowly:

'There wasn't any harm in Betty. I want you to understand that. She'd always go straight. She's not the weekending kind. Nothing of that sort. But she liked being taken out and dancing and – oh, cheap flattery and compliments and all that sort of thing.'

'And she was pretty – yes?'

This question, the third time I had heard it, met this time with a practical response.

Megan slipped off the table, went to her suitcase, snapped it open and extracted something which she handed to Poirot.

In a leather frame was a head and shoulders of a fair-haired, smiling girl. Her hair had evidently recently been permed, it stood out from her head in a mass of rather frizzy curls. The smile was arch and artificial. It was certainly not a face that you could call beautiful, but it had an obvious and cheap prettiness.

Poirot handed it back, saying:

'You and she do not resemble each other, mademoiselle.'

'Oh! I'm the plain one of the family. I've always known that.' She seemed to brush aside the fact as unimportant.

'In what way exactly do you consider your sister was behaving foolishly? Do you mean, perhaps, in relation to Mr Donald Fraser?'

'That's it, exactly. Don's a very quiet sort of person – but he – well, naturally he'd resent certain things – and then –'

'And then what, mademoiselle?'

His eyes were on her very steadily.

It may have been my fancy but it seemed to me that she hesitated a second before answering.

'I was afraid that he might – chuck her altogether. And that would have been a pity. He's a very steady and hard-working man and would have made her a good husband.'

Poirot continued to gaze at her. She did not flush under his glance but returned it with one of her own equally steady and with something else in it – something that reminded me of her first defiant, disdainful manner.

'So it is like that,' he said at last. 'We do not speak the truth any longer.'

She shrugged her shoulders and turned towards the door.

'Well,' she said. 'I've done what I could to help you.'

Poirot's voice arrested her.

'Wait, mademoiselle. I have something to tell you. Come back.'

Rather unwillingly, I thought, she obeyed.

Somewhat to my surprise, Poirot plunged into the whole story of the A B C letters, the murder of Andover, and the railway guide found by the bodies.

He had no reason to complain of any lack of interest on her part. Her lips parted, her eyes gleaming, she hung on his words.

'Is this all true, M. Poirot?'

'Yes, it is true.'

'You really mean that my sister was killed by some horrible homicidal maniac?'

'Precisely?'

She drew a deep breath.

'Oh! Betty – Betty – how – how *ghastly*!'

'You see, mademoiselle, that the information for which I ask you can give freely without wondering whether or not it will hurt anyone.'

'Yes, I see that now.'

'Then let us continue our conversation. I have formed the idea that this Donald Fraser has, perhaps, a violent and jealous temper, is that right?'

Megan Barnard said quietly:

380

'I'm trusting you now, M. Poirot. I'm going to give you the absolute truth. Don is, as I say, a very quiet person – a bottled-up person, if you know what I mean. He can't always express what he feels in words. But underneath it all he minds things terribly. And he's got a jealous nature. He was always jealous of Betty. He was devoted to her – and of course she was very fond of him, but it wasn't in Betty to be fond of one person and not notice anybody else. She wasn't made that way. She'd got a – well, an eye for any nice-looking man who'd pass the time of day with her. And of course, working in the Ginger Cat, she was always running up against men – especially in the summer holidays. She was always very pat with her tongue and if they chaffed her she'd chaff back again. And then perhaps she'd meet them and go to the pictures or something like that. Nothing serious – never anything of that kind – but she just liked her fun. She used to say that as she'd got to settle down with Don one day she might as well have her fun now while she could.'

Megan paused and Poirot said:

'I understand. Continue.'

'It was just that attitude of mind of hers that Don couldn't understand. If she was really keen on him he couldn't see why she wanted to go out with other people. And once or twice they had flaming big rows about it.'

'M. Don, he was no longer quiet?'

'It's like all those quiet people, when they do lose their tempers they lose them with a vengeance. Don was so violent that Betty was frightened.'

'When was this?'

'There was one row nearly a year ago and another – a worse one – just over a month ago. I was home for the weekend – and I got them to patch it up again, and it was then I tried to knock a little sense into Betty – told her she was a little fool. All she would say was that there hadn't been any harm in it. Well, that was true enough, but all the same she was riding for a fall. You see, after the row a year ago, she'd got into the habit of telling a few useful lies on the principle that what the mind doesn't know the heart doesn't grieve over. This last flare-up came because she'd told Don she was going to Hastings to see a girl pal – and he found out that she'd really been over to Eastbourne with some man. He was a married man, as it happened, and he'd been a bit secretive about the business anyway – and so that made it worse. They had an awful scene – Betty saying that she wasn't married to him yet and she had a right to go about with whom

381

she pleased and Don all white and shaking and saying that one day –
one day –'

'Yes?'

'He'd commit murder –' said Megan in a lowered voice.

She stopped and stared at Poirot.

He nodded his head gravely several times.

'And so, naturally you were afraid . . .'

'I didn't think he'd actually done it – not for a minute! But I was afraid it might be brought up – the quarrel and all that he'd said – several people knew about it.'

Again Poirot nodded his head gravely.

'Just so. And I may say, mademoiselle, that but for the egoistical vanity of a killer, that is just what would have happened. If Donald Fraser escapes suspicion, it will be thanks to A B C's maniacal boasting.'

He was silent for a minute or two, then he said:

'Do you know if your sister met this married man, or any other man, lately?'

Megan shook her head.

'I don't know. I've been away, you see.'

'But what do you think?'

'She mayn't have met that particular man again. He'd probably sheer off if he thought there was a chance of a row, but it wouldn't surprise me if Betty had – well, been telling Don a few lies again. You see, she did so enjoy dancing and the pictures, and of course, Don couldn't afford to take her all the time.'

'If so, is she likely to have confided in anyone? The girl at the café, for instance?'

'I don't think that's likely. Betty couldn't bear the Higley girl. She thought her common. And the others would be new. Betty wasn't the confiding sort anyway.'

An electric bell trilled sharply above the girl's head.

She went to the window and leaned out. She drew back her head sharply.

'It's Don . . .'

'Bring him in here,' said Poirot quickly. 'I would like a word with him before our good inspector takes him in hand.'

Like a flash Megan Barnard was out of the kitchen, and a couple of seconds later she was back again leading Donald Fraser by the hand.

CHAPTER TWELVE

Donald Fraser

I felt sorry at once for the young man. His white haggard face and bewildered eyes showed how great a shock he had had.

He was a well-made, fine-looking young fellow, standing close on six foot, not good-looking, but with a pleasant, freckled face, high cheek-bones and flaming red hair.

'What's this, Megan?' he said. 'Why in here? For God's sake, tell me – I've only just heard – Betty . . .'

His voice trailed away.

Poirot pushed forward a chair and he sank down on it.

My friend then extracted a small flask from his pocket, poured some of its contents into a convenient cup which was hanging on the dresser and said:

'Drink some of this, Mr Fraser. It will do you good.'

The young man obeyed. The brandy brought a little colour back into his face. He sat up straighter and turned once more to the girl. His manner was quite quiet and self-controlled.

'It's true, I suppose?' he said. 'Betty is – dead – killed?'

'It's true, Don.'

He said as though mechanically:

'Have you just come down from London?'

'Yes. Dad phoned me.'

'By the 9.30, I suppose?' said Donald Fraser.

His mind, shrinking from reality, ran for safety along those unimportant details.

'Yes.'

There was silence for a minute or two, then Fraser said:

'The police? Are they doing anything?'

'They're upstairs now. Looking through Betty's things, I suppose.'

'They've no idea who –? They don't know –?'

He stopped.

He had all a sensitive, shy person's dislike of putting violent facts into words.

Poirot moved forward a little and asked a question. He spoke in a businesslike, matter-of-fact voice as though what he asked was an unimportant detail.

'Did Miss Barnard tell you where she was going last night?'

Fraser replied to the question. He seemed to be speaking mechanically:

'She told me she was going with a girl friend to St Leonards.'

'Did you believe her?'

'I –' Suddenly the automaton came to life. 'What the devil do you mean?'

His face then, menacing, convulsed by sudden passion, made me understand that a girl might well be afraid of rousing his anger.

Poirot said crisply:

'Betty Barnard was killed by a homicidal murderer. Only by speaking the exact truth can you help us to get on his track.'

His glance for a minute turned to Megan.

'That's right, Don,' she said. 'It isn't a time for considering one's own feelings or anyone else's. You've got to come clean.'

Donald Fraser looked suspiciously at Poirot.

'Who are you? You don't belong to the police?'

'I am better than the police,' said Poirot. He said it without conscious arrogance. It was, to him, a simple statement of fact.

'Tell him,' said Megan.

Donald Fraser capitulated.

'I – wasn't sure,' he said. 'I believed her when she said it. Never thought of doing anything else. Afterwards – perhaps it was something in her manner. I – I, well, I began to wonder.'

'Yes?' said Poirot.

He had sat down opposite Donald Fraser. His eyes, fixed on the other man's, seemed to be exercising a mesmeric spell.

'I was ashamed of myself for being so suspicious. But – but I *was* suspicious . . . I thought of going to the front and watching her when she left the café. I actually went there. Then I felt I couldn't do that. Betty would see me and she'd be angry. She'd realize at once that I was watching her.'

'What did you do?'

'I went over to St Leonards. Got over there by eight o'clock. Then I watched the buses – to see if she were in them . . . But there was no sign of her . . .'

'And then?'

'I – I lost my head rather. I was convinced she was with some man. I thought it probable he had taken her in his car to Hastings. I went on there – looked in hotels and restaurants, hung round cinemas – went on the pier. All damn foolishness. Even if she was there I was unlikely to find her, and anyway, there were heaps of other places he might have taken her to instead of Hastings.'

He stopped. Precise as his tone had remained, I caught an undertone of that blind, bewildering misery and anger that had possessed him at the time he described.

'In the end I gave it up – came back.'

'At what time?'

'I don't know. I walked. It must have been midnight or after when I got home.'

'Then –'

The kitchen door opened.

'Oh, there you are,' said Inspector Kelsey.

Inspector Crome pushed past him, shot a glance at Poirot and a glance at the two strangers.

'Miss Megan Barnard and Mr Donald Fraser,' said Poirot, introducing them.

'This is Inspector Crome from London,' he explained.

Turning to the inspector, he said:

'While you pursued your investigations upstairs I have been conversing with Miss Barnard and Mr Fraser, endeavouring if I could to find something that will throw light upon the matter.'

'Oh, yes?' said Inspector Crome, his thoughts not upon Poirot but upon the two newcomers.

Poirot retreated to the hall. Inspector Kelsey said kindly as he passed:

'Get anything?'

But his attention was distracted by his colleague and he did not wait for a reply.

I joined Poirot in the hall.

'Did anything strike you, Poirot?' I inquired.

'Only the amazing magnanimity of the murderer, Hastings.'

I had not the courage to say that I had not the least idea what he meant.

CHAPTER THIRTEEN

A Conference

Conferences!

Much of my memories of the A B C case seem to be of conferences. Conferences at Scotland Yard. At Poirot's rooms. Official conferences. Unofficial conferences.

This particular conference was to decide whether or not the facts relative to the anonymous letters should or should not be made public in the press.

The Bexhill murder had attracted much more attention than the Andover one.

It had, of course, far more elements of popularity. To begin with the victim was a young and good-looking girl. Also, it had taken place at a popular seaside resort.

All the details of the crime were reported fully and rehashed daily in thin disguises. The A B C railway guide came in for its share of attention. The favourite theory was that it had been bought locally by the murderer and that it was a valuable clue to his identity. It also seemed to show that he had come to the place by train and was intending to leave for London.

The railway guide had not figured at all in the meagre accounts of the Andover murder, so there seemed at present little likelihood of the two crimes being connected in the public eye.

'We've got to decide upon a policy,' said the Assistant Commissioner. 'The thing is – which way will give us the best results? Shall we give the public the facts – enlist their co-operation – after all, it'll be the co-operation of several million people, looking out for a madman –'

'He won't look like a madman,' interjected Dr Thompson.

'– looking out for sales of A B C's – and so on. Against that I suppose there's the advantage of working in the dark – not letting our man know what we're up to, but then there's the fact that *he knows very well that we know*. He's drawn attention to himself deliberately by his letters. Eh, Crome, what's your opinion?'

'I look at it this way, sir. If you make it public, *you're playing A B C's game*. That's what he wants – publicity – notoriety. That's what he's out after. I'm right, aren't I, doctor? He wants to make a splash.'

Thompson nodded.

The Assistant Commissioner said thoughtfully:

'So you're for balking him. Refusing him the publicity he's hankering after. What about you, M. Poirot?'

Poirot did not speak for a minute. When he did it was with an air of choosing his words carefully.

'It is difficult for me, Sir Lionel,' he said. 'I am, as you might say, an interested party. The challenge was sent to me. If I say "Suppress that fact – do not make it public," may it not be thought that it is my vanity that speaks? That I am afraid for my reputation? It is difficult! To speak out – to tell all – that has its advantages. It is, at least, a warning . . . On the other hand, I am as convinced as Inspector Crome *that it is what the murderer wants us to do.*'

'H'm!' said the Assistant Commissioner, rubbing his chin. He looked across at Dr Thompson. 'Suppose we refuse our lunatic the satisfaction of the publicity he craves. What's he likely to do?'

'Commit another crime,' said the doctor promptly. 'Force your hand.'

'And if we splash the thing about in headlines. Then what's his reaction?'

'Same answer. One way you *feed* his megalomania, the other you *balk* it. The result's the same. Another crime.'

'What do you say, M. Poirot?'

'I agree with Dr Thompson.'

'A cleft stick – eh? How many crimes do you think this – lunatic has in mind?'

Dr Thompson looked across at Poirot.

'Looks like A to Z,' he said cheerfully.

'Of course,' he went on, 'he won't get there. Not nearly. You'll have him by the heels long before that. Interesting to know how he'd have dealt with the letter X.' He recalled himself guiltily from this purely enjoyable speculation. 'But you'll have him long before that. G or H, let's say.'

The Assistant Commissioner struck the table with his fist.

'My God, are you telling me we're going to have five more murders?'

'It won't be as much as that, sir,' said Inspector Crome. 'Trust me.'

He spoke with confidence.

'Which letter of the alphabet do you place it at, inspector?' asked Poirot.

There was a slight ironic note in his voice. Crome, I thought, looked at him with a tinge of dislike adulterating the usual calm superiority.

'Might get him next time, M. Poirot. At any rate, I'd guarantee to get him by the time he gets to F.'

He turned to the Assistant Commissioner.

'I think I've got the psychology of the case fairly clear. Dr Thompson will correct me if I'm wrong. I take it that every time A B C brings a crime off, his self-confidence increases about a hundred per cent. Every time he feels "I'm clever – they can't catch me!" he becomes so over-weeningly confident that he also becomes careless. He exaggerates his own cleverness and everyone else's stupidity. Very soon he'd be hardly bothering to take any precautions at all. That's right, isn't it doctor?'

Thompson nodded.

'That's usually the case. In non-medical terms it couldn't have been put better. You know something about such things, M. Poirot. Don't you agree?'

I don't think that Crome liked Thompson's appeal to Poirot. He considered that he and he only was the expert on this subject.

'It is as Inspector Crome says,' agreed Poirot.

'Paranoia,' murmured the doctor.

Poirot turned to Crome.

'Are there any material facts of interest in the Bexhill case?'

'Nothing very definite. A waiter at the Splendide at Eastbourne recognizes the dead girl's photograph as that of a young woman who dined there on the evening of the 24th in company with a middle-aged man in spectacles. It's also been recognised at a roadhouse place called the Scarlet Runner half-way between Bexhill and London. They say she was there about 9 pm on the 24th with a man who looked like a naval officer. They can't both be right, but either of them's probable. Of course, there's a host of other identifications, but most of them not good for much. We haven't been able to trace the A B C.'

'Well, you seem to be doing all that can be done, Crome,' said the Assistant Commissioner. 'What do you say, M. Poirot? Does any line of inquiry suggest itself to you?'

Poirot said slowly:

'It seems to me that there is one very important clue – the discovery of the motive.'

'Isn't that pretty obvious? An alphabetical complex. Isn't that what you called it, doctor?'

'*Ça, oui,*' said Poirot. 'There is an alphabetical complex. But why an alphabetical complex? A madman in particular has always a very strong reason for the crimes he commits.'

'Come, come, M. Poirot,' said Crome. 'Look at Stoneman in 1929. He ended by trying to do away with anyone who annoyed him in the slightest degree.'

Poirot turned to him.

'Quite so. But if you are a sufficiently great and important person, it is necessary that you should be spared small annoyances. If a fly settles on your forehead again and again, maddening you by its tickling – what do you do? You endeavour to kill that fly. You have no qualms about it. *You* are important – the fly is not. You kill the fly and the annoyance ceases. Your action appears to you sane and justifiable. Another reason for killing a fly is if you have a strong passion for hygiene. The fly is a potential source of danger to the community – the fly must go. So works the mind of the mentally deranged criminal. But consider now this case – *if the victims are alphabetically selected, then they are not being removed because they are a source of annoyance to the murderer personally.* It would be too much of a coincidence to combine the two.'

'That's a point,' said Dr Thompson. 'I remember a case where a woman's husband was condemned to death. She started killing the members of the jury one by one. Quite a time before the crimes were connected up. They seemed entirely haphazard. But as M. Poirot says, there isn't such a thing as a murderer who commits crimes at *random*. Either he removes people who stand (however insignificantly) in his path, or else he kills by *conviction*. He removes clergymen, or policemen, or prostitutes because he firmly believes that they *should* be removed. That doesn't apply here either as far as I can see. Mrs Ascher and Betty Barnard cannot be linked as members of the same class. Of course, it's possible that there is a sex complex. Both victims have been women. We can tell better, of course, after the next crime –'

'For God's sake, Thompson, don't speak so glibly of the next crime,' said Sir Lionel irritably. 'We're going to do all we can to prevent another crime.'

Dr Thompson held his peace and blew his nose with some violence.

'Have it your own way,' the noise seemed to say. 'If you won't face facts –'

The Assistant Commissioner turned to Poirot.

'I see what you're driving at, but I'm not quite clear yet.'

'I ask myself,' said Poirot, 'what passes exactly in the mind of the murderer? He kills, it would seem from his letters, *pour le sport* – to amuse himself. Can that really be true? And even if it is true, on what principle does he select his victims *apart from the merely alphabetical one*? If he kills merely to amuse himself he would not advertise the fact, since, otherwise, he could kill with impunity. But no, he seeks, as we all agree, to make the splash in the public eye – to assert his personality. In what way has his personality been suppressed that one can connect with the two victims he has so far selected? A final suggestion: Is his motive direct personal hatred of *me*, of Hercule Poirot? Does he challenge me in public because I have (unknown to myself) vanquished him somewhere in the course of my career? Or is his animosity impersonal – directed against a *foreigner*? And if so, what again has led to that? What injury has he suffered at a foreigner's hand?'

'All very suggestive questions,' said Dr Thompson.

Inspector Crome cleared his throat.

'Oh, yes? A little unanswerable at present, perhaps.'

'Nevertheless, my friend,' said Poirot, looking straight at him, '*It is there, in those questions, that the solution lies.* If we knew the exact reason – fantastic, perhaps, to us – but logical to him – of *why* our madman commits these crimes, we should know, perhaps, who the next victim is likely to be.'

Crome shook his head.

'He selects them haphazard – that's my opinion.'

'The magnanimous murderer,' said Poirot.

'What's that you say?'

'I said – the magnanimous murderer! Franz Ascher would have been arrested for the murder of his wife – Donald Fraser might have been arrested for the murder of Betty Barnard – if it had not been for the warning letter of A B C. Is he, then, so soft-hearted that he cannot bear others to suffer for something they did not do?'

'I've known stranger things happen,' said Dr Thompson. 'I've known men who've killed half a dozen victims all broken up because one of their victims didn't die instantaneously and suffered pain. All the same, I don't think that that is our fellow's reason. He wants the credit of these crimes for his own honour and glory. That's the explanation that fits best.'

'We've come to no decision about the publicity business,' said the Assistant Commissioner.

'If I may make a suggestion, sir,' said Crome. 'Why not wait till the receipt of the next letter? Make it public then – special editions, etc. It will make a bit of a panic in the particular town named, but it will put everyone whose name begins with C on their guard, and it'll put A B C on his mettle. He'll be determined to succeed. And that's when we'll get him.'

How little we knew what the future held.

CHAPTER FOURTEEN

The Third Letter

I well remember the arrival of A B C's third letter.

I may say that all precautions had been taken so that when A B C resumed his campaign there should be no unnecessary delays. A young sergeant from Scotland Yard was attached to the house and if Poirot and I was out it was his duty to open anything that came so as to be able to communicate with headquarters without loss of time.

As the days succeeded each other we had all grown more and more on edge. Inspector Crome's aloof and superior manner grew more and more aloof and superior as one by one his more hopeful clues petered out. The vague descriptions of men said to have been seen with Betty Barnard proved useless. Various cars noticed in the vicinity of Bexhill and Cooden were either accounted for or could not be traced. The investigation of purchases of A B C railway guides caused inconvenience and trouble to heaps of innocent people.

As for ourselves, each time the postman's familiar rat-tat sounded on the door, our hearts beat faster with apprehension. At least that was true for me, and I cannot but believe that Poirot experienced the same sensation.

He was, I knew, deeply unhappy over the case. He refused to leave London, preferring to be on the spot in case of emergency. In those hot dog days even his moustaches drooped – neglected for once by their owner.

It was on a Friday that A B C's third letter came. The evening post arrived about ten o'clock.

When we heard the familiar step and the brisk rat-tat, I rose and went along to the box. There were four or five letters, I remember. The last one I looked at was addressed in printed characters.

'Poirot,' I cried ... My voice died away.

'It has come? Open it, Hastings. Quickly. Every moment may be needed. We must make our plans.'

I tore open the letter (Poirot for once did not reproach me with untidiness) and extracted the printed sheet.

'Read it,' said Poirot.

I read aloud:

POOR MR POIROT, – Not so good at these little criminal matters as you thought yourself, are you? Rather past your prime, perhaps? Let us see if you can do any better this time. This time it's an easy one. Churston on the 30th. Do try and do something about it! It's a bit dull having it *all* my own way, you know!

Good hunting. Ever yours,

A B C

'Churston,' I said, jumping to our own copy of an A B C. 'Let's see where it is.'

'Hastings,' Poirot's voice came sharply and interrupted me. 'When was that letter written? Is there a date on it?'

I glanced at the letter in my hand.

'Written on the 27th,' I announced.

'Did I hear you aright, Hastings? Did he give the date of the murder as the *30th*?'

'That's right. Let me see, that's –'

'*Bon Dieu*, Hastings – do you not realise? *Today is the 30th.*'

His eloquent hand pointed to the calendar on the wall. I caught up the daily paper to confirm it.

'But why – how –' I stammered.

Poirot caught up the torn envelope from the floor. Something unusual about the address had registered itself vaguely in my brain, but I had been too anxious to get at the content of the letter to pay more than fleeting attention to it.

Poirot was at the time living in Whitehaven Mansions. The address ran: *M. Hercule Poirot, Whitehorse Mansions*, across the corner was scrawled: '*Not known at Whitehorse Mansions, EC1, nor at Whitehorse Court – try Whitehaven Mansions.*'

'*Mon Dieu!*' murmured Poirot. 'Does even chance aid this madman? *Vite – vite –* we must get on to Scotland Yard.'

A minute or two later was were speaking to Crome over the wire. For once the self-controlled inspector did not reply 'Oh, yes?' Instead a quickly stifled curse came to his lips. He heard what we had to say, then rang off in order to get a trunk connection to Churston as rapidly as possible.

'*C'est trop tard*,' murmured Poirot.

'You can't be sure of that,' I argued, though without any great hope.

He glanced at the clock.

'Twenty minutes past ten? An hour and forty minutes to go. Is it likely that A B C will have held his hand so long?'

393

I opened the railway guide I had previously taken from its shelf.

'Churston, Devon,' I read, 'from Paddington 204¾ miles. Population 656. It sounds a fairly small place. Surely our man will be bound to be noticed there.'

'Even so, another life will have been taken,' murmured Poirot. 'What are the trains? I imagine train will be quicker than car.'

'There's a midnight train – sleeping car to Newton Abbot – gets there 6.08 am, and then Churston at 7.15.'

'That is from Paddington?'

'Paddington, yes.'

'We will take that, Hastings.'

'You'll hardly have time to get news before we start.'

'If we receive bad news tonight or tomorrow morning does it matter which?'

'There's something in that.'

I put a few things together in a suitcase while Poirot once more rang up Scotland Yard.

A few minutes later he came into the bedroom and demanded:

'*Mais qu'est ce que vous faites là?*'

'I was packing for you. I thought it would save time.'

'*Vous éprouvez trop d'émotion, Hastings*. It affects your hands and your wits. Is that a way to fold a coat? And regard what you have done to my pyjamas. If the hairwash breaks what will befall them?'

'Good heavens, Poirot,' I cried, 'this is a matter of life and death. What does it matter what happens to our clothes?'

'You have no sense of proportion, Hastings. We cannot catch a train earlier than the time that it leaves, and to ruin one's clothes will not be the least helpful in preventing a murder.'

Taking his suitcase from me firmly, he took the packing into his own hands.

He explained that we were to take the letter and envelope to Paddington with us. Someone from Scotland Yard would meet us there.

When we arrived on the platform the first person we saw was Inspector Crome.

He answered Poirot's look of inquiry.

'No news as yet. All men available are on the look-out. All persons whose names begins with C are being warned by phone when possible. There's just a chance. Where's the letter?'.

Poirot gave it to him.

He examined it, swearing softly under his breath.

'Of all the damned luck. The stars in their courses fight for the fellow.'

'You don't think,' I suggested, 'that it was done on purpose?'

Crome shook his head.

'No. He's got his rules – crazy rules – and abides by them. Fair warning. He makes a point of that. 'That's where his boastfulness comes in. I wonder now – I'd almost bet the chap drinks White Horse whisky.'

'*Ah, c'est ingénieux, ça!*' said Poirot, driven to admiration in spite of himself. 'He prints the letter and the bottle is in front of him.'

'That's the way of it,' said Crome. 'We've all of us done much the same thing one time or another, unconsciously copied something that's just under the eye. He started off White and went on horse instead of haven . . .'

The inspector, we found, was also travelling by the train.

'Even if by some unbelievable luck nothing happened, Churston is the place to be. Our murderer is there, or has been there today. One of my men is on the phone here up to the last minute in case anything comes through.'

Just as the train was leaving the station we saw a man running down the platform. He reached the inspector's window and called up something.

As the train drew out of the station Poirot and I hurried along the corridor and tapped on the door of the inspector's sleeper.

'You have news – yes?' demanded Poirot.

Crome said quietly:

'It's about as bad as it can be. Sir Carmichael Clarke has been found with his head bashed in.'

Sir Carmichael Clarke, although his name was not very well known to the general public, was a man of some eminence. He had been in his time a very well-known throat specialist. Retiring from his profession very comfortably off, he had been able to indulge what had been one of the chief passions of his life – a collection of Chinese pottery and porcelain. A few years later, inheriting a considerable fortune from an elderly uncle, he had been able to indulge his passion to the full, and he was now the possessor of one of the best-known collections of Chinese art. He was married but had no children and lived in a house he had built for himself near the Devon coast, only coming to London on rare occasions such as when some important sale was on.

It did not require much reflection to realize that his death,

395

following that of the young and pretty Betty Barnard, would provide and best newspaper sensation for years. The fact that it was August and that the papers were hard up for subject matter would make matters worse.

'*Eh bien,*' said Poirot. 'It is possible that publicity may do what private efforts have failed to do. The whole country now will be looking for A B C.'

'Unfortunately,' I said, 'that's what he wants.'

'True. But it may, all the same, be his undoing. Gratified by success, he may become careless ... That is what I hope – that he may be drunk with his own cleverness.'

'How odd all this is, Poirot,' I exclaimed, struck suddenly by an idea. 'Do you know, this is the first crime of this kind that you and I have worked on together? All our murders have been – well, private murders, so to speak.'

'You are quite right, my friend. Always, up to now, it has fallen to our lot to work from the *inside*. It has been the history of the *victim* that was important. The important points have been: "Who benefited by the death? What opportunities had those round him to commit the crime?" It has always been the "*crime intime.*" Here, for the first time in our association, it is cold-blooded, impersonal murder. Murder from the *outside*.'

I shivered.

'It's rather horrible ...'

'Yes. I felt from the first, when I read the original letter, that there was something wrong – misshapen ...'

He made an impatient gesture.

'One must not give way to the nerves ... *This is no worse than any ordinary crime* ...'

'It is ... It is ...'

'Is it worse to take the life or lives of strangers than to take the life of someone near and dear to you – someone who trusts and believes in you, perhaps?'

'It's worse because it's *mad* ...'

'No, Hastings. It is not *worse*. It is only more *difficult*.'

'No, no, I do not agree with you. It's infinitely more frightening.'

Hercule Poirot said thoughtfully:

'It should be easier to discover because it is mad. A crime committed by someone shrewd and sane would be far more complicated. Here, if one could but hit on the *idea* ... This alphabetical business, it has discrepancies. If I could once see the *idea* – then everything would be clear and simple . . .'

He sighed and shook his head.

'These crimes must not go on. Soon, soon, I must see the truth . . . Go, Hastings. Get some sleep. There will be much to do tomorrow.'

Sir Carmichael Clarke

Churston, lying as it does between Brixham on the one side and
Paignton and Torquay on the other, occupies a position about
half-way round the curve of Torbay. Until about ten years ago it was
merely a golf links and below the links a green sweep of countryside
dropping down to the sea with only a farmhouse or two in the way of
human occupation. But of late years there had been big building
developments between Churston and Paignton and the coastline is
now dotted with small houses and bungalows, new roads, etc.

Sir Carmichael Clarke had purchased a site of some two acres
commanding an uninterrupted view of the sea. The house he had
built was of modern design – a white rectangle that was not
unpleasing to the eye. Apart from two big galleries that housed his
collection it was not a large house.

Our arrival there took place about 8 am. A local police officer had
met us at the station and had put us *au courant* of the situation.

Sir Carmichael Clarke, it seemed, had been in the habit of taking a
stroll after dinner every evening. When the police rang up – at some
time after eleven – it was ascertained that he had not returned. Since
his stroll usually followed the same course, it was not long before a
search-party discovered his body. Death was due to a crashing blow
with some heavy instrument on the back of the head. *An open A B C
had been placed face downwards on the dead body.*

We arrived at Combeside (as the house was called) at about eight
o'clock. The door was opened by an elderly butler whose shaking
hands and disturbed face showed how much the tragedy had affected
him.

'Good morning, Deveril,' said the police officer.

'Good morning, Mr Wells.'

'These are the gentlemen from London, Deveril.'

'This way, gentlemen.' He ushered us into a long dining-room
where breakfast was laid. 'I'll get Mr Franklin.'

A minute or two later a big fair-haired man with a sunburnt face
entered the room.

This was Franklin Clarke, the dead man's only brother.

He had the resolute competent manner of a man accustomed to
meeting with emergencies.

'Good morning, gentlemen.'

Inspector Wells made the introductions.

'This is Inspector Crome of the CID, Mr Hercule Poirot and – er – Captain Hayter.'

'Hastings,' I corrected coldly.

Franklin Clarke shook hands with each of us in turn and in each case the handshake was accompanied by a piercing look.

'Let me offer you some breakfast,' he said. 'We can discuss the position as we eat.'

There were no dissentient voices and we were soon doing justice to excellent eggs and bacon and coffee.

'Now for it,' said Franklin Clarke. 'Inspector Wells gave me a rough idea of the position last night – though I may say it seemed one of the wildest tales I have ever heard. Am I really to believe, Inspector Crome, that my poor brother is the victim of a homicidal maniac, that this is the third murder that has occurred and that *in each case an A B C railway guide has been deposited beside the body*?'

'That is substantially the position, Mr Clarke.'

'But *why*? What earthly benefit can accrue from such a crime – even in the most diseased imagination?'

Poirot nodded his head in approval.

'You go straight to the point, Mr Franklin,' he said.

'It's not much good looking for motives at this stage, Mr Clarke,' said Inspector Crome. 'That's a matter for an alienist – though I may say that I've had a certain experience of criminal lunacy and that the motives are usually grossly inadequate. There is a desire to assert one's personality, to make a splash in the public eye – in fact, to be a somebody instead of a nonentity.'

'Is that true, M. Poirot?'

Clarke seemed incredulous. His appeal to the older man was not too well received by Inspector Crome, who frowned.

'Absolutely true,' replied my friend.

'At any rate such a man cannot escape detection long,' said Clarke thoughtfully.

'*Vous croyez?* Ah, but they are cunning – *ces gens là!* And you must remember *such a type has usually all the outer signs of insignificance* – he belongs to the class of person who is usually passed over and ignored or even laughed at!'

'Will you let me have a few facts, please, Mr Clarke,' said Crome, breaking in on the conversation.

'Certainly.'

399

'Your brother, I take it, was in his usual health and spirits yesterday? He received no unexpected letters? Nothing to upset him?'

'No. I should say he was quite his usual self.'

'Not upset and worried in any way.'

'Excuse me, inspector. I didn't say that. To be upset and worried was my poor brother's normal condition.'

'Why was that?'

'You may not know that my sister-in-law, Lady Clarke, is in very bad health. Frankly, between ourselves, she is suffering from an incurable cancer, and cannot live very much longer. Her illness has preyed terribly on my brother's mind. I myself returned from the East not long ago and I was shocked at the change in him.'

Poirot interpolated a question.

'Supposing, Mr Clarke, that your brother had been found shot at the foot of a cliff – or shot with a revolver beside him. What would have been your first thought?'

'Quite frankly, I should have jumped to the conclusion that it was suicide,' said Clarke.

'*Encore!*' said Poirot.

'What is that?'

'A fact that repeats itself. It is of no matter.'

'Anyway, it *wasn't* suicide,' said Crome with a touch of curtness. 'Now I believe, Mr Clarke, that it was your brother's habit to go for a stroll every evening?'

'Quite right. He always did.'

'Every night?'

'Well, not if it was pouring with rain, naturally.'

'And everyone in the house knew of this habit?'

'Of course.'

'And outside?'

'I don't know what you mean by outside. The gardener may have been aware of it or not, I don't know.'

'And in the village?'

'Strictly speaking, we haven't got a village. There's a post office and cottages at Churston Ferrers – but there's no village or shops.'

'I suppose a stranger hanging round the place would be fairly easily noticed?'

'On the contrary. In August all this part of the world is a seething mass of strangers. They come over every day from Brixham and Torquay and Paignton in cars and buses and on foot. Broadsands, which is down there (he pointed), is a very popular beach and so is Elbury Cove – it's a well-known beauty spot and people come there and picnic. I wish they didn't! You've no idea how beautiful and peaceful this part of the world is in June and the beginning of July.'

'So you don't think a stranger would be noticed?'

'Not unless he looked – well, off his head.'

'This man doesn't look off his head,' said Crome with certainty. 'You see what I'm getting at, Mr Clarke. This man must have been spying out the land beforehand and discovered your brother's habit of taking an evening stroll. I suppose, by the way, that no strange man came up to the house and asked to see Sir Carmichael yesterday?'

'Not that I know of – but we'll ask Deveril.'

He rang the bell and put the question to the butler.

'No, sir, no one came to see Sir Carmichael. And I didn't notice anyone hanging about the house either. No more did the maids, because I've asked them.'

The butler waited a moment, then inquired: 'Is that all, sir?'

'Yes, Deveril, you can go.'

The butler withdrew, drawing back in the doorway to let a young woman pass.

Franklin Clarke rose as she came in.

'This is Miss Grey, gentlemen. My brother's secretary.'

My attention was caught at once by the girl's extraordinary Scandinavian fairness. She had the almost colourless ash hair – light-grey eyes – and transparent glowing pallor that one finds amongst Norwegians and Swedes. She looked about twenty-seven and seemed to be as efficient as she was decorative.

'Can I help you in any way?' she asked as she sat down.

Clarke brought her a cup of coffee, but she refused any food.

'Did you deal with Sir Carmichael's correspondence?' asked Crome.

'Yes, all of it.'

'I suppose he never received a letter or letters signed A B C?'

'A B C?' She shook her head. 'No, I'm sure he didn't.'

'He didn't mention having seen anyone hanging about during his evening walks lately?'

'No. He never mentioned anything of the kind.'

'And you yourself have noticed no strangers?'

'Not exactly hanging about. Of course, there are a lot of people what you might call *wandering* about at this time of year. One often

401

meets people strolling with an aimless look across the golf links or down the lanes to the sea. In the same way, practically everyone one sees this time of year is a stranger.'

Poirot nodded thoughtfully.

Inspector Crome asked to be taken over the ground of Sir Carmichael's nightly walk. Franklin Clarke led the way through the french window, and Miss Grey accompanied us.

She and I were a little behind the others.

'All this must have been a terrible shock to you all,' I said.

'It seems quite unbelievable. I had gone to bed last night when the police rang up. I heard voices downstairs and at last I came out and asked what was the matter. Deveril and Mr Clarke were just setting out with lanterns.'

'What time did Sir Carmichael usually come back from his walk?'

'About a quarter to ten. He used to let himself in by the side door and then sometimes he went straight to bed, sometimes to the gallery where his collections were. That is why, unless the police had rung up, he would probably not have been missed till they went to call him this morning.'

'It must have been a terrible shock to his wife?'

'Lady Clarke is kept under morphia a good deal. I think she is in too dazed a condition to appreciate what goes on round her.'

We had come out through a garden gate on to the golf links. Crossing a corner of them, we passed over a stile into a steep, winding lane.

'This leads down to Elbury Cove,' explained Franklin Clarke. 'But two years ago they made a new road leading from the main road to Broadsands and on to Elbury, so that now this lane is practically deserted.'

We went on down the lane. At the foot of it a path led between brambles and bracken down to the sea. Suddenly we came out on a grassy ridge overlooking the sea and a beach of glistening white stones. All round dark green trees ran down to the sea. It was an enchanting spot – white, deep green – and sapphire blue.

'How beautiful!' I exclaimed.

Clarke turned to me eagerly.

'Isn't it? Why people want to go abroad to the Riviera when they've got this! I've wandered all over the world in my time and, honest to God, I've never seen anything as beautiful.'

Then, as though ashamed of his eagerness, he said in a more matter-of-fact tone:

'This was my brother's evening walk. He came as far as here, then back up the path, and turning to the right instead of the left, went past the farm and across the fields back to the house.'

We proceeded on our way till we came to a spot near the hedge, half-way across the field where the body had been found.

Crome nodded.

'Easy enough. The man stood here in the shadow. Your brother would have noticed nothing till the blow fell.'

The girl at my side gave a quick shiver.

Franklin Clarke said:

'Hold up, Thora. It's pretty beastly, but it's no use shirking facts.'

Thora Grey – the name suited her.

We went back to the house where the body had been taken after being photographed.

As we mounted the wide staircase the doctor came out of a room, black bag in hand.

'Anything to tell us, doctor?' inquired Clarke.

The doctor shook his head.

'Perfectly simple case. I'll keep the technicalities for the inquest. Anyway, he didn't suffer. Death must have been instantaneous.'

He moved away.

'I'll just go in and see Lady Clarke.'

A hospital nurse came out of a room farther along the corridor and the doctor joined her.

We went into the room out of which the doctor had come.

I came out again rather quickly. Thora Grey was still standing at the head of the stairs.

There was a queer scared expression on her face.

'Miss Grey –' I stopped. 'Is anything the matter?'

She looked at me.

'I was thinking,' she said, 'about D.'

'About D?' I stared at her stupidly.

'Yes. The next murder. Something must be done. It's got to be stopped.'

Clarke came out of the room behind me.

He said:

'What's got to be stopped, Thora?'

'These awful murders.'

'Yes.' His jaw thrust itself out aggressively. 'I want to talk to M. Poirot some time ... Is Crome any good?' He shot the words out unexpectedly.

403

I replied that he was supposed to be a very clever officer.

My voice was perhaps not as enthusiastic as it might have been.

'He's got a damned offensive manner,' said Clarke. 'Looks as though he knows everything – and what *does* he know? Nothing at all as far as I can make out.'

He was silent for a minute or two. Then he said:

'M. Poirot's the man for my money. I've got a plan. But we'll talk of that later.'

He went along the passage and tapped at the same door as the doctor had entered.

I hesitated a moment. The girl was staring in front of her.

'What are you thinking of, Miss Grey?'

She turned her eyes towards me.

'I'm wondering *where he is now* . . . the murderer, I mean. It's not twelve hours yet since it happened . . . Oh! aren't there any *real* clairvoyants who could see where he is now and what he is doing . . .'

'The police are searching –' I began.

My commonplace words broke the spell. Thora Grey pulled herself together.

'Yes,' she said. 'Of course.'

In her turn she descended the staircase. I stood there a moment longer conning her words over in my mind.

A B C . . .

Where was he now . . .?

CHAPTER SIXTEEN

(Not from Captain Hastings' Personal Narrative)

Mr Alexander Bonaparte Cust came out with the rest of the audience from the Torquay Palladium, where he had been seeing and hearing that highly emotional film, *Not a Sparrow* ...

He blinked a little as he came out into the afternoon sunshine and peered round him in that lost-dog fashion that was characteristic of him.

He murmured to himself: 'It's an idea ...'

Newsboys passed along crying out:

'Latest ... Homicidal Maniac at Churston ...'

They carried placards on which was written:

CHURSTON MURDER. LATEST.

Mr Cust fumbled in his pocket, found a coin, and bought a paper. He did not open it at once.

Entering the Princess Gardens, he slowly made his way to a shelter facing Torquay harbour. He sat down and opened the paper.

There were big headlines:

SIR CARMICHAEL CLARKE MURDERED.
TERRIBLE TRAGEDY AT CHURSTON.
WORK OF A HOMICIDAL MANIAC.
And below them:

Only a month ago England was shocked and startled by the murder of a young girl, Elizabeth Barnard, at Bexhill. It may be remembered that an A B C railway guide figured in the case. An A B C was also found by the dead body of Sir Carmichael Clarke, and the police incline to the belief that both crimes were committed by the same person. Can it be possible that a homicidal murderer is going the round of our seaside resorts? ...

A young man in flannel trousers and a bright blue Aertex shirt who was sitting beside Mr Cust remarked:

'Nasty business – eh?'

Mr Cust jumped.

'Oh, very – very –'

His hands, the young man noticed, were trembling so that he

405

could hardly hold the paper.

'You never know with lunatics,' said the young man chattily. 'They don't always look barmy, you know. Often they seem just the same as you or me . . .'

'I suppose they do,' said Mr Cust.

'It's a fact. Sometimes it's the war what unhinged them – never been right since.'

'I – I expect you're right.'

'I don't hold with wars,' said the young man.

His companion turned on him.

'I don't hold with plague and sleeping sickness and famine and cancer . . . but they happen all the same!'

'War's preventable,' said the young man with assurance.

Mr Cust laughed. He laughed for some time.

The young man was slightly alarmed.

'He's a bit batty himself,' he thought.

Aloud he said:

'Sorry, sir, I expect you were in the war.'

'I was,' said Mr Cust. 'It – it – unsettled me. My head's never been right since. It aches, you know. Aches terribly.'

'Oh! I'm sorry about that,' said the young man awkwardly.

'Sometimes I hardly know what I'm doing . . .'

'Really? Well, I must be getting along,' said the young man and removed himself hurriedly. He knew what people were once they began to talk about their health.

Mr Cust remained with his paper.

He read and reread . . .

People passed to and fro in front of him.

Most of them were talking of the murder . . .

'Awful . . . do you think it was anything to do with the Chinese? Wasn't the waitress in a Chinese café . . .'

'Actually on the golf links . . .'

'I heard it was on the beach . . .'

'– but, darling, we took our tea to Elbury only *yesterday* . . .'

'– police are sure to get him . . .'

'– say he may be arrested any minute now . . .'

'– quite likely he's in Torquay . . . that other woman was who murdered the what do you call 'ems . . .'

Mr Cust folded up the paper very neatly and laid it on the seat. Then he rose and walked sedately along towards the town.

Girls passed him, girls in white and pink and blue, in summery frocks and pyjamas and shorts. They laughed and giggled. Their eyes appraised the men they passed.

Not once did their eyes linger for a second on Mr Cust . . .

He sat down at a little table and ordered tea and Devonshire cream . . .

CHAPTER SEVENTEEN

Marking Time

With the murder of Sir Carmichael Clarke the A B C mystery leaped into the fullest prominence.

The newspapers were full of nothing else. All sorts of 'clues' were reported to have been discovered. Arrests were announced to be imminent. There were photographs of every person or place remotely connected with the murder. There were interviews with anyone who would give interviews. There were questions asked in Parliament.

The Andover murder was now bracketed with the other two.

It was the belief of Scotland Yard that the fullest publicity was the best chance of laying the murderer by the heels. The population of Great Britain turned itself into an army of amateur sleuths.

The *Daily Flicker* had the grand inspiration of using the caption: HE MAY BE IN *YOUR* TOWN!

Poirot, of course, was in the thick of things. The letters sent to him were published and facsimiled. He was abused wholesale for not having prevented the crimes and defended on the ground that he was on the point of naming the murderer.

Reporters incessantly badgered him for interviews.

What M. Poirot Says Today.

Which was usually followed by a half-column of imbecilities.

M. Poirot Takes Grave View of Situation.

M. Poirot on the Eve of Success.

Captain Hastings, the great friend of M. Poirot, told our Special Representative ...

'Poirot,' I would cry. 'Pray believe me. I never said anything of the kind.'

My friend would reply kindly:

'I know, Hastings – I know. The spoken word and the written – there is an astonishing gulf between them. There is a way of turning sentences that completely reverses the original meaning.'

'I wouldn't like you to think I'd said –'

'But do not worry yourself. All this is of no importance. These imbecilities, even, may help.'

'How?'

'*Eh bien*,' said Poirot grimly. 'If our madman reads what I am

408

supposed to have said to the *Daily Blague* today, he will lose all respect for me as an opponent!'

I am, perhaps, giving the impression that nothing practical was being done in the way of investigations. On the contrary, Scotland Yard, and the local police of the various counties were indefatigable in following up the smallest clues.

Hotels, people who kept lodgings, boarding-houses – all those within a wide radius of the crimes were questioned minutely.

Hundreds of stories from imaginative people who had 'seen a man looking very queer and rolling his eyes,' or 'noticed a man with a sinister face slinking along', were sifted to the last detail. No information, even of the vaguest character, was neglected. Trains, buses, trams, railway porters, conductors, bookstalls, stationers – there was an indefatigable round of questions and verifications.

At least a score of people were detained and questioned until they could satisfy the police as to their movements on the night in question.

The net result was not entirely a blank. Certain statements were borne in mind and noted down as of possible value, but without further evidence they led nowhere.

If Crome and his colleagues were indefatigable, Poirot seemed to me strangely supine. We argued now and again.

'But what is it that you would have me do, my friend? The routine inquiries, the police make them better than I do. Always – always you want me to run about like the dog.'

'Instead of which you sit at home like – like –'

'A sensible man! My force, Hastings, is in my *brain*, not in my *feet*! All the time, whilst I seem to you idle, I am reflecting.'

'Reflecting?' I cried. 'Is this a time for reflection?'

'Yes, a thousand times yes.'

'But what can you possibly gain by reflection? You know the facts of the three cases by heart.'

'It is not the facts I reflect upon – but the mind of the murderer.'

'The mind of a madman!'

'Precisely. And therefore not to be arrived at in a minute. *When I know what the murderer is like, I shall be able to find out who he is*. And all the time I learn more. After the Andover crime, what did we know about the murderer? Next to nothing at all. After the Bexhill crime? A little more. After the Churston murder? More still. I begin to see – not what *you* would like to see – the outlines of *a face and form* but the outlines of a *mind*. A mind that moves and works in certain definite directions. After the next crime –'

'Poirot!'

My friend looked at me dispassionately.

'But, yes, Hastings, I think it is almost certain there will be another. A lot depends on *la chance*. So far our *inconnu* has been lucky. This time the luck may turn against him. But in any case, after another crime, we shall know infinitely more. Crime is terribly revealing. Try and vary your methods as you will, your tastes, your habits, your attitude of mind, and your soul is revealed by your actions. There are confusing indications – sometimes it is as though there were two intelligences at work – but soon the outline will clear itself, *I shall know*.'

'Who it is?'

'No, Hastings, I shall not know his name and address! I shall know *what kind of a man he is* . . .'

'And then? . . .'

'*Et alors, je vais à la pêche.*'

As I looked rather bewildered, he went on:

'You comprehend, Hastings, an expert fisherman knows exactly what flies to offer to what fish. I shall offer the right kind of fly.'

'And then?'

'And then? And then? You are as bad as the superior Crome with his eternal "Oh, yes?" *Eh bien*, and then he will take the bait and the hook and we will reel in the line . . .'

'In the meantime people are dying right and left.'

'Three people. And there are, what is it – about 120 – road deaths every week?'

'That is entirely different.'

'It is probably exactly the same to those who die. For the others, the relations, the friends – yes, there is a difference, but one thing at least rejoices me in this case.'

'By all means let us hear anything in the nature of rejoicing.'

'*Inutile* to be so sarcastic. It rejoices me that there is here no shadow of guilt to distress the innocent.'

'Isn't this worse?'

'No, no, a thousand times no! There is nothing so terrible as to live in an atmosphere of suspicion – to see eyes watching you and the love in them changing to fear – nothing so terrible as to suspect those near and dear to you – It is poisonous – a miasma. No, the poisoning of life for the innocent, that, at least, we cannot lay at A B C's door.'

'You'll soon be making excuses for the man!' I said bitterly.

'Why not? He may believe himself fully justified. We may, perhaps, end by having sympathy with his point of view.'

'Really, Poirot!'

'Alas! I have shocked you. First my inertia – and then my views.'

I shook my head without replying.

'All the same,' said Poirot after a minute or two. 'I have one project that will please you – since it is active and not passive. Also, it will entail a lot of conversation and practically no thought.'

I did not quite like his tone.

'What is it?' I asked cautiously.

'The extraction from the friends, relations and servants of the victims of all they know.'

'Do you suspect them of keeping things back, then?'

'Not intentionally. But telling everything you know always implies *selection*. If I were to say to you, recount me your day yesterday, you would perhaps reply: "I rose at nine, I breakfasted at half-past, I had eggs and bacon and coffee, I went to my club, etc." You would not include: "I tore my nail and had to cut it. I rang for shaving water. I spilt a little coffee on the tablecloth. I brushed my hat and put it on." One cannot tell *everything*. Therefore one *selects*. As the time of a murder people select what *they* think is important. But quite frequently they think wrong!'

'And how is one to get at the right things?'

'Simply, as I said just now, by conversation. By talking! By discussing a certain happening, or a certain person, or a certain day, over and over again, extra details are bound to arise.'

'What kind of details?'

'Naturally that I do not know or I should not want to find out. But enough time has passed now for ordinary things to reassume their value. It is against all mathematical laws that in three cases of murder there is no single fact nor sentence with a bearing on the case. Some trivial happening, some trivial remark there *must* be which would be a pointer! It is looking for the needle in the haystack, I grant – *but in the haystack there is a needle* – of that I am convinced!'

It seemed to me extremely vague and hazy.

'You do not see it? Your wits are not so sharp as those of a mere servant girl.'

He tossed me over a letter. It was neatly written in a sloping board-school hand.

'DEAR SIR, – I hope you will forgive the liberty I take in writing to

411

you. I have been thinking a lot since these awful two murders like poor auntie's. It seems as though we're all in the same boat, as it were. I saw the young lady's picture in the paper, the young lady, I mean, that is the sister of the young lady was killed at Bexhill. I made so bold as to write to her and tell her I was coming to London to get a place and asked if I could come to her or her mother as I said two heads might be better than one and I would not want much wages, but only to find out who this awful fiend is and perhaps we might get at it better if we could say what we knew something might come of it.

'The young lady wrote very nicely and said as how she worked in an office and lived in a hostel, but she suggested I might write to you and she said she'd been thinking something of the same kind as I had. And she said we were in the same trouble and we ought to stand together. So I am writing, sir to say I am coming to London and this is my address.

'Hoping I am not troubling you, Yours respectfully,

'MARY DROWER.'

'Mary Drower,' said Poirot, 'is a very intelligent girl.'

He picked up another letter.

'Read this.'

It was a line from Franklin Clarke, saying that he was coming to London and would call upon Poirot the following day if not inconvenient.

'Do not despair, *mon ami*,' said Poirot. 'Action is about to begin.'

CHAPTER EIGHTEEN

Poirot Makes a Speech

Franklin Clarke arrived at three o'clock on the following afternoon and came straight to the point without beating about the bush.

'M. Poirot,' he said, 'I'm not satisfied.'

'No, Mr Clarke?'

'I've no doubt that Crome is a very efficient officer, but, frankly, he puts my back up. That air of his of knowing best! I hinted something of what I had in mind to your friend here when he was down at Churston, but I've had all my brother's affairs to settle up and I haven't been free until now. My idea is, M. Poirot, that we oughtn't to let the grass grow under our feet –'

'Just what Hastings is always saying!'

'– but go right ahead. We've got to get ready for the next crime.'

'So you think there will be a next crime?'

'Don't you?'

'Certainly.'

'Very well, then. I want to get organized.'

'Tell me your idea exactly?'

'I propose, M. Poirot, a kind of special legion – to work under your orders – composed of the friends and relatives of the murdered people.'

'*Une bonne idée.*'

'I'm glad you approve. By putting our heads together I feel we might get at something. Also, when the next warning comes, by being on the spot, one of us might – I don't say it's probable – but we might recognize some person as having been near the scene of a previous crime.'

'I see your idea, and I approve, but you must remember, Mr Clarke, the relations and friends of the other victims are hardly in your sphere of life. They are employed persons and though they might be given a short vacation –'

Franklin Clarke interrupted.

'That's just it. I'm the only person in a position to foot the bill. Not that I'm particularly well off myself, but my brother died a rich man and it will eventually come to me. I propose, as I say, to enroll a special legion, the members to be paid for their services at the same rate as they get habitually, with, of course, the additional expenses.'

413

'Who do you propose should form this legion?'

'I've been into that. As a matter of fact, I wrote to Miss Megan Barnard – indeed, this is partly her idea. I suggest myself, Miss Barnard, Mr Donald Fraser, who was engaged to the dead girl. Then there is a niece of the Andover woman – Miss Barnard knows her address. I don't think the husband would be of any use to us – I hear he's usually drunk. I also think the Barnards – the father and mother – are a bit old for active campaigning.'

'Nobody else?'

'Well – er – Miss Grey.'

He flushed slightly as he spoke the name.

'Oh! Miss Grey?'

Nobody in the world could put a gentle nuance of irony into a couple of words better than Poirot. About thirty-five years fell away from Franklin Clarke. He looked suddenly like a shy schoolboy.

'Yes. You see, Miss Grey was with my brother for over two years. She knows the countryside and the people round, and everything. I've been away for a year and a half.'

Poirot took pity on him and turned the conversation.

'You have been in the East? In China?'

'Yes. I had a kind of roving commission to purchase things for my brother.'

'Very interesting it must have been. *Eh bien*, Mr Clarke, I approve very highly of your idea. I was saying to Hastings only yesterday that a *rapprochement* of the people concerned was needed. It is necessary to pool reminiscences, to compare notes – *enfin* to talk the thing over – to talk – to talk – and again to talk. Out of some innocent phrase may come enlightenment.'

A few days later the 'Special Legion' met at Poirot's rooms.

As they sat round looking obediently towards Poirot, who had his place, like the chairman at a board meeting, at the head of the table, I myself passed them, as it were, in review, confirming or revising my first impressions of them.

The three girls were all of them striking-looking – the extraordinary fair beauty of Thora Grey, the dark intensity of Megan Barnard, with her strange Red Indian immobility of face – Mary Drower, neatly dressed in a black coat and skirt, with her pretty, intelligent face. Of the two men, Franklin Clarke, big, bronzed and talkative, Donald Fraser, self-contained and quiet, made an interesting contrast to each other.

Poirot, unable, of course, to resist the occasion, made a

little speech.

'Mesdames and Messieurs, you know what we are here for. The police are doing their utmost to track down the criminal. I, too, in my different way. But it seems to me a reunion of those who have a personal interest in the matter – and also, I may say, a personal knowledge of the victims – might have results that an outside investigation cannot pretend to attain.

'Here we have three murders – an old woman, a young girl, an elderly man. Only one thing links these three people together – *the fact that the same person killed them*. That means that *the same person was present in three different localities* and was seen necessarily by a large number of people. That he is a madman in an advanced stage of mania goes without saying. That his appearance and behaviour give no suggestion of such a fact is equally certain. This person – and though I say *he*, remember it may be a man or a woman – has all the devilish cunning of insanity. He has succeeded so far in covering his traces completely. The police have certain vague indications but nothing upon which they can act.

'Nevertheless, there must exist indications which are not vague but certain. To take one particular point – this assassin, he did not arrive at Bexhill at midnight and find conveniently on the beach a young lady whose name began with B –'

'Must we go into that?'

It was Donald Fraser who spoke – the words wrung from him, it seemed, by some inner anguish.

'It is necessary to go into everything, monsieur,' said Poirot, turning to him. 'You are here, not to save your feelings by refusing to think of details, but if necessary to harrow them by going into the matter *au fond*. As I say, it was not *chance* that provided A B C with a victim in Betty Barnard. There must have been deliberate selection on his part – and therefore premeditation. That is to say, he must have reconnoitred the ground *beforehand*. There were facts of which he had informed himself – the best hour for the committing of the crime at Andover – the *mise en scène* at Bexhill – the habits of Sir Carmichael Clarke at Churston. Me, for one, I refuse to believe that there is *no* indication – no slightest hint – that might help to establish his identity.

'I make the assumption that one – or possibly *all* of you – *knows something that they do not know they know*.

'Sooner or later, by reason of your association with one another, something will come to light, will take on a significance as yet

415

undreamed of. It is like the jig-saw puzzle – each of you may have *a piece apparently without meaning, but which when reunited may show a definite portion of the picture as a whole.*'

'Words!' said Megan Barnard.

'Eh?' Poirot looked at her inquiringly.

'What you've been saying. It's just words. It doesn't mean anything.'

She spoke with that kind of desperate intensity that I had come to associate with her personality.

'Words, mademoiselle, are only the outer clothing of ideas.'

'Well, I think it's sense,' said Mary Drower. 'I do really, miss. It's often when you're talking over things that you seem to see your way clear. Your mind gets made up for you sometimes without your knowing how it's happened. Talking leads to a lot of things one way and other.'

'If "least said is soonest mended", it's the converse we want here,' said Franklin Clarke.

'What do you say, Mr Fraser?'

'I rather doubt the practical applicability of what you say, M. Poirot.'

'What do you think, Thora?' asked Clarke.

'I think the principle of talking things over is always sound.'

'Suppose,' suggested Poirot, 'that you all go over your own remembrances of the time preceding the murder. Perhaps you'll start, Mr Clarke.'

'Let me see, on the morning of the day Car was killed I went off sailing. Caught eight mackerel. Lovely out there on the bay. Lunch at home. Irish stew, I remember. Slept in the hammock. Tea. Wrote some letters, missed the post, and drove into Paignton to post them. Then dinner and – I'm not ashamed to say it – reread a book of E. Nesbit's that I used to love as a kid. Then the telephone rang –'

'No further. Now reflect, Mr Clarke, did you meet anyone on your way down to the sea in the morning?'

'Lots of people.'

'Can you remember anything about them?'

'Not a damned thing now.'

'Sure?'

'Well – let's see – I remember a remarkably fat woman – she wore a striped silk dress and I wondered why – had a couple of kids with her – two young men with a fox terrier on the beach throwing stones for it – Oh, yes, a girl with yellow hair squeaking as she bathed – funny

416

how things come back – like a photograph developing.'

'You are a good subject. Now later in the day – the garden – going to the post –'

'The gardener watering . . . Going to the post? Nearly ran down a bicyclist – silly woman wobbling and shouting to a friend. That's all, I'm afraid.'

Poirot turned to Thora Grey.

'Miss Grey?'

Thora Grey replied in her clear, positive voice:

'I did correspondence with Sir Carmichael in the morning – saw the housekeeper. I wrote letters and did needlework in the afternoon, I fancy. It is difficult to remember. It was quite an ordinary day. I went to bed early.'

Rather to my surprise, Poirot asked no further. He said:

'Miss Barnard – can you bring back your remembrances of the last time you saw your sister?'

'It would be about a fortnight before her death. I was down for Saturday and Sunday. It was fine weather. We went to Hastings to the swimming pool.'

'What did you talk about most of the time?'

'I gave her a piece of my mind,' said Megan.

'And what else? She conversed of what?'

The girl frowned in an effort of memory.

'She talked about being hard up – of a hat and a couple of summer frocks she'd just bought. And a little of Don . . . She also said she disliked Milly Higley – that's the girl at the café – and we laughed about the Merrion woman who keeps the café . . . I don't remember anything else . . .'

'She didn't mention any man – forgive me, Mr Fraser – she might be meeting?'

'She wouldn't to me,' said Megan dryly.

Poirot turned to the red-haired young man with the square jaw.

'Mr Fraser – I want you to cast your mind back. You went, you said, to the café on the fatal evening. Your first intention was to wait there and watch for Betty Barnard to come out. Can you remember anyone at all whom you noticed whilst you were waiting here?'

'There were a large number of people walking along the front. I can't remember any of them.'

'Excuse me, but are you trying? However preoccupied the mind may be, the eye notices mechanically – unintelligently but accurately . . .'

417

The young man repeated doggedly:

'I don't remember anybody.'

Poirot sighed and turned to Mary Drower.

'I suppose you got letters from your aunt?'

'Oh, yes, sir.'

'When was the last?'

Mary thought a minute.

'Two days before the murder, sir.'

'What did it say?'

'She said the old devil had been round and that she'd sent him off with a flea in the ear – excuse the expression, sir – said she expected me over on the Wednesday – that's my day out, sir – and she said we'd go to the pictures. It was going to be my birthday, sir.'

Something – the thought of the little festivity perhaps – suddenly brought the tears to Mary's eyes. She gulped down a sob. Then apologized for it.

'You must forgive me, sir. I don't want to be silly. Crying's no good. It was just the thought of her – and me – looking forward to our treat. It upset me somehow, sir.'

'I know just what you feel like,' said Franklin Clarke. 'It's always the little things that get one – and especially anything like a treat or a present – something jolly and natural. I remember seeing a woman run over once. She'd just bought some new shoes. I saw her lying there – and the burst parcel with the ridiculous little high-heeled slippers peeping out – it gave me a turn – they looked so pathetic.'

Megan said with a sudden eager warmth:

'That's true – that's awfully true. The same thing happened after Betty – died. Mum had bought some stockings for her as a present – bought them the very day it happened. Poor mum, she was all broken up. I found her crying over them. She kept saying: "I bought them for Betty – I bought them for Betty – and she never even saw them." '

Her own voice quivered a little. She leaned forward, looking straight at Franklin Clarke. There was between them a sudden sympathy – a fraternity in trouble.

'I know,' he said. 'I know exactly. Those are just the sort of things that are hell to remember.'

Donald Fraser stirred uneasily.

Thora Grey diverted the conversation.

'Aren't we going to make any plans – for the future?' she asked.

'Of course.' Franklin Clarke resumed his ordinary manner. 'I

418

think that when the moment comes – that is, when the fourth letter arrives – we ought to join forces. Until then, perhaps we might each try our luck on our own. I don't know whether there are any points M. Poirot thinks might repay investigation?'

'I could make some suggestions,' said Poirot.

'Good. I'll take them down.' He produced a notebook. 'Go ahead, M. Poirot. A –?'

'I consider it just possible that the waitress, Milly Higley, might know something useful.'

'A – Milly Higley,' wrote down Franklin Clarke.

'I suggest two methods of approach. You, Miss Barnard, might try what I call the offensive approach.'

'I suppose you think that suits my style?' said Megan dryly.

'Pick a quarrel with the girl – say you knew she never liked your sister – and that your sister had told you all about *her*. If I do not err, that will provoke a flood of recrimination. She will tell you just what she thought of your sister! Some useful fact may emerge.'

'And the second method?'

'May I suggest, Mr Fraser, that you should show signs of interest in the girl?'

'Is that necessary.'

'No, it is not necessary. It is just a possible line of exploration.'

'Shall I try my hand?' asked Franklin. 'I've – er – a pretty wide experience, M. Poirot. Let me see what I can do with the young lady.'

'You've got your own part of the world to attend to,' said Thora Grey rather sharply.

Franklin's face fell just a little.

'Yes,' he said. 'I have.'

'*Tout de même*, I do not think there is much you can do down there for the present,' said Poirot. 'Mademoiselle Grey now, she is far more fitted –'

Thora Grey interrupted him.

'But you see, M. Poirot, I have left Devon for good.'

'Ah? I did not understand.'

'Miss Grey very kindly stayed on to help me clear up things,' said Franklin. 'But naturally she prefers a post in London.'

Poirot directed a sharp glance from one to the other.

'How is Lady Clarke?' he demanded.

I was admiring the faint colour in Thora Grey's cheeks and almost missed Clarke's reply.

419

'Pretty bad. By the way, M. Poirot, I wonder if you could see your way to running down to Devon and paying her a visit? She expressed a desire to see you before I left. Of course, she often can't see people for a couple of days at a time, but if you would risk that – at my expense, of course.'

'Certainly, Mr Clarke. Shall we say the day after tomorrow?'

'Good. I'll let nurse know and she'll arrange the dope accordingly.'

'For you, my child,' said Poirot, turning to Mary, 'I think you might perhaps do good work in Andover. Try the children.'

'The children?'

'Yes. Children will not chat readily to outsiders. But you are known in the street where your aunt lived. There were a good many children playing about. They may have noticed who went in and out of your aunt's shop.'

'What about Miss Grey and myself?' asked Clarke. 'That is, if I'm not to go to Bexhill.'

'M. Poirot,' said Thora Grey, 'what was the postmark on the third letter?'

'Putney, mademoiselle.'

She said thoughtfully: 'SW15, Putney, that is right, is it not?'

'For a wonder, the newspapers printed it correctly.'

'That seems to point to A B C being a Londoner.'

'On the face of it, yes.'

'One ought to be able to draw him,' said Clarke. 'M. Poirot, how would it be if I inserted an advertisement – something after these lines: *A B C. Urgent, H.P. close on your track. A hundred for my silence. X Y Z.* Nothing quite so crude as that – but you see the idea. It might draw him.'

'It is a possibility – yes.'

'Might induce him to try and have a shot at me.'

'I think it's very dangerous and silly,' said Thora Grey sharply.

'What about it, M. Poirot?'

'It can do no harm to try. I think myself that A B C will be too cunning to reply.' Poirot smiled a little. 'I see, Mr Clarke, that you are – if I may say so without being offensive – still a boy at heart.'

Franklin Clarke looked a little abashed.

'Well,' he said, consulting his notebook. 'We're making a start.'

A – Miss Barnard and Milly Higley.
B – Mr Fraser and Miss Higley.

420

C – Children in Andover.
D – Advertisement.

I don't feel any of it is much good, but it will be something to do whilst waiting.'

He got up and a few minutes later the meeting had dispersed.

CHAPTER NINETEEN

By Way of Sweden

Poirot returned to his seat and sat humming a little tune to himself.

'Unfortunate that she is so intelligent,' he murmured.

'Who?'

'Megan Barnard. Mademoiselle Megan. "Words," she snaps out. At once she perceives that what I am saying means nothing to all. Everybody else was taken in.'

'I thought it sounded very plausible.'

'Plausible, yes. It was just that she perceived.'

'Didn't you mean what you said, then?'

'What I said could have been comprised into one short sentence. Instead I repeated myself *ad lib* without anyone but Mademoiselle Megan being aware of the fact.'

'But why?'

'*Eh bien* – to get things going! To imbue everyone with the impression that there was work to be done! To start – shall we say – the conversations!'

'Don't you think any of these lines will lead to anything?'

'Oh, it is always possible.'

He chuckled.

'In the midst of tragedy we start the comedy. It is so, is it not?'

'What *do* you mean?'

'The human drama, Hastings! Reflect a little minute. Here are three sets of human beings brought together by a common tragedy. Immediately a second drama commences – *tout à fait à part*. Do you remember my first case in England? Oh, so many years ago now. I brought together two people who loved one another – by the simple method of having one of them arrested for murder! Nothing less would have done it! In the midst of death we are in life, Hastings ... Murder, I have often noticed, is a great matchmaker.'

'Really, Poirot,' I cried scandalized. 'I'm sure none of those people was thinking of anything but –'

'Oh! my dear friend. And what about yourself?'

'I?'

'*Mais oui*, as they departed, did you not come back from the door humming a tune?'

'One may do that without being callous.'

'Certainly, but that tune told me your thoughts.'

'Indeed?'

'Yes. To hum a tune is extremely dangerous. It reveals the subconscious mind. The tune you hummed dates, I think, from the days of the war. *Comme ça,*' Poirot sang in an abominable falsetto voice:

'Some of the time I love a brunette,
Some of the time I love a blonde (Who comes from Eden by way of Sweden).

'What could be more revealing? *Mais je crois que la blonde l'emporte sur la brunette!*'

'Really, Poirot,' I cried, blushing slightly.

'*C'est tout naturel.* Did you observe how Franklin Clarke was suddenly at one and in sympathy with Mademoiselle Megan? How he leaned forward and looked at her? And did you also notice how very much annoyed Mademoiselle Thora Grey was about it? And Mr Donald Fraser, he –'

'Poirot,' I said. 'Your mind is incurably sentimental.'

'That is the last thing my mind is. You are the sentimental one, Hastings.'

I was about to argue the point hotly, but at the moment the door opened.

To my astonishment it was Thora Grey who entered.

'Forgive me for coming back,' she said composedly. 'But there was something that I think I would like to tell you, M. Poirot.'

'Certainly, mademoiselle. Sit down, will you not?'

She took a seat and hesitated for just a minute as though choosing her words.

'It is just this, M. Poirot. Mr Clarke very generously gave you to understand just now that I had left Combeside by my own wish. He is a very kind and loyal person. But as a matter of fact, it is not quite like that. I was quite prepared to stay on – there is any amount of work to be done in connection with the collections. It was Lady Clarke who wished me to leave! I can make allowances. She is a very ill woman, and her brain is somewhat muddled with the drugs they give her. It makes her suspicious and fanciful. She took an unreasoning dislike to me and insisted that I should leave the house.'

I could not but admire the girl's courage. She did not attempt to gloss over facts, as so many might have been tempted to do, but went

423

straight to the point with an admirable candour. My heart went out to her in admiration and sympathy.

'I call it splendid of you to come and tell us this,' I said.

'It's always better to have the truth,' she said with a little smile. 'I don't want to shelter behind Mr Clarke's chivalry. He is a very chivalrous man.'

There was a warm glow in her words. She evidently admired Franklin Clarke enormously.

'You have been very honest, mademoiselle,' said Poirot.

'It is rather a blow to me,' said Thora ruefully. 'I had no idea Lady Clarke disliked me so much. In fact, I always thought she was rather fond of me.' She made a wry face. 'One lives and learns.'

She rose.

'That is all I came to say. Goodbye.'

I accompanied her downstairs.

'I call that very sporting of her,' I said as I returned to the room. 'She has courage, that girl.'

'And calculation.'

'What do you mean – calculation?'

'I mean that she has the power of looking ahead.'

I looked at him doubtfully.

'She really is a lovely girl,' I said.

'And wears very lovely clothes. That crêpe marocain and the silver fox collar – *dernier cri*.'

'You're a man milliner, Poirot. I never notice what people have on.'

'You should join a nudist colony.'

As I was about to make an indignant rejoinder, he said, with a sudden change of subject:

'Do you know, Hastings, I cannot rid my mind of the impression that already, in our conversations this afternoon, something was said that was significant. It is odd – I cannot pin down exactly what it was ... Just an impression that passed through my mind ... *That reminds me of something I have already heard or seen or noted* ...'

'Something at Churston?'

'No – not at Churston ... Before that ... No matter, presently it will come to me ...'

He looked at me (perhaps I had not been attending very closely), laughed and began once more to hum.

'She is an angel, is she not? From Eden by way of Sweden ...'

'Poirot,' I said 'Go to the devil!'

CHAPTER TWENTY

Lady Clarke

There was an air of deep and settled melancholy over Combeside when we saw it again for the second time. This may, perhaps, have been partly due to the weather – it was a moist September day with a hint of autumn in the air, and partly, no doubt, it was the semi-shut-up state of the house. The downstairs rooms were closed and shuttered, and the small room into which we were shown smelt damp and airless.

A capable-looking hospital nurse came to us there pulling down her starched cuffs.

'M. Poirot?' she said briskly. 'I am Nurse Capstick. I got Mr Clarke's letter saying you were coming.'

Poirot inquired after Lady Clarke's health.

'Not at all bad really, all things considered.'

'All things considered,' I presumed, meant considering she was under sentence of death.

'One can't hope for much improvement, of course, but some new treatment has made things a little easier for her. Dr Logan is quite pleased with her condition.'

'But it is true, is it not, that she can never recover?'

'Oh, we never actually *say* that,' said Nurse Capstick, a little shocked by this plain speaking.

'I suppose her husband's death was a terrible shock to her?'

'Well, M. Poirot, if you understand what I mean, it wasn't as much of a shock as it would have been to anyone in full possession of her health and faculties. Things are *dimmed* for Lady Clarke in her condition.'

'Pardon my asking, but was she deeply attached to her husband and he to her?'

'Oh, yes, they were a very happy couple. He was very worried and upset about her, poor man. It's always worse for a doctor, you know. They can't buoy themselves up with false hopes. I'm afraid it preyed on his mind very much to begin with.'

'To begin with? Not so much afterwards?'

'One gets used to everything, doesn't one? And then Sir Carmichael had his collection. A hobby is a great consolation to a man. He used to run up to sales occasionally, and then he and Miss Grey

425

were busy recataloguing and rearranging the museum on a new system.'

'Oh, yes – Miss Grey. She has left, has she not?'

'Yes – I'm very sorry about it – but ladies do take these fancies sometimes when they're not well. And there's no arguing with them. It's better to give in. Miss Grey was very sensible about it.'

'Had Lady Clarke always disliked her?'

'No – that is to say, not *disliked*. As a matter of fact, I think she rather liked her to begin with. But there, I mustn't keep you gossiping. My patient will be wondering what has become of us.'

She led us upstairs to a room on the first floor. What had at one time been a bedroom had been turned into a cheerful-looking sitting-room.

Lady Clarke was sitting in a big armchair near the window. She was painfully thin, and her face had the grey, haggard look of one who suffers much pain. She had a slightly faraway, dreamy look, and I noticed that the pupils of her eyes were mere pin-points.

'This is M. Poirot whom you wanted to see,' said Nurse Capstick in her high, cheerful voice.

'Oh, yes, M. Poirot,' said Lady Clarke vaguely.

She extended her hand.

'My friend Captain Hastings, Lady Clarke.'

'How do you do? So good of you both to come.'

We sat down as her vague gesture directed. There was a silence. Lady Clarke seemed to have lapsed into a dream.

Presently with a slight effort she roused herself.

'It was about Car, wasn't it? About Car's death. Oh, yes.'

She sighed, but still in a faraway manner, shaking her head.

'We never thought it would be that way round . . . I was so sure I should be the first to go . . .' She mused a minute or two. 'Car was very strong – wonderful for his age. He was never ill. He was nearly sixty – but he seemed more like fifty . . . Yes, very strong . . .'

She relapsed again into her dream. Poirot, who was well acquainted with the effects of certain drugs and of how they give their taker the impression of endless time, said nothing.

Lady Clarke said suddenly:

'Yes – it was good of you to come. I told Franklin. He said he wouldn't forget to tell you. I hope Franklin isn't going to be foolish . . . he's so easily taken in, in spite of having knocked about the world so much. Men are like that . . . They remain boys . . . Franklin, in particular.'

426

'He has an impulsive nature,' said Poirot.

'Yes – yes . . . And very chivalrous. Men are so foolish that way. Even Car –' Her voice trailed off.

She shook her head with a febrile impatience.

'Everything's so dim . . . One's body is a nuisance, M. Poirot, especially when it gets the upper hand. One is conscious of nothing else – whether the pain will hold off or not – nothing else seems to matter.'

'I know, Lady Clarke. It is one of the tragedies of this life.'

'It makes me so stupid. I cannot even remember what it was I wanted to say to you.'

'Was it something about your husband's death?'

'Car's death? Yes, perhaps . . . Mad, poor creature – the murderer, I mean. It's all the noise and the speed nowadays – people can't stand it. I've always been sorry for mad people – their heads must feel so queer. And then, being shut up – it must be so terrible. But what else can one do? If they kill people . . .' She shook her head – gently pained. 'You haven't caught him yet?' she asked.

'No, not yet.'

'He must have been hanging round here that day.'

'There were so many strangers about, Lady Clarke. It is the holiday season.'

'Yes – I forgot . . . But they keep down by the beaches, they don't come up near the house.'

'No stranger came to the house that day.'

'Who says so?' demanded Lady Clarke, with a sudden vigour.

Poirot looked slightly taken aback.

'The servants,' he said. 'Miss Grey.'

Lady Clarke said very distinctly:

'That girl is a liar!'

I started on my chair. Poirot threw me a glance.

Lady Clarke was going on, speaking now rather feverishly.

'I didn't like her. I never liked her. Car thought all the world of her. Used to go on about her being an orphan and alone in the world. What's wrong with being an orphan? Sometimes it's a blessing in disguise. You might have a good-for-nothing father and a mother who drank – then you would have something to complain about. Said she was so brave and such a good worker. I dare say she did her work well! I don't know where all this bravery came in!'

'Now don't excite yourself, dear,' said Nurse Capstick, intervening. 'We mustn't have you getting tired.'

427

'I soon sent her packing! Franklin had the impertinence to suggest that she might be a comfort to me. Comfort to me indeed! The sooner I saw the last of her the better – that's what I said! Franklin's a fool! I didn't want him getting mixed up with her. He's a boy! No sense! "I'll give her three months' salary, if you like," I said. "But out she goes. I don't want her in the house a day longer." There's one thing about being ill – men can't argue with you. He did what I said and she went. Went like a martyr, I expect – with more sweetness and bravery!'

'Now, dear, don't get so excited. It's bad for you.'

Lady Clarke waved Nurse Capstick away.

'You were as much of a fool about her as anyone else.'

'Oh! Lady Clarke, you mustn't say that. I did think Miss Grey a very nice girl – so romantic-looking, like someone out of a novel.'

'I've no patience with the lot of you,' said Lady Clarke feebly.

'Well, she's gone now, my dear. Gone right away.'

Lady Clarke shook her head with feeble impatience but she did not answer.

Poirot said:

'Why did you say that Miss Grey was a liar?'

'Because she is. She told you no strangers came to the house, didn't she?'

'Yes.'

'Very well, then. I saw her – with my own eyes – out of this window – talking to a perfectly strange man on the front doorstep.'

'When was this?'

'In the morning of the day Car died – about eleven o'clock.'

'What did this man look like?'

'An ordinary sort of man. Nothing special.'

'A gentleman – or a tradesman?'

'Not a tradesman. A shabby sort of person. I can't remember.'

A sudden quiver of pain shot across her face.

'Please – you must go now – I'm a little tired – Nurse.'

We obeyed the cue and took our departure.

'That's an extraordinary story,' I said to Poirot as we journeyed back to London. 'About Miss Grey and a strange man.'

'You see, Hastings? It is, as I tell you: *there is always something to be found out.*'

'Why did the girl lie about it and say she had seen no one?'

'I can think of seven separate reasons – one of them an extremely simple one.'

428

'Is that a snub?' I asked.

'It is, perhaps, an invitation to use your ingenuity. But there is no need for us to perturb ourselves. The easiest way to answer the question is to ask her.'

'And suppose she tells us another lie.'

'That would indeed be interesting – and highly suggestive.'

'It is monstrous to suppose that a girl like that could be in league with a madman.'

'Precisely – so I do not suppose it.'

I thought for some minutes longer.

'A good-looking girl has a hard time of it,' I said at last with a sigh.

'*Du tout.* Disabuse your mind of that idea.'

'It's true,' I insisted, 'everyone's hand is against her simply because she is good-looking.'

'You speak the *bêtises*, my friend. Whose hand was against her at Combeside? Sir Carmichael's? Franklin's? Nurse Capstick's?'

'Lady Clarke was down on her, all right.'

'*Mon ami*, you are full of charitable feeling towards beautiful young girls. Me, I feel charitable to sick old ladies. It may be that Lady Clarke was the clear-sighted one – and that her husband, Mr Franklin Clarke and Nurse Capstick were all as blind as bats – and Captain Hastings.'

'You've got a grudge against that girl, Poirot.'

To my surprise his eyes twinkled suddenly.

'Perhaps it is that I like to mount you on your romantic high horse, Hastings. You are always the true knight – ready to come to the rescue of damsels in distress – good-looking damsels, *bien entendu*.'

'How ridiculous you are, Poirot,' I said, unable to keep from laughing.

'Ah, well, one cannot be tragic all the time. More and more I interest myself in the human developments that arise out of this tragedy. It is three dramas of family life that we have there. First there is Andover – the whole tragic life of Mrs Ascher, her struggles, her support of her German husband, the devotion of her niece. That alone would make a novel. Then you have Bexhill – the happy, easy-going father and mother, the two daughters so widely differing from each other – the pretty fluffy fool, and the intense, strong-willed Megan with her clear intelligence and her ruthless passion for truth. And the other figure – the self-controlled young Scotsman with his passionate jealousy and his worship of the dead girl. Finally you have the Churston household – the dying wife, and the husband absorbed in his collections, but with a growing tenderness and sympathy for the beautiful girl who helps him so sympathetically, and then the younger brother, vigorous, attractive, interesting, with a romantic glamour about him from his long travels.

'Realize, Hastings, that in the ordinary course of events *those three separate dramas would never have touched each other*. They would have pursued their course uninfluenced by each other. The permutations and combinations of life, Hastings – I never cease to be fascinated by them.'

'This is Paddington,' was the only answer I made.

It was time, I felt, that someone pricked the bubble.

On our arrival at Whitehaven Mansions we were told that a gentleman was waiting to see Poirot.

I expected it to be Franklin, or perhaps Japp, but to my astonishment it turned out to be none other than Donald Fraser.

He seemed very embarrassed and his inarticulateness was more noticeable than ever.

Poirot did not press him to come to the point of his visit, but instead suggested sandwiches and a glass of wine.

Until these made their appearance he monopolized the conversation, explaining where we had been, and speaking with kindliness and feeling of the invalid woman.

Not until we had finished the sandwiches and sipped the wine did he give the conversation a personal turn.

'You have come from Bexhill, Mr Fraser?'

'Yes.'

'Any success with Milly Higley?'

'Milly Higley? Milly Higley?' Fraser repeated the name wonderingly. 'Oh, that girl! No, I haven't done anything there yet. It's –'

He stopped. His hands twisted themselves together nervously.

'I don't know why I've come to you,' he burst out.

'I know,' said Poirot.

'You can't. How can you?'

'You have come to me because there is something that you must tell to someone. You were quite right. I am the proper person. Speak!'

Poirot's air of assurance had its effect. Fraser looked at him with a queer air of grateful obedience.

'You think so?'

'*Parbleu*, I am sure of it.'

'M. Poirot, do you know anything about dreams?'

430

It was the last thing I had expected him to say.

Poirot, however, seemed in no way surprised.

'I do,' he replied. 'You have been dreaming –?'

'Yes. I suppose you'll say it's only natural that I should – should dream about – It. But it isn't an ordinary dream.'

'No?'

'No?'

'I've dreamed it now three nights running, sir . . . I think I'm going mad . . .'

'Tell me –'

The man's face was livid. His eyes were staring out of his head. As a matter of fact, he *looked* mad.

'It's always the same. I'm on the beach. Looking for Betty. She's lost – only lost, you understand. I've got to find her. I've got to give her her belt. I'm carrying it in my hand. And then –'

'Yes?'

'The dream changes . . . I'm not looking any more. She's there in front of me – sitting on the beach. She doesn't see me coming – It's – oh, I can't –'

'Go on.'

Poirot's voice was authoritative – firm.

'I come up behind her . . . she doesn't hear me . . . I slip the belt round her neck and pull – oh – pull . . .'

The agony in his voice was frightful . . . I gripped the arms of my chair . . . The thing was too real.

'She's choking . . . she's dead . . . I've strangled her – and then her head falls back and I see her face . . . and it's *Megan* – not Betty!'

He leant back white and shaking. Poirot poured out another glass of wine and passed it over to him.

'What's the meaning of it, M. Poirot? Why does it come to me? Every night . . .'

'Drink up your wine,' ordered Poirot.

The young man did so, then he asked in a calmer voice:

'What does it mean? I – I didn't kill her, did I?'

What Poirot answered I do not know, for at that minute I heard the postman's knock and automatically I left the room.

What I took out of the letter-box banished all my interest in Donald Fraser's extraordinary revelations.

I raced back into the sitting-room.

'Poirot,' I cried. 'It's come. The fourth letter.'

He sprang up, seized it from me, caught up his paper-knife and slit

431

it open. He spread it out on the table.

The three of us read it together.

Still no success? Fie! Fie! What are you and the police doing? Well, well, isn't this fun? And where shall we go next for honey?

Poor Mr Poirot. I'm quite sorry for you.

If at first you don't succeed, try, try, try again.

We've a long way to go still.

Tipperary? No – that comes farther on. Letter T.

The next little incident will take place at Doncaster on September 11th.

So long.

A B C.

CHAPTER TWENTY-ONE

Description of a Murderer

It was at this moment, I think, that what Poirot called the human element began to fade out of the picture again. It was as though, the mind being unable to stand unadulterated horror, we had had an interval of normal human interests.

We had, one and all, felt the impossibility of doing anything until the fourth letter should come revealing the projected scene of the D murder. That atmosphere of waiting had brought a release of tension.

But now, with the printed words jeering from the white stiff paper, the hunt was up once more.

Inspector Crome had come round from the Yard, and while he was still there, Franklin Clarke and Megan Barnard came in.

The girl explained that she, too, had come up from Bexhill.

'I wanted to ask Mr Clarke something.'

She seemed rather anxious to excuse and explain her procedure. I just noted the fact without attaching much importance to it.

The letter naturally filled my mind to the exclusion of all else.

Crome was not, I think, any too pleased to see the various participants in the drama. He became extremely official and non-committal.

'I'll take this with me, M. Poirot. If you care to take a copy of it –'

'No, no, it is not necessary.'

'What are your plans, inspector?' asked Clarke.

'Fairly comprehensive ones, Mr Clarke.'

'This time we've got to get him,' said Clarke. 'I may tell you, inspector, that we've found an association of our own to deal with the matter. A legion of interested parties.'

Inspector Crome said in his best manner:

'Oh, yes?'

'I gather you don't think much of amateurs, inspector?'

'You've hardly the same resources at your command, have you, Mr Clarke?'

'We've got a personal axe to grind – and that's something.'

'Oh, yes?'

'I fancy your own task isn't going to be too easy, inspector. In fact, I rather fancy old A B C has done you again.'

Crome, I noticed, could often be goaded into speech when other methods would have failed.

'I don't fancy the public will have much to criticize in our arrangements this time,' he said. 'The fool has given us ample warning. The 11th isn't till Wednesday of next week. That gives ample time for a publicity campaign in the press. Doncaster will be thoroughly warned. Every soul whose name begins with a D will be on his or her guard – that's so much to the good. Also, we'll draft police into the town on a fairly large scale. That's already been arranged for by consent of all the Chief Constables in England. The whole of Doncaster, police and civilians, will be out to catch one man – and with reasonable luck, we ought to get him!'

Clarke said quietly:

'It's easy to see you're not a sporting man, inspector.'

Crome stared at him.

'What do you mean, Mr Clarke?'

'Man alive, don't you realize that on *next Wednesday the St Leger is being run at Doncaster?*'

The inspector's jaw dropped. For the life of him he could not bring out the familiar 'Oh, yes?' Instead he said:

'That's true. Yes, that complicates matters ...'

'A B C is no fool, even if he *is* a madman.'

We were all silent for a minute or two, taking in the situation. The crowds on the race-course – the passionate, sport-loving English public – the endless complications.

Poirot murmured:

'*C'est ingénieux. Tout de même c'est bien imaginé, ça.*'

'It's my belief,' said Clarke, 'that the murder will take place on the race-course – perhaps actually while the Leger is being run.'

For the moment his sporting instincts took a momentary pleasure in the thought ...

Inspector Crome rose, taking the letter with him.

'The St Leger is a complication,' he allowed. 'It's unfortunate.'

He went out. We heard a murmur of voices in the hallway. A minute later Thora Grey entered.

She said anxiously:

'The inspector told me there is another letter. Where this time?'

It was raining outside. Thora Grey was wearing a black coat and skirt and furs. A little black hat just perched itself on the side of her golden head.

It was to Franklin Clarke that she spoke and she came right up to

434

him and, with a hand on his arm, waited for his answer.

'Doncaster – and on the day of the St Leger.'

We settled down to a discussion. It went without saying that we all intended to be present, but the race-meeting undoubtedly complicated the plans we had made tentatively beforehand.

A feeling of discouragement swept over me. What could this little band of six people do, after all, however strong their personal interest in the matter might be? There would be innumerable police, keen-eyed and alert, watching all likely spots. What could six more pairs of eyes do?

As though in answer to my thought, Poirot raised his voice. He spoke rather like a schoolmaster or a priest.

'*Mes enfants*,' he said. 'We must not disperse the strength. We must approach this matter with method and order in our thoughts. We must look within and not without for the truth. We must say to ourselves – each one of us – what do *I* know about the murderer? And so we must build up a composite picture of the man we are going to seek.'

'We know nothing about him,' sighed Thora Grey helplessly.

'No, no, mademoiselle. That is not true. Each one of us knows something about him – *if we only knew what it is we know. I am convinced that the knowledge is there* if we could only get at it.'

Clarke shook his head.

'We don't know anything – whether he's old or young, fair or dark! None of us has ever seen him or spoken to him! We've gone over everything we all know again and again.'

'Not everything! For instance, Miss Grey here told us that she did not see or speak to any stranger on the day that Sir Carmichael Clarke was murdered.'

Thora Grey nodded.

'That's quite right.'

'Is it? *Lady Clarke told us, mademoiselle, that from her window she saw you standing on the front doorstep talking to a man.*'

'She saw *me* talking to a strange man?' The girl seemed genuinely astonished. Surely that pure, limpid look could not be anything but genuine.

She shook her head.

'Lady Clarke must have made a mistake. I never – Oh!'

The exclamation came suddenly – jerked out of her. A crimson wave flooded her cheeks.

'I remember now! How stupid! I'd forgotten all about it. But it

435

wasn't important. Just one of those men who come round selling stockings – you know, ex-army people. They're very persistent. I had to get rid of him. I was just crossing the hall when he came to the door. He spoke to me instead of ringing but he was quite a harmless sort of person. I suppose that's why I forgot about him.'

Poirot was swaying to and fro, his hands clasped to his head. He was muttering to himself with such vehemence that nobody else said anything, but stared at him instead.

'Stockings,' he was murmuring. 'Stockings ... stockings ... stockings ... *ça vient* ... stockings ... stockings ... it is the *motif* – yes ... three months ago ... and the other day ... and now. *Bon Dieu*, I have it!'

He sat upright and fixed me with an imperious eye.

'You remember, Hastings? Andover. The shop. We go upstairs. The bedroom. On a chair. *A pair of new silk stockings*. And now I know what it was that roused my attention two days ago. It was you, mademoiselle –' He turned on Megan. 'You spoke of your mother who wept *because she had bought your sister some new stockings on the very day of the murder* ...'

He looked round on us all.

'You see? *It is the same motif* three times repeated. That cannot be coincidence. When mademoiselle spoke I had the feeling that what she said linked up with something. I know now with what. The words spoken by Mrs Ascher's next-door neighbour, Mrs Fowler. About people who were always trying to *sell* you things – and she mentioned *stockings*. Tell me, mademoiselle, it is true, is it not, that your mother bought those stockings, not at a shop, but from someone who came to the door?'

'Yes – yes – she did ... I remember now. She said something about being sorry for these wretched men who go round and try to get orders.'

'But what's the connection?' cried Franklin. 'That a man came selling stockings proves nothing!'

'I tell you, my friends, it *cannot* be coincidence. Three crimes – and every time a man selling stockings and spying out the land.'

He wheeled round on Thora.

'*A vous la parole!* Describe this man.'

She looked at him blankly.

'I can't ... I don't know how ... He had glasses, I think – and a shabby overcoat ...'

'*Mieux que ça, mademoiselle.*'

436

'He stooped . . . I don't know. I hardly looked at him. He wasn't the sort of man you'd notice . . .'

Poirot said gravely:

'You are quite right, mademoiselle. The whole secret of the murders lies there in your description of the murderer – for without a doubt he *was* the murderer! *"He wasn't the sort of man you'd notice."* Yes – there is no doubt about it . . . You have described the murderer!'

CHAPTER TWENTY-TWO

(Not from Captain Hastings' Personal Narrative)

Mr Alexander Bonaparte Cust sat very still. His breakfast lay cold and untasted on his plate. A newspaper was propped up against the teapot and it was this newspaper that Mr Cust was reading with avid interest.

Suddenly he got up, paced to and fro for a minute, then sank back into a chair by the window. He buried his head in his hands with a stifled groan.

He did not hear the sound of the opening door. His landlady, Mrs Marbury, stood in the doorway.

'I was wondering, Mr Cust, if you'd fancy a nice – why, whatever is is? Aren't you feeling well?'

Mr Cust raised his head from his hands.

'Nothing. It's nothing at all, Mrs Marbury. I'm not – feeling very well this morning.'

Mrs Marbury inspected the breakfast tray.

'So I see. You haven't touched your breakfast. Is it your head troubling you again?'

'No. At least, yes ... I – I just feel a bit out of sorts.'

'Well, I'm sorry, I'm sure. You'll not be going away today, then?'

Mr Cust sprang up abruptly.

'No, no. I have to go. It's business. Important. Very important.'

His hands were shaking. Seeing him so agitated, Mrs Marbury tried to soothe him.

'Well, if you must – you must. Going far this time?'

'No. I'm going to' – he hesitated for a minute or two – 'Cheltenham.'

There was something so peculiar about the tentative way he said the word that Mrs Marbury looked at him in surprise.

'Cheltenham's a nice place,' she said conversationally. 'I went there from Bristol one year. The shops are ever so nice.'

'I suppose so – yes.'

Mrs Marbury stooped rather stiffly – for stooping did not suit her figure – to pick up the paper that was lying crumpled on the floor.

'Nothing but this murdering business in the papers nowadays,' she said as she glanced at the headlines before putting it back on the table. 'Give me the creeps, it does. I don't read it. It's like Jack the

Ripper all over again.'

Mr Cust's lips moved, but no sound came from them.

'Doncaster – that's the place he's going to do his next murder,' said Mrs Marbury. 'And tomorrow! Fairly makes your flesh creep, doesn't it? If I lived in Doncaster and my name began with a D, I'd take the first train away, that I would. I'd run no risks. What did you say, Mr Cust?'

'Nothing, Mrs Marbury – nothing.'

'It's the races and all. No doubt he thinks he'll get his opportunity there. Hundreds of police, they say, they're drafting in and – Why, Mr Cust, you *do* look bad. Hadn't you better have a little drop of something? Really, now, you oughtn't to go travelling today.'

Mr Cust drew himself up.

'It is necessary, Mrs Marbury. I have always been punctual in my – engagements. People must have – must have confidence in you! When I have undertaken to do a thing, I carry it through. It is the only way to get on in – in – business.'

'But if you're ill?'

'I am not ill, Mrs Marbury. Just a little worried over – various personal matters. I slept badly. I am really quite all right.'

His manner was so firm that Mrs Marbury gathered up the breakfast things and reluctantly left the room.

Mr Cust dragged out a suitcase from under the bed and began to pack. Pyjamas, sponge-bag, spare collar, leather slippers. Then unlocking a cupboard, he transfered a dozen or so flattish cardboard boxes about ten inches by seven from a shelf to the suitcase.

He just glanced at the railway guide on the table and then left the room, suitcase in hand.

Setting it down in the hall, he put on his hat and overcoat. As he did so he sighed deeply, so deeply that the girl who came out from a room at the side looked at him in concern.

'Anything the matter, Mr Cust?'

'Nothing, Miss Lily.'

'You were sighing so!'

Mr Cust said abruptly:

'Are you at all subject to premonitions, Miss Lily? To presentiments?'

'Well, I don't know that I am, really . . . Of course, there are days when you just feel everything's going wrong, and days when you feel everything's going right.'

'Quite,' said Mr Cust.

He sighed again.

'Well, goodbye, Miss Lily. Goodbye. I'm sure you've been very kind to me always here.'

'Well, don't say goodbye as though you were going away for ever,' laughed Lily.

'No, no, of course not.'

'See you Friday,' laughed the girl. 'Where are you going this time? Seaside again.'

'No, no – er – Cheltenham.'

'Well, that's nice, too. But not quite as nice as Torquay. That must have been lovely. I want to go there for my holiday next year. By the way, you must have been quite near where the murder was – that A B C murder. It happened while you were down there, didn't it?'

'Er – yes. But Churston's six or seven miles away.'

'All the same, it must have been exciting! Why, you may have passed the murderer in the street! You may have been quite near to him!'

'Yes, I may, of course,' said Mr Cust with such a ghastly and contorted smile that Lily Marbury noticed it.

'Oh, Mr Cust, you *don't* look well.'

'I'm quite all right, quite all right. Goodbye, Miss Marbury.'

He fumbled to raise his hat, caught up his suitcase and fairly hastened out of the front door.

'Funny old thing,' said Lily Marbury indulgently. 'Looks half batty to my mind.'

Inspector Crome said to his subordinate:

'Get me out a list of all stocking manufacturing firms and circularize them. I want a list of all their agents – you know, fellows who sell on commission and tout for orders.'

'This the A B C case, sir?'

'Yes. One of Mr Hercule Poirot's ideas.' The inspector's tone was disdainful. 'Probably nothing in it, but it doesn't do to neglect any chance, however faint.'

'Right, sir. Mr Poirot's done some good stuff in his time, but I think he's a bit gaga now, sir.'

'He's a mountebank,' said Inspector Crome. 'Always posing. Takes in some people. It doesn't take in *me*. Now then, about the arrangement for Doncaster . . .'

Tom Hartigan said to Lily Marbury:

440

'Saw your old dugout this morning.'

'Who? Mr Cust?'

'Cust it was. At Euston. Looking like a lost hen, as usual. I think the fellow's half loony. He needs someone to look after him. First he dropped his paper and then he dropped his ticket. I picked that up – he hadn't the faintest idea he'd lost it. Thanked me in an agitated sort of manner, but I don't think he recognized me.'

'Oh, well,' said Lily. 'He's only seen you passing in the hall, and not very often at that.'

They danced once round the floor.

'You dance something beautiful,' said Tom.

'Go on,' said Lily and wriggled yet a little closer.

They danced round again.

'Did you say Euston or Paddington?' asked Lily abruptly. 'Where you saw old Cust, I mean?'

'Euston.'

'Are you sure?'

'Of course I'm sure. What to you think?'

'Funny. I thought you went to Cheltenham from Paddington.'

'So you do. But old Cust wasn't going to Cheltenham. He was going to Doncaster.'

'Cheltenham.'

'Doncaster. I know, my girl! After all, I picked up his ticket, didn't I?'

'Well, he told *me* he was going to Cheltenham. I'm sure he did.'

'Oh, you've got it wrong. He was going to Doncaster all right. Some people have all the luck. I've got a bit on Firefly for the Leger and I'd love to see it run.'

'I shouldn't think Mr Cust went to race-meetings, he doesn't look the kind. Oh, Tom, I hope he won't get murdered. It's Doncaster the A B C murder's going to be.'

'Cust'll be all right. His name doesn't begin with a D.'

'He might have been murdered last time. He was down near Churston at Torquay when the last murder happened.'

'Was he? That's a bit of a coincidence, isn't it?'

He laughed.

'He wasn't at Bexhill the time before, was he?'

Lily crinkled her brows.

'He was away ... Yes, I remember he was away ... because he forgot his bathing-dress. Mother was mending it for him. And she said: "There – Mr Cust went away yesterday without his bathing-

441

dress after all," and I said: "Oh, never mind the old bathing-dress – there's been the most awful murder," I said, "a girl strangled at Bexhill." '

'Well, if he wanted his bathing-dress, he must have been going to the seaside. I say, Lily' – his face crinkled up with amusement. 'What price your old dugout being the murderer himself?'

'Poor Mr Cust? He wouldn't hurt a fly,' laughed Lily.

They danced on happily – in their conscious minds nothing but the pleasure of being together.

In their unconscious minds something stirred . . .

CHAPTER TWENTY-THREE

September 11th. Doncaster

Doncaster!

I shall, I think, remember that 11th of September all my life.

Indeed, whenever I see a mention of the St Leger my mind flies automatically not to horse-racing but to murder.

When I recall my own sensations, the thing that stands out most is a sickening sense of insufficiency. We were here – on the spot – Poirot, myself, Clarke, Fraser, Megan Barnard, Thora Grey and Mary Drower, and in the last resort *what could any of us do?*

We were building on a forlorn hope – on the chance of recognizing amongst a crowd of thousands of people a face or figure imperfectly seen on an occasion one, two or three months back.

The odds were in reality greater than that. Of us all, the only person likely to make such a recognition was Thora Grey.

Some of her serenity had broken down under the strain. Her calm, efficient manner was gone. She sat twisting her hands together, almost weeping, appealing incoherently to Poirot.

'I never really looked at him ... Why didn't I? What a fool I was. You're depending on me, all of you ... and I shall let you down. Because even if I did see him again I mightn't recognize him. I've got a bad memory for faces.'

Poirot, whatever he might say to me, and however harshly he might seem to criticize the girl, showed nothing but kindness now. His manner was tender in the extreme. It struck me that Poirot was no more indifferent to beauty in distress than I was.

He patted her shoulder kindly.

'Now then, *petite*, not the hysteria. We cannot have that. If you should see this man you would recognize him.'

'How do you know?'

'Oh, a great many reasons – for one, because the red succeeds the black.'

'What do you mean, Poirot?' I cried.

'I speak the language of the tables. At roulette there may be a long run on the black – but in the end *red must turn up*. It is the mathematical laws of chance.'

'You mean that luck turns?'

'Exactly, Hastings. And that is where the gambler (and the

443

murderer, who is, after all, only a supreme kind of gambler since what he risks is not his money but his life) often lacks intelligent anticipation. Because he *has* won he thinks he will *continue* to win! He does not leave the tables in good time with his pocket full. So in crime the murderer who is successful *cannot conceive the possibility of not being successful!* He takes to *himself* all the credit for a successful performance – but I tell you, my friends, however carefully planned, no crime can be successful without luck!'

'Isn't that going rather far?' demurred Franklin Clarke.

Poirot waved his hands excitedly.

'No, no. It is an even chance, if you like, but it *must* be in your favour. Consider! It might have happened that someone enters Mrs Ascher's shop just as the murderer is leaving. That person might have thought of looking behind the counter, have seen the dead woman – and either laid hands on the murderer straight away or else been able to give such an accurate description of him to the police that he would have been arrested forthwith.'

'Yes, of course, that's possible,' admitted Clarke. 'What it comes to is that a murderer's got to take a chance.'

'Precisely. A murderer is always a gambler. And, like many gamblers, a murderer often does not know when to stop. With each crime his opinion of his own abilities is strengthened. His sense of proportion is warped. He does not say "I have been clever *and lucky!*" No, he says only "I have been clever!" And his opinion of his cleverness grows and then, *mes amis*, the ball spins, and the run of colour is over – it drops into a new number and the croupier calls out "*Rouge.*" '

'You think that will happen in this case?' said Megan, drawing her brows together in a frown.

'It *must* happen sooner or later! So far *the luck has been with the criminal* – sooner or later it must turn and be with us. I believe that it *has* turned! The clue of the stockings is the beginning. Now, instead of everything going *right* for him, everything will go *wrong* for him! And he, too, will begin to make mistakes . . .'

'I will say you're heartening,' said Franklin Clarke. 'We all need a bit of comfort. I've had a paralysing feeling of helplessness ever since I woke up.'

'It seems to me highly problematical that we can accomplish anything of practical value,' said Donald Fraser.

Megan rapped out:

'Don't be a defeatist, Don.'

Mary Drower, flushing up a little, said:

'What I say is, you never know. That wicked fiend's in this place, and so are we – and after all, you do run up against people in the funniest way sometimes.'

I fumed:

'If only we could do something more.'

'You must remember, Hastings, that the police are doing everything reasonably possible. Special constables have been enrolled. The good Inspector Crome may have the irritating manner, but he is a very able police officer, and Colonel Anderson, the Chief Constable, is a man of action. They have taken the fullest measures for watching and patrolling the town and the race-course. There will be plain-clothes men everywhere. There is also the press campaign. The public is fully warned.'

Donald Fraser shook his head.

'He'll never attempt it, I'm thinking,' he said more hopefully. 'The man would just be mad!'

'Unfortunately,' said Clarke dryly, 'he is mad! What do you think, M. Poirot? Will he give it up or will he try to carry it through?'

'In my opinion the strength of his obsession is such that he *must* attempt to carry out his promise! Not to do so would be to admit failure, and that his insane egoism would never allow. That, I may say, is also Dr Thompson's opinion. Our hope is that he may be caught in the attempt.'

Donald shook his head again.

'He'll be very cunning.'

Poirot glanced at his watch. We took the hint. It had been agreed that we were to make an all-day session of it, patrolling as many streets as possible in the morning, and later, stationing ourselves at various likely points on the race-course.

I say 'we'. Of course, in my own case such a patrol was of little avail since I was never likely to have set eyes on A B C. However, as the idea was to separate so as to cover as wide an area as possible I had suggested that I should act as escort to one of the ladies.

Poirot had agreed – I am afraid with somewhat of a twinkle in his eye.

The girls went off to get their hats on. Donald Fraser was standing by the window looking out, apparently lost in thought.

Franklin Clarke glanced over at him, then evidently deciding that the other was too abstracted to count as a listener, he lowered his voice a little and addressed Poirot.

'Look here, M. Poirot. You went down to Churston, I know, and saw my sister-in-law. Did she say – or hint – I mean – did she suggest at all –?'

He stopped, embarrassed.

Poirot answered with a face of blank innocence that aroused my strongest suspicions.

'*Comment?* Did your sister-in-law say, hint, or suggest – what?'

Franklin Clarke got rather red.

'Perhaps you think this isn't a time for butting in with personal things –'

'*Du tout!*'

'But I feel I'd like to get things quite straight.'

'An admirable course.'

This time I think Clarke began to suspect Poirot's bland face of concealing some inner amusement. He ploughed on rather heavily.

'My sister-in-law's an awfully nice woman – I've been very fond of her always – but of course she's been ill some time – and in that kind of illness – being given drugs and all that – one tends to – well, to *fancy* things about people!'

'Ah?'

By now there was no mistaking the twinkle in Poirot's eye.

But Franklin Clarke, absorbed in his diplomatic task, was past noticing it.

'It's about Thora – Miss Grey,' he said.

'Oh, it is of Miss Grey you speak?' Poirot's tone held innocent surprise.

'Yes. Lady Clarke got certain ideas in her head. You see, Thora – Miss Grey is well, rather a good-looking girl –'

'Perhaps – yes,' conceded Poirot.

'And women, even the best of them, are a bit catty about other women. Of course, Thora was invaluable to my brother – he always said she was the best secretary he ever had – and he was very fond of her, too. But it was all perfectly straight and above-board. I mean, Thora isn't the sort of girl –'

'No?' said Poirot helpfully.

'But my sister-in-law got it into her head to be – well – jealous, I suppose. Not that she ever showed anything. But after Car's death, when there was a question of Miss Grey staying on – well, Charlotte cut up rough. Of course, it's partly the illness and the morphia and all that – Nurse Capstick says so – she says we mustn't blame Charlotte for getting these ideas into her head –'

He paused.

'Yes?'

'What I want you to understand, M. Poirot, is that there isn't anything in it at all. It's just a sick woman's imaginings. Look here' – he fumbled in his pocket – 'here's a letter I received from my brother when I was in the Malay States. I'd like you to read it because it shows exactly what terms they were on.'

Poirot took it. Franklin came over beside him and with a pointing finger read some of the extracts out loud.

' – *things go on here much as usual. Charlotte is moderately free from pain. I wish one could say more. You may remember Thora Grey? She is a dear girl and a greater comfort to me that I can tell you. I should not have known what to do through this bad time but for her. Her sympathy and interest are unfailing. She has an exquisite taste and flair for beautiful things and shares my passion for Chinese art. I was indeed lucky to find her. No daughter could be a closer or more sympathetic companion. Her life had been a difficult and not always a happy one, but I am glad to feel that here she has a home and true affection.*

'You see,' said Franklin, '*that's* how my brother felt to her. He thought of her like a daughter. What I feel so unfair is the fact that the moment my brother is dead, his wife practically turns her out of the house! Women really are devils, M. Poirot.'

'Your sister-in-law is ill and in pain, remember.'

'I know. That's what I keep saying to myself. One musn't judge her. All the same, I thought I'd show you this. I don't want you to get a false impression of Thora from anything Lady Clarke may have said.'

Poirot returned the letter.

'I can assure you,' he said, smiling, 'that I never permit myself to get false impressions from anything anyone tells me. I form my own judgments.'

'Well,' said Clarke, stowing away the letter. 'I'm glad I showed it to you anyway. Here come the girls. We'd better be off.'

As we left the room, Poirot called me back.

'You are determined to accompany the expedition, Hastings?'

'Oh, yes. I shouldn't be happy staying here inactive.'

'There is activity of mind as well as body, Hastings.'

'Well, you're better at it than I am,' I said.

'You are incontestably right, Hastings. Am I correct in supposing that you intend to be a cavalier to one of the ladies?'

'That was the idea.'

447

'And which lady did you propose to honour with your company?'

'Well – I – er – hadn't considered yet.'

'What about Miss Barnard?'

'She's rather the independent type,' I demurred.

'Miss Grey?'

'Yes. She's better.'

'I find you, Hastings, singularly though transparently dishonest! All along you had made up your mind to spend the day with your blonde angel!'

'Oh, really, Poirot!'

'I am sorry to upset your plans, but I must request you to give your escort elsewhere.'

'Oh, all right. I think you've got a weakness for that Dutch doll of a girl.'

'The person you are to escort is Mary Drower – and I must request you not to leave her.'

'But, Poirot, why?'

'Because, my dear friend, her name begins with a D. We must take no chances.'

I saw the justice of his remark. At first it seemed far-fetched. But then I realized that if A B C had a fanatical hatred of Poirot, he might very well be keeping himself informed of Poirot's movements. And in that case the elimination of Mary Drower might strike him as a very pat fourth stroke.

I promised to be faithful to my trust.

I went out leaving Poirot sitting in a chair near the window.

In front of him was a little roulette wheel. He spun it as I went out of the door and called after me:

'*Rouge* – that is a good omen, Hastings. The luck, it turns!'

CHAPTER TWENTY-FOUR

(Not from Captain Hastings' Personal Narrative)

Below his breath Mr Leadbetter uttered a grunt of impatience as his next-door neighbour got up and stumbled clumsily past him, dropping his hat over the seat in front, and leaning over to retrieve it.

All this at the culminating moment of *Not a Sparrow*, that all-star, thrilling drama of pathos and beauty that Mr Leadbetter had been looking forward to seeing for a whole week.

The golden-haired heroine, played by Katherine Royal (in Mr Leadbetter's opinion the leading film actress in the world), was just giving vent to a hoarse cry of indignation:

'Never. I would sooner starve. But I shan't starve. Remember those words: *not a sparrow falls –*'

Mr Leadbetter moved his head irritably from right to left. People! Why on earth people couldn't wait till the *end* of a film ... And to leave at this soul-stirring moment.

Ah, that was better. The annoying gentleman had passed on and out. Mr Leadbetter had a full view of the screen and of Katherine Royal standing by the window in the Van Schreiner Mansion in New York.

And now she was boarding the train – the child in her arms ... What curious trains they had in America – not at all like English trains.

Ah, there was Steve again in his shack in the mountains ...

The film pursued its course to its emotional and semi-religious end.

Mr Leadbetter breathed a sigh of satisfaction as the lights went up.

He rose slowly to his feet, blinking a little.

He never left the cinema very quickly. It always took him a moment or two to return to the prosaic reality of everyday life.

He glanced round. Not many people this afternoon – naturally. They were all at the races. Mr Leadbetter did not approve of racing nor of playing cards nor of drinking nor of smoking. This left him more energy to enjoy going to the pictures.

Everyone was hurrying towards the exit. Mr Leadbetter prepared to follow suit. The man in the seat in front of him was asleep – slumped down in his chair. Mr Leadbetter felt indignant to think that anyone could sleep with such a drama as *Not a Sparrow* going on.

449

An irate gentleman was saying to the sleeping man whose legs were stretched out blocking the way:

'Excuse *me*, sir.'

Mr Leadbetter reached the exit. He looked back.

There seemed to be some sort of commotion. A commissionaire ... a little knot of people ... Perhaps that man in front of him was dead drunk and not asleep ...

He hesitated and then passed out – and in so doing missed the sensation of the day – a greater sensation even than Not Half winning the St Leger at 85 to 1.

The commissionaire was saying:

'Believe you're right, sir ... He's ill ... Why – what's the matter, sir?'

The other had drawn away his hand with an exclamation and was examining a red sticky smear.

'Blood ...'

The commissionaire gave a stifled exclamation.

He had caught sight of the corner of something yellow projecting from under the seat.

'Gor blimey!' he said. *'It's a b – A B C.'*

CHAPTER TWENTY-FIVE

(Not from Captain Hastings' Personal Narrative)

Mr Cust came out of the Regal Cinema and looked up at the sky.

A beautiful evening . . . A really beautiful evening . . .

A quotation from Browning came into his head.

'God's in His heaven. All's right with the world.'

He had always been fond of that quotation.

Only there were times, very often, when he had felt it wasn't true . . .

He trotted along the street smiling to himself until he came to the Black Swan where he was staying.

He climbed the stairs to his bedroom, a stuffy little room on the second floor, giving over a paved inner court and garage.

As he entered the room his smile faded suddenly. There was a stain on his sleeve near the cuff. He touched it tentatively – wet and red – blood . . .

His hand dipped into his pocket and brought out something – a long slender knife. The blade of that, too, was sticky and red . . .

Mr Cust sat there a long time.

Once his eyes shot round the room like those of a hunted animal.

His tongue passed feverishly over his lips . . .

'It isn't my fault,' said Cust.

He sounded as though he were arguing with somebody – a schoolboy pleading to his headmaster.

He passed his tongue over his lips again . . .

Again, tentatively, he felt his coat sleeve.

His eyes crossed the room to the wash-basin.

A minute later he was pouring out water from the old-fashioned jug into the basin. Removing his coat, he rinsed the sleeve, carefully squeezing it out . . .

Ugh! The water was red now . . .

A tap on the door.

He stood there frozen into immobility – staring.

The door opened. A plump young woman – jug in hand.

'Oh, excuse me, sir. Your hot water, sir.'

He managed to speak then.

'Thank you . . . I've washed in cold . . .'

Why had he said that? Immediately her eyes went to the basin.

451

He said frenziedly: 'I – I've cut my hand . . .'

There was a pause – yes, surely a very long pause – before she said: 'Yes, sir.'

She went out, shutting the door.

Mr Cust stood as though turned to stone.

He listened.

It had come – at last . . .

Were there voices – exclamations – feet mounting the stairs?

He could hear nothing but the beating of his own heart . . .

Then, suddenly, from frozen immobility he leaped into activity.

He slipped on his coat, tiptoed to the door and opened it. No noises as yet except the familiar murmur arising from the bar. He crept down the stairs . . .

Still no one. That was luck. He paused at the foot of the stairs. Which way now?

He made up his mind, darted quickly along a passage and out by the door that gave into the yard. A couple of chauffeurs were there tinkering with cars and discussing winners and losers.

Mr Cust hurried across the yard and out into the street.

Round the first corner to the right – then to the left – right again . . .

Dare he risk the station?

Yes – there would be crowds there – special trains – if luck were on his side he would do it all right . . .

If only luck were with him . . .

CHAPTER TWENTY-SIX

(Not from Captain Hastings' Personal Narrative)

Inspector Crome was listening to the excited utterances of Mr Leadbetter.

'I assure you, inspector, my heart misses a beat when I think of it. He must actually have been sitting beside me all through the programme!'

Inspector Crome, completely indifferent to the behaviour of Mr Leadbetter's heart, said:

'Just let me have it quite clear? This man went out towards the close of the big picture –'

'*Not a Sparrow* – Katherine Royal,' murmured Mr Leadbetter automatically.

'He passed you and in doing so stumbled –'

'He *pretended* to stumble, I see it now. Then he leaned over the seat in front to pick up his hat. He must have stabbed the poor fellow then.'

'You didn't hear anything? A cry? Or groan?'

Mr Leadbetter had heard nothing but the loud, hoarse accents of Katherine Royal, but in the vividness of his imagination he invented a groan.

Inspector Crome took the groan at its face value and bade him proceed.

'And then he went out –'

'Can you describe him?'

'He was a very big man. Six foot at least. A giant.'

'Fair or dark?'

'I – well – I'm not exactly sure. I think he was bald. A sinister-looking fellow.'

'He didn't limp, did he?' asked Inspector Crome.

'Yes – yes, now you come to speak of it I think he did limp. Very dark, he might have been some kind of half-caste.'

'Was he in his seat the last time the lights came up?'

'No. He came in after the big picture began.'

Inspector Crome nodded, handed Mr Leadbetter a statement to sign and got rid of him.

'That's about as bad a witness as you'll find,' he remarked pessimistically. 'He'd say anything with a little leading. It's perfectly clear that he hasn't the faintest idea what our man looks like. Let's have the commissionaire back.'

The commissionaire, very stiff and military, came in and stood to attention, his eyes fixed on Colonel Anderson.

'Now, then, Jameson, let's hear your story.'

Jameson saluted.

'Yessir. Close of the performance, sir. I was told there was a gentleman taken ill, sir. Gentleman was in the two and fourpennies, slumped down in his seat like. Other gentlemen standing around. Gentleman looked bad to me, sir. One of the gentlemen standing by put his hand to the ill gentleman's coat and drew my attention. Blood, sir. It was clear the gentleman was dead – stabbed, sir. My attention was drawn to an A B C railway guide, sir, under the seat. Wishing to act correctly, I did not touch same, but reported to the police immediately that a tragedy had occurred.'

'Very good. Jameson, you acted very properly.'

'Thank you, sir.'

'Did you notice a man leaving the two and fourpennies about five minutes earlier?'

'There were several, sir.'

'Could you describe them?'

'Afraid not, sir. One was Mr Geoffrey Parnell. And there was a young fellow, Sam Baker, with his young lady. I didn't notice anybody else particular.'

'A pity. That'll do, Jameson.'

'Yessir.'

The commissionaire saluted and departed.

'The medical details we've got,' said Colonel Anderson. 'We'd better have the fellow that found him next.'

A police constable came in and saluted.

'Mr Hercule Poirot's here, sir, and another gentleman.'

Inspector Crome frowned.

'Oh, well,' he said. 'Better have 'em in, I suppose.'

454

CHAPTER TWENTY-SEVEN

The Doncaster Murder

Coming in hard on Poirot's heels, I just caught the fag end of Inspector Crome's remark.

Both he and the Chief Constable were looking worried and depressed.

Colonel Anderson greeted us with a nod of the head.

'Glad you've come, M. Poirot,' he said politely. I think he guessed that Crome's remark might have reached our ears. 'We've got it in the neck again, you see.'

'Another A B C murder?'

'Yes. Damned audacious bit of work. Man leaned over and stabbed the fellow in the back.'

'Stabbed this time?'

'Yes, varies his methods a bit, doesn't he? Biff on the head, strangled, now a knife. Versatile devil – what? Here are the medical details if you care to see 'em.'

He shoved a paper towards Poirot. 'A B C down on the floor between the dead man's feet,' he added.

'Has the dead man been identified?' asked Poirot.

'Yes. A B C's slipped up for once – if that's any satisfaction to us. Deceased's a man called Earlsfield – George Earlsfield. Barber by profession.'

'Curious,' commented Poirot.

'May have skipped a letter,' suggested the colonel.

My friend shook his head doubtfully.

'Shall we have in the next witness?' asked Crome. 'He's anxious to get home.'

'Yes, yes – let's get on.'

A middle-aged gentleman strongly resembling the frog footman in *Alice in Wonderland* was led in. He was highly excited and his voice was shrill with emotion.

'Most shocking experience I have ever known,' he squeaked. 'I have a weak heart, sir – a very weak heart, it might have been the death of me.'

'Your name, please,' said the inspector.

'Downes. Roger Emmanuel Downes.'

'Profession?'

455

'I am a master at Highfield School for boys.'

'Now, Mr Downes, will you tell us in your own words what happened.'

'I can tell you that very shortly, gentlemen. At the close of the performance I rose from my seat. The seat on my left was empty but in the one beyond a man was sitting, apparently asleep. I was unable to pass him to get out as his legs were stuck out in front of him. I asked him to allow me to pass. As he did not move I repeated my request in – a – er – slightly louder tone. He still made no response. I then took him by the shoulder to waken him. His body slumped down further and I became aware that he was either unconscious or seriously ill. I called out: "This gentleman is taken ill. Fetch the commissionaire." The commissionaire came. As I took my hand from the man's shoulder I found it was wet and red . . . I can assure you, gentlemen, the shock was terrific! Anything might have happened! For years I have suffered from cardiac weakness –'

Colonel Anderson was looking at Mr Downes with a very curious expression.

'You can consider that you're a lucky man, Mr Downes.'

'I do, sir. Not even a palpitation!'

'You don't quite take my meaning, Mr Downes. You were sitting two seats away, you say?'

'Actually I was sitting at first in the next seat to the murdered man – then I moved along so as to be behind an empty seat.'

'You're about the same height and build as the dead man, aren't you, and you were wearing a woollen scarf round your neck just as he was?'

'I fail to see –' began Mr Downes stiffly.

'I'm telling you, man,' said Colonel Anderson, 'just where your luck came in. Somehow or other, when the murderer followed you in, he got confused. *He picked on the wrong back.* I'll eat my hat, Mr Downes, if that knife wasn't meant for you!'

However well Mr Downes' heart had stood former tests, it was unable to stand up to this one. He sank on a chair, gasped, and turned purple in the face.

'Water,' he gasped. 'Water . . .'

A glass was brought him. He sipped it whilst his complexion gradually returned to the normal.

'Me?' he said. 'Why me?'

'It looks like it,' said Crome. 'In fact, it's the only explanation.'

'You mean that this man – this – this fiend incarnate – this

456

bloodthirsty madman has been following *me* about waiting for an opportunity?'

'I should say that was the way of it.'

'But in heaven's name, why *me*?' demanded the outraged schoolmaster.

Inspector Crome struggled with the temptation to reply: 'Why not?' and said instead: 'I'm afraid it's no good expecting a lunatic to have reasons for what he does.'

'God bless my soul,' said Mr Downes, sobered into whispering.

He got up. He looked suddenly old and shaken.

'If you don't want me any more, gentlemen, I think I'll go home. I – I don't feel very well.'

'That's quite all right, Mr Downes. I'll send a constable with you – just to see you're all right.'

'Oh, no – no, thank you. That's not necessary.'

'Might as well,' said Colonel Anderson gruffly.

His eyes slid sideways, asking an imperceptible question of the inspector. The latter gave an equally imperceptible nod.

Mr Downes went out shakily.

'Just as well he didn't tumble to it,' said Colonel Anderson. 'There'll be a couple of them – eh?'

'Yes, sir. Your Inspector Rice has made arrangements. The house will be watched.'

'You think,' said Poirot, 'that when A B C finds out his mistake he might try again?'

Anderson nodded.

'It's a possibility,' he said. 'Seems a methodical sort of chap, A B C. It will upset him if things don't go according to programme.'

Poirot nodded thoughtfully.

'Wish we could get a description of the fellow,' said Colonel Anderson irritably. 'We're as much in the dark as ever.'

'It may come,' said Poirot.

'Think so? Well, it's possible. Damn it all, hasn't anyone got eyes in their head?'

'Have patience,' said Poirot.

'You seem very confident, M. Poirot. Got any reason for this optimism?'

'Yes, Colonel Anderson. Up to now, the murderer has not made a mistake. He is bound to make one soon.'

'If that's all you've got to go on,' began the Chief Constable with a snort, but he was interrupted.

457

'Mr Ball of the Black Swan is here with a young woman, sir. He reckons he's got summat to say might help you.'

'Bring them along. Bring them along. We can do with anything helpful.'

Mr Ball of the Black Swan was a large, slow-thinking, heavily moving man. He exhaled a strong odour of beer. With him was a plump young woman with round eyes clearly in a state of high excitement.

'Hope I'm not intruding or wasting valuable time,' said Mr Ball in a slow, thick voice. 'But this wench, Mary here, reckons she's got something to tell as you ought to know.'

Mary giggled in a half-hearted way.

'Well, my girl, what is it?' said Anderson. 'What's your name?'

'Mary, sir, Mary Stroud.'

'Well, Mary, out with it.'

Mary turned her round eyes on her master.

'It's her business to take up hot water to the gents' bedrooms,' said Mr Ball, coming to the rescue. 'About half a dozen gentlemen we'd got staying. Some for the races and some just commercials.'

'Yes, yes,' said Anderson impatiently.

'Get on, lass,' said Mr Ball. 'Tell your tale. Nowt to be afraid of.'

Mary gasped, groaned and plunged in a breathless voice into her narrative.

'I knocked on door and there wasn't no answer, otherwise I wouldn't have gone in leastways not unless the gentleman had said "Come in," and as he didn't say nothing I went in and he was there washing his hands.'

She paused and breathed deeply.

'Go on, my girl,' said Anderson.

Mary looked sideways at her master and as though receiving inspiration from his slow nod, plunged on again.

' "It's your hot water, sir," I said, "and I did knock," but "Oh," he says, "I've washed in cold," he said, and so, naturally, I looks in basin, and oh! God help me, sir, *it were all red!*'

'Red?' said Anderson sharply.

Ball struck in.

'The lass told me that he had his coat off and that he was holding the sleeve of it, and it was all wet – that's right, eh, lass?'

'Yes, sir, that's right, sir.'

She plunged on:

'And his face, sir, it looked queer, mortal queer it looked. Gave me

458

quite a turn.'

'When was this?' asked Anderson sharply.

'About a quarter after five, so near as I can reckon.'

'Over three hours ago,' snapped Anderson. 'Why didn't you come at once?'

'Didn't hear about it at once,' said Ball. 'Not till news came along as there'd been another murder done. And then the lass she screams out as it might have been blood in the basin, and I asks her what she means, and she tells me. Well, it doesn't sound right to me and I went upstairs myself. Nobody in the room. I asks a few questions and one of the lads in courtyard says he saw a fellow sneaking out that way and by his description it was the right one. So I says to the missus as Mary here had best go to police. She doesn't like the idea, Mary doesn't, and I says I'll come along with her.'

Inspector Crome drew a sheet of paper towards him.

'Describe this man,' he said. 'As quick as you can. There's no time to be lost.'

'Medium-sized he were,' said Mary. 'And stooped and wore glasses.'

'His clothes?'

'A dark suit and a Homburg hat. Rather shabby-looking.'

She could add little to this description.

Inspector Crome did not insist unduly. The telephone wires were soon busy, but neither the inspector nor the Chief Constable were over-optimistic.

Crome elicited the fact that the man, when seen sneaking across the yard, had had no bag or suitcase.

'There's a chance there,' he said.

Two men were despatched to the Black Swan.

Mr Ball, swelling with pride and importance, and Mary, somewhat tearful, accompanied them.

The sergeant returned about ten minutes later.

'I've brought the register, sir,' he said. 'Here's the signature.'

We crowded round. The writing was small and cramped – not easy to read.

'A. B. Case – or is it Cash?' said the Chief Constable.

'A B C,' said Crome significantly.

'What about luggage?' asked Anderson.

'One good-sized suitcase, sir, full of small cardboard boxes.'

'Boxes? What was in 'em?'

'Stockings, sir. Silk stockings.'

459

Crome turned to Poirot.
'Congratulations,' he said. 'Your hunch was right.'

CHAPTER TWENTY-EIGHT

(Not from Captain Hastings' Personal Narrative)

Inspector Crome was in his office at Scotland Yard.

The telephone on his desk gave a discreet buzz and he picked it up.

'Jacobs speaking, sir. There's a young fellow come in with a story that I think you ought to hear.'

Inspector Crome sighed. On an average twenty people a day turned up with so-called important information about the A B C case. Some of them were harmless lunatics, some of them were well-meaning persons who genuinely believed that their information was of value. It was the duty of Sergeant Jacobs to act as a human sieve – retaining the grosser matter and passing on the residue to his superior.

'Very well, Jacobs,' said Crome. 'Send him along.'

A few minutes later there was a tap on the inspector's door and Sergeant Jacobs appeared, ushering in a tall, moderately good-looking young man.

'This is Mr Tom Hartigan, sir. He's got something to tell us which may have a possible bearing on the A B C case.'

The inspector rose pleasantly and shook hands.

'Good morning, Mr Hartigan. Sit down, won't you? Smoke? Have a cigarette?'

Tom Hartigan sat down awkwardly and looked with some awe at what he called in his own mind 'One of the big-wigs.' The appearance of the inspector vaguely disappointed him. He looked quite an ordinary person!

'Now then,' said Crome. 'You've got something to tell us that you think may have a bearing on the case. Fire ahead.'

Tom began nervously.

'Of course it may be nothing at all. It's just an idea of mine. I may be wasting your time.'

Again Inspector Crome sighed imperceptibly. The amount of time he had to waste in reassuring people!

'We're the best judge of that. Let's have the facts, Mr Hartigan.'

'Well, it's like this, sir. I've got a young lady, you see, and her mother lets rooms. Up Camden Town way. Their second-floor back has been let for over a year to a man called Cust.'

'Cust – eh?'

'That's right, sir. A sort of middle-aged bloke what's rather vague and soft – and come down in the world a bit, I should say. Sort of creature who wouldn't hurt a fly you'd say – and I'd never of dreamed of anything being wrong if it hadn't been for something rather odd.'

In a somewhat confused manner and repeating himself once or twice, Tom described his encounter with Mr Cust at Euston Station and the incident of the dropped ticket.

'You see, sir, look at it how you will, it's funny like. Lily – that's my young lady, sir – she was quite positive that it was Cheltenham he said, and her mother says the same – says she remembers distinct talking about it the morning he went off. Of course, I didn't pay much attention to it at the time. Lily – my young lady – said as how she hoped he wouldn't cop it from this A B C fellow going to Doncaster – and then she says it's rather a coincidence because he was down Churston way at the time of the last crime. Laughing like, I asks her whether he was at Bexhill the time before, and she says she don't know where he was, but he was away at the seaside – that she does know. And then I said to her it would be odd if he was the A B C himself and she said poor Mr Cust wouldn't hurt a fly – and that was all at the time. We didn't think no more about it. At least, in a sort of way I did, sir, underneath like. I began wondering about this Cust fellow and thinking that, after all, harmless as he seemed, he might be a bit batty.'

Tom took a breath and then went on. Inspector Crome was listening intently now.

'And then after the Doncaster murder, sir, it was in all the papers that information was wanted as to the whereabouts of a certain A B Case or Cash, and it gave a description that fitted well enough. First evening off I had, I went round to Lily's and asked her what her Mr Cust's initials were. She couldn't remember at first, but her mother did. Said they were A B right enough. Then we got down to it and tried to figure out if Cust had been away at the time of the first murder at Andover. Well, as you know, sir, it isn't too easy to remember things three months back. We had a job of it, but we got it fixed down in the end, because Mrs Marbury had a brother come from Canada to see her on June 21st. He arrived unexpected like and she wanted to give him a bed, and Lily suggested that as Mr Cust was away Bert Smith might have his bed. But Mrs Marbury wouldn't agree, because she said it wasn't acting right by her lodger, and she always liked to act fair and square. But we fixed the date all right because of Bert Smith's ship docking at Southampton that day.'

Inspector Crome had listened very attentively, jotting down an occasional note.

'That's all ?' he asked.

'That's all, sir. I hope you don't think I'm making a lot of nothing.' Tom flushed slightly.

'Not at all. You were quite right to come here. Of course, it's very slight evidence – these dates may be mere coincidence and the likeness of the name, too. But it certainly warrants my having an interview with your Mr Cust. Is he at home now?'

'Yes, sir.'

'When did he return?'

'The evening of the Doncaster murder, sir.'

'What's he been doing since?'

'He's stayed in mostly, sir. And he's been looking very queer, Mrs Marbury says. He buys a lot of newspapers – goes out early and gets the morning ones, and then after dark he goes out and gets the evening ones. Mrs Marbury says he talks a lot to himself, too. She thinks he's getting queerer.'

'What is this Mrs Marbury's address?'

Tom gave it to him.

'Thank you. I shall probably be calling round in the course of the day. I need hardly tell you to be careful of your manner if you come across this Cust.'

He rose and shook hands.

'You may be quite satisfied you did the right thing in coming to us. Good morning, Mr Hartigan.'

'Well, sir?' asked Jacobs, re-entering the room a few minutes later. 'Think it's the goods?'

'It's promising,' said Inspector Crome. 'That is, if the facts are as the boy stated them. We've had no luck with the stocking manufacturers yet. It was time we got hold of something. By the way, give me that file of the Churston case.'

He spent some minutes looking for what he wanted.

'Ah, here it is. It's amongst the statements made to the Torquay police. Young man of the name of Hill. Deposes he was leaving the Torquay Palladium after the film *Not a Sparrow* and noticed a man behaving queerly. He was talking to himself. Hill heard him say "That's an idea." *Not a Sparrow* – that's the film that was on at the Regal in Doncaster?'

'Yes, sir.'

463

'There may be something in that. Nothing to it at the time – but it's possible that the idea of the *modus operandi* for his next crime occurred to our man then. We've got Hill's name and address, I see. His description of the man is vague but it links up well enough with the descriptions of Mary Stroud and this Tom Hartigan . . .'

He nodded thoughtfully.

'We're getting warm,' said Inspector Crome – rather inaccurately, for he himself was always slightly chilly.

'Any instructions, sir?'

'Put on a couple of men to watch this Camden Town address, but I don't want our bird frightened. I must have a word with the A.C. Then I think it would be as well if Cust was brought along here and asked if he'd like to make a statement. It sounds as though he's quite ready to get rattled.'

Outside Tom Hartigan had rejoined Lily Marbury who was waiting for him on the Embankment.

'All right, Tom?'

Tom nodded.

'I saw Inspector Crome himself. The one who's in charge of the case.'

'What's he like?'

'A bit quiet and lah-di-dah – not my idea of a detective.'

'That's Lord Trenchard's new kind,' said Lily with respect. 'Some of them are ever so grand. Well, what did he say?'

Tom gave her a brief résumé of the interview.

'So they think as it really was him?'

'They think it might be. Anyway, they'll come along and ask him a question or two.'

'Poor Mr Cust.'

'It's no good saying poor Mr Cust, my girl. If he's A B C, he's committed four terrible murders.'

Lily sighed and shook her head.

'It does seem awful,' she observed.

'Well, now you're going to come and have a bite of lunch, my girl. Just you think that if we're right I expect my name will be in the papers!'

'Oh, Tom, will it?'

'Rather. And yours, too. *And* your mother's. And I dare say you'll have your picture in it, too.'

'Oh, Tom.' Lily squeezed his arm in an ecstasy.

'And in the meantime what do you say to a bite at the Corner

House?'

Lily squeezed tighter.

'Come on then!'

'All right – half a minute. I must just telephone from the station.'

'Who to?'

'A girl I was going to meet.'

She slipped across the road, and rejoined him three minutes later, looking rather flushed.

'Now then, Tom.'

She slipped her arm in his.

'Tell me more about Scotland Yard. You didn't see the other one there?'

'What other one?'

'The Belgian gentleman. The one that A B C writes to always.'

'No. He wasn't there.'

'Well, tell me all about it. What happened when you got inside? Who did you speak to and what did you say?'

Mr Cust put the receiver back very gently on the hook.

He turned to where Mrs Marbury was standing in the doorway of the room, clearly devoured with curiosity.

'Not often you have a telephone call, Mr Cust?'

'No – er – no, Mrs Marbury. It isn't.'

'Not bad news, I trust?'

'No – no.' How persistent the woman was. His eyes caught the legend on the newspaper he was carrying.

Births – Marriages – Deaths . . .

'My sister's just had a little boy,' he blurted out.

He – who had never had a sister!

'Oh, dear! Now – well, that *is* nice, I am sure. ("And never once mentioned a sister all these years," was her inward thought. "If that isn't just like a man!") I was surprised, I'll tell you, when the lady asked to speak to Mr Cust. Just at first I fancied it was my Lily's voice – something like hers, it was – but haughtier if you know what I mean – sort of high up in the air. Well, Mr Cust, my congratulations, I'm sure. Is it the first one, or have you other little nephews and nieces?'

'It's the only one,' said Mr Cust. 'The only one I've ever had or likely to have, and – er – I think I must go off at once. They – they want me to come. I – I think I can just catch a train if I hurry.'

'Will you be away long, Mr Cust?' called Mrs Marbury as he ran up the stairs.

'Oh, no – two or three days – that's all.'

He disappeared into his bedroom. Mrs Marbury retired into the kitchen, thinking sentimentally of 'the dear little mite'.

Her conscience gave her a sudden twinge.

Last night Tom and Lily and all the hunting back over dates! Trying to make out that Mr Cust was that dreadful monster, A B C. Just because of his initials and because of a few coincidences.

'I don't suppose they meant it seriously,' she thought comfortably. 'And now I hope they'll be ashamed of themselves.'

In some obscure way that she could not have explained, Mr Cust's statement that his sister had had a baby had effectually removed any doubts Mrs Marbury might have had of her lodger's *bona fides*.

'I hope she didn't have too hard a time of it, poor dear,' thought Mrs Marbury, testing an iron against her cheek before beginning to iron out Lily's silk slip.

Her mind ran comfortably on a well-worn obstetric track.

Mr Cust came quietly down the stairs, a bag in his hand. His eyes rested a minute on the telephone.

That brief conversation re-echoed in his brain.

'Is that you, Mr Cust? I thought you might like to know there's an inspector from Scotland Yard may be coming to see you . . .'

What had he said? He couldn't remember.

'Thank you – thank you, my dear . . . very kind of you . . .'

Something like that.

Why had she telephoned to him? Could she possibly have guessed? Or did she just want to make sure he would stay in for the inspector's visit?

But how did she know the inspector was coming?

And her voice – she'd disguised her voice from her mother . . .

It looked – it looked – as though she *knew* . . .

But surely if she knew, she wouldn't . . .

She might, though. Women were very queer. Unexpectedly cruel and unexpectedly kind. He's seen Lily once letting a mouse out of a mouse-trap.

A kind girl . . .

A kind, pretty girl . . .

He paused by the hall stand with its load of umbrellas and coats. Should he . . .?

A slight noise from the kitchen decided him . . .

No, there wasn't time . . .

Mrs Marbury might come out . . .

He opened the front door, passed through and closed it behind him . . .

Where . . .?

CHAPTER TWENTY-NINE

At Scotland Yard

Conference again.

The Assistant Commissioner, Inspector Crome, Poirot and myself.

The A.C. was saying:

'A good tip that of yours, M. Poirot, about checking a large sale of stockings.'

Poirot spread out his hands.

'It was indicated. This man could not be a regular agent. He sold outright instead of touting for orders.'

'Got everything clear so far, inspector?'

'I think so, sir.' Crome consulted a file. 'Shall I run over the position to date?'

'Yes, please.'

'I've checked up with Churston, Paignton and Torquay. Got a list of people where he went and offered stockings. I must say he did the thing thoroughly. Stayed at the Pitt, small hotel near Torre Station. Returned to the hotel at 10.30 on the night of the murder. Could have taken a train from Churston at 9.57, getting to Torre at 10.20. No one answering to his description noticed on train or at station, but that Friday was Dartmouth Regatta and the trains back from Kingswear were pretty full.

'Bexhill much the same. Stayed at the Globe under his own name. Offered stockings to about a dozen addresses, including Mrs Barnard and including the Ginger Cat. Left hotel early in the evening. Arrived back in London about 11.30 the following morning. As to Andover, same procedure. Stayed at the Feathers. Offered stockings to Mrs Fowler, next door to Mrs Ascher, and to half a dozen other people in the street. The pair Mrs Ascher had I got from the niece (name of Drower) – they're identical with Cust's supply.'

'So far, good,' said the A.C.

'Acting on information received,' said the inspector, 'I went to the address given me by Hartigan, but found that Cust had left the house about half an hour previously. He received a telephone message, I'm told. First time such a thing had happened to him, so his landlady told me.'

'An accomplice?' suggested the Assistant Commissioner.

'Hardly,' said Poirot. 'It is odd that – unless –'

We all looked at him inquiringly as he paused.

He shook his head, however, and the inspector proceeded.

'I made a thorough search of the room he had occupied. That search puts the matter beyond doubt. I found a block of notepaper similar to that on which the letters were written, a large quantity of hosiery and – at the back of the cupboard where the hosiery was stored – a parcel much the same shape and size but which turned out to contain – not hosiery – *but eight new A B C railway guides!*'

'Proof positive,' said the Assistant Commissioner.

'I've found something else, too,' said the inspector – his voice becoming suddenly almost human with triumph. 'Only found it this morning, sir. Not had time to report yet. There was no sign of the knife in his room –'

'It would be the act of an imbecile to bring that back with him,' remarked Poirot.

'After all, he's not a reasonable human being,' remarked the inspector. 'Anyway, it occurred to me that he might just possibly have brought it back to the house and then realized the danger of hiding it (as M. Poirot points out) in his room, and have looked about elsewhere. What place in the house would he be likely to select? I got it straight away. *The hall stand* – no one ever moves a hall stand. With a lot of trouble I got it moved out from the wall – and there it was!'

'The knife?'

'The knife. Not a doubt of it. The dried blood's still on it.'

'Good work, Crome,' said the A.C. approvingly. 'We only need one thing more now.'

'What's that?'

'The man himself.'

'We'll get him, sir. Never fear.'

The inspector's tone was confident.

'What do you say, M. Poirot?'

Poirot started out of a reverie.

'I beg your pardon?'

'We were saying that it was only a matter of time before we got our man. Do you agree?'

'Oh, that – yes. Without a doubt.'

His tone was so abstracted that the others looked at him curiously.

'Is there anything worrying you, M. Poirot?'

'There is something that worries me very much. It is the *why*? The *motive.*'

'But, my dear fellow, the man's crazy,' said the Assistant Commissioner impatiently.

'I understand what M. Poirot means,' said Crome, coming graciously to the rescue. 'He's quite right. There's got to be some definite obsession. I think we'll find the root of the matter in an intensified inferiority complex. There may be a persecution mania, too, and if so he may possibly associate M. Poirot with it. He may have the delusion that M. Poirot is a detective employed on purpose to hunt him down.'

'H'm,' said the A.C. 'That's the jargon that's talked nowadays. In my day if a man was mad he was mad and we didn't look about for scientific terms to soften it down. I suppose a thoroughly up-to-date doctor would suggest putting a man like A B C in a nursing home, telling him what a fine fellow he was for forty-five days on end and then letting him out as a responsible member of society.'

Poirot smiled but did not answer.

The conference broke up.

'Well,' said the Assistant Commissioner. 'As you say, Crome, pulling him in is only a matter of time.'

'We'd have had him before now,' said the inspector, 'if he wasn't so ordinary-looking. We've worried enough perfectly inoffensive citizens as it is.'

'I wonder where he is at this minute,' said the Assistant Commissioner.

CHAPTER THIRTY

(Not from Captain Hastings' Personal Narrative)

Mr Cust stood by a greengrocer's shop.

He stared across the road.

Yes, that was it.

Mrs Ascher. Newsagent and Tobacconist . . .

In the empty window was a sign.

To Let.

Empty . . .

Lifeless . . .

'Excuse me, sir.'

The greengrocer's wife, trying to get at some lemons.

He apologized, moved to one side.

Slowly he shuffled away – back towards the main street of the town . . .

It was difficult – very difficult – now that he hadn't any money left . . .

Not having had anything to eat all day made one feel very queer and light-headed . . .

He looked at a poster outside a newsagent's shop.

The A B C Case. Murderer Still at Large. Interviews with M. Hercule Poirot.

Mr Cust said to himself:

'Hercule Poirot. I wonder if *he* knows . . .'

He walked on again.

It wouldn't do to stand staring at that poster . . .

He thought:

'I can't go on much longer . . .'

Foot in front of foot . . . what an odd thing walking was . . .

Foot in front of foot – ridiculous.

Highly ridiculous . . .

But man was a ridiculous animal anyway . . .

And he, Alexander Bonaparte Cust, was particularly ridiculous.

He had always been . . .

People had always laughed at him . . .

He couldn't blame them . . .

Where was he going? He didn't know. He'd come to the end. He no longer looked anywhere but at his feet.

Foot in front of foot.

He looked up. Lights in front of him. And letters ...

Police Station.

'That's funny,' said Mr Cust. He gave a little giggle.

Then he stepped inside. Suddenly, as he did so, he swayed and fell forward.

CHAPTER THIRTY-ONE

Hercule Poirot Asks Questions

It was a clear November day. Dr Thompson and Chief Inspector Japp had come round to acquaint Poirot with the result of the police court proceedings in the case of Rex v. Alexander Bonaparte Cust.

Poirot himself had had a slight bronchial chill which had prevented his attending. Fortunately he had not insisted on having my company.

'Committed for trial,' said Japp. 'So that's that.'

'Isn't it unusual?' I asked, 'for a defence to be offered at this stage? I thought prisoners always reserved their defence.'

'It's the usual course,' said Japp. 'I suppose young Lucas thought he might rush it through. He's a trier, I will say. Insanity's the only defence possible.'

Poirot shrugged his shoulders.

'With insanity there can be no acquittal. Imprisonment during His Majesty's pleasure is hardly preferable to death.'

'I suppose Lucas thought there was a chance,' said Japp. 'With a first-class alibi for the Bexhill murder, the whole case might be weakened. I don't think he realized how strong our case is. Anyway, Lucas goes in for originality. He's a young man, and he wants to hit the public eye.'

Poirot turned to Thompson.

'What's your opinion, doctor?'

'Of Cust? Upon my soul, I don't know what to say. He's playing the sane man remarkably well. He's an epileptic, of course.'

'What an amazing dénouement that was,' I said.

'His falling into the Andover police station in a fit? Yes – it was a fitting dramatic curtain to the drama. A B C has always timed his effects well.'

'Is it possible to commit a crime and be unaware of it?' I asked. 'His denials seem to have a ring of truth in them.'

Dr Thompson smiled a little.

'You mustn't be taken in by that theatrical "I swear by God" pose. It's my opinion *that Cust knows perfectly well he committed the murders.*'

'When they're as fervent as that they usually do,' said Crome.

'As to your question,' went on Thompson, 'it's perfectly possible

473

for an epileptic subject in a state of somnambulism to commit an action and be entirely unaware of having done so. But it is the general opinion that such an action must "not be contrary to the will of the person in the waking state".'

He went on discussing the matter, speaking of *grand mal* and *petit mal* and, to tell the truth, confusing me hopelessly as is often the case when a learned person holds forth on his own subject.

'However, I'm against the theory that Cust committed these crimes without knowing he'd done them. You might put that theory forward if it weren't for the letters. The letters knock the theory on the head. They show premeditation and a careful planning of the crime.'

'And of the letters we have still no explanation,' said Poirot.

'That interests you?'

'Naturally – since they were written to me. And on the subject of the letters Cust is persistently dumb. Until I get at the reason for those letters being written to me, I shall not feel that the case is solved.'

'Yes – I can understand that from your point of view. There doesn't seem to be any reason to believe that the man ever came up against you in any way?'

'None whatever.'

'I might make a suggestion. Your name!'

'My name?'

'Yes. Cust is saddled – apparently by the whim of his mother (Oedipus complex there, I shouldn't wonder!) – with two extremely bombastic Christian names: Alexander and Bonaparte. You see the implications? Alexander – the popularly supposed undefeatable who sighed for more worlds to conquer. Bonaparte – the great Emperor of the French. He wants an adversary – an adversary, one might say, in his class. Well – there you are – Hercules the strong.'

'Your words are very suggestive, doctor. They foster ideas . . .'

'Oh, it's only a suggestion. Well, I must be off.'

Dr Thompson went out. Japp remained.

'Does this alibi worry you?' Poirot asked.

'It does a little,' admitted the inspector. 'Mind you, I don't believe in it, because I know it isn't true. But it is going to be the deuce to break it. This man Strange is a tough character.'

'Describe him to me.'

'He's a man of forty. A tough, confident, self-opinionated mining engineer. It's my opinion that it was he who insisted on his evidence being taken now. He wants to get off to Chile. He hoped the thing might be settled out of hand.'

'He's one of the most positive people I've ever seen,' I said.

'The type of man who would not like to admit he was mistaken,' said Poirot thoughtfully.

'He sticks to his story and he's not one to be heckled. He swears by all that's blue that he picked up Cust in the Whitecross Hotel at Eastbourne on the evening of July 24th. He was lonely and wanted someone to talk to. As far as I can see, Cust made an ideal listener. He didn't interrupt! After dinner he and Cust played dominoes. It appears Strange was a whale on dominoes and to his surprise Cust was pretty hot stuff too. Queer game, dominoes. People go mad about it. They'll play for hours. That's what Strange and Cust did apparently. Cust wanted to go to bed but Strange wouldn't hear of it – swore they'd keep it up until midnight at least. And that's what they did do. They separated at ten minutes past midnight. And if Cust was in the Whitecross Hotel at Eastbourne at ten minutes past midnight on the morning of the 25th he couldn't very well be strangling Betty Barnard on the beach at Bexhill between midnight and one o'clock.'

'The problem certainly seems insuperable,' said Poirot thoughtfully. 'Decidedly, it gives one to think.'

'It's given Crome something to think about,' said Japp.

'This man Strange is very positive?'

'Yes. He's an obstinate devil. And it's difficult to see just where the flaw is. Supposing Strange is making a mistake and the man wasn't Cust – why on earth should he *say* his name is Cust? And the writing in the hotel register is his all right. You can't say he's an accomplice – homicidal lunatics don't have accomplices! Did the girl die later? The doctor was quite firm in his evidence, and anyway it would take some time for Cust to get out of the hotel at Eastbourne without being seen and get over to Bexhill – about fourteen miles away –'

'It is a problem – yes,' said Poirot.

'Of course, strictly speaking, it oughtn't to matter. We've got Cust on the Doncaster murder – the blood-stained coat, the knife - not a loophole there. You couldn't bounce any jury into acquitting him. But it spoils a pretty case. He did the Doncaster murder. He did the Churston murder. He did the Andover murder. Then, by hell, he *must* have done the Bexhill murder. But I don't see how!'

He shook his head and got up.

'Now's your chance, M. Poirot,' he said. 'Crome's in a fog. Exert those cellular arrangements of yours I used to hear so much about. Show us the way he did it.'

Japp departed.

'What about it, Poirot?' I said. 'Are the little grey cells equal to the task?'

Poirot answered my question by another.

'Tell me, Hastings, do you consider the case ended?'

'Well – yes, practically speaking. We've got the man. And we've got most of the evidence. It's only the trimmings that are needed.'

Poirot shook his head.

'The case is ended! The case! The case is the *man*, Hastings. Until we know all about the man, the mystery is as deep as ever. It is not victory because we have put him in the dock!'

'We know a fair amount about him.'

'We know nothing at all! We know where he was born. We know he fought in the war and received a slight wound in the head and that he was discharged from the army owing to epilepsy. We know that he lodged with Mrs Marbury for nearly two years. We know that he was quiet and retiring – the sort of man that nobody notices. We know that he invented and carried out an intensely clever scheme of systemized murder. We know that he made certain incredibly stupid blunders. We know that he killed without pity and quite ruthlessly. We know, too, that he was kindly enough not to let blame rest on any other person for the crimes he committed. If he wanted to kill unmolested – how easy to let other persons suffer for his crimes. Do you not see, Hastings, that the man is a mass of contradictions? Stupid and cunning, ruthless and magnanimous – *and that there must be some dominating factor that reconciles his two natures*.'

'Of course, if you treat him like a psychological study,' I began.

'What else has this case been since the beginning? All along I have been groping my way – trying *to get to know the murderer*. And now I realize, Hastings, *that I do not know him at all!* I am at sea.'

'The lust for power –' I began.

'Yes – that might explain a good deal . . . But it does not satisfy me. There are things I want to know. *Why* did he commit these murders? *Why* did he choose those particular people –?'

'Alphabetically –' I began.

'Was Betty Barnard the only person in Bexhill whose name began with a B? Betty Barnard – I had an idea there. . . . It ought to be true – it must be true. But if so –'

476

He was silent for some time. I did not like to interrupt him. As a matter of fact, I believe I fell asleep.

I woke to find Poirot's hand on my shoulder.

'*Mon cher Hastings*,' he said affectionately. 'My good genius.'

I was quite confused by this sudden mark of esteem.

'It is true,' Poirot insisted. 'Always – always – you help me – you bring me luck. You inspire me.'

'How have I inspired you this time?' I asked.

'While I was asking myself certain questions I remembered a remark of yours – a remark absolutely shimmering in its clear vision. Did I not say to you once that you had a genius for stating the obvious. It is the obvious that I have neglected.'

'What is this brilliant remark of mine?' I asked.

'It makes everything as clear as crystal. I see the answers to all my questions. The reason for Mrs Ascher (that, it is true, I glimpsed long ago), the reason for Sir Carmichael Clarke, the reason for the Doncaster murder, and finally and supremely important, *the reason for Hercule Poirot*.'

'Could you kindly explain?' I asked.

'Not at the moment. I require first a little more information. That I can get from our Special Legion. And then – then, *when I have got the answer to a certain question, I will go and see ABC*. We will be face to face at last – A B C and Hercule Poirot – the adversaries.'

'And then?' I asked.

'And then,' said Poirot. 'We will talk! *Je vous assure, Hastings* – there is nothing so dangerous *for anyone who has something to hide* as conversation! Speech, so a wise old Frenchman said to me once, is an invention of man's to prevent him from thinking. It is also an infallible means of discovering that which he wishes to hide. A human being, Hastings, cannot resist the opportunity to reveal himself and express his personality which conversation gives him. Every time he will give himself away.'

'What do you expect Cust to tell you?'

Hercule Poirot smiled.

'A lie,' he said. 'And by it, I shall know the truth!'

CHAPTER THIRTY-TWO

And Catch a Fox

During the next few days Poirot was very busy. He made mysterious absences, talked very little, frowned to himself, and consistently refused to satisfy my natural curiosity as to the brilliance I had, according to him, displayed in the past.

I was not invited to accompany him on his mysterious comings and goings – a fact which I somewhat resented.

Towards the end of the week, however, he announced his intention of paying a visit to Bexhill and neighbourhood and suggested that I should come with him. Needless to say, I accepted with alacrity.

The invitation, I discovered, was not extended to me alone. The members of our Special Legion were also invited.

They were as intrigued by Poirot as I was. Nevertheless, by the end of the day, I had at any rate an idea as to the direction in which Poirot's thoughts were tending.

He first visited Mr and Mrs Barnard and got an exact account from her as to the hour at which Mr Cust had called on her and exactly what he had said. He then went to the hotel at which Cust had put up and extracted a minute description of that gentleman's departure. As far as I could judge, no new facts were elicited by his questions but he himself seemed quite satisfied.

Next he went to the beach – to the place where Betty Barnard's body had been discovered. Here he walked round in circles for some minutes studying the shingle attentively. I could see little point in this, since the tide covered the spot twice a day.

However I have learnt by this time that Poirot's actions are usually dictated by an idea – however meaningless they may seem.

He then walked from the beach to the nearest point at which a car could have been parked. From there again he went to the place where the Eastbourne buses waited before leaving Bexhill.

Finally he took us all to the Ginger Cat café, where we had a somewhat stale tea served by the plump waitress, Milly Higley.

Her he complimented in a flowing Gallic style on the shape of her ankles.

'The legs of the English – always they are too thin! But you, mademoiselle, have the perfect leg. It has shape – it has an ankle!'

Milly Higley giggled a good deal and told him not to go on so. She knew what French gentlemen were like.

Poirot did not trouble to contradict her mistake as to his nationality. He merely ogled her in such a way that I was startled and almost shocked.

'*Voilà*,' said Poirot, 'I have finished in Bexhill. Presently I go to Eastbourne. One little inquiry there – that is all. Unnecessary for you all to accompany me. In the meantime come back to the hotel and let us have a cocktail. That Carlton tea, it was abominable!'

As we were sipping our cocktails Franklin Clarke said curiously:

'I suppose we can guess what you are after? You're out to break that alibi. But I can't see what you're so pleased about. You haven't got a new fact of any kind.'

'No – that is true.'

'Well, then?'

'Patience. Everything arranges itself, given time.'

'You seem quite pleased with yourself anyway.'

'Nothing so far has contradicted my little idea – that is why.'

His face grew serious.

'My friend Hastings told me once that he had, as a young man, played a game called The Truth. It was a game where everyone in turn was asked three questions – two of which must be answered truthfully. The third one could be barred. The questions, naturally, were of the most indiscreet kind. But to begin with everyone had to swear that they would indeed speak the truth, and nothing but the truth.'

He paused.

'Well?' said Megan.

'*Eh bien* – me, I want to play that game. Only it is not necessary to have three questions. One will be enough. One question to each of you.'

'Of course,' said Clarke impatiently. 'We'll answer anything.'

'Ah, but I want it to be more serious than that. Do you all swear to speak the truth?'

He was so solemn about it that the others, puzzled, became solemn themselves. They all swore as he demanded.

'*Bon*,' said Poirot briskly. 'Let us begin –'

'I'm ready,' said Thora Grey.

'Ah, but ladies first – this time it would not be the politeness. We will start elsewhere.'

He turned to Franklin Clarke.

'What, *mon cher M. Clarke*, did you think of the hats the ladies wore at Ascot this year?'

Franklin Clarke stared at him.

'Is this a joke?'

'Certainly not.'

'Is that seriously your question?'

'It is.'

Clarke began to grin.

'Well, M. Poirot, I didn't actually go to Ascot, but from what I could see of them driving in cars, women's hats for Ascot were an even bigger joke than the hats they wear ordinarily.'

'Fantastic?'

'Quite fantastic.'

Poirot smiled and turned to Donald Fraser.

'When did you take your holiday this year, monsieur?'

It was Fraser's turn to stare.

'My holiday? The first two weeks in August.'

His face quivered suddenly. I guessed that the question had brought the loss of the girl he loved back to him.

Poirot, however, did not seem to pay much attention to the reply. He turned to Thora Grey and I heard the slight difference in his voice. It had tightened up. His question came sharp and clear.

'Mademoiselle, in the event of Lady Clarke's death, would you have married Sir Carmichael if he had asked you?'

The girl sprang up.

'How dare you ask me such a question. It's – it's insulting!'

'Perhaps. But you have sworn to speak the truth. *Eh bien* – Yes or no?'

'Sir Carmichael was wonderfully kind to me. He treated me almost like a daughter. And that's how I felt to him – just affectionate and grateful.'

'Pardon me, but that is not answering Yes or No, mademoiselle.'

She hesitated.

'The answer, of course, is no!'

He made no comment.

'Thank you, mademoiselle.'

He turned to Megan Barnard. The girl's face was very pale. She was breathing hard as though braced up for an ordeal.

Poirot's voice came out like the crack of a whiplash.

'Mademoiselle, what do you hope will be the result of my investigations? Do you want me to find out the truth – or not?'

480

Her head went back proudly. I was fairly sure of her answer. Megan, I knew, had a fanatical passion for truth.

Her answer came clearly – and it stupefied me.

'No!'

We all jumped. Poirot leant forward studying her face.

'Mademoiselle Megan,' he said, 'you may not want the truth but – *ma foi* – you can speak it!'

He turned towards the door, then, recollecting, went to Mary Drower.

'Tell me, *mon enfant*, have you a young man?'

Mary, who had been looking apprehensive, looked startled and blushed.

'Oh, Mr Poirot. I – I – well, I'm not sure.'

He smiled.

'*Alors c'est bien, mon enfant.*'

He looked round for me.

'Come, Hastings, we must start for Eastbourne.'

The car was waiting and soon we were driving along the coast road that leads through Pevensey to Eastbourne.

'Is it any use asking you anything, Poirot?'

'Not at this moment. Draw your own conclusions as to what I am doing.'

I relapsed into silence.

Poirot, who seemed pleased with himself, hummed a little tune. As we passed through Pevensey he suggested that we stop and have a look over the castle.

As we were returning towards the car, we paused a moment to watch a ring of children – Brownies, I guessed, by their get-up – who were singing a ditty in shrill, untuneful voices. . . .

'What is it that they say, Hastings? I cannot catch the words.'

I listened – till I caught one refrain.

> '– *And catch a fox*
> *And put him in a box*
> *And never let him go.*'

'And catch a fox and put him in a box and never let him go!' repeated Poirot.

His face had gone suddenly grave and stern.

'It is very terrible that, Hastings.' He was silent a minute. 'You hunt the fox here?'

481

'I don't. I've never been able to afford to hunt. And I don't think there's much hunting in this part of the world.'

'I meant in England generally. A strange sport. The waiting at the covert side – then they sound the tally-ho, do they not? – and the run begins – across the country – over the hedges and ditches – and the fox he runs – and sometimes he doubles back – but the dogs –'

'Hounds!'

'– hounds are on his trail, and at last they catch him and he dies – quickly and horribly.'

'I suppose it does sound cruel, but really –'

'The fox enjoys it? Do not say *les bêtises*, my friend. *Tout de même* – it is better that – the quick, cruel death – than what those children were singing . . .

'To be shut away – in a box – for ever . . . No, it is not good, that.'

He shook his head. Then he said, with a change of tone:

'Tomorrow, I am to visit the man Cust,' and he added to the chauffeur:

'Back to London.'

'Aren't you going to Eastbourne?' I cried.

'What need? I know – quite enough for my purpose.'

CHAPTER THIRTY-THREE

Alexander Bonaparte Cust

I was not present at the interview that took place between Poirot and that strange man – Alexander Bonaparte Cust. Owing to his association with the police and the peculiar circumstances of the case, Poirot had no difficulty in obtaining a Home Office order – but that order did not extend to me, and in any case it was essential, from Poirot's point of view, that that interview should be absolutely private – the two men face to face.

He has given me, however, such a detailed account of what passed between them that I set it down with as much confidence on paper as though I had actually been present.

Mr Cust seemed to have shrunk. His stoop was more apparent. His fingers plucked vaguely at his coat.

For some time, I gather, Poirot did not speak.

He sat and looked at the man opposite him.

The atmosphere became restful – soothing – full of infinite leisure . . .

It must have been a dramatic moment – this meeting of the two adversaries in the long drama. In Poirot's place I should have felt the dramatic thrill.

Poirot, however, is nothing if not matter-of-fact. He was absorbed in producing a certain effect upon the man opposite him.

At last he said gently:

'Do you know who I am?'

The other shook his head.

'No – no – I can't say I do. Unless you are Mr Lucas's – what do they call it? – junior. Or perhaps you come from Mr Maynard?'

(Maynard & Cole were the defending solicitors.)

His tone was polite but not very interested. He seemed absorbed in some inner abstraction.

'I am Hercule Poirot . . .'

Poirot said the words very gently . . . and watched for the effect.

Mr Cust raised his head a little.

'Oh, yes?'

He said it as naturally as Inspector Crome might have said it – but without the superciliousness.

Then, a minute later, he repeated his remark.

'Oh, yes?' he said, and this time his tone was different – it held an awakened interest. He raised his head and looked at Poirot.

Hercule Poirot met his gaze and nodded his own head gently once or twice.

'Yes,' he said. 'I am the man to whom you wrote the letters.'

At once the contact was broken. Mr Cust dropped his eyes and spoke irritably and fretfully.

'I never wrote to you. Those letters weren't written by me. I've said so again and again.'

'I know,' said Poirot. 'But if you did not write them, who did?'

'An enemy. I must have an enemy. They are all against me. The police – everyone – all against me. It's a gigantic conspiracy.'

Poirot did not reply.

Mr Cust said:

'Everyone's hand has been against me – always.'

'Even when you were a child?'

Mr Cust seemed to consider.

'No – no – not exactly then. My mother was very fond of me. But she was ambitious – terribly ambitious. That's why she gave me those ridiculous names. She had some absurd idea that I'd cut a figure in the world. She was always urging me to assert myself – talking about will-power . . . saying anyone could be master of his fate . . . she said I could do anything!'

He was silent for a minute.

'She was quite wrong, of course. I realized that myself quite soon. I wasn't the sort of person to get on in life. I was always doing foolish things – making myself look ridiculous. And I was timid – afraid of people. I had a bad time at school – the boys found out my Christian names – they used to tease me about them . . . I did very badly at school – in games and work and everything.'

He shook his head.

'Just as well poor mother died. She'd have been disappointed . . . Even when I was at the Commercial College I was stupid – it took me longer to learn typing and shorthand than anyone else. And yet I didn't *feel* stupid – if you know what I mean.'

He cast a sudden appealing look at the other man.

'I know what you mean,' said Poirot. 'Go on.'

'It was just the feeling that everybody else *thought* me stupid. Very paralysing. It was the same thing later in the office.'

'And later still in the war?' prompted Poirot.

Mr Cust's face lightened up suddenly.

484

'You know,' he said, 'I enjoyed the war. What I had of it, that was. I felt, for the first time, a man like anybody else. We were all in the same box. I was as good as anyone else.'

His smile faded.

'And then I got that wound on the head. Very slight. But they found out I had fits . . . I'd always known, of course, that there were times when I hadn't been quite sure what I was doing. Lapses, you know. And of course, once or twice I'd fallen down. But I don't really think they ought to have discharged me for that. No, I don't think it was right.'

'And afterwards?' asked Poirot.

'I got a place as a clerk. Of course there was good money to be got just then. And I didn't do so badly after the war. Of course, a smaller salary . . . And – I didn't seem to get on. I was always being passed over for promotion. I wasn't go-ahead enough. It grew very difficult – really very difficult. . . . Especially when the slump came. To tell you the truth, I'd got hardly enough to keep body and soul together (and you've got to look presentable as a clerk) when I got the offer of this stocking job. A salary and commission!'

Poirot said gently:

'But you are aware, are you not, that the firm whom you say employed you deny the fact?'

Mr Cust got excited again.

'That's because they're in the conspiracy – they must be in the conspiracy.'

He went on:

'I've got written evidence – written evidence. I've got their letters to me, giving me instructions as to what places to go to and a list of people to call on.'

'Not *written* evidence exactly – *typewritten* evidence.'

'It's the same thing. Naturally a big firm of wholesale manufacturers typewrite their letters.'

'Don't you know, Mr Cust, that a typewriter can be identified? All those letters were typed by one particular machine.'

'What of it?'

'And that machine was your own – the one found in your room.'

'It was sent me by the firm at the beginning of my job.'

'Yes, but these letters were received *afterwards*. So it looks, does it not, as though *you typed them yourself and posted them to yourself?*'

'No, no! It's all part of the plot against me!'

He added suddenly:

485

'Besides, their letters *would* be written on the same kind of machine.'

'The same *kind*, but not the same actual machine.'

Mr Cust repeated obstinately:

'It's a plot!'

'And the A B C's that were found in the cupboard?'

'I know nothing about them. I thought they were all stockings.'

'Why did you tick off the name of Mrs Ascher in that first list of people in Andover?'

'Because I decided to start with her. One must begin somewhere.'

'Yes, that is true. *One must begin somewhere.*'

'I don't mean that!' said Mr Cust. 'I don't mean what you mean!'

'*But you know what I meant?*'

Mr Cust said nothing. He was trembling:

'I didn't do it!' he said. 'I'm perfectly innocent! It's all a mistake. Why, look at that second crime – that Bexhill one. I was playing dominoes at Eastbourne. You've got to admit that!'

His voice was triumphant.

'Yes,' said Poirot. His voice was meditative – silky. 'But it's so easy, isn't it, to make a mistake of one day? And if you're an obstinate, positive man, like Mr Strange, you'll never consider the possibility of having been mistaken. What you've said you'll stick to . . . He's that kind of man. And the hotel register – it's very easy to put down the wrong date when you're signing it – probably no one will notice it at the time.'

'I was playing dominoes that evening!'

'You play dominoes very well, I believe.'

Mr Cust was a little flurried by this.

'I – I well, I believe I do.'

'It is a very absorbing game, is it not, with a lot of skill in it?'

'Oh, there's a lot of play in it – a lot of play! We used to play a lot in the city, in the lunch hour. You'd be surprised the way total strangers come together over a game of dominoes.'

He chuckled.

'I remember one man – I've never forgotten him because of something he told me – we just got talking over a cup of coffee, and we started dominoes. Well, I felt after twenty minutes that I'd known that man all my life.'

'What was it that he told you?' asked Poirot.

Mr Cust's face clouded over.

'It gave me a turn – a nasty turn. Talking of your fate being written

486

in your hand, he was. And he showed me his hand and the lines that showed he'd have two near escapes of being drowned – and he had had two near escapes. And then he looked at mine and he told me some amazing things. Said I was going to be one of the most celebrated men in England before I died. Said the whole country would be talking about me. But he said – he said . . .'

Mr Cust broke down – faltered . . .

'Yes?'

Poirot's gaze held a quiet magnetism. Mr Cust looked at him, looked away, then back again like a fascinated rabbit.

'He said – he said – that it looked as though I might die a violent death – and he laughed and said: "Almost looks as though you might die on the scaffold," and then he laughed and said that was only his joke . . .'

He was silent suddenly. His eyes left Poirot's face – they ran from side to side . . .

'My head – I suffer very badly with my head . . . the headaches are something cruel sometimes. And then there are times when I don't know – when I don't know . . .'

He broke down.

Poirot leant forward. He spoke very quietly but with great assurance.

'*But you do know, don't you,*' he said, '*that you committed the murders?*'

Mr Cust looked up. His glance was quite simple and direct. All resistance had left him. He looked strangely at peace.

'Yes,' he said, 'I know.'

'But – I am right, am I not? – *you don't know why you did them?*'

Mr Cust shook his head.

'No,' he said. 'I don't.'

CHAPTER THIRTY-FOUR

Poirot Explains

We were sitting in a state of tense attention to listen to Poirot's final explanation of the case.

'All along,' he said, 'I have been worried over the *why* of this case. Hastings said to me the other day that the case was ended. I replied to him that the case was the *man*! The mystery was *not the mystery of the murders*, but the *mystery of A B C*. Why did he find it necessary to commit these murders? Why did he select *me* as his adversary?

'It is no answer to say that the man was mentally unhinged. To say a man does mad things because he is mad is merely unintelligent and stupid. A madman is as logical and reasoned in his actions as a sane man – *given his peculiar biased point of view*. For example, if a man insists on going out and squatting about in nothing but a loin cloth his conduct seems eccentric in the extreme. But once you know *that the man himself is firmly convinced that he is Mahatma Gandhi*, then his conduct becomes perfectly reasonable and logical.

'What was necessary in this case was to imagine a mind so constituted *that it was logical and reasonable to commit four or more murders* and to announce them beforehand by letters written to Hercule Poirot.

'My friend Hastings will tell you that from the moment I received the first letter I was upset and disturbed. It seemed to me at once that there was something very wrong about the letter.'

'You were quite right,' said Franklin Clarke dryly.

'Yes. But there, at the very start, I made a grave error. I permitted my feeling – my very strong feeling about the letter – to remain a mere impression. I treated it as though it had been an intuition. In a well-balanced, reasoning mind there is no such thing as an intuition – an inspired guess! You *can* guess, of course – and a guess is either right or wrong. If it is right you call it an intuition. If it is wrong you usually do not speak of it again. But what is often called an intuition is really *an impression based on logical deduction or experience*. When an expert feels that there is something wrong about a picture or a piece of furniture or the signature on a cheque he is really basing that feeling on a host of small signs and details. He has no need to go into them minutely – his experience obviates that – the net result is *the definite impression that something is wrong*. But it is not a *guess*, it is an impression based on *experience*.

'*Eh bien*, I admit that I did not regard that first letter in the way I should. It just made me extremely uneasy. The police regarded it as a hoax. I myself took it seriously. I was convinced that a murder would take place in Andover as stated. As you know, a murder *did* take place.

'There was no means at that point, as I well realized, of knowing who the *person* was who had done the deed. The only course open to me was to try and understand just what kind of a person had done it.

'I had certain indications. The letter – the manner of the crime – the person murdered. What I had to discover was: the motive of the crime, the motive of the letter.'

'Publicity,' suggested Clarke.

'Surely an inferiority complex covers that,' added Thora Grey.

'That was, of course, the obvious line to take. But why *me*? *Why Hercule Poirot*? Greater publicity could be ensured by sending the letters to Scotland Yard. More again by sending them to a newspaper. A newspaper might not print the first letter, but by the time the second crime took place, A B C could have been assured of all the publicity the press could give. Why, then, Hercule Poirot? Was it for some *personal* reason? There was, discernible in the letter, a slight anti-foreign bias – but not enough to explain the matter to my satisfaction.

'Then the second letter arrived – and was followed by the murder of Betty Barnard at Bexhill. It became clear now (what I had already suspected) that the murders were to proceed on an alphabetical plan, but the fact, which seemed final to most people, left the main question unaltered to my mind. Why did A B C *need* to commit these murders?'

Megan Barnard stirred in her chair.

'Isn't there such a thing as – as a blood lust?' she said.

Poirot turned to her.

'You are quite right, mademoiselle. There *is* such a thing. The lust to kill. But that did not quite fit the facts of the case. A homicidal maniac who desires to kill usually desires to kill *as many victims as possible*. It is a recurring *craving*. The great idea of such a killer is to *hide his tracks* – not to *advertise* them. When we consider the four victims selected – or at any rate three of them (for I know very little of Mr Downes or Mr Earlsfield), we realize that *if he had chosen*, the murderer could have done away with them without incurring any suspicion. Franz Ascher, Donald Fraser or Megan Barnard, possibly

489

Mr Clarke – those are the people the police would have suspected even if they had been unable to get direct proof. An unknown homicidal murderer would not have been thought of! Why, then, did the murderer feel it necessary to call attention to himself? Was it the necessity of leaving on each body a copy of an A B C railway guide? Was *that* the compulsion? Was there some complex connected *with the railway guide?*'

'I found it quite inconceivable at this point *to enter into the mind of the murderer*. Surely it could not be magnanimity? A horror of responsibility for the crime being fastened on an innocent person?

'Although I could not answer the main question, certain things I did feel I was learning about the murderer.'

'Such as?' asked Fraser.

'To begin with – that he had a tabular mind. His crimes were listed by alphabetical progression – that was obviously important to him. On the other hand, he had no particular taste in victims – Mrs Ascher, Betty Barnard, Sir Carmichael Clarke, they all differed widely from each other. There was no sex complex – no particular age complex, and that seemed to me to be a very curious fact. If a man kills indiscriminately it is usually because he removes anyone who stands in his way or annoys him. *But the alphabetical progression showed that such was not the case here*. The other type of killer usually selects *a particular type of victim* – nearly always of the opposite sex. There was something haphazard about the procedure of A B C that seemed to me to be at war with the alphabetical selection.

'One slight inference I permitted myself to make. The choice of the A B C suggested to me what I may call a *railway-minded man*. This is more common in men than women. Small boys love trains better than small girls do. It might be the sign, too, of an in some ways undeveloped mind. The "boy" motif still predominated.

'The death of Betty Barnard and the manner of it gave me certain other indications. The manner of her death was particularly suggestive. (Forgive me, Mr Fraser.) To begin with, she was strangled with her own belt – therefore she must almost certainly have been killed by someone with whom she was on friendly or affectionate terms. When I learnt something of her character a picture grew up in my mind.

'Betty Barnard was a flirt. She liked attention from a personable male. Therefore A B C, to persuade her to come out with him, must have had a certain amount of attraction – of *le sex appeal!* He must be able, as you English say, to "get off". He must be capable of the click!

490

I visualize the scene on the beach thus: the man admires her belt. She takes it off, he passes it playfully round her neck – says, perhaps, "I shall strangle you." It is all very playful. She giggles – and he pulls –'

Donald Fraser sprang up. He was livid.

'M. Poirot – for God's sake.'

Poirot made a gesture.

'It is finished. I say no more. It is over. We pass to the next murder, that of Sir Carmichael Clarke. Here the murderer goes back to his first method – the blow on the head. The same alphabetical complex – but one fact worries me a little. To be consistent the murderer should have chosen his towns in some definite sequence.

'If Andover is the 155th name under A, then the B crime should be the 155th also – or it should be the 156th and the C the 157th. Here again the towns seemed to be chosen in rather too *haphazard* a fashion.'

'Isn't that because you're rather biased on that subject, Poirot?' I suggested. 'You yourself are normally methodical and orderly. It's almost a disease with you.'

'No, it is *not* a disease! *Quelle idée!* But I admit that I may be over-stressing that point. *Passons!*

'The Churston crime gave me very little extra help. We were unlucky over it, since the letter announcing it went astray, hence no preparations could be made.

'But by the time the D crime was announced, a very formidable system of defence had been evolved. It must have been obvious that A B C could not much longer hope to get away with his crimes.

'Moreover, it was at this point that the clue of the stockings came into my hand. It was perfectly clear that the presence of an individual selling stockings on and near the scene of each crime could not be a coincidence. Hence the stocking-seller must be the murderer. I may say that his description, as given me by Miss Grey, did not quite correspond with my own picture of the man who strangled Betty Barnard.

'I will pass over the next stages quickly. A fourth murder was committed – the murder of a man named George Earlsfield – it was supposed in mistake for a man named Downes, who was something of the same build and who was sitting near him in the cinema.

'*And now at last comes the turn of the tide*. Events play against A B C instead of into his hand. He is marked down – hunted – and at last arrested.

'The case, as Hastings says, is ended!

491

'True enough as far as the public is concerned. The man is in prison and will eventually, no doubt, go to Broadmoor. There will be no more murders. Exit! R.I.P.

'*But not for me!* I know nothing – nothing at all! Neither the *why* nor the *wherefore*.

'And there is one small vexing fact. The man Cust has an alibi for the night of the Bexhill crime.'

'That's been worrying me all along,' said Franklin Clarke.

'Yes. It worried me. For the alibi, it has the air of being *genuine*. But it cannot be genuine unless – and now we come to two very interesting speculations.

'Supposing, my friends, that while Cust committed *three* of the crimes – the A, C, and D crimes – *he did not commit the B crime*.'

'M. Poirot. It isn't –'

Poirot silenced Megan Barnard with a look.

'Be quiet, mademoiselle. I am for the truth, I am! I have done with lies. Supposing, I say, *that A B C did not commit the second crime*. It took place, remember, in the early hours of the 25th – the day he had arrived for the crime. Supposing someone had forestalled him? What in those circumstances would he do? Commit a *second* murder, or lie low and *accept the first as a kind of macabre present?*'

'M. Poirot!' said Megan. 'That's a fantastic thought! All the crimes *must* have been committed by the same person!'

He took no notice of her and went steadily on:

'Such a hypothesis had the merit of explaining one fact – *the discrepancy between the personality of Alexander Bonaparte Cust* (who could never have made the click with any girl) *and the personality of Betty Barnard's murderer*. And it has been known, before now, that would-be murderers *have* taken advantage of the crimes committed by other people. Not all the crimes of Jack the Ripper were committed by Jack the Ripper, for instance. So far, so good.

'But then I came up against a definite difficulty.

'Up to the time of the Barnard murder, *no facts about the A B C murders had been made public*. The Andover murder had created little interest. The incident of the open railway guide had not even been mentioned in the press. It therefore followed that whoever killed Betty Barnard *must have had access to facts known only to certain persons* – myself, the police, and certain relations and neighbours of Mrs Ascher.

'That line of research seemed to lead me up against a blank wall.'

The faces that looked at him were blank too. Blank and puzzled.

492

Donald Fraser said thoughtfully:

'The police, after all, are human beings. And they're good-looking men –'

He stopped, looking at Poirot inquiringly.

Poirot shook his head gently.

'No – it is simpler than that. I told you that there was a second speculation.

'Supposing that Cust was *not* responsible for the killing of Betty Barnard? Supposing that *someone else* killed her. Could that someone else have been responsible *for the other murders too*?'

'But that doesn't make sense!' cried Clarke.

'Doesn't it? I did then *what I ought to have done at first*. I examined the letters I had received from a totally different point of view. I had felt from the beginning that there was something wrong with them – just as a picture expert knows a picture is wrong . . .

'I had assumed, without pausing to consider, that what was wrong with them was the fact that they were written by a madman.

'Now I examined them again – and this time I came to a totally different conclusion. What was wrong with them was *the fact that they were written by a sane man*!'

'What?' I cried.

'But yes – just that precisely! They were wrong as a picture is wrong – *because they were a fake*! They pretended to be the letters of madman – of a homicidal lunatic, but in reality they were nothing of the kind.'

'It doesn't make sense,' Franklin Clarke repeated.

'*Mais si!* One must reason – reflect. What would be the object of writing such letters? To focus attention on the writer, to call attention to the murders! *En vérité*, it did not seem to make sense at first sight. And then I saw light. It was to focus attention on several murders – on a *group* of murders . . . Is it not your great Shakespeare who has said "You cannot see the trees for the wood." '

I did not correct Poirot's literary reminiscences. I was trying to see his point. A glimmer came to me. He went on:

'When do you notice a pin least? When it is in a pin-cushion! When do you notice an individual murder least? When it is one of *a series of related murders*.

'I had to deal with an intensely clever, resourceful murderer – reckless, daring and a thorough gambler. *Not* Mr Cust! He could never have committed these murders! No, I had to deal with a very different stamp of man – a man with a boyish temperament (witness

493

the schoolboy-like letters and the railway guide), an attractive man to women, and a man with a ruthless disregard for human life, a man who was necessarily a prominent person in *one* of the crimes!

'Consider when a man or woman is killed, what are the questions that the police ask? Opportunity. Where everybody was at the time of the crime? Motive. Who benefited by the deceased's death? If the motive and the opportunity are fairly obvious, what is a would-be murderer to do? Fake an alibi – that is, manipulate *time* in some way? But that is always a hazardous proceeding. Our murderer thought of a more fantastic defence. Create a *homicidal* murderer!

'I had now only to review the various crimes and find the possible guilty person. The Andover crime? The most likely suspect for that was Franz Ascher, but I could not imagine Ascher inventing and carrying out such an elaborate scheme, nor could I see him planning a premeditated murder. The Bexhill crime? Donald Fraser was a possibility. He had brains and ability, and a methodical turn of mind. But his motive for killing his sweetheart could only be jealousy – and jealousy does not tend to premeditation. Also I learned that he had his holidays *early* in August, which rendered it unlikely he had anything to do with the Churston crime. We come to the Churston crime next – and at once we are on infinitely more promising ground.

'Sir Carmichael Clarke was an immensely wealthy man. Who inherits his money? His wife, who is dying, has a life interest in it, and it then goes to *his brother Franklin*.'

Poirot turned slowly round till his eyes met those of Franklin Clarke.

'I was quite sure then. The man I had known a long time in my secret mind *was the same as the man whom I had known as a person. A B C and Franklin Clarke were one and the same!* The daring adventurous character, the roving life, the partiality for England that had showed itself, very faintly, in the jeer at foreigners. The attractive free and easy manner – nothing easier for him than to pick up a girl in a café. The methodical tabular mind – he made a list here one day, ticked off over the headings A B C – and finally, the boyish mind – mentioned by Lady Clarke and even shown by his taste in fiction – I have ascertained that there is a book in the library called *The Railway Children* by E. Nesbit. I had no further doubt in my own mind – A B C, the man who wrote the letters and committed the crimes, was *Franklin Clarke*.'

Clarke suddenly burst out laughing.

'Very ingenious! And what about our friend Cust, caught

494

red-handed? What about the blood on his coat? And the knife he hid in his lodgings? He may deny he committed the crimes –'

Poirot interrupted.

'You are quite wrong. He admits the fact.'

'What?' Clarke looked really startled.

'Oh, yes,' said Poirot gently. 'I had no sooner spoken to him than I was aware that Cust *believed himself to be guilty.*'

'And even that didn't satisfy M. Poirot?' said Clarke.

'No. Because as soon as I saw him *I also knew that he could not be guilty*! He has neither the nerve nor the daring – nor, I may add, the *brains* to plan! All along I have been aware of the dual personality of the murderer. Now I see wherein it consisted. Two people were involved – the real murderer, cunning, resourceful and daring – and the *pseudo* murderer, stupid, vacillating and suggestible.

'Suggestible – it is in that word that the mystery of Mr Cust consists! It was not enough for you, Mr Clarke, to devise this plan of a *series* to distract attention from a *single* crime. You had also to have a stalking horse.

'I think the idea first originated in your mind as the result of a chance encounter in a city coffee den with this odd personality with his bombastic Christian names. You were at that time turning over in your mind various plans for the murder of your brother.'

'Really? And why?'

'Because you were seriously alarmed for the future. I do not know whether you realize it, Mr Clarke, but you played into my hands when you showed me a certain letter written to you by your brother. In it he displayed very clearly his affection and absorption in Miss Thora Grey. His regard may have been a paternal one – or he may have preferred to think it so. Nevertheless, there was a very real danger that on the death of your sister-in-law he might, in his loneliness, turn to this beautiful girl for sympathy and comfort and it might end – as so often happens with elderly men – in his marrying her. Your fear was increased by your knowledge of Miss Grey. You are, I fancy, an excellent, if somewhat cynical judge of character. You judged, whether correctly or not, that Miss Grey was a type of young woman "on the make". You had no doubt that she would jump at the chance of becoming Lady Clarke. Your brother was an extremely healthy and vigorous man. There might be children and your chance of inheriting your brother's wealth would vanish.

'You have been, I fancy, in essence a disappointed man all your life. You have been the rolling stone – and you have gathered very little moss. You were bitterly jealous of your brother's wealth.

'I repeat then that, turning over various schemes in your mind, your meeting with Mr Cust gave you an idea. His bombastic Christian names, his account of his epileptic seizures and of his headaches, his whole shrinking and insignificant personality, struck you as fitting him for the tool you wanted. The whole alphabetical plan sprang into your mind – Cust's initials – the fact that your brother's name began with a C and that he lived at Churston were the nucleus of the scheme. You even went so far as to hint to Cust at his possible end – though you could hardly hope that that suggestion would bear the rich fruit that it did!

'Your arrangements were excellent. In Cust's name you wrote for a large consignment of hosiery to be sent to him. You yourself sent a number of A B C's looking like a similar parcel. You wrote to him – a typed letter purporting to be from the same firm offering him a good salary and commission. Your plans were so well laid beforehand that you typed all the letters that were sent subsequently, *and then presented him with the machine on which they had been typed*.

'You had now to look about for two victims whose names began with A and B respectively and who lived at places also beginning with those same letters.

'You hit on Andover as quite a likely spot and your preliminary reconnaissance there led you to select Mrs Ascher's shop as the scene of the first crime. Her name was written clearly over the door, and you found by experiment that she was usually alone in the shop. Her murder needed nerve, daring and reasonable luck.

'For the letter B you had to vary your tactics. Lonely women in shops might conceivably have been warned. I should imagine that you frequented a few cafés and teashops, laughing and joking with the girls there and finding out whose name began with the right letter and who would be suitable for your purpose.

'In Betty Barnard you found just the type of girl you were looking for. You took her out once or twice, explaining to her that you were a married man, and that outings must therefore take place in a somewhat hole-and-corner manner.

'Then, your preliminary plans completed, you set to work! You sent the Andover list to Cust, directing him to go there on a certain date, and you sent off the first A B C letter to me.

'On the appointed day you went to Andover – and killed Mrs Ascher – without anything occurring to damage your plans.

'Murder No. 1 was successfully accomplished.

'For the second murder, you took the precaution of committing it, in reality, *the day before*. I am fairly certain that Betty Barnard was killed well before midnight on the 24th July.

'We now come to murder No 3 – the important – in fact, the *real* murder from your point of view.

'And here a full meed of praise is due to Hastings, who made a simple and obvious remark to which no attention was paid.

'*He suggested that the third letter went astray intentionally!*

'And he was right! . . .

'In that one simple fact lies the answer to the question that has puzzled me so all along. Why were the letters addressed in the first place to Hercule Poirot, a private detective, and not to the police?

'Erroneously I imagined some personal reason.

'Not at all! The letters were sent to me because the essence of your plan was that one of them *should be wrongly addressed and go astray* – but you cannot arrange for a letter addressed to the Criminal Investigation Department of Scotland Yard to go astray! It is necessary to have a *private* address. You chose me as a fairly well-known person, and a person who was sure to take the letters to the police – and also, in your rather insular mind, you enjoyed scoring off a foreigner.

'You addressed your envelope very cleverly – Whitehaven – Whitehorse – quite a natural slip. Only Hastings was sufficiently perspicacious to disregard subtleties and go straight for the obvious!

'Of course the letter was *meant* to go astray! The police were to be set on the trail *only when the murder was safely over*. Your brother's nightly walk provided you with the opportunity. And so successfully had the A B C terror taken hold on the public mind that the possibility of your guilt never occurred to anyone.

'After the death of your brother, of course, your object was accomplished. You had no wish to commit any more murders. On the other hand, if the murders stopped without reason, a suspicion of the truth might come to someone.

'Your stalking horse, Mr Cust, had so successfully lived up to his role of the invisible – because insignificant – man, that so far no one had noticed that the same person had been seen in the vicinity of the three murders! To your annoyance, even his visit to Combeside had not been mentioned. The matter had passed completely out of Miss Grey's head.

'Always daring, you decided that one more murder must take place but this time the trail must be well blazed.

'You selected Doncaster for the scene of operations.

'Your plan was very simple. You yourself would be on the scene in the nature of things. Mr Cust would be ordered to Doncaster by his firm. Your plan was to follow him round and trust to opportunity. Everything fell out well. Mr Cust went to a cinema. That was simplicity itself. You sat a few seats away from him. When he got up to go, you did the same. You pretended to stumble, leaned over and stabbed a dozing man in the row in front, slid the A B C on to his knees and managed to collide heavily with Mr Cust in the darkened doorway, wiping the knife on his sleeve and slipping it into his pocket.

'You were not in the least at pains to choose a victim whose name began with D. Anyone would do! You assumed – and quite rightly – that it would be considered to be a *mistake*. There was sure to be someone whose name began with D not far off in the audience. It would be assumed that he had been intended to be the victim.

'And now, my friends, let us consider the matter from the point of view of Mr Cust.

'The Andover crime means nothing to him. He is shocked and surprised by the Bexhill crime – why, he himself was there about the time! Then comes the Churston crime and the headlines in the newspapers. An A B C crime at Andover when he was there, an A B C crime at Bexhill, and now another close by . . . Three crimes *and he has been at the scene of each of them*. Persons suffering from epilepsy often have blanks when they cannot remember what they have done . . . Remember that Cust was a nervous, highly neurotic subject and extremely suggestible.

'Then he receives the order to go to Doncaster.

'Doncaster! And the next A B C crime is to be in Doncaster. He must have felt as though it was fate. He loses his nerve, fancies his landlady is looking at him suspiciously, and tells her he is going to Cheltenham.

'He goes to Doncaster because it is his duty. In the afternoon he goes to a cinema. Possibly he dozes off for a minute or two.

'Imagine his feelings when on his return to his inn he discovers *that there is blood on his coat sleeve and a blood-stained knife in his pocket*. All his vague forebodings leap into certainty.

'*He – he himself – is the killer!* He remembers his headaches – his lapses of memory. He is quite sure of the truth – *he, Alexander Bonaparte Cust, is a homicidal lunatic*.

'His conduct after that is the conduct of a hunted animal. He gets back to his lodgings in London. He is safe there – known. They think he has been in Cheltenham. He has the knife with him still – a thoroughly stupid thing to do, of course. He hides it behind the hall stand.

'Then, one day, he is warned that the police are coming. It is the end! They *know*!

'The hunted animal does his last run . . .

'I don't know why he went to Andover – a morbid desire, I think, to go and look at the place where the crime was committed – the crime *he* committed though he can remember nothing about it . . .

'He has no money left – he is worn out . . . his feet lead him of his own accord to the police station.

'But even a cornered beast will fight. Mr Cust fully believes that he did the murders but he sticks strongly to his plea of innocence. And he holds with desperation to that alibi for the second murder. At least that cannot be laid to his door.

'As I say, when I saw him, I knew at once that he was *not* the murderer and that my name *meant* nothing to *him*. I knew, too, that he *thought* himself the murderer!

'After he had confessed his guilt to me, I knew more strongly than ever that my own theory was right.'

'Your theory,' said Franklin Clarke, 'is absurd!'

Poirot shook his head.

'No, Mr Clarke. You were safe enough *so long as no one suspected you*. Once you *were* suspected proofs were easy to obtain.'

'Proofs?'

'Yes. I found the stick that you used in the Andover and Churston murders in a cupboard at Combeside. An ordinary stick with a thick knob handle. A section of wood had been removed and melted lead poured in. Your photograph was picked out from half a dozen others by two people who saw you leaving the cinema when you were supposed to be on the racecourse at Doncaster. You were identified at Bexhill the other day by Milly Higley and a girl from the Scarlet Runner Roadhouse, where you took Betty Barnard to dine on the fatal evening. And finally – most damning of all – you *overlooked a most elementary precaution*. You left a fingerprint on Cust's typewriter – the typewriter that, if you are innocent, you *could never have handled*.'

Clarke sat quite still for a minute, then he said:

'*Rouge, impair, manque!* – you win, M. Poirot! But it was worth trying!'

With an incredibly rapid motion he whipped out a small automatic from his pocket and held it to his head.

I gave a cry and involuntarily flinched as I waited for the report. But no report came – the hammer clicked harmlessly.

Clarke stared at it in astonishment and uttered an oath.

'No, Mr Clarke,' said Poirot. 'You may have noticed I had a new manservant today – a friend of mine – an expert sneak thief. He removed your pistol from your pocket, unloaded it, and returned it, all without you being aware of the fact.'

'You unutterable little jackanapes of a foreigner!' cried Clarke, purple with rage.

'Yes, yes, that is how you feel. No, Mr Clarke, no easy death for you. You told Mr Cust that you had had near escapes from drowning. You know what that means – that you were born for another fate.'

'You –'

Words failed him. His face was livid. His fists clenched menacingly.

Two detectives from Scotland Yard emerged from the next room. One of them was Crome. He advanced and uttered his time-honoured formula: 'I warn you that anything you say may be used as evidence.'

'He has said quite enough,' said Poirot, and he added to Clarke: 'You are very full of an insular superiority, but for myself I consider your crime not an English crime at all – not above-board – not *sporting* –'

CHAPTER THIRTY-FIVE

Finale

I am sorry to relate that as the door closed behind Franklin Clarke I laughed hysterically.

Poirot looked at me in mild surprise.

'It's because you told him his crime was not sporting,' I gasped.

'It was quite true. It was abominable – not so much the murder of his brother – but the cruelty that condemned an unfortunate man to a living death. *To catch a fox and put him in a box and never let him go!* That is not *le sport*!'

Megan Barnard gave a deep sigh.

'I can't believe it – I can't. Is it true?'

'Yes, mademoiselle. The nightmare is over.'

She looked at him and her colour deepened.

Poirot turned to Fraser.

'Mademoiselle Megan, all along, was haunted by a fear that it was you who had committed the second crime.'

Donald Fraser said quietly:

'I fancied so myself at one time.'

'Because of your dream?' He drew a little nearer to the young man and dropped his voice confidentially. 'Your dream has a very natural explanation. It is that you find that already the image of one sister fades in your memory and that its place is taken by the other sister. Mademoiselle Megan replaces her sister in your heart, but since you cannot bear to think of yourself being unfaithful so soon to the dead, you strive to stifle the thought, to kill it! That is the explanation of the dream.'

Fraser's eyes went towards Megan.

'Do not be afraid to forget,' said Poirot gently. 'She was not so well worth remembering. In Mademoiselle Megan you have one in a hundred – *un coeur magnifique*!'

Donald Fraser's eyes lit up.

'I believe you are right.'

We all crowded round Poirot asking questions, elucidating this point and that.

'Those questions, Poirot? That you asked of everybody. Was there any point in them?'

'Some of them were *simplement une blague*. But I learnt one thing that I wanted to know – *that Franklin Clarke was in London when the first letter was posted* – and also I wanted to see his face when I asked my question of Mademoiselle Thora. He was off his guard. I saw all the malice and anger in his eyes.'

'You hardly spared my feelings,' said Thora Grey.

'I do not fancy you returned me a truthful answer, mademoiselle,' said Poirot dryly. 'And now your second expectation is disappointed. Franklin Clarke will not inherit his brother's money.'

She flung up her head.

'Is there any need for me to stay here and be insulted?'

'None whatever,' said Poirot and held the door open politely for her.

'That fingerprint clinched things, Poirot,' I said thoughtfully. 'He went all to pieces when you mentioned that.'

'Yes, they are useful – fingerprints.'

He added thoughtfully:

'I put that in to please you, my friend.'

'But, Poirot,' I cried, 'wasn't it *true*?'

'Not in the least, *mon ami*,' said Hercule Poirot.

I must mention a visit we had from Mr Alexander Bonaparte Cust a few days later. After wringing Poirot's hand and endeavouring very incoherently and unsuccessfully to thank him, Mr Cust drew himself up and said:

'Do you know, a newspaper has actually offered me a hundred pounds – *a hundred pounds* – for a brief account of my life and history – I – I really don't know what to do about it.'

'I should not accept a hundred,' said Poirot. 'Be firm. Say five hundred is your price. And do not confine yourself to one newspaper.'

'Do you really think – that I might –'

'You must realize,' said Poirot, smiling, 'that you are a very famous man. Practically the most famous man in England today.'

Mr Cust drew himself up still further. A beam of delight irradiated his face.

'Do you know, I believe you're right! Famous! In all the papers. I shall take your advice, M. Poirot. The money will be most agreeable – most agreeable. I shall have a little holiday . . . And then I want to give a nice wedding present to Lily Marbury – a dear girl – really a dear girl, M. Poirot.'

Poirot patted him encouragingly on the shoulder.

502

'You are quite right. Enjoy yourself. And – just a little word – what about a visit to an oculist? Those headaches, it is probably that you want new glasses.'

'You think that it may have been that all the time?'

'I do.'

Mr Cust shook him warmly by the hand.

'You're a very great man, M. Poirot.'

Poirot, as usual, did not disdain the compliment. He did not even succeed in looking modest.

When Mr Cust had strutted importantly out, my old friend smiled across at me.

'So, Hastings – we went hunting once more, did we not? *Vive le sport.*'

One, Two, Buckle My Shoe

One, two, buckle my shoe,
Three, four, shut the door,
Five, six, picking up sticks,
Seven, eight, lay them straight,
Nine, ten, a good fat hen,
Eleven, twelve, men must delve,
Thirteen, fourteen, maids are courting,
Fifteen, sixteen, maids in the kitchen,
Seventeen, eighteen, maids in waiting,
Nineteen, twenty, my plate's empty. . . . .

ONE, TWO, BUCKLE MY SHOE

I

Mr Morley was not in the best of tempers at breakfast.

He complained of the bacon, wondered why the coffee had to have
the appearance of liquid mud, and remarked that breakfast cereals
were each one worse than the last.

Mr Morley was a small man with a decided jaw and a pugnacious
chin. His sister, who kept house for him, was a large woman rather
like a female grenadier. She eyed her brother thoughtfully and asked
whether the bath water had been cold again.

Rather grudgingly, Mr Morley said it had not.

He glanced at the paper and remarked that the Government
seemed to be passing from a state of incompetence to one of positive
imbecility!

Miss Morley said in a deep bass voice that it was Disgraceful!

As a mere woman she had always found whatever Government
happened to be in power distinctly useful. She urged her brother on
to explain *why* the Government's present policy was inconclusive,
idiotic, imbecile and frankly suicidal!

When Mr Morley had expressed himself fully on these points, he
had a second cup of the despised coffee and unburdened himself of
his true grievance.

'These girls,' he said, 'are all the same! Unreliable, self-centred –
not to be depended on in any way.'

Miss Morley said interrogatively:

'Gladys?'

'I've just had the message. Her aunt's had a stroke and she's had to
go down to Somerset.'

Miss Morley said:

'Very trying, dear, but after all hardly the girl's *fault*.'

Mr Morley shook his head gloomily.

'How do I know the aunt *has* had a stroke? How do I know the
whole thing hasn't been arranged between the girl and that very
unsuitable young fellow she goes about with? That young man is a
wrong 'un if I ever saw one! They've probably planned some outing
together for today.'

'Oh, no, dear, I don't think Gladys would do a thing like that. You
know, you've always found her very conscientious.'

'Yes, yes.'

509

'An intelligent girl and really keen on her work, you said.'

'Yes, yes, Georgina, but that was before this undesirable young man came along. She's been quite different lately – *quite* different – absent-minded – upset – nervy.'

The Grenadier produced a deep sigh. She said:

'After all, Henry, girls do fall in love. It can't be helped.'

Mr Morley snapped:

'She oughtn't to let it affect her efficiency as my secretary. And today, in particular, I'm extremely busy! Several *very* important patients. It is *most* trying!'

'I'm sure it must be extremely vexing, Henry. How is the new boy shaping, by the way?'

Henry Morley said gloomily:

'He's the worst I've had yet! Can't get a single name right and has the most uncouth manners. If he doesn't improve I shall sack him and try again. I don't know what's the good of our education nowadays. It seems to turn out a collection of nit-wits who can't understand a single thing you say to them, let alone remember it.'

He glanced at his watch.

'I must be getting along. A full morning, and that Sainsbury Seale woman to fit in somewhere as she is in pain. I suggested that she should see Reilly, but she wouldn't hear of it.'

'Of course not,' said Georgina loyally.

'Reilly's very able – very able indeed. First-class diplomas. Thoroughly up-to-date in his work.'

'His hand shakes,' said Miss Morley. 'In my opinion he *drinks*.'

Her brother laughed, his good temper restored. He said:

'I'll be up for a sandwich at half-past one as usual.'

II

At the Savoy Hotel Mr Amberiotis was picking his teeth with a toothpick and grinning to himself.

Everything was going very nicely.

He had had his usual luck. Fancy those few kind words of his to that idiotic hen of a woman being so richly repaid. Oh! well – *cast your bread upon the waters*. He had always been a kind-hearted man. *And* generous! In the future he would be able to be even more generous. Benevolent visions floated before his eyes. Little Dimitri . . . And the good Constantopopolus struggling with his little restaurant . . . What

510

pleasant surprises for them . . .

The toothpick probed unguardedly and Mr Amberiotis winced. Rosy visions of the future faded and gave way to apprehensions of the immediate future. He explored tenderly with this tongue. He took out his notebook. Twelve o'clock. 58, Queen Charlotte Street.

He tried to recapture his former exultant mood. But in vain. The horizon had shrunk to six bare words:

'58, Queen Charlotte Street. Twelve o'clock.'

III

At the Glengowrie Court Hotel, South Kensington, breakfast was over. In the lounge, Miss Sainsbury Seale was sitting talking to Mrs Bolitho. They occupied adjacent tables in the dining-room and had made friends the day after Miss Sainsbury Seale's arrival a week ago.

Miss Sainsbury Seale said:

'You know, dear, it really *has* stopped aching! Not a twinge! I think perhaps I'll ring up –'

Mrs Bolitho interrupted her.

'Now don't be foolish, my dear. You go to the dentist and *get it over*.'

Mrs Bolitho was a tall, commanding female with a deep voice. Miss Sainsbury Seale was a woman of forty odd with indecisively bleached hair rolled up in untidy curls. Her clothes were shapeless and rather artistic, and her pince-nez were always dropping off. She was a great talker.

She said now wistfully:

'But really, you know, it doesn't ache *at all*.'

'Nonsense, you told me you hardly slept a wink last night.'

'No, I didn't – no, indeed – but perhaps, *now*, the nerve has actually *died*.'

'All the more reason to go to the dentist,' said Mrs Bolitho firmly. 'We all like to put it off, but that's just cowardice. Better make up one's mind and *get it over*!'

Something hovered on Miss Sainsbury Seale's lips. Was it the rebellious murmur of: 'Yes, but it's not *your* tooth!'

All she actually said, however, was:

'I expect you're right. And Mr Morley is such a careful man and really never hurts one *at all*.'

IV

The meeting of the Board of Directors was over. It had passed off smoothly. The report was good. There should have been no discordant note. Yet to the sensitive Mr Samuel Rotherstein there had been *something*, some nuance in the chairman's manner.

There had been, once or twice, a shortness, an acerbity, in his tone – quite uncalled for by the proceedings.

Some secret worry, perhaps? But somehow Rotherstein could not connect a secret worry with Alistair Blunt. He was such a unemotional man. He was so very normal. So essentially British.

There was, of course, always liver ... Mr Rotherstein's liver gave him a bit of trouble from time to time. But he'd never known Alistair complain of his liver. Alistair's health was as sound as his brain and his grasp of finance. It was not annoying heartiness – just quiet well-being.

And yet – there was *something* – once or twice the chairman's hand had wandered to his face. He had sat supporting his chin. Not his normal attitude. And once or twice he had seemed actually – yes, *distrait*.

They came out of the board room and passed down the stairs.

Rotherstein said:

'Can't give you a lift, I suppose?'

Alistair Blunt smiled and shook his head.

'My car's waiting.' He glanced at his watch. 'I'm not going back to the city.' He paused. 'As a matter of fact I've got an appointment with the dentist.'

The mystery was solved.

V

Hercule Poirot descended from his taxi, paid the man and rang the bell of 58, Queen Charlotte Street.

After a little delay it was opened by a boy in page-boy's uniform with a freckled face, red hair, and an earnest manner.

Hercule Poirot said:

'Mr Morley?'

There was in his heart a ridiculous hope that Mr Morley might have been called away, might be indisposed, might not be seeing patients today ... All in vain. The page-boy drew back, Hercule

512

Poirot stepped inside, and the door closed behind him with the quiet remorselessness of unalterable doom.

The boy said: 'Name, please?'

Poirot gave it to him, a door on the right of the hall was thrown open and he stepped into the waiting-room.

It was a room furnished in quiet good taste and, to Hercule Poirot, indescribably gloomy. On the polished (reproduction) Sheraton table were carefully arranged papers and periodicals. The (reproduction) Hepplewhite sideboard held two Sheffield plated candlesticks and an *épergne*. The mantelpiece held a bronze clock and two bronze vases. The windows were shrouded by curtains of blue velvet. The chairs were upholstered in a Jacobean design of red birds and flowers.

In one of them sat a military-looking gentleman with a fierce moustache and a yellow complexion. He looked at Poirot with an air of one considering some noxious insect. It was not so much his gun he looked as though he wished he had with him, as his Flit spray. Poirot, eyeing him with distaste said to himself, 'In verity, there are some Englishmen who are altogether so unpleasing and ridiculous that they should have been put out of their misery at birth.'

The military gentleman, after a prolonged glare, snatched up *The Times*, turned his chair so as to avoid seeing Poirot, and settled down to read it.

Poirot picked up *Punch*.

He went through it meticulously, but failed to find any of the jokes funny.

The page-boy came in and said, 'Colonel Arrow-bumby?' – and the military gentleman was led away.

Poirot was speculating on the probabilities of there really being such a name, when the door opened to admit a young man of about thirty.

As the young man stood by the table, restlessly flicking over the covers of magazines, Poirot looked at him sideways. An unpleasant and dangerous looking young man, he thought, and not impossibly a murderer. At any rate he looked far more like a murderer than any of the murderers Hercule Poirot had arrested in the course of his career.

The page-boy opened the door and said to mid-air:

'Mr Peerer.'

Rightly construing this as a summons to himself, Poirot rose. The boy led him to the back of the hall and round the corner to a small lift in which he took him up to the second floor. Here he led him along a passage, opened a door which led into a little anteroom, tapped at a second door; and without waiting for a reply opened it and stood back for Poirot to enter.

Poirot entered to a sound of running water and came round the back of the door to discover Mr Morley washing his hands with professional gusto at a basin on the wall.

VI

There are certain humiliating moments in the lives of the greatest of men. It has been said that no man is a hero to his valet. To that may be added that few men are heroes to themselves at the moment of visiting their dentist.

Hercule Poirot was morbidly conscious of this fact.

He was a man who was accustomed to have a good opinion of himself. He was Hercule Poirot, superior in most ways to other men. But in this moment he was unable to feel superior in any way whatever. His morale was down to zero. He was just that ordinary, craven figure, a man afraid of the dentist's chair.

Mr Morley had finished his personal ablutions. He was speaking now in his encouraging professional manner.

'Hardly as warm as it should be, is it, for the time of year?'

Gently he led the way to the appointed spot – to The Chair! Deftly he played with its head rest, running it up and down.

Hercule Poirot took a deep breath, stepped up, sat down and relaxed his head to Mr Morley's professional fiddlings.

'There,' said Mr Morley with hideous cheerfulness. 'That quite comfortable? Sure?'

In sepulchral tones Poirot said that it was quite comfortable.

Mr Morley swung his little table nearer, picked up his little mirror, seized an instrument and prepared to get on with the job.

Hercule Poirot grasped the arms of the chair, shut his eyes and opened his mouth.

'Any special trouble?' Mr Morley inquired.

Slightly indistinctly, owing to the difficulty of forming consonants while keeping the mouth open, Hercule Poirot was understood to say that there was no special trouble. This was, indeed, the twice yearly overhaul that his sense of order and neatness demanded. It was, of course, possible that there might be nothing to do ... Mr Morley might, perhaps, overlook that second tooth from the back from

514

which those twinges had come . . . He *might* – but it was unlikely – for Mr Morley was a very good dentist.

Mr Morley passed slowly from tooth to tooth, tapping and probing, murmuring little comments as he did so.

'That filling is wearing down a little – nothing serious, though. Gums are in pretty good condition, I'm glad to see.' A pause at a suspect, a twist of the probe – no, on again, false alarm. He passed to the lower side. One, two – on to three? – No – 'The dog,' Hercule Poirot thought in confused idiom, 'has seen the rabbit!'

'A little trouble here. Not been giving you any pain? Hm, I'm surprised.' The probe went on.

Finally Mr Morley drew back, satisfied.

'Nothing very serious. Just a couple of fillings – and a trace of decay on that upper molar. We can get it all done, I think, this morning.'

He turned on a switch and there was a hum. Mr Morley unhooked the drill and fitted a needle to it with loving care.

'Guide me,' he said briefly, and started the dread work.

It was not necessary for Poirot to avail himself of this permission, to raise a hand, to wince, or even to yell. At exactly the right moment, Mr Morley stopped the drill, gave the brief command 'Rinse,' applied a little dressing, selected a new needle and continued. The ordeal of the drill was terror rather than pain.

Presently, while Mr Morley was preparing the filling, conversation was resumed.

'Have to do this myself this morning,' he explained. 'Miss Nevill has been called away. You remember Miss Nevill?'

Poirot untruthfully assented.

'Called away to the country by the illness of a relative. Sort of thing that *does* happen on a busy day. I'm behind-hand already this morning. The patient before you was late. Very vexing when that happens. It throws the whole morning out. Then I was to fit in an extra patient because she is in pain. I always allow a quarter of an hour in the morning in case that happens. Still, it adds to the rush.'

Mr Morley peered into his little mortar as he ground. Then he resumed his discourse.

'I'll tell you something that I've always noticed, M. Poirot. The big people – the important people – they're always on time – never keep you waiting. Royalty, for instance. Most punctilious. And these big City men are the same. Now this morning I've got a most important man coming – Alistair Blunt!'

Mr Morley spoke the name in a voice of triumph.

Poirot, prohibited from speech by several rolls of cotton wool and a glass tube that gurgled under his tongue, made an indeterminate noise.

Alistair Blunt! Those were the names that thrilled nowadays. Not Dukes, not Earls, not Prime Ministers. No, plain Mr Alistair Blunt. A man whose face was almost unknown to the general public – a man who only figured in an occasional quiet paragraph. Not a spectacular person.

Just a quiet nondescript Englishman who was the head of the greatest banking firm in England. A man of vast wealth. A man who said Yes and No to Governments. A man who lived a quiet, unobtrusive life and never appeared on a public platform or made speeches. Yet a man in whose hands lay supreme power.

Mr Morley's voice still held a reverent tone as he stood over Poirot ramming the filling home.

'Always comes to his appointment absolutely on time. Often sends his car away and walks back to his office. Nice, quiet unassuming fellow. Fond of golf and keen on his garden. You'd never dream he could buy up half Europe! Just like you and me.'

A momentary resentment rose in Poirot at this off-hand coupling of names. Mr Morley was a good dentist, yes, but there *were* other good dentists in London. There was only *one* Hercule Poirot.

'Rinse, please,' said Mr Morley.

'It's the answer, you know, to their Hitlers and Mussolinis and all the rest of them,' went on Mr Morley, as he proceeded to tooth number two. 'We don't make a fuss over here. Look how democratic our King and Queen are. Of course, a Frenchman like you, accustomed to the Republican idea –'

'I ah nah a Frahah – I ah – ah a Benyon.'

'Tchut – tchut –' said Mr Morley sadly. 'We must have the cavity completely dry.' He puffed hot air relentlessly on it.

Then he went on:

'I didn't realize you were a Belgian. Very interesting. Very fine man, King Leopold, so I've always heard. I'm a great believer in the tradition of Royalty myself. The training is good, you know. Look at the remarkable way they remember names and faces. All the result of training – though of course some people have a natural aptitude for that sort of thing. I, myself, for instance. I don't remember names, but it's remarkable the way I never forget a face. One of my patients the other day, for instance – I've seen that patient before. The name

516

meant nothing to me – but I said to myself at once, "Now where have I met you before?" I've not remembered yet – but it will come back to me – I'm sure of it. Just another rinse, please.'

The rinse accomplished, Mr Morley peered critically into his patient's mouth.

'Well, I think that seems all right. Just close – very gently ... Quite comfortable? You don't feel the filling at all? Open again, please. No, that seems quite all right.'

Hercule Poirot descended, a free man.

'Well, goodbye, M. Poirot. Not detected any criminals in my house, I hope?'

Poirot said with a smile:

'Before I came up, every one looked to me like a criminal! Now, perhaps, it will be different!'

'Ah, yes, a great deal of difference between before and after! All the same, we dentists aren't such devils now as we used to be! Shall I ring for the lift for you?'

'No, no, I will walk down.'

'As you like – the lift is just by the stairs.'

Poirot went out. He heard the taps start to run as he closed the door behind him.

He walked down the two flights of stairs. As he came to the last bend, he saw the Anglo-Indian Colonel being shown out. Not at all a bad-looking man, Poirot reflected mellowly. Probably a fine shot who had killed many a tiger. A useful man – a regular outpost of Empire.

He went into the waiting-room to fetch his hat and stick which he had left there. The restless young man was still there somewhat to Poirot's surprise. Another patient, a man, was reading the *Field*.

Poirot studied the young man in his newborn spirit of kindliness. He still looked very fierce – and as though he wanted to do a murder – but not really a murderer – thought Poirot kindly. Doubtless, presently, this young man would come tripping down the stairs, his ordeal over, happy and smiling and wishing no ill to any one.

The page-boy entered and said firmly and distinctly:

'Mr Blunt.'

The man at the table laid down the *Field* and got up. A man of middle height, of middle age, neither fat nor thin. Well dressed, quiet.

He went out after the boy.

One of the richest and most powerful men in England – but he still had to go to the dentist just like anybody else, and no doubt felt just the same as anybody else about it!

These reflections passing through his mind, Hercule Poirot picked up his hat and stick and went to the door. He glanced back as he did so, and the startled thought went through his mind that that young man must have very bad toothache indeed.

In the hall Poirot paused before the mirror there to adjust his moustaches, slightly disarranged as the result of Mr Morley's ministrations.

He had just completed their arrangement to his satisfaction when the lift came down again and the page-boy emerged from the back of the hall whistling discordantly. He broke off abruptly at the sight of Poirot and came to open the front door for him.

A taxi had just drawn up before the house and a foot was protruding from it. Poirot surveyed the foot with gallant interest.

A neat ankle, quite a good quality stocking. Not a bad foot. But he didn't like the shoe. A brand new patent leather shoe with a large gleaming buckle. He shook his head.

Not chic – very provincial!

The lady got out of the taxi, but in doing so she caught her other foot in the door and the buckle was wrenched off. It fell tinkling on to the pavement. Gallantly, Poirot sprang forward and picked it up, restoring it with a bow.

Alas! Nearer fifty than forty. Pince-nez. Untidy yellow-grey hair – unbecoming clothes – those depressing art greens! She thanked him, dropping her pince-nez, then her handbag.

Poirot, polite if no longer gallant, picked them up for her.

She went up the steps of 58, Queen Charlotte Street, and Poirot interrupted the taxi-driver's disgusted contemplation of a meagre tip.

'You are free, *hein?*'

The taxi-driver said gloomily: 'Oh, I'm *free*.'

'So am I,' said Hercule Poirot. 'Free of care!'

He saw the taxi-man's air of deep suspicion.

'No, my friend, I am not drunk. It is that I have been to the dentist and I need not go again for six months. It is a beautiful thought.'

I

It was a quarter to three when the telephone rang.

Hercule Poirot was sitting in an easy-chair happily digesting an excellent lunch.

He did not move when the bell rang but waited for the faithful George to come and take the call.

'*Eh bien?*' he said, as George, with a 'Just a minute, sir,' lowered the receiver.

'It's Chief Inspector Japp, sir.'

'Aha?'

Poirot lifted the receiver to his ear.

'*Eh bien, mon vieux,*' he said. 'How goes it?'

'That you, Poirot?'

'Naturally.'

'I hear you went to the dentist this morning? Is that so?'

Poirot murmured:

'Scotland Yard knows everything!'

'Man of the name of Morley. 58, Queen Charlotte Street?'

'Yes.' Poirot's voice had changed. 'Why?'

'It was a genuine visit, was it? I mean you didn't go to put the wind up him or anything of that sort?'

'Certainly not. I had three teeth filled if you want to know.'

'What did he seem like to you – manner much as usual?'

'I should say so, yes. Why?'

Japp's voice was rigidly unemotional.

'Because not very much later he shot himself.'

'What?'

Japp said sharply:

'That surprises you?'

'Frankly, it does.'

Japp said:

'I'm not too happy about it myself . . . I'd like to have a talk with you. I suppose you wouldn't like to come round?'

'Where are you?'

'Queen Charlotte Street.'

Poirot said:

'I will join you immediately.'

It was a police constable who opened the door of 58. He said respectfully:

'M. Poirot?'

'It's I, myself.'

'The Chief Inspector is upstairs. Second floor – you know it?'

Hercule Poirot said:

'I was there this morning.'

There were three men in the room. Japp looked up as Poirot entered.

He said:

'Glad to see you, Poirot. We're just going to move him. Like to see him first?'

A man with a camera who had been kneeling near the body got up. Poirot came forward. The body was lying near the fireplace.

In death Mr Morley looked very much as he had looked in life. There was a little blackened hole just below his right temple. A small pistol lay on the floor near his outflung right hand.

Poirot shook his head gently.

Japp said:

'All right, you can move him now.'

They took Mr Morley away. Japp and Poirot were left alone.

Japp said:

'We're through all the routine. Finger-prints, etc.'

Poirot sat down. He said:

'Tell me.'

Japp pursed his lips. He said:

'He *could* have shot himself. He probably *did* shoot himself. There are only his finger-prints on the gun – but I'm not quite satisfied.'

'What are your objections?'

'Well, to begin with, there doesn't seem to be any reason *why* he should shoot himself ... He was in good health, he was making money, he hadn't any worries that any one knew of. He wasn't mixed up with a woman – at least,' Japp corrected himself cautiously, 'as far as we know he wasn't. He hasn't been moody or depressed or unlike himself. That's partly why I was anxious to hear what *you* said. You saw him this morning, and I wondered if you'd noticed anything.'

Poirot shook his head.

'Nothing at all. He was – what shall I say – normality itself.'

'Then that makes it odd, doesn't it? Anyway, you wouldn't think a man would shoot himself in the middle of business hours, so to speak. Why not wait till this evening? That would be the natural thing to do.'

Poirot agreed.

'When did the tragedy occur?'

'Can't say exactly. Nobody seems to have heard the shot. But I don't think they would. There are two doors between here and the passage and they have baize fitted round the edges – to deaden the noise from the victims of the dental chair, I imagine.'

'Very probably. Patients under gas sometimes make a lot of noise.'

'Quite. And outside, in the street, there's plenty of traffic, so you wouldn't be likely to hear it out there.'

'When was it discovered?'

'Round about one-thirty – by the page-boy, Alfred Biggs. Not a very bright specimen, by all accounts. It seems that Morley's twelve-thirty patient kicked up a bit of a row at being kept waiting. About one-ten the boy came up and knocked. There was no answer and apparently he didn't dare come in. He'd got in a few rows already from Morley and he was nervous of doing the wrong thing. He went down again and the patient walked out in a huff at one-fifteen. I don't blame her. She'd been kept waiting three-quarters of an hour and she wanted her lunch.'

'Who was she?'

Japp grinned.

'According to the boy she was Miss Shirty – but from the appointment book her name was Kirby.'

'What system was there for showing up patients?'

'When Morley was ready for his next patient he pressed the buzzer over there and the boy then showed the patient up.'

'And Morley pressed the buzzer last?'

'At five minutes past twelve, and the boy showed up the patient who was waiting. Mr Amberiotis, Savoy Hotel, according to the appointment book.'

A faint smile came to Poirot's lips. He murmured:

'I wonder what our page-boy made of *that* name!'

'A pretty hash, I should say. We'll ask him presently if we feel like a laugh.'

Poirot said:

'And at what time did this Mr Amberiotis leave?'

'The boy didn't show him out, so he doesn't know ... A good many patients just go down the stairs without ringing for the lift and

521

let themselves out.'

Poirot nodded.

Japp went on:

'But I rang up the Savoy Hotel. Mr Amberiotis was quite precise. He said he looked at his watch as he closed the front door and it was then twenty-five minutes past twelve.'

'He could tell you nothing of importance?'

'No, all he could say was that the dentist had seemed perfectly normal and calm in his manner.'

'*Eh bien,*' said Poirot. 'Then that seemed quite clear. Between five-and-twenty past twelve and half-past one something happened – and presumably nearer the former time.'

'Quite. Because otherwise –'

'Otherwise he would have pressed the buzzer for the next patient.'

'Exactly. The medical evidence agrees with that for what it's worth. The divisional surgeon examined the body – at twenty past two. He wouldn't commit himself – they never do nowadays – too many individual idiosyncrasies, they say. But Morley couldn't have been shot *later* than one o'clock, he says – probably considerably earlier – but he wouldn't be definite.'

Poirot said thoughtfully:

'Then at twenty-five minutes past twelve our dentist is a normal dentist, cheerful, urbane, competent. And after that? Despair – misery – what you will – and he shoots himself?'

'It's funny,' said Japp. 'You've got to admit, it's funny.'

'Funny,' said Poirot, 'is not the word.'

'I know it isn't really – but it's the sort of thing one says. It's odd, then, if you like that better.'

'Was it his own pistol?'

'No, it wasn't. He hadn't got a pistol. Never had had one. According to his sister there wasn't such a thing in the house. There isn't in most houses. Of course he *might* have *bought* it if he'd made up his mind to do away with himself. If so, we'll soon know about it.'

Poirot asked:

'Is there anything else that worries you?'

Japp rubbed his nose.

'Well, there was the way he was lying. I wouldn't say a man *couldn't* fall like that – but it wasn't quite *right* somehow! And there was just a trace or two on the carpet – as though something had been dragged along it.'

'That, then, is decidedly suggestive.'

522

'Yes, unless it was that dratted boy. I've a feeling that *he* may have tried to move Morley when he found him. He denies it, of course, but then he was scared. He's that kind of young ass. The kind that's always putting their foot in it and getting cursed, and so they come to lie about things almost automatically.'

Poirot looked thoughtfully round the room.

At the wash-basin on the wall behind the door, at the tall filing cabinet on the other side of the door. At the dental chair and surrounding apparatus near the window, then along to the fireplace and back to where the body lay, there was a second door in the wall near the fireplace.

Japp had followed his glance. 'Just a small office through there.' He flung open the door.

It was as he had said, a small room, with a desk, a table with a spirit lamp and tea apparatus and some chairs. There was no other door.

'This is where his secretary worked,' explained Japp. 'Miss Nevill. It seems she's away today.'

His eyes met Poirot's. The latter said:

'He told me, I remember. That again – might be a point against suicide?'

'You mean she was *got* out of the way?'

Japp paused. He said:

'If it *wasn't* suicide, he was murdered. But why? That solution seems almost as unlikely as the other. He seems to have been a quiet inoffensive sort of chap. Who would want to murder him?'

Poirot said:

'Who *could* have murdered him?'

Japp said:

'The answer to that is – almost anybody! His sister could have come down from their flat above and shot him, one of the servants could have come in and shot him. His partner, Reilly, could have shot him. The boy Alfred could have shot him. One of the patients could have shot him.' He paused and said, '*And Amberiotis could have shot him* – easiest of the lot.'

Poirot nodded.

'But in that case – we have to find out why?'

'Exactly. You've come round again to the original problem. Why? Amberiotis is staying at the Savoy. Why does a rich Greek want to come and shoot an inoffensive dentist?'

'That's really going to be our stumbling block. *Motive!*'

Poirot shrugged his shoulders. He said:

'It would seem that death selected, most inartistically, the wrong man. The Mysterious Greek, the Rich Banker, the Famous Detective – how natural that one of *them* should be shot! For mysterious foreigners may be mixed up in espionage and rich bankers have connections who will benefit by their deaths and famous detectives may be dangerous to criminals.'

'Whereas poor old Morley wasn't dangerous to anybody,' observed Japp gloomily.

'I wonder.'

Japp whirled round on him.

'What's up your sleeve now?'

'Nothing. A chance remark.'

He repeated to Japp those few casual words of Mr Morley's about recognizing faces, and his mention of a patient.

Japp looked doubtful.

'It's possible, I suppose. But it's a bit far-fetched. It might have been someone who wanted their identity kept dark. You didn't notice any of the other patients this morning?'

Poirot murmured:

'I noticed in the waiting-room a young man who looked exactly like a murderer!'

Japp said, startled: 'What's that?'

Poirot smiled:

'*Mon cher*, it was upon my arrival here! I was nervous, fanciful – *enfin*, in a *mood*. Everything seemed sinister to me, the waiting-room, the patients, the very carpet on the stairs! Actually, I think the young man had very bad toothache. That was all!'

'I know what it can be,' said Japp. 'However, we'll check up on your murderer all the same. We'll check up on *everybody* whether it's suicide or not. I think the first thing is to have another talk with Miss Morley. I've only had a word or two. It was a shock to her, of course, but she's the kind that doesn't break down. We'll go and see her now.'

III

Tall and grim, Georgina Morley listened to what the two men had said and answered their questions. She said with emphasis:

'It's incredible to me – *quite* incredible – that my brother should have committed suicide!'

Poirot said:

'You realize the alternative, Mademoiselle?'

'You mean – murder.' She paused. Then she said slowly: 'It is true – that alternative seems nearly as impossible as the other.'

'But not *quite* as impossible?'

'No – because – oh, in the first case, you see, I am speaking of *something I know* – that is: my brother's state of mind. I *know* he had nothing on his mind – I *know* that there was no reason – no reason *at all* why he should take his own life!'

'You saw him this morning – before he started work?'

'At breakfast – yes.'

'And he was quite as usual – not upset in any way?'

'He was upset – but not in the way you mean. He was just annoyed!'

'What was that?'

'He had a busy morning in front of him, and his secretary and assistant had been called away.'

'That is Miss Nevill?'

'Yes.'

'What used she to do for him?'

'She did all his correspondence, of course, and kept the appointment book, and filed all the charts. She also saw to the sterilizing of the instruments and ground up his fillings and handed them to him when he was working.'

'Had she been with him long?'

'Three years. She is a very reliable girl and we are – were both very fond of her.'

Poirot said:

'She was called away owing to the illness of a relative, so your brother told me.'

'Yes, she got a telegram to say her aunt had had a stroke. She went off to Somerset by an early train.'

'And that was what annoyed your brother so much?'

'Ye-es.' There was a faint hesitation in Miss Morley's answer. She went on rather hurriedly. 'You – you mustn't think my brother unfeeling. It was only that he thought – just for a moment –'

'Yes, Miss Morley?'

'Well, that she might have played truant on purpose. Oh! Please don't misunderstand me – I'm quite certain that Gladys would *never* do such a thing. I told Henry so. But the fact of the matter is, that she has got herself engaged to rather an unsuitable young man – Henry was very vexed about it – and it occurred to him that this young man *might* have persuaded her to take a day off.'

'Was that likely?'

'No, I'm sure it wasn't. Gladys is a very conscientious girl.'

'But it is the sort of thing the young man might have suggested?'

Miss Morley sniffed.

'Quite likely, I should say.'

'What does he do, this young fellow – what is his name, by the way?'

'Carter, Frank Carter. He is – or was – an insurance clerk, I believe. He lost his job some weeks ago and doesn't seem able to get another. Henry said – and I dare say he was right – that he is a complete rotter. Gladys had actually lent him some of her savings and Henry was very annoyed about it.'

Japp said sharply:

'Did your brother try to persuade her to break her engagement?'

'Yes, he did, I know.'

'Then this Frank Carter would, quite possibly, have a grudge against your brother.'

The Grenadier said robustly:

'Nonsense – that is if you are suggesting that Frank Carter shot Henry. Henry advised the girl against young Carter, certainly; but she didn't take his advice – she is foolishly devoted to Frank.'

'Is there any one else you can think of who had a grudge against your brother?'

Miss Morley shook her head.

'Did he get on well with his partner, Mr Reilly?'

Miss Morley replied acidly:

'As well as you can ever hope to get on with an Irishman!'

'What do you mean by that, Miss Morley?'

'Well, Irishmen have hot tempers and they thoroughly enjoy a row of any kind. Mr Reilly liked arguing about politics.'

'That was all?'

'That was all. Mr Reilly is unsatisfactory in many ways, but he was very skilled in his profession – or so my brother said.'

Japp persisted:

'How is he unsatisfactory?'

Miss Morley hesitated, then said acidly:

'He drinks too much – but please don't let that go any further.'

'Was there any trouble between him and your brother on that subject?'

'Henry gave him one or two hints. In dentistry,' continued Miss Morley didactically, 'a steady hand is needed, and an alcoholic breath does *not* inspire confidence.'

Japp bowed his head in agreement. Then he said:

'Can you tell us anything of your brother's financial position?'

'Henry was making a good income and he had a certain amount put by. We each had a small private income of our own left to us by our father.'

Japp murmured with a slight cough:

'You don't know, I suppose, if your brother left a will?'

'He did – and I can tell you its contents. He left a hundred pounds to Gladys Nevill, otherwise everything comes to me.'

'I see. Now –'

There was a fierce thump on the door. Alfred's face then appeared round it. His goggling eyes took in each detail of the two visitors as he ejaculated:

'It's Miss Nevill. She's back – and in a rare taking. Shall she come in, she wants to know?'

Japp nodded and Miss Morley said:

'Tell her to come here, Alfred.'

'O.K.,' said Alfred, and disappeared. Miss Morley said with a sigh and in obvious capital letters:

'That Boy is a Sad Trial.'

IV

Gladys Nevill was a tall, fair, somewhat anæmic girl of about twenty-eight. Though obviously very upset, she at once showed that she was capable and intelligent.

Under the pretext of looking through Mr Morley's papers, Japp got her away from Miss Morley down to the little office next door to the surgery.

She repeated more than once:

'I simply *cannot* believe it! It seems quite incredible that Mr Morley should do such a thing!'

She was emphatic that he had not seemed troubled or worried in any way.

Then Japp began:

'You were called away today, Miss Nevill –'

She interrupted him.

527

'Yes, and the whole thing was a wicked practical joke! I do think it's awful of people to do things like that. I really do.'

'What do you mean, Miss Nevill?'

'Why, there wasn't anything the matter with Aunt at all. She'd never been better. She couldn't understand it when I suddenly turned up. Of course I was ever so glad – but it did make me mad. Sending a telegram like that and upsetting me and everything.'

'Have you got that telegram, Miss Nevill?'

'I threw it away, I think, at the station. It just said, *Your aunt had a stroke last night. Please come at once.*'

'You are quite sure – well –' Japp coughed delicately – 'that it wasn't your friend, Mr Carter, who sent the telegram?'

'Frank? Whatever for? Oh! I see, you mean – a put-up job between us? No, indeed, Inspector – neither of us would do such a thing.'

Her indignation seemed genuine enough and Japp had a little trouble in soothing her down. But a question as to the patients on this particular morning restored her to her competent self.

'They are all here in the book. I dare say you have seen it already. I know about most of them. Ten o'clock, Miss Soames – that was about her new plate. Ten-thirty, Lady Grant – she's an elderly lady – lives in Lowndes Square. Eleven o'clock, M. Hercule Poirot, he comes regularly – oh, of courst this *is* him – sorry, M. Poirot, but I really am *so* upset! Eleven-thirty, Mr Alistair Blunt – that's the banker, you know – a short appointment, because Mr Morley had prepared the filling last time. Then Miss Sainsbury Seale – she rang up specially – had toothache and so Mr Morley fitted her in. A terrible talker, she is, never stops – the fussy kind, too. Then twelve o'clock, Mr Amberiotis – he was a new patient – made an appointment from the Savoy Hotel. Mr Morley gets quite a lot of foreigners and Americans. Then twelve-thirty, Miss Kirby. She comes up from Worthing.'

Poirot asked:

'There was here when I arrived a tall military gentleman. Who would he be?'

'One of Mr Reilly's patients, I expect. I'll just get his list for you, shall I?'

'Thank you, Miss Nevill.'

She was absent only a few minutes. She returned with a similar book to that of Mr Morley.

She read out:

'Ten o'clock, Betty Heath (that's a little girl of nine). Eleven o'clock, Colonel Abercrombie.'

'Abercrombie!' murmured Poirot. *'C'etait ça!'*

'Eleven thirty, Mr Howard Raikes. Twelve o'clock, Mr Barnes.'

'That was all the patients this morning. Mr Reilly isn't so booked up as Mr Morley, of course.'

'Can you tell us anything about any of these patients of Mr Reilly's?'

'Colonel Abercrombie has been a patient for a long time, and all Mrs Heath's children come to Mr Reilly. I can't tell you anything about Mr Raikes or Mr Barnes, though I fancy I have heard their names. I take all the telephone calls, you see –'

Japp said:

'We can ask Mr Reilly ourselves. I should like to see him as soon as possible.'

Miss Nevill went out. Japp said to Poirot:

'All old patients of Mr Morley's *except Amberiotis*. I'm going to have an interesting talk with Mr Amberiotis presently. He's the last person, as it stands, to see Morley alive, and we've got to make quite sure that when he last saw him, Morley *was* alive.'

Poirot said slowly, shaking his head.

'You have still to prove motive.'

'I know. That's what is going to be the teaser. But we may have something about Amberiotis at the Yard.' He added sharply: 'You're very thoughtful, Poirot!'

'I was wondering about something.'

'What was it?'

Poirot said with a faint smile:

'Why Chief Inspector Japp?'

'Eh?'

'I said, "Why Chief Inspector Japp?" An officer of your eminence – is he usually called in to a case of suicide?'

'As a matter of fact, I happened to be nearby at the time. At Lavenham's – in Wigmore Street. Rather an ingenious system of frauds they've had there. They telephoned me there to come on here.'

'But *why* did they telephone you?'

'Oh, that – that's simple enough. Alistair Blunt. As soon as the Divisional Inspector heard *he'd* been here this morning, he got on to the Yard. Mr Blunt is the kind of person we take care of in this country.'

'You mean that there are people who would like him – out of the way?'

'You bet there are. The Reds, to begin with – and our Blackshirted friends, too. It's Blunt and his group who are standing solid behind the present Government. Good sound Conservative finance. That's why, if there were the least chance that there was any funny stuff intended against him this morning, they wanted a thorough investigation.'

Poirot nodded.

'That is what I more or less guessed. And that is the feeling I have' – he waved his hands expressively – 'that there was, perhaps – a *hitch* of some kind. The proper victim was – should have been – Alistair Blunt. Or is this only a beginning – the beginning of a campaign of some kind? I smell – I smell' he sniffed the air, '– big money in this business!'

Japp said:

'You're assuming a lot, you know.'

'I am suggesting that *ce pauvre* Morley was only a pawn in the game. Perhaps he knew something – perhaps he told Blunt something – or they feared he *would* tell Blunt something –'

'He stopped as Gladys Nevill entered the room.

'Mr Reilly is busy on an extraction case,' she said. 'He will be free in about ten minutes if that will be all right?'

Japp said that it would. In the meantime, he said, he would have another talk to the boy Alfred.

v

Alfred was divided between nervousnss, enjoyment, and a morbid fear of being blamed for everything that had occurred! He had only been a fortnight in Mr Morley's employment, and during that fortnight he had consistently and unvaryingly done everything wrong. Persistent blame had sapped his self-confidence.

'He was a bit rattier than usual, perhaps,' said Alfred in answer to a question, 'nothing else as I can remember. I'd never have thought he was going to do himself in.'

Poirot interposed.

'You must tell us,' he said, 'everything that you can remember about this morning. You are a very important witness, and your recollections may be of immense service to us.'

Alfred's face was suffused by vivid crimson and his chest swelled.

He had already given Japp a brief account of the morning's happenings. He proposed now to spread himself. A comforting sense of importance oozed into him.

'I can tell you orl right,' he said. 'Just you ask me.'

'To begin with, did anything out of the way happen this morning?'

Alfred reflected a minute and then said rather sadly: 'Can't say as it did. It was orl just as usual.'

'Did any strangers come to the house?'

'No, sir.'

'Not even among the patients?'

'I didn't know as you meant the patients. Nobody come what hadn't got an appointment, if that's what you mean. They were all down in the book.'

Japp nodded. Poirot asked:

'Could anybody have walked in from outside?'

'No, they couldn't. They'd have to have a key, see?'

'But it was quite easy to leave the house?'

'Oh, yes, just turn the handle and go out and pull the door to after you. As I was saying most of 'em do. They often come down the stairs while I'm taking up the next party in the lift, see?'

'I see. Now just tell us who came first this morning and so on. Describe them if you can't remember their names.'

Alfred reflected a minute. Then he said: 'Lady with a little girl, that was for Mr Reilly and a Mrs Soap or some such name for Mr Morley.'

Poirot said:

'Quite right. Go on.'

'Then another elderly lady – bit of a toff she was – came in a Daimler. As she went out a tall military gent come in, and just after him, *you* came,' he nodded to Poirot.

'Right.'

'Then the American gent came –'.

Japp said sharply:

'American?'

'Yes, sir. Young fellow. He was American all right – you could tell by his voice. Come early, he did. His appointment wasn't till eleven-thirty – and what's more he didn't keep it – neither.'

Japp said sharply:

'What's that?'

'Not him. Come in for him when Mr Reilly's buzzer went at eleven-thirty – a bit later it was, as a matter of fact, might have been

531

twenty to twelve – and he wasn't there. Must have funked it and gone away.' He added with a knowledgeable air. 'They do sometimes.'

Poirot said:

'Then he might have gone out soon after me?'

'That's right, sir. You went out after I'd taken up a toff what come in a Rolls. Coo – it was a loverly car, Mr Blunt – eleven-thirty. Then I come down and let you out, and a lady in. Miss Some Berry Seal, or something like that – and then I – well, as a matter of fact I just nipped down to the kitchen to get my elevenses, and when I was down there the buzzer went – Mr Reilly's buzzer – so I came up and as I say, the American gentleman had hooked it. I went and told Mr Reilly and he swore a bit, as is his way.'

Poirot said:

'Continue.'

'Lemme see, what happened next? Oh, yes, Mr Morley's buzzer went for that Miss Seal, and the toff came down and went out as I took Miss Whatsername up in the lift. Then I came down again and two gentlemen came – one a little man with a funny squeaky voice – I can't remember his name. For Mr Reilly, he was. And a fat foreign gentleman for Mr Morley.

'Miss Seal wasn't very long – not above a quarter of an hour. I let her out and then I took up the foreign gentleman. I'd already taken the other gent into Mr Reilly right away as soon as he came.'

Japp said:

'And you didn't see Mr Amberiotis, the foreign gentleman, leave?'

'No, sir, I can't say as I did. He must have let himself out. I didn't see either of those two gentlemen go.'

'Where were you from twelve o'clock onwards?'

'I always sit in the lift, sir, waiting until the front-door bell or one of the buzzers goes.'

Poirot said:

'And you were perhaps reading?'

Alfred blushed again.

'There ain't no harm in that, sir. It's not as though I could be doing anything else.'

'Quite so. What were you reading?'

'*Death at Eleven-Forty-Five*, sir. It's an American detective story. It's a corker, sir, it really is! And about gunmen.'

Poirot smiled faintly. He said:

'Would you hear the front door close from where you were?'

'You mean any one going out? I don't think I should, sir. What I mean is I shouldn't *notice* it! You see, the lift is right at the back of the hall and a little round the corner. The bell rings just behind it, and the buzzers too. You can't miss *them*.'

Poirot nodded and Japp asked:

'What happened next?'

Alfred frowned in a supreme effort of memory.

'Only the last lady, Miss Shirty. I waited for Mr Morley's buzzer to go, but nothing happened and at one o'clock the lady who was waiting, she got rather ratty.'

'It did not occur to you to go up before and see if Mr Morley was ready?'

Alfred shook his head very positively.

'Not me, sir. I wouldn't have dreamed of it. For all I knew the last gentleman was still up there. I'd got to wait for the buzzer. Of course if I'd knowed as Mr Morley had done himself in –'

Alfred shook his head with morbid relish.

Poirot asked:

'Did the buzzer usually go before the patient came down, or the other way about?'

'Depends. Usually the patient would come down the stairs and then the buzzer would go. If they rang for the lift, that buzzer would go perhaps as I was bringing them down. But it wasn't fixed in anyway. Sometimes Mr Morley would be a few minutes before he rang for the next patient. If he was in a hurry, he'd ring as soon as they were out of the room.'

'I see –' Poirot paused and then went on:

'Were you surprised at Mr Morley's suicide, Alfred?'

'Knocked all of a heap, I was. He hadn't no call to go doing himself in as far as *I* can see – oh!' Alfred's eyes grew large and round. 'Oo – er – he wasn't *murdered*, was he?'

Poirot cut in before Japp could speak.

'Supposing he were, would it surprise you less?'

'Well, I don't know, sir, I'm sure. I can't see who'd want to murder Mr Morley. He was – well, he was a very *ordinary* gentleman, sir. Was he *really* murdered, sir?'

Poirot said gravely:

'We have to take every possibility into account. That is why I told you you would be a very important witness and that you must try and recollect everything that happened this morning.'

He stressed the words and Alfred frowned with a prodigious effort of memory.

'I can't think of anything else, sir. I can't indeed.'

Alfred's tone was rueful.

Very good, Alfred. And you are quite sure no one except patients came to the house this morning?'

'No *stranger* did, sir. That Miss Nevill's young man came round – and in a rare taking not to find her here.'

Japp said sharply:

'When was that?'

'Some time after twelve it was. When I told him Miss Nevill was away for the day, he seemed very put out and he said he'd wait and see Mr Morley. I told him Mr Morley was busy right up to lunch time, but he said: Never mind, he'd wait.'

Poirot asked:

'And did he wait?'

A startled look came into Alfred's eyes. He said:

'Cor – I never thought of that! He went into the waiting-room, *but he wasn't there later*. He must have got tired of waiting, and thought he'd come back another time.'

VI

When Alfred had gone out of the room, Japp said sharply:

'D'you think it wise to suggest murder to that lad?'

Poirot shrugged his shoulders.

'I think so – yes. Anything suggestive that he *may* have seen or heard will come back to him under the stimulus, and he will be keenly alert to everything that goes on here.'

'All the same, we don't want it to get about too soon.'

'*Mon cher*, it will not. Alfred reads detective stories – Alfred is enamoured of crime. Whatever Alfred lets slip will be put down to Alfred's morbid criminal imagination.'

'Well, perhaps you are right, Poirot. Now we've got to hear what Reilly has to say.'

Mr Reilly's surgery and office were on the first floor. They were as spacious as the ones above but had less light in them, and were not quite so richly appointed.

Mr Morley's partner was a tall, dark young man, with a plume of hair that fell untidily over his forehead. He had an attractive voice and a very shrewd eye.

'We're hoping, Mr Reilly,' said Japp, after introducing himself,

534

'that you can throw some light on this matter.'

'You're wrong then, because I can't,' replied the other. 'I'd say this – that Henry Morley was the last person to go taking his own life. *I* might have done it – but *he* wouldn't.'

'Why might you have done it?' asked Poirot.

'Because I've oceans of worries,' replied the other. 'Money troubles, for one! I've never yet been able to suit my expenditure to my income. But Morley was a careful man. You'll find no debts, nor money troubles, I'm sure of that.'

'Love affairs?' suggested Japp.

'Is it Morley you mean? He had no joy of living at all! Right under his sister's thumb he was, poor man.'

Japp went on to ask Reilly details about the patients he had seen that morning.

'Oh, I fancy they're all square and above-board. Little Betty Heath, she's a nice child – I've had the whole family one after another. Colonel Abercrombie's an old patient too.'

'What about Mr Howard Raikes?' asked Japp.

Reilly grinned broadly.

'The one who walked out on me? He's never been to me before. I know nothing about him. He rang up and particularly asked for an appointment this morning.'

'Where did he ring up from?'

'Holborn Palace Hotel. He's an American, I fancy.'

'So Alfred said.'

'Alfred should know,' said Mr Reilly. 'He's a film fan, our Alfred.'

'And your other patient?'

'Barnes? A funny precise little man. Retired Civil Servant. Lives out Ealing way.'

Japp paused a minute and then said:

'What can you tell us about Miss Nevill?'

Mr Reilly raised his eyebrows.

'The bee-yewtiful blonde secretary? Nothing doing, old boy! Her relations with old Morley were perfectly pewer – I'm sure of it.'

'I never suggested they weren't,' said Japp, reddening slightly.

'My fault,' said Reilly. 'Excuse me filthy mind, won't you? I thought it might be an attempt on your part to *cherchez la femme*.

'Excuse me for speaking your language,' he added parenthetically to Poirot. 'Beautiful accent, haven't I? It comes of being educated by nuns.'

Japp disapproved of this flippancy. He asked.

'Do you know anything about the young man she is engaged to? His name is Carter, I understand. Frank Carter.'

'Morley didn't think much of him,' said Reilly. 'He tried to get la Nevill to turn him down.'

'That might have annoyed Carter?'

'Probably annoyed him frightfully,' agreed Mr Reilly cheerfully. He paused and then added:

'Excuse me, this *is* a suicide you are investigating, not a murder?'

Japp said sharply:

'If it were a murder, would you have anything to suggest?'

'Not I! I'd like it to be Georgina! One of those grim females with temperance on the brain. But I'm afraid Georgina is full of moral rectitude. Of course I could easily have nipped upstairs and shot the old boy myself, but I didn't. In fact, I can't imagine *any one* wanting to kill Morley. But then I can't conceive of his killing himself.'

He added – in a different voice:

'As a matter of fact, I'm very sorry about it . . . You mustn't judge by my manner. That's just nervousness, you know. I was fond of old Morley and I shall miss him.'

VII

Japp put down the telephone receiver. His face, as he turned to Poirot, was rather grim.

He said:

'Mr Amberiotis isn't feeling very well – would rather not see any one this afternoon.

'He's going to see me – *and* he's not going to give me the slip either! I've got a man at the Savoy ready to trail him if he tries to make a get-away.'

Poirot said thoughtfully:

'You think Amberiotis shot Morley?'

'I don't know. *But he was the last person to see Morley alive.* And he was a new patient. According to *his* story, he left Morley alive and well at twenty-five minutes past twelve. That may be true or it may not. If Morley *was* all right then we've got to reconstruct what happened next. *There was still five minutes to go before his next appointment.* Did someone come in and see him during that five minutes? Carter, say? Or Reilly? What happened? Depend upon it, by half-past twelve, or five-and-twenty to one at the latest, *Morley*

536

was dead – otherwise he'd either have sounded his buzzer or else sent down word to Miss Kirby that he couldn't see her. No, either he was killed, or else somebody told him something which upset the whole tenor of his mind, and he took his own life.'

He paused.

'I'm going to have a word with every patient he saw this morning. There's just the possibility that he *may* have said something to one of them that will put us on the right track.'

He glanced at his watch.

'Mr Alistair Blunt said he could give me a few minutes at four-fifteen. We'll go to him first. His house is on Chelsea Embankment. Then we might take the Sainsbury Seale woman on our way to Amberiotis. I'd prefer to know all we can before tackling our Greek friend. After that, I'd like a word or two with the American who, according to you "looked like murder".'

Hercule Poirot shook his head.

'Not murder – toothache.'

'All the same, we'll see this Mr Raikes. His conduct was queer to say the least of it. And we'll check up on Miss Nevill's telegram *and* on her aunt *and* on her young man. In fact, we'll check up on everything and everybody!'

VIII

Alistair Blunt had never loomed large in the public eye. Possibly because he was himself a very quiet and retiring man. Possibly because for many years he had functioned as a Prince Consort rather than as a King.

Rebecca Sanseverato, *née* Arnholt, came to London a disillusioned woman of forty-five. On either side she came of the Royalty of wealth. Her mother was an heiress of the European family of Rothersteins. Her father was the head of the great American banking house of Arnholt. Rebecca Arnholt, owing to the calamitous deaths of two brothers and a cousin in an air accident, was sole heiress to immense wealth. She married a European aristocrat with a famous name, Prince Felipe di Sanseverato. Three years later she obtained a divorce and custody of the child of the marriage, having spent two years of wretchedness with a well-bred scoundrel whose conduct was notorious. A few years later her child died.

Embittered by her sufferings, Rebecca Arnholt turned her

537

undoubted brains to the business of finance – the aptitude for it ran in her blood. She associated herself with her father in banking.

After his death she continued to be a powerful figure in the financial world with her immense holdings. She came to London – and a junior partner of the London house was sent to Claridge's to see her with various documents. Six months later the world was electrified to hear that Rebecca Sanseverato was marrying Alistair Blunt, a man nearly twenty years younger than herself.

There were the usual jeers – and smiles. Rebecca, her friends said, was really an incurable fool where men were concerned! First Sanseverato – now this young man. Of course he was only marrying her for her money. She was in for a second disaster! But to everyone's surprise the marriage was a success. The people who prophesied that Alistair Blunt would spend her money on other women were wrong. He remained quietly devoted to his wife. Even after her death, ten years later, when as inheritor of her vast wealth he might have been supposed to cut loose, he did not marry again. He lived the same quiet and simple life. His genius for finance had been no less than his wife's. His judgements and dealings were sound – his integrity above question. He dominated the vast Arnholt and Rotherstein interests by his sheer ability.

He went very little into society, had a house in Kent and one in Norfolk where he spent week-ends – not with gay parties, but with a few quiet stodgy friends. He was fond of golf and played moderately well. He was interested in his garden.

This was the man towards whom Chief Inspéctor Japp and Hercule Poirot were bouncing along in a somewhat elderly taxi.

The Gothic House was a well-known feature on Chelsea Embankment. Inside it was luxurious with an expensive simplicity. It was not very modern but it was eminently comfortable.

Alistair Blunt did not keep them waiting. He came to them almost at once.

'Chief Inspector Japp?'

Japp came forward and introduced Hercule Poirot. Blunt looked at him with interest.

'I know your name, of course, M. Poirot. And surely – somewhere – quite recently –' he paused, frowning.

Poirot said:

'This morning, Monsieur, in the waiting-room of *ce pauvre M. Morley.*'

Alistair Blunt's brow cleared. He said:

'Of course. I knew I had seen you somewhere.' He turned to Japp. 'What can I do for you? I am extremely sorry to hear about poor Morley.'

'You were surprised, Mr Blunt?'

'Very surprised. Of course I knew very little about him, but I should have thought him a most unlikely person to commit suicide.'

'He seemed in good health and spirits then, this morning?'

'I think so – yes.' Alistair Blunt paused, then said with an almost boyish smile: 'To tell you the truth. I'm a most awful coward about going to the dentist. And I simply hate that beastly drill thing they run into you. That's why I really didn't notice anything much. Not till it was over, you know, and I got up to go. But I must say Morley seemed perfectly natural then. Cheerful and busy.'

'You have been to him often?'

'I think this was my third or fourth visit. I've never had much trouble with my teeth until the last year. Breaking up, I suppose.'

Hercule Poirot asked:

'Who recommended Mr Morley to you originally?'

Blunt drew his brows together in an effort of concentration.

'Let me see now – I had a twinge – somebody told me Morley of Queen Charlotte Street was the man to go to – no, I can't for the life of me remember who it was. Sorry.'

Poirot said:

'If it should come back to you, perhaps you will let one of us know?'

Alistair Blunt looked at him curiously.

He said:

'I will – certainly. Why? Does it matter?'

'I have an idea,' said Poirot, 'that it might matter very much.'

They were going down the steps of the house when a car drew up in front of it. It was a car of sporting build – one of those cars from which it is necessary to wriggle from under the wheel in sections.

The young woman who did so appeared to consist chiefly of arms and legs. She had finally dislodged herself as the men turned to walk down the street.

The girl stood on the pavement looking after them. Then, suddenly and vigorously, she ejaculated, 'Hi!'

Not realizing that the call was addressed to them, neither man turned, and the girl repeated: 'Hi! Hi! You there!'

They stopped and looked round inquiringly. The girl walked towards them. The impression of arms and legs remained. She was tall, thin, and her face had an intelligence and aliveness that redeemed its lack of actual beauty. She was dark with a deeply tanned skin.

She was addressing Poirot:

'I know who *you* are – you're the detective man, Hercule Poirot!' Her voice was warm and deep, with a trace of American accent.

Poirot said:

'At your service, Mademoiselle.'

Her eyes went on to his companion.

Poirot said:

'Chief Inspector Japp.'

Her eyes widened – almost it seemed with alarm. She said, and there was a slight breathlessness in her voice:

'What have you been doing here? Nothing – nothing has happened to Uncle Alistair, has it?'

Poirot said quickly:

'Why should you think so, Mademoiselle?'

'It hasn't? Good.'

Japp took up Poirot's question.

'Why should you think anything had happened to Mr Blunt, Miss –'

He paused inquiringly.

The girl said mechanically:

'Olivera. Jane Olivera.' Then she gave a slight and rather unconvincing laugh. 'Sleuths on the doorstep rather suggest bombs in the attic, don't they?'

'There's nothing wrong with Mr Blunt, I'm thankful to say, Miss Olivera.'

She looked directly at Poirot.

'Did he call you in about something?'

Japp said:

'*We* called on *him*, Miss Olivera, to see if he could throw any light on a case of suicide that occurred this morning.'

She said sharply:

'Suicide? Whose? Where?'

'A Mr Morley, a dentist, of 58, Queen Charlotte Street.'

'Oh!' said Jane Olivera blankly. 'Oh! –' She stared ahead of her, frowning. Then she said unexpectedly:

'Oh, but that's absurd!' And turning on her heel she left them abruptly, and without ceremony, running up the steps of the Gothic House and letting herself in with a key.

'Well!' said Japp staring after her, 'that's an extraordinary thing to say.'

'Interesting,' observed Poirot mildly.

Japp pulled himself together, glanced at his watch and hailed an approaching taxi.

'We'll have time to take the Sainsbury Seale on our way to the Savoy.'

IX

Miss Sainsbury Seale was in the dimly lit lounge of the Glengowrie Court Hotel having tea.

She was flustered by the appearance of a police officer in plain clothes – but her excitement was of a pleasurable nature, he observed. Poirot noticed, with sorrow, that she had not yet sewn the buckle on her shoe.

'Really, officer,' fluted Miss Sainsbury Seale, glancing round, 'I really don't know where we could go to be private. So difficult – just tea-time – but perhaps you would care for some tea – and – and your friend –'

'Not for me, Madam,' said Japp. 'This is M. Hercule Poirot.'

'Really?' said Miss Sainsbury Seale, 'then perhaps – you're sure – you won't either of you have tea? No. Well, perhaps we might try the drawing-room, though that's very often full – Oh, I see, there is a corner over there – in the recess. The people are just leaving. Shall we go there –'

She led the way to the comparative seclusion of a sofa and two chairs in an alcove. Poirot and Japp followed her, the former picking up a scarf and a handkerchief that Miss Sainsbury Seale had shed en route.

He restored them to her.

'Oh, thank you – so careless of me. Now please, Inspector – No, Chief Inspector, isn't it? – *do* ask me anything you like. So distressing the whole business. Poor man – I suppose he had something on his mind? Such worrying times we live in!'

'Did he seem to you worried, Miss Sainsbury Seale?'

'Well –' Miss Sainsbury Seale reflected, and finally said unwillingly:

'I can't really say, you know, that he *did*! But then perhaps I shouldn't notice – not under the *circumstances*. I'm afraid I'm rather a

541

coward, you know.' Miss Sainsbury Seale tittered a little and patted her bird's-nest-like curls.

'Can you tell us who else was in the waiting-room while you were there?'

'Now let me see – there was just one young man there when I went in. I think he was in pain because he was muttering to himself and looking quite wild and turning over the leaves of a magazine just anyhow. And then suddenly he jumped up and went out. Really *acute* toothache he must have had.'

'You don't know whether he left the house when he went out of the room?'

'I don't know at all. I imagined he just felt he couldn't wait any longer and *must* see the dentist. But it couldn't have been Mr Morley he was going to, because the boy came in and took me up to Mr Morley only a few minutes later.'

'Did you go into the waiting-room again on your way out?'

'No. Because, you see, I'd already put on my hat and straightened my hair up in Mr Morley's room. Some people,' went on Miss Sainsbury Seale, warming to her subject, 'take off their hats *downstairs* in the waiting-room, but I *never* do. A most distressing thing happened to a friend of mine who did that. It was a new hat and she put it very carefully on a chair, and when she came down, would you believe it, *a child had sat on it* and squashed it flat. Ruined! Absolutely ruined!'

'A catastrophe,' said Poirot politely.

'I blame the mother entirely,' said Miss Sainsbury Seale judicially. 'Mothers should keep an eye on their children. The little dears do not mean any harm, but they have to be *watched*.'

Japp said:

'Then this young man with toothache was the only other patient you noticed at 58, Queen Charlotte Street.'

'A gentleman came down the stairs and went out just as I went up to Mr Morley – Oh! and I remember – a very *peculiar* looking foreigner came *out* of the house just as I arrived.'

Japp coughed. Poirot said with dignity:

'That was I, Madame.'

'Oh dear!' Miss Sainsbury Seale peered at him. 'So it was! Do forgive – so short-sighted – and very dark here, isn't it?' She tailed off into incoherencies. 'And really, you know, I flatter myself that I have a *very* good memory for faces. But the light here *is* dim, isn't it? Do forgive my most unfortunate mistake!'

542

They soothed the lady down, and Japp asked:

'You are quite sure Mr Morley didn't say anything such as – for instance – that he was expecting a painful interview this morning? Anything of that kind?'

'No, indeed, I'm sure he didn't.'

'He didn't mention a patient by the name of Amberiotis?'

'No, no. He really said nothing – except, I mean, the things that dentists *have* to say.'

Through Poirot's mind there ran quickly: '*Rinse. Open a little wider, please, Now close gently.*'

Japp had proceeded to his next step. It would possibly be necessary for Miss Sainsbury Seale to give evidence at the inquest.

After a first scream of dismay, Miss Sainsbury Seale seemed to take kindly to the idea. A tentative inquiry from Japp produced Miss Sainsbury Seale's whole life history.

She had, it seemed, come from India to England six months ago. She had lived in various hotels and boarding-houses and had finally come to the Glengowrie Court which she liked very much because of its homely atmosphere; in India she had lived mostly in Calcutta where she had done Mission work and had also taught elocution.

'Pure, well enunciated English – most important, Chief Inspector. You see,' Miss Sainsbury Seale simpered and bridled, 'as a girl I was on the stage. Oh! only in small parts, you know. The provinces! But I had great ambitions. Repertory. Then I went on a world tour – Shakespeare, Bernard Shaw.' She sighed. 'The trouble with us poor women is *heart* – at the mercy of our *hearts*. A rash impulsive marriage. Alas! we parted almost immediately. I – I had been sadly deceived. I resumed my maiden name. A friend kindly provided me with a little capital and I started my elocution school. I helped to found a very good amateur dramatic society. I must show you some of our notices.'

Chief Inspector Japp knew the dangers of *that*! He escaped, Miss Sainsbury Seale's last words being: 'and if, by any chance, my name *should* be in the papers – as a witness at the inquest, I mean – you *will* be sure that it is spelt right. Mabelle Sainsbury Seale – Mabelle spelt M.A.B.E.L.L.E, and Seale S.E.A.L.E. And, of course, if they *did* care to mention that I appeared in *As You like It* at the Oxford Repertory Theatre –'

'Of course, of course.' Chief Inspector Japp fairly fled.

In the taxi, he sighed and wiped his forehead.

'If it's ever necessary, we ought to be able to check up on *her* all

543

right,' he observed, 'unless it was *all* lies – but that I *don't* believe!'

Poirot shook his head. 'Liars,' he said, 'are neither so circumstantial nor so inconsequential.'

Japp went on:

'I was afraid she'd jib at the inquest – most middle-aged spinsters do – but her having been an actress accounts for her being eager. Bit of limelight for her!'

Poirot said:

'Do you really want her at the inquest?'

'Probably not. It depends.' He paused and then said: 'I'm more than ever convinced, Poirot. *This wasn't suicide.*'

'And the motive?'

'Has us beat for the moment. Suppose Morley once seduced Amberiotis' daughter?'

Poirot was silent. He tried to visualize Mr Morley in the role of seducer to a luscious-eyed Greek maiden, but failed lamentably.

He reminded Japp that Mr Reilly had said his partner had had no joy of living.

Japp said vaguely: 'Oh well, you never know what may happen on a cruise!' and he added with satisfaction. 'We shall know better where we stand when we've talked to this fellow.'

They paid off the taxi and entered the Savoy.

Japp asked for Mr Amberiotis.

The clerk looked at them rather oddly. He said:

'Mr Amberiotis? I'm sorry, sir, I'm afraid you can't see him.'

'Oh, yes, I can, my lad,' Japp said grimly. He drew the other a little aside and showed him his credentials.

The clerk said:

'You don't understand, sir. *Mr Amberiotis died half an hour ago.*'

To Hercule Poirot it was as though a door had gently but firmly shut.

I

Twenty-four hours later Japp rang Poirot up. His tone was bitter.

'Wash-out! The whole thing!'

'What do you mean, my friend?'

'Morley committed suicide all right. We've got the motive.'

'What was it?'

'I've just had the doctor's report on Amberiotis' death. I won't give you the official jargon but in plain English he died as a result of an overdose of adrenaline and novocaine. It acted on his heart, I understand, and he collapsed. When the wretched devil said he was feeling bad yesterday afternoon, he was just speaking the truth. Well, there you are! Adrenaline and procaine is the stuff dentists inject into your gum – local anæsthetic. Morley made an error, injected an overdose, and then after Amberiotis left, he realized what he had done, couldn't face the music and shot himself.'

'With a pistol he was not known to possess?' queried Poirot.

'He *may* have possessed it all the same. Relations don't know everything. You'd be surprised sometimes, the things they *don't* know!'

'That is true, yes.'

Japp said:

'Well, there you are. It's a perfectly logical explanation of the whole thing.'

Poirot said:

'You know, my friend, it does not quite satisfy me. It is true that patients have been known to react unfavourably to these local anæsthetics. Adrenaline idiosyncrasy is well known. In combination with procaine toxic effects have followed quite small doses. *But* the doctor or dentist who employed the drug does not usually carry his concern as far as killing himself!'

'Yes, but you're talking of cases where the employment of the anæsthetic was normal. In that case no particular blame attaches to the surgeon concerned. It is the idiosyncrasy of the patient that has caused death. But in this case it's pretty clear that there was a definite overdose. They haven't got the exact amount yet – these quantitive analyses seem to take a month of Sundays – but it was definitely more than the normal dose. That means that Morley must have made a mistake.'

'Even then,' said Poirot, 'it *was* a mistake. It would not be a criminal matter.'

'No, but it wouldn't do him any good in his profession. In fact, it would pretty well ruin him. Nobody's going to go to a dentist who's likely to shoot lethal doses of poison into you just because he happened to be a bit absent-minded.'

'It was a curious thing to do, I admit.'

'These things happen – they happen to doctors – they happen to chemists . . . Careful and reliable for years, and then – one moment's inattention – and the mischief's done and the poor devils are for it. Morley was a sensitive man. In the case of a doctor, there's usually a chemist or a dispenser to share the blame – or to shoulder it altogether. In this case Morley was solely responsible.'

Poirot demurred.

'Would he not have left some message behind him? Saying what he had done? And that he could not face the consequences? Something of that kind? Just a word for his sister?'

'No, as I see it, he suddenly realized what had happened – and just lost his nerve and took the quickest way out.'

Poirot did not answer.

Japp said:

'I know you, old boy. Once you've got your teeth into a case of murder, you like it to *be* a case of murder! I admit I'm responsible for setting you on the track this time. Well, I made a mistake. I admit it freely.'

Poirot said:

'I still think, you know, that there might be another explanation.'

'Plenty of other explanations, I dare say. I've thought of them – but they're all too fantastic. Let's say that Amberiotis shot Morley, went home, was filled with remorse and committed suicide, using some stuff he'd pinched from Morley's surgery. If you thing *that's* likely, *I* think it's damned *un*likely. We've got a record of Amberiotis at the Yard. Quite interesting. Started as a little hotel-keeper in Greece, then he mixed himself up in politics. He's done espionage work in Germany and in France – and made very pretty little sums of money. But he wasn't getting rich quick enough that way, and he's believed to have done a spot or two of blackmail. Not a nice man, our Mr Amberiotis. He was out in India last year and is believed to have bled one of the native princes rather freely. The difficult thing has been ever to prove anything against him. Slippery as an eel! There is another possibility. He might have been blackmailing Morley over something or other. Morley, having a golden opportunity, plugs an overdose of adrenaline and novocaine into him, hoping that the verdict will be an unfortunate accident – adrenaline idiosyncrasy – something of that sort. Then, after the man's gone away Morley gets a fit of remorse and does himself in. That's possible, of course, but I can't somehow see Morley as a deliberate murderer. No, I'm pretty sure it was what I first said – a genuine mistake, made on a morning when he was overworked. We'll have to leave it at that, Poirot. I've talked to the A.C. and he's quite clear on it.'

'I see,' said Poirot, with a sigh. 'I see . . .'

Japp said kindly:

'I know what you feel, old boy. But you can't have a nice juicy murder *every* time! So long. All I can say by way of apology is the old phrase: "Sorry you have been troubled!" '

He rang off.

II

Hercule Poirot sat at his handsome modern desk. He liked modern furniture. It's squareness and solidity were more agreeable to him than the soft contours of antique models.

In front of him was a square sheet of paper with neat headings and comments. Against some of them were query marks.

First came:

Amberiotis. Espionage. In England for that purpose? Was in India last year. During period of riots and unrest. Could be a Communist agent.

There was a space, and then the next heading:

Frank Carter? Morley thought him unsatisfactory. Was discharged from his employment recently. Why?

After that came a name with merely a question mark:

Howard Raikes?

Next came a sentence in inverted commas.

'But that's absurd!' ???

Hercule Poirot's head was poised interrogatively. Outside the window a bird was carrying a twig to build its nest. Hercule Poirot looked rather like a bird as he sat there with his egg-shaped head cocked to one side.

He made another entry a little farther down:

Mr Barnes?

547

He paused and then wrote:

Morley's office? Mark on carpet. Possibilities.

He considered that last entry for some time.

Then he got up, called for his hat and stick and went out.

III

Three-quarters of an hour later Hercule Poirot came out of the underground station at Ealing Broadway and five minutes after that he had reached his destination – No. 88, Castlegardens Road.

It was a small semi-detached house, and the neatness of the front garden drew an admiring nod from Hercule Poirot.

'Admirably symmetrical,' he murmured to himself.

Mr Barnes was at home and Poirot was shown into a small precise dining-room and here presently Mr Barnes came to him.

Mr Barnes was a small man with twinkling eyes and a nearly bald head. He peeped over the top of his glasses at his visitor while in his left hand he twirled the card that Poirot had given the maid.

He said in a small prim almost falsetto voice:

'Well, well, M. Poirot? I am honoured, I am sure.'

'You must excuse my calling upon you in this informal manner,' said Poirot punctiliously.

'Much the best way,' said Mr Barnes. 'And the time is admirable, too. A quarter to seven – very sound time at this period of the year for catching any one at home.' He waved his hand. 'Sit down, M. Poirot. I've no doubt we've got a good deal to talk about. 58, Queen Charlotte Street, I suppose?'

Poirot said:

'You suppose rightly – but why should you suppose anything of the kind?'

'My dear sir,' said Mr Barnes, 'I've been retired from the Home Office for some time now – but I've not gone *quite* rusty yet. If there's any hush-hush business, it's far better not to use the police. Draws attention to it all!'

Poirot said:

'I will ask yet another question. Why should you suppose this is a hush-hush business?'

'Isn't it?' asked the other. 'Well, if it isn't, in my opinion it ought to be.' He leant forward and tapped with his pince-nez on the arm of the chair. 'In Secret Service work it's never the little fry you want –

it's the big bugs at the top – but to get them you've got to be careful not to alarm the little fry.'

'It seems to me, Mr Barnes, that you know more than I do,' said Hercule Poirot.

'Don't know anything at all,' replied the other, 'just put two and two together.'

'One of those two being?'

'Amberiotis,' said Mr Barnes promptly. 'You forget I sat opposite him in the waiting-room for a minute or two. *He* didn't know *me*. I was always an insignificant chap. Not a bad thing sometimes. But I knew *him* all right – and I could guess what he was up to over here.'

'Which was?'

Mr Barnes twinkled more than ever.

'We're very tiresome people in this country. We're conservative, you know, conservative to the backbone. We grumble a lot, but we don't really want to smash our democratic government and try new-fangled experiments. That's what's so heart-breaking to the wretched foreign agitator who's working full time and over! The whole trouble is – from their point of view – that we really *are*, as a country, comparatively solvent. Hardly any other country in Europe is at the moment! To upset England – really upset it – you've got to play hell with its finance – that's what it comes to! And you can't play hell with its finance when you've got men like Alistair Blunt at the helm.'

Mr Barnes paused and then went on:

'Blunt is the kind of man who in private life would always pay his bills and live within his income – whether he'd got twopence a year or several million makes no difference. He is that type of fellow. And he just simply thinks that there's no reason why a *country* shouldn't be the same! No costly experiments. No frenzied expenditure on possible Utopias. That's why' – he paused – 'that's why certain people have made up their minds that Blunt must go.'

'Ah,' said Poirot.

Mr Barnes nodded.

'Yes,' he said. 'I know what I'm talking about. Quite nice people some of 'em. Long-haired, earnest-eyed, and full of ideals of a better world. Others not so nice, rather nasty in fact. Furtive little rats with beards and foreign accents. And another lot again of the Big Bully type. But they've all got the same idea: Blunt Must Go!'

He tilted his chair gently back and forward again.

'Sweep away the old order! The Tories, the Conservatives, the

Diehards, the hard-headed suspicious Business Men, that's the idea. Perhaps these people are right – *I* don't know – but I know one thing – you've got to have something to put in place of the old order – something that will work – not just something that *sounds* all right. Well, we needn't go into that. We are dealing with concrete facts, not abstract theories. Take away the props and the building will come down. Blunt is one of the props of Things as They Are.'

He leaned forward.

'They're out after Blunt all right. That I *know.* And it's my opinion that yesterday morning *they nearly got him.* I may be wrong – but it's been tried before. The method, I mean.'

He paused and then quietly, circumspectly, he mentioned three names. An unusually able Chancellor of the Exchequer, a progressive and far-sighted manufacturer, and a hopeful young politician who had captured the public fancy. The first had died on the operating table, the second had succumbed to an obscure disease which had been recognized too late, the third had been run down by a car and killed.

'It's very easy,' said Mr Barnes. 'The anæsthetist muffed the giving of the anæsthetic – well, that does happen. In the second case the symptoms were puzzling. The doctor was just a well-meaning G.P., couldn't be expected to recognize them. In the third case, anxious mother was driving car in a hurry to get to her sick child. Sob stuff – the jury acquitted her of blame!'

He paused:

'All quite natural. And soon forgotten. But I'll just tell you *where those three people are now.* The anæsthetist is set up on his own with a first-class research laboratory – no expense spared. That G.P. has retired from practice. He's got a yacht, and a nice little place on the Broads. The mother is giving all her children a first-class education, ponies to ride in the holidays, nice house in the country with a big garden and paddocks.'

He nodded his head slowly.

'In every profession and walk of life there is *someone* who is vulnerable to temptation. The trouble in our case is that Morley *wasn't!*'

'You think it was like that?' said Hercule Poirot.

Mr Barnes said:

'I do. It's not easy to get at one of these big men, you know. They're fairly well protected. The car stunt is risky and doesn't always succeed. But a man is defenceless enough in a dentist's chair.'

He took off his pince-nez, polished them and put them on again.
He said:

'That's my theory! *Morley wouldn't do the job.* He knew too much,
though, so they had to put him out.'

'*They?*' asked Poirot.

'When I say *they* – I mean the organization that's behind all this.
Only one person actually did the job, of course.'

'Which person?'

'Well, I could make a guess,' said Mr Barnes, 'but it's only a guess
and I might be wrong.'

Poirot said quietly: 'Reilly?'

'Of course! He's the obvious person. I think that probably they
never asked Morley to do the job *himself*. What he *was* to do, was to
turn Blunt over to his partner at the last minute. Sudden illness,
something of that sort. Reilly would have done the actual business –
and there would have been another regrettable accident – death of a
famous banker – unhappy young dentist in court in such a state of
dither and misery that he would have been let down light. He'd have
given up dentistry afterwards – and settled down somewhere on a
nice income of several thousands a year.'

Mr Barnes looked across at Poirot.

'Don't think I'm romancing,' he said. 'These things happen.'

'Yes, yes, I know they happen.'

Mr Barnes went on, tapping a book with a lurid jacket that lay on a
table close at hand: 'I read a lot of these spy yarns. Fantastic, some of
them. But curiously enough *they're not any more fantastic than the real
thing*. There *are* beautiful adventuresses, and dark sinister men with
foreign accents, and gangs and international associations and super
crooks! I'd blush to see some of the things *I* know set down in print –
nobody would believe them for a minute!'

Poirot said:

'In your theory, *where does Amberiotis come in?*'

'I'm not quite sure. I *think* he was meant to take the rap. He's
played a double game more than once and I dare say he was framed.
That's only an idea, mind.'

Hercule Poirot said quietly:

'Granting that your ideas are correct – *what will happen next?*'

Mr Barnes rubbed his noise.

'They'll try to get him again,' he said. 'Oh, yes. They'll have
another try. Time's short. Blunt has got people looking after him, I
dare say. They'll have to be extra careful. It won't be a man hiding in

a bush with a pistol. Nothing so crude as that. You tell 'em to look out for the respectable people – the relations, the old servants, the chemist's assistant who makes up a medicine, the wine merchant who sells him his port. Getting Alistair Blunt out of the way is worth a great many millions, and it's wonderful what people will do for – say a nice little income of four thousand a year!'

'As much as that!'

'Possibly more. . . .'

Poirot was silent a moment, then he said:

'I have had Reilly in mind from the first.'

'Irish? I.R.A.?'

'Not that so much, but there was a mark, you see, on the carpet, as though the body had been dragged along it. But if Morley had been shot by a patient he would be shot in the surgery and there would be no need to move the body. That is why, from the first, I suspected that he had been shot, not in the surgery, but in his office – next door. That would mean that it was not a patient who shot him, but some member of his own household.'

'Neat,' said Mr Barnes appreciatively.

Hercule Poirot got up and held out a hand.

'Thank you,' he said. 'You have helped me a great deal.'

IV

On the way home, Poirot called in at the Glengowrie Court Hotel.

As a result of that visit he rang Japp up very early the following morning.

'*Bon jour, mon ami.* The inquest is today, is it not?'

'It is. Are you going to attend?'

'I do not think so.'

'It won't really be worth your while, I expect.'

'Are you calling Miss Sainsbury Seale as a witness?'

'The lovely Mabelle – why can't she just spell it plain Mabel. These women get my goat! I'm not calling her. There's no need.'

'You have heard nothing from her?'

'No, why should I?'

Hercule Poirot said:

'I wondered, that was all. Perhaps it may interest you to learn that Miss Sainsbury Seale walked out of the Glengowrie Court Hotel just before dinner the night before last – and did not come back.'

'*What?* She's hooked it?'

'That is a possible explanation.'

'But why should she? She's quite all right, you know. Perfectly genuine and above-board. I cabled Calcutta about her – that was before I knew the reason for Amberiotis' death, otherwise I shouldn't have bothered – and I got the reply last night. Everything O.K. She's been known there for years, and her whole account of herself is true – except that she's slurred over her marriage a bit. Married a Hindu student and then found he'd got a few attachments already. So she resumed her maiden name and took to good works. She's hand and glove with the missionaries – teaches elocution, and helps in amateur dramatic shows. In fact, what I call a terrible woman – but definitely above suspicion of being mixed up in a murder. And *now* you say she's walked out on us! I can't understand it.' He paused a minute and then went on doubtfully : 'Perhaps she just got fed up with that hotel? I could have easily.'

Poirot said:

'Her luggage is still there. She took nothing with her.'

Japp swore.

'When did she go?'

'About a quarter-to-seven.'

'What about the hotel people?'

'They're very upset. Manageress looked quite distraught.'

'Why didn't they report to the police?'

'Because, *mon cher*, supposing that a lady does happen to stay out for a night (however unlikely it may seem from her appearance) she will be justifiably annoyed by finding on her return that the police have been called in. Mrs Harrison, the manageress in question, called up various hospitals in case there had been an accident. She was considering notifying the police when I called. My appearance seemed to her like an answer to a prayer. I charged myself with everything, and explained that I would enlist the help of a very discreet police officer.'

'The discreet police officer being yours truly, I suppose?'

'You suppose rightly.'

Japp groaned:

'All right. I'll meet you at the Glengowrie Court Hotel after the inquest.'

553

Japp grumbled as they were waiting for the manageress.

'What does the woman want to disappear for?'

'It is curious, you admit?'

They had no time for more.

Mrs Harrison, proprietor of the Glengowrie Court, was with them.

Mrs Harrison was voluble and almost tearful. She was so worried about Miss Sainbury Seale. What *could* have happened to her? Rapidly she went over every possibility of disaster. Loss of memory, sudden illness, haemorrhage, run down by an omnibus, robbery and assault –

She paused at last for breath, murmuring:

'Such a nice type of woman – and she seemed so happy and comfortable here.'

She took them, at Japp's request, up to the chaste bedroom occupied by the missing lady. Everything was neat and orderly. Clothes hung in the wardrobe, nightclothes were folded ready on the bed, in a corner were Miss Sainsbury Seale's two modest suitcases. A row of shoes stood under the dressing-table – some serviceable Oxfords, two pairs of rather meretricious glacé fancy shoes with court heels and ornament with bows of leather, some plain black satin evening shoes practically new, and a pair of moccasins. Poirot noted that the evening shoes were a size smaller than the day ones – a fact that might be put down to corns or to vanity. He wondered whether Miss Sainsbury Seale had found time to sew the second buckle on her shoe before she went out. He hoped so. Slovenliness in dress always annoyed him.

Japp was busy looking through some letters in a drawer of the dressing-table. Hercule Poirot gingerly pulled open a drawer of the chest of drawers. It was full of underclothing. He shut it again modestly, murmuring that Miss Sainsbury Seale seemed to believe in wearing wool next to the skin, and opened another drawer which contained stockings.

Japp said:

'Got anything, Poirot?'

Poirot said sadly, as he dangled a pair: 'Ten inch, cheap shiny silk, price probably two-and-eleven.'

Japp said:

'You're not valuing for probate, old boy. Two letters here from

India, one or two receipts from charitable organizations, no bills. Most estimable character, our Miss Sainsbury Seale.'

'But very little taste in dress,' said Poirot sadly.

'Probably thought dress worldly.' Japp was noting down an address from an old letter dated two months back.

'These people may know something about her,' he said. 'Address up Hampstead way. Sound as though they were fairly intimate.'

There was nothing more to be gleaned at the Glengowrie Court Hotel except the negative fact that Miss Sainsbury Seale had not seemed excited or worried in any way when she went out, and it would appear that she had definitely intended to return since on passing her friend Mrs Bolitho in the hall, she had called out:

'After dinner I will show you that Patience I was telling you about.'

Moreover, it was the custom at the Glengowrie Court to give notice in the dining-room if you intended to be out for a meal. Miss Sainsbury Seale had not done so. Therefore it seemed clear that she had intended returning for dinner which was served from seven-thirty to eight-thirty.

But she had not returned. She had walked out into the Cromwell Road and disappeared.

Japp and Poirot called at the address in West Hampstead which had headed the letter found.

It was a pleasant house and the Adams were pleasant people with a large family. They had lived in India for many years and spoke warmly of Miss Sainsbury Seale. But they could not help.

They had not seen her lately, not for a month, not in fact, since they came back from their Easter holidays. She had been staying then at a hotel near Russell Square. Mrs Adams gave Poirot the address of it and also the address of some other Anglo-Indian friends of Miss Sainsbury Seale's who lived in Streatham.

But the two men drew a blank in both places. Miss Sainsbury Seale had stayed at the hotel in question, but they remembered very little about her and nothing that could be of any help. She was a nice quiet lady and had lived abroad. The people in Streatham were no help either. They had not seen Miss Sainsbury Seale since February.

There remained the possibility of an accident, but that possibility was dispelled too. No hospital had admitted any casualty answering to the description given.

Miss Sainsbury Seale had disappeared into space.

On the following morning, Poirot went to the Holborn Palace Hotel and asked for Mr Howard Raikes.

By this time it would hardly have surprised him to hear that Mr Howard Raikes, too, had stepped out one evening and had never returned.

Mr Howard Raikes, however, was still at the Holborn Palace and was said to be breakfasting.

The apparition of Hercule Poirot at the breakfast table seemed to give Mr Howard Raikes doubtful pleasure.

Though not looking so murderous as in Poirot's disordered recollection of him, his scowl was still formidable – he stared at his uninvited guest and said ungraciously:

'What the hell?'

'You permit?'

Hercule Poirot drew a chair from another table.

Mr Raikes said:

'Don't mind me! Sit down and make yourself at home!'

Poirot smiling availed himself of the permission.

Mr Raikes said ungraciously:

'Well, what do you want?'

'Do you remember me at all, Mr Raikes?

'Never set eyes on you in my life.'

'There you are wrong. You sat in the same room with me for at least five minutes not more than three days ago.'

'I can't remember every one I meet at some God-damned party or other.'

'It was not a party,' said Poirot. 'It was a dentist's waiting-room.'

Some swift emotion flashed into the young man's eyes and died again at once. His manner changed. It was no longer impatient and casual. It became suddenly wary. He looked across at Poirot and said:

'Well!'

Poirot studied him carefully before replying. He felt, quite positively, that this was indeed a dangerous young man. A lean hungry face, an aggressive jaw, the eyes of a fanatic. It was a face though, that women might find attractive. He was untidily, even shabbily dressed, and he ate with a careless voraciousness that was, so the man watching him thought, significant.

Poirot summed him up to himself.

'It is a wolf with ideas. ....'

Raikes said harshly:

'What the hell do you mean – coming here like this?'

'My visit is disagreeable to you?'

'I don't even know who you are.'

'I apologize.'

Dexterously Poirot whipped out his card case. He extracted a card and passed it across the table.

Again that emotion that he could not quite define showed upon Mr Raikes' lean face. It was not fear – it was more aggressive than fear. After it, quite unquestionably, came anger.

He tossed the card back.

'So that's who you are, is it? I've heard of you.'

'Most people have,' said Hercule Poirot modestly.

'You're a private dick, aren't you? The expensive kind. The kind people hire when money is no object – when its worth paying anything in order to save their miserable skins!'

'If you do not drink your coffee,' said Hercule Poirot, 'it will get cold.'

He spoke kindly and with authority.

Raikes stared at him.

'Say, just what kind of an insect are you?'

'The coffee in this country is very bad anyway –' said Poirot.

'I'll say it is,' agreed Mr Raikes with fervour.

'But if you allow it to get cold it is practically undrinkable.'

The young man leant forward.

'What are you getting at? What's the big idea in coming round here?'

Poirot shrugged his shoulders.

'I wanted to – see you.'

'Oh yes?' said Mr Raikes sceptically.

His eyes narrowed.

'If it's the money you're after, you've come to the wrong man! The people I'm in with can't afford to *buy* what they want. Better go back to the man who pays your salary.'

Poirot said, sighing:

'Nobody has paid me anything – yet.'

'You're telling me,' said Mr Raikes.

'It is the truth,' said Hercule Poirot. 'I am wasting a good deal of valuable time for no recompense whatsoever. Simply, shall we say, to assuage my curiosity.'

557

'And I suppose,' said Mr Raikes, 'you were just assuaging your curiosity at that darned dentist's the other day.'

Poirot shook his head. He said:

'You seem to overlook the most ordinary reason for being in a dentist's waiting-room – which is that one is waiting to have one's teeth attended to.'

'So that's what you were doing?' Mr Raikes' tone expressed contemptuous unbelief. 'Waiting to have your teeth seen to?'

'Certainly.'

'You'll excuse me if I say I don't believe it.'

'May I ask then, Mr Raikes, what *you* were doing there?'

Mr Raikes grinned suddenly. He said:

'Got you there! I was waiting to have my teeth seen to also.'

'You had perhaps the toothache?'

'That's right, big boy.'

'But all the same, you went away without having your teeth attended to?'

'What if I did? That's my business.'

He paused – then he said, with a quick savagery of tone: 'Oh, what the hell's the use of all this slick talking? You were there to look after your big shot. Well, he's all right, isn't he? Nothing happened to your precious Mr Alistair Blunt. You've nothing on me.'

Poirot said:

'Where did you go when you went so abruptly out of the waiting-room?'

'Left the house, of course.'

'Ah!' Poirot looked up at the ceiling. 'But nobody saw you leave, Mr Raikes.'

'Does that matter?'

'It might. Somebody died in that house not long afterwards, remember.'

Raikes said carelessly:

'Oh, you mean the dentist fellow.'

Poirot's tone was hard as he said:

'Yes, I mean the dentist fellow.'

Raikes stared. He said:

'You trying to pin that on me? Is that the game? Well, you can't do it. I've just read the account of the inquest yesterday. The poor devil shot himself because he'd made a mistake with a local anæsthetic and one of his patients died.'

Poirot went on unmoved: 'Can you prove that you left the house when you say you did? Is there any one who can say definitely where you were between twelve and one?'

The other's eyes narrowed.

'So you *are* trying to pin it on me? I suppose Blunt put you up to this?'

Poirot sighed. He said:

'You will pardon me, but it seems an obsession with you – this persistent harping on Mr Alistair Blunt. I am not employed by him, I never have been employed by him. I am concerned, not with his safety, but with the death of a man who did good work in his chosen profession.'

Raikes shook his head.

'Sorry,' he said, 'I don't believe you. You're Blunt's private dick all right.' His face darkened as he leaned across the table. 'But you can't save him, you know. He's got to go – he and everything he stands for! There's got to be a new deal – the old corrupt system of finance has got to go – this cursed net of bankers all over the world like a spider's web. They've go to be swept away. I've nothing against Blunt personally – but he's the type of man I hate. He's mediocre – he's smug. He's the sort you can't move unless you use dynamite. He's the sort of man who says, "You can't disrupt the foundations of civilization." Can't you, though? Let him wait and see! He's an obstruction in the way of Progress and he's got to be removed. There's no room in the world today for men like Blunt – men who hark back to the past – men who want to live as their fathers lived or even as their grandfathers lived! You've got a lot of them here in England – crusted old diehards – useless worn-out symbols of a decayed era. And, my God, they've got to go! There's got to be a new world. Do you get me – a new world, see?'

'I see, Mr Raikes, that you are an idealist.'

'What if I am?'

'Too much of an idealist to care about the death of a dentist.'

Mr Raikes said scornfully:

'What does the death of one miserable dentist matter?'

Hercule Poirot said:

'It does not matter to you. It matters to me. That is the difference between us.'

559

Poirot arrived home to be informed by George that a lady was waiting to see him.

'She is – ahem – a little nervous, sir,' said George.

Since the lady had given no name Poirot was at liberty to guess. He guessed wrong, for the young woman who rose agitatedly from the sofa as he entered was the late Mr Morley's secretary, Miss Gladys Nevill.

'Oh, dear, M. Poirot. I am *so* sorry to worry you like this – and really I don't know how I had the courage to come – I'm afraid you'll think it very bold of me – and I'm sure I don't want to take up your time – I know what time means to a busy professional man – but really I have been so unhappy – only I dare say you will think it all a waste of time –'

Profiting by a long experience of the English people, Poirot suggested a cup of tea. Miss Nevill's reaction was all that could be hoped for.

'Well, really, M. Poirot, that's *very* kind of you. Not that it's so very long since breakfast, but one can always do with a cup of tea, can't one?'

Poirot who could always do without one, assented mendaciously. George was instructed to this effect, and in a miraculously short time, Poirot and his visitor faced each other across a tea-tray.

'I must apologize to you,' said Miss Nevill, regaining her aplomb under the influence of the beverage, 'but as a matter of fact the inquest yesterday upset me a good deal.'

'I'm sure it must have done,' said Poirot kindly.

'There was no question of my giving evidence, or anything like *that*. But I felt somebody *ought* to go with Miss Morley. Mr Reilly was there, of course – but I meant a *woman*. Besides, Miss Morley doesn't *like* Mr Reilly. So I thought it was my duty to go.'

'That was very kind of you,' said Poirot encouragingly.

'Oh, no, I just felt I *had* to. You see, I have worked for Mr Morley for quite a number of years now – and the whole thing was a great shock to me – and of course the inquest made it worse –'

'I'm afraid it must have done.'

Miss Nevill leaned forward earnestly.

'*But it's all wrong, M. Poirot.* It really is all wrong.'

'What is wrong, Mademoiselle?'

'Well, it just couldn't have happened – not the way they make out

– giving a patient an overdose in injecting the gum, I mean.'

'You think not.'

'I'm sure about it. Occasionally patients do suffer ill effects, but that is because they are physiologically unfit subjects – their heart action isn't normal. But I'm sure that an overdose is a very rare thing. You see practitioners get so into the habit of giving the regulation amount that it is absolutely mechanical – they'd give the right dose automatically.'

Poirot nodded approvingly. He said:

'That is what I thought myself, yes.'

'It's so standardized, you see. It's not like a chemist who is making up different amounts the whole time, or multiplying dosage where an error might creep in through inattention, Or a doctor who writes a great many different prescriptions. But a dentist isn't like that at all.'

Poirot asked:

'You did not ask to be allowed to make these observations in the Coroner's Court?'

Gladys Nevill shook her head. She twisted her fingers uncertainly.

'You see,' she broke out at last, 'I was afraid of – of making things worse. Of course *I* know that Mr Morley wouldn't do such a thing – but it might make people think that he had done it deliberately.'

Poirot nodded.

Gladys Nevill said:

'That's why I came to you, M. Poirot. Because with you it – it wouldn't be *official* in any way. But I do think *somebody* ought to know how – how *unconvincing* the whole thing is!'

'Nobody wants to know,' said Poirot.

She stared at him, puzzled.

Poirot said:

'I should like to know a little more about that telegram you received, summoning you away that day.'

'Honestly, I don't know what to think about that, M. Poirot. It does seem so queer. You see, it must have been sent by someone who knew all about me – and Aunt – where she lived and everything.'

'Yes, it would seem as though it must have been sent by one of your intimate friends, or by someone who lived in the house and knew all about you.'

'None of my friends would do such a thing, M. Poirot.'

'You have no ideas yourself on the subject?'

The girl hesitated. She said slowly:

'Just at first, when I realized that Mr Morley had shot himself, I

561

wondered if *he* could possibly have sent it.'

'You mean, out of consideration for you, to get you out of the way?'

The girl nodded.

'But that really seemed a fantastic idea, even if he *had* got the idea of suicide in his mind that morning. It's really very odd. Frank – my friend, you know – was quite absurd at first about it. He accused me of wanting to go off for the day with somebody else – as though I would do such a thing.'

'Is there somebody else?'

'No, of course there isn't. But Frank has been so different lately – so moody and suspicious. Really, you know, it was losing his job and not being able to get another. Just hanging about is so bad for a man. I've been very worried about Frank.'

'He was upset, was he not, to find you had gone away that day?'

'Yes, you see, he came round to tell me he had got a new job – a marvellous job – ten pounds a week. And he couldn't wait. He wanted me to know right away. And I think he wanted Mr Morley to know, too, because he'd been very hurt at the way Mr Morley didn't appreciate him, and he suspected Mr Morley of trying to influence me against him.'

'Which was true, was it not?'

'Well, yes, it was, in a *way*! Of course, Frank *has* lost a good many jobs and he hasn't been, perhaps, what most people would call very *steady*. But it will be different now. I think one can do so much by influence, don't you, M. Poirot? If a man feels a woman expects a lot of him, he tries to live up to her ideal of him.'

Poirot sighed. But he did not argue. He had heard many hundreds of women produce that same argument, with the same blithe belief in the redeeming power of a woman's love. Once in a thousand times, he supposed, cynically, it *might* be true.

He merely said:

'I should like to meet this friend of yours.'

'I'd love to have you meet him, M. Poirot. But just at present Sunday is his only free day. He's away in the country all the week, you see.'

'Ah, on the new job. What is the job, by the way?'

'Well, I don't exactly know, M. Poirot. Something in the secretarial line, I imagine. Or some government department. I know I have to send letters to Frank's London address and they get forwarded.'

562

'That is a little odd, is it not?'

'Well, I thought so – but Frank says it is often done nowadays.'

Poirot looked at her for a moment or two without speaking.

Then he said deliberately:

'Tomorrow is Sunday, is it not? Perhaps you would both give me the pleasure of lunching with me – at Logan's Corner House? I should like to discuss this sad business with you both.'

'Well – thank you, M. Poirot. I – yes, I'm sure we'd like to lunch with you very much.'

VIII

Frank Carter was a fair young man of medium height. His appearance was cheaply smart. He talked readily and fluently. His eyes were set rather close together and they had a way of shifting uneasily from side to side when he was embarrassed.

He was inclined to be suspicious and slightly hostile.

'I'd no idea we were to have the pleasure of lunching with *you* M. Poirot. Gladys didn't tell me anything about it.'

He shot her a rather annoyed glance as he spoke.

'It was only arranged yesterday,' said Poirot, smiling. 'Miss Nevill is very upset by the circumstances of Mr Morley's death and I wondered if we put our heads together –'

Frank Carter interrupted him rudely.

'Morley's death? I'm sick of Morley's death! Why can't you forget him, Gladys? There wasn't anything so wonderful about him that *I* can see.'

'Oh, Frank, I don't think you ought to say *that*. Why, he left me a hundred pounds. I got the letter about it last night.'

'That's all right,' admitted Frank grudgingly. 'But after all, why shouldn't he? He worked you like a nigger – and who pocketed all the fat fees? Why, he did!'

'Well, of course he did – he paid me a very good salary.'

'Not according to *my* ideas! You're too humble altogether, Gladys, my girl, you let yourself be put upon, you know. I *sized* Morley up all right. You know as well as I do that he tried his best to get you to give me the chuck.'

'He didn't understand.'

'He understood all right. The man's dead now – otherwise I can tell you I'd have given him a piece of my mind.'

'You actually came round to do so on the morning of his death, did you not?' Hercule Poirot inquired gently.

Frank Carter said angrily:

'Who's been saying so?'

'You did come round, did you not?'

'What if I did? I wanted to see Miss Nevill here.'

'But they told you she was away.'

'Yes, and that made me pretty suspicious, I can tell you. I told that red-headed oaf I'd wait and see Morley myself. This business of putting Gladys against me had gone on long enough. I meant to tell Morley that instead of being a poor unemployed rotter, I'd landed a good job and that it was about time Gladys handed in her notice and thought about her trousseau.'

'But you did not actually tell him so?'

'No, I got tired of waiting in that dingy mausoleum. I went away.'

'What time did you leave?'

'I can't remember.'

'What time did you arrive then?'

'I don't know. Soon after twelve, I should imagine.'

'And you stayed half an hour – or longer – or less than half an hour?'

'I don't know, I tell you. I'm not the sort of chap who's always looking at a clock.'

'Was there any one in the waiting-room while you were there?'

'There was an oily fat bloke when I went in, but he wasn't there long. After that I was alone.'

'Then you must have left before half-past twelve – for at that time a lady arrived.'

'Dare say I did. The place got on my nerves as I tell you.'

Poirot eyed him thoughtfully.

The bluster was uneasy – it did not ring quite true. And yet that might be explained by mere nervousness.

Poirot's manner was simple and friendly as he said:

'Miss Nevill tells me that you have been very fortunate and have found a very good job indeed.'

'The pay's good.'

'Ten pounds a week, she tells me.'

'That's right. Not too dusty, is it? Shows I can pull it off when I set my mind to it.'

He swaggered a little.

'Yes, indeed. And the work is not too arduous?'

564

Frank Carter said shortly:

'Not too bad.'

'And interesting?'

'Oh, yes, quite interesting. Talking of jobs, I've always been interested to know how you private detectives go about things? I suppose there's not much of the Sherlock Holmes touch really, mostly divorce nowadays?'

'I do not concern myself with divorce.'

'Really? Then I don't see how you live.'

'I manage, my friend, I manage.'

'But you're right at the top of the tree, aren't you, M. Poirot?' put in Gladys Nevill. 'Mr Morley used to say so. I mean you're the sort of person Royalty calls in, or the Home Office or Duchesses.'

Poirot smiled upon her.

'You flatter me,' he said.

IX

Poirot walked home through the deserted streets in a thoughtful frame of mind.

When he got in, he rang up Japp.

'Forgive my troubling you, my friend, but did you ever do anything in the matter of tracing that telegram that was sent to Gladys Nevill?'

'Still harping on the subject? Yes, we did, as a matter of fact. There was a telegram and – rather clever – the aunt lives at Richbourne in Somerset. The telegram was handed in at Richbarn – you know, the London suburb.'

Hercule Poirot said appreciatively:

'That was clever – yes, that was clever. If the recipient happened to glance at where the telegram was handed in, the word would look sufficiently like Richbourne to carry conviction.'

He paused.

'Do you know what I think, Japp?'

'Well?'

'There are signs of brains in this business.'

'Hercule Poirot wants it to be murder, so it's got to be murder.'

'How do you explain that telegram?'

'Coincidence. Someone was hoaxing the girl.'

'Why should they?'

565

'Oh, my goodness, Poirot, why do people do things? Practical jokes, hoaxes. Misplaced sense of humour, that's all.'

'And somebody felt like being funny just on the day that Morley was going to make a mistake over an injection.'

'There may have been a certain amount of cause and effect. Because Miss Nevill was away, Morley was more rushed than usual and consequently was more likely to make a mistake.'

'I am still not satisfied.'

'I dare say – but don't you see where your view is leading you? If anybody got la Nevill out of the way, it was probably Morley himself. Making his killing of Amberiotis deliberate and not an accident.'

Poirot was silent. Japp said:

'You see?'

Poirot said:

'Amberiotis might have been killed in some other way.'

'Not he. Nobody came to see him at the Savoy. He lunched up in his room. And the doctors say the stuff was definitely injected, not taken by mouth – it wasn't in the stomach. So there you are. It's a clear case.'

'That is what we are meant to think.'

'The A.C. is satisfied anyway.'

'And he is satisfied with the disappearing lady?'

'The Case of the Vanishing Seal? No, I can tell you, we're still working on that. That woman's got to be somewhere. You just can't walk out into the street and disappear.'

'She seems to have done so.'

'For the moment. But she must be somewhere, alive or dead, and I don't think she is dead.'

'Why not?'

'Because we'd have found her body by now.'

'Oh, my Japp, do bodies always come to light so soon?'

'I suppose you're hinting that *she's* been murdered now and that we'll find her in a quarry, cut up in little pieces like Mrs Ruxton?'

'After all, *mon ami*, you *do* have missing persons who are not found.'

'Very seldom, old boy. Lots of women disappear, yes, but we usually find 'em, all right. Nine times out of ten it's a case of good old sex. They're somewhere with a man. But I don't think it could be that with our Mabelle, do you?'

'One never knows,' said Poirot cautiously. 'But I do not think it likely. So you are sure of finding her?'

566

'We'll find her all right. We're publishing a description of her to the Press and we're roping in the B.B.C.'

'Ah,' said Poirot, 'I fancy that may bring developments.'

'Don't worry, old boy. We'll find your missing beauty for you – woollen underwear and all.'

He rang off.

George entered the room with his usual noiseless tread. He set down on a little table a steaming pot of chocolate and some sugar biscuits.

'Will there be anything else, sir?'

'I am in great perplexity of mind, Georges.'

'Indeed sir? I am sorry to hear it.'

Hercule Poirot poured himself out some chocolate and stirred his cup thoughtfully.

George stood deferentially waiting, recognizing the signs. There were moments when Hercule Poirot discussed his cases with his valet. He always said that he found George's comments singularly helpful.

'You are aware, no doubt, Georges, of the death of my dentist?'

'Mr Morley, sir? Yes, sir. Very distressing, sir. He shot himself, I understand.'

'That is the general understanding. If he did not shoot himself, he was murdered.'

'Yes, sir.'

'The question is, if he was murdered, who murdered him?'

'Quite so, sir.'

'There are only a certain number of people, Georges, who *could* have murdered him. That is to say the people who were actually in, or *could have been in* the house at the time.'

'Quite so, sir.'

'Those people are: a cook and housemaid, amiable domestics and highly unlikely to do anything of the kind. A devoted sister, also highly unlikely, but who does inherit her brother's money such as it was – and one can never entirely neglect the financial aspect. An able and efficient partner – no motive known. A somewhat bone-headed page-boy addicted to cheap crime stories. And lastly, a Greek gentleman of somewhat doubtful antecedents.'

George coughed.

'These foreigners, sir –'

'Exactly. I agree perfectly. The Greek gentleman is decidedly indicated. But you see, Georges, the Greek gentleman also died and

567

apparently it was Mr Morley who killed him – whether by intention or as the result of an unfortunate error we cannot be sure.'

'It might be, sir, that they killed each other. I mean, sir, each gentleman had formed the idea of doing the other gentleman in, though of course each gentleman was unaware of the other gentleman's intention.'

Hercule Poirot purred approvingly.

'Very ingenious, Georges. The dentist murders the unfortunate gentleman who sits in the chair, not realizing that the said victim is at that moment meditating exactly at what moment to whip out his pistol. It could, of course, be so but it seems to me, Georges, extremely unlikely. And we have not come to the end of our list yet. There are still two other people who might possibly have been in the house at the given moment. Every patient, before Mr Amberiotis, was actually seen to leave the house with the exception of one – a young American gentleman. He left the waiting-room at about twenty minutes to twelve, but no one actually saw him leave the house. We must therefore count him as a possibility. The other possibility is a certain Mr Frank Carter (*not* a patient) who came to the house at a little after twelve with the intention of seeing Mr Morley. Nobody saw *him* leave, either. Those, my good Georges, are the facts; what do you think of them?'

'At what time was the murder committed, sir?'

'If the murder was committed by Mr Amberiotis, it was committed at any time between twelve and five-and-twenty past. If by somebody else, it was committed *after* twenty-five minutes past twelve, as otherwise Mr Amberiotis would have noticed the corpse.'

He looked encouragingly at George.

'Now, my good Georges, what have you to say about the matter?'

George pondered. He said:

'It strikes me, sir –'

'Yes, Georges?'

'You will have to find another dentist to attend to your teeth in future sir.'

Hercule Poirot said:

'You surpass yourself, Georges. That aspect of the matter had not as yet occurred to me!'

Looking gratified, George left the room.

Hercule Poirot remained sipping his chocolate and going over the facts he had just outlined. He felt satisfied that they were as he had stated them. Within that circle of persons was the hand that had

568

actually done the deed – no matter whose the inspiration had been.

Then his eyebrows shot up as he realized that the list was incomplete. He had left out one name.

And no one must be left out – not even the most unlikely person. There had been one other person in the house at the time of the murder.

He wrote down:

'Mr *Barnes.*'

x

George announced:

'A lady to speak to you on the telephone, sir.'

A week ago, Poirot had guessed wrongly the identity of a visitor. This time his guess was right.

He recognized her voice at once.

'M. Hercule Poirot?'

'Speaking.'

'This is Jane Olivera – Mr Alistair Blunt's niece.'

'Yes, Miss Olivera.'

'Could you come to the Gothic House, please? There is something I feel you ought to know.'

'Certainly. What time would be convenient?'

'At six-thirty, please.'

'I will be there.'

For a moment the autocratic note wavered:

'I – I hope I am not interrupting your work?'

'Not at all. I was expecting you to call me.'

He put down the receiver quickly. He moved away from it smiling. He wondered what excuse Jane Olivera had found for summoning him.

On arrival at the Gothic House he was shown straight into the big library overlooking the river. Alistair Blunt was sitting at the writing-table playing absent-mindedly with a paper-knife. He had the slightly harassed look of a man whose womenfolk have been too much for him.

Jane Olivera was standing by the mantelpiece. A plump middle-aged woman was speaking fretfully as Poirot entered – 'and I really think *my* feelings should be considered in the matter, Alistair.'

'Yes, Julia, of course, of course.'

Alistair Blunt spoke soothingly as he rose to greet Poirot.

'And if you're going to talk horrors I shall leave the room,' added the good lady.

'I should, mother,' said Jane Olivera.

Mrs Olivera swept from the room without condescending to take any notice of Poirot.

Alistair Blunt said:

'It's very good of you to come, M. Poirot. You've met Miss Olivera, I think? It was she who sent for you –'

Jane said abruptly:

'It's about this missing woman that the papers are full of. Miss Something Seale.'

'Sainsbury Seale? Yes?'

Jane turned once more to Poirot.

'It's such a pompous name, that's why I remember. Shall I tell him, or will you, Uncle Alistair?'

'My dear, it's your story.'

Jane turned once more to Poirot.

'It mayn't be important in the least – but I thought you ought to know.'

'Yes?'

'It was the last time Uncle Alistair went to the dentist's – I don't mean the other day – I mean about three months ago. I went with him to Queen Charlotte Street in the Rolls and it was to take me on to some friends in Regent's Park and come back for him. We stopped at 58, and Uncle got out, and just as he did, a woman came out of 58 – a middle-aged woman with fussy hair and rather arty clothes. She made a bee-line for Uncle and said (Jane Olivera's voice rose to an affected squeak): "Oh, Mr Blunt, you don't remember *me*, I'm *sure*!" Well, of course, I could see by Uncle's face that he *didn't* remember her in the slightest –'

Alistair Blunt sighed.

'I never do. People are always saying it –'

'He put on his special face,' went on Jane. 'I know it well. Kind of polite and make-believe. It wouldn't deceive a baby. He said in a most unconvincing voice: "Oh – er – of course." The terrible woman went on: "I was a *great* friend of your wife's, you know!"'

'They usually say that, too,' said Alistair Blunt in a voice of even deeper gloom.

He smiled rather ruefully.

'It always ends the same way! A subscription to something or other. I got off this time with five pounds to a Zenana Mission or something. Cheap!'

'Had she really known your wife?'

'Well, her being interested in Zenana Missions made me think that, if so, it would have been in India. We were there about ten years ago. But, of course, she couldn't have been a great friend or I'd have known about it. Probably met her once at a reception.'

Jane Olivera said:

'I don't believe she'd ever met Aunt Rebecca at all. I think it was just an excuse to speak to you.'

Alistair Blunt said tolerantly:

'Well, that's quite possible.'

Jane said:

'I mean, I think it's *queer* the way she tried to scrape an acquaintance with you, Uncle.'

Alistair Blunt said with the same tolerance:

'She did not try to follow it up in any way?'

Blunt shook his head.

'I never thought of her again. I'd even forgotten her name till Jane spotted it in the paper.'

Jane said a little unconvincingly:

'Well, *I* thought M. Poirot ought to be told!'

Poirot said politely:

'Thank you, Mademoiselle.'

He added:

'I must not keep you, Mr Blunt. You are a busy man.'

Jane said quickly:

'I'll come down with you.'

Under his moustaches, Hercule Poirot smiled to himself.

On the ground floor, Jane paused abruptly. She said:

'Come in here.'

They went into a small room off the hall.

She turned to face him.

'What did you mean on the telephone when you said that you had been expecting me to call you?'

Poirot smiled. He spread out his hands.

'Just that, Mademoiselle. I was expecting a call from you – and the call came.'

'You mean that you knew I'd ring up about this Sainsbury Seale woman.'

Poirot shook his head.

'That was only the pretext. You could have found something else if necessary.'

Jane said:

'Why the hell *should* I call you up?'

'Why should you deliver this titbit of information about Miss Sainsbury Seale to *me* instead of giving it to Scotland Yard? That would have been the natural thing to do.'

'All right, Mr Know All, how much exactly *do* you know?'

'I know that you are interested in me since you heard that I paid a visit to the Holborn Palace Hotel the other day.'

She went so white that it startled him. He had not believed that that deep tan could change to such a greenish hue.

He went on, quietly and steadily:

'You got me to come here today because you wanted to pump me – that is the expression, is it not? – yes, to *pump* me on the subject of Mr Howard Raikes.'

Jane Olivera said:

'Who's he, anyway?'

It was not a very successful parry.

Poirot said:

'You do not need to pump me, Mademoiselle. I will tell you what I know – or rather what I guessed. That first day that we came here, Inspector Japp and I, you were startled to see us – alarmed. You thought something had happened to your uncle. Why?'

'Well, he's the kind of man things might happen to. He had a bomb by post one day – after the Herjoslovakian Loan. And he gets lots of threatening letters.'

Poirot went on:

'Chief Inspector Japp told you that a certain dentist, Mr Morley, had been shot. You may recollect your answer. You said: "*But that's absurd.*"'

Jane bit her lip. She said:

'Did I? That was rather absurd of me, wasn't it?'

'It was a curious remark, Mademoiselle. It revealed that you knew of the existence of Mr Morley, that you had rather expected something to happen – not to happen to him – but possibly to happen in his house.'

'You do like telling yourself stories, don't you?'

Poirot paid no attention.

'You had expected – or rather you had feared – that something might happen at Mr Morley's house. You had feared that that something would have happened to your uncle. But if so, *you must know something that we did not know.* I reflected on the people who had been in Mr Morley's house that day, and I seized at once on the one person who might possibly have a connection with you – which was that young American, Mr Howard Raikes.'

'It's just like a serial, isn't it? What's the next thrilling instalment?'

'I went to see Mr Howard Raikes. He is a dangerous and attractive young man –'

Poirot paused expressively.

Jane said meditatively:

'He is, isn't he?' She smiled. 'All right! You win! I was scared stiff.'

She leaned forward.

'I'm going to tell you things, M. Poirot. You're not the kind one can just string along. I'd rather tell you than have you snooping around finding out. I love that man, Howard Raikes. I'm just crazy about him. My mother brought me over here just to get me away from him. Partly that and partly because she hopes Uncle Alistair might get fond enough of me to leave me his money when he dies.'

She went on:

'Mother is his niece by marriage. Her mother was Rebecca Arnholt's sister. He's my great-uncle-in-law. Only he hasn't got any near relatives of his own, so mother doesn't see why we shouldn't be his residuary legatees. She cadges off him pretty freely too.

'You see, I'm being frank with you, M. Poirot. That's the kind of people we are. Actually we've got plenty of money ourselves – an indecent amount according to Howard's ideas – but we're not in Uncle Alistair's class.'

She paused. She struck with one hand fiercely on the arm of her chair.

'How can I make you understand? Everything I've been brought up to believe in, Howard abominates and wants to do away with. And sometimes, you know, I feel like he does. I'm fond of Uncle Alistair, but he gets on my nerves sometimes. He's so *stodgy* – so British – so cautious and conservative. I feel sometimes that he and his kind *ought* to be swept away, that they are blocking progress – that without them we'd get things *done!*'

'You are a convert to Mr Raikes' ideas?'

'I am – and I'm not. Howard is – is wilder than most of his crowd. There are people, you know, who – who agree with Howard up to a point. They would be willing to – to try things – if Uncle Alistair and

573

his crowd would agree. But they never will! They just sit back and shake their heads and say: "We could never risk that." And "It wouldn't be sound economically." And "We've got to consider our responsibility." And "Look at history." But I think that one *mustn't* look at history. That's looking back. One must look *forward* all the time.'

Poirot said gently:

'It is an attractive vision.'

Jane looked at him scornfully.

'You say that too!'

'Perhaps because I am old. *Their old men have dreams* – only dreams, you see.'

He paused and then asked in a matter-of-fact voice:

'Why did Mr Howard Raikes make that appointment in Queen Charlotte Street?'

'Because *I* wanted him to meet Uncle Alistair and I couldn't see otherwise how to manage it. He'd been so bitter about Uncle Alistair – so full of – well, hate really, that I felt if he could only see him – see what a nice kindly unassuming person he was – that – that he would feel differently ... I couldn't arrange a meeting here because of mother – she would have spoilt everything.'

Poirot said:

'But after having made that arrangement, you were – afraid.'

Her eyes grew wide and dark. She said:

'Yes. Because – because – sometimes Howard gets carried away. He – he –'

Hercule Poirot said:

'He wants to take a short cut. To exterminate –'

Jane Olivera cried: '*Don't!*'

SEVEN, EIGHT, LAY THEM STRAIGHT

I

Time went on. It was over a month since Mr Morley's death, and there was still no news of Miss Sainsbury Seale.

Japp became increasingly wrathful on the subject.

'Dash it all, Poirot, the woman's got to be *somewhere*.'

'Indubitably, *mon cher*.'

'Either she's dead or alive. If she's dead, where's her body? Say, for instance, she committed suicide –'

'Another suicide?'

'Don't let's get back to that. *You* still say Morley was murdered – *I* say it was suicide.'

'You haven't traced the pistol?'

'No, it's a foreign make.'

'That is suggestive, is it not?'

'Not in the way you mean. Morley had been abroad. He went on cruises, he and his sister. Everybody in the British Isles goes on cruises. He may have picked it up abroad. They like to feel life's dangerous.'

He paused and said:

'Don't sidetrack me. I was saying that *if* – only if, mind you – that blasted woman committed suicide, if she'd drowned herself for instance, the body would have come ashore by now. If she was murdered, the same thing.'

'Not if a weight was attached to her body and it was put into the Thames.'

'From a cellar in Limehouse, I suppose! You're talking like a thriller by a lady novelist.'

'I know – I know. I blush when I say these things!'

'And she was done to death by an international gang of crooks, I suppose?'

Poirot sighed. He said:

'I have been told lately that there really are such things.'

'Who told you so?'

'Mr Reginald Barnes of Castlegarden Road, Ealing.'

'Well, he might know,' said Japp dubiously. 'He dealt with aliens when he was at the Home Office?'

'And you do not agree?'

'It isn't my branch – oh yes, there *are* such things – but they're

575

rather futile as a rule.'

There was a momentary silence as Poirot twirled his moustache.

Japp said:

'We've got one or two additional bits of information. She came home from India on the same boat as Amberiotis. But she was second class and he was first, so I don't suppose there's anything in that, although one of the waiters at the Savoy thinks she lunched there with him about a week or so before he died.'

'So there may have been a connection between them?'

'There may be – but I can't feel it's likely. I can't see a Missionary lady being mixed up in any funny business.'

'Was Amberiotis mixed up in any "funny business" as you term it?'

'Yes, he was. He was in close touch with some of our Central European friends. Espionage racket.'

'You are sure of that?'

'Yes. Oh, he wasn't doing any of the dirty work himself. We wouldn't have been able to touch him. Organizing and receiving reports – that was his lay.'

Japp paused and then went on:

'But that doesn't help us with the Sainsbury Seale. She wouldn't have been in on that racket.'

'She had lived in India, remember. There was a lot of unrest there last year.'

'Amberiotis and the excellent Miss Sainsbury Seale – I can't feel that they were team-mates.'

'Did you know that Miss Sainsbury Seale was a close friend of the late Mrs Alistair Blunt?'

'Who says so? I don't believe it. Not in the same class.'

'She said so.'

'Who'd she say that to?'

'Mr Alistair Blunt.'

'Oh! That sort of thing. He must be used to that lay. Do you mean that Amberiotis was using her that way? It wouldn't work. Blunt would get rid of her with a subscription. He wouldn't ask her down for a week-end or anything of that kind. He's not so unsophisticated as that.'

This was so palpably true that Poirot could only agree. After a minute or two, Japp went on with his summing up of the Sainsbury Seale situation.

'I suppose her body might have been lowered into a tank of acid by

576

a mad scientist – that's another solution they're very fond of in books! But take my word for it, these things are all my eye and Betty Martin. If the woman *is* dead, her body has just been quietly buried somewhere.'

'But where?'

'Exactly. She disappeared in London. Nobody's got a garden there – not a proper one. A lonely chicken farm, that's what we want!'

A garden! Poirot's mind flashed suddenly to that neat prim garden in Ealing with it's formal beds. How fantastic if a dead woman should be buried *there*! He told himself not to be absurd.

'And if she *isn't* dead,' went on Japp. 'Where is she? Over a month now, description published in the Press, circulated all over England –'

'And nobody has seen her?'

'Oh yes, practically *everybody* has seen her! You've no idea how many middle-aged faded-looking women wearing olive green cardigan suits there are. She's been seen on Yorkshire moors, and in Liverpool hotels, in guest houses in Devon and on the beach at Ramsgate! My men have spent their time patiently investigating all these reports – and one and all they've led nowhere, except to getting us in wrong with a number of perfectly respectable middle-aged ladies.'

Poirot clicked his tongue sympathetically.

'And yet,' went on Japp, 'She's a real person all right. I mean sometimes you come across a dummy, so to speak – someone who just comes to a place and poses as a Miss Spinks – when all the time there *isn't* a Miss Spinks. But this woman's *genuine* – she's got a past, a background! We know all about her from her childhood upwards! She's led a perfectly normal reasonable life – and suddenly hey presto – vanish!'

'There must be a reason,' said Poirot.

'She didn't shoot Morley, if that's what you mean. Amberiotis saw him alive after she left – and we've checked up on her movements after she left Queen Charlotte Street that morning.'

Poirot said impatiently:

'I am not suggesting for a moment that she shot Morley. Of course she did not. But all the same –'

Japp said:

'If you are right about Morley, then it's far more likely that he told her something which, although she doesn't suspect it, gives a clue to

577

his murderer. In that case, she *might* have been deliberately got out of the way.'

Poirot said:

'All this involves an organization, some big concern quite out of proportion to the death of a quiet dentist in Queen Charlotte Street.'

'Don't you believe everything Reginald Barnes tells you! He's a funny old bird – got spies and communists on the brain.'

Japp got up and Poirot said:

'Let me know if you have news.'

When Japp had gone out, Poirot sat frowning down at the table in front of him.

He had definitely the feeling of waiting for something. What was it?

He remembered how he had sat before, jotting down various unrelated facts and a series of names. A bird had flown past the window with a twig in its mouth.

He, too, had been collecting twigs. *Five, six, picking up sticks.* . . .

He had the sticks – quite a number of them now. They were all there, neatly pigeonholed in his orderly mind – but he had not as yet attempted to set them in order. That was the next step – lay them straight.

What was holding him up? He knew the answer. He was waiting for something.

Something inevitable, fore-ordained, the next link in the chain. When it came – then – *then* he could go on. . . .

II

It was late evening a week later when the summons came. Japp's voice was brusque over the telephone.

'That you, Poirot? *We've found her.* You'd better come round. King Leopold Mansions. Battersea Park. Number 45.'

A quarter of an hour later a taxi deposited Poirot outside King Leopold Mansions.

It was a big block of mansion flats looking out over Battersea Park. Number 45 was on the second floor. Japp himself opened the door.

His face was set in grim lines.

'Come in,' he said. 'It's not particularly pleasant, but I expect you'll want to see for yourself.'

Poirot said – but it was hardly a question:

578

'Dead?'

'What you might describe as very dead!'

Poirot cocked his head at a familiar sound coming from a door on his right.

'That's the porter,' said Japp. 'Being sick in the scullery sink! I had to get him here to see if he could identify her.'

He led the way down the passage and Poirot followed him. His nose wrinkled.

'Not nice,' said Japp. 'But what can you expect? She's been dead well over a month.'

The room they went into was a small lumber and box room. In the middle of it was a big metal chest of the kind used for storing furs. The lid was open.

Poirot stepped forward and looked inside.

He saw the foot first, with the shabby shoe on it and the ornate buckle. His first sight of Miss Sainsbury Seale had been, he remembered, a shoe buckle.

His gaze travelled up, over the green wool coat and skirt till it reached the head.

He made an inarticulate noise.

'I know,' said Japp. 'It's pretty horrible.'

The face had been battered out of all recognizable shape. Add to that the natural process of decomposition, and it was no wonder that both men looked a shade pea green as they turned away.

'Oh well,' said Japp. 'It's all in a day's work – our day's work. No doubt about it, ours is a lousy job sometimes. There's a spot of brandy in the other room. You'd better have some.'

The living-room was smartly furnished in an up-to-date style – a good deal of chromium and some large square-looking easy chairs upholstered in a pale fawn geometric fabric.

Poirot found the decanter and helped himself to some brandy. As he finished drinking, he said:

'It was not pretty, that! Now tell me, my friend, all about it.'

Japp said:

'This flat belongs to a Mrs Albert Chapman. Mrs Chapman is, I gather, a well-upholstered smart blonde of forty-odd. Pays her bills, fond of an occasional game of bridge with her neighbours but keeps herself to herself more or less. No children. Mr Chapman is a commercial traveller.

'Sainsbury Seale came here on the evening of our interview with her. About seven-fifteen. So she probably came straight here from the Glengowrie Court. She'd been here once before, so the porter says. You see, all perfectly clear and above-board – nice friendly call. The porter took Miss Sainsbury Seale up in the lift to this flat. The last he saw of her was standing on the mat pressing the bell.'

Poirot commented:

'He has taken his time to remember this!'

'He's had gastric trouble, it seems, been away in hospital while another man took on temporarily for him. It wasn't until about a week ago that he happened to notice in an old paper the description of a "wanted woman" and he said to his wife. "Sounds quite like that old cup of tea who came to see Mrs Chapman on the second floor. *She* had on a green wool dress and buckles on her shoes." And after about another hour he registered again – "Believe she had a name, too, something like that. Blimey, it *was* – Miss Something or other Seale!"'

'After that,' continued Japp, 'it took him about four days to overcome his natural distrust of getting mixed up with the police and come along with his information.

'We didn't really think it would lead to anything. You've no idea how many of these false alarms we've had. However, I sent Sergeant Beddoes along – he's a bright young fellow. A bit too much of this high-class education but he can't help that. It's fashionable now.

'Well, Beddoes got a hunch at once that we were on to something at last. For one thing this Mrs Chapman hadn't been seen about for over a month. She'd gone away without leaving any address. That was a bit odd. In fact everything he could learn about Mr and Mrs Chapman seemed odd.

'He found out the porter hadn't seen Miss Sainsbury Seale leave again. That in itself wasn't unusual. She might easily have come down the stairs and gone out without his seeing her. But then the porter told him that Mrs Chapman had gone away rather suddenly. There was just a big printed notice outside the door the next morning. "NO MILK. TELL NELLIE I AM CALLED AWAY."

'Nellie was the daily maid who did for her. Mrs Chapman had gone away suddenly once or twice before, so the girl didn't think it odd, but what *was* odd was the fact that she hadn't rung for the porter to take her luggage down or get her a taxi.

'Anyway, Beddoes decided to get into the flat. We got a search warrant and a pass key from the manager. Found nothing of interest except in the bathroom. There had been some hasty clearing up done there. There was a trace of blood on the linoleum – in the corners

580

where it had been missed when the floor was washed over. After that, it was just a question of finding the body. Mrs Chapman couldn't have left with any luggage with her or the porter would have known. Therefore the body *must* still be in the flat. We soon spotted that fur chest – airtight, you know – just the place. Keys were in the dressing-table drawer.'

'We opened it up – and there was the missing lady! Mistletoe Bough up-to-date.'

Poirot asked:

'What about Mrs Chapman?'

'What indeed? Who is Sylvia (her name's Sylvia, by the way), what is she? One thing is certain. Sylvia, or Sylvia's friends, murdered the lady and put her in the box.'

Poirot nodded.

He asked:

'But why was her face battered in? It is not nice, that.'

'I'll say it isn't nice! As to *why* – well, one can only guess. Sheer vindictiveness, perhaps. Or it may have been with the idea of concealing the woman's identity.'

'But it did *not* conceal her identity.'

'No, because not only had we got a pretty good description of what Mabelle Sainsbury Seale was wearing when she disappeared, but her handbag had been stuffed into the fur box too and inside the handbag there was actually an old letter addressed to her at her hotel in Russell Square.'

Poirot sat up. He said:

'But that – that does not make the common sense!'

'It certainly doesn't. I suppose it was a slip.'

'Yes – perhaps – a slip. But –'

He got up.

'You have been over the flat?'

'Pretty well. There's nothing illuminating.'

'I should like to see Mrs Chapman's bedroom.'

'Come along then.'

The bedroom showed no signs of a hasty departure. It was neat and tidy. The bed had not been slept in, but was turned down ready for the night. There was a thick coating of dust everywhere.

Japp said:

'No finger-prints, so far as we can see. There are some on the kitchen things, but I expect they'll turn out to be the maid's.'

'That means that the whole place was dusted very carefully after the murder?'

'Yes.'

Poirot's eyes swept slowly round the room. Like the sitting-room it was furnished in the modern style – and furnished, so he thought, by someone with a moderate income. The articles in it were expensive but not ultra expensive. They were showy but not first-class. The colour scheme was rose pink. He looked into the built-in wardrobe and handled the clothes – smart clothes but again not of first-class quality. His eyes fell to the shoes – they were largely of the sandal variety popular at the moment, some had exaggerated cork soles. He balanced one in his hand, registered the fact that Mrs Chapman had taken a 5 in shoes and put it down again. In another cupboard he found a pile of furs, shoved in a heap.

Japp said:

'Came out of the fur chest.'

Poirot nodded.

He was handling a grey squirrel coat. He remarked appreciatively: 'First-class skins.'

He went into the bathroom.

There was a lavish display of cosmetics. Poirot looked at them with interest. Powder, rouge, vanishing cream, skin food, two bottles of hair application.

Japp said:

'Not one of our natural platinum blondes, I gather.'

Poirot murmured:

'At forty, *mon ami*, the hair of most women has begun to go grey but Mrs Chapman was not one to yield to nature.'

'She's probably gone henna red by now for a change.'

'I wonder.'

Japp said:

'There's something worrying you, Poirot. What is it?'

Poirot said:

'But yes, I am worried. I am very seriously worried. There is here, you see, for me an insoluble problem.'

Resolutely, he went once more into the box-room. ....

He took hold of the shoe on the dead woman's foot. It resisted and came off with difficulty.

He examined the buckle. It had been clumsily sewn on by hand.

Hercule Poirot sighed. He said:

'It is that I am dreaming!'

Japp said curiously:

'What are you trying to do – make the thing more difficult?'

'Exactly that.'

Japp said:

'One patent leather shoe, complete with buckle. What's wrong with that?'

Hercule Poirot said:

'Nothing – absolutely nothing. But all the same – I do not understand.'

III

Mrs Merton of No. 82, King Leopold Mansions had been designated by the porter as Mrs Chapman's closest friend in the Mansions.

It was, therefore, to No. 82 that Japp and Poirot betook themselves next.

Mrs Merton was a loquacious lady, with snapping black eyes, and an elaborate coiffure.

It needed no pressure to make her talk. She was only too ready to rise to a dramatic situation.

'Sylvia Chapman – well, of course, I don't know her really well – not intimately, so to speak. We had a few bridge evenings occasionally and we went to the pictures together, and of course shopping sometimes. But oh, do tell me – she isn't *dead*, is she?'

Japp reassured her.

'Well, I'm sure I'm thankful to hear it! But the postman just now was all agog about a body having been found in one of the flats – but then one really can't believe half one hears, can one? I *never* do.'

Japp asked a further question.

'No, I haven't heard anything of Mrs Chapman – not since we had spoken about going to see the new Ginger Rogers and Fred Astaire the following week, and she said nothing about going away *then*.'

Mrs Merton had never heard a Miss Sainsbury Seale mentioned. Mrs Chapman had never spoken of any one of that name.

'And yet, you know, the name *is* familiar to me, distinctly familiar. I seem to have seen it somewhere quite *lately*.'

Japp said drily:

'It's been in all the papers for some weeks –'

'Of course – some missing person, wasn't it? And you thought Mrs Chapman might have known her? No, I'm sure I've never heard Sylvia mention *that* name.'

'Can you tell me anything about Mr Chapman, Mrs Merton?'

A rather curious expression came over Mrs Merton's face. She said:

'He was a commercial traveller, I believe, so Mrs Chapman told me. He travelled abroad for his firm – armaments, I believe. He went all over Europe.'

'Did you ever meet him?'

'No, never. He was at home so seldom, and when he was at home he and Mrs Chapman didn't want to bother with outsiders. Very naturally.'

'Do you know if Mrs Chapman had any near relations or friends?'

'I don't know about friends. I don't think she had any near relations. She never spoke of any.'

'Was she ever in India?'

'Not that I know of.'

Mrs Merton paused, and then broke out:

'But please tell me – why are you asking all these questions? I quite understand that you come from Scotland Yard and all that, but there must be some special reason?'

'Well, Mrs Merton, you are bound to know some time. As a matter of fact, a dead body *has* been found in Mrs Chapman's flat.'

'Oh –?' Mrs Merton looked for a moment like the dog whose eyes were as big as saucers.

'A dead body! It wasn't Mr Chapman, was it? Or perhaps some foreigner?'

Japp said:

'It wasn't a man at all – it was a woman.'

'A woman.' Mrs Merton seemed even more surprised.

Poirot said gently:

'Why should you think it was a man?'

'Oh, I don't know. It seemed more likely somehow.'

'But why? Was it because Mrs Chapman was in the habit of receiving gentleman visitors?'

'Oh no – oh no indeed.' Mrs Merton was indignant. 'I never meant anything of *that* kind. Sylvia Chapman wasn't in the least *that* kind of woman – not at all! It was just that, with Mr Chapman – I mean –'

She came to a stop.

Poirot said:

'I think, Madame, that you know a little more than you have told us.'

Mrs Merton said uncertainly:

584

'I don't know, I'm sure – *what* I ought to do! I mean, I don't exactly want to betray a confidence and of course I never have repeated what Sylvia told me – except just to one or two intimates whom I knew were really *safe* –'

Mrs Merton leaned forward and lowered her voice:

'It just – slipped out, as it were, one day. When we were seeing a film – about the Secret Service and Mrs Chapman said you could see that whoever had written it didn't know much about their subject, and then it came out – only she swore me to secrecy. Mr Chapman was in the Secret Service, I mean. That was the real reason he had to go abroad so much. The armament firm was only a blind. And it was terribly worrying for Mrs Chapman because she couldn't write to him or get letters from him while he was away. And, of course, it was terribly *dangerous*!'

IV

As they went down the stairs again to No. 42, Japp ejaculated with feeling: 'Shades of Phillips Oppenheim, Valentine Williams and William le Queux, I think I'm going mad!'

That smart young man, Sergeant Beddoes, was waiting for them. He said respectfully:

'Haven't been able to get anything helpful from the maid, sir. Mrs Chapman changed maids pretty often, it seems. This one only worked for her for a month or two. She says Mrs Chapman was a nice lady, fond of the radio and pleasant spoken. Girl was of the opinion the husband was a gay deceiver but that Mrs Chapman didn't suspect it. She got letters from abroad sometimes, some from Germany, two from America, and from Italy and one from Russia. The girl's young man collects stamps, and Mrs Chapman used to give them to her off the letters.'

'Anything among Mrs Chapman's papers?'

'Absolutely nothing, sir. She didn't keep much. A few bills and receipted accounts – all local. Some old theatre programmes, one or two cookery recipes cut out of the papers, and a pamphlet about Zenana Missions.'

'And we can guess who brought *that* here. She doesn't sound like a murderess, does she? And yet that's what it seems to be. She's bound to be an accomplice anyway. No strange men seen about that evening?'

'The porter doesn't remember any – but then I don't suppose he would by now, and anyway it's a big block of flats – people always going in and out. He can only fix the date of Miss Sainsbury Seale's visit because he was taken off to the hospital the next day and was actually feeling rather bad that evening.'

'Anybody in the other flats hear anything out of the way?'

The younger man shook his head.

'I've inquired at the flat above this and the one beiow. Nobody can remember hearing anything unusual. Both of them had their radios on, I gather.'

The divisional surgeon came out of the bathroom where he had been washing his hands.

'Most unsavoury corpse,' he said cheerfully. 'Send her along when you're ready and I'll get down to brass tacks.'

'No idea of the cause of death, doctor?'

'Impossible to say until I've done the autopsy. Those face injuries were definitely inflicted after death, I should say. But I shall know better when I've got her at the mortuary. Middle-aged woman, quite healthy – grey hair at the roots but tinted blonde. There may be distinguishing marks on the body – if there isn't, it may be a job to identify her – oh, you know who she is, splendid? What? Missing woman there's been all the fuss about? Well, you know, I never read the papers. Just do the crosswords.'

Japp said bitterly:

'And that's publicity for you!' as the doctor went out.

Poirot was hovering over the desk. He picked up a small brown address book.

The indefatigable Beddoes said:

'Nothing of special interest there – mostly hairdressers, dressmakers, etc. I've noted down any private names and addresses.'

Poirot opened the book at the letter D.

He read Dr Davis, 17, Prince Albert Road, Drake and Pomponetti, Fishmongers. And below it: *Dentist. Mr Morley, 58, Queen Charlotte Street.*

There was a green light in Poirot's eyes. He said:

'There will be no difficulty, I imagine, in positively identifying the body.'

Japp looked at him curiously. He said:

'Surely – you don't imagine –?'

Poirot said with vehemence:

'I want to be *sure*.'

Miss Morley had moved to the country. She was living in a small country cottage near Hertford.

The Grenadier greeted Poirot amicably. Since her brother's death her face had perhaps grown slightly grimmer, her carriage more upright, her general attitude towards life more unyielding. She resented bitterly the slur cast upon her brother's professional name by the findings of the inquest.

Poirot, she had reason to believe, shared the view that the verdict of the Coroner's inquest was untrue. Hence the Grenadier unbent a little.

She answered his questions readily enough and with competence. All Mr Morley's professional papers had been carefully filed by Miss Nevill and had been handed over by her to Mr Morley's successor. Some of the patients had transferred themselves to Mr Reilly, others had accepted the new partner, others again had gone to other dentists elsewhere.

Miss Morley, after she had given what information she could, said:

'So you have found that woman who was Henry's patient – Miss Sainsbury Seale – and *she* was murdered *too*.'

The 'too' was a little defiant. She stressed the word.

Poirot said:

'Your brother never mentioned Miss Sainsbury Seale particularly to you?'

'No, I don't remember his doing so. He would tell me if he had had a particularly trying patient, or if one of his patients had said something amusing he would pass it on to me, but we didn't usually talk about his work much. He was glad to forget it when the day was over. He was very tired sometimes.'

'Do you remember hearing of a Mrs Chapman amongst your brother's patients?'

'Chapman? No, I don't think so. Miss Nevill is really the person to help you over all this.'

'I am anxious to get in touch with her. Where is she now?'

'She has taken a post with a dentist in Ramsgate, I believe.'

'She has not married that young man Frank Carter yet?'

'No. I rather hope that will never come off. I don't like that young man, M. Poirot. I really don't. There is something wrong about him. I still feel that he hasn't really any proper moral sense.'

Poirot said:

'Do you think it is possible that *he* could have shot your brother?'

Miss Morley said slowly:

'I do feel perhaps that he would be *capable* of it – he has a very uncontrollable temper. But I don't really see that he had any motive – nor opportunity for that matter. You see, it wasn't as though Henry had succeeded in persuading Gladys to give him up. She was sticking to him in the most faithful way.'

'Could he have been bribed, do you think?'

'Bribed? To kill my brother? What an extraordinary idea!'

A nice-looking dark-haired girl brought in the tea at this moment. As she closed the door behind her again, Poirot said:

'That girl was with you in London, was she not?'

'Agnes? Yes, she was house-parlourmaid. I let the cook go – she didn't want to come to the country anyway – and Agnes does everything for me. She is turning into quite a nice little cook.'

Poirot nodded.

He knew very accurately the domestic arrangements of 58, Queen Charlotte Street. They had been thoroughly gone into at the time of the tragedy. Mr Morley and his sister had occupied the two top floors of the house as a maisonette. The basement had been shut up altogether except for a narrow passage leading from the area to the backyard where a wire cage ran up to the top floor with the tradesman's deliveries and where a speaking-tube was installed. Therefore the only entrance to the house was by the front door which it was Alfred's business to answer. This had enabled the police to be sure that no outsider could have entered the house on that particular morning.

Both cook and house-parlourmaid had been with the Morleys for some years and bore good characters. So, although it was theoretically possible that one or the other of them *might* have crept down to the second floor and shot her master, the possibility had never been taken seriously into account. Neither of the two had appeared unduly flustered or upset at being questioned, and there certainly seemed no possible reason for connecting either of them with his death.

Nevertheless, as Agnes handed Poirot his hat and stick on leaving, she asked him with an unusually nervous abruptness:

'Does – does any one know anything more about the master's death, sir?'

Poirot turned to look at her. He said:

'Nothing fresh has come to light.'

'They're still quite sure as he *did* shoot himself because he'd made a mistake with that drug?'

'Yes. Why do you ask?'

Agnes pleated her apron. Her face was averted. She said rather indistinctly:

'The – the mistress doesn't think so.'

'And you agree with her, perhaps?'

'Me? Oh, I don't know nothing, sir. I only – I only wanted to be *sure*.'

Hercule Poirot said in his most gentle voice:

'It would be a relief to you to feel beyond any possible doubt that it *was* suicide?'

'Oh, yes, sir,' Agnes agreed quickly, 'it would indeed.'

'For a special reason, perhaps?'

Her startled eyes met his. She shrank back a little.

'I – I don't know anything about it, sir. I only just asked.'

'But *why* did she ask?' Hercule Poirot demanded of himself, as he walked down the path to the gate.

He felt sure that there was an answer to that question. But as yet he could not guess what it was.

All the same, he felt a step nearer.

VI

When Poirot returned to his flat he was surprised to find an unexpected visitor waiting for him.

A bald head was visible above the back of a chair, and the small neat figure of Mr Barnes rose to his feet.

With eyes that twinkled as usual, he made a dry little apology.

He had come, he explained, to return M. Hercule Poirot's visit.

Poirot professed himself delighted to see Mr Barnes.

George was instructed to bring some coffee unless his visitor preferred tea or whisky and soda?

'Coffee will be admirable,' said Mr Barnes. 'I imagine that your manservant prepares it well. Most English servants do not.'

Presently, after a few interchanges of polite remarks, Mr Barnes gave a little cough and said:

'I will be frank with you, M. Poirot. It was sheer curiosity that brought me here. You, I imagined, would be well posted in all the details of this rather curious case. I see by the papers that the missing

Miss Sainsbury Seale has been found, that an inquest was held and adjourned for further evidence. Cause of death was stated to have been an overdose of medinal.'

'That is quite correct,' said Poirot.

There was a pause and then Poirot asked:

'Have you ever heard of Albert Chapman, Mr Barnes?'

'Ah, the husband of the lady in whose flat Miss Sainsbury Seale came to die? Rather an elusive person, it would seem.'

'But hardly non-existent?'

'Oh no,' said Mr Barnes. 'He exists. Oh yes, he exists – or *did* exist. I had heard he was dead. But you can't trust these rumours.'

'Who was he, Mr Barnes?'

'I don't suppose they'll say at the inquest. Not if they can help it. They'll trot out the armaments firm traveller story.'

'He *was* in the Secret Service then?'

'Of course he was. But he had no business to tell his wife so – no business at all. In fact he ought not to have continued in the Service after his marriage. It isn't usually done – not, that is, when you're one of the really hush-hush people.'

'And Albert Chapman was?'

'Yes. Q.X.912. That's what he was known as. Using a name is most irregular. Oh, I don't mean that Q.X.912 was specially important – or anything of that kind. But he was useful because he was an insignificant kind of chap – the kind whose face isn't easily remembered. He was used a lot as a messenger up and down Europe. You know the sort of thing. One dignified letter sent *via* our Ambassador in Ruritania – one unofficial ditto containing the dirt per Q.X.912 – that is to say: Mr Albert Chapman.'

'Then he knew a lot of useful information?'

'Probably didn't know a thing,' said Mr Barnes cheerfully. 'His job was just hopping in and out of trains and boats and aeroplanes and having the right story to explain *why* he was going *where* he was going!'

'And you heard he was dead?'

'That's what I heard,' said Mr Barnes. 'But you can't believe all you hear. I never do.'

Looking at Mr Barnes intently, Poirot asked:

'What do you think has happened to his wife?'

'I can't imagine,' said Mr Barnes. He looked, wide-eyed at Poirot. 'Can you?'

Poirot said:

590

'I had an idea –' He stopped.

He said slowly:

'It is very confusing.'

Mr Barnes murmured sympathetically: 'Anything worrying you in particular?'

Hercule Poirot said slowly:

'Yes. The evidence of my own eyes. ....'

VII

Japp came into Poirot's sitting-room and slammed down his bowler hat with such force that the table rocked.

He said:

'What the devil made you think of it?'

'My good Japp, I do not know what you are talking about.'

Japp said slowly and forcefully:

'What gave you the idea that the body wasn't Miss Sainsbury Seale's body?'

Poirot looked worried. He said:

'It was the face that worried me. Why smash up a dead woman's face?'

Japp said:

'My word, I hope old Morley's somewhere where he can know about it. It's just possible, you know, that he was put out of the way on purpose – so that he couldn't give evidence.'

'It would certainly be better if he could have given evidence himself.'

'Leatheran will be all right. Morley's successor. He's a thoroughly capable man with a good manner and the evidence is unmistakable.'

The evening papers came out with a sensation the next day. The dead body found in the Battersea flat, believed to be that of Miss Sainsbury Seale, was positively identified as that of Mrs Albert Chapman.

Mr Leatheran, of 58, Queen Charlotte Street, unhesitatingly pronounced it to be Mrs Chapman on the evidence of the teeth and jaw, full particulars of which were recorded in the late Mr Morley's professional chart.

Miss Sainsbury Seale's clothes had been found on the body and Miss Sainsbury Seale's handbag with the body – but where was Miss Sainsbury Seale herself?

As they came away from the inquest Japp said jubilantly to Poirot:

'A smart piece of work, that. Gave 'em a sensation!'

Poirot nodded.

'You tumbled to it first,' said Japp, 'but, you know, *I* wasn't happy about that body myself. After all, you don't go smashing a dead person's face and head about for nothing. It's messy, unpleasant work, and it was pretty plain there must be *some* reason for it. And there's only one reason there could be – to confuse the identity.' He added generously: 'But I shouldn't have tumbled so quickly to the fact that it actually was the other woman.'

Poirot said with a smile:

'And yet, my friend, the actual descriptions of the women were not unlike as regards fundamentals. Mrs Chapman was a smart, good-looking woman, well made up and fashionably turned out. Miss Sainsbury Seale was dowdy and innocent of lipstick or rouge. But the essentials were the same. Both were women of forty odd. Both were roughly about the same height and build. Both had hair turning grey which they touched up to make it appear golden.'

'Yes, of course, when you put it like *that*. One thing we've got to admit – the fair Mabelle put it over on both of us, good and proper. I'd have sworn she was the genuine article.'

'But, my friend, she *was* the genuine article. We know all about her past life.'

'We didn't know she was capable of murder – and that's what it looks like now. Sylvia didn't murder Mabelle. Mabelle murdered Sylvia.'

Hercule Poirot shook his head in a worried fashion. He still found it difficult to reconcile Mabelle Sainsbury Seale with murder. Yet in his ears he heard the small, ironic voice of Mr Barnes:

'Look among the respectable people. . . .'

Mabelle Sainsbury Seale had been eminently respectable.

Japp said with emphasis:

'I'm going to get to the bottom of this case, Poirot. That woman isn't going to put it over on me.'

The following day, Japp rang up. His voice held a curious note. He said:

'Poirot, do you want to hear a piece of news? It's Na Poo, my lad. Na Poo!'

'*Pardon?* – the line is perhaps not very clear. I did not quite catch –'

'It's off, my boy. O.F.F. Call it a day! Sit down and twiddle our thumbs!'

There was no mistaking the bitterness now. Poirot was startled.

'What is off?'

'The whole ruddy blinking thing! The hue and cry! The publicity! The whole bag of tricks!'

'But I still do not understand.'

'Well, listen. Listen carefully, because I can't mention names very well. You know our inquiry? You know we're combing the country for a performing fish?'

'Yes, yes, perfectly. I comprehend now.'

'Well, that's been called *off*. Hushed up – kept mum. *Now* do you understand?'

'Yes, yes. But *why*?'

'Orders from the ruddy Foreign Office.'

'Is not that very extraordinary?'

'Well, it does happen now and again.'

'Why should they be so forbearing to Miss— to the performing fish?'

'They're not. They don't care tuppence about her. It's the publicity – if she's brought to trial too much might come out about Mrs A. C. The corpse. That's the hush-hush side! I can only suppose that the ruddy husband – Mr A. C. – Get me?'

'Yes, yes.'

'That he's somewhere abroad in a ticklish spot and they don't want to queer his pitch.'

'Tchah!'

'What did you say?'

'I made, *mon ami*, an exclamation of annoyance!'

'Oh! that was it. I thought you'd caught cold. Annoyance is right! I could use a stronger word. Letting that dame get away with it makes me see red.'

Poirot said very softly:

'She will not get away with it.'

'Our hands are tied, I tell you!'

'Yours may be – *mine* are not!'

'Good old Poirot! Then you *are* going on with it?'

'*Mais oui* – to the death.'

'Well, don't let it be your death, old boy! If this business goes on as it has begun someone will probably send you a poisoned tarantula by post!'

As he replaced the receiver, Poirot said to himself:

'Now, why did I use that melodramatic phrase – "to the death"? *Vraiment*, it is absurd!'

III

The letter came by evening post. It was typewritten except for the signature.

'DEAR M. POIROT' (it ran),

'I should be greatly obliged if you would call upon me some time tomorrow. I may have a commission for you. I suggest twelve-thirty, at my house in Chelsea. If this is inconvenient to you, perhaps you would telephone my secretary? I apologize for giving you such short notice.

> 'Yours sincerely,
> 'ALISTAIR BLUNT.'

Poirot smoothed out the letter and read it a second time. At that moment the telephone rang.

Hercule Poirot occasionally indulged in the fancy that he knew by the ring of his telephone bell what kind of message was impending.

On this occasion he was at once quite sure that the call was significant. It was not a wrong number – not one of his friends.

He got up and took down the receiver. He said in his polite, foreign voice:

"*Allo?*"

An impersonal voice said: 'What number are you, please?'

'This is Whitehall 7272.'

There was a pause, a click, and then a voice spoke. It was a woman's voice.

'M. Poirot?'

'Yes.'

594

'M. Hercule Poirot?'

'Yes.'

'M. Poirot, you have either already received – or will shortly receive, a letter.'

'Who is speaking?'

'It is not necessary that you should know.'

'Very well. I have received, Madame, eight letters and three bills by the evening post.'

'Then you know which letter I mean. You will be wise, M. Poirot, to refuse the commission you have been offered.'

'That, Madame, is a matter I shall decide myself.'

The voice said coldly:

'I am warning you, M. Poirot. Your interference will no longer be tolerated. *Keep out of this business.*'

'And if I do not keep out of it?'

'Then we shall take steps to see that your interference is no longer to be feared. ....'

'That is a threat, Madame!'

'We are only asking you to be sensible. .... It is for your own good.'

'You are very magnanimous!'

'You cannot alter the course of events and what has been arranged. *So keep out of what doesn't concern you!* Do you understand?'

'Oh yes, I understand. But I consider that Mr Morley's death *is* my concern.'

The woman's voice said sharply:

'Morley's death was only an incident. He interfered with our plans.'

'He was a human being, Madame, and he died before his time.'

'He was of no importance.'

Poirot's voice was dangerous as he said very quietly:

'There you are wrong. ....'

'It was his own fault. He refused to be sensible.'

'I, too, refuse to be sensible.'

'Then you are a fool.'

There was a click the other end as the receiver was replaced.

Poirot said, '*Allo?*' then put down his receiver in turn. He did not trouble to ask the Exchange to trace the number. He was fairly sure that the call had been put through from a public telephone box.

What intrigued and puzzled him was the fact that he thought he had heard the voice somewhere before. He racked his brains, trying to bring the elusive memory back. Could it be the voice of Miss

Sainsbury Seale?

As he remembered it, Mabelle Sainsbury Seale's voice had been high-pitched and somewhat affected, with rather overemphasized diction. This voice was not at all like that, and yet – perhaps it might be Miss Sainsbury Seale with her voice disguised. After all, she had been an actress in her time. She could alter her voice, probably, easily enough. In actual timbre, the voice was not unlike what he remembered.

But he was not satisfied with that explanation. No, it was some other person that the voice brought back to him. It was not a voice he knew well – but he was still quite sure that he had heard it once, if not twice, before.

Why, he wondered, bother to ring up and threaten him? Could these people actually believe that threats would deter him? Apparently they did. It was poor psychology!

IV

There was some sensational news in the morning papers. The Prime Minister had been shot at when leaving 10, Downing Street with a friend yesterday evening. Fortunately the bullet had gone wide. The man, an Indian, had been taken into custody.

After reading this, Poirot took a taxi to Scotland Yard where he was shown up to Japp's room. The latter greeted him heartily.

'Ah, so the news has brought you along. Have any of the papers mentioned who "the friend" was with the P.M.?'

'No, who was it?'

'Alistair Blunt.'

'Really?'

'And,' went on Japp, 'we've every reason to believe that the bullet was meant for Blunt and not for the P.M. That is, unless the man was an even more thundering bad shot than he is already!'

'Who did it?'

'Some crazy Hindu student. Half baked, as usual. But he was put up to it. It wasn't all his own idea.'

Japp added:

'Quite a sound bit of work getting him. There's usually a small group of people, you know, watching No. 10. When the shot was fired, a young American grabbed hold of a little man with a beard. He held on to him like grim death and yelled to the police that he'd got the man. Meanwhile the Indian was quietly hooking it – but one of our people nabbed him all right.'

'Who was the American?' asked Poirot curiously.

'Young fellow by the name of Raikes. Why –' He stopped short, staring at Poirot. 'What's the matter?'

Poirot said:

'Howard Raikes, staying at the Holborn Palace Hotel?'

'That's right. Who – why, of course! I thought the name seemed familiar. He's the patient who ran away that morning when Morley shot himself. . . .'

He paused. He said slowly:

'Rum – how that old business keeps cropping up. You've still got your ideas about it, haven't you, Poirot?'

Hercule Poirot replied gravely:

'Yes. I still have my ideas. . . .'

V

At the Gothic House, Poirot was received by a secretary, a tall, limp young man with an accomplished social manner.

He was pleasantly apologetic.

'I am so sorry, M. Poirot – and so is Mr Blunt. He has been called to Downing Street. The result of this – er – incident last night. I rang your flat, but unfortunately you had already left.'

The young man went on rapidly:

'Mr Blunt commissioned me to ask you if it would be possible for you to spend the week-end with him at his house in Kent. Exsham, you know. If so, he would call for you in the car tomorrow evening.'

Poirot hesitated.

The young man said persuasively:

'Mr Blunt is really most anxious to see you.'

Hercule Poirot bowed his head.

He said: 'Thank you. I accept.'

'Oh, that's splendid. Mr Blunt will be delighted. If he calls for you about a quarter to six, will that – Oh, good morning, Mrs Olivera –'

Jane Olivera's mother had just entered. She was very smartly dressed, with a hat clinging to an eyebrow in the midst of a very soignée coiffure.

'Oh! Mr Selby, did Mr Blunt give you any instructions about those garden chairs? I meant to talk to him about them last night, because I knew we'd be going down this week-end and –'

Mrs Olivera took in Poirot and paused.

'Do you know Mrs Olivera, M. Poirot?'

'I have already had the pleasure of meeting Madame.'

Poirot bowed.

Mrs Olivera said vaguely:

'Oh? How do you do. Of course, Mr Selby, I know that Alistair is a very busy man and that these small domestic matters mayn't seem to him important –'

'It's quite all right, Mrs Olivera,' said the efficient Mr Selby. 'He told me about it and I rang up Messrs Deevers about them.'

'Well, now, that's a real load off my mind. Now, Mr Selby, can you tell me . . .'

Mrs Olivera clacked on. She was, thought Poirot, rather like a hen. A big, fat hen! Mrs Olivera, still clacking, moved majestically after her bust towards the door.

'. . . And if you're quite sure that there will only be ourselves this week-end –'

Mr Selby coughed.

'Er – M. Poirot is also coming down for the week-end.'

Mrs Olivera stopped. She turned round and surveyed Poirot with visible distaste.

'Is that really so?'

'Mr Blunt has been kind enough to invite me,' said Poirot.

'Well, I wonder – why, if that isn't *queer* of Alistair. You'll excuse me, M. Poirot, but Mr Blunt particularly told me that he wanted a quiet, *family* week-end!'

Selby said firmly:

'Mr Blunt is particularly anxious that M. Poirot should come.'

'Oh really? He didn't mention it to *me*.'

The door opened. Jane stood there. She said impatiently:

'Mother, aren't you coming? Our lunch appointment is at one-fifteen!'

'I'm coming, Jane. Don't be impatient.'

'Well, get a move on, for goodness sake – Hallo, M. Poirot.'

She was suddenly very still – her petulance frozen. Her eyes more wary.

Mrs Olivera said in a cold voice:

'M. Poirot is coming down to Exsham for the week-end.'

'Oh – I see.'

Jane Olivera stood back to let her mother pass her. On the point of

598

following her, she whirled back again.

'M. Poirot!'

Her voice was imperious.

Poirot crossed the room to her.

She said in a low voice: 'You're coming down to Exsham? Why?'

Poirot shrugged his shoulders. He said:

'It is a kind thought of your uncle's.'

Jane said:

'But he can't know ... He can't ... When did he ask you? Oh, there's no need –'

'Jane!'

Her mother was calling from the hall.

Jane said in a low, urgent tone:

'Stay away, Please don't come.'

She went out. Poirot heard the sounds of altercation. Heard Mrs Olivera's high, complaining, clucking voice. 'I really will not tolerate your rudeness, Jane ... I shall take steps to see that you do not interfere –'

The secretary said:

'Then at a little before six tomorrow, M. Poirot?'

Poirot nodded assent mechanically. He was standing like a man who has seen a ghost. But it was his ears, not his eyes, that had given him the shock.

Two of the sentences that had drifted in through the open door were almost identical with those he had heard last night through the telephone, and he knew why the voice had been faintly familiar.

As he walked out into the sunshine he shook his head blankly. Mrs Olivera?

But it was impossible! It could not have been *Mrs Olivera* who had spoken over the 'phone!

That empty-headed society woman – selfish, brainless, grasping, self-centred? What had he called her to himself just now?

'That good fat hen? *C'est ridicule!*' said Hercule Poirot.

His ears, he decided, must have deceived him. And yet –

VI

The Rolls called punctually for Poirot at a little before six.

Alistair Blunt and his secretary were the only occupants. Mrs Olivera and Jane had gone down in another car earlier, it seemed.

The drive was uneventful. Blunt talked a little, mostly of his garden and of a recent horticultural show.

Poirot congratulated him on his escape from death, at which Blunt demurred. He said:

'Oh, *that*! Don't think the fellow was shooting at me particularly. Anyway, the poor chap hadn't the first idea of how to aim! Just one of these half-crazed students. There's no harm in them really. They just get worked up and fancy a pot shot at the P.M. will alter the course of history. It's pathetic, really.'

'There have been other attempts on your life, have there not?'

'Sounds quite melodramatic,' said Blunt, with a slight twinkle. 'Someone sent me a bomb by post not long ago. It wasn't a very efficient bomb. You know, these fellows who want to take on the management of the world – what sort of an efficient business do they think they could make of it, when they can't even devise an effectual bomb?'

He shook his head.

'It's always the same thing – long-haired woolly idealists – without one practical bit of knowledge in their heads. I'm not a clever chap – never have been – but I can just read and write and do arithmetic. D'you understand what I mean by that?'

'I think so, but explain to me further.'

'Well, if I read something that is written down in English *I can understand what it means* – I am not talking of abstruse stuff, formulae or philosophy – just plain businesslike English – *most people can't*! If I want to write down something *I can write down what I mean* – I've discovered that quite a lot of people can't do that either! And, as I say, I can do plain arithmetic. If Jones has eight bananas and Brown takes ten away from him, how many will Jones have left? That's the kind of sum people like to pretend has a simple answer. They won't admit, first that Brown can't do it – and second that there won't be an answer in plus bananas!'

'They prefer the answer to be a conjuring trick?'

'Exactly. Politicians are just as bad. But I've always held out for plain common sense. You can't beat it, you know, in the end.'

He added with a slightly self-conscious laugh:

'But I mustn't talk shop. Bad habit. Besides, I like to leave business matters behind when I get away from London. I've been looking forward, M. Poirot, to hearing a few of *your* adventures. I read a lot of thrillers and detective stories, you know. Do you think any of them are true to life?'

The conversation dwelt for the rest of the journey on the more spectacular cases of Hercule Poirot. Alistair Blunt displayed himself as vivid as any schoolboy for details.

This pleasant atmosphere sustained a chill on arrival at Exsham, where behind her massive bust Mrs Olivera radiated a freezing disapproval. She ignored Poirot as far as possible, addressing herself exclusively to her host and to Mr Selby.

The latter showed Poirot to his room.

The house was a charming one, not very big, and furnished with the same quiet good taste that Poirot had noticed in London. Everything was costly but simple. The vast wealth that owned it was only indicated by the smoothness with which this apparent simplicity was produced. The service was admirable – the cooking, English, not Continental – the wines at dinner stirred Poirot to a passion of appreciation. They had a perfect clear soup, a grilled sole, saddle of lamb with tiny young garden peas and strawberries and cream.

Poirot was so enjoying these creature comforts that the continued frigid demeanour of Mrs Olivera and the brusque rudeness of her daughter hardly attracted his attention. Jane, for some reason, was regarding him with definite hostility. Hazily, towards the end of the dinner, Poirot wondered why!

Looking down the table with mild curiosity, Blunt asked:

'Helen not dining with us tonight?'

Julia Olivera's lips drew themselves in with a taut line. She said:

'Dear Helen has been over-tiring herself, I think, in the garden. I suggested it would be far better for her to go to bed and rest than to bother to dress herself up and come here. She quite saw my point.'

'Oh, I see.' Blunt looked vague and a little puzzled. 'I thought it made a bit of a change for her at week-ends.'

'Helen is such a simple soul. She likes turning in early,' said Mrs Olivera firmly.

When Poirot joined the ladies in the drawing-room, Blunt having remained behind for a few minutes' conversation with his secretary, he heard Jane Olivera say to her mother:

'Uncle Alistair didn't like the cool way you'd shelved Helen Montressor, Mother.'

'Nonsense,' said Mrs Olivera robustly. 'Alistair is too good-natured. Poor relations are all very well – very kind of him to let her have the cottage rent free, but to think he has to have her up to the house every week-end for dinner is absurd! She's only a second cousin or something. I don't think Alistair ought to be imposed upon!'

'I think she's proud in her way,' said Jane. 'She does an awful lot in the garden.'

'That shows a proper spirit,' said Mrs Olivera comfortably. 'The Scotch are very independent and one respects them for it.'

She settled herself comfortably on the sofa and, still not taking any notice of Poirot, added:

'Just bring me the *Low Down Review*, dear. There's something about Lois Van Schuyler in it and that Moroccan guide of hers.'

Alistair Blunt appeared in the doorway. He said:

'Now M. Poirot, come into my room.'

Alistair Blunt's own sanctum was a low, long room at the back of the house, with windows opening upon the garden. It was comfortable, with deep armchairs and settees and just enough pleasant untidiness to make it livable.

(Needless to say, Hercule Poirot would have preferred a greater symmetry!)

After offering his guest a cigarette and lighting his own pipe, Alistair Blunt came to the point quite simply and directly.

He said:

'There's a good deal that I'm not satisfied about. I'm referring, of course, to this Sainsbury Seale woman. For reasons of their own – reasons no doubt which are perfectly justified – the authorities have called off the hunt. I don't know exactly who Albert Chapman is or what he's doing – but whatever it is, it's something pretty vital and it's the sort of business that might land him in a tight spot. I don't know the ins and outs of it, but the P.M. did just mention that they can't afford any publicity whatever about this case and that the sooner it fades out of the public's memory the better.

'That's quite O.K. That's the official view, and they know what's necessary. So the police have got their hands tied.'

He leaned forward in his chair.

'*But I want to know the truth, M. Poirot.* And you're the man to find it out for me. *You* aren't hampered by officialdom.'

'What do you want me to do, M. Blunt?'

'I want you to find this woman – Sainsbury Seale.'

'Alive or dead?'

Alistair Blunt's eyebrows rose.

'You think it's possible that she is dead?'

Hercule Poirot was silent for a minute or two, then he said, speaking slowly and with weight:

'If you want my opinion – but it is only an opinion, remember – then, yes, I think she is dead. ....'

'Why do you think so?'

Hercule Poirot smiled slightly.

He said:

'It would not make sense to you if I said it was because of a pair of unworn stockings in a drawer.'

Alistair Blunt stared at him curiously.

'You're an odd man, M. Poirot.'

'I am very odd. That is to say, I am methodical, orderly and logical – and I do not like distorting facts to support a theory – that, I find – *is* unusual!'

Alistair Blunt said:

'I've been turning the whole thing over in my mind – it takes me a little time always to think a thing out. And the whole business is deuced odd! I mean – that dentist chap shooting himself, and then this Chapman woman packed away in her own fur chest with her face smashed in. It's nasty! It's damned nasty! I can't help feeling that there's something *behind* it all.'

Poirot nodded.

Blunt said:

'And you know – the more I think of it – I'm quite sure that woman never knew my wife. It was just a pretext to speak to *me*. But why? What good did it do her? I mean – bar a small subscription – and even that was made out to the society, not to her personally. And yet I do feel – that – that it was engineered – just meeting me on the steps of the house. It was all so pat. So suspiciously well-timed! But *why*? That's what I keep asking myself – *why*?'

'It is indeed the word – why? I too ask myself – and I cannot see it – no, I cannot see it.'

'You've no ideas at all on the subject?'

Poirot waved an exasperated hand.

'My ideas are childish in the extreme. I tell myself, it was perhaps a ruse to indicate you to someone – to point you out. But that again is absurd – you are quite a well-known man – and anyway how much more simple to say "See, that is he – the man who entered now by that door."'

'And anyway,' said Blunt, 'why *should* any one want to point me out?'

'Mr Blunt, think back once more on your time that morning in the dentist's chair. Did nothing that Morley said strike an unusual note? Is there nothing at all that you can remember which might help as a clue?'

Alistair Blunt frowned in an effort of memory. Then he shook his head.

'I'm sorry. I can't think of anything.'

'You're quite sure he didn't mention this woman – this Miss Sainsbury Seale?'

'No.'

'Or the other woman – Mrs Chapman?'

'No – no – we didn't speak of people at all. We mentioned roses, gardens needing rain, holidays – nothing else.'

'And no one came into the room while you were there?'

'Let me see – no, I don't think so. On other occasions I seem to remember a young woman being there – fair-haired girl. But she wasn't there this time. Oh, another dentist fellow came in, I remember – the fellow with an Irish accent.'

'What did he say or do?'

'Just asked Morley some question and went out again. Morley was a bit short with him, I fancy. He was only there a minute or so.'

'And there is nothing else you can remember? Nothing at all?'

'No. He was absolutely normal.'

Hercule Poirot said thoughtfully:

'I, too, found him absolutely normal.'

There was a long pause. Then Poirot said:

'Do you happen to remember, Monsieur, a young man who was in the waiting-room downstairs with you that morning?'

Alistair Blunt frowned.

'Let me see – yes, there was a young man – rather restless he was. I don't remember him particularly, though. Why?'

'Would you know him again if you saw him?'

Blunt shook his head.

'I hardly glanced at him.'

'He didn't try to enter into conversation with you at all?'

'No.'

Blunt looked with frank curiosity at the other.

'What's the point? Who is this young man?'

'His name is Howard Raikes.'

Poirot watched keenly for any reaction, but he saw none.

'Ought I to know his name? Have I met him elsewhere?'

'I do not think you have met him. He is a friend of your niece, Miss

Olivera's.'

'Oh, one of Jane's friends.'

'Her mother, I gather, does not approve of the friendship.'

Alistair Blunt said absently:

'I don't suppose that will cut any ice with Jane.'

'So seriously does her mother regard the friendship that I gather she brought her daughter over from the States on purpose to get her away from this young man.'

'Oh!' Blunt's face registered comprehension. 'It's *that* fellow, is it?'

'Aha, you become more interested now.'

'He's a most undesirable young fellow in every way, I believe. Mixed up in a lot of subversive activities.'

'I understand from Miss Olivera that he made an appointment that morning in Queen Charlotte Street, solely in order to get a look at you.'

'To try and get me to approve of him?'

'Well – no – I understand the idea was that *he* should be induced to approve of *you*.'

'Well, of all the damned cheek!'

Poirot concealed a smile.

'It appears you are everything that he most disapproves of.'

'He's certainly the kind of young man *I* disapprove of! Spends his time tub-thumping and talking hot air, instead of doing a decent job of work!'

Poirot was silent for a minute, then he said:

'Will you forgive me if I ask you an impertinent and very personal question?'

'Fire ahead.'

'In the event of your death, what are your testamentary dispositions?'

Blunt stared. He said sharply:

'Why do you want to know that?'

'Because, it is just possible,' he shrugged his shoulders – 'that it might be relevant to this case.'

'Nonsense!'

'Perhaps. But perhaps not.'

Alistair Blunt said coldly:

'I think you are being unduly melodramatic, M. Poirot. Nobody has been trying to murder *me* – or anything like that!'

'A bomb on your breakfast table – a shot in the street –'

'Oh those! Any man who deals in the world's finance in a big way is liable to that kind of attention from some crazy fanatic!'

'It might possibly be a case of someone who is not a fanatic and not crazy.'

Blunt stared.

'What are you driving at?'

'In plain language, I want to know who benefits by your death.'

Blunt grinned.

'Chiefly the St Edward's Hospital, the Cancer Hospital, and the Royal Institute for the Blind.'

'Ah!'

'In addition, I have left a sum of money to my niece by marriage, Mrs Julia Olivera; an equivalent sum, but in trust, to her daughter, Jane Olivera, and also a substantial provision for my only surviving relative, a second cousin, Helen Montressor, who was left very badly off and who occupies a small cottage on the estate here.'

He paused and then said:

'This, M. Poirot, is strictly in confidence.'

'Naturally, Monsieur, naturally.'

Alistair Blunt added sarcastically:

'I suppose you do not suggest, M. Poirot, that either Julia or Jane Olivera or my cousin Helen Montressor, are planning to murder me for my money?'

'I suggest nothing – nothing at all.'

Blunt's slight irritation subsided. He said:

'And you'll take on that other commission for me?'

'The finding of Miss Sainsbury Seale? Yes, I will.'

Alistair Blunt said heartily:

'Good man.'

VII

In leaving the room Poirot almost cannoned into a tall figure outside the door.

He said: 'I beg your pardon, Mademoiselle.'

Jane Olivera drew apart a little.

She said. 'Do you know what I think of you, M. Poirot?'

'*Eh bien* – Mademoiselle –'

She did not give time to finish. The question, indeed, had but a rhetorical value. All that it meant was that Jane Olivera was about to answer it herself.

'You're a spy, that's what you are! A miserable, low, snooping spy, nosing round and making trouble!'

'I assure you, Mademoiselle –'

'I know just what you're after! And I know now just what lies you tell! Why don't you admit it straight out? Well, I'll tell you this – you won't find out *anything – anything* at all! There's nothing to find out! No one's going to harm a hair on my precious uncle's head. *He's* safe enough. He'll always be safe. Safe and smug and prosperous – and full of platitudes! He's just a stodgy John Bull, that's what he is – without an ounce of imagination or vision.'

She paused, then, her agreeable, husky voice deepening, she said venomously: 'I loathe the sight of you – you bloody little *bourgeois* detective!'

She swept away from him in a whirl of expensive model drapery.

Hercule Poirot remained, his eyes very wide open, his eyebrows raised and his hand thoughtfully caressing his moustaches.

The epithet *bourgeois* was, he admitted, well applied to him. His outlook on life was essentially *bourgeois*, and always had been, but the employment of it as an epithet of contempt by the exquisitely turned out Jane Olivera gave him, as he expressed it to himself, furiously to think.

He went, still thinking, into the drawing room.

Mrs Olivera was playing patience.

She looked up as Poirot entered, surveyed him with the cold look she might have bestowed upon a black-beetle and murmured distantly:

'Red knave on black queen.'

Chilled, Poirot retreated. He reflected mournfully:

'Alas, it would seem that nobody loves me!'

He strolled out of the window into the garden. It was an enchanting evening with a smell of night-scented stocks in the air. Poirot sniffed happily and strolled along a path that ran between two herbaceous borders.

He turned a corner and two dimly-seen figures sprang apart.

It would seem that he had interrupted a pair of lovers.

Poirot hastily turned and retraced his steps.

Even out here, it would seem, his presence was *de trop*.

He passed Alistair Blunt's window and Alistair Blunt was dictating to Mr Selby.

There seemed definitely only one place for Hercule Poirot.

He went up to his bedroom.

He pondered for some time on various fantastic aspects of the situation.

Had he or had he not made a mistake in believing the voice on the telephone to be that of Mrs Olivera? Surely the idea was absurd!

He recalled the melodramatic revelations of quiet little Mr Barnes. He speculated on the mysterious whereabouts of Mr Q.X.912, alias Albert Chapman. He remembered, with a spasm of annoyance, the anxious look in the eyes of the maidservant, Agnes –

It was always the same way – people *would* keep things back! Usually quite unimportant things, but until they were cleared out of the way, impossible to pursue a straight path.

At the moment the path was anything but straight!

And the most unaccountable obstacle in the way of clear thinking and orderly progress was what he described to himself as the contradictory and impossible problem of Miss Sainsbury Seale. For, if the facts that Hercule Poirot had observed were true facts – then nothing whatever made sense!

Hercule Poirot said to himself, with astonishment in the thought: 'Is it possible that I am growing old?'

After passing a troubled night, Hercule Poirot was up and about early on the next day. The weather was perfect and he retraced his steps of last night.

The herbaceous borders were in full beauty and though Poirot himself leaned to a more orderly type of flower arrangement – a neat arrangement of beds of scarlet geraniums such as are seen at Ostend – he nevertheless realized that here was the perfection of the English garden spirit.

He pursued his way through a rose garden, where the neat lay-out of the beds delighted him – and through the winding ways of an alpine rock garden, coming at last to the walled kitchen gardens.

Here he observed a sturdy woman clad in a tweed coat and skirt, black browed, with short cropped black hair who was talking in a slow, emphatic Scots voice to what was evidently the head gardener. The head gardener, Poirot observed did not appear to be enjoying the conversation.

A sarcastic inflection made itself heard in Miss Helen Montressor's voice, and Poirot escaped nimbly down a side path.

A gardener who had been, Poirot shrewdly suspected, resting on his spade, began digging with fervour. Poirot approached nearer. The man, a young fellow, dug with ardour, his back to Poirot who paused to observe him.

'Good-morning,' said Poirot amiably.

A muttered 'Morning, sir,' was the response, but the man did not stop working.

Poirot was a little surprised. In his experience a gardener, though anxious to appear zealously at work as you approached, was usually only too willing to pause and pass the time of day when directly addressed.

It seemed, he thought, a little unnatural. He stood there for some minutes, watching the toiling figure. Was there, or was there not, something a little familiar about the turn of those shoulders? Or could it be, thought Hercule Poirot, that he was getting into a habit of thinking that both voices and shoulders were familiar when they were really nothing of the kind? Was he, as he had feared last night, growing old?

He passed thoughtfully onward out of the walled garden and

609

paused to regard a rising slope of shrubbery outside.

Presently, like some fantastic moon, a round object rose gently over the top of the kitchen garden wall. It was the egg-shaped head of Hercule Poirot, and the eyes of Hercule Poirot regarded with a good deal of interest the face of the young gardener who had now stopped digging and was passing a sleeve across his wet face.

'Very curious and very interesting,' murmured Hercule Poirot as he discreetly lowered his head once more.

He emerged from the shrubbery and brushed off some twigs and leaves that were spoiling the neatness of his apparel.

Yes, indeed, very curious and interesting that Frank Carter, who had a secretarial job in the country, should be working as a gardener in the employment of Alistair Blunt.

Reflecting on these points, Hercule Poirot heard a gong in the distance and retraced his steps towards the house.

On the way there he encountered his host talking to Miss Montressor who had just emerged from the kitchen garden by the farther door.

Her voice rose clear and distinct:

'It's verra kind of you, Alistairr, but I would preferr not to accept any invitations this week while your Amerrican relations are with you!'

Blunt said:

'Julia's rather a tactless woman, but she doesn't mean –'

Miss Montressor said calmly:

'In my opinion her manner to me is verra insolent, and I will not put up with insolence – from Amerrican women or any others!'

Miss Montressor moved away, Poirot came up to find Alistair Blunt looking as sheepish as most men look who are having trouble with their female relations. He said ruefully:

'Women really are the devil! Good-morning, M. Poirot. Lovely day, isn't it?'

They turned towards the house and Blunt said with a sigh: 'I do miss my wife!'

In the dining-room, he remarked to the redoubtable Julia:

'I'm afraid, Julia, you've rather hurt Helen's feelings.'

Mrs Olivera said grimly:

'The Scotch are always touchy.'

Alistair Blunt looked unhappy.

Hercule Poirot said:

'You have a young gardener, I noticed, whom I think you must

610

have taken on recently.'

'I dare say,' said Blunt. 'Yes, Burton, my third gardener, left about three weeks ago, and we took this fellow on instead.'

'Do you remember where he came from?'

'I really don't. MacAlister engaged him. Somebody or other asked me to give him a trial, I think. Recommended him warmly. I'm rather surprised, because MacAlister says he isn't much good. He wants to sack him again.'

'What is his name?'

'Dunning – Sunbury – something like that.'

'Would it be a great impertinence to ask what you pay him?'

'Not at all. Two pounds fifteen, I think it is.'

'Not more?'

'Certainly not more – might be a bit less.'

'Now that,' said Poirot, 'is very curious.'

Alistair Blunt looked at him inquiringly.

But Jane Olivera, rustling the paper, distracted the conversation.

'A lot of people seem to be out for your blood, Uncle Alistair!'

'Oh, you're reading the debate in the House. That's all right. Only Archerton – he's always tilting at windmills. And he's got the most crazy ideas of finance. If we let him have his way, England would be bankrupt in a week.'

Jane said:

'Don't you ever *want* to try anything new?'

'Not unless it's an improvement to the old, my dear.'

'But you'd never think it would be. You'd always say, "This would never work" – without even trying.'

'Experimentalists can do a lot of harm.'

'Yes, but how can you be satisfied with things as they are. All the waste and the inequality and the unfairness. Something *must* be done about it!'

'We get along pretty well in this country, Jane, all things considered.'

Jane said passionately:

'What's needed is a new heaven and a new earth! And you sit there eating kidneys!'

She got up and went out by the french window into the garden.

Alistair looked mildly surprised and a little uncomfortable.

He said: 'Jane has changed a lot lately. Where does she get all these ideas?'

'Take no notice of what Jane says,' said Mrs Olivera. 'Jane's a very

611

silly girl. You know what girls are – they go to these queer parties in studios where the young men have funny ties and they come home and talk a lot of nonsense.'

'Yes, but Jane was always rather a hardboiled young woman.'

'It's just a fashion, Alistair, these things are in the air!'

Alistair Blunt said:

'Yes, they're in the air all right.'

He looked a little worried.

Mrs Olivera rose and Poirot opened the door for her. She swept out frowning to herself.

Alistair Blunt said suddenly:

'I don't like it, you know! Everybody's talking this sort of stuff! And it doesn't mean anything! It's all hot air! I find myself up against it the whole time – a new heaven and a new earth. What does it *mean*? They can't tell you themselves! They're just drunk on words.'

He smiled suddenly, rather ruefully.

'I'm one of the last of the Old Guard, you know.'

Poirot said curiously:

'If you were – removed, what would happen?'

'Removed! What a way of putting it!' His face grew suddenly grave. 'I'll tell you. A lot of damned fools would try a lot of very costly experiments. And that would be the end of stability – of common sense, of solvency. In fact, of this England of ours as we know it. . . .'

Poirot nodded his head. He was essentially in sympathy with the banker. He, too, approved of solvency. And he began to realize with a new meaning just exactly what Alistair Blunt stood for. Mr Barnes had told him, but he had hardly taken it in then. Quite suddenly, he was afraid. . . .

.

II

'I've finished my letters,' said Blunt, appearing later in the morning. 'Now, M. Poirot, I'm going to show you my garden.'

The two men went out together and Blunt talked eagerly of his hobby.

The rock garden, with its rare alpine plants, was his greatest joy and they spent some time there while Blunt pointed out certain minute and rare species.

Hercule Poirot, his feet encased in his best patent leather shoes, listened patiently, shifting his weight tenderly from one foot to the other and wincing slightly as the heat of the sun caused the illusion that his feet were gigantic puddings!

His host strolled on, pointing out various plants in the wide border. Bees were humming and from near at hand came the monotonous clicking of a pair of shears trimming a laurel hedge.

It was all very drowsy and peaceful.

Blunt paused at the end of the border, looking back. The clip of the shears was quite close by, though the clipper was concealed from view.

'Look at the vista down from here, Poirot. The Sweet Williams are particularly fine this year. I don't know when I've seen them so good – and those are Russell lupins. Marvellous colours.'

Crack! The shot broke the peace of the morning. Something sang angrily through the air. Alistair Blunt turned bewildered to where a faint thread of smoke was rising from the middle of the laurels.

There was a sudden outcry of angry voices, the laurels heaved as two men struggled together. A high-pitched American voice sang out resolutely:

'I've got you, you damned scoundrel! Drop that gun!'

Two men struggled out into the open. The young gardener who had dug so industriously that morning was writhing in the powerful grip of a man nearly a head taller.

Poirot recognized the latter at once. He had already guessed from the voice.

Frank Carter snarled:

'Let go of me! It wasn't me, I tell you! I never did.'

Howard Raikes said:

'Oh, no? Just shooting at the birds, I suppose!'

He stopped – looking at the newcomers.

'Mr Alistair Blunt? This guy here has just taken a pot-shot at you. I caught him right in the act.'

Frank Carter cried out:

'It's a lie! I was clipping the hedge. I heard a shot and the gun fell right here at my feet. I picked it up – that's only natural, that is, and then this bloke jumped on me.'

Howard Raikes said grimly:

'The gun was in your hand and it had just been fired!'

With a final gesture, he tossed the pistol to Poirot.

'Let's see what the dick's got to say about it! Lucky I got hold of you in time. I guess there are several more shots in that automatic of yours.'

Poirot murmured:

'Precisely.'

Blunt was frowning angrily. He said sharply:

'Now then Dunnon – Dunbury – what's your name?'

Hercule Poirot interrupted. He said:

'This man's name is Frank Carter.'

Carter turned on him furiously:

'You've had it in for me all along! You came spying on me that Sunday. I tell you, it's not true. I never shot at him.'

Hercule Poirot said gently:

'Then, in that case, *who did?*'

He added:

'There is no one else here but ourselves, you see.'

III

Jane Olivera came running along the path. Her hair streamlined back behind her. Her eyes were wide with fear. She gasped: 'Howard?'

Howard Raikes said lightly:

'Hallo, Jane. I've just been saving your uncle's life.'

'Oh!' She stopped. '*You* have?'

'Your arrival certainly seems to have been very opportune, Mr – er –' Blunt hesitated.

'This is Howard Raikes, Uncle Alistair. He's a friend of mine.'

Blunt looked at Raikes – he smiled.

'Oh!' he said. 'So you are Jane's young man! I must thank you.'

With a puffing noise as of a steam engine at high pressure Julia Olivera appeared on the scene. She panted out:

'I heard a shot. Is Alistair – Why –' she stared blankly at Howard Raikes. '*You?* Why, why, how *dare* you?'

Jane said in an icy voice:

'Howard has just saved Uncle Alistair's life, mother.'

'What? I – I –'

'This man tried to shoot Uncle Alistair and Howard grabbed him and took the pistol away from him.'

Frank Carter said violently:

614

'You're bloody liars, all of you.'

Mrs Olivera, her jaw dropping, said blankly:

'Oh!' It took her a minute or two to readjust her poise. She turned first to Blunt.

'My dear Alistair! How *awful*! Thank God you're safe. But it must have been a frightful shock. I – I feel quite faint myself. I wonder – do you think I could have just a *little* brandy?'

Blunt said quickly:

'Of course. Come back to the house.'

She took his arm, leaning on it heavily.

Blunt looked over his shoulder at Poirot and Howard Raikes.

'Can you bring that fellow along?' he asked. 'We'll ring up the police and hand him over.'

Frank Carter opened his mouth, but no words came. He was dead white, and his knees were wilting. Howard Raikes hauled him along with an unsympathetic hand.

'Come on, *you*,' he said.

Frank Carter murmured hoarsely and unconvincingly:

'It's all a lie. . . .'

Howard Raikes looked at Poirot.

'You've got precious little to say for yourself for a high-toned sleuth! Why don't you throw your weight about a bit?'

'I am reflecting, Mr Raikes.'

'I guess you'll need to reflect! I should say you'll lose your job over this! It isn't thanks to *you* that Alistair Blunt is still alive at this minute.'

'This is your second good deed of the kind, is it not, Mr Raikes?'

'What the hell do you mean?'

'It was only yesterday, was it not, that you caught and held the man whom you believed to have shot at Mr Blunt and the Prime Minister?'

Howard Raikes said:

'Er – yes. I seem to be making a kind of habit of it.'

'But there is a difference,' Hercule Poirot pointed out. 'Yesterday, the man you caught and held was *not* the man who fired the shot in question. You made a mistake.'

Frank Carter said sullenly:

'He's made a mistake now.'

'Quiet, you,' said Raikes.

Hercule Poirot murmured to himself:

'I wonder. . . .'

Dressing for dinner, adjusting his tie to an exact symmetry, Hercule Poirot frowned at his reflection in the mirror.

He was dissatisfied – but he would have been at a loss to explain why. For the case, as he owned to himself, was so very clear. Frank Carter had indeed been caught red-handed.

It was not as though he had any particular belief in, or liking for, Frank Carter. Carter, he thought dispassionately, was definitely what the English call a 'wrong 'un'. He was an unpleasant young bully of the kind that appeals to women, so that they are reluctant to believe the worst, however plain the evidence.

And Carter's whole story was weak in the extreme. This tale of having been approached by agents of the 'Secret Service' – and offered a plummy job. To take the post of gardener and report on the conversations and actions of the other gardeners. It was a story that was disproved easily enough – there was no foundation for it.

A particularly weak invention – the kind of thing. Poirot reflected, that a man like Carter *would* invent.

And on Carter's side, there was nothing at all to be said. He could offer no explanation, except that somebody else must have shot off the revolver. He kept repeating that. It was a frame-up.

No, there was nothing to be said for Carter except, perhaps, that it seemed an odd coincidence that Howard Raikes should have been present two days running at the moment when a bullet had just missed Alistair Blunt.

But presumably there wasn't anything in that. Raikes certainly hadn't fired the shot in Downing Street. And his presence down here was fully accounted for – he had come down to be near his girl. No, there was nothing definitely improbable in *his* story.

It had turned out, of course, very fortunately for Howard Raikes. When a man has just saved you from a bullet, you cannot forbid him the house. The least you can do is to show friendliness and extend hospitality. Mrs Olivera didn't like it, obviously, but even she saw that there was nothing to be done about it.

Jane's undesirable young man had got his foot in and he meant to keep it there!

Poirot watched him speculatively during the evening.

He was playing his part with a good deal of astuteness. He did not air any subversive views, he kept off politics. He told amusing stories of his hitch-hikes and tramps in wild places.

'He is no longer the wolf,' thought Poirot. 'No, he has put on the sheep's clothing. But underneath? I wonder. . . .'

As Poirot was preparing for bed that night, there was a rap on the door. Poirot called, 'Come in,' and Howard Raikes entered.

He laughed at Poirot's expression.

'Surprised to see me? I've had my eye on you all evening. I didn't like the way you were looking. Kind of thoughtful.'

'Why should that worry you, my friend?'

'I don't know why, but it did. I thought maybe that you were finding certain things just a bit hard to swallow.'

'*Eh bien?* And if so?'

'Well, I decided that I'd best come clean. About yesterday, I mean. That was a fake show all right! You see, I was watching his lordship come out of 10, Downing Street and I saw Ram Lal fire at him. I know Ram Lal. He's a nice kid. A bit excitable but he feels the wrongs of India very keenly. Well, there was no harm done, that precious pair of stuffed shirts weren't harmed – the bullet had missed 'em both by miles – so I decided to put up a show and hope the Indian kid would get clear. I grabbed hold of a shabby little guy just by me and called out that I'd got the villain and hoped Ram Lal was beating it all right. But the dicks were too smart. They were on to him in a flash. That's just how it was. See?'

Hercule Poirot said:

'And today?'

'That's different. There weren't any Ram Lals about today. Carter was the only man on the spot. *He* fired that pistol all right! It was still in his hand when I jumped on him. He was going to try a second shot, I expect.'

Poirot said:

'You were very anxious to preserve the safety of M. Blunt?'

Raikes grinned – an engaging grin.

'A bit odd, you think, after all I've said? Oh, I admit it. I think Blunt is a guy who *ought* to be shot – for the sake of Progress and Humanity – I don't mean personally – he's a nice enough old boy in his British way. I think that, and yet when I saw someone taking a pot shot at him I leap in and interfere. That shows you how illogical the human animal is. It's crazy, isn't it?'

'The gap between theory and practice is a wide one.'

'I'll say it is!' Mr Raikes got up from the bed where he had been sitting.

His smile was easy and confiding.

617

'I just thought,' he said, 'that I'd come along and explain the thing to you.'

He went out shutting the door carefully behind him.

v

'*Deliver me, O Lord, from the evil man: and preserve me from the wicked man,*' sang Mrs Olivera in a firm voice, slightly off the note.

There was a relentlessness about her enunciation of the sentiment which made Hercule Poirot deduce that Mr Howard Raikes was the wicked man immediately in her mind.

Hercule Poirot had accompanied his host and the family to the morning service in the village church.

Howard Raikes had said with a faint sneer: 'So you always go to church, Mr Blunt?'

And Alistair had murmured vaguely something about it being expected of you in the country – can't let the parson down, you know – which typically English sentiment had merely bewildered the young man, and had made Hercule Poirot smile comprehendingly.

Mrs Olivera had tactfully accompanied her host and commanded Jane to do likewise.

'*They have sharpened their tongues like a serpent,*' sang the choir boys in shrill treble, '*adder's poison is under their lips.*'

The tenors and basses demanded with gusto:

'*Keep me, O Lord, from the hands of the ungodly. Preserve me from the wicked men who are purposed to overthrow my goings.*'

Hercule Poirot essayed in a hesitant baritone.

'*The proud have laid a snare for me,*' he sang, '*and spread a net with cords: yea, and set traps in my way. . . .*'

His mouth remained open.

He saw it – saw clearly the trap into which he had so nearly fallen!

Like a man in a trance Hercule Poirot remained, mouth open, staring into space. He remained there as the congregation seated themselves with a rustle; until Jane Olivera tugged at his arm and murmured a sharp, 'Sit down.'

Hercule Poirot sat down. An aged clergyman with a beard intoned: '*Here beginneth the fifteenth chapter of the First Book of Samuel,*' and began to read.

But Poirot heard nothing of the smiting of the Amalekites.

A snare cunningly laid – a net with cords – a pit open at his feet –

618

dug carefully so that he should fall into it.

He was in a daze – a glorious daze where isolated facts spun wildly round before settling neatly into their appointed places.

It was like a kaleidoscope – shoe buckles, 10-inch stockings, a damaged face, the low tastes in literature of Alfred the page-boy, the activities of Mr Amberiotis, and the part played by the late Mr Morley, all rose up and whirled and settled themselves down into a coherent pattern.

For the first time, Hercule Poirot was looking at the case *the right way up*.

'*For rebellion is as the sin of witchcraft and stubborness is as iniquity and idolatry. Because thou has rejected the word of the Lord he hath also rejected thee from being king. Here endeth the first lesson,*' quavered the aged clergyman all in one breath.

As one in a dream, Hercule Poirot rose to praise the Lord in the Te Deum.

I

'M. Reilly, is it not?'

The young Irishman started as the voice spoke at his elbow.

He turned.

Standing next to him at the counter of the Shipping Co. was a small man with large moustaches and an egg-shaped head.

'You do not remember me, perhaps?'

'You do yourself injustice, M. Poirot. You're not a man that's easily forgotten.'

He turned back to speak to the clerk behind the counter who was waiting.

The voice at his elbow murmured:

'You are going abroad for a holiday?'

'It's not a holiday I'm taking. And you yourself, M. Poirot? You're not turning your back on this country, I hope?'

'Sometimes,' said Hercule Poirot, 'I return for a short while to my own country – Belgium.'

'I'm going farther than that,' said Reilly. 'It's America for me.' He added: 'And I don't think I'll be coming back, either.'

'I'm sorry to hear that, Mr Reilly. You are then, abandoning your practice in Queen Charlotte Street.'

'If you'd say it was abandoning me, you'd be nearer the mark.'

'Indeed? That is very sad.'

'It doesn't worry me. When I think of the debts I shall leave behind me unpaid, I'm a happy man.'

He grinned engagingly.

'It's not I who'll be shooting myself because of money troubles. Leave them behind you, I say, and start afresh. I've got my qualifications and they're good ones if I say so myself.'

Poirot murmured:

'I saw Miss Morley the other day.'

'Was that a pleasure to you? I'd say it was not. A more sour-faced woman never lived. I've often wondered what she'd be like drunk – but that's what no one will know.'

Poirot said:

'Did you agree with the verdict of the Coroner's Court on your partner's death?'

'I did not,' said Reilly emphatically.

'You don't think he made a mistake in the injection?'

Reilly said:

'If Morley injected that Greek with the amount that they say he did, he was either drunk or else he meant to kill the man. And I've never seen Morley drink.'

'So you think it was deliberate?'

'I'd not like to be saying that. It's a grave accusation to be making. Truly now, I don't believe it.'

'There must be some explanation.'

'There must indeed – but I've not thought of it yet.'

Poirot said:

'When did you last actually see Mr Morley alive?'

'Let me see now. It's a long time after to be asking me a thing like that. It would be the night before – about a quarter to seven.'

'You didn't see him on the actual day of the murder?'

Reilly shook his head.

'You are sure?' Poirot persisted.

'Oh, I'd not say that. But I don't remember –'

'You did not, for instance, go up to his room about eleven-thirty-five when he had a patient there?'

'You're right now. I did. There was a technical question I had to ask him about some instruments I was ordering. They'd rung me up about it. But I was only there for a minute, so it slipped my memory. He had a patient there at the time.'

Poirot nodded. He said.

'There is another question I always meant to ask you. Your patient, Mr Raikes, cancelled his appointment by walking out. What did you do during that half-hour's leisure?'

'What I always do when I have any leisure. Mixed myself a drink. And as I've been telling you, I put through a telephone call and ran up to see Morley for a minute.'

Poirot said:

'And I also understand that you had no patient from half-past twelve to one after Mr Barnes left. When did he leave, by the way?'

'Oh! Just after half-past twelve.'

'And what did you do then?'

'The same as before. Mixed myself another drink!'

'And went up to see Morley again?'

Mr Reilly smiled.

'Are you meaning did I go up and shoot him? I've told you already, long ago, that I did not. But you've only my word for it.'

Poirot said:

'What did you think of the house-parlourmaid, Agnes?'

Reilly stared:

'Now that's a funny question to be asking.'

'But I should like to know.'

'I'll answer you. I didn't think about her. Georgina kept a strict eye on the maids – and quite right too. The girl never looked my way once – which was bad taste on her part.'

'I have a feeling,' said Hercule Poirot, 'that that girl knows something.'

He looked inquiringly at Mr Reilly. The latter smiled and shook his head.

'Don't ask me,' he said. 'I know nothing about it. I can't help you at all.'

He gathered up the tickets which were lying in front of him and went off with a nod and a smile.

Poirot explained to a disillusioned clerk that he would not make up his mind about that cruise to the Northern Capitals after all.

II

Poirot paid another visit to Hampstead. Mrs Adams was a little surprised, perhaps, to see him. Though he had been vouched for, so to speak, by a Chief Inspector of Scotland Yard, she nevertheless regarded him as a 'quaint little foreigner' and had not taken his pretentions very seriously. She was, however, very willing to talk.

After the first sensational announcement about the identity of the victim, the finding of the inquest had received very little publicity. It had been a case of mistaken identity – the body of Mrs Chapman had been mistaken for that of Miss Sainsbury Seale. That was all that the public knew. The fact that Miss Sainsbury Seale had been probably the last person to see the unfortunate Mrs Chapman alive was not stressed. There had been no hint in the Press that Miss Sainsbury Seale might possibly be wanted by the police on a criminal charge.

Mrs Adams had been very relieved when she knew that it was not her friend's body which had been discovered so dramatically. She appeared to have no idea that any suspicion might attach to Mabelle Sainsbury Seale.

'But it is so extraordinary that she has disappeared like this. I feel sure, M. Poirot, that it *must* be loss of memory.'

622

Poirot said that it was very probable. He had known cases of the kind.

'Yes – I remember a friend of one my cousins. She'd had a lot of nursing and worry, and it brought it on. Amnesia, I think they called it.'

Poirot said that he believed that that was the technical term.

He paused and then asked if Mrs Adams had ever heard Miss Sainsbury Seale speak of a Mrs Albert Chapman?

No, Mrs Adams never remembered her friend mentioning any one of that name. But then, of course, it wasn't likely that Miss Sainsbury Seale should happen to mention every one with whom she was acquainted. Who was this Mrs Chapman? Had the police any idea who could have murdered her?

'It is still a mystery, Madame.' Poirot shook his head and then asked if it was Mrs Adams who had recommended Mr Morley as a dentist to Miss Sainsbury Seale.

Mrs Adams replied in the negative. She herself went to a Mr French in Harley Street, and if Mabelle had asked her about a dentist she would have sent her to him.

Possibly, Poirot thought, it might have been this Mrs Chapman who recommended Miss Sainsbury Seale to go to Mr Morley.

Mrs Adams agreed that it might have been. Didn't they know at the dentist's?

But Poirot had already asked Miss Nevill that question and Miss Nevill had not known or had not remembered. She recollected Mrs Chapman, but did not think the latter had ever mentioned a Miss Sainsbury Seale – the name being an odd one, she would have remembered it had she heard it then.

Poirot persevered with his questions.

Mrs Adams had known Miss Sainsbury Seale first in India, had she not? Mrs Adams agreed.

Did Mrs Adams know if Miss Sainsbury Seale had met Mr or Mrs Alistair Blunt at any time out there?

'Oh, I don't think so, M. Poirot. You mean the big banker? They were out some years ago staying with the Viceroy, but I'm sure if Mabelle had met them at all, she would have talked about it or mentioned them.'

'I'm afraid,' added Mrs Adams, with a faint smile, 'one does usually mention the important people. We're all such snobs at heart.'

'She never did mention the Blunts – Mrs Blunt in particular?'

'Never.'

623

'If she had been a close friend of Mrs Blunt's probably you would have known?'

'Oh yes. I don't believe she knew any one like that. Mabelle's friends were all very ordinary people – like us.'

'That, Madame, I cannot allow,' said Poirot gallantly.

Mrs Adams went on talking of Mabelle Sainsbury Seale as one talks of a friend who has recently died. She recalled all Mabelle's good works, her kindnesses, her indefatigable work for the mission, her zeal, her earnestness.

Hercule Poirot listened. As Japp had said, Mabelle Sainsbury Seale was a real person. She had lived in Calcutta and taught elocution and worked amongst the native population. She had been respectable, well meaning, a little fussy and stupid perhaps, but also what is termed a woman with a heart of gold.

And Mrs Adams' voice ran on: 'She was so much in *earnest* over everything, M. Poirot. And she found people so apathetic – so hard to rouse. It was very difficult to get subscriptions out of people – worse every year, with the income tax rising and the cost of living and everything. She said to me once: "When one knows what money can do – the wonderful good you can accomplish with it – well, really sometimes, Alice, I feel I would commit a *crime* to get it." That shows, doesn't it, M. Poirot, how strongly she felt?'

'She said that, did she?' said Poirot thoughtfully.

He asked, casually, when Miss Sainsbury Seale had enunciated this particular statement, and learned that it had been about three months ago.

He left the house and walked away lost in thought.

He was considering the character of Mabelle Sainsbury Seale.

A nice woman – an earnest and kindly woman – a respectable decent type of woman. It was amongst that type of person that Mr Barnes had suggested a potential criminal could be found.

She had travelled back on the same boat from India as Mr Amberiotis. There seemed reason to believe that she had lunched with him at the Savoy.

She had accosted and claimed acquaintance with Alistair Blunt and laid claim to an intimacy with his wife.

She had twice visited King Leopold Mansions where, later, a dead body had been found dressed in her clothes and with her handbag conveniently identifying it.

A little *too* convenient, that!

She had left the Glengowrie Court Hotel suddenly after an

interview with the police.

Could the theory that Hercule Poirot believed to be true account for and explain all those facts?

He thought it could.

III

These meditations had occupied Hercule Poirot on his homeward way until reaching Regent's Park. He decided to traverse a part of the Park before taking a taxi on. By experience, he knew to a nicety the moment when his smart patent leather shoes began to press painfully on his feet.

It was a lovely summer's day and Poirot looked indulgently on courting nursemaids and their swains, laughing and giggling while their chubby charges profited by nurse's inattention.

Dogs barked and romped.

Little boys sailed boats.

And under nearly every tree was a couple sitting close together. . . . 'Ah! *Jeunesse, Jeunesse*,' murmured Hercule Poirot, pleasurably affected by the sight.

They were *chic*, these little London girls. They wore their tawdry clothes with an air.

Their figures, however, he considered lamentably deficient. Where were the rich curves, the voluptuous lines that had formerly delighted the eye of an admirer?

He, Hercule Poirot, remembered women . . . One woman, in particular – what a sumptuous creature – Bird of Paradise – a Venus. . . .

What woman was there amongst these pretty chits nowadays, who could hold a candle to Countess Vera Rossakoff? A genuine Russian aristocrat, an aristocrat to her fingertips! And also, he remembered, a most accomplished thief . . . One of those natural geniuses. . . .

With a sigh, Poirot wrenched his thoughts away from the flamboyant creature of his dreams.

It was not only, he noted, the little nursemaids and their like who were being wooed under the trees of Regent's Park.

That was a Schiaparelli creation there, under that lime tree, with the young man who bent his head so close to hers, who was pleading so earnestly.

One must not yield too soon! He hoped the girl understood that.

The pleasure of the chase must be extended as long as possible. . . .

His beneficent eye still on them, he became suddenly aware of a familiarity in those two figures.

So Jane Olivera had come to Regent's Park to meet her young American revolutionary?

His face grew suddenly sad and rather stern.

After only a brief hesitation he crossed the grass to them. Sweeping off his hat with a flourish, he said:

'*Bonjour, Mademoiselle.*'

Jane Olivera, he thought, was not entirely displeased to see him.

Howard Raikes, on the other hand, was a good deal annoyed at the interruption.

He growled: 'Oh, so it's *you* again!'

'Good afternoon, M. Poirot,' said Jane. 'How unexpectedly you always pop up, don't you?'

'Kind of a Jack in the Box,' said Raikes, still eyeing Poirot with a considerable coldness.

'I do not intrude?' Poirot asked anxiously.

Jane Olivera said kindly:

'Not at all.'

Howard Raikes said nothing.

'It is a pleasant spot you have found here,' said Poirot.

'It was,' said Mr Raikes.

Jane said:

'Be quiet, Howard. You need to learn manners!'

Howard Raikes snorted and asked:

'What's the good of manners?'

'You'll find they kind of help you along,' said Jane. '*I* haven't got any myself, but that doesn't matter so much. To begin with I'm rich, and I'm moderately good-looking, and I've got a lot of influential friends – and none of those unfortunate disabilities they talk about so freely in the advertisements nowadays. I can get along all right without manners.'

Raikes said:

'I'm not in the mood for small talk, Jane. I guess I'll take myself off.'

He got up, nodded curtly to Poirot and strode away.

Jane Olivera stared after him, her chin cupped in her palm.

Poirot said with a sigh:

'Alas, the proverb is true. When you are courting, two is company, is it not, three is none?'

Jane said:

'Courting? What a word!'

'But yes, it is the right word, is it not? For a young man who pays attention to a young lady before asking her hand in marriage? They say, do they not, a courting couple?'

'Your friends seem to say some very funny things.'

Hercule Poirot chanted softly:

'Thirteen, fourteen, maids are courting. See, all around us they are doing it.'

Jane said sharply:

'Yes – I'm just one of the crowd, I suppose. . . .'

She turned suddenly to Poirot.

'I want to apologize to you. I made a mistake the other day. I thought you had wormed your way in and come down to Exsham just to spy on Howard. But afterwards Uncle Alistair told me that he had definitely asked you because he wanted you to clear up this business of that missing woman – Sainsbury Seale. That's right, isn't it?'

'Absolutely.'

'So I'm sorry for what I said to you that evening. But it did look like it, you know. I mean – as though you *were* just following Howard and spying on us both.'

'Even if it were true, Mademoiselle – I was an excellent witness to the fact that Mr Raikes bravely saved your uncle's life by springing on his assailant and preventing him from firing another shot.'

'You've got a funny way of saying things, M. Poirot. I never know whether you're serious or not.'

Poirot said gravely:

'At the moment I am very serious, Miss Olivera.'

Jane said with a slight break in her voice:

'Why do you look at me like that? As though – as though you were sorry for me?'

'Perhaps because I am sorry, Mademoiselle, for the things that I shall have to do so soon. . . .'

'Well, then – don't do them!'

'Alas, Mademoiselle, but I must. . . .'

She stared at him for a minute or two, then she said:

'Have you – found that woman?'

Poirot said:

'Let us say – *that I know where she is.*'

'Is she dead?'

'I have not said so.'

627

'She's alive, then?'

'I have not said that either.'

Jane looked at him with irritation. She exclaimed:

'Well, she's got to be one or the other, hasn't she?'

'Actually, it's not quite so simple.'

'I believe you just *like* making things difficult!'

'It has been said of me,' admitted Hercule Poirot.

Jane shivered. She said:

'Isn't it funny? It's a lovely warm day – and yet I suddenly feel cold. . . .'

'Perhaps you had better walk on, Mademoiselle.'

Jane rose to her feet. She stood a minute irresolute. She said abruptly:

'Howard wants me to marry him. At once. Without letting any one know. He says – he says it's the only way I'll ever do it – that I'm weak –' She broke off, then with one hand she gripped Poirot's arm with surprising strength. 'What shall I do about it, M. Poirot?'

'Why ask me to advise you? There are those who are nearer!'

'Mother? She'd scream the house down at the bare idea! Uncle Alistair? He'd be cautious and prosy. Plenty of time, my dear. Got to make quite sure, you know. Bit of an odd fish – this young man of yours. No sense in rushing things –'

'Your friends?' suggested Poirot.

'I haven't got any friends. Only a silly crowd I drink and dance and talk inane catchwords with! Howard's the only *real* person I've ever come up against.'

'Still – why ask *me*, Miss Olivera?'

Jane said:

'Because you've got a queer look on your face – as though you were sorry about something – as though you knew something that – that – was – *coming*. . . .'

She stopped.

'Well?' she demanded. 'What do you say?'

Hercule Poirot slowly shook his head.

IV

When Poirot reached home, George said:

'Chief Inspector Japp is here, sir.'

Japp grinned in a rueful way as Poirot came into the room.

'Here I am, old boy. Come round to say: "Aren't you a marvel? How do you do it? What makes you think of these things?"'

'All this meaning –? But *pardon*, you will have some refreshment? A sirop? Or perhaps the whisky?'

'The whisky is good enough for me.'

A few minutes later he raised his glass, observing:

'Here's to Hercule Poirot who is always right!'

'No, no, *mon ami*.'

'Here we had a lovely case of suicide. H.P. says it's murder – wants it to be murder – and dash it all, it *is* murder!'

'Ah? So you agree at last?'

'Well, nobody can say I'm pig-headed. I don't fly in the face of evidence. The trouble was there *wasn't* any evidence before.'

'But there is now?'

'Yes, and I've come round to make the amend honourable, as you call it, and present the titbit to you on toast, as it were.'

'I am all agog, my good Japp.'

'All right. Here goes. The pistol that Frank Carter tried to shoot Blunt with on Saturday is a twin pistol to the one that killed Morley!'

Poirot stared: 'But this is extraordinary!'

'Yes, it makes it look rather black for Master Frank.'

'It is not conclusive.'

'No, but it's enough to make us reconsider the suicide verdict. They're a foreign make of pistol and rather an uncommon one at that!'

Hercule Poirot stared. His eyebrows looked like crescent moons. He said at last:

'Frank Carter? No – surely not!'

Japp breathed a sigh of exasperation.

'What's the matter with you, Poirot? First you will have it that Morley was murdered and that it wasn't suicide. Then when I come and tell you we're inclined to come round to your views you hem and ha and don't seem to like it.'

'You really believe that Morley was murdered by Frank Carter?'

'It fits. Carter had got a grudge against Morley – that we knew all along. He came to Queen Charlotte Street that morning – and he pretended afterwards that he had come along to tell his young woman he'd got a job – but we've now discovered that he *hadn't* got the job then. He didn't get it till later in the day. He admits that now. So there's lie No. 1. He can't account for where he was at twenty-five past twelve onwards. Says he was walking in the Marylebone Road, but the first thing he can prove is having a drink in a pub at five past one. And the barman says he was in a regular state – his hand shaking and his face as white as a sheet!'

Hercule Poirot sighed and shook his head. He murmured:

'It does not accord with my ideas.'

'What are these ideas of yours?'

'It is very disturbing what you tell me. Very disturbing indeed. Because, you see, if you are right. . . .'

The door opened softly and George murmured deferentially:

'Excuse me, sir, but . . .'

He got no further. Miss Gladys Nevill thrust him aside and came agitatedly into the room. She was crying.

'Oh, M. Poirot –'

'Here, I'll be off,' said Japp hurriedly.

He left the room precipitately.

Gladys Nevill paid his back the tribute of a venomous look.

'That's the man – that horrid Inspector from Scotland Yard – it's he who has trumped up a whole case against poor Frank.'

'Now, now, you must not agitate yourself.'

'But he has. First they pretend that he tried to murder this Mr Blunt and not content with that they've accused him of murdering poor Mr Morley.'

Hercule Poirot coughed. He said:

'I was down there, you know, at Exsham, when the shot was fired at Mr Blunt.'

Gladys Nevill said with a somewhat confusing use of pronouns:

'But even if Frank did – did do a foolish thing like that – and he's one of those Imperial Shirts, you know – they march with banners and have a ridiculous salute, and of course I suppose Mr Blunt's wife *was* a very notorious Jewess, and they just work up these poor young men – quite harmless ones like Frank – until they think they are doing something wonderful and patriotic.'

'Is that Mr Carter's defence?' asked Hercule Poirot.

'Oh *no*. Frank just swears he didn't do anything and had never seen the pistol before. I haven't spoken to him, of course – they wouldn't let me – but he's got a solicitor acting for him and he told me what Frank had said. Frank just says it's all a frame-up.'

Poirot murmured:

'And the solicitor is of opinion that his client had better think of a more plausible story?'

'Lawyers are so difficult. They won't say anything *straight out*. But

630

it's the murder charge I'm worrying about. Oh! Mr Poirot, I'm sure Frank *couldn't* have killed Mr Morley. I mean really – he hadn't any reason to.'

'Is it true,' said Poirot, 'that when he came round that morning he had not yet got a job of any kind?'

'Well, really, M. Poirot, I don't see what difference *that* makes. Whether he got the job in the morning or the afternoon can't matter.'

Poirot said:

'But his story was that he came to tell you about his good luck. Now, it seems he had as yet had no luck. Why, then, did he come?'

'Well, M. Poirot, the poor boy was dispirited and upset, and to tell the truth I believe he'd been drinking a little. Poor Frank has rather a weak head – and the drink upset him and so he felt like – like making a row, and he came round to Queen Charlotte Street to have it out with Mr Morley, because, you see, Frank is awfully sensitive and it had upset him a lot to feel that Mr Morley disapproved of him, and was what he called poisoning my mind.'

'So he conceived the idea of making a scene in business hours?'

'Well – yes – I suppose that *was* his idea. Of course it was very wrong of Frank to think of such a thing.'

Poirot looked thoughtfully at the tearful blonde young woman in front of him. He said:

'Did you know that Frank Carter had a pistol – or a pair of pistols?'

'Oh no, M. Poirot. I swear I didn't. And I don't believe it's true, either.'

Poirot shook his head slowly in a perplexed manner.

'Oh! M. Poirot, do help us. If I could only feel that you were on our side –'

Poirot said:

'I do not take sides. I am on the side only of the truth.'

v

After he had got rid of the girl, Poirot rang up Scotland Yard. Japp had not yet returned but Detective Sergeant Beddoes was obliging and informative.

The police had not as yet found any evidence to prove Frank Carter's possession of the pistol before the assault at Exsham.

Poirot hung up the receiver thoughtfully. It was a point in Carter's favour. But so far it was the only one.

He had also learned from Beddoes a few more details as to the statement Frank Carter had made about his employment as gardener at Exsham. He stuck to his story of a Secret Service job. He had been given money in advance and some testimonials as to his gardening abilities and been told to apply to Mr MacAlister, the head gardener, for the post.

His instructions were to listen to the other gardeners' conversations and sound them as to their 'red' tendencies, and to pretend to be a bit of a 'red' himself. He had been interviewed and instructed in his task by a woman who had told him that she was known as Q.H.56, and that he had been recommended to her as a strong anti-communist. She had interviewed him in a dim light and he did not think he would know her again. She was a red-haired lady with a lot of make-up on.

Poirot groaned. The Phillips Oppenheim touch seemed to be reappearing.

He was tempted to consult Mr Barnes on the subject.

According to Mr Barnes these things happened.

The last post brought him something which disturbed him more still.

A cheap envelope in an unformed handwriting, post-marked Hertfordshire.

Poirot opened it and read:

'DEAR SIR, –

'Hoping as you will forgive me for troubling you, but I am very worried and do not know what to do. I do not want to be mixed up with the police in any way. I know that perhaps I ought to have told something I know before, but as they said the master had shot himself it was all right I thought and I wouldn't have liked to get Miss Nevill's young man into trouble and never thought really for one moment as he had done it but now I see he has been took up for shooting at a gentleman in the country and so perhaps he isn't quite all there and I ought to say but I thought I would write to you, you being a friend of the mistress and asking me so particular the other day if there was anything and of course I wish now I had told you then. But I do hope it won't mean getting mixed up with the police because I shouldn't like that and my mother wouldn't like it either. She has always been most particular.

'Yours respectfully
'AGNES FLETCHER.'

632

Poirot murmured:

'I always knew it was something to do with some man. I guessed the wrong man, that is all.'

I

The interview with Agnes Fletcher took place in Hertford, in a somewhat derelict teashop, for Agnes had been anxious not to tell her story under Miss Morley's critical eye.

The first quarter of an hour was taken up listening to exactly how particular Agnes' mother had always been. Also how Agnes' father, though a proprietor of licensed premises, had never once had any friction with the police, closing time being strictly observed to the second, and indeed Agnes' father and mother were universally respected and looked up to in Little Darlingham, Gloucestershire, and none of Mrs Fletcher's family of six (two having died in infancy) had ever occasioned their parents the least anxiety. And if Agnes, now, were to get mixed up with the police in any way, Mum and Dad would probably die of it, because as she'd been saying, they'd always held their heads high, and never had no trouble of any kind with the police.

After this had been repeated, *da capo*, and with various embellishments, several times, Agnes drew a little nearer to the subject of the interview.

'I wouldn't like to say anything to Miss Morley, sir, because it might be, you see, that she'd say as how I ought to have said something before, but me and cook, we talked it over and we didn't see as it was any business of ours, because we'd read quite clear and plain in the paper as how the master had made a mistake in the drug he was giving and that he'd shot himself and the pistol was in his hands and everything, so it did seem quite clear, didn't it, sir?'

'When did you begin to feel differently?' Poirot hoped to get a little nearer the promised revelation by an encouraging but not too direct question.

Agnes replied promptly.

'Seeing it in the paper about that Frank Carter – Miss Nevill's young man as was. When I read as he'd shot at that gentleman where he was gardener, well, I thought, it looks as if he *might* be queer in the head, because I do know there's people it takes like that, think they're being persecuted, or something, and that they're ringed round by enemies, and in the end it's dangerous to keep them at home and they have to be took away to the asylum. And I thought that maybe that Frank Carter was like that, because I did remember that he used to go on about Mr Morley and say as Mr Morley was against him and trying to separate him from Miss Nevill, but of course she wouldn't hear a word against him, and quite right too we thought – Emma and me, because you couldn't deny as Mr Carter was very nice-looking and quite the gentleman. But, of course, neither of us thought he'd really done anything to Mr Morley. We just thought it was a bit queer if you know what I mean.'

Poirot said patiently:

'What was queer?'

'It was that morning, sir, the morning Mr Morley shot himself. I'd been wondering if I dared run down and get the post. The postman had come but that Alfred hadn't brought up the letters, which he wouldn't do, not unless there was some for Miss Morley or Mr Morley, but if it was just for Emma and me he wouldn't bother to bring them up till lunch time.

'So I went out on the landing and I looked down over the stairs. Miss Morley didn't like us going down to the hall, not during the master's business hours, but I thought maybe as I'd see Alfred taking in a patient to the master and I'd call down to him as he came back.'

Agnes gasped, took a deep breath and went on: 'And it was then I saw him – that Frank Carter, I mean. Halfway up the stairs he was – our stairs, I mean, above the master's floor. And he was standing there waiting and looking down – and I've come to feel more and more as though there was something *queer* about it. He seemed to be listening very intent, if you know what I mean?'

'What time was this?'

'It must have been getting on for half-past twelve, sir. And just as I was thinking: There now, it's Frank Carter, and Miss Nevill's away for the day and *won't* he be disappointed, and I was wondering if I ought to run down and tell him because it looked as though that lump of an Alfred had forgot, otherwise I thought he wouldn't have been waiting for her. And just as I was hesitating, Mr Carter, he seemed to make up his mind, and he slipped down the stairs very quick and went along the passage towards the master's surgery, and I thought to myself, the master won't like *that*, and I wondered if there was going to be a row, but just then Emma called me, said whatever was I up to? and I went up again and then, afterwards, I heard the master had shot himself and, of course, it was so awful it just drove everything out of my head. But later, when that Police Inspector had gone I said to Emma, I said, I didn't say anything about Mr Carter having been up with the master this morning, and she said was he?

635

and I told her, and she said well, perhaps I *ought* to tell, but anyway I said I'd better wait a bit, and she agreed, because neither of us didn't want to get Frank Carter into trouble if we could help. And then, when it came to the inquest and it come out that the master had made that mistake in a drug and really had got the wind up and shot himself, quite natural-like – well, then, of course, there was no call to say anything. But reading that piece in the paper two days ago – Oh! it did give me a turn! And I said to myself "If he's one of those loonies that thinks they're persecuted and goes round shooting people, well, then maybe he *did* shoot the master after all!" '

Her eyes, anxious and scared, looked hopefully at Hercule Poirot. He put as much reassurance into his voice as he could.

'You may be sure that you have done absolutely the right thing in telling me, Agnes,' he said.

'Well, I must say, sir, it does take a load off my mind. You see, I've kept saying to myself as perhaps I *ought* to tell. And then, you see, I thought of getting mixed up with the police and what mother would say. She's always been so particular about us all. . . .'

'Yes, yes,' said Hercule Poirot hastily.

He had had, he felt, as much of Agnes' mother as he could stand for one afternoon.

II

Poirot called at Scotland Yard and asked for Japp. When he was taken up to the Chief Inspector's room: 'I want to see Carter,' said Hercule Poirot.

Japp shot him a quick, sideways glance.

He said.

'What's the big idea?'

'You are unwilling?'

Japp shrugged his shoulders. He said:

'Oh, *I* shan't make objections. No good if I did. Who's the Home Secretary's little pet? You are. Who's got half the Cabinet in his pocket? You have. Hushing up their scandals for them.'

Poirot's mind flew for a moment to that case that he had named the Case of the Augean Stables. He murmured, not without complacence:

'It was ingenious, yes? You must admit it. Well imagined, let us say.'

636

'Nobody but you would ever have thought of such a thing! Sometimes, Poirot, I think you haven't any scruples at all!'

Poirot's face became suddenly grave. He said:

'That is not true.'

'Oh, all right, Poirot, I didn't mean it. But you're so pleased sometimes with your damned ingenuity. What do you want to see Carter for? To ask him whether he really murdered Morley?'

'To Japp's surprise, Poirot nodded his head emphatically.

'Yes, my friend, that is exactly the reason.'

'And I suppose you think he'll tell you if he did?'

Japp laughed as he spoke. But Hercule Poirot remained grave. He said:

'He might tell me – yes.'

Japp looked at him curiously. He said:

'You know, I've known you a long time – twenty years? Something like that. But I still don't always catch on to what you're driving at. I know you've got a bee in your bonnet about young Frank Carter. For some reason or other, you don't *want* him to be guilty –'

Hercule Poirot shook his head energetically.

'No, no, there you are wrong. It is the other way about –'

'I thought perhaps it was on account of that girl of his – the blonde piece. You're a sentimental old buzzard in some ways –'

Poirot was immediately indignant.

'It is not I who am sentimental! That is an English failing! It is in England that they weep over young sweethearts and dying mothers and devoted children. Me, I am logical. If Frank Carter is a killer, then I am certainly not sentimental enough to wish to unite him in marriage to a nice but commonplace girl who, if he is hanged, will forget him in a year or two and find someone else?'

'Then why don't you want to believe he is guilty?'

'I *do* want to believe he is guilty.'

'I suppose you mean that you've got hold of something which more or less conclusively proves him to be innocent? Why hold it up, then? You ought to play fair with us, Poirot.'

'I *am* playing fair with you. Presently, very shortly, I will give you the name and address of a witness who will be invaluable to you for the prosecution. Her evidence ought to clinch the case against him.'

'But then – Oh! You've got me all tangled up. Why are you so anxious to see him.'

'To satisfy *myself*,' said Hercule Poirot.

And he would say no more.

III

Frank Carter, haggard, white-faced, still feebly inclined to bluster, looked on his unexpected visitor with unconcealed disfavour. He said rudely:

'So it's you, you ruddy little foreigner? What do *you* want?'

'I want to see you and talk to you.'

'Well, you see me all right. But I won't talk. Not without my lawyer. That's right, isn't it? You can't go against that. I've got the right to have my solicitor present before I say a word.'

'Certainly you have. You can send for him if you like – but I should prefer that you did not.'

'I dare say. Think you're going to trap me into making some damaging admissions, eh?'

'We are quite alone, remember.'

'That's a bit unusual, isn't it? Got your police pals listening-in, no doubt.'

'You are wrong. This is a private interview between you and me.'

Frank Carter laughed. He looked cunning and unpleasant. He said:

'Come off it! You don't take me in with the old gag.'

'Do you remember a girl called Agnes Fletcher?'

'Never heard of her.'

'I think you will remember her, though you may never have taken much notice of her. She was house-parlourmaid at 58, Queen Charlotte Street.'

'Well, what of it?'

Hercule Poirot said slowly:

'On the morning of the day that Mr Morley was shot, this girl Agnes happened to look over the banisters from the top floor. She saw you on the stairs – waiting and listening. Presently she saw you go along to Mr Morley's room. The time was then twenty-six minutes or thereabouts past twelve.'

Frank Carter trembled violently. Sweat came out on his brow. His eyes, more furtive than ever, went wildly from side to side. He shouted angrily:

'It's a lie! It's a damned lie! You've paid her – the police have paid her – to say she saw me.'

'At that time,' said Hercule Poirot, 'by your own account, you had left the house and were walking in the Marylebone Road.'

'So I was. That girl's lying. She couldn't have seen me. It's a dirty

638

plot. If it's true, why didn't she say so before?'

Hercule Poirot said quietly:

'She did mention it at the time to her friend and colleague the cook. They were worried and puzzled and didn't know what to do. When a verdict of suicide was brought in they were much relieved and decided that it wasn't necessary for them to say anything.'

'I don't believe a word of it! They're in it together, that's all. A couple of dirty, lying little . . .'

He tailed off into furious profanity.

Hercule Poirot waited.

When Carter's voice at last ceased, Poirot spoke again, still in the same calm, measured voice.

'Anger and foolish abuse will not help you. These girls are going to tell their story and it is going to be believed. Because, you see, they are telling the truth. The girl, Agnes Fletcher, *did* see you. You *were* there, on the stairs, at that time. You had *not* left the house. And you *did* go into Mr Morley's room.'

He paused and then asked quietly:

'What happened then?'

'It's a lie, I tell you!'

Hercule Poirot felt very tired – very old. He did not like Frank Carter. He disliked him very much. In his opinion Frank Carter was a bully, a liar, a swindler – altogether the type of young man the world could well do without. He, Hercule Poirot, had only to stand back and let this young man persist in his lies and the world would be rid of one of its more unpleasant inhabitants. . . .

Hercule Poirot said:

'I suggest you tell me the truth. . . .'

He realized the issue very clearly. Frank Carter was stupid – but he wasn't so stupid as not to see that to persist in his denial was his best and safest course. Let him once admit that he *had* gone into that room at twenty-six minutes past twelve and he was taking a step into grave danger. For after that, any story he told would have a good chance of being considered a lie.

Let him persist in his denial, then. If so, Hercule Poirot's duty would be over. Frank Carter would in all probability be hanged for the murder of Henry Morley – and it might be, justly hanged.

Hercule Poirot had only to get up and go.

Frank Carter said again:

'It's a lie!'

There was a pause. Hercule Poirot did not get up and go. He

639

would have liked to do so – very much. Nevertheless, he remained.

He leaned forward. He said – and his voice held all the compelling power of his powerful personality –

'I am not lying to you. I ask you to believe me. If you did not kill Morley your only hope is to tell me the *exact truth* of what happened that morning.'

The mean, treacherous face looking at him, wavered, became uncertain. Frank Carter pulled at his lip. His eyes went from side to side, terrified, frankly animal eyes.

It was touch and go now. . . .

Then suddenly, overborne by the strength of the personality confronting him, Frank Carter surrendered.

He said hoarsely:

'All right then – I'll tell you. God curse you if you let me down now! I did go in . . . I went up the stairs and waited till I could be sure of getting him alone. Waited there, up above Morley's landing. Then a gent came out and went down – fat gent. I was just making up my mind to go – when another gent came out of Morley's room and went down too. I knew I'd got to be quick. I went along and nipped into his room without knocking. I was all set to have it out with him. Mucking about, putting my girl against me – damn him –'

He stopped.

'Yes?' said Hercule Poirot: and his voice was still urgent – compelling –

Carter's voice croaked uncertainly.

'*And he was lying there – dead. It's true!* I swear it's true! Lying just as they said at the inquest. I couldn't believe it at first. I stooped over him. But he was dead all right. His hand was stone cold and I saw the bullet hole in his head with a hard black crust of blood round it. . . .'

At the memory of it, sweat broke out on his forehead again.

'I saw then I was in a jam. They'd go and say *I'd* done it. I hadn't touched anything except his hand and the door handle. I wiped that with my handkerchief, both sides, as I went out, and I stole downstairs as quickly as I could. There was nobody in the hall and I let myself out and legged it away as fast as I could. No wonder I felt queer.'

He paused. His scared eyes went to Poirot.

'That's the truth. *I swear that's the truth . . . He was dead already.* You've got to believe me!'

Poirot got up. He said – and his voice was tired and sad – 'I believe you.'

He moved towards the door.

Frank Carter cried out:

'They'll hang me – they'll hang me for a cert if they know I was in there.'

Poirot said:

'By telling the truth you have saved yourself from being hang 1.'

'I don't see it. They'll say –'

Poirot interrupted him.

'Your story has confirmed what I knew to be the truth. You can leave it now to me.'

He went out.

He was not at all happy.

IV

He reached Mr Barnes' House at Ealing at 6.45. He remembered that Mr Barnes had called that a good time of day.

Mr Barnes was at work in his garden.

He said by way of greeting:

'We need rain, M. Poirot – need it badly.'

He looked thoughtfully at his guest. He said:

'You don't look very well, M. Poirot?'

'Sometimes,' said Hercule Poirot, 'I do not like the things I have to do.'

Mr Barnes nodded his head sympathetically.

He said:

'I know.'

Hercule Poirot looked vaguely round at the neat arrangement of the small beds. He murmured:

'It is well-planned, this garden. Everything is to scale. It is small but exact.'

Mr Barnes said:

'When you have only a small place you've got to make the most of it. You can't afford to make mistakes in the planning.'

Hercule Poirot nodded.

Barnes went on:

'I see you've got your man?'

'Frank Carter?'

'Yes. I'm rather surprised, really.'

'You did not think that it was, so to speak, a private murder?'

641

'No. Frankly I didn't. What with Amberiotis and Alistair Blunt – I made sure that it was one of these Espionage or Counter-Espionage mix-ups.'

'That is the view you expounded to me at our first meeting.'

'I know. I was quite sure of it at the time.'

Poirot said slowly:

'But you were wrong.'

'Yes. Don't rub it in. The trouble is, one goes by one's own experience. I've been mixed up in that sort of thing so much I suppose I'm inclined to see it everywhere.'

Poirot said:

'You have observed in your time a conjurer offer a card, have you not? What is called – forcing a card?'

'Yes, of course.'

'That is what was done here. Every time that one thinks of a private reason for Morley's death, hey presto – the card is forced on one. Amberiotis, Alistair Blunt, the unsettled state of politics – of the country –' He shrugged his shoulder. 'As for you, Mr Barnes, you did more to mislead me than anybody.'

'Oh, I say, Poirot, I'm sorry. I suppose that's true.'

'You were in a position to *know*, you see. So your words carried weight.'

'Well – I believed what I said. That's the only apology I can make.'

He paused and sighed.

'And all the time, it was a purely private motive?'

'Exactly. It has taken me a long time to see the reason for the murder – although I had one very definite piece of luck.'

'What was that?'

'A fragment of conversation. Really a very illuminating fragment if only I had had the sense to realize its significance at the time.'

Mr Barnes scratched his nose thoughtfully with the trowel. A small piece of earth adhered to the side of his nose.

'Being rather cryptic, aren't you?' he asked genially.

Hercule Poirot shrugged his shoulders. He said:

'I am, perhaps, aggrieved that you were not more frank with me.'

'I?'

'Yes.'

'My dear fellow – I never had the least idea of Carter's guilt. As far as I knew he'd left the house long before Morley was killed. I suppose now they've found he didn't leave when he said he did?'

Poirot said:

'Carter was in the house at twenty-six minutes past twelve. He actually *saw* the murderer.'

'Then Carter didn't –'

'Carter saw the murderer, I tell you!'

Mr Barnes said:

'Did he recognize him?'

Slowly Hercule Poirot shook his head.

On the following day Hercule Poirot spent some hours with a theatrical agent of his acquaintance. In the afternoon he went to Oxford. On the day after that he drove down to the country – it was late when he returned.

He had telephoned before he left to make an appointment with Mr Alistair Blunt for that same evening.

It was half-past nine when he reached the Gothic House.

Alistair Blunt was alone in the library when Poirot was shown in.

He looked an eager question at his visitor as he shook hands.

He said:

'Well?'

Slowly, Hercule Poirot nodded his head.

Blunt looked at him in almost incredulous appreciation.

'Have you found her?'

'Yes. Yes, I have found her.'

He sat down. And he sighed.

Alistair Blunt said:

'You are tired?'

'Yes. I am tired. And it is not pretty – what I have to tell you.'

Blunt said:

'Is she dead?'

'That depends,' said Hercule Poirot slowly, 'on how you like to look at it.'

Blunt frowned.

He said:

'My dear man, a person *must* be dead or alive. Miss Sainsbury Seale must be one or the other?'

'Ah, but who is Miss Sainsbury Seale?'

Alistair Blunt said:

'You don't mean that – that there isn't any such person?'

'Oh, no, no. There was such a person. She lived in Calcutta. She taught elocution. She busied herself with good works. She came to England in the *Maharanah* – the same boat in which Mr Amberiotis travelled. Although they were not in the same class, he helped her over something – some fuss about her luggage. He was, it would seem, a kindly man in little ways. And sometimes, M. Blunt, kindness is repaid in an unexpected fashion. It was so, you know, with M. Amberiotis. He chanced to meet the lady again in the streets of London. He was feeling expansive, he good naturedly invited her to lunch with him at the Savoy. An unexpected treat for her. And an unexpected windfall for M. Amberiotis! For his kindness was not pre-meditated – he had no idea that this faded, middle-aged lady was going to present him with the equivalent of a gold mine. But nevertheless, that is what she did, though she never suspected the fact herself.

'She was never, you see, of the first order of intelligence. A good, well-meaning soul, but the brain, I should say, of a hen.'

Blunt said:

'Then it wasn't she who killed the Chapman woman?'

Poirot said slowly:

'It is difficult to know just how to present the matter. I shall begin, I think, where the matter began for me. With a *shoe*!'

Blunt said blankly:

'With a *shoe*?'

Hercule Poirot nodded.

'Yes, a buckled shoe. I came out from my *séance* at the dentists and as I stood on the steps of 58, Queen Charlotte Street, a taxi stopped outside, the door opened and a woman's foot prepared to descend. I am a man who notices a woman's foot and ankle. It was a well-shaped foot, with a good ankle and an expensive stocking, but I did not like the shoe. It was a new, shining patent leather shoe with a large ornate buckle. Not chic – not at all chic!

'And whilst I was observing this, the rest of the lady came into sight – and frankly it was a disappointment – a middle-aged lady without charm and badly dressed.'

'Miss Sainsbury Seale?'

'Precisely. As she descended a *contretemps* occurred – she caught the buckle of her shoe in the door and it was wrenched off. I picked it up and returned it to her. That was all. The incident was closed.

'Later, on that same day, I went with Chief Inspector Japp to interview the lady. (She had not as yet sewn on the buckle, by the way.)

'On that same evening, Miss Sainsbury Seale walked out of her hotel and vanished. That, shall we say, is the end of Part One.

'Part Two began when Chief Inspector Japp summoned me to King Leopold Mansions. There was a fur chest in a flat there, and in that fur chest there had been found a body. I went into the room, I walked up to the chest – and the first thing I saw was a shabby buckled shoe!'

'Well?'

'You have not appreciated the point. It was a *shabby* shoe – a *well-worn* shoe. But you see, Miss Sainsbury Seale had come to King Leopold Mansions on the evening of that same day – the day of Mr Morley's murder. In the morning the shoes were *new* shoes – in the evening they were *old* shoes. One does not wear out a pair of shoes in a day, you comprehend.'

Alistair Blunt said without much interest:

'She could have two pairs of shoes, I suppose?'

'Ah, *but that was not so.* For Japp and I had gone up to her room at the Glengowrie Court and had looked at all her possessions – and there was no pair of buckled shoes there. She might have had an old pair of shoes, yes. She might have changed into them after a tiring day to go out in the evening, yes? But if so, the other pair would have been at the hotel. It was curious, you will admit?'

'I can't see that it is important.'

'No, not important. Not at all important. But one does not like things that one cannot explain. I stood by the fur chest and I looked at the shoe – the buckle had recently been sewn on by hand. I will confess that I had had a moment of doubt – of myself. Yes, I said to myself, Hercule Poirot, you were a little light-headed perhaps this morning. You saw the world through rosy spectacles. Even the old shoes looked like new ones to you?'

'Perhaps that *was* the explanation?'

'But no, it was *not*. My eyes do not deceive me! To continue, I studied the dead body of this woman and I did not like what I saw. Why had the face been wantonly, deliberately smashed and rendered unrecognizable?'

Alistair Blunt moved restlessly. He said:

'Must we go over that again? We know –'

Hercule Poirot said firmly:

'It is necessary. I have to take you over the steps that led me at last to the truth. I said to myself: "Something is wrong here. Here is a dead woman in the clothes of Miss Sainsbury Seale (except, perhaps, the shoes?) and with the handbag of Miss Sainsbury Seale – but why is her face unrecognizable? Is it, perhaps, because the face is not the face of Miss Sainsbury Seale?" And immediately I begin to put together what I have heard of the appearance of the *other* woman – the woman to whom the flat belongs, and I ask myself – Might it not perhaps be *this other woman* who lies dead here? I go then and look at

647

the other woman's bedroom. I try to picture to myself what sort of woman she is. In superficial appearance, very different to the other. Smart, showily dressed, very much made up. But in essentials, *not unlike*. Hair, build, age ... But there is one difference. Mrs Albert Chapman took a five in shoes. Miss Sainsbury Seale, I knew, took a 10-inch stocking – that is to say she would take at least a 6 in shoes. Mrs Chapman, then, had smaller feet than Miss Sainsbury Seale. I went back to the body. If my half-formed idea was right, and the body was that of Mrs Chapman wearing Miss Sainsbury Seale's clothes, *then the shoes should be too big.* I took hold of one. But it was not loose. It fitted tightly. That looked as though it *were* the body of Miss Sainsbury Seale after all! But in that case, *why* was the face disfigured? Her identity was already proved by the handbag, which could easily have been removed, but which had *not* been removed.

'It was a puzzle – a tangle. In desperation I seized on Mrs Chapman's address book – a dentist was the only person who could prove definitely who the dead woman was – or was not. By coincidence, Mrs Chapman's dentist was Mr Morley. Morley was dead, but identification was still possible. You know the result. The body was identified in the Coroner's Court by Mr Morley's successor as that of Mrs Albert Chapman.'

Blunt was fidgeting with some impatience, but Poirot took no notice. He went on:

'I was left now with a psychological problem. What sort of a woman was Mabelle Sainsbury Seale? There were two answers to that question. The first was the obvious one borne out by her whole life in India and by the testimony of her personal friends. That depicted her as an earnest, conscientious, slightly stupid woman. Was there another Miss Sainsbury Seale? Apparently there was. There was a woman who had lunched with a well-known foreign agent, who had accosted you in the street and claimed to be a close friend of your wife's (a statement that was almost certainly untrue) a woman who had left a man's house very shortly before a murder had been committed, a woman who had visited another woman on the evening when in all probability that other woman had been murdered, and who had since disappeared although she must be aware that the police force of England was looking for her. Were all these actions compatible with the character which her friends gave her? It would seem that they were not. Therefore, if Miss Sainsbury Seale was *not* the good, amiable creature she seemed, then it would appear that she was quite possibly a cold-blooded murderess or

648

almost certainly an accomplice after the fact.

'I had one more criterion – my own personal impression. I had talked to Mabelle Sainsbury Seale myself. How had she struck *me*? And that, M. Blunt, was the most difficult question to answer of all. Everything that she said, her way of talking, her manner, her gestures, all were perfectly in accord with her given character. *But they were equally in accord with a clever actress playing a part*. And, after all, Mabelle Sainsbury Seale had started life as an actress.

'I had been much impressed by a conversation I had had with Mr Barnes of Ealing who had also been a patient at 58, Queen Charlotte Street on that particular day. His theory, expressed very forcibly, was that the deaths of Morley and of Amberiotis were only incidental, so to speak – that the intended victim was *you*.'

Alistair Blunt said:

'Oh, come now – that's a bit far-fetched.'

'Is it, M. Blunt? Is it not that at this moment there are various groups of people to whom it is vital that you should be – removed, shall we say? Shall be no longer capable of exerting your influence?'

Blunt said:

'Oh yes, that's true enough. But why mix up this business of Morley's death with that?'

Poirot said:

'Because there is a certain – how shall I put it? – lavishness about the case – Expense is no object – human life is no object. Yes, there is a recklessness, a lavishness – that points to a *big* crime!'

'You don't think Morley shot himself because of a mistake?'

'I never thought so – not for a minute. No, Morley was murdered, Amberiotis was murdered, an unrecognizable woman was murdered – Why? For some big stake. Barnes' theory was that somebody had tried to bribe Morley or his partner to put you out of the way.'

Alistair Blunt said sharply:

'Nonsense!'

'Ah, but is it nonsense? Say one wishes to put someone out of the way. Yes, but that someone is forewarned, forearmed, difficult of access. To kill that person it is necessary to be able to approach him without awakening his suspicions – and where would a man be less suspicious than in the dentist's chair.'

'Well, that's true, I suppose. I never thought of it like that.'

'It *is* true. And once I realized it I had my first vague glimmering of the truth.'

'So you accepted Barnes' theory? Who is Barnes, by the way?'

'Barnes was Reilly's twelve o'clock patient. He is retired from the Home Office and lives in Ealing. An insignificant little man. But you are wrong when you say I accepted his theory. I did not. I only accepted the *principle* of it.'

'What do you mean?'

Hercule Poirot said:

'All along, all the way through, I have been led astray – sometimes unwittingly, sometimes deliberately and for a purpose. All along it was presented to me, *forced* upon me, that this was what you might call a *public* crime. That is to say, that you, M. Blunt, were the focus of it all, in your *public* character. You, the banker, you the controller of finance, you, the upholder of conservative tradition!

'But every public character has a *private* life also. That was my mistake, *I forgot the private life.* There existed *private* reasons for killing Morley – Frank Carter's for instance.

'There could also exist private reasons for killing *you* . . . You had relations who would inherit money when you died. You had people who loved and hated you – as a *man* – not as a public figure.

'And so I came to the supreme instance of what I call "the forced card." The purported attack upon you by Frank Carter. If that attack was genuine – then it *was* a political crime. But was there any other explanation? *There could be.* There was a second man in the shrubbery. The man who rushed up and seized Carter. A man who could easily have fired that shot and then tossed the pistol to Carter's feet so that the latter would almost inevitably pick it up and be found with it in this hand. . . .

'I considered the problem of Howard Raikes. Raikes had been at Queen Charlotte Street that morning of Morley's death. Raikes was a bitter enemy of all that you stood for and were. Yes, but Raikes was something more. *Raikes was the man who might marry your niece,* and with you dead, your niece would inherit a very handsome income, even though you had prudently arranged that she could not touch the principal.

'Was the whole thing, after all, a *private* crime – a crime for *private* gain, for *private* satisfaction? Why had I thought it a *public* crime? *Because, not once, but many times, that idea had been suggested to me, had been forced upon me like a forced card.* . . .

'It was then, when that idea occurred to me, that I had my first glimmering of the truth. I was in church at the time and singing a verse of a psalm. It spoke of a snare laid with cords. . . .

'A snare? Laid for me? Yes, it could be . . . But in that case *who* had

650

laid it? *There was only one person who could have laid it* ... And that did not make sense – or *did* it? Had I been looking at the case *upside down*? Money no object? Exactly! Reckless disregard of human life? Yes again. For the stakes for which the guilty person was playing were *enormous*. ...

'But if this new, strange idea of mine were right, it must explain *everything*. I must explain, for instance, the mystery of the dual nature of Miss Sainsbury Seale. It must solve the riddle of the buckled shoe. And it must answer the question: *Where is Miss Sainsbury Seale now?*

'*Eh bien* – it did all that and more. It showed me that Miss Sainsbury Seale was the beginning and middle and end of the case. No wonder it had seemed to me that there were two Mabelle Sainsbury Seales. There *were* two Mabelle Sainsbury Seales. There was the good, stupid, amiable woman who was vouched for so confidently by her friends. And there was the other – the woman who was mixed up with two murders and who told lies and who vanished mysteriously.

'Remember, the porter at King Leopold Mansions said that Miss Sainsbury Seale had been there once before. ...

'In my reconstruction of the case, that first time was the only time. She never left King Leopold Mansions. *The other Miss Sainsbury Seale took her place*. That other Mabelle Sainsbury Seale, dressed in clothes of the same type and wearing a new pair of shoes with buckles because the others were too large for her, went to the Russell Square Hotel at a busy time of day, packed up the dead woman's clothes, paid the bill and left. She went to the Glengowrie Court Hotel. None of the real Miss Sainsbury Seale's friends saw her after that time, remember. She played the part of Mabelle Sainsbury Seale there for over a week. She wore Mabelle Sainsbury Seale's clothes, she talked in Mabelle Sainsbury Seale's voice, but she had to buy a smaller pair of evening shoes, too. And then – she vanished, her last appearance being when she was seen re-entering King Leopold Mansions on the evening of the day Morley was killed.'

'Are you trying to say,' demanded Alistair Blunt, 'that it *was* Mabelle Sainsbury Seale's dead body in that flat, after all.'

'Of course it was! It was a very clever double bluff – the smashed face was *meant* to raise a question of the woman's identity!'

'But the dental evidence?'

'Ah! Now we come to it. It was not the *dentist himself* who gave evidence. Morley was dead. He couldn't give evidence as to his own work. *He* would have known who the dead woman was. It was the *charts* that were put in as evidence – and the charts were faked. Both women were his patients, remember. All that had to be done was to relabel the charts, exchanging the names.'

Hercule Poirot added:

'And now you see what I meant when you asked me if the woman was dead and I replied, "That depends." For when you say "Miss Sainsbury Seale" – *which woman do you mean*? The woman who disappeared from the Glengowrie Court Hotel or the real Mabelle Sainsbury Seale.'

Alistair Blunt said:

'I know, M. Poirot, that you have a great reputation. Therefore I accept that you must have some grounds for this extraordinary assumption – for it is an assumption, nothing more. But all I can see is the fantastic improbability of the whole thing. You are saying, are you not, that Mabelle Sainsbury Seale was deliberately murdered and that Morley was also murdered to prevent his identifying her dead body. But *why*? That's what I want to know? Here's this woman – a perfectly harmless, middle-aged woman – with plenty of friends and apparently no enemies. Why on earth all this elaborate plot to get rid of her?'

'Why? Yes, that is the question? *Why*? As you say, Mabelle Sainsbury Seale was a perfectly harmless creature who wouldn't hurt a fly! Why, then, was she deliberately and brutally murdered? Well, I will tell you that I think.'

'Yes?'

Hercule Poirot leaned forward. He said:

'It is my belief that Mabelle Sainsbury Seale was murdered because she happened to have too good a memory for faces.'

'What do you mean?'

Hercule Poirot said:

'We have separated the dual personality. There is the harmless lady from India. But there is one incident that falls between the two roles. Which Miss Sainsbury Seale was it who spoke to you on the doorstep of Mr Morley's house? She claimed, you will remember, to be "a great friend of your wife's." Now that claim was adjudged by her friends and by the light of ordinary probability to be untrue. So we can say: "That was a lie. The real Miss Sainsbury Seale does not tell lies." So it was a lie uttered by the imposter for a purpose of her own.'

Alistair Blunt nodded.

'Yes, that reasoning is quite clear. Though I still don't know what the purpose was.'

Poirot said:

'Ah, *pardon* – but let us first look at it *the other way round*. It was the *real* Miss Sainsbury Seale. She does *not* tell lies. *So the story must be true.*'

'I suppose you *can* look at it that way – but it seems very unlikely –'

'Of course it is unlikely! But taking that second hypothesis as fact – the story is *true*. Therefore Miss Sainsbury Seale *did* know your wife. She knew her *well*. Therefore – *your wife must have been the type of person Miss Sainsbury Seale would have known well*. Someone in her own station of life. An Anglo-Indian – a missionary – or, to go back farther still – an actress – Therefore – *not* Rebecca Arnholt!

'Now, M. Blunt, do you see what I meant when I talked of a private and a public life? You are the great banker. But you are also a man who married a rich wife. And before you married her you were only a junior partner in the firm – not very long down from Oxford.

'You comprehend – I began to look at the case the *right way up*. Expense no object? Naturally not – to you. Reckless of human life – that, too, since for a long time you have been virtually a dictator and to a dictator his own life becomes unduly important and those of others unimportant.'

Alistair Blunt said:

'What are you suggesting, M. Poirot?'

Poirot said quietly:

'I am suggesting, M. Blunt, that when you married Rebecca Arnholt, *you were married already*. That, dazzled by the vista, not so much of wealth, as of power, you suppressed that fact and deliberately committed bigamy. That your real wife acquiesced in the situation.'

'And who was this real wife?'

'Mrs Albert Chapman was the name she went under at King Leopold Mansions – a handy spot, not five minutes' walk from your house on the Chelsea Embankment. You borrowed the name of a real secret agent, realizing that it would give support to her hints of a husband engaged in intelligence work. Your scheme succeeded perfectly. No suspicion was ever aroused. Nevertheless, the fact remained, *you have never been legally married to Rebecca Arnholt* and you were guilty of bigamy. You never dreamt of danger after so many years. It came out of the blue – in the form of a tiresome woman who remembered you after nearly twenty years, as her friend's husband.

Chance brought her back to this country, chance let her meet you in Queen Charlotte Street – it was chance that your niece was with you and heard what she said to you. Otherwise I might never have guessed.'

'I told you about that myself, my dear Poirot.'

'No, it was your niece who insisted on telling me and you could not very well protest too violently in case it might arouse suspicions. And after that meeting, one more evil chance (from your point of view) occurred. Mabelle Sainsbury Seale met Amberiotis, went to lunch with him and babbled to him of this meeting with a friend's husband – "after all these years"! – "Looked older, of course, but had hardly changed!" That, I admit, is pure guess-work on my part but I believe it is what happened. I do not think that Mabelle Sainsbury Seale realized for a moment that the Mr Blunt her friend had married was the shadowy figure behind the finance of the world. The name, after all, is not an uncommon one. But Amberiotis, remember, in addition to his espionage activities, was a blackmailer. Blackmailers have an uncanny nose for a secret. Amberiotis wondered. Easy to find out just who the Mr Blunt was. And then, I have no doubt, he wrote to you or telephoned . . . Oh, yes – a gold mine for Amberiotis.'

Poirot paused. He went on:

'There is only one effectual method of dealing with a really efficient and experienced blackmailer. Silence him.

'It was not a case, as I had had erroneously suggested to me, of "Blunt must go." It was, on the contrary, "Amberiotis must go." But the answer was the same! The easiest way to get at a man is when he is off his guard, and when is a man more off his guard than in the dentist's chair?'

Poirot paused again. A faint smile came to his lips. He said:

'The truth about the case was mentioned very early. The page-boy, Alfred, was reading a crime story called *Death at Eleven Forty-Five*. We should have taken that as an omen. For, of course, that is just about the time when Morley was killed. You shot him just as you were leaving. Then you pressed his buzzer, turned on the taps of the wash basin and left the room. You timed it so that you came down the stairs just as Alfred was taking the false Mabelle Sainsbury Seale to the lift. You actually opened the front door, perhaps you passed out, but as the lift doors shut and the lift went up you slipped inside again and went up the stairs.

'I know, from my own visits, just what Alfred did when he took up a patient. He knocked on the door, opened it, and stood back to let

654

the patient pass in. Inside the water was running – inference, Morley was washing his hands as usual. But Alfred couldn't actually *see* him.

'As soon as Alfred had gone down again in the lift, you slipped along into the surgery. Together you and your accomplice lifted the body and carried it into the adjoining office. Then a quick hunt through the files, and the charts of Mrs Chapman and Miss Sainsbury Seale were cleverly falsified. You put on a white linen coat, perhaps your wife applied a trace of make-up. But nothing much was needed. It was Amberiotis' first visit to Morley. He had never met you. And your photograph seldom appears in the papers. Besides, why should he have suspicions? A blackmailer does not fear his dentist. Miss Sainsbury Seale goes down and Alfred shows her out. The buzzer goes and Amberiotis is taken up. He finds the dentist washing his hands behind the door in approved fashion. He is conducted to the chair. He indicates the painful tooth. You talk the accustomed patter. You explain it will be best to freeze the gum. The procaine and adrenalin are there. You inject a big enough dose to kill. And incidently he will not feel any lack of skill in your dentistry!

'Completely unsuspicious, Amberiotis leaves. You bring out Morley's body and arrange it on the floor, dragging it slightly on the carpet now that you have to manage it single-handed. You wipe the pistol and put it in his hand – wipe the door handle so that your prints shall not be the last. The instruments you used have all been passed into the sterilizer. You leave the room, go down the stairs and slip out of the front door at a suitable moment. That is your only moment of danger.

'It should all have passed off so well! Two people who threatened your safety – both dead. A third person also dead – but that, from your point of view, was unavoidable. And all so easily explained. Morley's suicide explained by the mistake he had made over Amberiotis. The two deaths cancel out. One of these regrettable accidents.

'But alas for you, *I* am on the scene. *I* have doubts. *I* make objections. All is not going as easily as you hoped. So there must be a second line of defences. There must be, if necessary, a scapegoat. You have already informed yourself minutely, of Morley's household. There is this man, Frank Carter, he will do. So your accomplice arranges that he shall be engaged in a mysterious fashion as gardener. If, later, he tells such a ridiculous story no one will believe it. In due course, the body in the fur chest will come to light. At first it will be thought to be that of Miss Sainsbury Seale, then the

655

dental evidence will be taken. Big sensation! It may seem a needless complication, but it was *necessary*. You do not want the police force of England to be looking for a missing Mrs Albert Chapman. No, let Mrs Chapman be dead – and let it be Mabelle Sainsbury Seale for whom the police look. Since they can never find her. Besides, through your influence, you can arrange to have the case dropped.

'You did do that, but since it was necessary that you should know just what *I* was doing, you sent for me and urged me to find the missing woman for you. And you continued, steadily, to "force a card" upon me. Your accomplice rang me up with a melodramatic warning – the same idea – espionage – the *public* aspect. She is a clever actress, this wife of yours, but to disguise one's voice the natural tendency is to imitate another voice. Your wife imitated the intonation of Mrs Olivera. That puzzled me, I may say, a good deal.

'Then I was taken down to Exsham – the final performance was staged. How easy to arrange a loaded pistol amongst laurels so that a man, clipping them, shall unwittingly cause it to go off. The pistol falls at his feet. Startled, he picks it up. What more do you want? He is caught red-handed – with a ridiculous story and with a pistol which is a twin to the one with which Morley was shot.

'And all a snare for the feet of Hercule Poirot.'

Alistair Blunt stirred a little in his chair. His face was grave and a little sad. He said:

'Don't misunderstand me, M. Poirot. How much do you guess? And how much do you actually *know*?'

Poirot said:

'I have a certificate of the marriage – at a registry office near Oxford – of Martin Alistair Blunt and Gerda Grant. Frank Carter saw two men leave Morley's surgery just after twenty-five past twelve. The first was a fat man – Amberiotis. The second was, of course, you. Frank Carter did not recognize you. He only saw you from above.'

'How fair of you to mention that!'

'He went into the surgery and found Morley's body. The hands were cold and there was dried blood round the wound. That meant that Morley had been dead some time. Therefore the dentist who attended to Amberiotis could not have been Morley and must have been Morley's murderer.'

'Anything else?'

'Yes. *Helen Montressor was arrested this afternoon.*'

Alistair Blunt gave one sharp movement. Then he sat very still. He said:

'That – rather tears it.'

Hercule Poirot said:

'Yes. The real Helen Montressor, your distant cousin, died in Canada seven years ago. You suppressed that fact, and took advantage of it.'

A smile came to Alistair Blunt's lips. He spoke naturally and with a kind of boyish enjoyment.

'Gerda got a kick out of it all, you know. I'd like to make you understand. You're such a clever fellow. I married her without letting my people know. She was acting in repertory at the time. My people were the strait-laced kind, and I was going into the firm. We agreed to keep it dark. She went on acting. Mabelle Sainsbury Seale was in the company too. She knew about us. Then she went abroad with a touring company. Gerda heard of her once or twice from India. Then she stopped writing. Mabelle got mixed up with some Hindu. She was always a stupid, credulous girl.

'I wish I could make you understand about my meeting with Rebecca and my marriage. Gerda understood. The only way I can put it is that it was like Royalty. I had the chance of marrying a Queen and playing the part of Prince Consort or even King. I looked on my marriage to Gerda as morganatic. I loved her. I didn't want to get rid of her. And the whole thing worked splendidly. I liked Rebecca immensely. She was a woman with a first-class financial brain and mine was just as good. We were good at team work. It was supremely exciting. She was an excellent companion and I think I made her happy. I was genuinely sorry when she died. The queer thing was that Gerda and I grew to enjoy the secret thrill of our meetings. We had all sorts of ingenious devices. She was an actress by nature. She had a repertoire of seven or eight characters – Mrs Albert Chapman was only one of them. She was an American widow in Paris. I met her there when I went over on business. And she used to go to Norway with painting things as an artist. I went there for the fishing. And then, later, I passed her off as my cousin. Helen Montressor. It was great fun for us both, and it kept romance alive, I suppose. We could have married officially after Rebecca died – but we didn't want to. Gerda would have found it hard to live my official life and, of course, something from the past *might* have been raked up, but I think the real reason we went on more or less the same was that we *enjoyed* the secrecy of it. We should have found open domesticity dull.'

Blunt paused. He said, and his voice changed and hardened:

'And then that damned fool of a woman messed up everything. Recognizing me – after all those years! And she told Amberiotis. You see – you *must* see – that something had to be done! It wasn't only myself – not only the selfish point of view. If I was ruined and disgraced – the country, *my* country was hit as well. For I've done something for England, M. Poirot. I've held it firm and kept it solvent. It's free from Dictators – from Fascism and from Communism. I don't really care for money as money. I do like power – I like to rule – but I don't want to tyrannize. We *are* democratic in England – truly democratic. We can grumble and say what we think and laugh at our politicians. We're *free*. I care for all that – it's been my life-work. But if *I* went – well, you know what would probably happen. I'm *needed*, M. Poirot. And a damned double-crossing, blackmailing rogue of a Greek was going to destroy my life work. Something *had* to be done. Gerda saw it, too. We were sorry about the Sainsbury Seale woman – but it was no good. We'd got to silence her. She couldn't be trusted to hold her tongue. Gerda went to see her, asked her to tea, told her to ask for Mrs Chapman, said she was staying in Mr Chapman's flat. Mabelle Sainsbury Seale came, quite unsuspecting. She never knew anything – the medinal was in the tea – it's quite painless. You just sleep and don't wake up. The face business was done afterwards – rather sickening, but we felt it was necessary. Mrs Chapman was to exit for good. I had given my "cousin" Helen a cottage to live in. We decided that after a while we would get married. But first we had to get Amberiotis out of the way. It worked beautifully. He hadn't a suspicion that I wasn't a real dentist. I did my stuff with the hand-pricks rather well. I didn't risk the drill. Of course, after the injection he couldn't feel what I was doing. Probably just as well!'

Poirot asked:

'The pistols?'

'Actually they belonged to a secretary I once had in America. He bought them abroad somewhere. When he left he forgot to take them.'

There was a pause. Then Alistair Blunt asked:

'Is there anything else you want to know?'

Hercule Poirot said:

'What about Morley?'

Alistair Blunt said simply:

'I was sorry about Morley.'

Hercule Poirot said:

'Yes, I see. . . .'

There was a long pause, then Blunt said:

'Well, M. Poirot, what about it?'

Poirot said:

'Helen Montressor is arrested already.'

'And now its my turn?'

'That was my meaning, yes.'

Blunt said gently.

'But you are not happy about it, eh?'

'No, I am not at all happy.'

Alistair Blunt said:

'I've killed three people. So presumably I *ought* to be hanged. But you've heard my defence.'

'Which is – exactly?'

'That I believe, with all my heart and soul, that I am necessary to the continued peace and well-being of this country.'

Hercule Poirot allowed:

'That may be – yes.'

'You agree, don't you?'

'I agree, yes. You stand for all the things that to my mind are important. For sanity and balance and stability and honest dealing.'

Alistair Blunt said quietly:

'Thanks.'

He added:

'Well, what about it?'

'You suggest that I – retire from the case?'

'Yes.'

'And your wife?'

'I've got a good deal of pull. Mistaken identity, that's the line to take.'

'And if I refuse?'

'Then,' said Alistair Blunt simply, 'I'm for it.'

He went on:

'It's in your hands, Poirot. It's up to you. But I tell you this – and it's not just self-preservation – I'm needed in the world. And do you know why? Because I'm an honest man. And because I've got common sense – and no particular axe of my own to grind.'

Poirot nodded. Strangely enough, he believed all that.

He said:

'Yes, that is one side. You are the right man in the right place. You have sanity, judgment, balance. But there is the other side. Three

659

human beings who are dead.'

'Yes, but think of them! Mabelle Sainsbury Seale – you said yourself – a woman with the brains of a hen! Amberiotis – a crook and a blackmailer!'

'And Morley?'

'I've told you before. I'm sorry about Morley. But after all – he was a decent fellow and a good dentist – but there *are* other dentists.'

'Yes,' said Poirot, 'there are other dentists. And Frank Carter? You would have let him die, too, without regret?'

Blunt said:

'I don't waste any pity on *him*. He's no good. An utter rotter.'

Poirot said:

'But a human being. ...'

'Oh well, we're all human beings. ...'

'Yes, we are all human beings. That is what you have not remembered. You have said that Mabelle Sainsbury Seale was a foolish human being and Amberiotis an evil one, and Frank Carter a wastrel – and Morley – Morley was only a dentist and there are other dentists. That is where you and I, M. Blunt, do not see alike. For to me the lives of those four people are just as important as your life.'

'You're wrong.'

'No, I am not wrong. You are a man of great natural honesty and rectitude. You took one step aside – and outwardly it has not affected you. Publicly you have continued the same, upright, trustworthy, honest. But within you the love of power grew to overwhelming heights. So you sacrificed four human lives and thought them of no account.'

'Don't you realize, Poirot, that the safety and happiness of the whole nation depends on me?'

'I am not concerned with nations, Monsieur. I am concerned with the lives of private individuals who have the right not to have their lives taken from them.'

He got up.

'So that's your answer,' said Alistair Blunt.

Hercule Poirot said in a tired voice:

'Yes – that is my answer. ...'

He went to the door and opened it. Two men came in.

II

Hercule Poirot went down to where a girl was waiting.

Jane Olivera, her face white and strained, stood against the mantelpiece. Beside her was Howard Raikes.

She said:

'Well?'

Poirot said gently:

'It is all over.'

Raikes said harshly:

'What do you mean?'

Poirot said:

'Mr Alistair Blunt has been arrested for murder.'

Raikes said:

'I thought he'd buy you off. ...'

Jane said:

'No. *I* never thought that.'

Poirot sighed. He said:

'The world is yours. The New Heaven and the New Earth. In your new world, my children, let there be freedom and let there be pity ... That is all I ask.'

Hercule Poirot walked home along the deserted streets.

An unobtrusive figure joined him.

'Well?' said Mr Barnes.

Hercule Poirot shrugged his shoulders and spread out his hands. Barnes said:

'What line did he take?'

'He admitted everything and pleaded justification. He said that this country needed him.'

'So it does,' said Mr Barnes.

He added after a minute or two:

'Don't you think so?'

'Yes, I do.'

'Well, then –'

'We may be wrong,' said Hercule Poirot.

'I never thought of that,' said Mr Barnes. 'So we may.'

They walked on for a little way, then Barnes asked curiously:

'What are you thinking about?'

Hercule Poirot quoted:

'*Because thou hast rejected the word of the Lord, he hath also rejected thee from being king.*'

'Hm – I see –' said Mr Barnes. 'Saul – after the Amalekites. Yes, you could think of it that way.'

They walked on a little farther, then Barnes said:

'I take the tube here. Good-night, Poirot.' He paused, then said awkwardly: 'You know – there's something I'd like to tell you.'

'Yes, *mon ami?*'

'Feel I owe it to you. Led you astray unintentionally. Fact of the matter is, Albert Chapman, Q.X.912.'

'Yes?'

'I'm Albert Chapman. That's partly why I was interested. I knew, you see, that I'd never had a wife.'

He hurried away, chuckling.

Poirot stood stock still. Then his eyes opened, his eyebrows rose. He said to himself:

'*Nineteen, twenty, my plate's empty –*'

And went home.